The
Collected
Short Fiction
of
C.J. CHERRYH

DAW BOOKS, INC.

DONALD A. WOLLHEIM, FOUNDER
375 Hudson Street, New York, NY 10014
ELIZABETH R. WOLLHEIM
SHEILA E. GILBERT
PUBLISHERS
http://www.dawbooks.com

First Printing, February 2004
1   2   3   4   5   6   7   8   9   10

The
Collected
Short Fiction
of
C.J. CHERRYH

Table of Contents

▼

OTHER STORIES

INTRODUCTION

I started writing when I was ten, when I hadn't read any short stories—or if I had, I didn't think of them as short stories. Stories are as long as stories need to be, and no longer, and I'd never read one that wasn't, from Poe to Pyle. So it never occurred to me that there were classes and classifications of stories. I read stories that appealed to me. I wrote stories until I satisfied the story. Mostly my stories, the ones I wrote, worked out to about two hundred pages handwritten. When I learned to type (self-taught) the stories (also self-taught) blossomed to five hundred pages single-spaced.

The typing picked up to a high speed. The stories, fortunately, did not proportionately increase in length. I sold professionally—my first novel went to DAW Books, which has graciously proposed this collection of short stories.

But at the time I was writing that first novel, common wisdom said that the route to professional writing lay through short stories and the magazines.

I just didn't think of stories that short. Novels it was. Novels it stayed—until I had several on the stands.

Then I began to say to myself that I could write short stories, if I figured out how they worked.

Now, be it understood, a short story is really not a novel that takes place in three to five thousand words. It's a very different sort of creature, compressed in time and space (usually), and limited in characterization (almost inevitably).

Since characters and near archaeological scope are a really driving element of my story-telling, I began to see why I'd never quite written short.

But when I began thinking of the problem in that light, I began to see that the tales I'd used to tell aloud on certain occasions, whether around the campfire or in the classroom, tolerably well fit the description. So I wrote one out: the Sisyphos legend. And a modern take on Cassandra. The latter won the Hugo Award for Best Short Story, surprising its creator no end, and I have since written short stories mostly on request, and when some concept occurs to me which just doesn't find itself a whole novel.

It's rare that I'm not working on a novel. Short stories often happen between novels. Consequently my output is fairly small. But I love the tale-telling concept, the notion that I can spin a yarn, rather than construct something architectural and precise. So I think most of my short stories are more organic than not. I became aware, when I thought closely about it, that that Poe fellow I liked was a short story writer—in fact, I'd learned he was the father of the short story—but I'd just never analyzed what he did; and to me it still seems more like tales than architectural structure. You fall into them. Same with Fritz Leiber's wonderful Mouser stories. I never counted the words in them. I just lapped them up for what they were—and then analyzed just how he did it, because it seemed to me, and still seems, that he was one of the most natural, seamless tale-tellers of the last two centuries. I like that kind of story. I hope I can do a few.

I enjoy the chance to do them. I write the kind I like to read. Or the kind the idea of which starts to nag me, so I have to write it, or it begins to occupy my subconscious to such an extent I get nothing else done.

But most are because someone asks me to. The first question writers ever get asked by the general public is "Where do you get your ideas?" Just imagine, if someone said, "Write a story about—an island. People stranded on an island." Well, that would work. Being a science fiction writer, I can think of various definitions of "island" and various definitions of "people," from ship in trouble to stuck elevator to real tract of sand. Then you tell me that it has to be short—and I have to say, well, we can't go too deeply into the people, but we can have a situation. We can have a compression of time and a really dire necessity. That's a source of ideas. If I were set down on an island in a crisis, I can assure you I'd have ideas . . . as I think my readers would have, themselves. So Ideas aren't the be-all and end-all. The question that drives the short story is—what's unique about your situation? What's the question, what's the problem? And how are you going to fix it?

It's not the only way to do it, but it's one way to do it. It's not a formula, it's a set of questions. And I hope if anything a few of my tales leave you thinking of your own solutions.

Thanks to Betsy Wollheim, my extremely patient and dedicated publisher, who thought of doing this volume, and who kept after the project until it all worked. You have the result of her persistence in your hands.

—CJ Cherryh, Spokane, 2003

SUNFALL

I've always thought well of cities. They're ecological (think of all those millions turned loose with axes to burn firewood in the forest, each with an acre or two, and contemplate the footprint they'd leave in, say, the Adirondacks or the Rockies.) And they're a library of our culture and our past (consider Rome, Osaka, Los Angeles, and Chattanooga, as history and cuisine and human psychology.) Might all cities be haunted—repositories of the restless spirits of all the lives that have ever passed there? Might they shape their modern inhabitants subtly and constantly, as new individuals tread old, old paths and cross old, old bridges for the same reasons as thousands of years ago?

Sunfall is the wonder and the power of cities. I take it as one of the highest compliments that Fritz Lieber, whose writing I greatly admired, loved it, and troubled to tell me so—he was a kindred soul on this point. Myself, I love the woods. I love the wild places. Ask me where I'd go for a vacation and it invariably involves the open country. Ask me where I'd live, however, and it would always be in the center, in the beating heart of a city. And I'm very happy with these stories. I'm delighted to see them in another edition.

CJC

▼

PROLOGUE

▲

On the whole land surface of the Earth and on much of the seas, humankind had lived and died. In the world's youth the species had drawn together in the basins of its great rivers, the Nile, the Euphrates, the Indus; had come together in valleys to till the land; hunted the rich forests and teeming plains; herded; fished; wandered and built. In the river lands, villages grew from families; irrigated; grew; joined. Systems grew up for efficiency; and systems wanted written records; villages became towns; and towns swallowed villages and became cities.

Cities swallowed cities and became nations; nations combined into empires; conquerors were followed by law-givers who regulated the growth into new systems; systems functioned until grandsons proved less able to rule and the systems failed: again to chaos and the rise of new conquerors; endless pattern. There was no place where foot had not trod; or armies fought; and lovers sighed; and human dust settled, all unnoticed.

It was simply old, this world; had scattered its seed like a flower yielding to the winds. They had gone to the stars and gained . . . new worlds. Those who visited Earth in its great age had their own reasons . . . but those born here remained for that most ancient of reasons: it was home.

There were the cities, microcosms of human polity, great entities with much the character of individuals, which bound their residents by habit and by love and by the invisible threads that bound the first of the species to stay together, because outside the warmth of the firelit circle there was dark, and the unknown watched with wolfen eyes.

In all of human experience there was no word which encompassed this urge in all its aspects: it might have been love, but it was too often hate; it might have been community, but there was too little commonality; it might have been unity but there was much of diversity. It was in one sense remarkable that mankind had never found a word apt for it, and in another sense not remarkable at all. There had always been such things too vast and too human to name: like the reason of love and the logic in climbing mountains.

It was home, that was all.

And the cities were the last flourishing of this tendency, as they had been its beginning.

1981

THE ONLY DEATH IN THE CITY

(Paris)

It was named the City of Lights. It had known other names in the long history of Earth, in the years before the sun turned wan and plague-ridden, before the moon hung vast and lurid in the sky, before the ships from the stars grew few and the reasons for ambition grew fewer still. It stretched as far as the eye could see . . . if one saw it from the outside, as the inhabitants never did. It was so vast that a river flowed through it, named the Sin, which in the unthinkable past had flowed through a forest of primeval beauty, and then through a countless succession of cities, through ancient ages of empires. The City grew about the Sin, and enveloped it, so that, stone-channeled, it flowed now through the halls of the City, thundering from the tenth to the fourteenth level in a free fall, and flowing meekly along the channel within the fourteenth, a grand canal which supplied the City and made it self-sufficient. The Sin came from the outside, but it was so changed and channeled that no one remembered that this was so. No one remembered the outside. No one cared. The City was sealed, and had been so for thousands of years.

There *were* windows, but they were on the uppermost levels, and they were tightly shuttered. The inhabitants feared the sun, for popular rumor held that the sun was a source of vile radiations, unhealthful, a source of plagues. There were windows, but no doors, for no one would choose to leave. No one ever had, from the day the outer walls were built. When the City must build in this age, it built downward, digging a twentieth and twenty-first level for the burial of the dead . . . for the dead of the City were transients, in stone coffins, which might always be shifted lower still when the living needed room.

Once, it had been a major pastime of the City, to tour the lower levels, to seek out the painted sarcophagi of ancestors, to seek the resemblances of living face to dead so common in this long self-contained city. But now those levels were full of dust, and few were interested in going there save for funerals.

Once, it had been a delight to the inhabitants of the City to search the vast libraries and halls of art for histories, for the City lived much in the past, and reveled in old glories . . . but now the libraries went unused save for the very lightest of fictions, and those were very abstract and full of drug-dream fancies.

More and more . . . the inhabitants *remembered*.

There were a few at first who were troubled with recollections and a thorough familiarity with the halls—when once it was not uncommon to spend one's time touring the vast expanse of the City, seeing new sights. These visionaries sank into ennui . . . or into fear, when the recollections grew quite vivid.

There was no need to go to the lower levels seeking ancestors. They lived . . . incarnate in the sealed halls of the City, in the persons of their descendants, souls so long immured within the megalopolis that they began to wake to former pasts, for dying, they were reborn, and remembered, eventually. So keenly did they recall that now mere infants did not cry, but lay patiently dreaming in their cradles, or, waking, stared out from haunted eyes, gazing into mothers' eyes with millennia of accumulated lives, *aware*, and waiting on adulthood, for body to overtake memory.

Children played . . . various games, wrought of former lives.

The people lived in a curious mixture of caution and recklessness: caution, for they surrounded themselves with the present, knowing the danger of entanglements; recklessness, for past ceased to fascinate them as an unknown and nothing had permanent meaning. There was only pleasure, and the future, which held the certainty of more lives, which would remember the ones they presently lived. For a very long time, death was absent from the halls of the City of Lights.

Until one was born to them.

Only rarely there were those born new, new souls which had not made previous journeys within the City, babes which cried, children who grew up conscious of their affliction, true children among the reborn.

Such was Alain.

He was born in one of the greatest of families—those families of associations dictated more by previous lives than by blood, for while it was

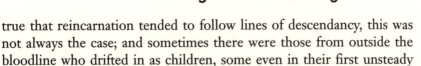

true that reincarnation tended to follow lines of descendancy, this was not always the case; and sometimes there were those from outside the bloodline who drifted in as children, some even in their first unsteady steps, seeking old loves, old connections. But Alain was new. He was born to the Jade Palace Family, which occupied the tenth level nearest the stairs, although he was not *of* that family or indeed of any family, and therefore grew up less civilized.

He tried. He was horribly conscious of his lack of taste, his lack of discrimination which he could not excuse as originality: originality was for—older—minds and memories. His behavior was simply awkward, and he stayed much in the shadows in Jade Palace, enduring this life and thinking that his next would surely be better.

But Jade was neighbor to Onyx Palace, and it was inevitable that these two houses mix upon occasion of anniversaries. These times were Alain's torment when he was a child, when his naïve and real childhood was exposed to outsiders; they became torment of a different kind in his fourteenth year, when suddenly his newly maturing discrimination settled upon a certain face, a certain pale loveliness in the Onyx House.

"Only to be expected," his mother sighed. He had embarrassed her many times, and diffidently came to her now with this confession . . . that he had seen in this Onyx princess what others saw within their own houses; an acuteness of longing possessed him which others claimed only for old recognitions and old lovers of former lives. He was new, and it was for the first time. "Her name," his mother asked.

"Ermine," he whispered, his eyes downcast upon the patterns of the carpets, which his aunt had loomed herself in a long-past life. "Her name is Ermine."

"Boy," his mother said, "you are a droplet in the canal of *her* lives. Forget her."

It was genuine pity he heard in his mother's voice, and this was very rare. *You entertain me*, was the kindest thing she had yet said to him, high compliment, implying he might yet attain to novelty. Now her kind advice brought tears to his eyes, but he shook his head, looked up into her eyes, which he did seldom: they were very old and very wise and he sensed them forever comparing him to memories ages past.

"Does anyone," he asked, "ever forget?"

"Boy, I give you good advice. Of course I can't stop you. You'll be born a thousand times and so will she, and you'll never make up for your youth. But such longings come out again if they're not checked, in this life or the next, and they make misery. Sleep with many; make good friends, who may be born in your next life; no knowing whether you'll be man or woman or if they'll be what they are. Make many friends, that's my advice to you, so that whether some are born ahead of you and some behind, whether sexes are what they are . . . there'll be *some* who'll be glad to see you among them. That's how one makes a place for one's self. I did it ages ago before I began to remember my lives. But I've every confidence you'll remember yours at once; that's the way things are, now. And when you've a chance to choose intelligently as you do in these days, why, lad, be very glad for good advice. Don't set your affections strongly in your very first life. Make no enemies either. Think of your uncle Legran and Pertito, who kill each other in every life they live, whatever they are. Never set strong patterns. Be wise. A pattern set so early could make all your lives tragedy."

"I love her," he said with all the hopeless fervor of his fourteen unprefaced years.

"Oh, my dear," his mother said, and sadly shook her head. She was about to tell him one of her lives, he knew, and he looked again at the carpet, doomed to endure it.

He did not see Onyx Ermine again that year, not the next nor the two succeeding: his mother maneuvered the matter very delicately and he was thwarted. But in his eighteenth year the quarrel Pertito had with uncle Legran broke into feud, and his mother died, stabbed in the midst of the argument.

Complications, she had warned him. He stood looking at her coffin the day of the funeral and fretted bitterly for the loss of her who had been his best and friendliest adviser, fretted also for her sake, that she had been woven into a pattern she had warned him to avoid. Pertito and Legran were both there, looking hate at one another. "You've involved Claudette," Pertito had shouted at Legran while she lay dying on the carpet between them; and the feud was more bitter between the two than it had ever been, for they had both loved Claudette, his mother. It would not be long, he thought with the limits of his experience in such matters, before Pertito and Legran would follow her. He was wise and did not hate them, wrenched himself away from the small gathering of family and wider collection of curious outside Jade Palace, for he had other things to do with his lives, and he thought that his mother would much applaud his good sense.

But while he was walking away from the gathering he saw Ermine standing there among her kin of Onyx.

And if she had been beautiful when they were both fourteen, she was more so now. He stood and stared at her, a vision of white silk and pearls from the Sin, of pale hair and pink flushed skin. It was Ermine who drew him back to his mother's funeral . . . Claudette, he must think of his mother now, by her true name, for she had stopped being his mother, and might at this moment be born far across the City, to begin her journey back to them. This mourning was only ceremony, a farewell of sorts, excuse for a party. It grew, as they walked the stairs past the thundering waters of the Sin, as more and more curious attached themselves and asked who had died, and how, and the tale was told and retold at other levels. But it was the kin who really knew her who did the telling; in his own low estate he kept silent and soon grew disaffected from all the empty show . . . his eyes were only for Ermine.

He moved to her side as they walked constantly down the long stairs which wrapped the chute of the Sin. "Might we meet after?" he asked, not looking at her, for shyness was the rule of his life.

He felt her look at him; at least he perceived a movement, a certain silence, and the heat crept to his face. "I think we might," she said, and his heart pounded in his breast

Never set strong patterns, Claudette had warned him; and before her body was entombed her voice seemed far away, and her advice less wise than it had seemed. After all, *she* had passed that way, and he was about to live life on his own.

I shall be wise, he promised her ghost. Claudette would be a child of his generation, surely . . . perhaps . . . the thought stunned him, perhaps his own with Ermine's. She would be very welcome if she were. He would tell her so many things that he would have learned by then. It would be one of those rare, forever marriages, himself with Ermine; Ermine would love him . . . such a drawing could not be one-sided. The feeling soaring in him was the whole world and it was unreasonable to him that Ermine could go unmoved.

He was four years wiser than he had been, and filled with all the history he had been able to consume by reading and listening.

Pertito and Legran argued loudly near him. He paid them no heed. They reached the level of the tombs, far below the course of the Sin, and with great solemnity—all of them loved pomp when there was excuse for it—conveyed Claudette to her tomb. The populace was delighted when Pertito accused Legran of the murder; was elated when the whole funeral degenerated into a brawl, and the Pertito/Legran quarrel embroiled others. It found grand climax when knives were drawn, and uncle Legran and Pertito vowed suicide to expiate the wrong done

Claudette. This was a grand new turn to the centuries-old drama, and the crowd gasped and applauded, profoundly delighted by a variation in a vendetta more than thirty centuries old. The two walked ahead of the returning crowd, and from the tenth level, leaped into the chute of the Sin, to the thunderous applause of much of the City. Everyone was cheerful, anticipating a change in the drama in their next lives. Novelty—it was so rarely achieved, and so to be savored. The souls of Pertito and Legran would be welcomed wherever they incarnated, and there would be an orgy to commemorate the day's grand events, in the fond hope of hastening the return of the three most delightsome participants in the cycles of the City.

And Jade Alain fairly skipped up the long, long stairs above the thundering flood of the Sin, to change his garments for festal clothes, his very best, and to attend on Onyx Ermine.

He decked himself in sable and the green and white stones of his name, and with a smile on his face and a lightness in his step he walked to the doors of Onyx Palace.

There were no locks, of course, nor guards. The criminals of the City were centuries adept and not so crude. He walked in quite freely as he had come in company to the great anniversaries of the houses, asked of an Onyx child where might be the princess Ermine. The wise-eyed child looked him up and down and solemnly led him through the maze of corridors, into a white and yellow hall, where Ermine sat in a cluster of young friends.

"Why, it's the Jade youth," she said delightedly.

"It's Jade Alain," another yawned. "He's very new."

"Go away," Ermine bade them all. They departed in no great haste. The bored one paused to look Alain up and down, but Alain avoided the eyes . . . looked up only when he was alone with Ermine.

"Come here," she said. He came and knelt and pressed her hand.

"I've come," he said, "to pay you court, Onyx Ermine."

"To sleep with me?"

"To pay you court," he said. "To marry you."

She gave a little laugh. "I'm not wont to marry. I have very seldom married."

"I love you," he said. "I've loved you for four years."

"Only that?" Her laugh was sweet. He looked up into her eyes and wished that he had not, for the age that was there. "Four years," she mocked him. "But how old are you, Jade Alain?"

"It's," he said in a faint voice, "my first life. And I've never loved anyone but you."

"Charming," she said, and leaned and kissed him on the lips, took both his hands and drew them to her heart. "And shall we be lovers this afternoon?"

He accepted. It was a delirium, a dream half true. She brought him through halls of white and yellow stone and into a room with a bed of saffron satin. They made love there all the afternoon, though he was naïve and she sometimes laughed at his innocence; though sometimes he would look by mistake into her eyes and see all the ages of the City looking back at him. And at last they slept; and at last they woke.

"Come back again," she said, "when you're reborn. We shall find pleasure in it."

"Ermine," he cried. "Ermine!"

But she left the bed and shrugged into her gown, called attendants and lingered there among the maids, laughter in her aged eyes. "In Onyx Palace, newborn lover, the likes of you are servants . . . like these, even after several lifetimes. What decadences Jade tolerates to bring one up a prince! You have diverted me, put a crown on a memorable day. Now begone. I sense myself about to be bored."

He was stunned. He sat a good long moment after she had left in the company of her maids, heart-wounded and with heat flaming in his face. But then, the reborn were accustomed to speak to him and to each other with the utmost arrogance. He thought it a testing, as his mother had tested him, as Pertito and Legran had called him hopelessly young, but not without affection . . . He thought, sitting there, and thought, when he had dressed to leave . . . and concluded that he had not utterly failed to amuse. It was novelty he lacked.

He might achieve this by some flamboyance, a fourth Jade death . . . hastening into that next life . . . but he would miss Onyx Ermine by the years that she would continue to live, and he would suffer through lifetimes before they were matched in age again.

He despaired. He dressed again and walked out to seek her in the halls, found her at last in the company of Onyx friends, and the room echoing with laughter.

At him.

It died for a moment when she saw him standing there. She held out her hand to him with displeasure in her eyes, and he came to her, stood among them.

There was a soft titter from those around her.

"You should have sent him to me," a woman older than the others whispered, and there was general laughter.

"For you there *is* no novelty," Ermine laughed. She lolled carelessly upon her chair and looked up at Alain. "Do go now, before you become still more distressed. Shall I introduce you to my last husband?" She stroked the arm of the young woman nearest her. "She was. But that was very long ago. And already you are dangerously predictable. I fear I shall be bored."

"Oh, how can we be?" the woman who had been her husband laughed. "We shall be entertained at Jade's expense for years. He's very determined. Just look at him. This is the sort of fellow who can make a pattern, isn't he? Dear Ermine, he'll plague us all before he's done, create some nasty scandal and we shall all be like Legran and Pertito and poor Claudette . . . or whatever their names will be. We shall be sitting in this room cycle after cycle fending away this impertinent fellow."

"How distressing," someone yawned.

The laughter rippled round again, and Ermine rose from her chair, took his burning face in her two hands and smiled at him. "I cannot even remember being the creature you are. There is no hope for you. Don't you know that I'm one of the oldest in Onyx? You've had your education. Begone."

"Four years," someone laughed. "She won't look at me after thirty lifetimes."

"Good-bye," she said.

"What might I do," he asked quietly, "to convince you of novelty and persuade you, in this life or the next?"

Then she did laugh, and thought a moment. "Die the death for love of me. No one has done that."

"And will you marry me before that? It's certain there's no bargain after."

There was a shocked murmur among her friends, and the flush drained from the cheeks of Onyx Ermine.

"He's quite mad," someone said.

"Onyx offered a wager," he said. "Jade would never say what it doesn't mean. Shall I tell this in Jade, and amuse my elders with the tale?"

"I shall give you four years," she said, "since you reckon that a very long time."

"You will marry me."

"You will die the death after that fourth year, and I shall not be bothered with you in the next life."

"No," he said. "You will not be bothered."

There was no more laughter. He had achieved novelty. The older woman clapped her hands solemnly, and the others joined the applause. Ermine inclined her head to them, and to him; he bowed to all of them in turn.

"Arrange it," she said.

It was a grand wedding, the more so because weddings were rare, on the banks of the Sin where alone in the City there was room enough to contain the crowd. Alain wore black with white stones; Ermine wore white with yellow gold. There was dancing and feasting and the dark waters of the Sin glistened with the lights of lanterns and sparkling fires, with jewel-lights and the glowing colors of the various palaces of the City.

And afterward there was long, slow lovemaking, while the celebrants outside the doors of Jade Palace drank themselves giddy and feted a thing no one had ever seen, so bizarre a bargain, with all honor to the pair which had contrived it.

In days following the wedding all the City filed into Jade to pay courtesy, and to see the wedded couple . . . to applaud politely the innovation of the youngest and most tragic prince of the City. It was the more poignant because it was real tragedy. It eclipsed that of the Grand Cyclics. It was one of the marks of the age, an event unduplicatable, and no one wished to miss it.

Even the Death came, almost the last of the visitors, and that was an event which crowned all the outré affair, an arrival which struck dumb those who were in line to pay their respects and rewarded those who happened to be there that day with the most bizarre and terrible vision of all.

She had come far, up all the many turnings of the stairs from the nether depths of the City, where she kept her solitary lair near the tombs. She came robed and veiled in black, a spot of darkness in the line. At first no one realized the nature of this guest, but all at once the oldest did, and whispered to the others.

Onyx Ermine knew, being among the oldest, and rose from her throne in sudden horror. Alain stood and held Ermine's hand, with a sinking in his heart.

Their guest came closer, swathed in her robes . . . she, rumor held it, had a right to Jade, who had been born here—not born at all, others said, but engendered of all the deaths the City never died. She drank souls and lives. She had prowled among them in the ancient past like a beast, taking the unwilling, appearing where she would in the shadows.

But at last she established herself by the tombs below, for she found some who sought her, those miserable in their incarnations, those whose every life had become intolerable pain. She was the only death in the City from which there was no rebirth.

She was the one by whom the irreverent swore, lacking other terrors.

"Go away," the eldest of Jade said to her.

"But I have come to the wedding," the Death said. It was a woman's voice beneath the veils. "Am I not party to this? I was not consulted, but shall I not agree?"

"We have heard," said Onyx Ermine, who was of too many lifetimes to be set back for long, "we have heard that you are not selective."

"Ah," said the Death. "Not lately indeed; so few have come to me. But shall I not seal the bargain?"

There was silence, dread silence. And with a soft whispering of her robes the Death walked forward, held out her hands to Jade Alain, leaned forward for a kiss.

He bent, shut his eyes, for the veil was gauze, and he had no wish to see. It was hard enough to bear the eyes of the many-lived; he had no wish at all to gaze into hers, to see what rumor whispered he should find there, all the souls she had ever drunk. Her lips were warm through the gauze, touched lightly, and her hands on his were delicate and kind.

She walked away then. He felt Ermine's hand take his, cold and sweating. He settled again into the presence hall throne and Ermine took her seat beside him. There was awe on faces around them, but no applause.

"She has come out again," someone whispered. "And she hasn't done that in ages. But I remember the old days. She may hunt again. She's *awake*, and interested."

"It's Onyx's doing," another voice whispered. And in that coldness the last of the wedding guests drifted out.

The doors of Jade Palace closed. "Bar them," the eldest said. It was for the first time in centuries.

And Ermine's hand lay very cold in Alain's.

"Madam," he said, "are you satisfied?"

She gave no answer, nor spoke of it after.

There were seasons in the City. They were marked in anniversaries of the Palaces, in exquisite entertainments, in births and deaths.

The return of Claudette was one such event, when a year-old child with wise blue eyes announced his former name, and old friends came to toast the occasion.

The return of Legran and Pertito was another, for they were twin girls in Onyx, and this complication titillated the whole City with speculations which would take years to prove.

The presence of Jade Alain at each of these events was remarked with a poignancy which satisfied everyone with sensitivity, in the remarkable realization that Onyx Ermine, who hid in disgrace, would inevitably return to them, and this most exquisite of youths would not.

One of the greatest Cycles and one of the briefest lives existed in intimate connection. It promised change.

And as for the Death, she had no need to hunt, for the lesser souls, seeking to imitate fashion in this drama, flocked to her lair in unusual number . . . some curious and some self-destructive, seeking their one great moment of passion and notoriety, when a thousand thousand years had failed to give them fame.

They failed of it, of course, for such demises were only following a fashion, not setting one; and they lacked inventiveness in their endings as in their lives.

It was for the fourth year the City waited.

And in its beginning:

"It is three-fourths gone," Onyx Ermine said. She had grown paler still in her shamed confinement within Jade Palace. In days before this anniversary of their wedding she had received old friends from Onyx, the first time in their wedded life she had received callers. He had remarked then a change in her lovemaking, that what had been pleasantly indifferent acquired . . . passion. It was perhaps the rise in her spirits. There were other possibilities, involving a former lover. He was twenty-two and saw things more clearly than once he had.

"You will be losing something," he reminded her coldly, "beyond recall and without repetition. That should enliven your long life."

"Ah," she said, "don't speak of it. I repent the bargain. I don't want this horrid thing, I don't; I don't want you to die."

"It's late for that," he said.

"I love you."

That surprised him, brought a frown to his brow and almost a warmth to his heart, but he could muster only sadness. "You don't," he said. "You love the novelty I've brought. You have never loved a living being, not in all your lifetimes. You never could have loved. That is the nature of Onyx."

"No. You don't know. Please. Jade depresses me. Please let's go and spend the year in Onyx, among my friends. I must recover them, build back my old associations. I shall be all alone otherwise. If you care anything at all for my happiness, let's go home to Onyx."

"If you wish," he said, for it was the first time that she had shown him her heart, and he imagined that it might be very fearsome for one so long incarnate in one place to spend too much time apart from it. His own attachments were ephemeral. "Will it make you content?"

"I shall be very grateful," she said, and put her arms about his neck and kissed him tenderly.

They went that day, and Onyx received them, a restrained but festive occasion as befitted Ermine's public disfavor . . . but she fairly glowed with life, as if all the shadows she had dreaded in Jade were gone. "Let us make love," she said, "oh, now!" And they lay all afternoon in the saffron bed, a slow and pleasant time.

"You're happy," he said to her. "You're finally happy."

"I love you," she whispered in his ear as they dressed for dinner, she in her white and pearls and he in his black and his green jade. "Oh, let us stay here and not think of other things."

"Or of year's end?" he asked, finding that thought incredibly difficult, this day, to bear.

"Hush," she said, and gave him white wine to drink.

They drank together from opposite sides of one goblet, sat down on the bed and mingled wine and kisses. He felt strangely numb, lay back, with the first intimation of betrayal. He watched her cross the room, open the door. A tear slipped from his eye, but it was anger as much as pain.

"Take him away," Onyx Ermine whispered to her friends. "Oh, take him quickly and end this. *She* will not care if he comes early."

"The risk we run . . ."

"Would you have her come *here?* For three years I have lived in misery, seeing *her* in every shadow. I can't bear it longer. I can't bear touching what I'm going to lose. Take him there. Now."

He tried to speak. He could not. They wrapped him in the sheets and satin cover and carried him, a short distance at first, and then to the stairs, by many stages. He heard finally the thunder of the falls of the Sin, and the echoes of the lower levels . . . heard the murmur of spectators near him at times, and knew that none but Jade might have interfered. They were all merely spectators. That was all they wished to be, to avoid complications.

Even, perhaps, Jade itself . . . observed.

They laid him down at last in a place where feet scuffed dryly on dust, and fled, and left silence and dark. He lay long still, until a tingling in his fingers turned to pain, which traveled all his limbs and left him able again to move. He stirred, and staggered to his feet, cold in a bitter wind, chilled by the lonely dark. From before him came the dim light of lamps, and a shadow sat between them.

"You are betrayed," the Death said.

He wrapped his arms about him against the chill and stared at her.

"She doesn't love you," said the Death. "Don't you know that?"

"I knew," he said. "But then, no one ever did. They've forgotten how."

The Death lifted her hands to the veils and let them fall. She was beautiful, pale of skin, with ebon hair and a blood-red stain of rubies at her brow. She held out hands to him, rising. And when she came to him, he did not look away. "Some change their minds," she said. "Even those who come of their own will."

The eyes were strange, constantly shifting in subtle tones . . . the fires, perhaps, or all the souls she had drunk, all the torment. "I bring peace," she said. "If I did not exist, there would be no way out. And they would all go mad. I am their choice. I am possibility. I am change in the cycles."

He gazed into the flickerings, the all-too-tenanted eyes. "How is it done?" he asked, fearing to know.

She embraced him, and laid her head at his shoulder. He flinched from a tiny sharp pain at his throat, quickly done. A chill grew in his limbs, a slight giddiness like love.

"Go back," she said releasing him. "Run away until your time."

He stumbled back, found the door, realized belatedly her words.

"Go," she said. "I'll come for you . . . in my agreed time. I at least keep my word, Jade Alain."

And when he would have gone. . . .

"Jade Alain," she said. "I know you have moved to Onyx. I know most things in the City. Tell your wife . . . I keep my promises."

"She fears you."

"She is nothing," the Death said. "Do you fear me?"

He considered. The question found him numb. And for all his numbness he walked back to her, faced the dreadful eyes. He tested his courage by it. He tested it further, took the Death's face between his hands and returned the kiss she had given three years before.

"Ah," she said. "That was kind."

"You are gentle," he said. "I shall not mind."

"Sad Jade prince. Go. Go away just now."

He turned away, walked out the grim doorway into the light, walked up the stairs, a long, long walk, in which there were few passersby, for it was what passed for night in the City now, and of that he was very glad, because of the shame which Onyx had dealt him and the anger he felt. Those who did see him stared, and muttered behind their hands and shrank away. So did those at the doors of Onyx, who blanched and began to bar his way.

But the doors opened, and Ermine's several friends stood with knives.

"Go away," they said.

"That was not the bargain," he replied.

"Your wife is the bargain," the oldest woman said. "Take Ermine back to Jade. Don't involve us."

"*No,*" Ermine wailed from the hall beyond; but they brought her to him, and he took her by the hand and dragged her along to his own doors. She ceased struggling. They entered within the ornate halls of Jade Palace, and under the fearful eyes of his own kin, he drew her through the maze of corridors to his own apartments, and sealed the door fast behind them.

She was there. There was no possible means that she could be . . . but there the Death stood, clothed in black, among the green draperies by the bed. Ermine flung about and cried aloud, stopped by his opposing arms.

"Go," the Death said. "I've nothing to do with you yet. Your wife and I have business."

He held Ermine still, she shivering and holding to him and burying her face against him. He shook his head. "No," he said, "I can't. I can't give her to you."

"I've been offended," the Death said. "How am I to be paid for such an offense against my dignity?"

He thought a moment. Smoothed Ermine's pale hair. "The year that I have left. What is that to me? Don't take Ermine's lives. She cares so much to save them."

"Does Ermine agree?" the Death asked.

"Yes," Ermine sobbed, refusing to look back.

He sighed, hurt at last, shook his head and put Ermine from him. The Death reached out her hand, and he came to her, embraced her,

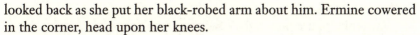

looked back as she put her black-robed arm about him. Ermine cowered in the corner, head upon her knees.

"Cousin," the Death whispered to him, for she was once of Jade. He looked into the shifting eyes, and she touched her finger first to her lips and to his; it bled, and left the blood on his lips. "Mine," she said. "As you are."

He was. He felt cold, and hungry for life, desired it more than ever he had desired it in his youth.

"I also," the Death said, "am once-born . . . and never die. Nor shall you. Nor have a name again. Nor care."

"Ermine," he whispered, to have the sight of her face again. She looked.

And screamed, and hid her face in her hands.

"When the lives grow too many," the Death said, "and you grow weary, Ermine . . . we will be waiting."

"Whenever you wish," he said to Ermine, and slipped his hand within the Death's warm hand, and went with her, the hidden ways.

Pertito shook his head sadly, poured more wine, stroked the cheek of Legran, who was his lover this cycle, and Claudette's sister. Below their vantage, beyond the balcony, a pale figure wavered on the tenth level stairs, where the Sin began its dizzying fall. "I'll wager she's on the verge again," he said. "Poor Ermine. Thousands of years and no invention left. Never more years than twenty-two. When she reaches that age . . . she's gone."

"Not this time," Legran said.

"Ah. Look. She's on the edge."

Legran stretched her neck to see, remained tranquil. "A wager?"

"Has she whispered things in your brother's ear, perhaps? Lovers' confidences?"

Legran sighed, smiled lazily, settling again. She sipped at her cup and her smoky eyes danced above the rim. A crowd was gathering to watch the impending leap.

"Do you know something?" Pertito asked.

"Ah, my tragic brother, to be in love with Ermine. Three lifetimes now he could not hold her. . . . Wager on it, my love?"

Pertito hesitated. A hundred lifetimes without variance. It was a small crowd, observing the suicide indifferently, expecting no novelty from Ermine.

"This time," Legran said, eyes dancing more, "there is a rival."

"A second lover?"

The white figure poised delicately on the topmost step of the chute. There were sighs, a polite rippling of applause.

"A very old one," Legran said. "For some months now. Ah. There she goes."

There were gasps, a dazed silence from the crowd.

Past the falls, this time, and down and down the stairs, a gleam of white and pearls.

THE HAUNTED TOWER

(London)

There were ghosts in old London, that part of London outside the walls and along the river, or at least the townsfolk outside the walls believed in them: mostly they were attributed to the fringes of the city, and the unbelievers inside the walls insisted they were manifestations of sun-struck brains, of senses deceived by the radiations of the dying star and the fogs which tended to gather near the Thames. Ghosts were certainly unfashionable for a city management which prided itself on technology, which confined most of its bulk to a well-ordered cube (geometrically perfect except for the central arch which let the Thames flow through) in which most of the inhabitants lived precisely ordered lives. London had its own spaceport, maintained offices for important offworld com-panies, and it thrived on trade. It pointed at other cities in its vicinity as declined and degenerate, but held itself as an excellent and enlightened government: since the Restoration and the New Mayoralty, reason reigned in London, and traditions were cultivated only so far as they added to the comfort of the city and those who ruled it. If the governed of the city believed in ghosts and other intangibles, well enough; re-liance on astrology and luck and ectoplasmic utterances made it less likely that the governed would seek to analyze the governors upstairs.

There were some individuals who analyzed the nature of things, and reached certain conclusions, and who made their attempts on power.

For them the Tower existed, a second cube some distance down the river, which had very old foundations and very old traditions. The use of it was an inspiration on the part of the New Mayoralty, which studied its records and found itself a way to dispose of unwanted opinion. The city was self-contained. So was the Tower. What disappeared into the Tower only rarely reappeared . . . and the river ran between, a private, unassailable highway for the damned, so that there was no untidy publicity.

Usually the voyagers were the fallen powerful, setting out from that dire river doorway of the city of London.

On this occasion one Bettine Maunfry came down the steps toward the rusty iron boat and the waters of old Thames. She had her baggage (three big boxes) brought along by the police, and though the police were grim, they did not insult her, because of who she had been, and might be again if the unseen stars favored her.

She boarded the boat in a state of shock, sat with her hands clenched in her lap and stared at something other than the police as they loaded her baggage aboard and finally closed the door of the cabin. This part of the city was an arch above the water, a darksome tunnel agleam with lights which seemed far too few; and she swallowed and clenched her hands the more tightly as the engines began to chug their way downriver toward the daylight which showed at the end.

They came finally into the wan light of the sun, colors which spread themselves amber and orange across the dirty glass of the cabin windows. The ancient ruins of old London appeared along the banks, upthrust monoliths and pillars and ruined bits of wall which no one ever had to look at but those born outside—as she had been, but she had tried to forget that.

In not so long a time there was a smooth modern wall on the left side, which was the wall of the Tower, and the boat ground and bumped its way to the landing.

Then she must get out again, and, being frightened and unsteady, she reached out her hand for the police to help her across the narrow ramp to the shore and the open gate of that wall. They helped her and passed her on to the soldier/warders, who brought her within the gates; she stood on stones which were among the most ancient things in all of ancient London, and the steel gates, which were not at all ancient, and very solid, gaped and hissed and snicked shut with ominous authority. The chief warder, a gray-haired man, led her beyond the gatehouse and into the ulterior of the Tower which, to her surprise, was not a building, but a wall, girding many buildings, many of them crumbling brick and very, very old-seeming. Guards followed with her baggage as she walked this strange, barren courtyard among the crumbling buildings.

"What are these stones?" she asked the older man who led the way, proper and militarily slim. "What are they?"

But he would not answer her, as none of them spoke to her. They escorted her to the steps of a modern Tower, which bestraddled ancient stones and made them a part of its structure, old brick with gleaming steel. The older man showed her through the gateway and up the steps, while the others followed after. It was a long climb—no lift, nothing of the sort; the lights were all shielded and the doors which they passed were all without handles.

Third level; the chief warder motioned her through a doorway just at the top of the stairs, which led to a hall ending in a closed door. She found the guards pushing her luggage past her into that short corridor, and when she did not move, the chief warder took her arm and put her through the archway, himself staying behind. "Wait," she cried, "wait," but no one waited and no one cared. The door shut. She wept, she beat at the closed door with her fists, she kicked the door and kicked it again for good measure, and finally she tried the door at the other end of the hall, pushed the only door switch she had, which let her into a grim, one-room apartment, part brick and part steel, a bed which did not look comfortable, thinly mattressed; a bathroom at least separate from the single room, a window, a wall console: she immediately and in panic pushed buttons there, but it was dead, quite dead. Tears streamed down her face and she wiped them with the back of her hand and snuffled because there was no one to see the inelegance.

She went to the window then and looked out, saw the courtyard and in it the guards who had brought her heading to the gates; and the gates opening on the river and closing again.

Fear came over her, dread that perhaps she was alone in this place and the stones and the machines might be all there was. She ran to the panel and punched buttons and pleaded, and there was nothing; then she grew anxious that the apartment door might close on its own. She scurried out into the short hallway and dragged her three cases in and sat down on the thin mattress and cried.

Tears ran out after a time; she had done a great deal of crying and none of it had helped, so she sat with her hands in her lap and hoped earnestly that the screen and the phone would come on and it would be Richard, his honor Richard Collier the Mayor, to say he had frightened her enough, and he had.

The screen did not come on. Finally she began to snuffle again and wiped her eyes and realized that she was staying at least . . . at least a little time. She gathered her clothes out of the boxes and hung them; laid out her magazines and her books and her knitting and sewing and her jewelry and her cosmetics and all the things she had packed. . . . At least they had let her pack. She went into the bath and sat down and repaired her makeup, painting on a perfectly insouciant face, and finding in this mundane act a little comfort.

She was not the sort of person who was sent to the Tower; she was only a girl, (though thirty) the Mayor's girl. She was plain Bettine Maunfry. His Honor's wife knew about her and had no resentments; it just could not be that Marge had turned on her; she was not the first girl his Honor had had, and not the only even at the moment. Richard was jealous, that was all, angry when he had found out there might be someone else, and he had power and he was using it to frighten her. It had to be. Richard had other girls and a wife, and there was no reason for him to be jealous. He had no right to be jealous. But he was; and he was vindictive. And because he was an important man, and she was no one, she was more frightened now than she had ever been in her life.

The Tower was for dangerous criminals. But Richard had been able to do this and get away with it, which she would never have dreamed; it was all too cruel a joke. He had some kind of power and the judges did what he wanted; or he never even bothered to get a court involved.

The tears threatened again, and she sniffed and stared without blinking at her reflected image until the tears dried. Her face was her defense, her beauty her protection. She had always known how to please others. She had worked all her life at it. She had learned that this was power, from the time she was a tiny girl, that she must let others have control of things, but that she could play on them and get them to do most things that she wanted. *I like people*, was the way she put it, in a dozen variants; all of which meant that as much as she hated technical things she liked to know all about different types of personalities; it sounded altruistic, and it also gave her power of the kind she wanted. Most of the time she even believed in the altruism . . . until a thing like this, until this dreadful grim joke. This time it had not worked, and none of this should be happening.

It would still work, if she could get face-to-face with Richard, and not Richard the Lord Mayor. She tested a deliberate and winning smile in the mirror, perfect teeth, a bewitching little twitch of a shoulder.

Downy lashes rimming blue eyes, a mouth which could pout and tremble and reflect emotions like the breathing of air over water, so fine, so responsive, to make a man like His Honor feel powerful . . . that was all very well: she knew how to do that. He *loved* her . . . after a possessive fashion; he had never said so, but she fed his middle-aged vanity, and that was what was hurt; that had to be it, that she had wounded him more than she had thought and he had done this, to show her he was powerful.

But he would have to come, and see how chastened she was and then he would feel sorry for what he had done, and they would make up and she would be back safe in the city again.

He would come.

She changed to her lounging gown, with a very deep neckline, and went back and combed her dark masses of hair just so, just perfect with the ruby gown with the deep plunge and the little bit of ruby glitter paler than the blood-red fabric. . . . He had given that to her. He would remember that evening when he saw her wearing it.

She waited. The silence here was deep, so, so deep. Somewhere in this great building there should be *someone* else. It was night outside the window now, and she looked out and could not bear to look out again, because it was only blackness, and reminded her she was alone. She wished that she could curtain it; she might have hung something over it, but that would make the place look shabby, and she lived by beauty. Survived by it. She sat down in the chair and turned on the light and read her magazines, articles on beauty and being desirable which now, while they had entertained her before, seemed shatteringly *important*.

Her horoscope was good; it said she should have luck in romance. She tried to take this for hopeful. She was a Pisces. Richard had given her this lovely charm which she wore about her neck; the fish had real diamond eyes. He laughed at her horoscopes, but she knew they were right.

They must be this time. *My little outsider*, he called her, because like most who believed in horoscopes, she came from outside; but she had overcome her origins. She had been a beautiful child, and because her father had worked Inside, she had gotten herself educated . . . was educated, absolutely, in all those things proper for a girl, nothing serious or studious, nothing of expertise unless it was in Working With People, because she knew that it was just not smart at all for a girl to be too obviously clever . . . modesty got a girl much further . . . that and the luck of being beautiful, which let her cry prettily. Her childish tantrums had gotten swift comfort and a chuck under the chin, while her brothers got spanked, and that was the first time she had learned about *that* kind of power, which she had always had. It was luck, and that was in the stars. And her magazines told her how to be even more pleasing and pleasant and that she succeeded in what she thought she did. That it worked was self-evident: a girl like her, from the outside, and a receptionist in His Honor the Mayor's office, and kept by him in style people Outside could not imagine. . . .

Only there were bad parts to it too, and being here was one, that she had never planned for—

A door opened somewhere below. Her heart jumped. She started to spring up and then thought that she should seem casual and then that she should not, that she should seem anxious and worried, which was why Richard had sent her here. Perhaps she should cry. Perhaps it was Richard. It *must* be Richard.

She put the magazine away and fretted with her hands, for once in her life not knowing what to do with them, but even this was a pretty gesture and she knew that it was.

The door opened. It was the military warden, with dinner.

"I can't eat," she said. It seemed upon the instant that intense depression was the ploy to use. She turned her face away, but he walked in and set it on the table.

"That's your business," he said, and started to leave.

"Wait." He stopped and she turned her best pleading look on him . . . an older man and the kind who could be intensely flattered by beauty . . . flattered, if she seemed vulnerable, and she put on that air. "Please. Is there any word . . . from Richard?"

"No," he said, distressingly impervious. "Don't expect any."

"Please. Please tell him that I want to talk to him."

"If he asks."

"Please. My phone doesn't work."

"Not supposed to. It doesn't work for all prisoners. Just those with privileges. You don't have any."

"*Tell* him I want to see him. Tell him. It's his message. Won't *he* decide whether he wants to hear it?"

That got through. She saw the mouth indecisive. The man closed the door; she heard the steps going away. She clutched her hands together, finding them shaking.

And she ignored the food, got out her magazine again and tried to read, but it hardly occupied her mind. She dared not sit on the bed and prop her knees up and read; or sit down to eat; it was too informal, too unlovely. She started to run her hand through her hair, but that would disarrange it. She fretted back and forth across the floor, back and forth, and finally she decided she could put on her negligee and if His Honor walked in on her that was to the better.

She took out not the bright orange one, but the white, lace-trimmed, transparent only here and there, innocent; innocence seemed precious at the moment. She went to the mirror in the bath, wiped off the lipstick and washed her face and did it all over again, in soft pinks and rosy blushes; she felt braver then. But when she came out again to go to bed, there was that black window, void and cold and without any curtain against the night. It was very lonely to sleep in this place. She could not bear to be alone.

And she had slept alone many a night until Tom had come into her life. Tom Ash was a clerk in the Mayor's office in just the next office over from hers; and he was sweet and kind . . . after all, she was beautiful, and still young, only thirty, and seven years she had given to Richard, who was not handsome, though he was attractive after the fashion of older, powerful men; but Tom was . . . Tom was handsome, and a good lover and all those things romances said she was due, and he loved her moreover. He had said so.

Richard did not know about him. Only suspected. Tom had got out the door before Richard arrived, and there was no way in the world Richard could know who it was; more to the point, Richard had asked who it was.

And if Richard had power to put her here despite all the laws, he had power to put Tom here too, and maybe to do worse things.

She was not going to confess to Richard, that was all. She was not going to confess, or she would tell him some other name and let Richard try to figure it all out.

Richard had no proof of anything.

And besides, he did not own her.

Only she liked the good things and the pretty clothes and the nice apartment Tom could never give her. Even her jewelry . . . Richard could figure out a way to take that back. Could blacklist her so she could never find a job, so that she would end up outside the walls, exiled.

She was reading a romance about a woman who had gotten herself into a similar romantic triangle, and it was all too very much like her situation. She was almost afraid to find out how it ended. Light reading. She had always liked light reading, about real, *involved* people, but of a sudden it was much too dramatic and involved her.

But it had to have a happy ending; all such stories did, which was why she kept reading them, to assure herself that she would, and that beautiful women could go on being clever and having happy endings.

Whoever *wanted* tragedy?

She grew weary of reading, having lost the thread of it many times, and arranged the pillows, and having arranged herself as decorously as she could, pushed the light switch by the head of the bed and closed her eyes.

She did sleep a time, more exhausted than she had known, and came to herself with the distinct impression that there had been someone whispering nearby, two someones, in very light voices.

Children, of all things; children in the Tower.

She opened her eyes, gaped upon candlelight, and saw to her wonder two little boys against the brick wall, boys dressed in red and blue brocades, with pale faces, tousled hair and marvelous bright eyes.

"Oh," said one, "she's awake."

"Who are you?" she demanded.

"She's beautiful," said the other. "I wonder if she's nice."

She sat bolt upright, and they held each other as if *she* had frightened them . . . they could hardly be much more than twelve . . . and stared at her wide-eyed.

"Who *are* you?" she asked.

"I'm Edward," said one; "I'm Richard," said the other.

"And how did you get in here?"

Edward let go Richard's arm, pointed vaguely down. "We live here," said young Edward, and part of his hand seemed to go right through the wall.

Then she realized what they must be if they were not a dream, and the hair rose on the back of her neck and she drew the sheet up to cover her, for they *were* children, and she was little covered by the gown. They were quaint and somewhat wise-eyed children, in grown-up clothes which seemed old and dusty.

"How did you get here?" Richard echoed her own question. "Who sent you here? Are you Queen?"

"Richard Collier. The Lord Mayor."

"Ah, said Edward. "A Richard sent us here too. He's supposed to have murdered us both. But he didn't, you know."

She shook her head. She did not know. She never bothered with history. She kept clinging to the idea that they were a dream, some old school lesson come out of her subconscious, for while she believed in ghosts and horoscopes, her mind was reeling under the previous shocks.

"We always come first," said Edward. "I am a king, you know."

"First? What *are* you? What are you doing here?"

"Why, much the same as everyone else," young Edward laughed, and his eyes, while his face was that of a child, now seemed fearsomely old. "We live here, that's all. What's your name?"

"Bettine."

"Bettine? How strange a name. But most are strange now. And so few come here, after all. Do you think he will let you go?"

"Of course he'll let me go."

"Very few ever leave. And no one leaves . . . lately."

"You're dead," she cried. "Go away. Go away."

"We've been dead longer than you've been alive," said Richard.

"Longer than this London's stood here," said Edward. "I liked my London better. It was brighter. I shall always prefer it. Do you play cards?"

She sat and shivered, and Richard tugged at Edward's sleeve.

"I think we should go," said Richard. "I think she's about to be afraid."

"She's very pretty," said Edward. "But I don't think it's going to do her any good."

"It never does," said Richard.

"I go first," said Edward, "being King."

And he vanished, right through the wall; and Richard followed; and the candle glow went out, leaving dark.

Bettine sat still, and held the bedclothes about her, and finally reached for the light button, feverishly, madly, and blinked in the white glare that showed nothing wrong, nothing at all wrong. But there was a deathly chill in the air.

She had dreamed. This strange old place gave her nightmares. It had to be that. Tears ran from her eyes. She shivered and finally she got up and picked at her cold dinner because she wanted something to take her mind off the solitude. She would not look up at the window over the table, not while there was night outside.

She would have shadows beneath her eyes in the morning, and she would not be beautiful, and she had to be. At last she gathered the courage to go back to bed, and lay wrapped in her nightrobe and shivering, in the full light, which she refused to turn out.

She tried the phone again in the morning, and it still refused to work. She found everything saner with the daylight coming in through the window again and the room seemed warmer because of it. She bathed and washed her hair and dried it, brushing it meticulously. It had natural curl and she fashioned it in ringlets and tried it this way and that about her face.

Suddenly the door open on the short hallway closed; she sprang up and looked toward it in consternation, heard footsteps downstairs and dithered about in panic, finally flung on a dress and fluffed her hair and while she heard footsteps coming up the long stairs, leaned near the mirror in the bath and put on her makeup with swift, sure strokes, not the full job, which she had no time for, but at least the touch of definition to the eyes, the blush to lips and cheeks. . . .

It was Richard come to see her, come to ask if she had had enough, and she had, oh, she had. . . .

The far-side door opened. She ran to the door on her side, waited, hands clasped, anxious, meaning to appear anxious and contrite and everything and anything that he should want.

Then the outer door closed again; and hers opened. She rushed to meet her visitor.

There was only a breakfast tray, left on the floor, and the door closed, the footsteps receding.

"Come back!" she cried, wept, wailed.

The steps went on, down the stairs.

She stood there and cried a good long time; and then because she found nothing else to do, she gathered up the tray. She had to bend down to do it, which disarranged her hair and upset her and humiliated her even with no one to see it. She was angry and frightened and wanted to throw the tray and break all the things in sight; but that would make a terrible mess of food and she reckoned that she would have to live in it if she did that, or clean it up herself, so she spared herself such labor and carried it meekly back to the table. She was sick to her stomach, and there was the old food tray which was smelling by now, and the new one which brought new, heavy aromas. She considered them both with her stomach tight with fear and her throat so constricted with anger and frustration that she could not swallow her breaths, let alone the food.

She carried the old tray to the anteroom and set it on the floor, and suddenly, with inspiration, began to search through her belongings for paper . . . she *had* brought some, with the sewing kit, because she made patterns for her embroideries and for her knitting. She searched through the needles and the yarns and found it at the bottom, found the pen, sat down at the desk and chewed the pen's cap, trying to think.

"Richard," she wrote, not "Dearest Richard," which she thought might not be the right approach to an angry man. "I am frightened here. I must see you. Please. Bettine."

That was right, she thought. To be restrained, to be calm, and at the same time dissuade him from doing worse to frighten her. Pathos. That was the tone of it. She folded it up, and with a clever impulse, stitched thread through it to seal it, so that the jailer should not be getting curious without making it obvious. "To His Honor Richard Collier," she wrote on the outside, in the beautiful letters she had practiced making again and again. And then she took it and set it in the supper tray, out in the hall, so that it should leave with the dishes and whoever got it would have to think what to do with it. And throwing away a letter to the Mayor was not a wise thing to do.

She sniffed then, satisfied, and sat down and ate her breakfast, which did fill a little bit of the loneliness in her stomach, and made her feel guilty and miserable afterward, because she had eaten too much; she would get fat, that was what they wanted, feeding her all that and leaving her nothing to do but eat; she would soon be fat and unlovely if there was nothing to do here but eat and pace the floor.

And maybe she would be here a long time. That began to penetrate her with a force it had not until now. A second day in this place . . . and how many days; and she would run out of things to read and to do . . . she set the second tray in the hall too, to be rid of the smell of the food, and punched buttons trying to close the door from inside; the whole console was complicated, and she started punching buttons at random. There were controls she did not know; she punched buttons in different combinations and only succeeded in getting the lights out in a way in which she could not get them on again, not from any combination of buttons until finally she punched the one by the bed. That frightened her, that she might cut off the heating or lose the lighting entirely and be alone in the dark when the sun should go down. She stopped punching buttons, knowing nothing of what she was doing with them, although when she had been in school there had been a course in managing the computers . . . but that was something the other girls did, who had plain long faces and fastened their hair back and had flat bodies and thought of nothing but studying and working. She hated them. Hated the whole thing. Hated prisons that could be made of such things.

She picked up her knitting and thought of Tom, of his eyes, his body, his voice . . . he *loved* her; and Richard did not, perhaps, but used her because she was beautiful, and one had to put up with that. It brought things. Would buy her way out of here. Richard might be proud and angry and have his feelings hurt, but ultimately he would want his pride salved, and she could do that, abundantly, assuring him that she was contrite, which was all she had to do, ultimately.

It was Tom she daydreamed of, wondering where he was and if he was in the Tower too. Oh, surely, surely not; but the books she read seemed so frighteningly real, and dire things happened for jealousy. She began to think of Tom in that kind of trouble, while her hands plied the colored yarns, knitting click, click, click, measuring out the time, stitch by stitch and row by row. Women did such things and went on doing them while the sun died because in all of women's lives there were so many moments that would kill the mind if one thought about them, which would suck the heart and the life out of one, and engrave lines in the face and put gray in the hair if ever one let one's mind work; but there was in the rhythm and the fascination of the stitches a loss of thought, a void, a blank, that was only numbers and not even that, because the mind did not need to count, the fingers did, the length of a thread against the finger measured evenly as a ruler could divide it, the slight difference in tension sensed finely as a machine could sense, the exact *number* of stitches keeping pattern without really the need to count, but something inward and regular as the beat of a heart, as the slow passing of time which could be frozen in such acts, or speeded past.

So the day passed; and click, click, click the needles went, using up the yarn, when she did not read; and she wound more and knitted more, row upon row, not thinking.

There was no noon meal; the sun began to fade, and the room grew more chill. I shall have to ask for more yarn someday, she thought with surprising placidity, and realized what that thought implied and refused to think anymore. At last she heard the steps coming up to the door and this time she refused to spring up and expect it to be Richard. She went right on with her knitting, click, click, while the steps came up and opened the door and closed it again.

Then quite calmly she went out and retrieved the new tray, saw with a little surge of hope that the message and the trays had gone. So, she thought; so, it will get to him; and she sat down and had her dinner, but not all of it. She took the tray out to the anteroom after, and went back and prepared herself for bed.

The light faded from the window, and the outside became black again; again she avoided looking toward it, because it so depressed her, and made the little room on the third level so lonely and so isolated.

And again she went to bed with the light on, because she was not willing to suffer more such illusions . . . they *were* illusions, and she put her mind from them all day long. She *believed* in supernatural things, but it had stopped being something which happened to someone else, and something which waited to happen to her, which was not shivery-entertaining, not in the least. It rather made her fear she was losing touch with things and losing control of her imagination, and she refused to have that happen.

She put on her white negligee again, reckoning that she just could be summoned out of bed by a phone call . . . after all, the message *could* be carried to His Honor Richard Collier direct. But it was more likely that it would go to his office instead, and that the call would come to-morrow, so she could relax just a bit and get some sleep, which she really needed. She was not actually afraid this second night and so long as lights were on, there was no likelihood that she would have silly dreams about dead children.

Dead children. She shuddered, appalled that such a dream could have come out of her own imagination; it was not at all the kind of thing that a girl wanted to think about

Tom . . . now *he* was worth thinking about.

She read her story; and the woman in the story had problems *not* direr than hers, which made her own seem worse and the story seem trivial; but it was going to be a happy ending. She was sure that it would, which would cheer her up.

Would they give her more books, she wondered, when these ran out? She thought that in the morning she would put another note on the tray and ask for books for herself; and maybe she should not, because that would admit to the jailer that she thought she was staying; and *that* would get to Richard too, who would ask how she was bearing up. She was sure that he would ask.

No. She would not ask for things to indicate a long stay here. They might give them to her, and she could not bear that.

Again she found she was losing the thread of the story, and she laid the book down against the side of the bed. She tried to think of Tom and could not, losing the thread of him too. She dreamed only the needles, back and forth, in and out, click.

The light dimmed . . . to candlelight; she felt it dim through her closed lids; and she cracked a lid very carefully, her muscles rigid and near to shivering. The dream was back; she heard the children laughing together.

"Well," said Edward's voice, "hello, Bettine."

She looked; she had to, not knowing how near they were, afraid they might touch her. They were standing against the bricks again, both of them, solemn-faced like boys holding some great joke confined for the briefest of moments.

"Of course we're back," said the boy Richard. "How are you, lady Bettine?"

"Go away," she said; and then the least little part of her heart said that she did not really want them to go. She blinked and sat up, and there was a woman walking toward her out of the wall, who became larger and larger as the boys retreated. The newcomer was beautiful, in an ancient mode, wearing a golden brocade gown. The visitor dipped a curtsy to the boy king Edward, who bowed to her. "Madam," the boy-king said; and "Majesty," said the stranger, and turned curious eyes on *her*. "She is Bettine," said Edward. "Be polite, Bettine: Anne is one of the queens."

"Queen Anne?" asked Bettine, wishing that she knew a little more of the ancient Tower. If one was to be haunted, it would be at least helpful to know by whom; but she had paid very little attention to history— there was so much of it.

"Boleyn," said the queen, and spread her skirts and sat on the end of her bed, narrowly missing her feet, very forthright for a dream. "And how are you, my dear?"

"Very well, thank you, Majesty."

The boys laughed. "She only half believes in us, but she plays the game, doesn't she? They don't have queens now."

"How pretty she is," said the queen. "So was I."

"I'm not staying here," Bettine said. It seemed important in this web of illusions to have that clear. "I don't really believe in you entirely. I'm dreaming this anyway."

"You're not, my dear, but there, there, believe what you like." The queen turned, looked back; the children had gone, and another was coming through, a handsome man in elegant brocade. "Robert Devereaux," said Anne. "Robert, her name is Bettine."

"Who is he?" Bettine asked. "Is he the king?"

The man named Robert laughed gently and swept a bow; "I might have been," he said. "But things went wrong."

"Earl of Essex," said Anne softly, and stood up and took his hand. "The boys said that there was someone who believed in us, all the same. How nice. It's been so long."

"You make me very nervous," she said. "If you were real I think you'd talk differently; something old. You're just like me."

Robert laughed. "But we aren't like the walls, Bettine. We do change. We listen and we learn and we watch all the passing time."

"Even the children," said Anne.

"You died here."

"Indeed we did. And the same way."

"Murdered?" she asked with a shiver.

Anne frowned. "Beheaded, my dear. Quite a few had a hand in arranging it. I was maneuvered, you see; and how should I know we were spied on?"

"You and Essex?"

"Ah, no," said Robert. "*We* weren't lovers, then."

"Only now," said Anne. "We met . . . posthumously on my part. And how are you here, my dear?"

"I'm the Mayor's girl," Bettine said. It was good to talk, to have even shadows to talk to. She sat forward, embracing her knees in her arms. Suddenly the tears began to flow, and she daubed at her eyes with the sheet, feeling a little silly to be talking to ectoplasms, which all the fashionable folk denied existed; and yet it helped. "We quarreled and he put me here."

"Oh dear," said Anne.

"Indeed," said Lord Essex, patting Anne's hand. "That's why the boys said we should come. It's very like us."

"You died for love?"

"Politics," said Anne. "So will you."

She shook her head furiously. This dream of hers was not in her control, and she tried to drag things her own way. "But it's a silly quarrel. And I don't die. They don't kill people here, they don't."

"They do," Anne whispered. "Just like they did."

"Well," said Essex, "not axes, any more. They're much neater than they were."

"Go away," Bettine cried. "Go away, go away, go away."

"You'd do well to talk with us," said Anne. "We could make you understand what you're really up against. And there's really so much you don't seem to see, Bettine."

"Don't think of love," said Essex. "It's not love, you know, that sends people here. It's only politics. I know that. And Anne does. Besides, you don't sound like someone in love, do you? You don't sound like someone in love, Bettine."

She shrugged and looked down, expecting that they would be gone when she looked up. "There *is* someone I love," she said in the faintest of whispers when she saw they were not gone.

Anne snorted delicately. "That's not worth much here. Eternity is long, Bettine. And there's love and love, Bettine." She wound insubstantial fingers with the earl's. "You mustn't think of it being love. That's not the reason you're here. Be wise, Bettine. These stones have seen a great deal come and go. So have we; and you don't have the face of one who loves."

"What do *you* know?" she cried. "You're nothing. I know *people*, believe me. And I know Richard."

"Good night, Bettine," Anne said.

"Good night," Essex said very softly and patiently, so that she did not seem to have ruffled either of them at all. And the children were back, who bowed with departing irony and faded. The lights brightened.

She flounced down among the bedclothes sulking at such depressing ideas and no small bit frightened, but not of the ghosts—of her situation. Of things they said. There was a chill in the air, and a whiff of dried old flowers and spices . . . the flowers, she thought, was Anne; and the spice must be Essex. Or maybe it was the children Edward and Richard. The apparitions did not threaten her; they only spoke her fears. That was what they really were, after all. Ectoplasms, indeed. She burrowed into the covers and punched out the lights, having dispensed with fear of ghosts; her eyes hurt and she was tired. She lay down with utter abandon, which she had really not done since she came, burrowed among the pillows and tried not to think or dream at all.

In the morning the phone came on and the screen lit up.

"Bettine," said Richard's voice, stern and angry.

She sprang up out of the covers, went blank for a moment and then assumed one of her bedroom looks, pushed her thick masses of hair looser on her head, stood up with a sinuous twist of her body and looked into the camera, moue'd into a worried frown, a tremble, a look near tears.

"Richard. Richard, I was so afraid. Please." Keep him feeling superior, keep him feeling great and powerful, which was what she was *for* in the world, after all, and how she lived. She came and stood before the camera, leaned there. "I want out of here, Richard. I don't understand this place." Naïveté always helped, helplessness; and it was, besides, truth. "The jailer was terrible." Jealousy, if she could provoke it. "Please, let me come back. I never meant to do anything wrong . . . what is it I've *done*, Richard?"

"Who was he?"

Her heart was beating very fast. Indignation now; set him off balance. "No one. I mean, it was just a small thing and he wasn't anyone in particular, and I never did anything like that before, Richard, but you left me alone and what's a girl to do, after all? Two weeks and you hadn't called me or talked to me—?"

"What's the *name*, Bettine? And where's the grade-fifty file? Where is it, Bettine?"

She was the one off balance. She put a shaking hand to her lips, blinked, shook her head in real disorganization. "I don't know anything about the file." This wasn't it, this wasn't what it was supposed to be about. "Honestly, Richard, I don't know. What file? Is *that* what this is? That you think I *stole* something? Richard, I never, I never stole anything."

"Someone got into the office. Someone who didn't belong there, Bettine; and you have the key, and I do, and that's a pretty limited range, isn't it? My office. My private office. Who did that, Bettine?"

"I don't know," she wailed, and pushed her hair aside—the pretty gestures were lifelong-learned and automatic. "Richard, I've gotten caught in something I don't understand at all, I don't understand, I don't, and I never let anyone in there." (But Tom had gotten in there; *he* could have, any time, since he was in the next office.) "Maybe the door . . . maybe I left it open and I shouldn't have, but Richard, I don't even know what was in that file, I swear I don't."

"Who was in your apartment that night?"

"I—it wasn't connected to that, it wasn't, Richard, and I wish you'd understand that. It wasn't anything, but that I was lonely and it was a complete mistake, and now if I gave you somebody's name then it would get somebody in trouble who just never was involved; I mean, I might have been careless, Richard, I guess I was; I'm terribly sorry about the file; but I did leave the door open sometimes, and you were gone a lot. I mean . . . it was possible someone could have gotten in there, but you never told me there was any kind of trouble like that . . ."

"The access numbers. You understand?"

"I don't. I never saw that file."

"Who was in your apartment?"

She remained silent, thinking of Tom, and her lip trembled. It went on trembling while Richard glared at her, because she could not make up her mind what she ought to do and what was safe. She could *handle* Richard. She was sure that she could. And then he blinked out on her.

"Richard!" she screamed. She punched buttons in vain. The screen was dead. She paced the floor and wrung her hands and stared out the window.

She heard the guard coming, and her door closed and the outer door opened for the exchange of the tray. Then the door gave back again and she went out into the anteroom after it. She carried the tray back and set it on the table, finally went to the bath and looked at herself, at sleep-tangled hair and shadowed eyes and the stain of old cosmetic. She was appalled at the face she had shown to Richard, at what she had been surprised into showing him. She scrubbed her face at once and brushed her hair and put slippers on her bare feet, which were chilled to numbness on the tiles.

Then she ate her breakfast, sparingly, careful of her figure, and dressed and sat and knitted. The silence seemed twice as heavy as before. She hummed to herself and tried to fill the void. She sang—she had a beautiful voice, and she sang until she feared she would grow hoarse, while the pattern grew. She read some of the time, and, bored, she found a new way to do her hair; but then she thought after she had done it that if Richard should call back he might not like it, and it was important that he like the way she looked. She combed it back the old way, all the while mistrusting this instinct, this reliance on a look which had already failed.

So the day passed, and Richard did not call again.

They wanted Tom. There was the chance that if she did give Richard Tom's name, it could be the right one, because it was all too obvious who *could* have gotten a file out of Richard's office, because there had been many times Richard had been gone and Tom had followed her about her duties, teasing her.

Safest not to ask and not to know. She was determined not to. She resented the thing that had happened—politics—politics. She hated politics.

Tom . . . was someone to love. Who loved her; and Richard had reasons which were Richard's, but it came down to two men being jealous. And Tom, being innocent, had no idea what he was up against . . . Tom could be hurt, but Richard would never hurt her; and while she did not tell Richard, she still had the power to perplex him. While he was perplexed, he would do nothing.

She was not totally confident . . . of Tom's innocence, or of Richard's attitude. She was not accustomed to saying no. She was not accustomed to being put in difficult positions. Tom should not have asked it of her. He should have known. It was not fair what he did, whatever he had gotten himself involved in—some petty little record-juggling—to have put her in this position.

The pattern grew, delicate rows of stitches, complex designs which needed no thinking, only seeing, and she wept sometimes and wiped at her eyes while she worked.

Light faded from the window. Supper came and she ate, and this night she did not prepare for bed, but wrapped her night robe about her for warmth and sat in the chair and waited, lacking all fear, expecting the children, looking forward to them in a strangely keen longing, because they were at least company, and laughter was good to hear in this grim place. Even the laughter of murdered children.

There began to be a great stillness. And not the laughter of children this time, but the tread of heavier feet, the muffled clank of metal. A grim, shadowed face materialized in dimming light.

She stood up, alarmed, and warmed her chilling hands before her lips. "Edward," she cried aloud. "Edward, Richard . . . are you there?" But what was coming toward her was taller and bare of face and arm and leg, bronze elsewhere, and wearing a *sword*, of all things. She wanted the children; wanted Anne or Robert Devereaux, any of the others. This one . . . was different.

"Bettine," he said in a voice which echoed in far distances. "Bettine."

"I don't think I like you," she said.

The ghost stopped with a little clank of armor, kept fading in and out. He was young, even handsome in a foreign way. He took off his helmet and held it under his arm. "I'm Marc," he said. "Marcus Atilius Regulus. They said I should come. Could you see your way, Bettine, to prick your finger?"

"Why should I do that?"

"I am oldest," he said. "Well—almost, and of a different persuasion, and perhaps it is old-fashioned, but it would make our speaking easier."

She picked up a sewing needle and jabbed her cold finger, once and hard, and the blood welled up black in the dim light and fell onto the stones. She put the injured finger in her mouth, and stared quite bewildered, for the visitor was very much brighter, and seemed to draw a living breath.

"Ah," he said. "Thank you with all my heart, Bettine."

"I'm not sure at all I should have done that. I think you might be dangerous."

"Ah, no, Bettine."

"Were you a soldier, some kind of knight?"

"A soldier, yes; and a knight, but not the kind you think of. I think you mean of the kind born to this land. I came from Tiberside. I am Roman, Bettine. We laid some of the oldest stones just . . ." he lifted a braceleted arm, rather confusedly toward one of the steel walls. "But most of the old work is gone now. There are older levels; all the surly ones tend to gather down there. Even new ones, and some that never were civilized, really, or never quite accepted being dead, all of them—" He made a vague and deprecating gesture. "But we don't get many now, because there hasn't been anyone in here who could believe in us . . . in so very long . . . does the finger hurt?"

"No." She sucked at it and rubbed the moisture off and looked at him more closely. "I'm not sure *I* believe in you."

"You're not sure you don't, and that's enough."

"Why are you here? Where are the others?"

"Oh, they're back there."

"But why you? Why wouldn't they come? I expected the children."

"Oh. They're there. Nice boys."

"And why did *you* come? What has a soldier to do with me?"

"I—come for the dead. I'm the psychopomp."

"The what?"

"Psychopomp. Soul-guider. When you die."

"But I'm not going to die," she wailed, hugging her arms about her and looking without wanting to at the ancient sword he wore. "There's a mistake, that's all. I've been trying to explain to the others, but they don't understand. We're civilized. We don't go around killing people in here, whatever *used* to happen. . . ."

"Oh, they *do*, Bettine; but we don't get them, because they're very stubborn, and they believe in nothing, and they can't see us. Last month I lost one. I almost had him to see me, but at the last he just couldn't; and he slipped away and I'm not sure where. It looked hopelessly drear. I try with all of them. I'm glad you're not like them."

"But you're wrong. I'm not going to die."

He shrugged, and his dark eyes looked very sad.

"I can get out of here," she said, unnerved at his lack of belief in her. "If I have to, there's always a way. I can just tell them what they want to know and they'll let me go."

"Ah," he said.

"It's true."

His young face, so lean and serious, looked sadder still. "Oh, Bettine."

"It *is* true; what do *you* know?"

"Why haven't you given them what they want before now?"

"Because. . . ." She made a gesture to explain and then shook her head. "Because I think I can get out of it without doing that."

"For pride? Or for honor?"

It sounded like something *he* should say, after all, all done up in ancient armor and carrying a sword. "You've been dead a long time," she said.

"Almost the longest of all. *Superbia*, we said. That's the wrong kind of pride; that's being puffed up and too important and not really seeing things right. And there's *exemplum*. That's a thing you do because the world needs it, like setting up something for people to look at, a little marker, to say Marcus Regulus stood here."

"And what if no one sees it? What good is it then, if I never get out of here? There's being brave and being stupid."

He shook his head very calmly. "An *exemplum* is an *exemplum* even if no one sees it. They're just markers, where someone was."

"Look outside, old ghost. The sun's going out and the world's dying."

"Still," he said, "*exempla* last . . . because there's nothing anyone can do to erase them."

"What, like old stones?"

"No. Just moments. Moments are the important thing. Not every moment, but more than some think."

"Well," she said, perplexed and bothered. "Well, that's all very well for men who go around fighting ancient wars, but I don't fight anyone. I don't like violence at all, and I'll do what I can for Tom but I'm not brave and there's a limit."

"Where, Bettine?"

The next time Richard asks me, that's where. I want out of here."

He looked sad.

"Stop that," she snapped. "I suppose you think you're superior."

"No."

"I'm just a girl who has to live and they can take my job away and I can end up outside the walls starving, that's what could happen to me."

"Yes, sometimes *exempla* just aren't quick. Mine would have been. And I failed it."

"You're a soldier. I'm a woman."

"Don't you think about honor at all, Bettine?"

"You're out of date. I stopped being a virgin when I was thirteen."

"No. *Honor*, Bettine."

"I'll bet you were some kind of hero, weren't you, some old war hero?"

"Oh no, Bettine. I wasn't. I ran away. That's why I'm the psychopomp. Because the old Tower's a terrible place; and a good many of the dead do break down as they die. There were others who could have taken the job: the children come first, usually, just to get the prisoners used to the idea of ghosts, but I come at the last . . . because I know what it is to be afraid, and what it is to want to run. I'm an Atilius Regulus, and there were heroes in my house, oh, there was a great one . . . I could tell you the story. I will, someday. But in the same family there was myself, and they were never so noble after me. *Exemplum* had something to do with it. I wish I could have left a better one. It came on me so quickly . . . a moment; one lives all one's life to be ready for moments when they come. I used to tell myself, you know, that if mine had just— crept up slowly, then I should have thought it out; I always did think. But I've seen so much, so very much, and I know human beings, and do you know . . . quick or slow in coming, it was what I *was* that made the difference, thinking or not; and I just wasn't then what I am now."

"Dead," she said vengefully.

He laughed silently. "And eons wiser." Then his face went sober. "Oh, Bettine, courage comes from being ready whenever the moment comes, not with the mind . . . I don't think anyone ever is. But what you *are* . . . can be ready."

"What happened to you?"

"I was an officer, you understand. . . ." He gestured at the armor he wore. "And when the Britons got over the rampart . . . I ran, and took all my unit with me—I didn't think what I was doing; *I* was getting clear. But a wise old centurion met me coming his way and ran me through right there. The men stopped running then and put the enemy back over the wall, indeed they did. And a lot of men were saved and discipline held. So I was an *exemplum*, after all; even if I was someone else's. It hurt. I don't mean the wound—those never do quite the way you think, I can tell you that—but I mean really hurt, so that it was a long long time before I came out in the open again—after the Tower got to be a prison. After I saw so many lives pass here. Then I decided I should come out. May I touch you?"

She drew back, bumped the chair, shivered. "That's not how you . . . ?"

"Oh, no. *I* don't take lives. May I touch you?"

She nodded mistrustingly, kept her eyes wide open as he drifted nearer and a braceleted hand came toward her face, beringed and masculine and only slightly transparent. It was like a breath of cool wind, and his young face grew wistful. Because she was beautiful, she thought, with a little rush of pride, and he was young and very handsome and very long dead.

She wondered. . . .

"Warmth," he said, his face very near and his dark eyes very beautiful. "I had gone into my melancholy again . . . in all these last long centuries, that there was no more for me to do, no souls for me to meet, no special one who believed, no one at all. I thought it was all done. Are there more who still believe?"

"Yes," she said. And started, for there were Anne and Essex holding hands within the brickwork or behind it or somewhere; and other shadowy figures. The children were there, and a man who looked very wet, with a slight reek of alcohol, and more and more and more, shadows which went from brocades to metals to leather to furs and strange helmets.

"Go away," she cried at that flood, and fled back, overturning the tray and crowding into the corner. "Get out of here. I'm not going to die. I'm not brave and I'm not going to. Let someone else do the dying. I don't want to die."

They murmured softly and faded; and there came a touch at her cheek like a cool breeze.

"Go away!" she shrieked, and she was left with only the echoes. "I'm going mad," she said then to herself, and dropped into the chair and bowed her head into her hands. When she finally went to bed, she sat fully dressed in the corner and kept the lights on.

Breakfast came, and she bathed and dressed, and read her book, which began to come to its empty and happy ending. She threw it aside, because her life was not coming out that way, and she kept thinking of Tom, and crying, not sobs, just a patient slow leaking of tears, which made her makeup run and kept her eyes swollen. She was not powerful. She had lost all illusion of that. She just wanted out of this alive, and to live and to forget it. She tried again to use the phone and she could not figure out the keyboard which she thought might give her access to *someone*, if she knew anything about such systems, and she did not.

For the first time she became convinced that she was in danger of dying here, and that, instead, Tom was going to, and she would be in a way responsible. She was no one, no one against all the anger that swirled about her. She was quite, quite helpless; and not brave at all, and nothing in her life had ever prepared her to be. She thought back to days when she was a child, and in school, and all kinds of knowledge had been laid out in front of her. She had found it useless . . . which it was, to a ten-year-old girl who thought she had the world all neatly wrapped around her finger. Who thought at that age that she knew all the things that were important, that if she went on pleasing others that the world would always be all right.

Besides, the past was about dead people and she liked living ones; and learning about science was learning that the world was in the process of ending, and there was no cheer in that. She wanted to be Bettine Maunfry who had all that she would ever need. Never think, never think about days too far ahead, or things too far to either side, or understand things, which made it necessary to decide, and prepare.

Moments. She had never wanted to imagine such moments would come. There was no time she could have looked down the long currents of her life, which had *not* been so long after all, and when she could have predicted that Bettine Maunfry would have gotten herself into a situation like this. People were supposed to take care of her. There had always been someone to take care of her. That was what it was being female and beautiful and young. It was just not supposed to happen this way.

Tom, she thought Oh, Tom, now what do I do, what am I supposed to do?

But of course the doing was hers.

To him.

She had no idea what her horoscope or his was on this date, but she thought that it must be disaster, and she fingered the little fishes which she wore still in her décolletage for His Honor Richard Collier to see.

And she waited, to bend as she had learned to bend; only . . . she began to think with the versatility of the old Bettine . . . never give up an advantage. *Never.*

She went in and washed her face and put on her makeup again, and stopped her crying and repaired all the subtle damages of her tears.

She dressed in her handsomest dress and waited.

And toward sundown the call came.

"Bettine," His Honor said. "Have you thought better of it, Bettine?"

She came and faced the screen and stood there with her lips quivering and her chin trembling because weakness worked for those who knew how to use it.

"I might," she said.

"There's no 'might' about it, Bettine," said Richard Collier, his broad face suffused with red. "Either you do or you don't."

"When you're here," she said, "when you come here and see me yourself, I'll tell you." '

"Before I come."

"No," she said, letting the tremor become very visible. "I'm *afraid*, Richard; I'm afraid. If you'll come here and take me out of here yourself, I promise I'll tell you anything I know, which isn't much, but I'll tell you. I'll give you his name, but he's not involved with anything besides that he had a silly infatuation and I was lonely. But I won't tell anything if you don't come and get me out of here. This has gone far enough, Richard. I'm frightened. Bring me home."

He stared at her, frowning. "If I come over there and you change your mind, Bettine, you can forget any favors you think I owe you. I won't be played with. You understand me, girl?"

She nodded.

"All right," he said. "You'll tell me his name, and you'll be thinking up any other detail that might explain how he could have gotten to that office, and you do it tonight. I'm sure there's some sense in that pretty head, there's a girl. You just think about it, Bettine, and you think hard, about where you want to be. Home, with all the comforts . . . or where you are, which isn't comfortable at all, is it, Bettine?"

"No," she said, crying. She shook her head. "No. It's not comfortable, Richard."

"See you in the morning, Bettine. And you can pack, if you have the right name."

"Richard—" But he had winked out, and she leaned there against the wall shivering, with her hands made into fists and the feeling that she was very small indeed. She did not want to be in the Tower another night, did not want to face the ghosts, who would stare at her with sad eyes and talk to her about honor, about things that were not for Bettine Maunfry.

I'm sorry, she thought for them. I won't be staying and dying here after all.

But Tom would. That thought depressed her enormously. She felt somehow responsible, and that was a serious burden, more serious than anything she had ever gotten herself into except the time she had thought for ten days that she was pregnant. Maybe Tom would—lie to them; maybe Tom would try to tell them she was somehow to blame in something which was not her fault.

That frightened her. But Tom loved her. He truly did. Tom would not hurt her by anything he would say, being a man, and braver, and motivated by some vaguely different drives, which had to do with pride and being strong, qualities which she had avoided all her life.

She went through the day's routines, such of the day as was left, and packed all but her dress that Richard said matched her eyes. She put that one on, to sit up all the night, because she was determined that Richard should not surprise her looking other than beautiful, and it would be like him to try that mean trick. She would simply sleep sitting up and keep her skirts from wrinkling, all propped with pillows: that way she could both be beautiful and get some sleep.

And she kept the lights on because of the ghosts, who were going to feel cheated.

Had he really died that way, she wondered of the Roman, the young Roman, who talked about battles from forgotten ages. Had he really died that way or did he only make it up to make her listen to him? She thought about battles which might have been fought right where this building stood, all the many, many ages.

And the lights faded.

The children came, grave and sober, Edward and then Richard, who stood and stared with liquid, disapproving eyes.

"I'm sorry," she said shortly. "I'm going to be leaving."

The others then, Anne and Robert, Anne with her heart-shaped face and dark hair and lovely manners, Essex tall and elegant, neither looking at her quite the way she expected—not disapproving, more as if they had swallowed secrets. "It was politics after all," asked Anne, "wasn't it, Bettine?"

"Maybe it was," she said shortly, hating to be proved wrong. "But what's that to me? I'm still getting out of here."

"What if your lover accuses you?" asked Essex, "Loves do end."

"He won't," she said. "He wouldn't. He's not likely to."

"*Exemplum,*" said a mournful voice. "Oh, Bettine, is this yours?"

"Shut up," she told Marc. He was hardest to face, because his sad, dark gaze seemed to expect something special of her. She was instantly sorry to have been rude; he looked as if his heart was breaking. He wavered, and she saw him covered in dust, the armor split, and bloody, and tears washing down his face. She put her hands to her face, horrified.

"You've hurt him," said Anne. "We go back to the worst moment when we're hurt like that."

"Oh, Marc," she said, "I'm sorry. I don't want to hurt you. But I want to be *alive*, you understand . . . can't you remember that? Wouldn't you have traded anything for that? And you had so much . . . when the sun was young and everything was new. Oh, Marc, do you blame me?"

"There is only one question," he said, his eyes melting-sad. "It's your moment, Bettine. Your moment."

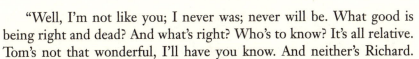

"Well, I'm not like you; I never was; never will be. What good is being right and dead? And what's right? Who's to know? It's all relative. Tom's not that wonderful, I'll have you know. And neither's Richard. And a girl gets along the best she can."

A wind blew, and there was a stirring among the others, an intaken breath. Essex caught at Anne's slim form, and the children withdrew to Anne's skirts. "It's *her*," said young Edward. "*She's* come."

Only Marc refused the panic which took the others; bright again, he moved with military precision to one side, cast a look back through the impeding wall where a tiny figure advanced.

"She didn't die here," he said quietly. "But she has many ties to this place. She is one of the queens, Bettine, a great one. And very seldom does *she* come out."

"For me?"

"Because you are one of the last, perhaps."

She shook her head, looked again in bewilderment as Anne and Robert and young Richard bowed; and Edward inclined his head. Marc only touched his heart and stepped further aside. "Marc," Bettine protested, not wanting to lose him, the one she trusted.

"Well," said the visitor, a voice like the snap of ice. She seemed less woman than small monument, in a red and gold gown covered with embroideries and pearls, and ropes of pearls and pearls in crisp red hair; she had a pinched face out of which two eyes stared like living cinder. "Well?"

Bettine bowed like the others; she thought she ought. The Queen paced slowly, diverted herself for a look at Essex, and a slow nod at Anne. "Well."

"My daughter," said Anne. "The first Elizabeth."

"Indeed," said the Queen. "And Marc, good evening. Marc, how do you fare? And the young princes. Quite a stir, my dear, indeed, quite a stir you've made. I have my spies; no need to reiterate."

"I'm not dying," she said. "You're all mistaken. I've told them I'm not dying. I'm going back to Richard."

The Queen looked at Essex, offered her hand. Essex kissed it, held it, smiled wryly. "Didn't you once say something of the kind?" asked the Queen.

"He did," said Anne. "It was, after all, your mistake, daughter."

"At the time," said Elizabeth. "But it was very stupid of you, Robert, to have relied on old lovers as messengers."

Essex shrugged, smiled again. "If not that year, the next. We were doomed to disagree."

"Of course," Elizabeth said. "There's love and there's power, and we all three wanted that, didn't we? And you . . ." Again that burning look turned on Bettine. "What sort are you? Not a holder. A seeker after power?"

"Neither one. I'm the Lord Mayor's girl and I'm going home."

"The Lord Mayor's girl." Elizabeth snorted. "The Lord Mayor's girl. I have spies, I tell you; all London's haunted. I've asked questions. The fellow gulled you, this Tom Ash. Ah, he himself's nothing; he works for others. He needs the numbers, that's all, for which he's paid. And with that list in others' hands your precious Lord Mayor's in dire trouble. Revolution, my dear, the fall of princes. Are you so blind? Your Lord Mayor's none so secure, tyrant that he is . . . if not this group of men, this year, then others, next. They'll have him; London Town's never cared for despots, crowned or plain. Not even in its old age has it grown soft-witted. Just patient."

"I don't want to hear any of it. Tom loved me, that's all. Whatever he's involved in . . ."

Elizabeth laughed. "I was born to power. Was it accident? Ask my mother here what she paid. Ask Robert here what he paid to try for mine, and how I held it all the same . . . no hard feelings, none. But do you think your Lord Mayor gained his by accident? You move in dark waters, with your eyes *shut*. You've wanted power all your life, and you thought there was an easy way. But you don't have it, because you don't understand what you want. If they gave you all of London on a platter, you'd see only the baubles. You'd look for some other hands to put the real power in; you're helpless. You've trained all your life to be, I'll warrant. I know the type. Bettine. What name is that? Abbreviated and diminished. *E-liz-a-beth* is our name, in fine round tones. You're tall; you try to seem otherwise. You dress to please everyone else; I pleased *Elizabeth*, and others copied me. If I was fond, it was that I liked men, but by all reason, I never handed my crown to one, no. However painful the decision . . . however many the self-serving ministers urging me this way and that, I did my own thinking; yes, Essex, even with you. Of course I'd hesitate, of course let the ministers urge me, of course I'd grieve—I'm not unhuman—but at the same time they could seem heartless and I merciful. And the deed got done, didn't it, Robert?"

"Indeed," he said.

"You were one of my favorites; much as you did, I always liked you; loved you, of course, but liked you, and there weren't as many of those. And you, Mother, another of the breed. But this modern bearer of my name—you have none of it, no backbone at all."

"I'm not in your class," Bettine said. "It's not fair."

"Whine and whimper. You're a born victim. I could make you a queen and you'd be a dead one in a fortnight."

"I just want to be comfortable and I want to be happy."

"Well, look at you."

"I will be again. I'm not going to be dead; I'm going to get out of this."

"Ah. You want, want, want; never look to see how things *are*. You spend all your life reacting to what others do. Ever thought about getting in the first stroke? No, of course not. I'm Elizabeth. You're just Bettine."

"I wasn't born with your advantages."

Elizabeth laughed. "I was a bastard . . . pardon me, Mother. And what were you? Why aren't *you* the Mayor? Ever wonder that?"

Bettine turned away, lips trembling.

"Look at me," said the Queen.

She did so, not wanting to. But the voice was commanding.

"Why did you?"

"What?"

"Look at me."

"You asked."

"Do you do everything people ask? You're everyone's victim, that's all. The Mayor's girl. You choose to be, no getting out of it. You *choose*, even by choosing not to choose. You'll go back and you'll give His Honor what he wants, and you'll go back to your apartment . . . maybe."

"What do you mean maybe?"

"Think, my girl, think. Girl you are; you've spent your whole majority trying to be nothing. I think you may achieve it."

"There's the Thames," said Essex.

"It's not what they take from you," said Anne, "it's what you give up."

"The water," said Edward, "is awfully cold, so I've heard."

"What do you know? You didn't have any life."

"But I did," said the boy, his eyes dancing. "I had my years . . . like you said, when the sun was very good."

"I had a pony," said Richard. "Boys don't, now."

"Be proud," said Elizabeth.

"I know something about you," Bettine said. "You got old and you had no family and no children, and I'm sure pride was cold comfort then."

Elizabeth smiled. "I hate to disillusion you, my dear, but I *was* happy. Ah, I shed a few tears, who doesn't in a lifetime? But I had exactly what I chose; and what I traded I knew I traded. I did precisely as I wanted. Not always the story book I would have had it, but for all that, within my circumstances, precisely as I chose, for all my life to its end. I lived and I was curious; there was nothing I thought foreign to me. I saw more of the world in a glance than you've wondered about lifelong. I was ahead of my times, never caught by the outrageously unanticipated; but your whole life's an accident, isn't it, little Elizabeth?"

"*Bettine,*" she said, setting her chin. "My *name* is Bettine."

"Good," laughed the Queen, slapping her skirted thigh. "Excellent. Go *on* thinking; and straighten your back, woman. Look at the eyes. Always look at the eyes."

The Queen vanished in a little thunderclap, and Essex swore and Anne patted his arm. "She was never comfortable," Anne said. "I would have brought her up with gentler manners."

"If I'd been your son—" said Essex.

"If," said Anne.

"They'll all be disturbed downstairs," said young Edward. "They *are*, when she comes through."

They faded . . . all but Marc.

"They don't change my mind," said Bettine. "The Queen was rude."

"No," said Marc. "Queens aren't. She's just what she is."

"Rude," she repeated, still smarting.

"Be what you are," said Marc, "I'll go. It's your moment."

"Marc?" She reached after him, forgetting. Touched nothing. She was alone then, and it was too quiet. She would have wanted Marc to stay. Marc understood fear.

Be what she was. She laughed sorrowfully, wiped at her eyes, and went to the bath to begin to be beautiful, looked at eyes which had puffed and which were habitually reddened from want of sleep. And from crying. She found herself crying now, and did not know why, except maybe at the sight of Bettine Maunfry as she was, little slim hands that had never done anything and a face which was all sex and a voice that no one would ever obey or take seriously . . . just for games, was Bettine. In all this great place which had held desperate criminals and fallen queens and heroes and lords, just Bettine, who was going to do the practical thing and turn in Tom who had never loved her, but only wanted something.

Tom's another, she thought with curiously clear insight, a *beautiful* person who was good at what he did, but it was not Tom who was going to be important, he was just smooth and good and all hollow, nothing behind the smiling white teeth and clear blue eyes. If you cracked him, it would be like a china doll, nothing in the middle.

So with Bettine.

"I love you," he had protested. As far as she had known, no one had ever really loved Bettine Maunfry, though she had sold everything she had to keep people pleased and smiling at her all her life. She was not, in thinking about it, sure what she would do *if* someone loved her, or if she would know it if he did. She looked about at the magazines with the pictures of eyes and lips and the articles on how to sell one's soul.

Articles on love.

There's love and love, Anne had said.

Pleasing people. Pleasing everyone, so that they would please Bettine. Pretty children got rewards for crying and boys got spanked. While the world was pacified, it would not hurt Bettine.

Eyes and lips, primal symbols.

She made up carefully, did her hair, added the last items to her packing.

Except her handwork, which kept her sane. Click, click. Mindless sanity, rhythms and patterns. There was light from the window now. Probably breakfast would arrive soon, but she was not hungry.

And finally came the noise of the doors, and the steps ascending the tower.

Richard Collier came. He shut the door behind him and looked down at her frowning; and she stood up in front of the only window.

Look them in the eyes, the Queen had said. She looked at Richard that way, the Queen's way, and he evidently did not like it.

"The name," he said.

She came to him, her eyes filling with tears in spite of herself. "I don't want to tell you," she said. "It would hurt somebody; and if you trusted me, you'd let me straighten it out. I can get your file back for you."

"You leave that to me," Richard said. "The name, girl, and no more—"

She had no idea why she did it. Certainly Richard's expression was one of surprise, as if he had calculated something completely wrong. There was blood on her, and the long needle buried between his ribs, and he slid down to lie on the floor screaming and rolling about, or trying to. It was a very soundproof room; and no one came. She stood and watched, quite numb in that part of her which ought to have been conscience; if anything feeling mild vindication.

"Bettine," she said quietly, and sat down and waited for him to die and for someone who had brought him to the Tower to miss him. Whoever had the numbers was free to use them now; there would be a new order in the city; there would be a great number of changes. She reckoned that if she had ordered her life better she might have been better prepared, and perhaps in a position to escape. She was not. She had not planned. It's not the moments that can be planned, the Roman would say; it's the lives . . . that lead to them.

And did London's life . . . lead to Bettine Maunfry? She suspected herself of a profound thought. She was even proud of it. Richard's eyes stared blankly now. There had not been a great deal of pain. She had not wanted that, particularly, although she would not have shrunk from it. In a moment, there was not time to shrink.

There was power and there was love, and she had gotten through life with neither. She did not see what one had to do with the other; nothing, she decided, except in the sense that there really never had been a Bettine Maunfry, only a doll which responded to everyone else's impulses. And there had been nothing of her to love.

She would not unchoose what she had done; that was Elizabeth's test of happiness. She wondered if Richard would.

Probably not, when one got down to moments; but Richard had not been particularly smart in some things.

I wonder if I could have been Mayor, she thought. Somewhere I decided about that, and never knew I was deciding.

There was a noise on the stairs now. They were coming. She sat still, wondering if she shought fight them too, but decided against it. She was not, after all, insane. It was politics. It had to do with the politics of His Honor the Mayor and of one Bettine, a girl, who had decided not to give a name.

They broke in, soldiers, who discovered the Mayor's body with great consternation. They laid hands on her and shouted questions.

"I killed him," she said. They waved rifles at her, accusing her of being part of the revolution.

"I led my own," she said.

They looked very uncertain then, and talked among themselves and made calls to the city. She sat guarded by rifles, and they carried the Mayor out, poor dead Richard. They talked out the murder and wondered that she could have had the strength to drive the needle so deep.

Finally—incredibly—they questioned the jailer as to what kind of prisoner she was, as if they believed that she had been more than the records showed, the imprisoned leader of some cause, the center of the movement they had been hunting. They talked about more guards. Eventually she had them, in great number, and by evening, all the Tower was ringed with soldiery, and heavy guns moved into position, great batteries of them in the inner court. Two days later she looked out the window and saw smoke where outer London was, and knew there was riot in the town.

The guards treated her with respect. Bettine Maunfry, they called her when they had to deal with her, not girl, and not Bettine. They called on her—of all things, to issue a taped call for a cease-fire.

But of her nightly companions . . . nothing. Perhaps they were shy, for at night a guard stood outside in the anteroom. Perhaps, after all, she was a little mad. She grieved for their absence, not for Richard and not for Tom, living in this limbo of tragic comedy. She watched the city burn and listened to the tread of soldiers in the court and watched the gun crews from her single window. It was the time before supper, when they left her a little to herself—if a guard at the stairside door was privacy; they had closed off the anteroom as they usually did, preparing to deliver her dinner.

"Quite a turmoil you've created."

She turned from the window, stared at Marc in amazement. "But it's daytime."

"I *am* a little faded," he said, looking at his hand, and looked up again. "How are you, Bettine?"

"It's ridiculous, isn't it?" She gestured toward the courtyard and the guns. "They think I'm dangerous."

"But you are."

She thought about it, how frightened they were and what was going on in London. "They keep asking me for names. Today they threatened me. I'm not sure I'm *that* brave, Marc, I'm really not."

"But you don't know any."

"No," she said. "Of course I don't. So I'll be counted as brave, won't I?"

"The other side needs a martyr, and you're it, you know that."

"How does it go out there? Do the Queen's spies tell her?"

"Oh, it's violent, quite. If I were alive, I'd be out there; it's a business for soldiers. The starships are hanging off just waiting. The old Mayor was dealing under the table in favoring a particular company, and the company that supported him had its offices wrecked. . . . others just standing by waiting to move in and give support to the rebels, to out-maneuver their own rivals. The ripple goes on to stars you've never seen."

"That's amazing."

"You're not frightened."

"Of course I'm frightened."

"There was a time a day ago when you might have ended up in power; a mob headed this way to get you out, but the troops got them turned."

"We'll it's probably good they didn't get to me. I'm afraid I wouldn't know what to do with London if they gave it to me. Elizabeth was right."

"But the real leaders of the revolution have come into the light now; they use your name as a cause. It's the spark they needed so long. Your name is their weapon."

She shrugged.

"They've a man inside the walls, Bettine . . . do you understand me?"

"No. I don't."

"I couldn't come before; it was still your moment . . . these last few days. None of us could interfere. It wouldn't be right. But I'm edging the mark . . . just a little. I always do. Do you understand me now, Bettine?"

"I'm going to die?"

"He's on his way. It's one of the revolutionaries . . . not the loyalists. The revolution needs a martyr; and they're afraid you *could* get out. They can't have their own movement taken away from their control by some mob. You'll die, yes. And they'll claim the soldiers killed you to stop a rescue. Either way, they win."

She looked toward the door, bit her lip. She heard a door open, heard steps ascending; a moment's scuffle.

"I'm here," Marc said.

"Don't you have to go away again? Isn't this . . . something I have to do?"

"Only if you wish."

The inner door opened. A wild-eyed man stood there, with a gun, which fired, right for her face. It *hurt*. It seemed too quick, too ill-timed; she was not ready, had not said all she wanted to say.

"There are things I wanted to do," she protested.

"There always are."

She had not known Marc was still there; the place was undefined and strange.

"Is it over? Marc, I wasn't through. I'd just figured things out."

He laughed and held out his hand. "Then you're ahead of most."

He was clear and solid to her eyes; it was the world which had hazed. She looked about her. There were voices, a busy hum of accumulated ages, time so heavy the world could scarcely bear it.

"I could have done better."

The hand stayed extended, as if it were important She reached out hers, and his was warm.

"Till the sun dies," he said.

"Then what?" It was the first question.

He told her.

ICE

(Moscow)

Beauty was all about ancient Moskva, in the vast whiteness at world's end. Moskva lived through the final ages wrapped in snows, while forests advanced and retreated, and the ships from the stars stopped coming. The City lost contact with other cities, caring little, for its struggle was its own, and peculiar to itself, a struggle of the soul, an inward and endless war which each citizen fought in his or her own way. In that struggle Moskva became as it was, a city no longer stone, not in its greater part, but wood, which it had been at its beginning. Ah, ancient, ancient monuments lay beneath, frozen, warped and changed, serving as mere foundations. Here and there throughout the city vast heads of statues and the tops of ancient buildings still thrust up at strange angles, but the features and the corners were blurred, scoured white and round and clean by the winds, stones become one with the snows, as the snows had lapped all the past in purest white and blurred all past and all to come.

But the present buildings, gaily colored, carved, embellished, the warmhearted buildings in which the people lived, were made of wood from the last and retreating forest, wood on which the people had shown their last and highest artistry. On every inch of the surfaces and columns, flowers twined, human faces stared out, vines and designs of bright colors entangled the gaze. Skins of animals adorned the floors, and bunches of dried flowers, memories of brief summer, sat on tables which were likewise carved and painted red and green and gold and blue. Hearths in every home burned bright, sending up cheery dark smoke which the winds carried away as soon as it touched the sky.

The people walked the snowy streets done up in furs edged with bright felt embroideries, reds and blues and greens, with border patterns in the most intricate stitchery, lilies and flowers and golden ears of grain; with scarves hand-stitched in convolute vine patterns, all jewel-bright, each garment a glory, a memory of color, a delight to the eye. All the soul of the people who lived in Moskva was poured into the making of this polychrome beauty, all the rich heritage of the lands and the fields and the passion of their hearts, both into the wooden buildings within Moskva's wooden walls, and into the gay colors they wore. There were dances, celebrations of life . . . dancing and singing, from which the participants fell down exhausted and full of warmth and joy, celebrations in which they danced life itself, to the bright whirling of cloth and tassels and scarves and the stamp of broidered boots, all picked out with flowers and reindeer and horses. Music of strings and music of voices rose from Moskva into the winds.

But above the city the songs changed, and the voice of the winds overpowered them, changing the brave words into wailing, and the wailing at last into a whisper of snow powdering along the rough ice of Moskva's interior skein of rivers, which were thawed only for a few weeks a year, and most times were frozen deep and solid . . . grains hissed along icy ridges outside the walls, and whispered of the north, of ground endlessly covered with snow, pure of any foot's imprint, forever.

White . . . but seldom truly white . . . was the world outside the wooden walls. Above it, the sun died its slow eons-long death, in glorious flarings of radiations which brought nightly curtains of moving light across the skies; it brought days of strange color, apricot and lavenders and oranges and eerie minglings of subtler shades, which touched the snows and the ice and streamed across them with glories and flares that made a thousand delicate shades of light and shadowings. The snows knew many subtleties—nights when the opal moon hung frighteningly low, in a sky sometimes violet and sometimes approaching blue, and very rarely black and dusted with ancient stars. At such times the snows went bright and pale and so, so still, with the black bristling shades of pines southward and the endless stillness of snow northward. Or starker pallor, storm . . . when the clouds went gray and strange and the wind took on an eerie voice, and the snow began to fly, for days and days of white as if the world had stopped being, and there was only white and wind.

This was the struggle, the reason for the bright fires, the bright colors, the noisy celebrations, the images of flowers and vines. Other cities round about might already have perished. No travelers came. But the soul of Moskva held firm, and their busyness about their own affairs saved them, because they refused to look up, or out, and their bright colors held against the snows, and their rough, man-made beauty prevailed against the terrible shifting beauty of the ice.

Bravest of all in Moskva were those who *could* venture outside the walls, who wrapped themselves in their bright furs and their courage and ventured out into the frozen wastes—the hunters, the loggers, the farers-forth, who could look out into the cold whiteness and keep the colors in their hearts.

But even to them sometimes the sickness came, which began to fade them, and which set their eyes to staring out into the horizons; for once that coldness did come on them, their lives were not long. There were wolves outside the walls, there were dire dangers, and deaths waiting always, but the white death was inward and quiet and direst of all.

Andrei Gorodin had no fear in him. Winter did not daunt him, and when the snows came and the foxes and ermines turned their coats to snowiest white, he was one of the rare ones who continued to go out, he and his piebald pony, a shaggy beast as gay in its coat as the city with its painting, looking out on the icy world through a shag of yellow mane and forelock that let all the world wonder whether there was a horse within it. Like Andrei, the pony had no fear, immune to the terrors which seized on other beasts allied to man, terrors which turned their ribs gaunt and their eyes stark, so that eventually they fell to pining and died. Not Umnik, who jogged along the snows surefooted and regarding the world with a seldom-seen and mistrustful eye.

His master, Andrei Vasilyevitch Gorodin, returning home after a day's good hunt, rode wrapped in lynx fur, with belts and boots of bright embroidered leather; and about his face a flowered leather scarf, which Anna Ivanovna had made for him (who made him other fine, bright gifts, storing them up in a carven chest beneath her bed . . . she was his bride-to-be this spring, when spring should come, when weddings were lucky). A brace of fat hares hung frozen from his saddle. His bow, from which gay tassels fluttered, hung at his back; and from his traps he had a snow fox which he planned to give Anna to make her an edging for a cape. He whistled as he rode, with Umnik's breath puffing merrily on the still air, with the crunch of hooves on crusted snow and the creak of the harness to keep the time. He had a flask with him, and from time to time he drank lightly from it, warming his belly. About him the snow gleamed pure white, for clouds veiled the sun, and he had no present need of the carved eyeshields which hung about his neck, and which, worn with the flower-broidered scarf, made him look like some strange bright-patterned beast atop a piebald shaggy one. It was one of the rare calm days, so quiet that he and Umnik seemed alone in the world; and when he stopped the pony to rest, savoring the quiet air, he could hear the crack of ice in the cold, and the fall of a branchload of snow in the lightest breath of air. He listened to such sounds, and just a slight touch of the silence came into his heart, which was dangerous. He gathered his courage and whistled to the pony, urged him on. He began to sing, louder and louder in the vast silence of the white world, and Umnik moved along right merrily, flicking his ears to the song.

But the song did not last, and the silence returned, seeming to muffle even the crunch of ice under Umnik's hooves. And all at once Umnik stopped, and his head turned to the north: his ears pricked up and his nostrils strained to drink the air. The pony began to tremble then, and Andrei quickly slid his bow from off his shoulder and strung it, and took a red-fletched arrow from his broidered quiver, then looked about, north, at the white vastness and its gentle rolls, south at the edge of pine forest beside which they rode. The pony looked fixedly toward a narrow view of the open land beyond two hills. He stood rigid, his mane lifting in a little cold wind, gathering crystals of blowing snow in its coarse yellow hairs.

There was nothing. Andrei tapped Umnik with his heels. Sometimes horses saw ghosts, so the old hunters said, and then the wasting began, and they would die, but this was not like Umnik, a plain-minded beast, not given to fancies. Umnik moved forward feather-footed and skittish. Andrei believed the horse, which had never yet played him false, and he kept his bow in hand and an arrow on the string, his eyes toward the north, as the horse gazed while it moved, though its course was westerly and homeward.

For a moment the gray clouds parted and the sun shone through, gilding the drifts with flaring colors. Umnik sidestepped and shied, throwing his head. A white shape was in the glare, slow and slinking . . . a wolf, white as a winter wind. Andrei's heart clenched; and he raised and bent his bow, between fear of it and desire for its beauty, for he had never seen such a beast. The arrow sped as horse and wolf moved, and the wolf was gone, over the rim of a drift. He clapped heels to Umnik's sides, once and again, and the brave pony went through the drift and off the way, reluctantly and warily. The clouds had closed again, the sun was gone, and a sudden gust of wind whipped off the snows of the right-hand hill, carrying stinging particles into his eyes.

Umnik shied, and Andrei reined him around, patted the pony's shaggy neck, and rode him back again. There was nothing, not wolf or so much as a footprint or the tiny wound of an arrow's feathers in the snowbanks. He cast about for the arrow, trampling the whole area with Umnik's hooves, for it was a well-made shaft and he was not pleased to lose it, or to be so puzzled. He thought perhaps it had gone into a deep drift, and surely it had, for try as he would he could not turn it up. He gave up finally, turned the pony about and set him on his way, trying to pretend that nothing had happened—the sun was always deceptive, and he had looked with eyes unshielded, never wise; he might have dreamed the wolf. But the arrow itself was gone. As he rode, the world seemed colder, the snow starker white, and now, like the piebald pony, he longed for the city and the bright and busy streets of human measure. He rode along with the frozen carcasses of his hunt dangling at his knee, now and again looking over his shoulder to mark how the east was darkening. He wished he had not delayed so long for the arrow, nor trifled with wolves, because it was a long ride yet.

He tried again to whistle, but his lips were dry, and the noise Umnik made in moving seemed muffled and not as loud as it ought. The wind gusted violently at his back.

Snow began to fall, when never in the morning had it looked as if it could, so white the clouds had been; but the day had gotten fouler and fouler since he had delayed, and now he began to be much concerned. The wind blew, sighing, whistling, picking up the snow it had just laid down as well, to drive it in fine streams along the crusted surface and off the crests of frozen drifts. Umnik knew the hazard; the little horse kept moving steadily, but he threw his head as the wind seemed to acquire voices, and those voices seemed to howl on this side and on that of them.

"Go," Andrei asked of the pony, "go, my clever one, haste, haste," for the wind came now harder at their backs, a wind with many voices, like the voices of wolves. But the pony kept his head, saving his strength. Umnik passed the last hill, then, halfway down the downward slope, began to run with all his might, the homeward stretch which should, round the hill and beyond, bring them to the city wall. Howls behind them now were unmistakable, coming off the hillside on the left. Umnik cleared the hillside at an all-out pace, with Moskva now in sight, and Andrei lifted up the horn which hung at his belt and blew it now with all that was in him, a sound all but lost in the wind; again and again he blew . . . and to his joy the great wooden gates of Moskva began to open for him in the white veil of snow.

Umnik's flying hooves thundered over the icy bridge, up to the gates and through, over new snow at the gateway and onto the trampled streets of the city; the doors swung shut. Andrei reined in, circled Umnik as he put on a brave face, waved a jaunty salute at old Pyotr and son Fedor who kept the gates. Then he trotted Umnik on into the narrow streets, past citizens bundled against the falling snow, folk who knew him, bright-cheeked children who looked up in delight and waved at a hunter's passing.

He turned in toward the cozy house of Ivan Nikolaev, two houses, in truth, which, neighbors, had leaned together for warmth and companionship years ago and finally grown together the year his own parents died, leaving him to the Nikolaevs and their kin. The carven-fenced yards had become one, the houses joined, and so did the painted stables where the Nikolaevs' bay pony and the Orlovs' three goats waited, Umnik's stay-at-home stablemates.

The household had been waiting for him; the side door opened, and Katya his foster mother came out bundled against the cold, to take Umnik's reins. He dropped to the snowy yard and tugged down the scarf to kiss her brow and hug her a welcome, cheerfully then slung the frozen game over his shoulder while he stripped off the pony's harness to carry it indoors. Umnik shook himself thoroughly and trotted away on his own to the grain and the warm stall waiting, and Andrei, slinging the saddle to his shoulder with one hand and hugging mother Katya with the other arm, headed for the porch. She would have worried for him, with the hour late and the snow beginning; she was all smiles now. And with a second slam of the door Anna was coming out too, her cheeks burned red by the wind, her eyes bright. She came running to him, her fair braids flying bare, her embroidered coat and skirts turned pale in the blowing snow; he dropped the gear and clapped her in his arms and swung her about as he had done when they were children of the same year; he kissed her (lightly, for her mother stood by laughing) then dragged the harness up again and walked with his arm about her and Katya along beside, lifted his hand from Anna's shoulder to wave at her brother Ilya, who had come outside still bundling up.

The oldest Nikolaev was a woodcutter, and his son Ivan a woodcutter; but young Ilya, Anna's twin, of no stout frame, was an artist, a carver, whose work was all about them, the bright posts of the porch, the flowered shutters . . . "Ah," Ilya said to him cheerfully, "back safe—what else could he be? I told her so." He hugged Ilya a snowy welcome too, stamped his boots clean and hung the game on the porch, then whisked inside with all the rest, into warmth like a wall. He hung the bow and harness in the inner porch, stripped off snowy furs and changed to his indoor boots. Katya bustled off and brought him back tepid water to drink, and mistress Orlov met them all at the inside door with hot tea. There was the smell of the women's delightsome cooking, and the cheer of the mingled families who beamed and gave him welcome as he came into the common room, a babble of children inevitable and inescapable in the house. Young Ivan came running to be picked up and flung about, and Andrei lifted him gladly, tired as he was. Fire crackled in the hearth and they all were gathered, settled finally for a meal, himself . . . a Gorodin; and Nikolaevs and Orlovs young and old, with the warm air smelling as the house always smelled, of wood chips and resins and leathers and furs and good cooking.

Then the fear seemed very far away.

He rested, with a full belly, and they drank steaming tea and a little vodka. Old Nikolaev and son Ivan talked their craft, where they should cut in the spring to come; and grandfather Orlov and his son, carpenters, talked of the porch they were going to repair down the street on the city hall. Grandmother Orlov sat in her chair which was always near the fire, tucked up with flowered pillows and quilts; the children—there were seven, among the prolific Orlovs—played by the warm hearth; and the women talked and stitched and invented patterns. "Tell stories," the children begged of any who would; drink passed about again, and it was that pleasant hour. The young would begin the tale-telling, and the elders would finish, for they had always seen deeper snows and stranger sights and colder winters.

"Tell us," little Ivan asked, bouncing against Andrei's knee, "ah, tell us about the hunt today." Andrei sighed, taking his arm from about Anna's waist, and smiled at the round little face and bounced Ivan on his foot, holding two small hands, joked with him, and drew squeals. He told the tale with flair and flourish, warmed to the telling while the children settled in a half-ring about his feet; his friend Ilya picked up a fresh block of pine and his favorite knife, a blade very fine and keen. . . . Most of all Anna listened, looked up at him when he looked down, her eyes very bright and soft. The wind still howled outside, but they were all warmed by each other, while the timbers cracked and boomed now and again with the cold. He told of the wild ride home, of the wolves . . . *wolves*, for something in him flinched at telling of the Wolf, and of the lost arrow. Little Ivan's eyes grew round as buttons, and when he came to the part about the closed gate, and how it had opened, the children all clapped their hands but Ivan, who sat with his eyes still round and his mouth wide agape.

"For shame," said his grandmother, sweeping the child against her quilt-wrapped knees. "You've frightened him, Andrei."

"I'm not afraid," the child exclaimed, and shrugged free to mime a bowshot. "I shall grow up and be a hunter outside the walls, like Andrei."

"What, not a carpenter?" his grandfather asked.

"No, I shall be *brave*," the little boy said, and there was a sudden silence in the room, a hurt, a loneliness that Andrei felt to the heart—alone of Gorodins, of hunters in this house, and a guest, living on parents' ancient friendship. He had never meant to steal a son's heart away. Then a timber cracked quite loudly, and the roof shed a few icicles and everyone laughed at the silence, to drive it away.

"That you shall be," said Ilya, and reached to ruffle the little boy's hair. "Braver than I. I shall make you a wolf, how will you like that?"

The child's eyes danced, and quickly he deserted to Ilya's knee, and hung there watching Ilya's deft blade peel fragrant curls from the pine—Ilya, who was Anna's very likeness, woman-beautiful, whose delicate hands likewise had no aptitude for his father's work, but who made beauty in wood, most skilled in all Moskva. Andrei watched as the child did, and with amazing swiftness the wood took on a wolf's dire shape. "I remember wolves," grandfather Orlov began, and childish eyes diverted again, traveled back and forth from Ilya's fingers to the old man's face, delightfully frightened.

Andrei held Anna's hand, and drew her against him, a bundle of furs and skirts beside the crackling fire. He listened to this tale he had heard before, and grandfather Orlov's voice seemed far from him; even Anna, against his side, seemed distant from him. He watched Ilya's razor-edged blade winking in the firelight and more and more surely saw the wolf emerge from the wood. He heard the snow fall; he had never truly *heard* it before: it needed silence, and the sense of the night outside, as the flakes settled thicker and thicker like goose down upon the roof, and their voices went up against the wind and fled away into the cold.

They spoke each of wolves that evening, and he did not hear with all his heart, nor even shiver now. He watched at last as the stories ended, and Ilya handed the wolf to the boy Ivan, with all the children crowded jealously about, a clamor swiftly dismissed for bed, blanket-heaped cots in the farthest room of the loft, and deep down mattresses and coziness and the rush of the wind at the shutters.

"Good night," he bade mother Katya and father Ivan, and "Good night," he kissed Anna. Then he and Ilya sought their room in the loft as well, bedded down together as they had slept since they were boys like Ivan, snugged down in piles of quilts and a deep down mattress.

"I was afraid," he confessed to Ilya when they had been some time settled, side by side in the dark. "I should have told the boy."

"Boys grow up," Ilya said. "And boys grow wiser. Do not we all?"

He thought of that, and lay there awake, staring at the beams and listening, hearing the wind above them, very close. It seemed to him that the down beneath him was like the snowdrifts, endlessly deep and soft; and if he shut his eyes, he could see the blue darkness of the night and a ghost-white form which loped over the snows, with beauty in its running. Deep soft drifts, and lupine eyes full of night . . . a triangular face and blowing snow, and wolf-eyes holding secrets—a shape which coursed the winds, drifts which became other wolves, snow-cold and coursing down upon his hapless dreams like hunters upon prey.

Then he was afraid with a deep fear, remembering the arrow, for the foremost wolf bore a wound which dropped blood from its heart, and the droplets became ruby ice, which fell without a sound.

He woke the next morning in an inner silence deeper than the day before, though the timbers groaned, and snow had slid upon the roof, tumbling down the eaves, and this had wakened him and Ilya. "No hunting this day," said Ilya, hearing the wind. He said nothing, but listened to the storm.

And as the children wakened and shivered downstairs, and the women stirred about, and there was no more lying abed, Ilya stirred out, quickly pulling his boots on, and so did Andrei, hearing the great town bell ringing, muted and soft in the storm which lapped the morning.

He and Ilya and Anna and the other Nikolaevs and Orlovs with strength to help dressed in their warmest clothing and ventured out into a town gone white. Drifts lay man-high in the streets; they hitched up the ponies, and worked . . . like ghosts, moving through the pale driving snow; worked until backs ached, cleared paths, braced roofs, braced the wall itself. The market opened, very quickly empty, and the winds kept a fury which sang through the air, and carried the snow back as swiftly as they could move it. They surrendered at last and returned to their homes, to warm meals and warm fires and patient cheer.

But within the house the silence gained yet a deeper hold, as snow piled about the walls and the windsong grew more distant. It was that manner of storm which could set in and last for days; in which the white loneliness settled close about the town. Andrei tied a rope about himself and went out in the last of day, fearing for Umnik's safety and that of the other beasts; but he found them well, snug in their stable and warm with the snow about. He started back again, into the white drifts, following the rope which he had tied about him, which vanished into white. Not even the shadow of the house was visible in the storm; and when he looked back, he could not see the stable.

White. All was white. He looked all about, suddenly dreading the slinking form that might be within that whiteness, itself immaculate and swift as the northwind. He imagined that he might see suddenly two strange darknesses staring at him, wolfish slanted; pink lolling tongue, and white, white teeth.

He looked behind him, turning with a start. With haste he seized hard upon the rope and followed it, pushed through a wall of blowing snow, stumbled against the buried porch and climbed to the door, found it frozen shut. His nape prickled, and he would not look back. Something breathed there, in the silence of the howling wind, and he would not turn to see. He rapped at the door, called those inside, refusing panic. But the silence grew, and he could hardly move from the chill in his bones when the door opened and Anna and Ilya snatched him inside.

"Oh, he is cold," Anna said, and they hastened him to the fire in the inmost hall, sitting him there to strip off his furs; they heated blankets before the fire and wrapped him in them, then brought him tea. All the house gathered, murmuring at some vast distance, and the children came and touched his cold hands, as did Anna and Ilya's mother, who hugged him and chafed his fingers and kissed his brow, greatly concerned. But from the mantle above the fire Ilya's wolf stared back at him.

They danced that night, and drank and sang; he drank much and laughed and yet—the silence was there.

He lay in bed that night and dreamed of blue nights and still snows, and that white shape which ran with the wind, amid moon-twinkling snowflakes and over drifts, never leaving a mark upon them.

The next day dawned clear and bright.

The whole of Moskva seemed to smile in the day, colored eaves peeking out from the deep drifts which lay between the houses, children and elders bundled like thick-limbed and thickly mittened dolls out breaking through the drifts to walk the streets and visit kin and friends. The Orlov children squealed with delight, breaking up the drifts to the stables, and breaking icicles off the eaves of the porch. Some children had sleds out on the streets, and the children clamored for their own.

But Andrei met the morning with less cheer, quietly put on his outdoor boots and his warm furs, took his gear out and saddled Umnik, who was restive and full of argument. He said no word to Anna or her parents, none to Ilya, only smiled bleakly at the children who grew quieter looking at him, and, stopping their sledding, stood like a row of huddled birds by the fence as he rode through the gate and passed down the street.

"Good morning," the neighbors said cheerfully, pausing in their snow-shoveling. "A good morning to you, Andrei Vasilyevitch." He nodded absently and kept going. "Good morning," said white-bearded Pyotr by the gatehouse, and he forgot to return the greeting, but got down off Umnik and helped the gate wardens heave the gates inward, got up again on Umnik's back. The pony tossed his shaggy head and advanced on the drift which barred their way, lurched through it and onto smoother going, toward the bridge and the open land, snuffing the cold crisp air with red-veined nostrils and pricking up his ears as he thumped across the bridge and jogged toward the hills.

The sun climbed higher still, until it passed noon. Andrei wrapped his scarf about his face to warm his breath, and omitted the eyeshields, for there was still haze in the heavens, and the snow lay white and thick everywhere. There were few tracks, no promise of good hunting; the snow had not been long enough to turn the beasts desperate and reckless . . . nor was the day warm enough to tempt them out of hiding. He should have waited a day, but the thought of the dark loft and sitting before the fire with nothing to do oppressed him. In idleness he had evil memory for company. He came out to deny it, to laugh at it, to hunt and to win this time.

He was afraid. He had never felt the like before. Even in the bright, clear daylight he felt what he had felt in that ride to the gates, with the wolves baying at his back. He was afraid of fear . . . for the hunt was his livelihood, and when he feared too much, he could not come outside the walls.

He rose in his stirrups and looked back, settled forward again as he rode. They were long out of sight of the city's wooden walls; snowy hills and snowy fields stretched in all directions but the south, where forest stood thickly whited and iced. There was no sound but Umnik's regular moving, the creak of harness, and the whuff of breath.

Umnik moved more slowly now, having run out his first wind, wading almost knee-deep along the trail. And there was such beauty in the white snow that his fear grew less. He stopped the horse and turned and looked all about him, heard a rapid, doggish panting at his back.

He spun, hauling at the reins, and Umnik shied in the deep drift, rose on hind legs, almost falling.

Nothing was there. He steadied the horse and patted it, and nothing was there. The light grew; the clouds parted. He reached for the eyeshields as the snows gathered the sunflares, misted gold and rose and amber; Umnik stood still, and Andrei stopped with the eyeshields in his hand . . . feeling a fascination for that light—for light had concealed the Wolf. He looked to the far hills—and to the sky, into the sun. He had never looked up in his life, save a furtive glance to know the condition of the sky—but not to see it. It smote his heart. And he looked north. The wolf was there, standing watchfully on the surface of a new drift, and its eyes were like the sun, and its coat was touched with the subtle shifting colors.

He whipped Umnik and rode; he never remembered beginning . . . but he and Umnik skimmed the snows in terror, the white wolf never far.

At last the city was before them, and he took the horn from his side to blow, but the sound of it seemed dim. Umnik faltered, and he whipped the pony, drove him, up to the approach to the city, across the wooden bridge and to the southern gate, while white shapes leaped and plunged about him and voices howled, far and still, as if his hearing were dulled, and all the world was wrapped in cold. Umnik slowed as they came to the opening gates, but he whipped the pony harder, and rode upon the streets, hooves skidding on the snow, and startled citizens and children with a sled scurried from the horse's path. He stopped, looked about, and the gates were closing slowly. "The wolves," he cried, but Pyotr the gate warden looked strangely at him, continuing to heave at the gates.

Nothing had been there. The wolves were in his own eyes. He knew this suddenly, and the cold grew deeper in his heart

"Are you all right, Andrei?" Pyotr asked.

He nodded, cold and shamed by the death he saw for himself. He reached vaguely for Umnik's reins, remembered how he had beaten the pony, and patted his neck as he led Umnik away down the street. Umnik shook himself, walked slowly and with head hanging, as if perhaps a bit of the coldness had come into his heart too, as if it had been driven there with blows.

He did not go home. He went to the house of old Mischa the hunter, which huddled small and antlered and not so bright as others between the market stalls and the public baths. Snow had drifted heavily there, almost buried it to the eaves on one side. The stone head of a forgotten hero loomed up, peering out of the snow with only the dimmest impression of features. He walked upon the porch and tied Umnik to its rail, stamped his boots and opened the first door, walked across the inner porch and rapped at the second.

There was no answer, no forbidding. "Mischa," he called, "it's Andrei Gorodin." He walked in, sweltering already in the warmth within, redolent with the smell of boiling oils and burned grease and dried herbs that was Mischa's house; antlers were everywhere, and feathers and a clutter of oddments. And a huddle of blankets before the fire . . . that was Mischa himself, a wrinkled face and dark narrow eyes and a skein of grizzled hair trailing from his hood. One hand held a bundle of herbs which he had been crumbling into a saucer; there was no left hand: a wolf had gotten that, when Mischa had been a hunter himself . . . but that was before Andrei had been born. Andrei crouched down and met Mischa's sightless eyes.

"So?" asked Mischa.

The question stopped behind his lips. And slowly Mischa's hand lifted, touched his face spiderwise, drifted to his chest as if it searched for something there as well.

"A visit with no questions, Andrei Vasilyevitch?"

"I have lost my luck, Mischa."

"So." Mischa dipped up water from the kettle, ladled it into the bowl, passed it to him. He took the bowl in gloved hands, inhaled the vapor, sipped the surface, for there was danger in heat so intense after the cold outside. He drank more after a moment, but the cold did not leave, nor the veil on the world diminish.

"I see wolves," Andrei said.

The darkened eyes rested on his, wrinkle-girt as though they were set in cracked stone.

"A white wolf," Andrei said. "Snow white. Ice white."

Old Mischa crumbled more herbs into yet another bowl, ladled in more water, drank, black eyes hooded.

"I shot at it," Andrei said. "But it was there again today. I've looked into the sun, Mischa."

Mischa stared at him as if the eyes could see.

"What shall I *do*, old hunter?"

Mischa moved his left hand, showing the stump. "Appease it," he said. "That is all you can hope to do."

Andrei set down the bowl, wrapped his furred arms the tighter about him, gazed at the old hunter. Wizard. Seer of visions . . . who had had the white sickness—and lived.

"You have looked," the seer said. "You have talked to the wind and heard it answer; you have run ahead of the wolf. And the light has got into your eyes, as it did your father's, my old friend. It took all of him. I gave it part of me. And I am still alive, Andrei Vasilyevitch. Your mother birthed you and pined away; and so they both went. But I am still alive, friend's son."

Andrei stumbled up and hurried for the door, looked back at the wizened face shrouded in gray hood, single hand cupping the bowl. He felt the cold even greater than before, on face and in heart, wherever the blind hunter's fingers had touched. "I will bring your fee," he said, "on my next hunt, a fat rabbit or two, Mischa."

"I take nothing," the old man said. "Not from you, until you see, Andrei Vasilyevitch."

He fled the house, stamped outside and closed the outer door. Umnik waited. He walked down the step to the pony, and noticed for the first time how the paint was peeling on the house opposite, how all the colors of Moskva looked gaudy, how stained the snow and how disarrayed the people, bundled in mismatched furs.

Slowly, with a squinting of his eye and a turning of his shoulder, he looked *up*. Colors shifted in the sky, danced along the rooftops, ran the ridges, streaming glories of pink and gold. *This* was beauty. About him was painted ugliness.

All his heart longed to go on looking, to go out to the ice and ride into the north, into the pure fair beauty.

But the Wolf was there. And the beauty killed.

He shuddered, took Umnik's reins and walked slowly into the street, walked down it among people who stared curiously and whispered behind their hands. This was the wasting. He knew now . . . what drank up the souls of those who took ill with the sickness. It was vision. It was looking on all that hands made and knowing that one had only to look up—and having looked, to yield to that blankness which would exist after all the world was done. To measure one's self and one's acts against that white sheet, and to find them small, and unlovely after all.

Beauty waited, outside the walls, near as a look at the unguarded sky; beauty waited . . . and the Wolf did.

Appease it, the old hunter said, no longer a hunter, Mischa who saw no more sunrises, who had given a part of himself to the wolves . . . to the Wolf.

He went home. Ilya and Ivan Nikolaev ran outside to meet him, and the women and children too, concerned for him. Anna came, and Katya, each hugging him. Quietly he took the harness from Umnik and expected he should go away to his stable . . . but Umnik stood. "Take him," he bade little Ivan, and the boy led the pony away. Andrei looked after the plodding horse and shivered. He felt within his gloved hand another hand, felt a touch upon his arm. . . . He looked into Anna's loving eyes, into her face, saw flaws which he had never seen before, the length of nose, the breadth of cheek, the imperfection of her brow. On it was the tiny fleck of a scar, not centered, and her hair, which he had always thought bright as the sunset on snow, was dull, the braids lusterless against the snowflakes blowing upon them, tiny stars sticking in the loose hair. . . . This was beauty, recalling cold, and fear.

"Come in," Anna urged him, and he surrendered the harness to Ilya, walked with Anna's hand in his, before them all to the house and the inner porch. He shed his outdoor boots and furs, and greeted the children indoors with a touch of his hand and greeted the old ones by the hearth with a kiss, seeing everywhere mortality, man's short span, and smallness.

"Andrei?" Anna sat by him, near the fireside, taking his hand again. He kissed and held hers because it was kind, but love and hope were dried up in him . . . a hunter who could not go outside the walls again, who sat with his soul withering within him.

There was nothing beautiful among men. There was only that beauty above and about Moskva. It would draw the mind from him, or cost the light of his eyes. He stared into the fire, and it was nothing to the brilliance of the sun on ice.

A silence settled about him, whether it was the silence of the house, that they knew there was something amiss with him, or the silence in his soul. He thought how easy it should be, how direly easy tomorrow noon, to walk outside, to stare at the sun until he had no more sight, but even then, there would be the memory.

He thought again and again of old Mischa, who had lost his eyes and lost his hand . . . appease it: but which had gone first, which availed against the Wolf? He should have asked.

"Andrei?" Ilya took his arm. He heard someone weeping by him, perhaps Anna, or some other one who loved him. Perhaps it was himself. He saw Ilya's face before his, much concerned, saw a hand pass before his eyes, heard them all discussing his plight, but he could not come back from that far place and argue with them. He had no desire in him.

They fed him, set food into his hands; and he ate, hardly tasting it. At last Anna took his face between her soft hands and kissed him on the brow; as mother Katya did. "What is *wrong* with Andrei?" a child's voice asked. He would have explained to the child, but someone else did: "He is ill. He is hurt. Go to bed, child."

"His hands are cold," said another; and Anna's voice: "Lock the doors. Oh, lock the doors, don't let him stray." Some did walk away to die, taken with the wasting, who sought the night, and frozen death.

"I shall not go," he said, great effort to speak; and no easier when he had done it. It cheered them all. They hugged him and chafed his hands.

"Perhaps," said Anna's still, faraway voice, "he only looked up a little moment. Perhaps he will get well."

"He will," someone vowed, but he was not sure who. Easier to retreat, back into that far place, but they gave him no peace.

"I will see him to bed," Ilya said. "Go, sleep. I will take care of him. No, Anna—Anna, please go."

Someone kissed him, gently, sadly. The house fell then slowly into silence. He rested, staring at the fire, disturbed only when Ilya would reach to stir the embers. "Will you go upstairs?" Ilya asked at last. "Dare you sleep?"

He roused himself out of kindness to them who loved him, rose, and rising, caught at the mantlepiece, stared fixedly at the face of Ilya's carven wolf, which seemed starker and truer than all else in the room. He looked at the other work which Ilya had made, the carven mantle itself, ran his fingers over the writhing wooden vines and leaves, touched the carven flowers, traced the gaudy, garish colors.

"I have seen beauty," he said. "Ilya, you do not know. It waits out there—"

"Andrei," Ilya said.

"I have seen colors . . . you have never seen."

Ilya reached out and turned his face toward him, lightly slapped his cheek. There was a terrible pain in Ilya's face, like Anna's pain.

"Tell me," Ilya said.

He thought of it, and would not.

"Andrei, if you go, Anna will follow. Do you understand? Anna loves you; and you will never go alone."

He thought of this too, and deep within, tainted by self and small, there was a kindness where love had been, that was the other pole which drew him. The death outside pulled at him, but within the walls there was a bond to living souls, so that at last he knew what he ought to choose, which was Mischa's way. He would not wish this torment on those who loved him. Not on Anna.

"Is there still sun?" he asked.

"No," Ilya said softly. "The sun has gone."

"Tomorrow, then."

"What, tomorrow?" Ilya asked. "What will be tomorrow?"

It was hard to resist Ilya, close to him—so long his friend. Brother. Other self. "There was a wolf," he said slowly, leaning there against the mantel, and fingering the carvings Ilya's hand had made. "I hunted it . . . and it hunts me. I have talked with old Mischa, do you know, Ilya? And Mischa knows that beast. Mischa said I must appease it, and then I shall be free; and so I shall. You love beauty, Ilya, and I hunted it, and I have seen it . . . out there, I have seen the sun, and the light, and the ice, and I am cold, Ilya. I shall look now by little stolen moments and sooner or later I will have to go outside the walls. Then it will be waiting there."

"Anna—would follow you. Do you understand that, Andrei? How much she loves you?"

He nodded. "So," he said, still staring at the wolf, "so I shall not wish to go. I shall try not to, Ilya."

"What . . . did you see?"

He looked into Ilya's eyes, and saw there a touch of that same cold. Of furtive desire. "No," he said. "Let be. Don't stay near me. Let me be."

"So that you can go, and die?"

He shrugged. Ilya stared at him, distraught. He patted Ilya's shoulder, walked away to the ladder to the loft. Stopped, for he could hear the wind outside, calling him, to the wolf. "It's there," he said. "Just outside."

"I shall watch you," Ilya said. "I shall; Anna will, one and then the other of us. We will not let you go."

He looked toward the door, seeing beyond it, into the blue night. Ilya took his arm, had a burning candle with him, to light them to the loft. "Come," Ilya bade him, and he climbed the wooden ladder that was carved with flowers, up among the painted columns and posts of the loft, quietly passed the roomful of sleeping children. There was their own nook; Ilya shut the door, touched the candle to the night lamp and blew the wick out, small ordinary acts, done every night of their lives, comforting now. Andrei moved of lifelong habit, undid his belt and hung it on the bedpost on his side, took off his boots, crawled beneath the cold, heavy bedclothes. Ilya tucked him in when he had lain down, as once

Katya had nightly climbed the stairs to do; and he feigned quick sleep. Ilya stood there a moment, walked around then with a creaking of the aged boards, climbed in the other side.

The bed was like ice; it remained so, but Andrei did not shiver. He lay still, and listened to the wind, listened to footsteps around the door downstairs, soft, padding steps that would never print the snow. Listened to the blowing of flakes from off the rooftree, and the fall of those particles onto drifts. Timbers boomed, like lightning strikes, and he would jump, and lie still again.

At last he could resist it no more, and stirred, thrust a foot for the cold air and the floor. "Andrei," Ilya said at once, turned, rose on an elbow, reached out to take his shoulder. "Are you all right, Andrei?"

He lay back. "Let me go," he said finally. "Ilya, the wolf is out there. It will always be."

"Hush, be still." And when he moved, hardly aware that he moved to rise, Ilya held him back. "It waits," he said, protesting. "It waits, Ilya, and the cold will spread, more than to me alone. You know that."

"Hush." Ilya quietly rolled from the bed, and went around to his side, sat down there. "I shall get no sleep," Ilya said. "I shall never know if you are not walking in yours. How shall I rest, Andrei? I promised Anna I would watch you."

He did not want to listen to this, but it touched through the numbness that possessed him. "You should let me go," he said. "I shall go . . . tomorrow or the next day. It will never be far, just outside the door. Umnik and me—it will have us."

"Hush." Ilya wrapped his wrist in his belt, then attached it to the bedpost; this he allowed, because it was Ilya, and he knew how greatly Ilya grieved; it was not fair that Ilya should worry so. Ilya took great pains, with this and with the other one, sat there, straightened his hair, his hand very gentle. "Sleep now," Ilya said. "Go to sleep; you will not wander in your dreams. You are safe."

He shut his eyes, thinking that the day would come, and other nights, and when he shut his eyes, the wolf was there, no less than he had been before, eyes like the sun, a white wolf in blue night, invisible against the snow which lay thick in the yard. The horses whickered softly, disturbed. Goats bleated . . . no need of alarm for them. They were safe in their warm stable, where the cold would never come . . . and it was the cold which waited.

He felt Ilya draw back, heard the creak of boards, the door open, heard Ilya go down the ladder. He felt a little distress then and pulled to be free, but Ilya's knots were snug, and the vision drank him back again, the blue night, the pale snows. Somewhere he heard the softest of sounds, and he dreamed the wolf retreated, standing warily out by the fence. And others were there, white and gaunt with famine. A vision came to him, of the house door opening softly in the dark and a figure in his furs, who carried his bow and his shafts. Umnik nickered softly, came out from the stable on his own, and his ears were pricked up and his eyes were full of the moving curtains of light which leapt and danced and flowed across the blue heavens. . . . The aurora, uncommonly bright and strange. The horse walked forward, nuzzled an offered hand and the two of them stood together, man and pony, beneath the glory of the sky. Slowly the man looked up, his face to the light, and it was Ilya, whose eyes, angry, showed the least fatal quickness as they gazed at the heavens . . . curiosity, and openness,

"There," Ilya said, tugging at Umnik's long mane, whispering and stretching out the bow like a wand toward the northern sky. "We shall hunt it, we two; we shall try at the least, shall we not?" And he opened the gate, swung up to Umnik's bare back, and the bridleless horse started to move, with eyes as fixed as Ilya's, down trampled streets, past shuttered, eyeless buildings.

And the wolves fled, like the wind, which swept over the eaves and the roofs and went its way, leaving a gate banging dully.

"No," Andrei cried, but that was in his dream; and tugged at the knots, but they were sound, and the strength was gone from him, his soul fled away with the winds, where he watched all the town spread beneath him, all of Moskva embracing her knot of rivers, frozen and cracked and frozen again nigh to the bottom. He saw the gates, through a dust of blowing snow, saw old Pyotr and young Fedor's house shut up tight and the lights out. There Umnik paused, and Ilya dropped down, unbarred the gates and dragged one valve back in the obstructing snow until there was room enough for pony and rider to pass through. He climbed again to Umnik's bare back and Umnik tossed his shaggy head and jogged away in the skirl of blown snow and the glory of the northern lights. "Come back," Andrei wailed, but he spoke with the wind's voice, and the wind carried him, powerless. . . . He skimmed the surface of the snows as if his soul were a flitting bird, racing along before horse and rider, growing small again as wind swept him up. The wolves ran beside, pale movement on pale snow. . . . "They are there," he tried to shout. "Ilya, they are there."

But Ilya was no hunter to understand the bow, had not so much as strung it. Andrei swept nearer, horror in his heart, and saw Ilya's face, the image of Anna's, saw fair hair astream in the wind, snow-dusted, saw his hands . . . Ilya's delicate hands, which were his life and livelihood, bare of gloves despite the cold. And Ilya's eyes, heedless of the wolves, roved the horizon and the sky where the curtaining lights streamed and touched the snows.

Ilya rode north, and north still, with the lights ever receding to the horizon, with the wolves coursing the drifts beside, waiting their time. And the bow at last tumbled from his hand, to lie in the snow, and he never seemed to notice. The quiver slid after. "He is caught," Andrei thought, and the drawing grew dimmer and dimmer within himself, like ice melting away. Pain came back. He dreamed, helpless now, and hurting, saw Ilya slide down from Umnik's back, saw his bare hands caress the shaggy piebald coat as if in farewell, but when Ilya began to walk alone, Umnik followed after. "Oh, go with him," Andrei wished the pony, which was part of him as Ilya had almost stopped being. "Do not let him go alone out there." And Umnik tossed his head as if, after all, he heard, and followed patiently, soundlessly in the powder snow and in the glory of the lights which played across the skies. Horror walked beside, four-footed, tongues lolling, sun-filled eyes glinting slantwise in the night, out of white, triangular faces, and teeth like shards of clear ice. Umnik threw up his head and blew a frosty breath, and his eyes slowly took on that strangeness too, a sunflare gleaming, as if he were no longer one with man; and now an unsuspected enemy trod at Ilya's back.

"Ah," Andrei thought, "let me see his face," and sought in his dream to come round before him, to warn him, to tell him, to know if that same change was yet worked on him. *Ilya*, he thought with all the strength left in him. *Ilya, I am here; oh, look at me.*

Ilya stopped, and turned, his face only vaguely troubled, as if he had heard some strange far voice.

Ilya, O my friend.

"Andrei?' he asked, his pale lips scarcely moving, and put out his hand as if he could see him standing there. "Is it this you saw? I have never been outside the walls; I was always too sickly. But it is beautiful, Andrei."

He had no answer. The beauty which he had seen in the sky was gone; it was all dulled in his eyes, save what he saw reflected in Ilya's.

"I thought," Ilya said, "that I knew what beauty was. . . . I make beauty, Andrei, at least I thought that I made beauty; but I have never seen it until now. I should fear it, I think, but I do not. Only to kill it—Andrei, how can I? How could you?"

"Do not," he whispered. "Come back. Set me free, Ilya. Come home. Let me go."

"I have gone too far," Ilya said. "Don't look, Andrei, go back to your bed; you are dreaming. Go back."

So a dream might speak to him, his own mind's reasoning in a phantom's mouth. It made him disbelieve for a moment, and in that moment Ilya turned and walked on, toward the north. "Wait," he cried, and followed, finding it harder and harder to go, for the wind no longer carried him. "Ilya, wait."

A second time the face turned to him, still Ilya's eyes, though unnaturally calm. And now the wolves ranged themselves upon a low ridge, slitted eyes agleam. "Come back from them," Andrei pleaded. "Do you not see them?"

Ilya looked on him with that look which he must once have turned on those who loved him, which reckoned him very distantly, and dismissed him, finding all the flaws in him.

"The wolves," he wept. "Ilya, do you not see them?"

"No," Ilya said slowly and considerately, looked about at them, and turned back. "There's nothing there. Go back. I've done this so you *could* go back, don't you understand?"

"I'll hunt them," he vowed. "I'll hunt them every one."

"No," Ilya said softly, and behind him stood the pony with eyes full of the sun; indeed the sun was rising, a thin line and bead, with glimmerings and streamings across the ice, ribbons and shafts of light which swept the snowy plain with rose and lavenders and opal odors. Ilya looked toward that sudden brilliance, turning his back. A shape was there, one with the light, robed in light, white like the snows.

"Ilya," Andrei murmured, but Ilya walked away. Andrei caught Umnik by the mane, but no more could he hold the pony . . . Umnik walked too. The wolves glided and flowed to that shape, becoming one with it, which was woman or man, and intolerably bright "Ilya," it whispered, and opened its arms.

Andrei caught at Ilya's sleeve, and received another distant look, turned him, hugged him, to keep his face from that shape, which became woman, and chill, and ineffably beautiful. "It is your Wolf," he said, holding Ilya's face between his hands. "No more real than mine."

"As real," Ilya said. "Never less real than yours." Ilya hugged him, slightly, and without love, with only the memory of it. "You gave it what you give to beauty, Andrei; and so do I. And so do I."

He walked away, and Andrei stood, as if there were a bond holding him that had yielded all it could: he could not go further. He watched Ilya and the pony, one after the other, reach that light, saw the semblance of arms reach from it, and enfold Ilya, so that for a moment they seemed two lovers entwined; saw Umnik blurred likewise into that streaming beauty, and saw it spread with coming morning.

Of a sudden as the light came Umnik was coming back, with a rider on his back, out of the sun which streamed about him and shot rays where his hooves touched the drifts. His rider was a like vision, in the moving of his hair and the lifting of his hand as the pony stopped . . . a fair cold face which had been Ilya's, the hair drifting in the winds, and the eyes, the eyes ablaze with opal gold, like lamps making his glowing face dark.

"Come," Ilya whispered. "O my friend."

Andrei turned and fled, raced with the retreating night, fled with other shadows, mounted the winds, naked and alone. He crossed the rivers, and saw the bridge, saw Moskva embracing the frozen ice with its wooden walls, and staining the purity of the world with its dark buildings. He found the open gate and whisked in, skimmed the well-trodden street, found the least chink in the wall of the house and gained entry, into warmth and stillness, into the loft, where he rested, trapped as before.

He woke, turned his head, found the place by him empty.

"*Ilya!*" he cried, and woke the house.

They found him by the gate, by the corner of the front-yard fence, partly covered by the blowing snow, frozen and with tiny ice crystals clinging to clothes and face . . . not terrible, as some of the dead were which the cold killed, but rather as one gazing into some fair dream, and smiling. Andrei touched his face as Anna held him, shedding tears which melted ice upon his cheek; and suddenly in his agony he sprang up and ran to the stable, with the others calling out after him.

Umnik lay there, quite stiff and dead. The other pony looked at him reproachfully, and the goats bleated, and he turned away, walked back to the others, gathered Anna into his arms.

The spring was then not long in coming; the winds shifted and the snows shrank and the rivers began to groan with breaking ice.

Andrei rode the other pony in the trodden street, the bay, the younger, a beast which would never be what Umnik had been. The drifts within the city yielded up the white wind-blasted pillars which had been statues, turned up small and pitiful discoveries, small animals which had been frozen the winter long; and an old woman had been found near the Moskva river. But such tragedies came with every winter; and spring came and the white retreated.

He passed the gates and the bridge, and neglected his eye-shields as he rode along. He had a new bow and quiver ... the old ones, from Ilya's dead hand, had seemed unlucky to him ... and he rode out along the edge of the retreating woods, where trees shed their burdens of snow, where the tracks of deer were visible.

He and Anna had begun their living together before the spring; he wore work of her stitchery, and she swelled with child, and the dull scar of winter past seemed bearable. He had taken a free gift to the old wizard, Mischa, who had now lived yet another winter—a pair of fat hares, paying for truth he had gotten, and bearing no resentments.

The bay pony's hooves broke melting snow, cracked ice, and there was a glistening on it from the sun, but the day was still overcast. He shielded his eyes with a gloved hand and looked at the drifts of gray-centered cloud, shivered somewhat later as the cloud blew athwart the sun, and a chill came into the air.

There were only ordinary days, forever. He saw the places in Moskva where the paint peeled, saw cracks in the images of Moskva; the patterns which Anna made to clothe him seemed garish and far less lovely than once they had; he had seen beauty once, and aimed at it and wounded it.

Now he saw truth.

"Was it your sight you gave the Wolf?" he had asked Mischa finally. "Or was it the hand?"

"I destroyed my sight," Mischa had said, "—after."

Mischa had had no one. He had three families; had Anna; had a growing child.

Had had a friend.

Ilya's carvings faded; would crack; would decay with the age of Moskva. Ilya had made nothing lasting. Nor did any man.

The colors would fade and the ice would come; he knew that, but looked at the colors and the patterns men made, because he had seared the other from his heart and from his eyes; and he went on looking at it because others needed him.

Cold touched the side of his face and pushed at his body, a touch of deep chill, a breathing of sleet and snowflakes. The bay pony threw her head and snorted in unease.

What had Ilya seen? he wondered again and again. What, if not the Wolf?

What had it been, that drew him away?

Snowflakes dusted the pony's black mane, smallish stars, each different, each delicate and white and in the world's long age, surely duplicated again and again. As human grief was.

He looked toward the north, toward the gleam of ice and sunlight, opal and orange and rose and gold, melting-bright.

There was nothing there.

Forever.

NIGHTGAME

(Rome)

They offered him food and drink. He accepted, although by all his codes he should not. He was no one. They had taken his name with his totem and his weapons, and they had killed Ta'in, who was his heart. A warrior of the *netang*, he would have refused food and drink offered from an enemy's hand, and died of it, but they had forced it into him during the long traveling that had brought him to this place, and taken from him all that he was, and he was tired. His weapons, had he had them, could never have fought the like of them, with their machines and their mocking smiles. He would have killed them all if he could, but that was while he had been a warrior, and while he had had a name. Now he sat listlessly and waited what more would happen, and what he would be, which was something of their purposing.

Belat switched the vid off and smiled at the portly executive who rested in the bowl-chair in the offices of the Earth Trade Center, next to the crumbling port. "*Netang* tribesman, off Phoenix IV. That's what I've gotten us."

Ginar folded his hands across his paunch and nodded slowly to Belat the trader. Grinned, in rising amusement "The Tyrant will be vastly surprised. You go as planned . . . tonight?"

"I've advised the usual contacts," Belat said, "that I have a special surprise for the evening. I've permission to cross the bridge. I even detected a spark of enthusiasm."

"A special surprise." Ginar chuckled again. It would be that. "You'll not," he said, "mention *my* name in the City, as sponsor of this . . .

should something go wrong. *Your* risk. After all—it's your risk. I only provide you . . . opportunity."

The City was old as Earth was old, in the waning chill of its plague-spotted sun.

The Eternal City . . . under the latest of its many names, in the reign of the latest of its Tyrants. It sat on its seven hills by its sluggish, miasmic river, and dreamed dreams.

That was the passion of its Tyrant, and of all the nobles of the City—dreams. The apparatus (which might have originated here, or perhaps on one of the colonial worlds: no one remembered) existed in the Palace which dominated the City; it gave substance to dreams, and by that substance consoled the violet nights and the oppressive days of the sickly star. There was nothing left to *do* on Earth, nothing at all, for the vanities were all exposed, the ambitions, the conceits of empire, the meaningless nature of power on one world, when greater powers now spanned the void and embraced worlds in the plural, when those powers themselves had had time to grow old and to decay many times. Earth had seen it all. The Eternal City had seen such eras pass . . . too often to be amused by the exercise of power or the pursuit of empire. It had no hopes left, being merely old, as the sun was old, and the moon looming large and sickly in the sky, lurid with the reflected glow of the ailing sun. Earth and the City could have no ambitions. Ambitions were for younger worlds. For the City there was only pleasure.

And the dreaming.

Exquisite decadence, the dreams . . . in which some lost themselves and failed to return—dreams which, in the strange power of the machine, could become too real, which for those that fell too far within their power wrought real consequences on fleshly bodies.

The days the Eternal City gave to mundane pursuits, for those who waked . . . the supervision of the dullard laborers who toiled in the catacomb depths of the City. The sun was a fearsome thing, and during most of the day the City stirred only beneath the ground, in the far-reaching windings of the tunnels, where mushrooms grew, and blind fishes, and yeasts and other such things; and by mornings and evenings, when the sun was kinder, the laborers tended the crops which still flourished on the edges of the sluggish River. Such men chose to work, and not to dream, amid the fearsome cruelties of their lords. The day belonged to them, and to the lesser nobles whose tedious duty it was to oversee, and to tally, and to arrange trade with the few ships which might chance to touch at the port across the River. The City had some mundane concerns, and labor existed, not because it had to, but because some men knew themselves doomed to be victims, and knew themselves less imaginative, and less fierce, and made themselves beasts of burden, because beasts toiled their little share and so fed themselves and so lived. Such were the days of the City.

But the nights, the violet nights . . . then, up on the Palace hill, the delicate dreamers sank into the many-colored deviances, the eldritch pleasures, the past of the City which had been, empires long lost—the past which might have been; the true future and the future which could never be.

The City exported dreams. This alone was enough to sustain its nobles, the glittering crowd which attended on the Tyrant. They dreamed; and when it pleased them, they sold those dreams, recorded tapes of a flavor and nature which alone could satisfy the jaded dreamtrippers of the Limb's decadent First Colonies (where law had long ago faded) or the illicit trade on younger worlds elsewhere. They were a commodity unique among expensive vices . . . expensive because they came from Earth, which was remote from important worlds; because they were rare (seldom would the Tyrant consent); and because they were purchased with lives.

The Port of the City remained open for this trade alone, bringing in the mere food and drink and precious objects which kept the nobles of the City well-disposed and luxurious—bringing in, more rarely, that prize victim which could open the iron gates of the seventh hill, and secure a tape of such sport as would echo wealth across the stars, enriching the hands through which it passed.

Hence Ginar, who lived in affluence in his mansion by the Port, served by countless servants who found tending Ginar more comfortable than toiling for the lords of the City . . . lapped in the luxury of goods he siphoned off from those lords, who hardly missed them. Presidency of such a post had to offer some recompense in luxury, physically, for it meant exile from the civilized worlds, the young worlds, where life was, and some could not have endured that. But there was one luxury Ginar had here, besides his fine foods and his servants: he was himself of one of the First Colonies, and for many years he had been an addict, a dreamtripper, who lived for that pleasure which was nearer here than anywhere—and across the River, out of reach save when some tape could be brought from out of the City, bought at price.

Hence Belat, who made the long ship runs, who had been very long in the trade, and whose well-being presently trembled on the brink.

Belat started now across the bridge, when the sun was still at dawning, and safe—across the bridge which was the oldest and the last of the bridges of the City. On it, monoliths which had been statues stared down, marble pillars deprived by time of all feature, only hints of faces, like wide-mouthed screams and sunken eyes, and handless, outstretched arms.

And beyond that . . . a slow walk through the City itself, through the catacombs, which were ruin piled on ruin, untended, for no one cared to repair what time had always, eternally, destroyed. Workers stared from eyes like those of the statues, pits of shadow, fear-haunted. Sometimes one would dart away, but most would stand wherever they were caught, trying, perhaps, to seem dull—for nightly what time there was no special game, the lords walked out among them and chose one of them for that fate, whatever one the lords judged guilty of imagination, whatever one promised sport.

He never saw one defiant. Those who offered such looks would have been first chosen, most savored.

He walked on, paying no great attention to them, not liking their eyes; he never had, in the many times he had walked this path.

Seven hills, and the centermost was a cloven hill, where lightnings played most frequently in storms, a hill poised above ruins and split by the seam of an ancient fault. Gods had dwelt here once, and now the Tyrant did, at the end of a road which walked the ancient line of destruction, sleeping now, as the City slept, huddled on its hills. In this place had been an ancient ruin, and bits of white marble worked up like broken bone from the seam of this old wound, the only bare ground in all the City, surrounded by catacombs, the heaped up ruins of the millennia of the City's old age.

An iron gate began that valley, where a Keeper stood, a lesser lord, on daywatch, with a shelter from the sun when it should rise, a gatehouse of jumbled bits of marble, aged and smooth, and twined about with vines. The Keeper's interest pricked at this visitation—which came but so very seldom, and Belat stood before the gates without touching them, hands folded, matching the hauteur of the guard himself.

"I've a gift," Belat said. The Keeper regarded him a moment more from kohl-rimmed eyes, gave a languid, deadly smile.

And with a touch the young lord loosed the gate. "Go on," he whispered, in that hoarse, hushed tone of the aristocracy of the City. None of the nobles spoke loudly; it was the mark of their peculiar art.

He passed through, walked that way among the ruins. He felt the smile behind his back, a feral smile which followed him with lazy, kohl-rimmed eyes, and lusted for him, in one way or the other.

The road wound on, over that field of broken bits of antiquity, with the catacombs looming down on the left, with a slow tide of them seeming to lap at this valley on his right. The road wound, for no apparent reason, but there might have been, once, in the long ago past, buildings which lay buried now. The Games were very old here. It was told that this place had known man's oldest and most dire vices, the ultimate sport of a species once hunters . . . to hunt itself.

"I've a gift," he informed the Keeper of the second gate, who stood behind the iron grill, before a gatehouse likewise sheltered from the sun. Behind this rose the Way of a Thousand Steps, and the inmost gates. "Then," that one whispered, opening wide the gates, "there will be a good hunt tonight, won't there?"

He climbed on, panting now, and with a weakness in his knees that was not all his lack of exercise, his habitude of ships. Above him the Lotus Dome of the Palace loomed against the morning, far, far up the steps worn into hollows by the passage of feet, of the Keepers up and down, and of the victims . . . up.

"I've a gift," he informed the Keeper of the third gate, the very doors.

That one merely grinned, showing sharp blue teeth, and let him pass.

Belat walked on, into the long inner halls of lotus-stem columns, which twisted their way up and writhed across vaulted ceilings; and far, into yet another hall, where the stems rose to stone lily pads and marble lotuses on the ceiling, stems behind which coy golden-scaled fishes lurked . . . beneath which a throne like one alabaster lotus flower, and languid golden limbs disposed upon it, and dark, kohl-smeared eyes regarding him. The Tyrant frowned at him, a cloud upon the youthful brow, a sudden quick movement of a jewel-nailed hand, a gesture to begone—mercy now twice given. Twelve years old was Elio DCCLII, petulant, spoiled . . . dangerous. "Go away," the boy whispered, "—*foreigner*. We sent you away last time. Do you think we forget? Do you think we forgive?"

"I've brought you a gift," Belat said, and watched the old interest grow unwillingly in the Tyrant's eyes . . . interests like pleasures which quickly came and quickly fled, which made this handsome, golden child the ruler he was—most skilled of dreamers, worker of finesses and deadly dangers the most jaded could not match, a coolness which insulated him from shocks and let him shape the dreams his way. Assassinations had been tried before—in vain.

"Your last gift," the boy said, "failed."

"This one," Belat said, venturing a step closer, "this one will not."

"What have you brought us?" the boy-Tyrant whispered, leaning forward on the Lotus Throne. "Something—new?"

"A dreamer," Belat whispered back, and before the pouting, painted lips could frame a word . . . "A *different* dreamer. A wild dreamer. Something you've not hunted, Majesty, something Earth has never seen."

The familiar petulance trembled on the childish lips, the frown gathered, deadly shadow in the kohl-smeared eyes . . . fresh from the night's hunt was Elio, and perhaps sated, or perhaps—disappointed. "You mean to stay," the Tyrant lisped, "and record this . . . with your machines. We should submit to this—distasteful intrusion in our sport. And you *sell* these things, do you not?"

"I have to travel far," he said, cautious on this point. "Consider only, Majesty, that I search the worlds for you . . . to bring you such a gift. And the record makes it possible again."

"You intrude."

"Don't I bring you the rarest treasures, Majesty? Can the dull creatures out there match mine? Don't I bring you always the most unusual, the greatest sport?"

"You *bored* us, dream-stealer. You raised our hopes, and you failed them, and are there not others—seller of our pleasures—who would fill your place more cleverly? Ships would still come and go at the port. The factor would still be there. And perhaps the next trader would be more careful . . . might he not? You *bored* us. So long we waited for what you promised, and it *failed*. We let you go once. Not again."

Belat sweated, resisted temptation to mop at his face and admit it. Ruin was on the one side. On the other—"You'll take my gift," he whispered. "It's my expense, Majesty. And if it pleases, the tape . . . to take with me."

"I'll take it," the boy said ever so softly. "And let you make your tape; but, Belat, this time there will be no forgiving. We'll hunt *you* if it fails to please."

He shivered, stared into the boyish eyes, and hated, smothering that hate, striving to smile. "I am confident," he said. "Would I risk coming here again—without cause to be?"

The eyes took on suspicion, the least suspicion, quickly fled, and a childish hand waved him gone. Belat took his cue, gathered his life and his sanity into his two hands and walked velvet footed from the lotus-stem hall—walked the long way down, past curiosity borning in the Keepers' eyes, curiosity which itself was, in the Eternal City, a commodity precious more than gold.

The sun climbed higher, and outside, the City sank into its daytime burrowings; and the Lotus Palace sank into its daily hush. Elio bathed, a lingering immersion in a golden bowl only slightly more gleaming than the limbs which curled in it, serpent-lithe and slender. He walked the cool, lily-stemmed halls, and stared restlessly out upon the only unshielded view in the Palace, upon the ruin-flecked valley below the hill, upon the catacombs sheened by the daystar's terrible radiations, and behind him his attendant lesser lords observed this madness with languid-lidded eyes, hoping for something bizarre. But he was not struck by the sun, nor did he leap to his death, as four Tyrants before him had done, when amusements failed; and he turned on them a look which in itself gave them a prized thrill of terror . . . remembering that to assuage the pangs of the last failed hunt—a minor lord had fallen to him in the Games, rare, rare sport.

But he passed them by with that deadly look and walked on, absorbed in his anticipations, often raised, ever disappointed.

The kill was always too swift. And he knew the whispers, that such power as his always burned itself out, that it grew more and more inward, lacking challenge, until at last nothing should suffice to stir him.

He imagined. Such talent was rare. The sickness was on him, that came on the talented, the brilliant dreamers, who found no further challenges. At twelve, he foresaw a day not far removed when his own death would seem the only excitement yet untried. He knew the halls, each lotus stem and startled, golden fish. He knew the lords and ladies, knew them, not alone the faces, but the very souls, and drank in all their pleasures, fed by them, nourished on their darkest fantasies, and was bored.

He probed the deaths of victims, and found even that tedious.

He grew thin, pacing the halls by day, and exhausting his body in dreams at night.

He terrorized captured laborers, but that waking sport palled, for the dreams were more, and deeper, and more colorful, unlimited in fantasy, save by the limits of the mind.

And these he had paced and plumbed as well.

At twelve he knew the limits of all about him, and had experienced all the pleasures, heritor of a thousand thousands of his sort, all of whom died young, in a City which found its Eternity a slow, slow death.

Perhaps tonight, he thought, savoring the thought, I die.

He sat much, in the cell. This day—if it was day—he knew that they were watching him, and they had not, before. This they were free to do, and he could not protest. He sat, and stared at his hands, and waited. There would come a time that they would insist he must eat and drink; or they would make him sleep and force this upon him. He sat still now, not betraying that he knew that they were there. He had had dignity once. They had none, who peeped and pried and did not come before his face, but that was his shame, who had fallen to the like of these. One day they must tire of this, he thought, when he let himself think at all, and then they must decide what they would do. Perhaps today, he thought, but did not let himself hold that thought, for that was ultimately to put himself in their power, and he would neither react nor think of them. He was alone. They had made him so. More than this they had to come and do to him. He would not help them.

And then the weariness came on his limbs, and he sat, still possessed of his little dignity, while his limbs loosed, and he began to yield. They did this to him when they wished to handle him. They wished so now.

But this time the limbs alone failed, and consciousness did not.

The dying sun was sinking, and the engorged moon rose over the marshes by the River, touched the catacombs of the common hills and the Lotus Dome of the seventh.

It was the hour.

The procession left the port, a slow line of the servants of Ginar, bearing the recording devices, bearing a black plastic coffin. They crossed the bridge of featureless statues; by the time the last rim of the diseased sun was sinking, they were treading the ways of the catacombs, where laborers watched like statues, fearing, perhaps, for the direst dreams sometimes spilled beyond, and worked terror even here, a miasma from the Palace that infected even the City.

They reached the first of the gates, and crossed the field of ruin; reached the second, and passed to the Way of the Thousand Steps, and up that height to the third. There the servants stayed, and set down the apparatus, and the coffin. Belat took up the apparatus, struggling with the weight; the Keepers and lords took up the coffin and bore it further, within the forbidden perimeters of the Lotus Palace, where only the privileged might go.

And victims.

Some, brought here, struggled at the last; some cried or cursed. This one did not, drugged, but not too far: Belat was sure of that. The coffin went ahead through the lotus-stem hall, and Belat walked last, incongruously like a mourner, head bowed with his load, panting after the measured steps of the Keepers who bore the case—into the inmost hall, of the lily-pad ceiling and the Lotus Throne.

The dreams were prepared. The apparatus which *was* the Lotus Dome was soon to be engaged. And the Tyrant would have his precious surprise, a manic *netang* . . . a trap neatly laid, even legally: a primitive mind this, without the softness of the dreamtrippers who were his usual gifts, the addicts of the First Colonies who fell into his hands and disappeared, seeking the ultimate thrill—and finding it here, themselves become material for the City and its dreams, recorded, sold in turn, to lure others.

Not this time . . . this time a surprise for His Majesty Elio DCCLII, one which might serve a double turn. Belat's breath came short with more than the burden he carried, and his skin had a deathly clamminess; he grinned, a grimace round his panting—for it was the Tyrant who was the focus of the dreams, the Tyrant who led . . . who died, if things went wrong.

Revenge, on the one hand, for the terrors he had suffered; and most of all—a new Tyrant to trade with, one more manageable, whereby he could keep his post. No more threats. No more humiliations. There were no more talents such as Elio's here—or the earlier assassinations would have succeeded. A manageable tyrant . . . well worth the price and risk.

Or on the other hand . . . *gratitude*, if that word had currency here. Pleasure, a hunt the Tyrant would much savor. And ask another, and another, until he died.

In either case a dream of special flavor, a unique prize which was his alone. Delicious murder, the wild *netang* with his savagery among these hunters, primitive innocence loosed among the jaded minds of the oldest city of man . . .

Or the death of a Tyrant of this City, with all its sensitive agonies, for when Elio should falter, they would all turn on him, all.

And the machines would capture it for him.

*   *   *

There was no fighting, as there had been none before. They bore him where they chose, to do what they chose. He wept in his narrow prison . . . not violent weeping, only the helpless flow of a tear down his cheek, but his body was paralyzed and he could not wipe it away. It shamed him, but he had encountered many shames since he lost his name and himself.

He felt movement, knew himself carried, had perceived them near water, in a closed echoing place, climbing . . . perhaps to hurl him to his death; but that seemed a small act after all the others. Now he heard echoes as of some great cavern . . . smelled thick scents of rot and of flowers, where before the climbing the air had been cold and clean.

Perhaps he had already died. He was no longer sure.

Belat bowed, smiled at the great Tyrant, who lounged on the Lotus Throne, in the inmost chamber of stone flowers. The whole court was about him, fantastical in their array, their painted skins and kohl-rimmed eyes, their nodding plumes and gossamer robes . . . like living flowers about the stone lotus-stems and golden fishes.

The boy Tyrant moved his fingers, which flashed amethyst from jeweled nails. The Keepers set down the coffin before him on the floor, opened it, exposing the brown, still body within. A whisper of displeasure went up, disappointment, but the tribesman's eyes opened, and glared, and a titter of anticipation ran round the room. Elio leaned forward on his throne, elbow against a lily-petal arm, chin propped on fist. His amethyst-dusted lids blinked; rouged lips smiled; and Belat who had gone rigid with fear—relaxed and smiled as well. The Tyrant flicked that look in his direction and the smile froze.

"The agreement, Majesty."

"Haste," the boy said.

Belat made haste, found himself a corner the disdainful lords and ladies allowed, set up his recorder, hands trembling in anxiety. He did not share the dreams—observed only.

When he had made the few adjustments, he made feverish speed to shield himself, to inject into his veins a stimulant that would keep him as much as possible—awake. He observed. When he entered into the dreams at all, it was always as a mere spectator, distant: he was not, himself, an addict. He preserved that remoteness as he valued his life, for the dreamtrippers were not without humor.

Elio smiled, amethyst-lidded eyes intent upon his prize. Others of his lords and ladies gathered close about him, a pastel ring of painted faces intent to stare at the tribesman within his coffin, savoring what they saw.

The boy Tyrant moved his hand once. The lights in all the dome dimmed. A second gesture. The apparatus engaged.

He stood. He could move again, and that sudden freedom shocked him. He was knee-deep, naked, in rotting marsh. The whole world was flat and the sun was barely able to provide a murky twilight.

"It's the end of the world," a voice whispered within him. "Where all the land has worn away. It's *old*."

A bird hovered against the sickly disk of the sun, watching. He tried to walk, but there was nowhere to walk to, for the marsh stretched as far as the eye could see in all directions, and he had no memory of how he had got there. The flatness was sinister. He walked toward the sun, that being the only object there was in all the world, walked until he tired, and stopped, still knee-deep in water.

A movement brushed against his ankle. He started and looked down. A serpent with amethyst scales, bright in all that brown, wound round his calf and lifted its head against his thigh—stared at him with wise and knowing eyes.

"I am young," it said.

No, he thought, refusing such madness, and it was a brown bit of weed.

He stood in a cave, where water dripped in blackness. He moved, and his steps echoed in far darkness. The cold bit into him. There was water before his feet, and fish hung glowing in it, and upon the wall, a worm spun a glowing web."

"It's the heart of the world," the voice whispered. "And it's hollow."

Water fell, plopped in tinkling echoes. Something moved, and breathed, and came toward him, dragging vast bulk among the rocks, which rattled and shifted in the dark.

"I have no heart," it said.

No, he thought again, but he would not run, and light broke about him, white and blinding.

He stood atop a mountain higher than all mountains, in snow, with mountain peaks about it, thrusting out of cloud; and the sun turned red and stained the white with blood. The bird was back, an inky blot, hovering on rowing wings against the gales which shook his naked limbs and streamed his hair into his eyes. The winds turned warm. He looked about him, and a languor stole over him.

"It's the height of the world," the voice whispered. "The sky is very near this place."

The warmth increased, melting down the drifts, and a woman lay naked in the snow, violet-lidded and seeming asleep. Her eyes began to open.

No, he thought at once, for he trusted nothing in this place. The lips parted and laughed; and the sleeper became a grinning skull, became a beast, became woman and man and goddess and god, became a machine which walked in the likeness of a man, and a demon which at last became the serpent again, and danced for him, hood spread, tongue flickering, violet-scaled against the ruddy snow.

"I am desire," it said, hissing. In the clouds about the peak, towers rose, and became what he knew for a city, and time flowed backward into an ancient past, of wars and armies and conquests, of horrors and of greatness of its kings. All of this he was offered, and all the while the black bird hovered in the winds. White beasts had gathered, and there came a faint, threatening laughter.

"Run," they taunted him. He tried to stand, but he was a beast hooved and made to be their prey. He whirled on slender legs, stretched out and ran, and they howled after him, across the snow, among the rocks. He skidded on ice, recovered and ran, bursting his heart in his running, leaping and bounding where he might till the air tore his lungs and his belly ached, till limbs quivered with the shocks of his leaps and he ran slower and slower, among crags echoing with laughter. The rocks closed before him, a cul de sac. He turned, his four legs trembling, and lowered his horned head, gasping.

But they were men, like those of the ancient city, and bore bows. They pierced him with arrows and his blood stained the snow and the rocks and ran in great smears down the sky.

No! he thought, refusing to die. He looked up at the bird which was always there, and saw among the rocks the violet-eyed serpent, which coiled with head uplifted, watching him.

It shaped itself. He made up his mind and did the same. He was a man again, on two feet. The bird screamed in the sky, and he gave it a cold look, and healed himself of his wounds. He glanced again at the serpent, but a whole host of polychrome serpents had taken its place, and the rocks had acquired a pair of eyes, amethyst-rimmed.

They were lively with interest. "What is your name?" the voice asked.

He shaped his totem again. It hung about his neck. He drew a great breath, suffused with power, and named them his name. He extended the ground at his feet, and made it golden grass, stretched it wide and pushed back the mountain peaks, until his own mountains stood there again. He made the sky blue overhead, and the sun, young and yellow. He stretched wide his arms, embracing the world, and looked again toward the rocks. A naked boy stood there, among the serpents, which hissed and threatened. The boy looked frightened, a frowning, sullen fear, with will to fight. He approved that, respected it.

"Elio," he said, for he knew that name among the others. He ignored the frown and made game in the land, and more and better birds to fly in the heavens, made the great river, and fish to swim in it, made it all as it had been, and himself as he had been, and lifted his hand and looked about him, showing it all to the boy who was a king.

"*No!*" the bird cried; and the serpents, far away now, wove into a man of metal which started at the horizon and clicked toward them.

"They will kill you," the boy said. "They will kill me too if I stand here. Let me out of your dream. Let me go. I should not have stepped so far apart from them."

"Do you want to leave?" he asked the boy, who, naked, looked about at the blue sky and the bright young sun and all the grasslands, and shook his head, his eyes shining violet to the depths.

"It is young," he said. "What else is it?"

He shut his eyes a moment, and dreamed Ta'in, whose vast slit eyes and scaly nose took shape for him, head and great amber-scaled body . . . huge, fierce Ta'in, who had carried *him* from boyhood. The dragon rubbed against him and nosed the boy, lifted a wide slit-eyed gaze at the edge of the land, which with every step of the metal creature, turned to metal and cities, and over that creeping change, a ship hovered, bristling with offworlders' weapons.

"We must run," the boy said.

He paid no heed, swung up to Ta'in's back, faced the metal edge which was growing wider and nearer, and reckoned well that this was the last time, that if he lost Ta'in again, Ta'in was truly lost, and so was he. He had his weapons again, drew bow and fired at the advancing edge, fired shaft after shaft, and saw the machines and the guns bearing down on him as they had before.

He was not alone. Another dragon whipped up beside him, with a young rider in the saddle. The boy drew bow and fired, shouted for joy to see the metal edge retreat ever so slightly.

And then there was another dragon, and another rider, on the boy's left.

"Mahin!" the boy cried, naming him. Three bows launched arrows now, and yet for all they took back, the metal edge still struggled forward.

And stopped its advance, for another and another dragon appeared, a hissing thunder. He saw them, shrieked a war cry, ordered attack, and the riders were still joining them, while dragon bodies surged forward, and Ta'in's power rippled between his knees. The arrows became a storm. The metal edge retreated, and the ship, last of all, began to shiver in a sky gone blue, plummeted down, grew feathers, shed them and died.

He looked about him, at the bright familiar land, at the keen-eyed warriors who had joined him, men and women, at the brave boy who was his once-lost son. Pride welled up in him.

"Your dream," his son said, love burning in his eyes, "is best of all."

"Let me in," Ginar said. He had walked far to the iron gates, and his bulk made walking difficult. Two days and Belat had not returned. It was a desperate act, to cross the bridge unbidden, to venture the catacombs . . . all but deserted now, but he had seen the movement from the hill by the port, the drift of peasants going where they would not have dared to go, the gradual desertion of the fringes of the City, the long silence . . . and Ginar, who was an addict of the dream, could no longer bear the question. "Let me in," he begged of the Keeper, who did not *look* like the legendary Keepers, but more like one of the peasants. He hoped for the tape at least, to have that, to savor the dream for which he had been longing with feverish desire.

The Keeper let him in. He walked, panting, the long road through the field of ruin, where peasants sat with placid eyes. Walked, with long, painful pauses, to the inner gates, and found them open; climbed, which took him very long, the Way of the Thousand Steps, sweating and panting; but he was driven by his addiction, and not by any rational impulse. Belat had promised him—promised him the most unique of all dreams. He had imagined this, savored this, desired it with a desire that consumed all sense . . . to have this one greatest dream . . . to experience such a death, and live—

At long last he reached the doors, which stood ajar, where peasants sat along the corridors . . . he stumbled among their bodies, pushed and forced his way in gathering shadow, for the lamps were dimmed. He entered the Lotus Hall at last, where peasants sat among the lords of dream, where a boy sat on a flower throne.

And a weariness came on his limbs so that they could no longer move, for it was night and the dream was strong. He sank down, no longer conscious of his bulk, forgetful of such desires, and the pleasures he had come to find.

He sat down in the council ring among the tents, and smiled, while the dragons stamped and shuffled outside the camp, and the wind whispered in the grass beyond, and the three moons were young.

1981

▼

HIGHLINER

▲

(New York City)

The city soared, a single spire aimed at the clouds, concave-curved from sprawling base to needle heights. It had gone through many phases in its long history. Wars had come and gone. Hammered into ruin, it rebuilt on that ruin, stubbornly rising as if up were the only direction it knew. How it had begun to build after that fashion no one remembered, only that it grew, and in the sun's old age, when the days of Earth turned strange, it grew into its last madness, becoming a windowed mountain, a tower, a latter-day Babel aimed at the sullen heavens. Its expanse at the base was enormous, and it crumbled continually under its own weight, but its growth outpaced that ruin, growing broader and broader below and more and more solid at its base and core, with walls crazily angled to absorb the stresses.

Climate had changed many times over the course of its life. Ice came now and froze on its crest, and even in summers, evening mists iced on the windward side, crumbling it more; but still it grew, constantly webbed with scaffolding at one point or the other, even at the extreme heights; and the smaller towers of its suburbs followed its example, so that on its peripheries, bases touching and joining its base, strange concave cones lifted against the sky, a circle of spires around the greater and impossible spire of the City itself, on all sides but the sea.

At night the City and its smaller companions gleamed with lighted windows, a spectacle the occupants of the outlying city-mountains could see from their uppermost windows, looking out with awe on the greatest and tallest structure man had ever built on Earth . . . or ever would. And from the much higher windows of the City itself, the occupants might look out on a perspective to take the senses away, towering over all the world. Even with windows tinted and shielded against the dying sun's radiations, the reflections off the surface of the land and the windows of other buildings flared and glared with disturbing brightness; and by night the cities rose like jeweled spires of the crown of the world, towering mounds which one day might be absorbed as their bases had already been.

It was alone, the City and its surrounding companions, on a land grown wild between; on an Earth severed from the younger inhabited worlds, with its aged and untrustworthy star.

The tower was for the elite, the artists, the analysts, the corporate directors and governors; the makers and builders and laborers lived at the sprawling, labyrinthine base, and worked there, in the filling of the core, or outward, in the quarrying of still more and more stone which came up the passages, from sources ever farther away; and some worked the outer shell, adding to it. It was mountain and city at once; and powerful yet. It had pride, in the hands of its workers and the soaring height of it.

And the highliners walked with a special share of that pride, proud in their trade and in the badges of it, among which were a smallish size and a unique courage.

Johnny and Sarah Tallfeather were such, brother and sister; and Polly Din and Sam Kenny were two others. They were of the East Face, of the 48th sector (only they worked everywhere) and when they were at the Bottom, in the domain of the Builders, they walked with that special arrogance of their breed, which could hang suspended on a thread in the great cold winds of Outside, and look down on the city-mountains, and wield a torch or manage the erection of the cranes, which had to be hoisted up from the smallest web of beginning lines and winches, which, assembled, hoisted up more scaffolding and stone and mortar. They could handle vast weights in the winds by patience and skill, but most of all, they could dare the heights and the ledges.

Others might follow them, on the platforms they made, creep about on those platforms anchored by their lines, Builders brave enough compared to others, who found it all their hearts could bear just to go up above the two hundreds and look down from the outer-shell windows; but those who worked the high open face on lines alone were a special breed, the few who could bear that fearful fascination, who could work between the dying sun and the lesser cities, who could step out on nothing and swing spiderwise in the howling winds and freezing mists; and rarer still, those with the nerve and with the skill of engineers as well. They were the first teams on any site, the elite of a special breed.

That was the 48th.

The order was out: the city would grow eastward, toward the Queens Tower; the work was well under way, the Bottom skylights covered on that side, because the high work required it. There was a burst of prosperity in the eastside Bottom, establishments which fed and housed the Builders who were being shifted there.

"It's going to *change*," some higher up muttered, less happy, for it meant that favorite and favored real estate would lose its view, and accesses, pass into the core, ultimately to be filled, and their windows would be taken out and carefully, lovingly transferred to the Outside as the building progressed: the computers ruled, dictated the cost-effective procedures; and the highliners moved in.

They began by walking the lower levels, work which made them impatient, mostly leaving that to Builders, who were skilled enough; then their real work began, mounting the East Face itself, floor by floor, swinging out in the winds and seeking with their eyes for any weaknesses in structure or stone which deviated from what the computers predicted. Small cracks were abundant and ordinary; they noted them on charts and the regular liner crews would fill them.

The liners worked higher and higher; came to the Bottom each night in increasing numbers, for the scaffolding had begun now, far across the Bottom, and new joy dens and sleeps had opened up to accommodate them in the sprawl of the base.

There were, of course, deeper levels than the liners ever saw: and they too were worked by a special breed that was doing its own job, men who probed the foundations which were going to bear that new weight, who crawled the narrow tunnels still left deep in the stonework heart of the base. Rivers, it was rumored, still flowed down there, but long ago the City had enclosed them, channeled them, dug down to rock beneath and settled her broad bottomside against the deep rocks, perched there for the ages to come. That great weight cracked supports from time to time, and precious conduits of power and water had to be adjusted against the sideways slippage which did happen, fractional inches year by year, or sometimes more, when the earth protested the enormous weight it had to bear. The sea was down there on one side, but those edges were filled and braced; the dead were down there, the ashes of all the ordinary dead, and many a Builder too, who had not gotten out of the way of a collapsing passage . . . but the dead served like other dust, to fill the cracks, so it was true that the living built upon the dead.

So the city grew.

"Go up to the nineties tomorrow," the liner boss said, and the four other members of 48 East, tired from the day and bone-chilled from the mist and anxious to head for the Bottom and its dens, took Jino Brown's instructions and handed in their charts. "So where were you, bossman?" Sam Kenny asked. Sometimes Jino went out with them and sometimes not; and it was a cold, bone-freezing day out there.

"Yeah," said Johnny. "The wind starts up, Jino, and where were you?"

"Meeting," Jino said; fill-in for their retired boss, he took such jokes with a sour frown, not the good humor they tried with him. "You worry too much," Johnny said, and unbelted the harness about his hips, last in, still shivering and bouncing to warm his muscles. He started peeling out of the black rubber suit, hung up his gear beside the others in the narrow Access Room, with the big hatch to Outside firmly and safely sealed at the end; they had a shower there: Sarah and Poll had first use of it. They came out looking happier and Johnny peeled out of the last of his rig, grabbed a towel and headed in with Sam, howled for the temperature the women had left it, which on their chilled bodies felt scalding. Sam dialed it down, and they lathered and soused themselves and came out again, rubbing down.

The women were dressed already, waiting. "Where's Jino gone now?" Sam asked. The women shrugged.

"Got to be careful of him," Sarah said. "Think we hurt his feelings."

"Ah," Johnny said, which was what that deserved. He grabbed his clothes and pulled them on; and Sam did, while the women waited. Then, "Going Down," Sarah sang, linking her arm in his, linking left arm to Sam's and laughing; he snagged Polly and they snaked their way out and down the hall, laughing for the deviltry of it, here in this carpeted, fine place of the tower, quiet, expensive apartments of the Residents. They used the service lift, their privilege . . . better, because *it* stopped very seldom, and not at all this time, shot them down and down while they leaned against the walls and grinned at each other in anticipation.

"Worm," Sarah proposed, a favorite haunt.

"Pillar," Poll said.

"Go your way; we'll go ours."

"Right," Sam said; and that was well enough: Sam and Sarah had business; and he and Poll did, and he was already thinking on it with a warm glow . . . on that and dinner, both of which seemed at the moment equally desirable. The lift slammed to its hard-braking halt on second and the door opened, let them out into the narrow maze, the window-less windings of stairs and passages, granite which seeped water squeezed out of the stones by the vast mass above their heads.

And music—music played here constantly, echoing madly through the deep stone halls. There was other music too, conduits, which came up from the rivers, and these sang softly when the hand touched them, with the force of the water surging in them up or down. There were power conduits, shielded and painted; there were areas posted with yel-low signs and DANGER and KEEP OUT, subterranean mysteries which were the business of the Deep Builders, and not for liners, and never for the soft-handed Residents of the high tower who came slumming here, thrill-seeking.

"Going my way?" Sarah asked of Sam, and off they went, by the stairs to the next level down, to the ancient Worm; but Johnny hugged Poll against him and took the corridor that snaked its way with one of the waterpipes, toward the core of second level; the Pillar was liner even to its decor, which was old tackle and scrawled signatures . . . they walked in through an arch that distinguished itself only by louder music—one had to know where one was down at the Bottom, or have a guide, and pay; and no Residents got shown to the Pillar, or to the Worm, not on the guides' lives. He found his favored table; next to the big support that gave the place its name, around which the tables wound, a curve which gave privacy, and, within the heartbeat throb of the music, calm and warmth after the shrieking winds.

He and Poll ordered dinner from the boy who did the waiting; a tiny—"tiny," he said, measuring a span with his fingers—glass of brew, because they were going out on the lines again tomorrow, and they needed their heads unswollen.

They had, of course, other pleasures in mind, because there was more to the Pillar than this smoky, music-pulsing den, and the food and drink; there were the rooms below, down the stairs beyond, for such rest as they had deserved.

He finished his good meal, and Poll did, and they sat there sipping their brew and eyeing one another with the anticipation of long ac-quaintance, but the brew was good too, and what they had been waiting for all day, with the world swinging under their feet and exertion suck-ing the juices out of them. They were that, old friends, and it could wait on the drink, slow love, and slow quiet sleep in the Bottom, with all the comforting weight of the City on their backs, where the world was solid and warm.

"Tallfeather."

He looked about, in the music and the smoke. No one used his last name, not among the highliners; but it was not a voice he knew . . . a thin man in Builders' blue coveralls and without a Builders' drawling accent either.

"Tallfeather, I'd like to talk with you. Privately."

He frowned, looked at Poll, who looked worried, tilted his head to one side. "Rude man, that."

"Mr. Tallfeather."

No one said Mister in the Bottom. That intrigued him. "Poll, you mind? This man doesn't get much of my time."

"I'll leave," Poll said. There was a shadow in Poll's eyes, the least hint of fear, he would have said, but there was no cause of it that he could reckon.

"No matter," the man said, hooking his arm to pull him up. "We've a place to go."

"No." He rose to his feet all right, and planted them, glared up at the man's face. Shook his arm free. "You're begging trouble. What's your name? Let me see your card."

The man reached for his pocket and took one out. *Manley*, it said, *Joseph*, and identified him as an East Face Builder, and that was a lie, with that accent. Company number 687. Private employ.

So money was behind this, that could get false cards. He looked for Poll's opinion, but she had slipped away, and he was alone with this man. He sat down at the table again, pointed to the other chair. "I'd be crazy to walk out of here with you. You sit down there and talk sense or I do some talking to security, and I don't think you'd like that, would you?"

Manley sat down, held out his hand for the card. Johnny gave it to him. "So who are you?" Johnny prodded.

There was no one, at the moment, near them. The huge pillar cut them off from sight and sound of others, and the serving boy was gone into the kitchen or round the bend.

"You're of the 48 East," Manley said, "and this project you're on . . . you know what kind of money that throws around. You want to stay on the lines all your life, Tallfeather, or do you think about old age?"

"I don't mind the lines," he said. "That's what I do."

"It's worth your while to come with me. Not far. No tricks. I have a friend of yours will confirm what I say. You'll trust him."

"What friend?"

"Jino Brown."

That disturbed him. Jino. Jino involved with something that had to sneak about like this. Jino had money troubles. Gambled. This was something else again. "Got a witness of my own, remember? My teammate's going to know who you are, just in case you have ideas."

"Oh, she does know me, Mr. Tallfeather."

That shook his confidence further, because he had known Poll all his life, and Poll was honest.

And scared.

"All right. Suppose we take that walk."

"Good," Manley said, and got to his feet. Johnny rose and walked with him to the door, caught the young waiter before he went out it "Tommy, lad, I'm going with Mr. Manley here." He took the order sheet from the boy's pocket and wrote the name down and the company number, probably false. "And you comp my bill and put your tip on it, and you remember who I left with, all right?"

"Right," the boy said. Builder by birth, Tommy Pratt, but small and unhealthy and sadly pale. "You in some kind of trouble, Johnny?"

"Just remember the name and drop it in the liners' ears if I don't come back before morning; otherwise forget it."

"Yes, sir."

Manley was not pleased. Johnny smiled a taut, hard smile and walked with him then, out the winding ways where the man wanted to lead him. In fact it was curiosity and nerves that brought him with Manley, an ugly kind of curiosity. He was no Resident to go rubber-kneed at the sight of the lines, but this had something to do with those he was going out there with, and where their minds were, and this he wanted to know.

There was another dive a good distance beyond, down a series of windings and up and down stairs, on the very margin of the territory he knew in the Bottom; and being that close to lost made him nervous too.

But Jino was there, at the table nearest the door, stood up to meet him, but did not take him back to the table; walked him with his hand on his shoulder, back into one of the rooms most of these places had, where the pounding music and the maze gave privacy for anything.

"What is this?" Johnny asked, trusting no one now; but Jino urged him toward a chair at the round table that occupied this place, that was likely for gambling—Jino *would* know such places. Manley had sat down there as if he owned the place, and stared at both of them as they sat down. "'I'll tell you what it is," Manley said. "There's a flaw on the East Face 90th, you understand?"

"There's not a flaw."

"Big one," said Manley. "Going to deviate the whole project a degree over."

"Going to miss some important property," Jino said, "whatever the computers projected. *We're* the ones go out there; the computers don't. We say."

He looked at Jino, getting the whole drift of it and not at all liking it.

"Mr. Tallfeather," Manley said. "Property rides on this. *Big* money. And it gets spread around. There is, you see, a company that needs some help; that's going to be hurt bad by things the way they're going; and maybe some other companies have an in with the comp operators, eh? Maybe this just balances the books. You understand that?"

"What company? That ATELCORP thing that made the fuss?"

"You don't need to know names, Mr. Tallfeather. Just play along with the rest of your team. They'll all be in on it. All. And all it takes is your cooperative—silence."

"Sure, and maybe you're telling that to all of them, that I went with it."

Manley frowned deeply. "You're the last holdout, Tallfeather, you and your sister. You two are the sticking point, the ones we knew would have been hard to convince. But it's a team play. You respect that. You don't want to cut your three partners out of that company's gratitude. Think of your old age, Tallfeather. Think how it is when you stop being young, when you still have to go out there. And this company's gratitude— can go a long way."

"Money," Jino said. "Enough to set us up. Influence. We're set, you understand that, Johnny? It's not crooked; just what he said, balancing the influence the others have on the computer input. So both sides are bought. This goes *high*, Johnny; the Council, the companies they run . . . this is a power grab."

"Mr. Brown," Manley cautioned.

"Johnny's reasonable. It's a matter of explaining."

"I think I see it," Johnny said in a flat voice.

Trust the company," Manley said. "Someone's talking to your sister too."

Panic settled over him. He settled back in his chair. He went out on the lines with these people. Had to. It was all he had. "Sarah will go with it if I do. Who's financing this? What company? If we're in it, I figure we should know."

"Never mind that."

"Just shut up and take it," Jino said. "And agree with the charts. I do that part of it. You just keep your mouth shut and take your cut."

"All right," he said. "All right. No problem from me." He pushed back from the table. "I'd better get back, you mind? I left some instructions if I didn't get back quick."

Jino frowned and motioned him gone. He gathered himself up, walked out, through the main room and down the corridors, with an increasingly leaden feeling at his gut.

Tommy's face lit with relief to see him; he clapped the boy on the shoulder. "Poll?" he asked, and Tommy blinked and looked about.

"I think she left," Tommy said.

He checked. She was not in the room they had rented. Not upstairs. He frowned and left, hunting Sarah, down in the Worm.

She was gone too. So was Sam Kenny.

He sat down, ordered a drink to occupy a table by the door of the Worm, a den as dark and loud and smoky as the Pillar, but smaller and older, and he asked a few questions, but not too many, not enough to raise brows either among the liners there or with the management. The drink gradually disappeared. He sat with a sick feeling at his stomach and ordered another.

Finally she came in. He restrained himself from jumping up, sat cool and silent while Sarah spotted him and walked over with a distressed look that told where she had been. She pulled up another chair and sat down.

"I know," he said. "They got to you and Sam?"

"What do we do, Johnny?"

"What did you tell them we'd do?"

"I told them we'd think about it."

"I told them we'd go with it," he said. "What do you think we are, Sarah?"

Her shoulders fell and she sat and looked morose. His drink came and he pushed it over to her, ordered one for himself. "I don't think," she said when they were alone, "I don't think they trust us, Johnny, whatever they promise."

He thought about that, and it frightened him, agreeing with his own thought. "We go along with it. It's all we can do. Report it . . . we don't know what it would stir up, or how high; or what enemies we'd have."

She nodded.

They took rooms in the Worm. He took a bottle with him, and Sarah did, and he at least slept. Sam never did come back, to his knowledge.

And came late morning, he and Sarah walked together to the service lift, got on it with two other liners not of their team who were making the ride up to tenth; they exchanged no words. The other liners got off, and they said nothing to each other, the whole long ride to the ninetieth.

Down the carpeted hall to the access hall: they were first to arrive. They stripped and put on the suits, waited around with hoods back and gloves off. Sam showed up, and Poll, avoiding their eyes. There was poison in the air. There had never been that, quarrels yes, but not this. Jino showed, clipboard in hand, and the silence continued. "Blast you," Jino said. "Look up, look alive. Get your minds on it. Who's been talking?"

Johnny shook his head. Jino looked from one to the other of them. "What's wrong?" Johnny asked. "Jino, maybe we and you better get this all straight. Or maybe we don't go out there today."

"Questions, that's all." Jino took his suit and harness off the hook and started stripping like the rest of them. "Had the man back, you understand me? Stopped me, asking . . . asking whether any of the team might have had second thoughts. Any of you been talking?"

Heads shook, one by one.

"Right, then." Jino climbed into the suit, zipped up, and the rest of them starting getting hoods up and masks hung in place. "It's all right," Jino said. He belted the harness about his chest and up through his legs, took the clipboard and hung it from his belt. "It's started, anyway. I've got the figures. All we have to do is keep developing this data; and it's all figured; they gave it to me the way we have to turn it in. Is that hard?"

They shook their heads again. There was a bitter taste in Johnny's mouth. He shrugged into his own harness, pulled it up, hooked it, checked the precious line, coiled in its case, to be sure it rolled and that the brake held as it should.

"So get moving," Jino said. "Go, get out there."

They moved. Sam opened the access door, a round hatch; and wind howled in, nothing to what it would do if the back door were open. Poll swore and bounced slightly, nervousness; it was always this way, going out. Sam went first, hooked his first line to the access eye, eased out of sight, bowed in the wind, facing outward for a moment and then turning to face the building. Sarah moved up next, as soon as that eye was free.

His turn. He hooked on, looked out into the blasting wind, at the view Residents never saw unshielded. He pulled his tinted mask down, and the sunglare resolved itself into the far dizzying horizon. He stepped to the ledge, jerked to be sure the brake was holding on his line before he trusted his weight to it. This was the part the groundlings could never take, that first trusting move in which he swung out with all the dizzy curve of the city-mountain at his feet, windows and ledges . . . shielded ledges below, as the curve increased, and finally mere glass tiles, thick and solid, the windows of the Bottom, which were skylights, thick because there was always the chance of getting something dropped through one . . . winter ice, which built up and crashed like spears weighing hundreds of pounds; or the falling body of a liner, which had happened; or something a liner dropped, which was enough to send a man to the Bottom for a month: even a bolt dropped from these heights became a deadly missile.

Ninety floors down.

The insulated suits protected from the cold, barely. The masks did, or the windchill would have frozen their eyes and membranes and robbed them of breath; every inch of their bodies was covered. He clipped his line to another bolt and let the last retract, dropping and traversing in a wide arc that made all the stones blur past, caught the most convenient ledge with a practiced reach that disdained the novice's straightline drop and laborious climb back; he had his line of ascent above him now, the number ten; Sarah had the eleventh; Sam the twelfth; Poll, coming after him, number nine; Jino number eight, near the access. Climb and map and watch for cracks, real ones, which was their proper job; and swear to a lie. He tried not to think of that. They still had a job to do, the routine that kept the building in repair; and out here at least, the air was clean and minds had one steady job to occupy all their attention—one small move after another, eyes straight ahead and wits about them.

They checked and climbed, steady work now, feet braced, backs leaning against the harness. They had come out after the sun was well up; paused often for rests. He felt the day's heat increasing on his back, felt the trickle of sweat down his sides. The ice was burned off, at least. None of that to make feet slip and line slip its brake in slides that could stop even a liner's heart. His mask kept the air warm and defogged itself immaculately, a breathing that those who spent their lives in the City never experienced, sharp and cold and cleansing. He got near the windows as the day wore on toward afternoon. He could see his own monstrous reflection in the tinted glass he passed, like some black spider with a blank, reflective face; and dimly, dimly, the interiors of the offices of ATELCORP: he recognized the logo.

He was out of love with them. But a woman at the desk nearest the glass looked up at him with bright innocent eyes. She smiled; he smiled, uselessly, behind his mask—freed a hand and waved, and watched her re-action, which looked like a gasp. He grinned, let go the other and then, businesslike, reached for the next clip and edged higher, to spider over a bit onto the blank wall. But the woman mouthed him something. He motioned with his hand and she said it again. He lipread, like many a liner, used to the high winds, the same as they used handsigns. He mimed a laugh, slapped his hand on his gut. Her half-mirrored face took on a little shock. She laughed then. The invitation had been coarse.

He let go again, mimed writing with his hand, teasing her for her number. She laughed and shook her head, and he reckoned it time to move on.

He had fallen behind. Poll and Sam and Sarah were ahead, two floors above, Jino about even with him. He made a little haste on the blank wall, like them, where there were no windows to be careful of, reach and clip, adjust the feet, reach and clip, never quite loose. They reached the ledge of the hundred, and stopped for a breather, eyed the clouds that had come in on the east, beyond the ringlet of other towers. "Going to have to call it soon," Sam said.

"We just move it over," Jino said. "Traverse five over, work it down, come back to the 90 access."

They nodded. That was what they wanted, no long one with that moving in. It boded ice.

And when they had worked the kinks from backs and shoulders and legs, they lined along the ledge, the easy way, and dropped into their new tracks, a windowless area and quick going. Johnny leaned over and bounced as he hit the wall, started working downward with enthusiasm. It faded. Muscles tired. He looked up, where Sam and Sarah seemed occupied about some charting; so maybe they had found something, or they were doing a little of the minor repair they could do on the spot.

It was a good route up; the computers were right, and it was the best place. He looked down between his feet at the hazy Bottom, where the ground prep had already been done with so much labor, tried not to let his mind dwell on the lie. It was getting toward the hour they should come in anyway, and the wind was picking up, shadows going the other way now, making the tower a little treacherous if he kept looking down, a dizzying prospect even to one accustomed to it.

Wind hit; he felt the cold and the lift carried him almost loose from his footing.

Suddenly something dark plummeted past. He flinched and fell inward against the stone, instinct. Something dropped—but big; it had been. . . . He looked up in the shadow, squinted against the flaring sky, saw the channel next to him vacant; Sarah's channel, a broken line flying.

He flung himself outward with his legs, looked down, but she had fallen all the way by now, spun down the long slow fall.

Sarah.

It hit him then, the grief, the loss. He hung there against the harness. By now the rest of the team had stopped, frozen in their places. He stayed put, in the windy silence, and the belt cutting into his back and hips, his legs numb and braced.

His hands were on his lines. He caressed the clip that was between him and such a fall, and was aware of a shadow, of someone traversing over to him.

Poll. She hung there on her lines' extension, touched his shoulder, shook at him and pointed up and over. Shouted in the wind and the muffling of the mask. *Access,* he lipread. *Get to the access.*

He began, the automatic series of moves that were so easy, so thoughtless, because the equipment held, but Sarah's had not. Sarah was down there, his own flesh and bone spattered over all the protected skylights on the mountain's long, slow curve.

He began shaking. He hung there against the flat stone, out in the wind, and his legs started shaking so that he could not make the next step, and hands froze so that he could not make the next release, could not make the swing across to the next track, suspended over that.

Another came. Sam, and Poll. He felt them more than saw, bodies hurtling near him on their lines, and he hung there, clinging with his fingers, flinched, shuddering as a third plummeted and came against him from the back, spider fashion.

They lined to him. He knew what they were doing and would do, but he was frozen, teeth chattering. The cold had gotten to him, and he clung desperately to the wall, trying to see nothing else, felt them hooking to him, felt them release his lines.

He screamed, hurled free by the wind, swung down and stopped against the lines as they jerked taut against his body harness. He hung there, swinging free in the wind gusts, while the twilit city spun and flared in streaks and spirals before his blurring eyes. He heard a scream, a chorus of them, and there was another body plummeting past him, an impact that hit his shoulder and spun him. He tried to catch it, but the body got past him as he spun, and he watched, watched downward as it spread itself like a star on the winds and whirled away, in slow, terrible falling. Vanished in perspective. He never saw it hit. Tried to convince his mind to see it soar away, safe, unharmed; but it had hit; and it was a terrible way to die. Like Sarah.

His stomach heaved. He swayed in the buffets of the wind. Two of their team fallen. *Two.* He hung there, thinking of the line, that never gave, never; it was beyond thought that it should give. But two had, and he hung there with his body flying loose from the building in the gusts.

He twisted his head, tried to help himself, but his arms were too chilled to move accurately and his hands fumbled in trying to turn himself against the stone. He managed to look up, saw the two other survivors of the team working at the latch of the access three stories above. They would winch him in, once safe themselves. But it was not opening.

Jammed. Locked. Someone had locked them out here.

And two of their lines had broken.

He moved again as a gust of wind caught him, slammed him against the building. The impact numbed that arm. He manipulated the extension hook with the right arm, shot it out, and even when the wind swayed him farthest that way, it was short of the next hook. He retracted it finally, let it swing from its cord again and his aching arm fall as he sank in his harness. He struggled to lift his head finally, saw his teammates likewise still. Their lines had tangled. They were in trouble, twisted in the wind, exhausted. Now and again, when he would look up, one of them would be striking at the hatch, but there was no sound; the wind swallowed it. There were no windows where they were, in this blind recess. No one saw; no one heard.

The light waned, wrapped in advancing cloud in a streaming of last colors. The wind kept blowing, and mist began to spit at them, icing lines, icing the suits, chilling to the bone. He watched the lights come on in the far, far tower of Queens, thinking that perhaps someone might be looking out, that someone might see a skein of figures, that someone might grow curious, make a call.

No. There was no way they could see so far. He could unclip, die early. That was all.

He did not. He hung there with his body growing number, and the chill working into his bones. How many hours until someone missed them? Until the other liners started asking questions?

He looked up, immense effort, saw what looked like the lift of an arm to the hatch in the dusk. They were still trying. "Who fell?" he tried to ask. He could not; waved a feeble hand to let them know he was alive. In the masks, in the dark suits, there was no seeing who it was in that tangle of line and bodies.

It darkened further into night, and he felt ice building up on his right side, flexed, and cracked it off his suit. The harness about his chest and waist and groin was stressed at an angle, gravity and the buffeting of the wind cutting off the blood to one side. He struggled, and began, when the wind would sway him far out and then slam him back against the building, to think of the thin line fraying with every move. It was not supposed to.

Was not supposed to. They had been murdered.

Were dying out here because of it.

Out and back. He moaned from the pain, a numb whimper, having had enough, and having no one to tell it to. Again . . . out and against the wall.

It went on and on, and the clouds cut off even the stars from view, leaving just the city lights, that streaked and spun and danced like jewels. He got a sliver of ice in his fingers, slipped it under his mask and into his mouth to relieve the thirst that tormented him; his arm dropped like lead. He stopped moving, aware only of the shriek of the wind, of battering like being taken up by a giant and slammed down again.

Release the catch, a tiny voice whispered to him. *Give up. Let go.*

Someone did. A body hurtled past, a thin, protesting cry—mind changed, perhaps? Grief? Outrage?

He could not see it fall. It went into the dark and the distance, a shadow for a moment against the light below, and then gone, kited on the winds.

Don't they find us down there? he wondered. *Don't they know?* But all the Bottom down there was shielded over for construction. No one would know, unless someone looked out at the moment of falling, unless someone just chanced to see.

There was one of his team left up there. One companion in the dark. "Who are you?" he cried. "Who?"

His voice was lost. No answer came to him.

He sank against the harness, let his head fall, exhausted, senses ebbing.

Came to again at the apex of a swing, screamed as he hung free a moment; but he was still lined. The jerk came, and he slammed against the stone, sobbed with the battering. The night was black, and the corner where they were was black. He dangled and twisted, his lines long since fouled, saw the whole world black, just a few lights showing in the Bottom, the tower of Queens a black, upsweeping point of darkness.

Early morning? How many hours until daylight?

"Who's still up there?" he called in a lull in the wind.

No answer. He dropped his head to his chest, tautened his muscles as a random gust got between him and the building, flying him almost at a right angle to the building, so that the city and the sky spun dizzyingly. The gust stopped. He swung back, hit, went limp, knowing the next such might break his back.

Let it go, the inner voice urged him. *Stop the pain.*

The line might break soon. Might save him the effort. Surely his harness had been tampered with like all the others, while it hung there in the access room.

Jino, he thought, Jino, who had stayed nearest the access. But the door had jammed.

Get rid of this team, get another one assigned more compatible with someone's interests.

He thought about that. Thought about it while the wind slammed and spun at him and the cold sank deeper.

Light flared above. He tried to look up, saw the hatch open, black figures in it against the light. A beam played down, caught him in the face.

The line slipped. He went hot and cold all over at that sickening drop. He twisted, tried to lift an arm, raised it a little. The light centered on him. The wind caught him, a brutal slam out and across the beam. And then the light moved off him. He shouted, hoarse and helpless. Then he felt one of the lines begin to shorten, pulling him in. The winch inside the access; they had that on it, a steady pull, dragging the line over the stone, one line, up and up. He hung still, hardly daring breathe, more frightened now than before . . . to live through this, and to have the line break at the last moment. . . . The wind kept catching him and swinging him far out so that he could see the lights below him.

Almost there. He twisted to see. Hands plucked at the taut line, seized his collar, his shoulders, his chest harness, dragged him backward over the sill of the access. One last sinking into human hands, an embrace which let his cold body to the floor, faces which ringed about him. Someone pulled his mask off, and he flinched at the white light.

"Alive," that one said. Liners. The hatchway was still open. He tried to move, rolled over, looked and saw his teammate, first recovered on the tangled lines, lying on the floor by him, open-eyed and dead.

Jino. It was Jino. He lay there, staring at the dead face. Jino tampered with the harness . . . maybe; or someone else—who locked the door and left them all out there . . . to die.

"There's no more," he heard someone shout; and the hatch boomed shut, mercifully cutting off the wind. His rescuers lifted his head, unzipped the tight suit. "Harness," he said. "Someone tampered with the lines." They were brothers. They had to know.

"Lock that door," one of them said. He let his breath go then, and let them strip the suit off him, winced as one of them brought wet towels that were probably only cold water; it felt scalding. He lived. He lay and shivered, with the floor under him and not the empty air and the dark. Someone seized his face between burning hands while continuing to soak the rest of his body. Dan Hardesty: he knew the team, four men and a woman; the 50 East. "What do you mean, tampered? What happened?"

"Tried to fake the reports," he said. "Someone wanted the reports doctored, and didn't trust us. They killed us. They—or the other side. Tampered with the harness. Lines broke. *Two lines broke out there.*"

They hovered about him, listening, grim-faced. His mind began to work with horrid clarity, two and two together; it took more than one team bought off. Took buying all that worked this section; them too. The 50th. He lay there, shivering as the water started to cool, thinking ugly thoughts, how easy it was to drop a body back out there.

"Someone," he said, "jammed the latch. Locked us out there."

Dan Hardesty stared at him. Finally scowled, looked above him at one of his own, looked down again. "Bring that water up to warm," he said. "Move it. We've got to get him out of here."

He shivered convulsively, stomach knotting up, limbs jerking; they set him up. They got the warmer cloths on him and he flinched, tried to control his limbs. His left leg and his right were blackening on the sides; his left arm already black. "Look at his back," the woman Maggie said, and he reckoned it was good he could not see it. They sponged at it, trying to get him back to room temperature.

"Tommy Pratt got worried," Dan said. "Started asking questions—where were you, what was going on—other questions got asked. So we figured to come up to your site and check. Wish we'd come sooner, Johnny. Wish we had."

He nodded, squeezed his eyes shut, remembering his friends. Sarah. Part of him. It was not grief, for Sarah. It was being cut in half.

Someone pounded at the door. "Security," someone called from outside.

"Hang Tommy," Dan said.

They were unlocking the door. "Help me up," he begged of them; and they did, held him on his feet, wrapped one of the towels about him. The door opened, and security was there, with drawn guns.

"Got an accident," Dan said. "Team went out, lines fouled, wind broke them. We got two in; one live, one dead; the others dropped."

"Call the meds," the officer in charge said. Johnny shook his head, panicked; the hospital—corporation-financed. He did not want to put himself in their hands.

"I'm not going," he said, while the call went out. "Going to the Bottom. Get myself a drink. That's what I want. That's all I want."

The officer pulled out a recorder. "You up to making a statement, Mr.—"

"Tallfeather. Johnny." His voice broke, abused by the cold, by fright. He leaned against the men holding him up. "I'll make your statement. We were out on the 90s, going down. My sister Sarah . . . her line broke. The others tried to spider me down, to come back, and the lines fouled. Hours out there. Lines broke, or maybe one suicided. The wind—"

"Man would," Dan said. "You ever been Outside, officer?"

"Names. IDs."

Dan handed his over. Another searched Johnny's out of his coveralls, turned everyone's over, dead and living. The officer read them off into the recorder. Returned them, to the living. "Dead man here?"

"Team boss," Johnny said, moistening his lips. "Jino Brown. The others dropped."

The officer looked at Dan Hardesty and his team. "Your part in this?"

"Friends. They didn't show and we came checking. Boy named Tommy Pratt in the Pillar, he put us onto it. Let the man go, Mister. He's had enough."

The officer bent down and checked Jino's corpse, touched the skin, flexed the fingers.

"Frosted," Dan said. "Pulled his mask off, you understand? No mask out there, you die quick. Painless, for those afraid of falling."

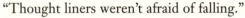

"Thought liners weren't afraid of falling."

"Lot of us are," Dan said levelly. "Come on, officer, this man's *sister* died out there."

"Think he'd be more upset about it, wouldn't you?"

Johnny swung; they stopped him, and the officer stepped back a pace.

"All right," the officer said carefully. "All right, all right. Easy."

Johnny sucked air, leaned there, glaring at the officer, cooled his mind slowly, thinking of what he wanted—to be out, down, away from them—alive.

The officer thumbed his mike. "Got an accident here," he said. "Liners fouled, one survivor, Tallfeather, John Ames, city employee."

Noise came back. The officer touched the plug in his ear and his eyes flickered, looking at them. The door opened, the rest of the security officers showing two meds in. "Get him out," the officer said with a gesture at Jino's body. "The other one says he's walking."

The meds ignored the body, turned on him. Johnny shook them off, shook his head while one of them told him about massive contusions and blood clots and his brain. "Get me my clothes," he told the liners. One did.

"Somebody," Dan was saying, "needs to go out there and get those bodies in off the Bottom."

He heard. Maybe he should protest, give way to grief, insist to be one to go even if there was no chance of his walking that far. He had no interest in finding Sarah's body, or Poll's, or Sam's. He had only one interest and that was to get his clothes on, to get out of here. He managed it, wincing, while the meds conferred with the police and wondered if there were not some way to arrest him to get him to the hospital.

"Get out of here," Dan warned them. There was sullen silence.

"Mr. Tallfeather," one of the medics appealed to him.

He shook his head. It hurt. He stared hatefully at them, and they devoted their attention to Jino, who was beyond protest.

"Free to go?" Dan asked the police.

"We've got your numbers," the officer said.

Dan said nothing. Johnny walked for the door between two of them, trying not to let his knees give under him.

They got him to the service lift, got a better grip on him once inside, because he gave way when the car dropped, and he came near to fainting. They went down, down as far as they would go, got out in the passages, walked the way to the Worm.

He fainted. He woke up in a bed with no recollection of how he had gotten there; and then he did remember, and lay staring at the ceiling. An old woman waited on him, fed him; labored over him. Others came in to look at him, liners and Builders both. When he was conscious and could get his legs under him, he tottered out into the Worm itself and sat down and had the drink he had promised himself, remembering Sarah, who had sat with him—over there. And the word whispered through the Worm that there was a strike on, that none of the liners were going out; that there was a Builder slowdown, and the name of Manley and ATELCORP was mentioned.

There was a quiet about the place, that day, the next. There were police, who came and took photographs inside the Worm and read a court order in dead silence, ordering the Builders back to work. But the silence hung there, and the police were very quiet and left, because no one wanted to go Outside but liners and the whole City would die if the Builders shut things down. Up in the towers they knew their computers. A lot was automated; a lot was not. The computers were all their knowledge.

There was talk of an investigation. The Mayor came on vid and appealed for calm; said there was an investigation proceeding about gang activity, about bribes; about corruption in certain echelons far down the corporation lists. There was a lot of talk. It all moved very quickly.

"We'll get something," Dan Hardesty told him. "We got the one that went by Manley. Fellow named George Bettin. ATELCORP's man. Flunky; but we got him."

"They'll hang him out," he said quietly, hollowly. "So much for Manley. Yes. We got him."

And that day the Bettin trial started he rode the lift up to the hundredth, and walked to one of the observation windows, but when he got close to it, with the far blue distance and the Newark spire rising in his view, he stopped.

It was a long time before a passerby happened to see him there, against the wall; before a woman took him by the arm and coaxed him away from the wall, down the corridor. They called the meds; and they offered him sedatives.

He took them. Rode the lift down. That itself was terror. He had had dreams at night; wakened with the world hanging under him and the sky above and screamed until the Worm echoed with it.

The drugs stopped that. But he stayed below, refused to go near the windows. Three, four days, while the Manley/Bettin trial dragged on. They never called him to testify; never called any of the liners.

But a message came to the Worm, signed with big names in ATEL-CORP; and that failed to surprise him. He went, up the far, far distance to the nineties.

He walked in, looked about him, flinched from the windows, a mere turning of his head. They wanted him to go into an office with windows. Paul Mason, the door said, President.

"Mr. Tallfeather," someone said, trying to coax him. He turned his back to the windows.

"He comes out here," he said, staring at the blank wall in front of him, the fancy wallpaper, the civic contribution citations. "He comes out to *me*."

He stood there. Eventually someone came, and a hand rested on his shoulder. "The windows. I understand, Mr. Tallfeather. I'm terribly sorry. Paul Mason. I called you here. You want to walk back this way, please?"

He walked, trembling, until they were in the hallway, in the safe, stone-veneer hall, and Mason drew him into a small windowless office, a desk, a few bookshelves, some chairs, immaculate, expensive. "Sit down," Mason urged him. "Sit down, Mr. Tallfeather."

He did so, sank into a chair. A secretary scurried in with an offer of hot tea.

"No," Johnny said quietly.

"Please," Mason said. "Something else."

"Tea," he said. The secretary left in haste. Mason sat in another chair, staring at him . . . a thin man, white-haired, with hard lines.

"Mr. Tallfeather," Mason said. "I've been briefed on your case. My staff came across with it. I've heard what happened."

"Heard," he echoed. Maybe there was still a craziness to his eyes. Mason looked uneasy.

"It was a man of ours, George Bettin. That's as far as it went; you've followed the trial."

He nodded, staring at Mason all the while.

"ATELCORP has no legal liability—certainly no criminal fault—but we want to make amends for this. To do right by you."

"To get the liners working again," he said bitterly.

"That, too, Mr. Tallfeather. I think your case, more than the end of the trial—I think justice done on this level may do more to heal the breach. We want to offer you a position. This office. A job."

"Only I stop talking. I stop saying what happened."

"Mr. Tallfeather, the public welfare is at stake. You understand that; it's more than the project. The strike . . . is illegal. We can't have that."

He sat still a moment. "Yes, sir," he said, very, very softly. Wiped at his face. He looked about him. "Thoughtful of you. No windows."

"We're terribly sorry, Mr. Tallfeather. Our extreme condolences. Sincerely."

"Yes, sir."

"You just come to the office when you like. The door . . . doesn't go past the windows out there. You come when you like."

"Doing what, Mr. Mason?"

"We'll develop that."

"And I don't talk about my sister; about my team."

"We'd prefer not."

"You're scared," he said.

Mason's face went hard.

"I'll take the job," he said. The tea had just arrived. Mason put on a smile and rose, offered him a hand and clapped him on a still-bruised shoulder. "Your own secretary, you choose from the pool. Anything you want in the way of decor . . ."

"Yes, sir."

Mason smiled, which was not a smile. The secretary stood there with the tea, and stepped aside as Mason left. Johnny walked over and took the tray, set it down himself. "That's enough," he said. "Go away."

And that afternoon the press came, escorted by Mason.

"What do you think of the investigation, Mr. Tallfeather?"

"What was it like, Mr. Tallfeather?"

He gave it to them, all the titillation the vid addicts could ask for, how it felt, dangling in air like that, watching the others die. He was steady; he was heroic, quiet, tragic; appealed for the liners to go to work, for an end to the civic agony.

They left, satisfied; Mason was satisfied, smiled at him. Clapped him on the shoulder and offered him a drink. He took it, and sat while Mason tried to be affable. He was pleasant in turn. "Yes, Mr. Mason. Yes, sir."

He went back to his office, which had no work, and no duties.

He was back in the morning. Sat in his office and stared at the walls.

Listened to vid. The liners went back to work. The strike was over. The whole City complex breathed easier.

He stayed all the day, and left by his own door, when Mason left; used a liner's key to prep the service elevator; waited in the hall outside.

"Mr. Mason."

"Hello, Johnny."

He smiled, walked to join Mason, and Mason looked uncomfortable there in the hall, the quite lonely hall, in front of ATELCORP's big sound-proof doors.

"Want you to come with me," he said to Mason.

"I'm sorry—" Mason started to say, headed for the doors.

Johnny whipped the hand and the razor from his pocket, encircled his neck, let it prick just a little. "Just want you to come with me," he said. "Don't yell."

Mason started to. The razor bit, Mason stopped, and yielded backward when he pulled him, down the hall, which at this time just before quitting time, with the Man in the hall—was very quiet.

"You're crazy," Mason said.

"Move." He jerked Mason backward, to the service elevator. Someone *had* come out. Saw. Darted back into the office. Mason started resisting and stopped at another nick.

"Look here," Mason gasped. "You're sick. It won't go bad for you; a hospital stay, a little rest . . . the company won't hold grudges; I won't. I understand—"

He dragged Mason backward into the lift; pushed TOP; and PRIORITY, with the key in. The door closed. The car shot up with a solid lift, that long, impossible climb. He let Mason loose, while he stood by the lift controls.

Mason stood against the wall and stared at him.

"I just want you," Johnny said ever so softly, "to go *with* me."

Mason's lips were trembling. He screamed aloud for help. It echoed in the small car.

"We have a head start," Johnny said. "Of course they'll come. But it takes the computers to override a service key. It'll take them a moment to realize that."

Mason stood and shivered. The car rose higher and higher, lurched at last to a stomach-wrenching stop. The door opened on a concrete room, and he took Mason by the arm and walked him outside the car. It left again. "I think they've called it," he said calmly. Used his left hand to pull the hatch lever.

The door slammed open, echoing; the wind hit them like a hammer blow, and Mason flinched. There was a wide balcony outside, heavy pipe from which lines were strung. Mason clung to the door and Johnny dragged him forward by the arm. All the world stretched about them in the twilight, and there was ice underfoot, a fine mist blowing, bitter cold, making muscles shake. Mason slipped, and Johnny caught his elbow, walked a step farther.

"I can't go out on the lines," Johnny said. "Can't look out the windows. But company helps. Doesn't it?" He walked him far out across the paving, his eyes on the horizon haze, and Mason came, shivering convulsively within the circle of his left arm. The wind hit them hard, staggered them both, made them slip a little on the ice. His right side was numb. He kept his arm about Mason, walked to the very railing, "No view like it, Mr. Mason. I dream of it. It's cold. And it's far. Look *down*, Mr. Mason."

Mason clutched at the railing, white-knuckled. Johnny let him go, moved back from him, turned and walked back toward the lift doors.

The hatch opened. Police were there, with guns drawn. And they stayed within the doorway, leaned there, sickness in their eyes, hands clenched together on the levelled guns.

He laughed, noiseless in the wind, motioned toward the edge, toward Mason. None of the police moved. The world was naked about them. The soaring height of the other towers was nothing to this, to the City itself, the great Manhattan tower. He grinned at them, while the wind leached warmth from him.

"Go get him," he shouted at the police. "Go out and get him."

One tried, got a step out, froze and fell.

And slowly, carefully, holding up hands they could see as empty, he walked back to Mason, took his right hand and pried it from the icy rail; took the other, stared almost compassionately into a face which had become a frozen mask of horror, mouth wide and dried, eyes stark and wild. He put his arm about Mason like a brother, and slowly walked with him back to the police. "Mr. Mason," he said to them, "seems to have gotten himself out where he can't get back. But he'll be all right now." Mason's hands clung to him, and would not let go. He walked into the housing and into the lift with the police, still with his arm about Mason, and Mason clutched at him as the lift shot down. He smoothed Mason's hair as he had once smoothed Sarah's. "I had a sister," he said in Mason's ear. "But someone shut a door. On all of us. They'll convict Bettin, of course. And it'll all be forgotten. Won't it?"

The lift stopped at a lower floor. The police pushed him out, carefully because of Mason; and there were windows there, wide windows, and the twilight gleaming on the other buildings on the horizon. Mason sobbed and turned his face away, holding to him, but the police pulled them apart; and Mason held to the wall, clung there, his face averted from the glass.

"I don't think I want your job, Mr. Mason," Johnny said. "I'm going back out on the lines. I don't think I belong in your offices."

He started to leave. The police stopped him, twisted his arm.

"Do you really want *me* on trial?" he asked Mason. "Does the Mayor, or the Council?"

"Let him go," Mason said hoarsely. The police hesitated. *"Let him go."* They did. Johnny smiled.

"My lines won't break," he said. "There won't be any misunderstandings. No more jammed doors. I'll go back to the Bottom now. I'll talk where I choose. I'll talk to whom I choose. Or have me killed. And then be ready to go on killing. Dan Hardesty and the 50 East know where I am; and why; and you kill them and there'll be more and more to kill. And it'll all come apart, Mr. Mason, all the tower will come apart, the liners on strike; the Builders . . . no more cooling, no more water, no more power. Just dark. And no peace at all."

He turned. He walked back into the lift.

No one stopped him. He rode down through all the levels of the City, to the Bottom itself, and walked out into its crooked ways. Men and women stopped, turned curious eyes on him.

"That's Johnny Tallfeather," they whispered. "That's *him*."

He walked where he chose.

There was peace, thin-stretched as a wire. The liners walked where they chose too; and the Builders; and the Residents stayed out of the lower levels. There was from all the upper floors a fearful hush.

So the City grew.

THE GENERAL

(Peking)

Man was old in this land. His dust was one with the dust which blew over the land, which had blown yellow and unstoppable from antiquity . . . which stained the great river and covered the land and settled again. The Forbidden City looked out on a land which moved, which shifted in this latter age of the world, beneath a lowering moon and the aging sun. Northward lay the vast ice sheet, but southern winds fended away that ancient enemy. Eastward lay the sea and southward the strangeness of the peninsulas and the isles; westward lay the plains, the endless plains, across which men and beasts moved again as they had moved in ages before . . . men wrapped and shielded against the sun, strange and shaggy as the beasts they rode.

In the Forbidden City, life was abundant, sheltered by walls. There was beauty in the seasons, there was art from the cultivation of rare flowers to the intricate symbolism of gestures and nuances of dress; they had had time to grow elaborate and refined. The inhabitants named the city the City of Heaven and its beauty was beyond dreaming. It had soldiers . . . necessary when the impoverished plains tribes came with the winter winds, tribes which traded with them in good times, but which—rarely—turned, and beat themselves desperately and futilely against the walls.

The interior, which raiders never saw, was tranquillity. Even the soldiers who defended the city were armed with beauty; weapons were works of art; and those were the only outward show permitted, for the walls were plain. The interior was as beautiful as the accumulated treasure of ages could make it. Not all the beauty was of gold and jewels and jade, although there was a great deal of such work; but the quiet, patient work of ordinary objects, a sense of place and permanence and above all of time . . . for while the City of Heaven was not the oldest in the Earth, still it was conscious of its passing years, and stored them up like treasures. It loved its age. It found life good. It found no great ambition, for it had been very long since its last outward motion; it rested at the end of days. Its quality now was patience, and meticulous loveliness, the contemplation of age and absorption in its private thoughts. Even the weather had been kind in the years of younger memory, only lately turning drier.

Only the season finally came of the yellow wind, and the dust, the worst dust of living memory.

Some whispered that it foretold a worse winter than any living had seen.

Some whispered that it foretokened invasion, for the grass must be dry and the hordes would move, and war among themselves.

But a tribe tamer than the others came for the season's trading and said, before departing again into the plains, that in the years of green grass and little dust, the hordes had multiplied, both man and beast; which meant greater numbers coming. And they told the City what the tribes had known for years, that the City had known peace because the hordes had massed for wars far to the west . . . that a single horde had dominated all the others, and a leader had risen, under whose horsetail banner all the hordes of the world-plain moved. They themselves, said the more peaceful tribe, prepared to go far away: so did all the friendly tribes, the city's friends, who could not resist such a force. But the city suspected otherwise, knowing that the tribes did not love them. It was mere rumor, they said in council, some clever trick to weaken their courage when these very peaceful tribes ran out of trade goods and turned to brigandage.

But the dust storms grew worse, and the tribes did vanish.

The City of Heaven searched its records and its long memory in more earnest. Indeed all these signs were confirmed, that one thing tended to lead to the other: they ought to have mistrusted the green years and laid in greater store of weapons.

Perhaps, some said now, they should call in the strangers their children, who would come with their machines and their starfarers' weapons and aid them to drive back the invaders. But the citizens would not, because the strangers their children were rough-handed and sudden and liked to manage things their own way, which—again ancient experience of them forewarned—led to strangers seeing the beauties of the city; and seeing led to desiring; and desiring led to quarrelsome threats and to disturbances in the city. To call in the starfarers was to invite a horde far greater than that which might gather on the vast plains; and to invite plunder as grievous.

So they did not.

After all, the records indicated that many times in the eons past such intrusion had come, and the City, when well prepared and well led, had prevailed.

Only when the dust took on a stronger color in the west did they take clear alarm. This plume amid the blowing clouds was indeed broader than it had been in living memory and darker. It was their sole warning, with the tribes of the surrounding area gone: they were without eyes and ears now . . . but they were prepared in mind. The soldiers of the Forbidden City decorated their armor with ribbons, and polished their weapons and saw to their supplies of gunpowder . . . for more deadly weapons again involved the thankless and rowdy starfarers, and they would have none of it, as the enemy, they fully trusted, had no such arms. They filed out, great in number, footsoldiers, for the folk of the Forbidden City no longer traveled and preferred the stability of infantry in such few wars as they fought. They prepared to fight as they lived, with precision and elegance, ribbons streaming from armor and weapons and flowers decking their helms.

All the city turned out to see the soldiers on their way, waved gaily embroidered kerchiefs from the beautiful walls, danced dragons in the streets, threw flowers, and cheered for the brave defenders of the city.

It was an event, not a crisis. Ah, they knew their danger, but the danger was remote, and their long tranquillity behind their walls had made them philosophical and happy.

Nowhere near the whole of the city's young folk marched out. It was in fact only half, the Lion and Phoenix regiments, which went, those forces which this year's turn made active. The rest were spectators.

Such were Tao Hua and Kan Te, of the Dragon. Kan Te was a tall young son of the Guardian of the Morning Gate, an excellent youth of straight limbs and a bright glance, and a brave heart; and Tao Hua, as splendid a young woman as Kan Te was a fine youth, daughter to renowned artists in inks. They were soon to be married. All the world was good to Tao Hua and Kan Te, and along with the rest of the cheering city, they turned out in optimism, standing on the walls by the western gate to wave cheer to their comrades and to take in the spectacle.

Their hearts lifted for the brave display. The fighting was something beyond their imaginations, for while they were soldiers, they had never fought in earnest. Usually there were shots fired at a great distance and a few of the barbarians would fall and that would be the end of the war. It was all very tidy and none of the flower-decked armor was sullied; in fact, in the last encounter, much before Tao Hua and Kan Te were born, the army had come back with its flowers unwilted, unstained and victorious.

There were drums and cymbals, and the dragon dancers chained along at the army's side as they passed the gate.

"Perhaps we will be called up," said Tao Hua.

"Perhaps," said Kan Te, marking the size of the cloud; and the least fear was in his heart, for he had heard his great-grandfather talking with his grandparents and parents after coming from council. "The council was divided about whether to send more."

"Lion and Phoenix are very brave," said Tao Hua.

"They are not enough," said Kan Te, surer and surer of this. He should not bear tales, things heard in family, but Tao Hua bore them no further. He took her hand in his and they watched the dust with the light of the dying sun piercing it with strange colors. "Some wanted to defend the walls from inside and some wanted to march out in all our strength; and the result . . . the council sent only half, and left half behind. To send more, they said, would panic the people unnecessarily."

Tao Hua looked up at him, her face quite serene and golden in the sun, and he thought again how he loved her. He was afraid, perceiving a shaking in his world, as if it were the tramp of hooves and feet, foretold in the dust.

"I dreamed," he said further, "that all the grass of the plains was gone; I dreamed that the Earth swarmed with men and beasts and that they were much alike; I dreamed of tents and campfires like stars across all the plain of the world; I dreamed that the moon fell, and the moon was the hope of the city."

Tao Hua gazed at him, her black eyes reflecting the shifting clouds, and he thought again of the moon which fell, no bit comforted to have told his dream. There had always seemed time enough: the end of the world crept on at a leisurely pace, and in its ending there were beauties enough. There was no ambition left, but there was time . . . all the time human lives needed: it was only the Earth which had grown old. Love had not.

For the first time the thought of death came between them.

* * *

The column moved slowly, inexorable in its flow across the plain of the world, a flow which had begun years ago in the Tarim and surged to the western rim of the world-plain; which now flowed back again multiplied until the eye could not span its breadth, let alone its length.

The general rode at the head of the column: Yilan Baba, his men called him, Father Serpent, but snake he had been from his youth, cunning and deadly in his strike. Now he was very old, braced in the saddle with furs and the habit of years on horseback. It was an old pony that carried him, a beast he called Horse, which was one in a long succession of shaggy high-tempered beasts of similar bay color . . . how many, Yilan had forgotten; and this one had grown patient over the long traveling, and quiet of manner, tired, perhaps, as Yilan was tired, and old, as Yilan had gotten old . . . but that was not the complaint which gnawed at Yilan. He was thin beneath the quilted coats and leathers and furs, thin to the point of gauntness. His mustaches were grizzled; his braids were gray, his narrow eyes were lost in sun-wrinkles and his cheeks were seamed and hollowed by age and by the wasting disease which had come on him in this last year.

But if he looked, squinting, through the sun-colored dust which swirled about them, it seemed that he could see this place of his dreams, the Forbidden City, the City of Heaven. He imagined that he could see it, as he imagined it each dawning, when the sun rose out of the east and the colors streamed through the dusty wind. The wind out of the east breathed of green lands, of beauty, of wealth . . .

. . . of ending. A place to rest. Beyond, was only the sea.

"Give me the city," he had asked of the hordes which he had gathered. For all of a lifetime he had gathered them, he, Yilan, the Snake, from his mastery of his own tribe to mastery of all the tribes which rode the world-plain.

They came with tents and with wagons, with oxen and with swift horses and with patient feet, men and women and children of the hordes. With the drought on the plains he might have lost them, but he stirred them now with visions of final paradise, with a dream which he had prised from the lips of a man who had actually seen the City of Heaven.

He had gathered power all his life, which had been fifty-nine seasons, and which—he knew—would not be another. He wanted this thing, he wanted it—ah, beyond telling.

And the flesh grew thinner and the pain of his bones against the saddle grew all but unbearable; he bled from the saddlegalls, he was so thin, and his eyes watered so that much of the time he rode with the shame of tears on his cheeks.

"Drink, Yilan Baba," said a voice by his side. He looked into the young face of Shimshek, dark and fierce as a kite, who offered him ku-miss and rode his pony close to Horse, so that he might steady him. He drank, and the liquor warmed him, but his hand was now so weak that he could not stopper the skin or long hold it. Shimshek caught it from him in time, and reached to grip his shoulder as they rode knee against knee. "Hold firm, Father, we will stop soon."

"The City will be in sight," he said, and comforted by the presence of his young lieutenant, he focused his mind and his eyes, and thought how long by now the plume of their dust might have been seen. "Hawk and Fox will go out with all others you can persuade," he said, his voice cracking; he steadied it and lifted his hand eastward, where he would send the forces. "And you must lead them. I no longer can, Shimshek."

"Father," Shimshek mourned. There was great sadness in his eyes, a genuine sorrow.

"I have taught you," said Yilan. Shimshek was not, in fact, his son; he had no son, though his wife's belly swelled with life. He loved this man as if he were a son, and trusted him with all that mattered. "Go," he said. "This time you lead."

Shimshek looked behind them, at the column of wagons which groaned after them, having in his eyes that look which was for the woman they both loved, and for things he could not say. There was fear in Shimshek's eyes that was not for the enemy, not for anything that he would yet name. Good, thought Yilan. Good, he knows; and yet Shimshek said nothing, because there was nothing which could be said. The task was for doing, and there was no help for it: he had himself fought his last battle, and knew it; and Horse knew it, who was also aging . . . by now Horse would have known the enemy, would have flared his nostrils and thrown his head and walked warily and eagerly with the scent of strangers and strange land coming on the winds. But he plodded, head hanging.

"Go," he said again, and Shimshek pressed his shoulder and then raced off full tilt, drumming his heels into his pony's side, shouting and kicking up the dust. "Hai hai hai," he yelled, and the Wolf standard moved to Shimshek's summons, for Wolf was Shimshek's clan. Hawk and Fox moved when Yilan lifted his arm and waved those units forward; the warriors thundered past to the Wolf banner. More couriers went out on their swift ponies, rallying the others, a vast horde gathering to the command of Shimshek the Wolf in this the first skirmish of the campaign.

Another horseman rode to be near Yilan, dour and frowning, of Yilan's own years, but hale and powerful. Yilan envied him the power and the years yet left to him and looked him in the eyes. Boga was this one's name, gray and broad: *bull* was his name, and he had led all the hordes of the Danube.

Once.

"You send the Wolf . . . where?"

"To command." Again the hoarseness, which robbed his voice of the command it had once had. He was doubly grateful for the loyalty of Shimshek: his back would be cold indeed with Boga at it. "To *lead*, Boga. And your men will guard the column."

Hate burned in the old man's eyes, deep and vengeful. Yes, Yilan thought, and now even Shimshek fears this man. Advisedly, if yet without knowledge.

Boga rode away. Yilan watched the gathering of chiefs which instantly surrounded him. "Come on, Horse," he said, and thumped the bony sides and rode toward the group, rode among them, gaining guilty looks as he shouldered in. "Move," he said, "back to your troops," he ordered some; and "Go with Shimshek," he ordered others. He commanded, and heads bowed and riders hurried off, and Boga was left to ride beside him. The gesture had tired him. He stared into the shifting light and the dust raised by Shimshek's swirling horsemen, and knew that hate was beside him.

"We camp in another degree of the sun," he said. He knew for a certainty what Shimshek had perhaps come to suspect in recent days, that he was dying quickly. That Boga wished the process hastened. "We have the City all but in sight," he said, to prod at Boga, for a perversity that he himself did not understand, except that in war, too, he had had such a habit, to draw the enemy out, and never to let him be concealed.

"I did not believe you could do it, Yilan Baba. I did not, but you've proved me wrong."

Boga had resisted. He followed because his tribe could not hold apart from the other tribes; because he had commanded the Danube hordes and could still, if he went where they went. Inevitably in council there was Boga standing up and saying that the tribes must keep their independence each from the other. It sounded noble and traditional. It meant another thing; for the more he weakened, the more Boga had stopped saying such things. The more he began to die, the more a look was born in Boga's slitted eyes, like the look of a hungry beast.

"I know you," Yilan Baba said hoarsely.

"You should know me well by these many years, Father. We have had our differences, but indeed, have I not followed you?"

"I know you," Yilan said again, turning his head to look into Boga's eyes a second time; and this time something in Boga looked out of those eyes and seemed to go very cold. "We are old," said Yilan. "Very old, Boga. I know you."

The look became fear. Perhaps he should have feared in turn, but instead he smiled at Boga, and watched the fear grow, the certainty in Boga's mind that he was indeed known, and that the whispers which Boga whispered with others in the far places of the column were heard.

They rode side by side, he and his murderer, while Shimshek and much of the vanguard rode away to crush the forces which the city might send against them, which could not possibly stand against the might of all the tribes of the plain of the world.

His eyes wept, and this time not from the wind. He cherished a selfish hope that he might be able to see the City before he died. He did not speak of it in those terms, far from it. He acknowledged no weakness to Boga and his lot. He knew, in fact, that by challenging Boga he had just hastened the hour of his death. He should not have done it, perhaps, but he had commanded all his life, and he would not allow another to choose for him. Tonight, then, likely tonight. Boga was thinking and planning and when Boga was sure, then Boga would strike.

He thought of Gunesh riding behind him in the wagon, thought of her with the only pain he felt. Gunesh loved him; Shimshek did; and they were all the world. A baby grew in Gunesh's belly . . . not his son, but Shimshek's. He knew that. Of course he knew it. His health made other answers impossible. That even Shimshek and Gunesh betrayed him in this regard did not matter, because they were the two he loved best, and he could not wish better for her than she had for that young man, or he in her, or himself, in them. Sex had never been a matter of pride with him. It had never been, from his youth. He had gone through the motions, enjoyed a bawdy joke—but that part of his instincts was subordinated to his obsessions: not power, not precisely that—in fact, power bored him—hunger, perhaps, but he never wanted it sated. Nor was it vague or formless; He knew himself, ah, very well—and loved, and even hurt for the pain he caused, but he went on causing it.

Had prepared more of it, maneuvering Shimshek into command

above Boga. But it was the right thing. Shimshek now had troops with him, tribe upon tribe . . . so it would be disaster for them to present Shimshek and the returning troops with the murdered body of Yilan Baba. Ah, no. They would do that only if they must.

He smiled to himself and stared into the dust with the wind cold on his cheeks, feeling the brush of Boga's knee against his as the ponies walked side by side, and the standard of the conquering hordes went before, the banner of the dying sun.

He still ruled, even making them kill him when he chose. That was always his power, that he chose everything he could, and gambled the rest.

And by the hour of camp the City appeared to them. A cry went up from the column which stretched as far as the mind could imagine. Ah, the tribes moaned. Ah, the women and children said, and it was the sighing of the rumored sea, and the rush of wind, and the breaking of thunder. *Ah.* The City shimmered like a mirage, its roofs shone with gold and with beauty in the light, and dust veiled it, which was the place of Shimshek and the others, where battle raged. Yilan had no doubt of the battle; had these not sufficed, he could have sent more. They might crush the City with the wagons of women and children alone, if they simply moved forward.

He wept, which he did continually, but it had meaning in this moment; and in truth many of the warriors wept, and waved their lances and raced their ponies. Here and there a rider wasted precious gunpowder, which he did not reprimand, for after this there were no more battles for the horde, because they should have conquered the whole of the known world, and there was nothing more but the sea.

"Do we camp?" asked a young rider from Fox. He nodded and looked at Boga. "Give the orders," he said. Boga rode off to do so. The column halted, the wagons were unhitched, the animals picketed. Yilan sat his horse and waited as he would do every evening, until all was in order, until firepots were brought from the wagons and cooking began.

The place of the wagon-tents was not chance; it was a matter of precedence. His own was central to the camp; and those of his chieftains of the Hawk and Fox touching his . . . but they were with Shimshek; and those of the Wolf himself, but Shimshek was not there, and his underchiefs were gone, so that there were only the families, wagons without defenders. Indeed, on his left was Boga's lynx standard, and near it the standards of chiefs who had not gone with Shimshek—all his enemies.

Boga's hour at last, Yilan thought to himself, riding slowly into the trap, that harmless-looking area by his own wagon, where Gunesh should be waiting. But there indeed Boga and the others, who stood with their horses, dismounted, beside the ladder of his wagon. He watched for blades, his heart paining him for Gunesh, who might be dead; but no, not yet, not until he should die. They would not dare, for fear of having all misfire. Cut off the snake's head before risking other provocations. Boga was not stupid; thus, he was predictable.

It was a simple drink they gave him, a skin of kumiss, and from Boga's own hand, while he was still in the saddle. He looked at Boga, and there was a fearsome silence despite all the noise and bustle of the camp . . . a silence and stark fear in the faces all about that circle as he sat Horse with that deadly gift in hand and looked from Boga to the rest of them.

"I know you," he said again, and watched the hate in Boga's eyes grow and the fear in the others' eyes increase.

He drank. He looked at them afterwards. Saw the fear no whit abated. It was a different fear, perhaps, that of men who suddenly felt transparent, and wondered if they had not walked into some unnamed trap in which the stakes were not quite as they had thought

"Help me down," he said, and swung a leg over, used Boga's arms to steady him, let Boga help him to the steps of his wagon. Boga helped him up slowly, into the carpeted, dark interior. "Light the lamps," he ordered, and Boga uncovered the firepot and did so, a servant's duty; but Boga let him exact this of him, enduring anything he might wish . . . this night.

Then Yilan leaned back among the embroidered leather cushions and rested his body on the carpets and the yellow lamplight shone down on him. He shut his eyes and dreamed of the City, and saw, from the slit of his eyes when he heard a step departing, and felt the wagon quake, that Boga had gone his way.

To lay traps and ambushes, doubtless.

O Shimshek, have a care!

"Husband?"

It was quite another step which came from behind the curtains, from the door by the forward chamber. A breath of herbs came with her, a hint of sweetness unlike the dust and the stink of urine that was the outside world. He opened his eyes smiling, for Gunesh was by him, beautiful, brave Gunesh, who had seen it all; there was terror in her eyes as she knelt by him. He reached up and touched a gloved hand to her cheek, for comfort.

"Will you eat, Yilan?"

He shook his head, made an effort to tug off his gloves. She helped him; even that exertion tired him now. "I shall smoke," he said. "And then I want you to go and pack a little food, Gunesh. It may be necessary. You saw that out there?"

She nodded. Her lips were pressed tight.

"Well," he said. "Go pack the food."

She said nothing. He was a great king, and she a captive once and long ago. She had the habit of doing as she was told, and then of saying her mind, and he waited while she brought him the long-stemmed pipe and his bowl, and filled it and set the stem between his lips. A tear rolled down her face. It was perhaps of his death she thought, and perhaps of her own, and perhaps of Shimshek's. They were all in their way doomed; he knew so and he thought she might.

And still she had nothing to say. By this he was sure that she was aware of what went on. "They wait," he said plainly, "because they wish to trap Shimshek too. I gave him power and now they have to contrive to get it away from him. If I grow too weak, Gunesh, my brave Gunesh, you will tell him how I passed. Have you your dagger?"

She nodded, touched the hilt at her belt, among the furs.

"Shimshek will take care of you."

Her chin weakened. "*Why*, Yilan? Why did you let them?"

"Stop that. Trust Shimshek, I say. I know you have in other things. Ah, do you think I don't know whose baby you're carrying? You're nothing to me—in that way—everything in my heart of hearts, Gunesh. You know that everything had to come before you, but no one can take your place."

"I don't understand you," she said.

"You're going to deny it. Don't. I know the truth."

Now her composure almost left her. "I don't understand. I don't."

"You do."

"I love you."

"You always have. And I you, Gunesh, forever and ever. Go away. Leave me. Whatever Boga's fed me, I doubt it will be painful. He'd like that, but he won't want whispers of poison. Ah no. He gave me this with his own hand."

"Yilan, why did you?"

"To save Shimshek. And you. And the child; him too. I'm dying— are a few weeks much to me? No. Not in my pain. I've seen the City. But even that ceases to matter, Gunesh. Don't be sad. I have all that I meant to do. I'm finished. Call Shimshek to me if he comes in time, and remember that I love you both."

"Yilan—"

"*Go,*" he said, in *that* voice which had moved armies and made chieftains flinch. But Gunesh drew in a breath and garnered her serenity like a robe of state, nodded with satisfaction. He chuckled, for the smoke was killing the pain, and he was pleased: he could never affright Gunesh, not that way.

"I shall be back," she said.

"Yes."

She pressed her lips to his then, and stroked his hand and withdrew.

He inhaled deeply of the smoke, clearer and clearer in his mind, his eyes hazed with far perspectives.

The riders came from the dust of evening, black swift shapes. "Look," the citizens watching from the walls had cried, waving kerchiefs, when first the shapes appeared; they had thought them their own returning soldiers, one of the units come back, perhaps, in victory. But all too quickly the truth became clear, and then a great wailing went up from the City of Heaven, and the citizens rushed to bring spears and whatever things they could to defend it.

"Here! O here!" Kan Te exclaimed, thrusting into Tao Hua's hands a bundle of lances as he reached her atop the wall. The armory and the museum had passed them out to any man who would stand atop the wall and throw them, and he suffered a terrible vision, Tao Hua's pale bewildered face, as the dusty wind caught her braids and her tassels and stirred the flower petals of the bloom she wore beside her cheek. She clutched the warlike burden, and passed one to him, as the stronger arm, as all about them citizens were taking positions, the weaker to hold and pass, the stronger to hurl the weapons, and tears were on the faces of both men and women who looked on the advancing riders. "O where are they?" they heard asked down the wind, for Phoenix and Lion had not returned, and here was the enemy upon them. Kan Te picked up the lance which Tao Hua gave him, bright and needle-keen. The ribbons fluttered bravely from the weapon and she thought as she watched him leaning above the parapet, his robes aflurry in the dust, his face set in a grimace of resolution, how very much they loved. She turned her face toward the enemy, the hordes which killed and burned and destroyed. She leaned the bundle of javelins against the wall, and took one in her own tiny hand, a weapon which trailed paper flowers from scarlet rib-

bons, and she leaned beside Kan Te to wait, copying his hold on the
weapon, though all along the city wall were a dozen different grips, people who had not the least idea of the use of such things, as they themselves did not. They had trained with long rifles, but there were not
enough left.

The riders drew nigh like thunder, and premature lances hurled
from the walls trailing ribbons. "Wait, wait," the two cried among the
others, chiding comrades to patience. In a moment more the riders were
in range, a stream of them, who hurled dark objects which battered at
the gate below; lances streamed down with their ribbons and their flowers and some few hit home, sending either horse or rider down, but
many whose horses fell scrambled up behind comrades, swept up never
so much as faltering; and the objects kept coming, thudding against the
gate like stones.

"They are heads!" someone near the gate cried, and the horrid cry
echoed round the walls.

The hail of javelins continued from above and the objects thrown by
the riders continued to strike the gate, each riding up to hurl his missile
and riding away, most unscathed. Before the riders had stopped coming,
they were out of weapons; the last riders coursed in unchecked, hurled
the heads they bore at the gate and rode off with shouted taunts.

There was weeping. Here and there a scream rang out as some new
viewer reached that place in the wall from which they could see the
gates.

And toward twilight they dared unbar the gate, where a heap of
thousands of heads stood, and some tumbled inward and rolled across
the beautiful stones of the road, heads of comrades of the Phoenix and
the Lion, sons and daughters of the city . . . and one living man, who had
been of the Phoenix. Cries of relatives split the night. Friends gathered
up the remains and bore them when parents and mates were too stunned
or horrified. They made a pyre in the city and burned them, because
there was nothing else to do.

And Kan Te and Tao Hua clung together, weeping for friends and
shivering. The Phoenix soldier wept news of enemies as many as the
grains of sand, of a living wind which threatened to pour over them.
Only a portion of that horde had bestirred itself to deal with them.

The City then knew it was doomed. The fever spread; lovers and be-
reaved leaped onto the pyre which destroyed what was left of Phoenix
and Lion; the last Phoenix soldier threw himself after.

Others simply stared, bewildered, at the death and the madness, and the smoke went up from the square of the City of Heaven, to mingle with the dust.

"He is back." Gunesh shook the wagon in climbing down, as the sound of several riders thundered up to the wagon. "Ah," said Yilan Baba to no one in particular, and sucked at the pipe and leaned among his cushions, pleased in the cessation of pain the drag had brought . . . or the poison. No need to have been concerned; Shimshek had won his battle, and Boga and his cronies let Shimshek and a few of his men get through to him. How could they gracefully prevent it?

And surely they did not want to prevent it, to have both their victims in one place at one time.

They came in together, his dear friends, Gunesh first up the ladder, and Shimshek hard after her, even yet covered with the dust of his riding and the blood of his enemies. Gunesh had got an early word in his ear out there. He saw the anguish in Shimshek's face. "Sit," he said. "Gunesh, not you—go forward."

Her eyes flashed.

"Go," he said in a gentle voice. "Give me a little private time with this young man. It regards you both, but give me the time to talk to him."

"When it regards me—"

"Out," he said. She went, perhaps sensing him too weak for dispute. A pain hit him; he clamped his jaw against it, turned out his pipe, packed it again with trembling hands. He reached for the light and Shimshek hastened feverishly to help him, to do anything for him, lingered in that moment's closeness, full of pain. Yilan looked and had a moment's vision of what Gunesh saw of them—a grayed, seamed old man, and Shimshek's godlike beauty, dark and strong. He sucked the smoke, reached and touched Shimshek's face, a father's touch this time.

Tears broke from Shimshek's eyes, flowed down his face unchecked.

"They have killed me," he said. "Gunesh told you, of course. If I'm not dead quickly, they'll see to it; and next you, and her. Most of all the baby she's carrying, yours or mine, no difference . . . oh, Shimshek, of course I know; how do you think not?"

Shimshek bowed his head, and he reached out and lifted his face.

"Prideful nonsense. You think the old man is blind? Sit with me a moment. Just a little time."

"For all of time, Father, if you wish."

He darted the youth a piercing glance, leaned back in the cushions, looked at him from hooded eyes. "You've said nothing about how it went. Wasn't that the news you came to tell me? Isn't that important?"

"They fell like grass under our hooves. We'll take the City tomorrow, Yilan Baba; we'll give you that."

He grinned faintly, grew sober again, sucked at the pleasing smoke. "Brave friend. Rome and Carthage, Thebes and Ur . . . how many, how many more . . . ?"

Shimshek shook his head, bewildered.

"Oh, my young friend," he sighed, "I'm tired, I'm tired this time, and it doesn't matter. I've done all that's needful; I know that. It's why I sit and smoke. There's no more of Yilan; only of you, of Gunesh. I have some small hope for you, if you're quick."

"I'll rouse the tribe. I'll get Boga's lot away from you. . . ."

"No. You'll take the tribes that will follow you and you'll ride, you and Gunesh. Get out of here."

"To break the hordes now . . ."

"It doesn't matter, do you understand me? No, of course you don't." He drew upon the pipe, passed it to Shimshek and let the calming smoke envelope him. "Do as I tell you. That's all I want."

"I'll have Boga's head on a pole."

"No. Not that either."

"Then tell me what I have to do."

"Just obey me. Go. The city means nothing."

"You struggled so many years—"

"I'm here. I'm here, that's all." He took back the pipe and inhaled. The smoke curled up and wreathed about them in the murk of the low-hanging lights, and the smoke made shapes, walls of cities, strange towers and distant lands, barren desert, high mountains, lush hills and trafficked streets, beasts and fantastical machines, men of many a shade and some who were not human at all. "I'm many lives old, Shimshek; and I know you . . . ah, my old, old friend. I remember . . . I've gotten to remembering since I've been sick; dreaming dreams . . . They're in the smoke, do you see them?"

"Only smoke, Yilan Baba."

"Solid as ever. I know your heart, and it's loyal, indeed it is. We've been through many a war, Shimshek. Fill the other pipe, will you; fill it and dream with me."

"Outside—"

"Do as I say."

Shimshek reached for the bowl, filled the other pipe, lit it and leaned back in attempted leisure, obedient though, Yilan saw with sudden clarity, his wounds were untreated. Poor Shimshek, bewildered indeed. At length a shiver went through him.

"Better?" Yilan asked.

"Numb," said Shimshek. Yilan chuckled. "Can you laugh, Baba?"

"I think I've done well," Yilan said. "Spent my life well."

"No one else could have united the tribes—no one—and when you're gone . . . it goes. I can't hold them, Baba."

"True," said Yilan. "Ah, Boga might. He has the strength. But I think not; not this time."

"Not this time?"

Yilan smiled and watched the cities in the smoke, and the passing shapes of friends. Enkindu, Patroclus, Hephestion, and Antony and a thousand others. "Patroclus," he called him. "And Lancelot. And Roland. O my friend . . . do you see, do you yet see? Sometimes we meet so late . . . you're always with me, but so often born late, my great, good friend. Most of my life I knew I was missing something, and then I found you, and Gunesh, and I was whole. Then it could begin. I didn't know in those years what I was waiting for, but I knew it when it came, and now I know why."

Shimshek's eyes lifted to his, spilling tears and dreams, dark as night his eyes now, but they had been green and blue and gray and brown, narrow and wide, and all shades between. "I don't know what you're talking about."

"Yes. Now I think you do. Cities more than this one . . . , And Gunesh . . . she's always there . . . through all the ages."

"You're like my father, Yilan Baba; more father than my own. Tell me what to believe and I believe it."

He shook his head. "You've only known me longer; give your father his honor. There was not always such a gap of years, sometimes we were brothers."

"In other lives, Baba? Is that what you mean?"

"There was a city named Dur-sharrunkin; I was Sargon; I was Menes, by a river called Nile; I was Hammurabi; and you were always there; I was Gilgamesh; we watched the birth of cities, my friend, the first stone piled on stone in this world."

Shimshek shivered, and looked into his eyes. "Achilles," he murmured. "You had that name once. Did you not?"

"And Cyrus the Persian; and Alexander. You were Hephestion, and I lost you first that round—ah, that hurt—and the generals murdered me then, not wanting to go on. How I needed you."

"O God," Shimshek wept.

Yilan reached out and caught Shimshek's strong young arm. "I was Hannibal, hear me? And you Hasdrubal my brother; Caesar, and you Antony; I was Germanicus and Arthur and Attila; Charlemagne and William; Saladin and Genghis. I fight; I fight the world's wars, and this one is finished as far as it must go, do you hear me, my son, my brother, my friend? Am I not always the same? Do I ever hold long what I win?"

"Yilan Baba—"

"Do I ever truly win? Or lose? Only you and Gunesh . . . Roxane and Cleopatra; Guenevere and Helen . . . as many shapes as mine and yours; and always you love her."

Terror was in Shimshek's eyes, and grief.

"Do you think I care?" Yilan asked. "I love you and her; and in all my lives—it's never mattered. Do you yet understand? No. For you it's love; for Gunesh it's sex . . . strange, is it not? For her it's sex that drives so many in this world, but you've always been moved by love and I—I've no strong interest there—but love, ah, a different kind of love; the love of true friends. I *love* you both, but sex . . . was never there. Listen to me. I'm talking frankly because there's no time. That there'll be a child . . . makes me happy, can you understand that? You've been so careful not to wound me; but I knew before you began. I did, my friend. Whenever you're young, children have happened if there was half a chance . . . and I don't begrudge a one, no, never."

"They haven't lived," Shimshek breathed, as if memory had shot through him. His grief was terrible, and Yilan reached out again and patted his arm.

"But some have lived. Some. That's always our destiny . . . you've begotten more of my heirs than I ever have. Mine are murdered. . . . Perhaps it's that which gives me so little enthusiasm in begetting them. But you've been more fortunate: have hope. Your heirs followed me in Rome. Have more confidence."

"And they brought down the empire, didn't they? I'm unlucky, Baba."

"Don't you yet understand that it doesn't matter?"

"But I can't stop hurting, Baba." He looked at the pipe cupped in his hand, and up again. "I can't."

"That's the way of it, isn't it?"

"Has Gunesh remembered?"

He shook his head. "I've thought so sometimes; and sometimes not. I have . . . for all this year, and more and more of late. That's why I'm sure it's close. That's why I didn't fight any further. I remember other times I remembered, isn't that odd? The conspirators in Rome . . . I knew they were coming long before they knew themselves. I felt that one coming. Modred too. I saw in his eyes. They'll accuse you of adultery this time too, do you reckon? They'll say Gunesh is carrying your child, and they'll demand your death with hers. And Boga of course will expect to lead when we're all dead."

"I'll kill him."

Yilan shook his head. "You can't save me. Save yourselves. It's only good sense . . . Boga has other names too, you know. Agamemnon, Xerxes, Bessus . . . don't sell him short."

"Modred."

"Him too."

"A curse on him!"

"There is. Like ours."

"Baba?"

"He's the dark force. The check on me. Lest I grow too powerful. I might myself be ill for the world, if there were not Boga. He reminds me . . . of what I might be. And often enough he has killed me. That is his function. Only woe to the world when we're apart. Hitler was a case like that. I was half the world away; we both were. He had the power to himself."

"Lawrence."

"That was the name. Bitterest when we two miss each other; hardest the world when Boga and I do. Pity Boga, he has no Patroclus, no Guenevere."

Shimshek smoked a time, and his eyes traveled around the padded interior of the wagon, which was only a wagon, perched on the world-plain, and smoky and deeply shadowed. But there seemed no limits and no walls, as if much of time hinged here.

"Sometimes," said Yilan slowly, "I live my whole life without seeing the pattern of what I do; sometimes . . . there is no design evident, and Boga and I and you and Gunesh . . . live apart and lost; sometimes in little lives and sometimes in great ones; sometimes I've been a baby that died before a year, only marking time till my soul could be elsewhere. Or resting, perhaps, just resting. Some of my deaths are hard."

"I'll go out with you this time. I've no fear of it."

Yilan chuckled and winced, a little twinge of pain in the gut. "Shimshek, you lie; you are afraid."

"Yes."

"And losing Gunesh would break your heart and mine; take care of her."

"Ah, Baba."

"You're the one who loves, you understand. My dear friend, I do think this time you may outlive me. You'll see a measure of revenge if you wait and watch."

"What is revenge if it never ends?"

"Indeed. Indeed, old friend. I'll tell you something I've begun to see. The balance swings. I move men only so far in a lifetime; only so much help to any side. I was Akkadian, Sumerian, Egyptian, Kushite, Greek, Macedonian. . . . I brought Persia to birth; defended Greece against it at Thermopylae; built an eastern empire as Alexander; and a western one as Hannibal; checked both as Caesar, and drove north and south; was Chinese and Indian and African . . . side against side. We live by balances; there is no revenge, and there is. Point of view, Shimshek."

Shimshek only stared.

"Love Gunesh," Yilan said. "Live. I want you out of here before the dawn; slip her into your camp. When I am dead, there will be a bit of noise. Then sound the horn and ride. Probably there'll be great confusion—some attacking the city, some coming this way; you see the old man's still thinking. It's one of my best stratagems."

"No, Baba. I'll not leave you here to be killed."

"Don't be obstinate. You'll only hasten your death. And hers."

"Shall I tell her . . . what you've told me?"

"Is it peace to you, to know what I've told you?"

"No," Shimshek said heavily. "No, Father; no peace— There's no ending, is there?"

"As to that, I don't know. But from the world's dawn to the world's ending . . . we're the same. Unchangeable."

"Boga and you are the great ones," Shimshek said, "Isn't it so . . . that she and I are powerless?"

"Mostly," he said and watched pride vastly hurt. "Only—Shimshek, if it weren't for you—I might *be* Boga. Think of that. If not for you . . . and for her. Because I love you."

"Baba," Shimshek murmured, and laid down the pipe and put gentle arms about him, kissed his brow.

"Go," he said. "Go now, and when you hear the uproar that will follow when I'm dead . . . ride with Gunesh."

"I will not leave you, Baba. Not to die in your bed."

"Can you not? Do you grudge me a quiet death? Even Boga has

chosen that for me this time, and I am tired, young firebrand; the old man is tired."

The curtain drew back. Shimshek reached frantically after his sword, but it was Gunesh.

"How much time must I give you?" she asked.

"Sit," Yilan said, patting the rug beside him, and she sat down there on her heels. "You have some persuasion in you, woman. Move this young man."

"To leave you?"

Yilan nodded grimly, motioned with the bowl of his pipe toward the peripheries of the camp. "How does it look out there?"

"Like stars," she said. "If the sky could hold so many."

"Like the old sky," he said. "So many, many more than now. Do you ever dream of such stars, Gunesh? I do. And I tell you that you have to go with this mad young man, and not to lose that baby of yours and his. Can you ride, Gunesh?"

She nodded, moist-eyed; he had had enough of tears from Shimshek.

"No nonsense," he said.

"I have dreamed," she said, "that we've said this before."

"Indeed," he said. "Indeed. And shall again. Someday Shimshek will tell you."

"They're *true*," she said, and shivered violently.

"Yes," he admitted finally, knowing full well what they she meant. "Yes, Gunesh. The dreams. Perhaps we all three have them."

Shimshek shut his eyes and turned his face away.

"Yilan," Gunesh wept.

"So there'll not be argument. You two have to get out of here. That's the pattern this time. I've ceased to need you."

"Have you?" Shimshek asked.

"Not in that way," he admitted. He could never bear to hurt them. And it began to have the flavor of something they had often done, a movement like ritual to which they knew the words; had known them for all the age of the Earth. "Hold me," he said, and opened his arms. It was the only real thing left, the thing they all wanted most of all. They made one embrace, he and she and he, and it was reward of all the pain, more than cities, more than empires—it was very rare that they understood one another so well; Montmorency and Dunstan and Kuwei; Arslan and Kemal; so many, many shapes. They were given nothing to take with them, but the memory, and the love and the knowledge—that the pattern went on.

"I love you," he told them. "The night is half done and there's nothing more for you to do. I'll see you again. Can you doubt it?"

The smoke of the pyres had died to a steady ascending plume, which the wind whipped away. A great number of the people of the City of Heaven gathered in the darkened square to mourn; white bones showed in that pathetic tangle, in the embers of that fire into which much of the wealth of the city had been cast, to keep the hands of barbarians from it.

It was much of the past which died, more bitter loss than the lives. It was the city's beauty which had died.

And some prayed and some were drunken, anticipating death.

And some sought their own places, and their familiar homes.

And lovers touched, mute. There were no words for what was happening, though it had been happening since the first army raided the first straw village. There were no words because it was happening to them, and it was tomorrow, and they were numb in that part of the mind which should understand their situation; and all too quick in that part of the heart which felt it.

They touched, Kan Te and Tao Hua, and touches became caresses; then caresses became infinitely pleasurable, a means to deny death existed. They were not wed—it was not lawful—but there was no time left for weddings. The ashes of the dead settled on their roof and drifted in the open window to settle on their bed.

They loved; and spent themselves, and slept with tears on their lashes, the exhausted sleep of lovers who had no tomorrow.

"No," said Gunesh, and touched Yilan's face in that secret, loving way. There were, for them, too many tomorrows. "This time . . . we stay. This time—after all the world's ages—we might make the difference. We might, mightn't we? If we've been trapped before, can't we fight, this time?"

A strange warmth pricked Yilan's cold heart. He turned, painful as it was, and cupped Gunesh's fair face between his scarred hands. "I have thought . . . perhaps . . . someday—you might have some part to play."

"Then let us," exlcaimed Lancelot/Shimshek/Antony. "O Yilan, let us."

He thought. "We proceed slowly, my friends. O so slowly; perhaps the old pattern is for changing; perhaps it does resolve itself, in the long ages. I grow wiser; and Boga . . . perhaps wiser too. It may be, someday, that you can change what is. Perhaps we've gained more than an empire in that, my friends; and maybe you *are* the ones . . . someday. But not this time. Not this time, I think; it's too late; we've lost too much."

"Do we *know* that?"

He looked at Shimshek, smiled with a sudden shedding of the fears which had made him old. Laughed, as he had laughed when he was young, and the world was, and they knew nothing of what would be. "No. No. Hai, my friends, my dear friends, there *is* something left we don't know."

"Tell me what we shall do," said Shimshek. "Tell me, Yilan, and I'll do it."

"Remember," he said. "Remember! We'll fight, my old friends; we'll fight each time. We'll change the pattern on him; and you'll be by me; and you'll . . . someday . . . tip the scales. I believe that. O my friends, I do believe it."

"*I* shall fight now," said Gunesh, drawing her small dagger.

"We are all drunk with the smoke," Yilan laughed. "We dream of old heroes and old wars. But the dreams are true. And we are those heroes."

He strove to rise, to walk, the last time, and Shimshek put his sword into his hand. Together they helped him down the steps, and Gunesh had gotten herself his second sword. Old Horse was standing there, with Shimshek's beast. Poor Horse, no one had attended him. And some of Shimshek's guard were there . . . and some of Boga's. "*Kill them!*" Shimshek commanded, and quick as sword could clear sheath the battle was joined: no honor there—Boga's men fell in their blood, and all about them men boiled from wagons clutching swords. "Get me up," Yilan raged; and Shimshek's guards gave them horses. Horse was left, to die of age.

He hit the saddle, winced, tautened his grip on the sword. "A curse on Boga," he shouted. "Death to Boga! *Traitor!*"

The cry spread, breaking the peace of the night, and the whole camp broke up into chaos, wagons pouring out men and men screaming for horses.

And Shimshek rode like a man demented, Yilan and Gunesh riding behind him, the night muddled before them, dark shapes of men and horses plunging this way and that, the tide of shouts and rumors sweeping the plain for miles. Fires were doused like all the stars of heaven going out, and men rushed inward to fight they knew not what night attack.

Straight past Boga's lynx standard they rode, Shimshek in his fury cutting down the standard-guard. Leaning from the saddle, he seized up the banner and bore it like a lance, for the heart of Boga's men who had rallied to defense.

He tore through them. There was slaughter done; and Gunesh swept through, wielding an unaccustomed sword on the heads of any in her way; Yilan last . . . he struck with feeble fury, with longing, with a rage of ages frustrated.

"Traitor!" he screamed.

And a spear, swifter than poison, found his belly. He saw Boga who had hurled it, saw Shimshek's blade arc down to kill Boga as he had killed him a thousand thousand tunes; saw Gunesh fall.

"My friends," he mourned, and tears blinded his eyes before death did.

They butchered him; but he knew nothing of that.

They had done it at Pompey's statue, and at Thermopylae, and a thousand times before.

Shimshek died, and Gunesh died beneath her horse, a son within her.

The fighting spread among the great horde; horde split from horde; bodies littered the plain. Some, leaderless, drew away in confusion. Boga's was one such tribe; and Yilan's; and Shimshek's. And a hundred others followed. Those left fought for Supremacy, killing and killing, until the sun showed them what they had done.

The sun rose on a calm day, in the strange sanity of this waiting. The City of Heaven waited, madness purged, men and women standing on the walls, holding the spears they had gathered from the ground outside, with the doors closed fast and barred, with their courage regathered in their hearts. No more flowers, no more ribbons; they were there to defend their home, a toughened, determined crew.

But the dust diminished; it went toward the west and diminished. When scouts went out they saw at a great distance the carrion birds circling and the slaughtered remnant of a great host, and the trampled trail of a retreat.

They found the broken banner of Yilan the conqueror, but his body they never found; they brought the banner back in triumph, and the spirit of the City swelled with pride, for they were great, and suspected it, in a fiercer, warlike spirit.

"We have turned them," said Kan Te, when the news came, clutching his spear the tighter. "We shall tell the story," said Tao Hua. "We shall never forget this day."

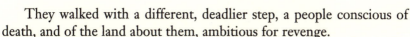

They walked with a different, deadlier step, a people conscious of death, and of the land about them, ambitious for revenge.

A new, fell spirit had gotten through the gates, clinging with the stink of the smoke.

"We shall wed properly," Kan Te said. "I don't think it matters; there must have been many who did what we did. There is no shame, but we shall wed properly."

"I am not ashamed," she said.

"Nor am I," he said. He kissed her, there atop the walls, in the sight of folk who had ceased to be shocked by anything, and she kissed him. They walked away together, and she set her hand to her belly, struck with a recollection of pain and pleasure and a lingering warmth . . . she could have become pregnant, she realized. She had not thought of that before, had not thought in terms of living long enough, and life was good. The warmth was strange, as if some vitality had gotten into her, some strange force of desire and will.

As if some stranger had come to dwell there, born of the death and the shaking of their world.

He had.

2004

I was happy when my editor wanted another Sunfall story for this volume, and the request gave me the chance to do a city I particularly love, which I hadn't done in the first volume. So Venice now joins the company—a city of unique history and constantly shifting perspectives, a city of romance and a particular stubborn courage in its long dealings with the sea. Maybe that's why it so attracts me, this city at war between sea and land, a city that has found a unique way to be modern, and still to remain so perfectly ancient.

CJC

MASKS

(Venice)

Venezia of the canals, queen of the Adriatic, Venezia: a city built and rebuilt, while the sun starts to fail and the Earth grows strange.

She was never meant to be an eternal city—only a refuge from danger. She was never planned to become one of the last great cities on Earth, but here she sits, behind her immense sea gates. The great tides of this latter age rush in and out while, outside the city lagoon, the heatborn Adriatic storms howl and hammer the ancient metal, cleverly-worked tidal gates a thousand times renewed and enlarged. The sea is the city's passionate admirer, a ruinous suitor who brings her gifts of ships and wealth when he smiles, and threatens to overwhelm her when his temper darkens.

While her gates hold, the sea observes his gentlemanly limits. So long as her gates hold, he will bring her his gifts as he always has, and he will bide his time, having had, as all her people know, no change of heart or character at all.

Timbers bear the city up, the oldest pilings long decayed into quaking ooze, so that her newest pilings float, rather than rest, in the accumulated detritus of ages. The natives say there exist places where, if an unfortunate fool, well-weighted, should fall into the canal, he would sink for a year before he reached bottom, down amid bronze age pots and Roman armor of the Iron Age. So they say. Venezia loves her legends.

Venezia loves two things more than her legends: her unique liberty, and her internal peace.

She has cherished her liberty from oldest times. While other cities bled under dukes and potentates, when other cities burned their dissenters and dressed all in black and gray, their citizens pretending deep, grim piety to survive, Venezia elected doges, civil leaders, who made humane laws.

Her ancient liberty gives her a joyous spirit. She prefaces her solemn days of sacrifice with days of *carnevale*, for masques and dream and glittering splendor, a furious few days, a luscious farewell to pleasures, and that only for a season. She is Venezia, la Repubblica Serenissima, and her pleasures like her lovers, will surely come again.

At this wildest time of year, at the *carnevale*, they all wear masks. They trade them about with no regard to class. They are all princes, all thieves, all harlequins, all pulcinellas behind the masks, since Venezia knows this truth about her citizens, that one man, a cobbler, is very like the clerk, and either one might be mistaken for their lord. A courtesan can become a lady for a night, and a virgin again by daybreak. If a citizen wearies of one mask, why, change the mask again. *Carnevale* encourages it. God has blessed it. Has He not been patient with *carnevale* forever? And does not Venezia endure?

Beyond her slender link to the dry land, out in the higher, rolling hills, people put their faith in lords again, strong warlords, wielders of dependable power—lords, so they hope, that may make them safe. But they pay a price for this. One might say that in Venezia people only wear their masks for the season. But in the cities to the west, people wear them forever, the dukes, the laborers, the artisans all doomed to their roles for life.

They lack humor and romance, those outsiders, Venetians say; but Venezia possesses both. Even if the powers of the world come in with heavy boots and rules as tyrants for a season—why, as philosophically and easily as they observe their annual interval of sacrifice, Venetians accept that things might be grim for the while, but Venetians always have their will, and their ways, interlopers and sojourners be damned, Venezia is confident she will choose her doge again. She will hold her masques again and build back her realm of glittering glass, her power like the glassworkers' art, like a bubble of air, of glowing heat. Sometimes it fails, but most times it hardens and shines like the sun.

Venezia is mercantile, more than regal, more glass than gems. Her days rest, like her foundations, on quaking ground, her eternal ideals of equality, and freedom. Everything is for sale in her markets. And nothing she sells is irreplaceable. When outsiders come to rule her, Venezia changes them, or, if they refuse, allows them a space to parade and make a show. When the show ceases to amuse—then Venezia can change her masks, oh, so quickly, and the interloper finds nothing quite as it had seemed.

Venezia is no friendlier to immigrants than to conquerors, alas: she is so tiny a city compared to, say, Milano, or ancient Ravenna, or Verona. She exists on a set of isles. She can scarcely expand her boundaries, or build up, or outward. She is what she is and has been and will be. Those families who live here have lived here forever. Those who come here come on family connections, or on the charity of residents, or find no place to lodge. There is simply no room.

Yet over millennia, family bloodlines run thin, and a few great houses stand vacant—a few, at least, as the age advances, as the floods grow more frequent.

In that particular circumstance, a very few newcomers find a foothold. Giovanna Sforza is one of these—la duchesa, she calls herself, this bitter old woman, la duchesa di Milano.

Whether she is, in fact truly titled in Milan, no one can ascertain, or greatly cares. The necessary matter is that she came with sufficient money, and the Venetian Montefiori, who might know the truth of her claim, has rented her an elegant house in a cluster of buildings overarching the Calle Corrente. Four canals border this clump of buildings, and bridges bring foot traffic along the Priuli margin, and back along the calles. It is, in short, a place where shops spread their wares, where tabernas set out tables, on the rare walkway beside a lesser canal. It is thus not a grand palazzo, this little house with its water-stairs on the Racheta waterway. It has been run down and let go, its last owner having died in penury and the current one, who inherited it, himself reputed as mad. But the little house possesses one glory, one amazing glory that would have made many wealthy families envy it, before it fell to ruin— and this was a garden, run entirely to weeds. Land was so precious in Venezia, that not to build on it and install a dozen persons on it was a token of wealth, of truly great wealth and standing. But this garden was simply neglected by the mad Montefiori, who took to religious orders, and lived in the upstairs.

Some said later that the duchesa was a distant Montefiori herself. Some said her fortunes had fallen so low that she had no income, but to serve as nurse and caretaker to this mad old man.

Whatever the truth of it, la duchesa came by boat, bringing no furniture at all, so far as anyone remembered. She came with a young granddaughter and three servants, the servants with six valises which they hired ported through the calles, and which they zealously followed afoot, as if they feared the porters were thieves. The duchesa and the young girl went by gondola to the water-stairs of the little house—such were the details afterward gossiped at the edge of the lagoon, where the gondoliers gathered, and on the Serpentine, by the offended porters. La duchesa's arrival was a moment's buzz in the city: the fact that she had leased from the odd Montefiori—that was itself a delicious oddity. But the gossip among the gondoliers and the porters was thin, beyond the fact that la duchesa had arrived with one very heavy valise among the others. Gold was the common and natural guess, and in three days thieves made two attempts on the little house, in vain; the servants were quick, and efficient.

The merchants of the city knew nothing, except that la duchesa, through her servants, purchased new furnishings, a dining table and two stout chairs of classical taste, three carpets of good quality, and excellent dinnerware, with, of course, blown glass. She also, through her servants, bought extravagant fabrics, and engaged seamstresses, who reported that the young girl, Giacinta, about twelve, was a lovely if solemn child, and that la duchesa was elegant and clearly of exquisite taste.

There was early speculation as to when la duchesa might invade society, and society underwent a slight stir of preparation and a shudder of fortification. Venezia did not readily admit foreigners—anyone not born in Venezia was, by definition, foreign—least of all welcomed foreign aristocrats, who might expect to be bowed to and deferred to by the merchant princes of the Adriatic. And no one wanted to admit that an acquaintance with the mad Montefiori constituted native standing. Venezia drew a deep breath and closed ranks behind its doge and its council, its mercantile elite, and its own sense of proprieties. It waited for the assault.

In vain. La duchesa did not enter society, and the mad Montefioro languished and died, taken in the black funerary barge to the sea, without relatives to lament him, only that la duchesa provided him a decent funerary procession, and watched from the windows as he was taken away, with what emotion no one could tell. She stayed quiet in her rented house afterward, engaged a gardener, and gossip about the gowns and the furnishings faded in favor of a grudging acceptance, since she never came out. The gossip that surrounded the house grew uninteresting, providing no amusement and no scandal.

So they caused no difficulties. They became a known quantity, and in their self-imposed isolation, respectable, even considered in invitations—but never quite invited, for fear of everyone else's opinion. The Montefiori house became an address, a location, an odd tidbit of knowledge. Fashionable people never saw the duchesa, except that gondoliers noted the beautiful child that looked out from the waterside windows, and from time to time merchants received requests to bring goods for inspection and purchase. The merchants thus favored reported the house as exquisite inside, and the gardener, who ate his lunch at a certain café on the Priuli, said the duchesa and her daughter spent hour upon hour in their little garden, that they had rooted out the weeds with their own hands, and discovered greenery and flowers under the neglect.

Three years passed, in which more important matters than la duchesa di Milano pressed on Venezia. In the first of those three years, a far more extravagant visitor arrived, noisily, with abundant baggage and a train of servants. His name was Cesare di Verona, exiled and outcast from his own city in a recent coup, but, it seemed, far from penniless. In fact, he had long supported Venetian mercantile interests, through intermediaries—not quite idle enough a nobleman to rule Verona, perhaps, but an easier fit within Venetian society than the duchesa from farther west, since he spread gold about, liberally. More, Cesare di Verona owned ships. Society therefore understood how he derived his money. It was apt to increase. It employed and it built, it traded and therefore it could be traced, by those who knew such things, by those whose business it was to know.

That meant it could be courted. The dark and handsome Cesare di Verona, unlike the duchesa, was invited to the houses of merchant princes, and did attend their parties, and ingratiated himself with certain ones by means of charity, by his relief to a merchant who had lost a ship and cargo, by his support and rescue of a foundering palazzo, with its historic treasures. Such an aristocrat found his way into ancient and inner circles, paving his way with good works. Could anyone disapprove of such generosity? And did anyone notice the comings and goings among his servants?

Venezia absorbed both arrivals, and went about its own affairs in peace, its life regulated by the tides, by the arrival and departure of ships from the deepwater port, the Porto Nuovo, beyond the great sea gates— and of course by the flow of trade to and from the port causeway, and goods likewise flowing on the western causeway, the sole landward connection of the city to the rest of the countryside.

Two things disturbed that peace. First event and least likely, a great quake struck remote Cairo, and the consequent tide, as it rushed inland, had flooded the Cairo harborside, wrecked ships at dock, and destroyed almost all the warehouses.

To certain merchants in Venezia, Cairo's misfortune seemed more opportunity than disaster, since it had happened to a trading partner, not to them, and since their ships had not been in port, they might sell to a city in dire need of goods. But the debate of the Council, whether to send assistance gratis to the stricken city, was the news of two days only. On the third day, while the city was still abuzz, with disputes over the matter of Cairo, the Doge slipped on the stairs of his own house and died—a careless servant, a previously spilled tray, a spot of oil, on the uncompromising marble steps of the Palazzo Ducale.

In an instant the benevolent and honest man who had ruled Venezia for two decades now was dead. The fate of Cairo entangled itself in the debate over his succession.

The Council, after loud argument and the purveying of every favor and counterfavor wealth could manage, deadlocked, and finally chose as the Doge's replacement a young man, an astonishingly young man, in fact: one Antonio Raffeto, remote relative by marriage of the lamented Doge, a scholar, and reputedly honest. His election came as a third-round compromise between the pro and the con of the relief effort. The Raffeti owned no ships, nor did they trade. In fact the Rafetti of the last five generations had been respected historians, professors, and scholars of the great library, though this young man was said to be very knowledgeable in practical matters. In fact, as people about town now said, the Raffeti finally held power openly, through this quiet young man, when, through the centuries, they had only stood behind the Doges and told them step by step what to do.

Antonio Raffeto's first official act was to send aid to Cairo. His second was to oppose Cesare di Verona in his bid to gain the long-vacant Montefiori seat on the Council—a bid against precedent, but supported by several still angry families who had voted against Antonio Raffeto.

It was straight into the boiling water of politics for the young Doge, but he withstood this storm, and gained from it a reputation, when several merchant princes found their own accounts audited, and Cesare di Verona was found to have entertained them extravagantly.

Audit the newcomer Cesare, as well? Di Verona was not quite implicated. And since he was a foreigner, though his position was precarious, his behavior, ordinarily benevolent, did not fall under the prohibitions of the city.

So nothing changed and everything changed, which was business as ordinary in Venezia. The tides came and lapped at the walls. The young Doge proved canny and immune to blandishments and threats from inside and out, and Cesare's enemies in Verona, a city which had attempted its own intrigues aimed at bringing Venezia under its control, did not prosper. Far from it—certain foreigners left Venezia hastily, and in disarray. Cesare di Verona gifted the city with a treasure of books for its library, and made peace with the young Doge, as the man who had pointed out this scheme.

Cairo thrived again and reopened trade. The city, relieved of its worries inside and out, drew a wide breath and celebrated.

Spring came as it always did, with its storms and its *carnevale*.

The young girl had disappeared from the barred window on the canalside this winter. In her place, a young woman of extraordinary beauty came and went freely on the streets, attended by one servant, or completely on her own. The gondoliers called to her, below the Ponte Vele, and along the walk, among the shops.

"Bella! Bellissima, oh, take pity."

She bought fine silks and grand plumes, this granddaughter of la duchesa. She also purchased—oh, yes—mauve silk and ribbons and beautiful leather shoes. She had come outside the walls of the little house. She bought, yes, masks, this spring, oh, indeed, una bauta, the common white mask of *carnevale*. And whispers took wing. She would join in the festivities. Young men sighed. She was beautiful, dark-haired dark-eyed, and oh, so quick in wit and soft of voice. Dared young gentlemen ask her name?

It was, she said softly, Giacinta.

Giacinta, like the upright flower that bloomed in spring gardens, the rare gardens of Venezia.

Giacinta, young men sighed.

Invitations suddenly came to the long-unvisited door, beautiful invitations, borne by liveried servants of this house and that. One such came from di Verona, who intended a ball in his beautiful palazzo. There were flowers sent, rare and beautiful. And the days of *carnevale* came on them.

The dress fitting went on, and the dress itself became like armor, such a weight of thick amethyst silk and cording and purple velvet that it could stand by itself. Giacinta drew in her breath as the servant drew in the laces, everything traditional, everything authentic, from the layers of lace petticoats to the beautiful black lace cuffs and the high-heeled shoes that lifted her up so the hem no longer swept the floor . . . or the watery edges of the canals.

The seamstress, on her knees, surveyed the hem, that it hung well, checked a spot, and stood up to take and pin a tuck at her rigid waist, to be dealt with after she shed the dress.

La duchesa sat in her chair across the room, her walking stick resting against her dark blue skirts, a pile of sweets beside her, untouched, in a silver bowl.

"I looked like you, once," la duchesa said wistfully.

Giacinta looked at her, wondering in what decade this was, but never doubting Nonna's word. Nonna never tolerated doubt, or contradiction.

"In Milano," Giacinta ventured.

"In Milano," Nonna said, "before there were fools in charge there. Before I met your grandfather. You look beautiful. Like your mother."

The comparison lanced like a knife. Giacinta had lost her parents and all the family but Nonna. They had died one autumn when the fever had swept the west, and Nonna had been immune, and had sheltered her, and brought her up, somehow blaming the people of Milano for this disaster. Giacinta never understood why. To this day she feared to question, somehow reading into Nonna's silence something Nonna had no wish for her to know, and what Nonna forbade her for her own good covered a world of dark things. Nonna would not, for instance, tell her why they had left Milano in the dead of night, or why they had ventured here. She knew that things had happened in the upstairs room with Signore Montefiori, terrible things, that had broken china and shaken the locks in the dark of night, when the Signore had cried out that devils were in the upstairs hall, and that they hunted little girls. Things had happened between Nonna and Signore Montefiori, when she had gone into that room, and the noise had very soon stopped. And Nonna did not talk about that night either.

So there were many, many things that she never asked Nonna. She came and went about the house and garden like the servants, in silence. If ever they entertained, it was di Verona, who called nearly every week, and sometimes walked in the garden with Nonna, or worse, sat and talked with them both in the gallery.

Di Verona came visiting during this last fitting, and Giacinta was mortified, being, as it were, incompletely dressed, but Nonna thought nothing of it.

"Hyacinth for Giacinta," di Verona said. He was in his thirties or his forties, if handsome, and came and fingered the damask silk of her skirt as if he were buying it. "How becoming."

Giacinta blushed furiously and looked only at the white and black tiles of the salon until di Verona strolled aside and spoke to Nonna.

"Gossip in the town is," di Verona said, "that she will wear mauve, and the white mask."

"Your gift," Nonna said, "will deceive these young scoundrels."

Then Giacinta knew where the hyacinth fabric had come from, and that Nonna approved this man. She had liked the dress until then.

"I do not like him," she confessed to Nonna, when di Verona had gone away. It took courage, to express an opinion while she wore the hyacinth dress, but it was the truth, and she had endured their one visitor too often since the signore had died, endured, because he was their only visitor, and pleased Nonna.

But, oh, she had gotten the taste of freedom, when, this year, having come by a little money, Nonna sent her out to the calles and the shops along the Serpentine to buy necessities and even fripperies. She had breathed the air and walked farther than ever the little garden permitted, and her steps had grown wider and surer every passing day. More, she had seen choices spread everywhere, choices in fabric and in glass, in trinkets and foods and wines and oils, and every sort of thing the merchants had. She had the choice to laugh or not to laugh. She had the choice to stare at a young man who stared at her, or not to stare; or to return a wink, or not, from a young gentleman in russet velvet, who followed her all the way to the Ponte Vela.

She had made such choices, and realizing that she had them, now she said to Nonna, her greatest act of rebellion, her greatest choice of all: "I don't like him at all, Nonna."

"Hush, silly girl. Would you have the servants gossip?"

"But, Nonna, I want my pretty mauve silk." It was what she had bought for her gown, before this fabric turned up. "I most of all don't want to wear his gift. He's an old man."

This amused la duchesa, who rose and leaned on her walking staff. "And what am I? Am I old?"

"You're my dear Nonna," Giacinta said, unhesitating: that was forever the coin that paid for quiet, and for getting her way. "You're always my Nonna, and you're always beautiful."

"Dear child." Nonna walked close and touched her cheek. La duchesa went, as usual, stiff-braced in an old-fashioned gown—such tight lacings helped her back, Nonna maintained; but Giacinta found the hyacinth silk dress, low cut, similarly rigid, exposed and emphasized far too much of her bosom, and the lacings made her ribs creak. She felt strangely undressed, to have had di Verona passing judgment on her. Most of all, she detested the way he looked at her, walking all around her, like a buyer contemplating a table at the market.

"Il duco is a good friend," Nonna said, "and a protector for you. He's a warlord, with claims to a wealthy city. Men follow him. And who knows? He may soon became a greater man than he is."

That word *soon* troubled Giacinta, who had no possible interest in di Verona's future. She walked to the diamond-pane windows that looked out on the Priuli's dark chasm, above the water where traffic passed. The sound of shops and restaurants down on the walkway always disturbed the peace in this room. The days of *carnevale* were approaching, beginning this evening, and already there was a scattering of festive traffic, despite the dimming of the sun and a spatter of rain. Thunder murmured in the distance.

"Il duco Cesare is our very powerful friend," Nonna said.

"He's not my friend," Giacinta said sharply. She wanted not to think about Cesare di Verona. She wanted the *carnevale* to break out now. All the spectacles of previous years she had viewed only from the windows, but this year, this year Nonna said she might go to one of the balls, di Verona's, unfortunately, on the fourth day of the festival, but it was the price she had to pay. "I don't want to think of him. I want only to think about the festival. I want my dress to be finished. I want to go to the Serpentine and see the barge parades."

"Listen to me, child. These pretty things you enjoy all have a source. Do you not care where?"

She was not a stupid girl. Nor was la duchesa a stupid woman. Giacinta looked at her grandmother sharply, with great apprehension now. A source? A source, for her party finery? Before now, only this or that trinket had been a gift from di Verona to her grandmother, not to her. But Nonna had talked of liquidating certain properties in Milano, of being sent a sum of gold.

"This man," her grandmother said, "this man you so lightly dismiss, mark me, will rule Venezia."

A moment of rash rebellion. "The Doge rules Venezia."

"The Doge," Nonna scoffed. "The Doge, the son of a professor, with the mind of an accountant. *We* are the nobili, *we* are the ones burdened and privileged to rule, for centuries."

Giacinta knew that speech. She had heard di Verona and Nonna talking together about old times.

"Come." Nonna took a bracelet from her own wrist, and put it on her. "You will go to il duco's ball, and dance with him, and perhaps . . . perhaps two great houses may make common cause."

"What are you saying?"

"That a union of our houses is to our good. I depend on you, my girl, my bella. I depend on you to make that union possible."

"To marry him, are you saying, Nonna? To *marry* him?"

"If you can manage to please him. If you are a good and clever girl, who thinks most of her Nonna, and make a good impression on this man."

He throat seemed too narrow, breath too short. She struggled for argument. 'Why should I marry? Why should I ever leave you?"

"Because—" Nonna always had a lace handkerchief, it was always perfumed, always slightly damp and warm, and, being magical, as she had once said, it dried tears even before they were shed. "Because, my sweet, my treasure, if you marry Cesare di Verona, you will become the most powerful woman in Venezia."

"How should I be?"

"Because Cesare is a clever man, and the Doge will soon fall, and the divided Council will find itself in chaos, with riot in the city. Cesare will be at hand with a strong presence, to save Venezia from civil disorder. When ever could an accountant rule a city like this? It's only to the good of the city that he fall. And you will be a grand duchesa yourself, la duchesa di Venezia, respected among all the other cities."

One could never argue with Nonna when she spoke like this, so soft, so close and so intimately. It began to sound reasonable and necessary, whatever Nonna said.

But this year she was seventeen, and thought her own thoughts, and had been promised the *carnevale*, and Nonna could not persuade her. She said, however, obediently, "What shall I do?" because there was only one way to have peace from Nonna, and to get out the door.

So Nonna told her how she must go to the duke's ball in three more days and dance with him, and he would dance with her the next day after that in the great Piazza di San Marco, declaring their engagement to the crowds. They would become the talk of Venezia, how handsome they were, how well matched.

"Then the people will applaud the match, and you will be in the public eye as his fiancée, and when someday soon some mischance befalls the Doge, as, who knows? it might, why, then, then, bella, you will be protected and well-situated. Il duco will take firm charge of the city and prevent public disorder with a strong show of force. As, who knows? such wild events might easily happen, in the license of festival."

It was a warning what Nonna wanted to happen, what Nonna expected to happen. She knew Nonna hated the Doge, for what reason she never had understood, except that he was common. Nonna had never shown hatred for the citizens of the Repubblica, only regarded as disgraceful the notion that commoners should rule when their betters wondered where their next meal might be coming from.

She had been happy before di Verona's visit. Now the sun seemed dimmed outside the diamond panes, and the thunder walking above the tiled roofs seemed full of omen. Her first *carnevale*, her *carnevale*, was to be full of Nonna's plans, of a betrothal, and to di Verona. Of a sudden her perspective was not of days of celebration, but a little stolen time before the holiday celebrations met di Verona's ambition, and before her own life forever took a turn she never wanted.

She let herself be unlaced, shed the dress to the seamstress for a final few tucks, and told the seamstress, when Nonna had left the room, "I shall want it in my room in an hour."

In fact, she had formed a deep resolution, that what *carnevale* she had left, she would enjoy with all her might.

She went to her room, she took out all the coins she had saved in secret, coins of Milano, coins of Verona, coins of Venezia, and put them all in the little purse she used when she went to the shops. She laid out her jewels, and when the seamstress came with the dress, she had the seamstress lace it up, lace it tight.

She did her hair up, she put on her jewelry, the amethyst necklace, and her pearls. Her mother's ring, all she had of her parents, she always wore, a gold circlet with a chased design and a band of diamonds. She put on the beautiful headdress, nodding with plumes of gray and hyacinth. Last of all she took her masks, the white bauta, the common mask, and the black moretta, the mask of silence—she tied them by long ribbons to a velvet belt, and put it on so they hung among the folds of her skirts. Outside the window, twilight came early, in storm.

Yet through the windows, from the walk outside, on the Priuli, came increasing squeals and laughter. She could not see what the cause was, but she resolved she would miss not a moment more of festival, nor think of di Verona a minute for the rest of her freedom. She slid her stockinged feet into the high-heeled, high-soled shoes, then fled downstairs to the front door and out under the sky, alone, free until the sunset. She put on the white bauta, beneath her plumes, the half-mask that let one eat and drink, and hurried along the Pruili and to the bridge, a young woman alone, dodging importunate young celebrants. She danced across the bridge, and so to the narrow shadow of the calles, then out again where she had longed to go, onto the great Serpentine, where the gold and fading sun speared the broad canal through massive gray cloud.

Here was spectacle. Here people went about in wonderful costumes, wondrous gowns flashing with paste jewels. Men and women alike squealed and fled the cloaked mattacino, who flung eggs at festivalgoers, targeting particularly the women, but his eggs when they burst were full of perfumed water, and left a sweet smell where they struck. Giacinta wished he would fling one her way, and she would try to catch it. But the mattacino only bowed, out of missiles, and went his way, seeking more eggs, it was sure.

Oh, and the gondolas, with their festival passengers, and, far down the canal, the great barges, proceeded along dark, sun-gilded water under a stormy sky. Musicians played, vying with one another across the Grand Canal, and sweet-sellers called out, becoming part of the music.

She bought a sweet from a stand, and watched a pair of harlequins walk down the edge of the canal. She followed them, and joined the rear of the crowd at a puppet show, dismissing from her mind what Nonna would say when Nonna found she would miss supper.

She would come back by full dark, well-fed, and her eyes brimming with sights—oh, so many sights—and her ears filled with music, so she would not dream of di Verona at all. She clapped for the puppets, she watched the dancers, she walked past shops and through traffic of festival-goers, all the way to the great square, the Piazza di San Marco, which was choked with celebrants. Musicians at every permanent café vied with one another for territory, making a no man's land of discord between. Sweet-sellers abounded, and a great red and gold tent had been set up in the middle of the square, where actors offered plays to make a girl blush.

She stayed through half a performance, and then, fearing she was missing something outside, went to look at the glasswares at the corner shop, and wandered afterward as far as the great cathedral, which was undergoing surely its thousandth renovation, all done up in scaffolding. A harlequin had climbed up above the entry and sat hurling flowers at all comers.

She caught one.

"Bella!" the harlequin called out, and she waved it back.

It was so grand an evening.

But all at once the thunder cracked fit to rattle the scaffoldings, and the rain pelted down. Festival-goers shrieked and screamed and pressed this way and that to find shelter for their finery, and Giacinta, pushed and shoved, found refuge inside the cathedral, inside its gold, lamplit sanctity, while the thunder cracked and boomed above.

The storm, some said, was no ordinary storm. A great storm had brewed up in the Adriatic, to come crashing against the sea gates, and a greater storm than any before it. The gates might fail, some said, and some had come here to pray they held.

When she heard this, a cold feeling crept through the ancient cathedral with its disapproving saints. The sea gates were vast, ancient, and saved Venezia from the flood, but now the rising sea backed up behind those gates in storm, so high the storm surges of recent years that if the gates were to fail, then all Venezia would drown.

"All the more reason for *carnevale!*" a pulcinella cried then, waving his hat, gallant against the threat, and people around him cheered, and laughed. Soon the crowd sheltering in the echoing cathedral shouted down the doomsayers, saying the gate would never fail.

"It will come," a prophet of disaster shouted.

"Be still, mantico doloroso!" someone shouted, and another, "Look, the storm has passed already!"

Indeed, the storm had swept past with uncommon speed, was in its last stages outside, and the crowd pressed the other way, to exit the cathedral into the vast piazza, which was all in stormlight, clouds as black as old sin. The gray stone of the piazza gleamed with moisture, reflecting black and silver off the puddles, little mirrors now and again flashing with the reflection of lightning, now and again gleaming gold with the sweep of a festival torch as people rushed back to their revels. The air was washed clean. The canal would run higher, perhaps, but not disastrously so. The day seemed not so late after all, now that the clouds had lightened.

The prophets of doom, Giacinta thought, were wrong. The only threat was that of her ball finery getting soaked, and Nonna in despair, forbidding her to go out again.

She thought it time to be tending homeward, at least, if not getting there, and she crossed the piazza, seeking the route that offered the most awnings on her way. Her high-soled shoes kept her hem clear. Her plumes were only a little draggled, and would dry good as new in the brisk wind. She was not the only one leaving the piazza; no few, inebriated, plied the rain-swollen canal in gondolas, waving lanterns and laughing.

A flash of lightning, a clap of thunder. The whole Serpentine flashed white, and Giacinta ran, ran, in deepening gloom, until a low place in the walk stopped her in utter doubt. The walk had flooded there. Another band of storm was coming on.

"Bella!" a young man called out, behind her, and another, joining him in rushing toward her, called something rude. They rushed down on her, picked her up by the elbows and carried her across, splashing through the shallow water. And did not let her go.

"Let me down!" she cried. "Let me down!" They reeked of wine, and one swept her entirely up in his arms. "Let go!" She kicked, she struggled. A huge gondola nosed close to the shore here, and she thought they meant to carry her off in it. "Let me down!"

"Citizen," another man said. A young gold-and-white harlequin in a white bauta stood in the path of her abductors, like a prince of the fairy tales, and two strong black and white harlequins stood behind him. "Set the lady down."

The man did, laughing—set her down in the edge of the puddle before he took the better part of valor and ran.

"Fools!" the white harlequin said, and offered his hand and pulled her to dry pavement. Both fools fled, splashing, down a narrow calle. "Madonna."

"Sir." She was not easily frightened, but she had been so close to disaster, so close to losing everything. She pulled away from his hand and went to the shelter of an awning, not so far from other traffic, within sight of it, at least.

He stayed, he and his two companions. He made no pursuit of her. "Would you have us deliver you to your house, madonna?"

She was not sure. She hesitated. Another man might have left in disgust, his kind offer rejected. But he stayed, and held out his hand.

She turned her back, hidden in the shadows. She pulled off the bauta and assumed instead the moretta, the silent mask, that, held by a button behind the teeth, would not let her betray herself.

"Ah," he said. "La moretta. But you must somehow tell me where you lodge."

There was an unfortunate fact she had not thought of. She felt foolish. But she grandly gestured down the walk before them, and he took her hand and stayed beside her. The two black harlequins stepped lightly back into the gondola and the boat began to turn, to pace them along the Serpentine, while lightnings danced and whitened the water.

His hand was warm and comforting. Her heart still beat hard and her hands trembled from the fright she had had.

"Such a fine hand," the young harlequin said, in possession of that hand, "it must belong to a beautiful young lady."

La moretta must say nothing—could say nothing. They simply walked, and he held that hand ever so gently, seeing her safely along. She gestured that they should turn aside from the Grand, and they did, though his young men wanted otherwise. He bade them stay with the gondola—a very grand one, it was, with curtains, more a nobleman's barge than not.

And, oh, why could Nonna not be content with this young gentleman, whose clothing was satin and brocade, whose hand was warm and strong and gentle, and whose chin beneath the bauta, was very fine? She would bring home her young knight of the festival and say to Nonna, Forget il duco—I have found my own young gentleman. I shall marry him, not di Verona. Never di Verona, so long as I live!

They walked through the calles. He delayed by a sweet-vendor, but of course, he seemed to recall mid-offer, la moretta could no more eat or drink than she could speak. He mimed realization to her, as if her silence was catching, and she took his arm, miming laughter. They walked on together, across the Ponte Vela, and on to her very door.

"Ah," he said, looking at the house, and at her, as if he knew, then, everything there was to know. Her heart sank. She was not among the highest of the city.

She turned to go inside, to end her fantasy, to be done with adventures for all her life, forever.

But he caught her hand, and pulled her about, lifting her hand to his lips.

"Madonna, when shall I see you again? Tomorrow? Please say tomorrow."

She was caught unable to speak, between longing and knowledge of her fate. Tomorrow. Tomorrow, her heart said. One more adventure. One more time, to see the sights of the festival—this time safer than before, escorted. Surely it was her best, her last chance in her life. And his voice was so kind, so persuasive. He, and not di Verona, was a gentleman.

She turned away, her face to the door, let fall the moretta and snatched the bauta to her face, holding it in place with her hand. Then she faced him.

"At afternoon." That was her best chance to get away. Nonna napped then, and might not come out of her bedroom for hours. "I shall be here after noon, about one. By the water-stairs, on the Racheta."

"I shall be there," he said, her harlequin, flashing a broad grin, and kissed her hand before she slipped into her own front doorway and dropped the mask.

All that night she courted sleep, thinking of him, and not of di Verona, but she found no rest until late, and did not wake until the sunlight came full through her window.

Then the servants brought her breakfast, since she had not come down, and she dressed in light fabric, and wrapped up in a shawl, and walked in Nonna's precious garden, thinking, building cloud-castles far more pleasant than any of Nonna's plans for her life—though she knew Nonna's plans would win, after all. Di Verona was her fate. Her harlequin was the fantasy.

Nonna came out to sit in the noon sun, and said not a word. They shared a light luncheon out in the sun, and Nonna remarked how, when they had money again, she would make a fountain in the garden.

"If there is not money soon," said Nonna, "I shall tell you the bitter truth. We shall lose this garden. We shall lose the house."

Her dreams all faltered and trembled. "What about the gold, Nonna?" But when she asked that question, she knew there had been no property in Milano. Everything was a deception, all Nonna's stories, if she had been taking gifts from di Verona.

"Never worry," Nonna said. "You will win di Verona's heart. And very soon after, you will live in the Palazzo Ducale, where you belong, and I shall have title to this house. You will give it to me, will you not, my darling, my precious girl? I am too old to find another fortune. I've taken care of you; now you must take care of me."

It was the softest and saddest and most desperate she had ever heard her Nonna. It struck her heart. And she had the most dire feeling that Montefiori's will had not, as Nonna had said, granted the house to them. Nothing else of Nonna's assurances seemed to have been the truth.

And amid Nonna's deceptions, weighed against greater lies, it was only a little rebellion she intended. Only one evening.

So, after noon, when all the city abandoned its business for an hour or so, when young and old took to their rooms for naps, and when the more energetic went out to enjoy the cafes, she put on her finery and the white bauta and tiptoed down the stairs to the canalside door, to the little steps where the water lapped.

Just as soon as she stood there, a sleek, curtained gondola, waiting silently down by the intersection of the Racheta with the Caterina, came to life. Its gondolier poled softly up, and a fine masculine hand drew back the curtain, and invited her aboard.

Her white harlequin was alone this time, but for his gondolier. He settled her onto the cushions opposite him, and smiled at her.

"My lady keeps her word," he said.

"So do you," she said. She had never seen a gondola so fine as this, with its black leather and red brocade cushions, nothing of faded splendor like Nonna's house, but all bright and new. Her harlequin was no poor man, not at all. He had such fine hands, carefully kept. His hair was dark, and curled beside his white half-mask. His smile was very kind.

"I should never fail madonna," he said. "What misadventures might she take to, without me?"

"I would have escaped those two," she said, self-defensive.

"Of course you would," he said, ignoring truth. "You were well on your way. But you would have splashed that lovely gown."

She thought he mocked her. But she looked at him and thought not. It was a day as bright as yesterday had been stormy.

And they ran the bull. They ran the black bull through the walkways from the far northern section of Venezia, once having to pull it from the canal, and chased it to the great piazza, to the very front of the holy cathedral, where it met its fate.

Giacinta hid her eyes. "It's cruel," she said.

"The bulls pay the penalty," her harlequin said.

"What penalty?"

"For our sins. But listen," he said, slipping an arm about her as they walked, "I shall tell you the real reason for the bull-running, which not many know. Once upon a time, when the sun was much younger, when there were no storms and no need of sea gates, we were off fighting the Paduans. Our neighbor Ulric of Aquileia attacked us. We attacked him back, and we won. And instead of plundering his city, we were, of course, moderate. We fined him in cattle. And that year we held *carnevale* for the first time, and slaughtered beef instead of our neighbors, and held festival instead of war. We were even then an enlightened city, you see. And every year since, we remember our civilized act, even when the Aquileians ceased paying us the thirteen sacrifices. Every year we hold *carnevale*. And we risk our lives only with the bulls, which feed the poorest of our citizens. We are merchants. The sacrifice reminds us that nothing comes free."

"You are no merchant."

"Would it matter to madonna if I were?"

She had never quite asked herself. She had assumed. Now she made up her mind. "No. Never."

He kissed her fingers, held them close, and a tingle went up from them, right to her heart.

They walked, the gondola long abandoned. They dodged the egg-throwers, whose porcelain eggs burst with petals and perfume. They ate savory pastries from a strolling peddler, and drank wine from the public barrel in the piazza, and danced, oh, they danced and skipped to the songs of strolling violins and flutes, among crowds well-gone with wine.

Then the square began to glow with lights from unshuttered windows, and the canals to shimmer with light from lanterns on the gondolas, and all the city was alive with music and laughter, with pranks and simpering gnagas, with foolish pantalones and balanzones, and black and white harlequins less dignified than hers.

"I must get home," she said at last.

"No, stay," he said. "*Carnevale* only truly lives at night."

"My Nonna," she said, "will never forgive me. Please let me go."

"Then I shall walk you home," he said, and took her to the place where the curtained gondola waited.

So they glided in grand safety up the Serpentine, with its firefly glows, lit by their own lantern, and with the curtains drawn back, in the privacy of night.

Then he kissed her, gently, quietly, and touched her cheek below the mask. For a moment she could hardly breathe.

"Set me ashore," she said. "I mustn't."

"No, no, madonna. I beg your pardon. I'm taking you straight home."

Don't, she thought, but held it secret. She caught her breath. "Tomorrow," she said. "Tomorrow I'll come out again."

He held her hand. He kissed it. "You have caught my heart, madonna."

"Tomorrow," was all she could say.

Nonna was, of course, cross with her, slipping in late. But by next noon Nonna took her nap, and she met her harlequin on the water-stairs. They went to watch the day's bull-chase, and to have crustata in the piazza, and to watch a puppet show, before the clouds darkened, and the whole afternoon became thunderous and lightning-shot. There were frightening rumors abroad, as there always were, in dark storms.

"The gates will hold," her harlequin assured her, as they sheltered in the gondola, rain beating on the canopy, and the gondolier quite drenched. "I saw them this morning."

"Are you a merchant, then?" The port was out there, and the ships.

He ignored her question. "Pietro," he said to the gondolier, "The Ca d'Oro, if you please."

Without a word the gondolier swung their bow over, and they tended toward the Grand.

"Why there?" Giacinta asked, grown anxious. It was a famous place, but shut, long shut, since the last owner gave it up, so the story was, two centuries ago.

"Why not there?" her harlequin said lightly. "Do you trust me?"

"Yes," she said, only a little lie, and the gondolier delivered them to the water-stairs of the Ca d'Oro, that ancient palace. The door there was bound with corroded brass, and eaten with moss and rot at its bottom, where the water lapped up against the wood. It looked entirely forbidding, desolate.

Thunder cracked as her harlequin skipped out onto the steps, and proved to have a large and ornate key. He opened the ancient water-stairs door, and held out a hand to her.

Rain was falling by now. The gondolier had made fast to the ring-bolt there, and pulled the storm-cover across the well. She was doubtful and afraid, but her harlequin had never been other than courteous and protective of her. It made sense to go somewhere out of the rain, and she gave him her hand, and carefully negotiated the water-stairs, up, through the mossy doors and into a stucco hall with an immediate upward stairs.

An aged candlestick sat dusty, in a nook. Her harlequin found a match somewhere about his person and lit the candle, which sent a wind-fluttered light up to a barrel vault above their heads, and to ancient ormolu on faded azure walls in the hall above. Cobwebs were much in evidence.

"I shall show you the ballroom," he said. "Few have seen this sight, this century."

He ascended the stairs, holding his light carefully, so that she could see her way, and led her up to a chamber so vast their light did little but spark off an array of mirrors.

"Stand still," he said, and went the circuit of the hall, touching light to candles, indeed, many of them new candles.

Light glittered about them, reflecting their images in a hundred mirrors, across a well-swept and polished floor. At the side of the room stood a table, and on that table a sweating pitcher, and blown-glass goblets, and a platter of crusted bread and cheese and meat, with two chairs.

"Supper," he said. "I had it laid, and the floor swept, in hopes you would join me here."

She feared he meant her to become his lover, and the whole tale wanted to burst from her lips, how she was to marry di Verona, how important it was to Nonna, how she had only just escaped for a last holiday, a last breath of freedom. But it did not rush out. She said nothing. She looked around her, stunned to silence.

"And now you are here," he said, and drew back a chair for her. "Do sit. Please."

She sat, stiff and fearful. By degrees, by a cup of wine, a morsel of bread and cheese and sweet pastry, she accepted his strange hospitality while the storm raged and thundered. She was alone, and shut behind walls, and wished she were home.

But he asked no more than to kiss her hand, when all was done, and to hold it in his, and to say he hoped she would have no fear of him, or of this place.

"I know who you are," he said. "And I know di Verona has asked you to his ball. May I ask you to mine?"

"Who are you?" she asked, that brutal, all-ending question of her dream.

"Hush," he said, and stopped her lips with a touch of his finger. "Hush. In *carnevale*, deceptions are allowed, between lovers. The mask is the moment. Never question."

"I can't be your lover," she protested. "Let me go."

"I would never hold you against your will," he said, and pressed something into her hand. It was his key. "Come here, come here for safety, any time you need it. Come here tomorrow, and trust no harm will come to you, ever in this world, while I can protect you." He tipped her face up, and kissed her a second time and lingeringly on the lips, and this time she felt nothing but safety in his arms—safety of a sort she had never felt in anyone.

But he would not pursue his advantage.

"If you come tomorrow," he said, "if you come here tomorrow, I shall tell you I love you, madonna. But I would never take advantage of your trust."

"I will come back," she promised him.

"Will you dance?" he asked, and she looked about, wondering if he had hid musicians, too.

But there was no music. The rest was a dream, dancing in silence in a glittering hall all their own, and looking down from the fretted windows, afterward, onto the lights on the Grand Canal. She would have gone to bed with him, she knew she would have, if he had asked, but after they had drunk, and danced, and stood there, arms about each other, he pressed her hand and said he should get her home, straightway, or he might, after all, break his word.

She remembered her promise to Nonna, the invitation to di Verona's ball, only when he had, in a moderate rain, set her safely on her own water-stairs, and she was halfway up the steps inside.

She turned back, she opened the water-stairs door onto the dark rush of rain, the lapping water, to tell him, to change their rendezvous. But he was gone, the curtained gondola disappearing into the dark down the Raceta.

She could not tell him she had made a terrible mistake.

She could not tell Nonna, or fail her attendance at di Verona's ball. Nonna had asked nothing but this of her, after sheltering her all her life. And she had never failed a promise to her Nonna, never since she was in pigtails.

What can I do? she asked herself. *What else can I do but what nonna wants? He says he will tell me he loves me. We would become lovers. But where is a choice for me?*

At noon the following day, Nonna took no nap. Nonna sat all afternoon and supervised her hair, her dressing in her finery, with new petticoats, and with a great deal of fuss among the servants to clean splashes of mud from the violet silk. But it was good, thick fabric. It had dried spotless, and the black lace and the white petticoats were fresh-pressed and crisp. The plumes were renewed, her hair coiffed to perfection around the festival bonnet.

"No more foolishness this evening," Nonna said sternly. "You have had your days of folly. Now attend to a woman's duty, and please this man. It is essential. It is life to us."

"Yes, Nonna," she said, hiding all bitterness. There was no slipping away, no explanation. And the storm that had broken yesterday still rumbled and flashed in her windows, the heavens as roiled as her heart.

It was still raining, and the canals were running high, when she went to the stairs to wait. There would be a gondola, Nonna said, and Nonna set the servants to watch down by the front door, while she waited and took a cup of tea standing, so as not to crush the newly-freshened gown.

"It is here," the servants reported, in awe, running up from below. "With gold curtains, and servants, and umbrellas against the rain."

She wished the gondola and its finery might sink to the bottom of the Priuli. But she went down, and boarded it, and sat miserably inside as it took its gliding way toward the Acqua Dolce.

Onward then. Lightning flashed through the curtains and thunder crashed. She wished a sudden bolt from the heavens might strike the gondola, a death unexpected, and she might never have to attend this wretched ball.

But in due time it swerved over, knocked against buffers, and with halloos and cursing the gondolier handed her to the duke's servants bearing umbrellas, who brought her under a wind-billowed awning, and so up into a brightly lighted passage to a reception hall.

There was sparkling wine, there was white wine and red wine, there were sweets heaped up, the sight and smell of which disgusted her. There were very many attendees whose colors she knew, and the banners of Sienna and Verona were displayed, and the banner of Milano, which was her own.

Music began, signaling the processional, and a young man presented himself, a man in il duco's azure blue.

"Il duco has wished me to lead the lady in," he said. "I am his cousin, Fedorico."

A handsome young man, but *not* the rank of il duco himself, and not to Nonna's wishes.

"I shall stand here," she said haughtily. "And you may say to il duco that I am stranded here, for want of courtesy."

"Signorina," the young man said, scandalized.

"Signore," she said, "shall I write down my message, or can you possibly remember it?"

It was what Nonna would say, when a servant failed her expectations, and she was angry, by now, and judged that if Nonna could deal with people in such a way, so could she, on Nonna's business.

"Signorina," the young man said, bowed, and walked stiffly off.

So she stood, and stood, until the foyer was empty of incoming guests, and at last the same young man came back.

"Il duco wishes you to come," the young man said.

"I should have written it down," she said, in mock regret, but now with a little qualm of fear she refused to show. "Try again, signore."

That brought Cesare himself, a Cesare as frowning as herself, a Cesare who snatched her hand and hurt it, leading her toward the stairs.

"I provided you an escort," he said.

"One that let you disclaim inviting me," she said, her back stiff in her tight lacings, and the moving air wafting chill on her exposed bosom. She might have felt naked, a few days ago, before her young harlequin had kissed her. Now she was armored in steel and anger. "Now I have you for escort, as promised."

"Damn you."

"I am la duchesa's granddaughter," she said. "Did you ever think I was not?"

He tightened his grip, crushing her hand. "Never defy me."

"I have choices," she said, "and you do not. To have my grandmother's name, you do not have a choice, signore."

"You have her tongue, that's very clear."

"I do," she said, and smiled dazzlingly at all about her, weeping and sick inside, as she came down into the hall.

The storm crashed outside. Certain fools drank too much too early and languished by the serpentine pillars of the grand ballroom, saying, like the prophets in the cathedral, that soon there would be no Venezia to rule, that the sea gates were doomed to fail, and that the flood would rise, and that they would all be swept away if they took di Verona's coin and settled here. Certain fools talked of the floods to come, and how they would set out the choice of their wine cellars and drink them all, when the flood began to rise. Others said that the failure would be catastrophic, and there would be no sipping of wine at all, that wise men would go back to higher ground—such fragments of conversation she heard, while she danced with di Verona, who held her hand too tightly, and who said that he would rule the city before it drowned. He would take back Verona, and she would be an apt bride for a conqueror, full of spite and fury.

"How should you ever rule?" she challenged him, hating him the deeper the more intimately she faced him, the more their bodies grazed each other. She wore the bauta, white, anyone's mask. He wore a lion's mask, in gold and azure and sable, and plumes were its mane, a heraldic creature, snarling at the world.

"By blood," he said. "Here, and then Verona, I promise you. Have faith, Sforza, in your husband to be."

"You have not courted me," she said, a fading defiance.

"I need not. You're bought and paid for. Your grandmother will have her fine furnishings, and her garden. She cares for nothing else, believe me. We announce it tomorrow, and you have no appeal."

It was true. It was all too true. In all the world she had met only one kindly creature. Everyone else only pretended kindness, even her servants, because it was bought and paid for, and they had no choice.

"I want some chilled wine," she said, out of breath from dancing. Others dutifully applauded their duke, as they left the floor for the side of the room. "It's far too warm."

He wrenched her hand to his lips. "Command me, dare you, to fetch your wine?"

"Shall I fetch it myself, and have every servant stare?"

"Shameless girl."

"Utterly," she said, protected behind her mask. "One who must be won. Like the city."

She felt his body heat, greater than her own, and sensed she had just challenged a predator, a cruel and determined predator, and by so doing, had set the harsh conditions of the rest of her life.

Unless . . . she said to herself as he walked away and snapped his fingers at a servant, who brought her the wine. Unless, she thought, she could not be won at all.

"Three days," she heard as she sipped her wine. She stood near the group of the duke's men. "In three more days, at the Palazzo," but it was all part of the dizzy, overheated room, until, again, her wine finished, di Verona set her cup down and brought her up against him, face to face.

"What will happen three days from now?" she asked, challenging him.

"Where did your hear this three days?"

"Oh, I have ears, signore."

"In three days, in three days, the Doge's ball. And you will have an invitation," he said in a low voice. "I shall give it to you. And I shall escort you there. Do you understand me?"

She understood too much, from far back, now that she understood things she had heard, having heard him and Nonna plotting together, when they regarded her as part of the furnishings. She stared into the lion's face, confronted its gleaming white grin inches from her face, and said, because she had not chosen to be meek: "Perhaps. Perhaps I shall."

"You will, fool woman. And you will appear with me tomorrow, in the grand processional, and in the square, where we shall announce our wedding. Remember your function. You are nothing necessary. An ornament. People love a wedding. A public betrothal. It will quite seduce them."

"Shall I? I might if you please me."

His hand wounded her arm. "Think of your grandmother. Think of her comforts, and of your own future. You can end, or you can begin."

She could not meet her harlequin. She would not bring him into so great a danger. This man would kill him, if she fled tonight to their trysting place, and tried to find him, tried to explain her failure of their rendezvous.

She had no choice but drink di Verona's wine and dance with him, in a room packed with foreigners, all foreigners, like herself, like Nonna. She danced until her feet hurt, and tried to think what she dared do. She found no answer.

And when the ball was done and the men were down to steady drinking, the ladies began to leave, and di Verona called his own gondoliers, and had her carried home to her own water-stairs, on the Raceta. It seemed dark, and ominous. The whole city felt in peril of the lightnings and the threats she had seen in that room.

And she only pretended to go inside. The moment the gondolas pulled away onto the Priuli, she slipped along the foundations, the merest precarious ledge above the rising flood, clinging here and there to the mooring-rings, perilously advancing crabwise, until she reached the broad walkway along the Priuli.

Then, weaving in and out among rain-spattered revelers cavorting along that frontage, she raced up and over the Ponte Vela, and on through the calles until she came to the Grand, and then down the Serpentine until she had reached the Ca d'Oro itself.

She hoped for lights to show from its windows. She hoped he would have been patient enough to go on waiting for her no matter how late the hour. But there was no hint of light to welcome her. She only had her key, which he had given her, and she found the waterside door, down a difficult and precarious ledge that soaked her feet.

Inside, she saw dimly, by the lightnings reflected off the water, the candle they had left, and a small pile of matches.

She lit that candle, and shut the door and climbed the stairs, up and up until the candlelight blazed out like a hundred stars in so many mirrors.

"Harlequin?" she asked the dark and the silence, but the echoes of her voice were distant and frightening, suggesting dark and deserted halls far beyond the reach of her candle. When she stopped moving, there was only silence.

Silence, to her ears, but for her eyes, a rose, left on the dusty sideboard—a red rose, a difficult and costly thing in Venezia, in its storm and its floods.

He had waited, but lost faith and left too early.

Still, he had left her a token of his presence.

She searched her possessions for what she might leave for him in turn, and settled on the most precious, the best thing she had: her ring, her mother's gift. She laid the small gold circlet on the marble tabletop. In the dust of abandonment she wrote, Your Giacinta, and laid the rose beneath.

Then, exhausted, sick at heart and cold, she took her light and went back to the water-stairs, and retraced all the difficult way home.

The servants met her at the top of the inner stairs. She went up to her room, gave her clothing to the maids, and fell into bed, in the freedom of breath and residual ache of the ribs that came with unlacing.

She slept the night by fits and starts, and waked all tangled in the bedclothes at noon. Her hair was so tangled that her unhappy maid had to comb and comb it, painfully. Nonna came in, with the maid looking for her shoes, which turned out to have half-dried, badly soaked, and suffered from mud and scrapes. A great to-do erupted, when Nonna knew it. "How can you have come in with wet shoes?" Nonna asked. "Where have you been walking?"

"The gondola moved," she said, a lie. "While I was getting out. The gondolier was a fool. I nearly fell in. I'm sure the duke doesn't care."

"Never speak badly of him."

"I find nothing good," she said, disrespectfully.

"Hush. Take the shoes away. Dry them in the kitchen, Anna." This to the maid. And Nonna insisted she eat a biscuit and take sweet tea.

"You're nervous, of course, you're only nervous, my dear. It's the day, the very important day ahead of us. He'll come himself, in the barge, in just two hours, and you'll do us proud. So grand, so beautiful a bride you'll be."

There was no escape, no escape she could see. She sat and let herself be coiffed, and her feet stockinged in spotless silk and set in restored and fire-warmed shoes.

Then, with no choice but Nonna's before her, she let herself be laced into the amethyst silk gown, and hung her two masks, dangling from silk ribbons, among its folds.

By then the time had run out, and Nonna saw her down not to the water-stairs on the Raceta, as she had come in last night, like a thief, but to the public walk, on the Priuli, where the whole city might see. A maid waited below to watch out the door, and soon the maid said the duke's gondola was coming.

Giacinta kissed her Nonna, and started to leave.

"The mask," Nonna said agitatedly, "the mask, Giacinta!" just as she went out the doors.

It was not the white half-face she put on. It was the moretta, the black mask of silence, a reproach to di Verona, a caution to herself, that she would say nothing, nothing at all, nor eat, and especially not drink. She clamped the button behind her teeth, and that was the end of converse and compromise and the foolish warfare she had chosen with il duco.

The gondola took her aboard and drew away down the lesser canals to the Grand, under a stormy sky, and there to the shore. Di Verona's grand barge was there, and he stood on the bank to meet her, with the passersby all curious to see the passenger for whom a foreign duke waited.

He was perhaps surprised, a little set aback by the mask she wore—he, the lion down to the lips, which at first frowned, then grinned at her with nothing of cheerfulness. "A mystery, are you, today?"

She did not, could not answer him, only inclined her head, took his hand, let herself be set into the barge, gilt and azure canopied, among other barges and other colors of the more grand and glorious of La Repubblica, on the great Serpentine.

"An improvement," il duco said, "over last night. Perhaps you should always wear it, as a wife."

She turned her black-masked face to the water, gray water, reflecting the leaden sunlight that pierced the clouds. Rain fell in sporadic drops, and thunder muttered. He spoke, thinking himself a cutting wit, and she thought only of her rose in the Ca d'Oro, and the candle re-flected in a hundred mirrors.

It was armor, her silence. She could not answer, so she need not lis-ten to him, or to anything in the world. She could not find excitement in the festival any longer, so she need not regard the parade of wealth and power: she only stared bleakly at the passing buildings, and the leaden sky and the dull gray surface of the canal.

Trumpets blew. The great barges moved with oars, and occupied the center of the Serpentine, the sort of parade she would have loved to watch, safe on shore. They made their way to the landing nearest the great piazza, and there, amid a cheering throng, the barges disgorged their grandly-costumed occupants in what became a foot processional.

There was music. Banners waved. Giacinta moved where her captor dictated, her hand locked in his, and everything was a confusion of color and noise, swirling faster and faster.

Cheers, then, and il duco demonstrated her to the masked, festive crowd, and with gallantry lifted up their joined hands, and shouts and pushing and shoving followed, for il duco's servants had cast fistfuls of coins into the crowd, all along their way.

"Share my happiness!" he cried to the onlookers, parading her along the edge of the crowd. "My bride, Venezia, my bride!" And his servants called out, "Giacinta Sforza is the bride-to-be of Cesare di Verona! Bring her flowers! Bring her joy and music!"

Flowers rained down, costly flowers, from his own servants, it was likely, and the music shrilled and piped. Di Verona seized her about the waist and swept her out across the crowd of celebrants. They danced, oh, they danced, and afterward, she was so thirsty, but wearing the moretta, she could not drink, or scarcely breathe. She felt faint, but still cherished her isolation. She stared blankly at the congratulating crowd, and then—

Then she saw a man among the others, a white and gold harlequin like her harlequin, who appeared just behind the first fringes of the crowd. She blinked, and he was gone.

Then she could not get her breath. She could not speak. She wanted to tear off the moretta and run through the crowd crying out to anyone who would hear that she belonged to the harlequin, not di Verona. But the harlequin was gone, fled from the sight of the celebration, and she was not such a fool. She found herself swept up again to dance, and dance, and dance, and never a sip of water, never relief from the mask which she would not shed, not now. It hid tears as well as anger, and she was too proud to shed them for the crowd.

Only afterward, when they had repaired to the barges, and di Verona brought her to his palace for another round of drink and dancing, he opened her hand and pressed into it a small scroll.

"Your invitation to the Doge's ball," he said, "as my betrothed. But we shall not become separated, shall we, love?"

She mimed exhaustion, and he closed her hand over the little scroll until it crumpled, until her hand hurt.

"You will dance," he said, "While I please."

It was past midnight that di Verona's gondola delivered her to her own water-stairs, and she closed the water-stairs door. Then and only then, she took off the mask, and wiped her tear-streaked face with the back of her hand, and took off her shoes. Her white silk stockings were bloodstained, where the once-soaked leather had galled her heels and pinched her toes.

She padded upstairs, and tried in her silence to evade Nonna. In vain. Nonna met her and hugged her, and with that strangely potent handkerchief, dried her tears.

"There, there, my sweet, all our informers say it went so well. The whole city approves il duco's bride, this shapely mystery, they say, this so silent, so proper, so mysterious girl. La moretta! You could not have done better for us."

"I want a drink of water, Nonna," she said, trembling, and had that, and a cup of wine, and a biscuit, which, besides the other biscuit at noon, was all she had had to eat that day. She wanted to go out again, to go back out into the calles to look for the harlequin who had haunted her day at the piazza, but she had hardly the strength, and the wine, unsupported by anything of substance in her stomach, quite undid her. She could scarcely climb the stairs or suffer the maids to undress her and wash and salve her feet.

She still had the invitation, crumpled as it was, in the bodice of her gown. The maids laid it aside on the nightstand, and she fell onto the soft mattress between the cool sheets, half-sensible, and then not sensible at all.

Thunder waked her. She heard the renewed pounding of rain against the roof, and heard the maids talking, how the rumor was the sea-gates were nearly overwhelmed, that water had risen into the back of the cathedral, and that the great waves, wind-driven, were splashing down over the great gates into the lagoon. "We'll all drown," one wailed, and the other said that the cathedral had lit candles and prayed for the city's salvation.

She went back to sleep and dreamed that the water came, that it rose up and up above the banks of the canals, and that they all drifted, dancing beneath the waves, the *carnevale* carried on forever, and they all were ghosts, she and her white harlequin.

But morning came, and a shaft of sun broke through, and the canals had not flooded last night after all. She sat listlessly, refusing her breakfast, now with a notion of starving herself, of fainting senseless from hunger before the wedding, which Nonna said would be within the month. Could one possibly starve to death, within a month?

"You will learn to love him," Nonna said, in their little breakfast room.

"I never shall. I will not marry him, Nonna. I will not!"

"And what will you choose, else? For us to be poor, in Venezia? To be turned out penniless? There's no worse fate."

"There is. Di Verona is worse. I don't care about being poor. I'd rather be poor, than face him for the rest of my days."

"Don't say such things."

Nonna was vastly upset. And she had had enough, suddenly. She stood up, her feet protesting even then. "He is cruel and spiteful, Nonna. He has a cruel nature, and cruel hands, and I detest him more the longer I spend in his company. I will never live with him."

"Let me show you something," Nonna said, and went to the cupboard drawer, and took out a little glass bottle, stoppered with waxed cork. Its contents were black, and left a brown stain on the glass.

Nonna set it on the table beneath them. "This is my alternative," Nonna said. "This is what I will choose, if you fail to secure our place here."

"Poison? Is it *poison*, Nonna?"

"Rather than poverty. Yes, it's poison. I want my garden, my girl, I want my garden and my house and my servants. I have earned them, in my old age. I have brought you up to use your wits and think like a practical woman. I have taught you to be practical. I have arranged the best marriage you could make, an alliance that will make you rich beyond anything I ever asked for myself, beyond anything your father had. You will be splendid, la duchesa in your own right. You will never, never be so foolish as to make me use this."

"Put it away," Giacinta said, sick at heart. "Put it away, Nonna."

Nonna took the little bottle back to the cupboard, and shut it in the drawer. "You will go with il duco to the Doge's ball. You will, of course, stay well aside from any matters there. Stay with il duco himself. He will see you come to no harm, and his men will let no harm come near him."

"I don't know why he should care whether he marries me. I don't know why I should matter."

"Legitimacy. Legitimacy, dear girl. You are your father's daughter, as I am mine, but Cesare di Verona—lacks a certain *certainty* in that matter, and you are the most beautiful, the most eligible—"

She was struck to bitter laughter. "So il duco is common! He is commonborn as the Doge, as the Council, as any of the merchant princes!"

"Common is as common does," nonna said stiffly, "and he has nobility of spirit, and he is, whatever they say, di Verona."

"He has *money*, Nonna, oh, say it! He has money, and he *wants* nobility, which our name can provide him."

"He wants Verona, which rejected him."

"Oh, is *that* the key to his passion? Reject him and he immediately must have you? Go reject him, Nonna, and he will become your passionate suitor."

She had never used such a tone to her grandmother. But she had reached the end of her endurance last night, and Nonna only bit her lip and shook her head at ingratitude.

"He is cruel, Nonna. He has no heart. I found none."

"If he had more legitimacy, if he had a noble wife, it would be easier for him. If he ruled Venezia, ruling Verona would be certain. And then Milano. Never forget Milano, granddaughter."

Oh, Nonna could never forget Milano, from which they themselves were exiles, her father's rights overthrown, and Nonna unable to prevent it. The fall of their family gave Nonna no peace, and di Verona was as much la duchesa's means to revenge on her enemies as she was di Verona's means to regain his city. It was all la vendetta. It was all revenge, and blood.

She lost all interest in her breakfast, but she forced it down, foreseeing she would need her strength. She only half heard Nonna's talk about the old days, and the house, and the garden, and how they would plant a flowering plum, which loved to have its feet in water. Then they would have fresh fruit in late spring. Nonna was happy in her imaginings. But it was all nonsense to her ears. Everything had become clangor and nonsense.

She had one night, one night left before this disastrous ball at the Palazzo Ducale, when di Verona's plan would set itself in motion. And she had one recourse. She had her key. She had her one escape.

She went upstairs by midafternoon, when Nonna had taken to her bed, and had her maid lace her into her party gown.

She put on the shoes, never minding the pain of her bandaged feet, and slipped downstairs. And from the drawer she took Nonna's little bottle, and slipped it into her reticule, with her few holiday coins.

Then, wearing the white mask, the bauta, she went out the front door of their little house on the Priuli, and walked down the margin among the revelers, looking, looking, hoping her forlorn harlequin might have lingered somewhere near. The music echoed off the opposing walls, sounding out of key to her, and the laughter and the revelry she met were sadly distant to her ears.

She thought perhaps she should go down to the Palazzo Ducale, and ask to see the Doge, and warn him of di Verona's intentions in the plainest words. The consequences of that brazen action were unforeseeable, but she feared for Nonna if she did so, and yet she did not know why she cared for Nonna's safety, when Nonna had arranged this all for her. She was angry, and bitter, and so full of plots and possibilities that an angry mind could hardly sort through the consequences. She was young. She was new to connivance and conspiracy. The affairs of three states had gone on over her head. Never worry, Nonna would say to her. It doesn't concern you.

Now it did. Now she wished she knew.

The sky commiserated with her, gray and thunderous, and the water lapped high about the foundations and crept onto the walkways in thin sheets. *Carnevale* struggled to be merry despite the storm, despite the rumors, but the sights all paled for her, and when she made her way to the great piazza, the sight of the dancers reminded her of her public humiliation. She stood a while, contemplating the Palazzo, and how she could manage to pass the door. She started in that direction, and got as far as sight of the guards, and lost her nerve.

All these things she did, evading the one venture she most wanted and feared to make.

But when the day began to decline, still leaden and rainy, and with no sight of her harlequin among the crowds, she had found no courage to dare the Doge's guards, and walked back through the calles, immune to the pranks of pantalones and pulcinellas, one white mask among many.

It was the Ca d'Oro she sought, and the door, which, with the flooding, she could scarcely manage. She soaked her shoes again, and her hem, with a slip on mossy rock. But she gained the still, silent inner stairs, where she had left the matches and the candle.

Thunder boomed above the city. The storm, threatening day-long, had broken. She lit the candle stub with difficulty in the wind, and shut the door against the rain and the world.

Then she suffered the greatest fear, ascending, candle flickering on walls and ceiling, until she came to the hall of mirrors, where her candle became a hundred candles, lost in a dark that the windows beyond the arched alcove did little to relieve.

The table had changed. On it stood a bouquet of drooping roses. Her ring was gone.

His was there, a more massive golden round, a signet. It must be his. She set down her candle, and picked it up, and turned it to the light. It bore a coat of arms engraved in flat gold, the divided shield, and above it not a helmet, but a cap, a common cap, and not at all common. She had seen it emblazoned on banners in the piazza, that divided shield and the unwarlike red cap.

The arms of the Doge himself.

All the blood fled her limbs. She plumped straight down in the shadow, in the mockery of a hundred mirrors, and turned the ring in her fingers, the arms faint in shadow and glittering in candlelight.

It was long before she found the will to move, and by then she found it difficult, her limbs gone to sleep among her crumpled skirts. She was no more warlike than the Doge. She had never been encouraged to contest her fate. But she had learned fire, all the same, from la duchesa's temper. She had learned la duchesa's stubborn endurance. She had learned la vendetta, and the will, when challenged, to stiffen the backbone when she had a choice before her.

Oh, that, above all else. And now she knew her footing—at least who she dealt with. But what he might now do, and why he had courted her, and if he already knew about Nonna's plot—these still were questions.

She rose. She took her candle. The ring clenched in one fist, she went to light candle stubs in the candelabra, and found them all renewed, long, fresh tapers, half-burned, marking the limit of his patience. She lit one candelabrum after another, until all the mirrored hall was aglow in the gathering dusk, until it would shine outward onto the canal, until, if he were near, he might see.

She took the diminishing candle stub, then, and explored the halls above, the forgotten, fading murals, the rotting tapestries in all the passages and the long disused bedrooms, clear to the attic.

She knew his name now, her harlequin. Everyone knew it. She said it to herself, while she waited: "Antonio." She whispered it to the empty halls, to see if it was friend or enemy. "Antonio Raffeto."

And when the light had utterly faded from the windows, while storm battered the roof tiles, and the candle stub she held began to gutter and burn close to her fingers, she went down again to the ballroom.

Every candle flame bent as she arrived, but she had opened no door. The wind sighed through the halls, and a cold air moved her skirts.

And ceased. The water-stairs door had opened. And it had just shut.

She stopped still, her eyes fixed on the opposing hall. There was no candle below. She had taken it. She held it in her hand.

But he needed no help to find the blaze of light in the grand ballroom. And he climbed into view—her harlequin, white and gold in the candleglow. He wore a gold domino, only that, and had a rose in his hand.

"My harlequin," she said faintly.

"Giacinta," he said, and gestured toward the stairs, toward the outside. "They say the Ca d'Oro is haunted now. We've made a legend, I fear."

"I'm its ghost. I've become its ghost." In her purse she had the little black bottle, her escape from Nonna's plans, and her betrayal of Nonna's own escape. But that was for the morning. "I shall live here forever."

"You were with di Verona," he said, accusingly, "in the square."

"You *were* there. I wished you'd rescued me. But I knew you couldn't."

"Did you think so? You might have called out for help."

"I wish I had. But I was afraid you would die."

He walked closer. Proffered her the rose. She ignored it and flung herself into his arms, crushing out the dying candle in her fist. The hot wax burned her, and tears welled up beneath the mask, but she hardly felt the pain. The ring was in her other hand, and it was cold as ice as lips met, as he took care for the candle, and found how she had burned herself.

"Foolish girl," he cried, and pried the wax from her fingers. He kissed the burn, and kissed her lips again before he set her back and looked at her. Dark eyes glittered behind the gold domino. "And faithless, I fear."

"No. I will not be. I shall never be." She spoke in pain, in pain that transcended the burn on her palm. "I swear," she said, "I will never marry that man."

"You accepted his betrothal. You stood in view of all the Repubblica and the great cathedral, and you accepted to be his bride."

"Under threat."

"What threat?"

Dared she imagine indignation, and that it might wake on her behalf?

"The threat to my grandmother. She is old. She is foolish, my Nonna. He gave her promises, di Verona did, that she could have her house and her garden, if I married him. And he—" Here was the thing she must say, and must not incriminate Nonna, must not, no matter the anger the Doge might direct elsewhere. "Defend yourself tomorrow, that is what I wanted to say, what I came to say today, but I had no courage. La Duchesa is no part of this, understand this first and foremost. But go protected, tomorrow, and don't let di Verona or his men come near you."

"You recognize my seal."

"I knew it once I saw it." She knew he would take back the ring. She clenched her hand on it a moment, and carried that fist to her heart, then stretched it toward him and opened her hand. "And I know di Verona is your enemy."

"Are you?" He had not taken the ring. "Are you my enemy, Sforza?"

"Never."

He took off his mask. The eyes had been wicked and dark behind it. Without it, they were brown and kind. She took off the white bauta, and let it fall.

"No more la moretta?" he asked her.

"No more mysteries," she said, looking only into his eyes, and willing, oh, very willing, if he were willing, too.

He took her hand and closed it on the ring, and pulled her to him and kissed her, oh, very long, while the thunder walked above the roof, and the water lapped about the walls. They danced to their silent music, they danced all about the vast mirrored hall until the candles spun and their heads were giddy.

He spread out his cloak on the floor, and she spread hers. He set her diamond circlet on his littlest finger, and set his heavy signet on her forefinger, with a solemn kiss. They made love, then, and she asked no questions at all, what would happen in the morning, what would become of her. He might go away in the morning, but she had warned him in as plain words as she could, to save his life.

They made love and slept, and the candles burned down to darkness.

Dark became dawn through the windows, and the pale day crept in, bringing detail into the shadows. They kissed. They gathered up their scattered garments, and spoke very little, casting glances at one another, grown strangely shy as the cold, gray light of day invaded the ballroom and reflected them in every mirror.

Then the bells began, from high up the Serpentine, faint and far.

"Come," her lover said, and took her by the hand, and led her out to the windows that offered a view of the Grand Canal and its beginning traffic. The farthest church rang out, and then the next, and the next, and the next, pealing all at once, until the nearest tolled, and the sound enveloped them, mad, and glorious, rolling down the Serpentine under a golden, clouded sunrise. It was his city, the Doge's city, all the bells of his city joining together for a special day, until, last, the great bells of San Marco itself joined in, deep and joyous.

It stole the senses. And it left such silence when it was done. She remembered to breathe. Remembered that she might soon die.

She found his arms about her, holding her warm and close, leaning back against him.

"I have to go soon," he said, his breath stirring the curls beside her neck. "And will you only haunt this old palace, or might you come to haunt mine?"

"I am la Sforza," she said, with a deep sigh, that old, proud name that was Nonna's, too. "I could never be your mistress."

"I have no wife."

That was true. Dared she think—dared she hope it was his offer? She pressed his hand against her heart, and drew a deep breath.

"Come with me," he said. "Come with me. You say you don't love him."

"It will embarrass him," she said, thinking of it, imagining di Verona's desires, fiercest for what defied him. "It would ruin him. It will drive him to war with you. Is *that* your plan, after all?"

"I have no plan at all," he said, against her neck, his arms pressing her close. "But I can make plans very quickly."

"So can I," she said. And let go a deep breath. "Let me go."

He released her, as if astonished, and his face frowned, wounded.

"I could love you," she said. "I do. And I never will marry him. I swear that. But let me go. My Nonna will be beside herself with worry."

"I will call my guards," he said, "and take you up to the Palazzo in safety. Send for your grandmother."

"No," she said, and laid a hand on his heart. "You will trust me. You will trust me in this, and let me go. And if something should happen to me, you will care for my grandmother. Let her have her little house, and her garden, and her pride. Promise me. It's all she cares for."

"How can I let you go?"

"Easily," she said, "if you trust me, as I trust you, and tell you the truth. Admit Cesare di Verona to the ball. Don't let him or his men near you. And don't let him or his men leave again. There's to be riot in the city. Division in the council—when the Doge is dead."

He gazed at her eye to eye a moment, not all a lover's gaze, but the Doge's as well—full of concern, and with a sure knowledge of the world's hard choices.

"I must get home now," she said.

"I will take you there," he said, and added, holding her arm, but never bruising, always gentle in his touch: "But, Sforza, if you betray me, you will break my heart. You broke it two days ago at San Marco. Last night you put it together again. I don't think you could do it twice."

"Mine was half dead," she said, "and I had nowhere in the world to go. Now I do. Only trust me, Antonio Raffeto."

It was down the stairs after that. Masked again, they went down to the water-stairs, where a gondolier and two of the Doge's guards had spent the stormy night cloaked and shaded in canvas.

The harder thing was to get to her own door. She imagined Nonna at watch at the windows, and she asked him to let her ashore well down the walk.

He let her go. She hurried, high heels striking the pavings, until she reached her own door. She tucked the signet into her purse, then opened it, and braved the storm inside.

"Shameless girl!" Nonna cried as she ran upstairs.

"I was caught by the storm," she said, which was true, "and I slept in a dry nook." Which was also true. "I was already chilled. I had no wish to take the fever."

"Shameless girl! Look at your shoes!"

"They're mostly dry now, Nonna. " She kicked them off for the maids to attend, and sped barefoot off to her room, to bathe and dress again.

The dress was the maids' complete despair. They heated irons and brushed it, they straightened the braid and curled the wind-tangled feathers, all these little touches. They brushed her cloak. They exclaimed most over her burned hand.

"It was one of the sweet-stands," she said. "I touched the stove."

They dressed it with herbs, they wrapped it in black lace so it would not show beneath the lace of her gown, but the pain was nothing to her today. She smiled through her bath, smiled while they pulled and tugged and curled her hair. She was the soul of patience while they applied her powders and her rouge. She put the freshened dress on again and stood arrayed as crisp and new as she had first ventured out to *carnevale*.

"You are so good," she said to Nonna's maids, and gave them each a coin, for luck.

She slipped a little dagger into the belt that held her ribbon-tethered masks. She put on her cloak, and fussed the lace at her cuffs into place over her burned hand. She smiled at Nonna.

"See? No damage, Nonna."

"Only because you're very, very lucky," Nonna said fiercely.

"I am clever, like my Nonna," she said, and kissed her Nonna on the forehead, to Nonna's great annoyance. She had never noticed before, how tall she had gotten, and how small Nonna was these days. And she saw that Nonna had grown small in all the world, too, and afraid, in these last years, when small and afraid was the last thing her fierce Nonna wanted to be. "I love you," she said, "I love you, Nonna."

"Pah," Nonna said, and waved her attentions away with great fierceness. "Il duco will be here any moment."

"Will he?" She hardly cared. But she went down to the landing above the front door. Night was falling, already rendering the shadows on the Priuli's margin dark and ominous. "I shall stand and wait outside."

"You shall do no such thing," Nonna cried, pursuing her downstairs, step at a time, aided by her cane. "What has possessed you, girl?"

He has, she thought to herself, and sighed deeply, and waited by the door until the maid, watching through the portal, signaled excitedly that il duco's gondola had arrived.

She descended the stairs like a duchess, exited the door, walked to the gondola and stepped aboard, with the gondolier's hand hardly needed to steady her. The gondolier boarded, fended off, and poled down the Priuli, nosing over into the Acqua Dolce, and carried her on and on to the Grand, where il duco's barge waited, its silver oars poised, its azure blue canopy tied back to show silver and gold cushions.

He had on, this time, the half-mask of a triton, plumed in azure and extravagant, overshadowing his cruel, beard-shadowed jaw. He stepped out and showed her aboard the barge with every grace, handing her down to the well, among the silver satin cushions.

He plucked the dagger from her waist, and flung it over the side, down, down into the opaque water. And smiled that predator's smile at her.

The oarsmen fended off smoothly and rowed down the Grand, past the Ca d'Oro and its silent windows, that kept secret their memories.

All the town looked on when they joined the processional of barges that led toward the Palazzo Ducale, the Doge's residence. And in her purse she still carried the Doge's ring, and the small black vial, her one recourse, in case everything went amiss.

She smiled her own smile at Cesare di Verona as they exited the barge and walked, grandly, across the great piazza.

"What amuses you?" he asked, holding her good hand fiercely, twisting it just a little. "What amuses you, girl?"

"Nonna," she said. "Nonna has such ideas."

They approached the doors of the Palazzo, with cheering townsmen on either hand, come to see the grand costumes of the rich and powerful. They joined the train of other guests, entered into the doors of the powerful, and, still in processional, mounted the stairs behind the rich merchant princes and their attendants. She imagined di Verona's thoughts—that he deserved to be first: no, that he deserved to own this palace. A bastard duke who planned to own the whole city walked tamely, with his men all in matching azure and silver, all costumed as lesser tritons.

Up and up the steps, into the gold and glitter of the Doge's entertainment, where the primary guests waited, the oldest heads of merchant houses, their brightly-dressed sons and daughters, all in masks, a full score of harlequins, no few pantalones, and two gnagas, with a mocking falsetto, men masquerading as ladies—one of them in the duke's own exact azure, who saluted him with a curtsy as they came in.

The duke stopped cold. He need not have. Everyone in la Republica Serenissima understood clowns made jokes. But il duco abruptly changed his course, snatching Giacinta with him, and hurting her hand.

"Oh!" she said, protesting.

"Fool," he said. "This will be the last joke, I promise you."

His men, his bodyguard, immediately deserted him, moving out along the edges of the hall. She saw it happen, so suddenly, so purposefully, she had no time to think, and her heart doubled its beats. Di Verona had no intention of waiting. The moment he was in the hall, his men were moving out, positioning themselves to strike, to take advantage of the panic that di Verona knew would come. And would the assassin who struck the Doge even wear di Verona's colors?

No, never, she thought, things coming clear in the reality of the moment. No, di Verona meant to be the avenger of the Doge, to size power. There were surely others, less obvious, in the crowd, men the Doge's guards could not spot, while his own men disposed of supposed traitors.

"You're hurting me," she protested when he pulled at her, and stumbled on her skirts. "You're making us a spectacle!"

That stopped him, when no other reason would. She saw it.

"They're laughing at us," she said. "Oh, I *hate* this."

She had seized power now. She suddenly knew il duco's weakness, and it was fear. He snatched her away, near one of the tables piled high with food. A fountain there spilled wine red as blood. Its vinous smell nauseated her. So did he. But now at least she could wholly despise him.

She snatched a sweetmeat with her wounded hand, and popped it into her mouth, then snatched a cup, and let a servant fill it with wine. She sipped, then delved into her purse, slipping items into the black lace bandages of her hand.

Di Verona took another cup himself, drank, and set it down empty as trumpets sounded, as the Doge, Antonio Rafetto, came in, no longer the white harlequin, but wearing black, with his red cap, and his cloak, and lifting his hands to welcome his guests. Only one thing was not the Doge's. His littlest finger sparked white fire, the diamonds of her ring, their pledge.

For a moment il Duce looked toward his prey. And quickly, slipping the little bottle into her fingers, Giacinta pulled the waxed stopper and poured the black liquid into her own cup, a little black swirl which immediately vanished in the deep, dark red. Onto her thumb she slid the Doge's ring, asking herself desperately how to warn him of what she saw, and knowing, if things went wrong, that this cup was her only rescue. She took it up and carried it against her heart, a heart that beat like a hammer.

"My guests," Antonio called out. "Welcome! Eat, drink, dance, everyone!"

People moved forward to meet him, a surge like the tide against the gates, but the Doge's guards prevented them, to universal chagrin. The wave broke in confusion, and milled aside.

She saw di Verona's face, saw him bite his lip. So one approach was frustrated. The musicians struck up a tune. Couples took to the floor. Di Verona, however, did not. She pretended to sip her wine, and di Verona looked about the edges of the room. She began to edge away, thinking she might make an escape, even warn Antonio's guards, using Antonio's ring, but di Verona seized her wrist.

"What will your men do now?" she asked him fiercely, and the triton-mask turned toward that challenge. "Oh, come, come, signore. I know. Do you think I'm a fool?"

"Don't risk being a dead fool."

"Shall I not? They failed to get near him." A wild, spur of the moment plan rose up in her mind, a last brazen chance, even with her hand held prisoner, and she took it. "Signore Rafetto!" she called out above the music. "Signore Rafetto! Di Verona hates you! But you know that. His assassins are in the crowd!"

'Fool!" di Verona cried, and the music died in discord, frightened couples seeking the edges of the ballroom, places less in a line between her voice and the Doge and his men.

"You asked me to marry you, Signore Rafetto! And I accept!"

It was embarrassment, public embarrassment, that deadliest thing to di Verona, that thing he could not survive. The crowd murmured in fear and astonishment as the Doge stepped forward a pace.

"Giacinta!"

"Fool, I say!" Di Verona wrenched her arm, making her spill a little of the wine. It splashed, dark, on her bosom. And suddenly there was racket on the sides of the hall, armed conflict that sent guests fleeing back to the floor, and toward the shelter of the foyer. But city police were there, armed, and in force, sealing the doors.

Di Verona saw it, too, and his grip faltered. Giacinta turned and smiled at him, Nonna's kind of smile, when they had left Milano, Nonna's smile when they had faced the rundown house and the weed-choked garden.

"Drink to the Doge," she said, cold as the depths of the canals. "Take my cup. It's your escape. They won't laugh, if you drink it."

"Damn you," di Verona said. Silence had fallen about the edges of the hall. There were other police, one might think, behind the masks in the crowd. There were weapons in this hall besides those di Verona had brought.

She offered the cup up to him. "They won't laugh," she said, as she would have said it to herself. "They won't arrest you, or take you to the prison."

Di Verona seized it from her hand, wine slipping over its edge. His hand was white-knuckled on the cup, as if he would crush it. She thought he would fling it at her. Black and red harlequins were moving toward them both, shouldering guests aside.

But he drank, all at a draft, and flung the cup at them instead. The harlequins pulled his hand from her, and began to take him away. A bridge led from the Palazzo to the prisons. This hall was sometimes a court, so she heard.

He did not go beyond a few steps before he fell, and they carried him. There was, she had promised it, no laughter, only stunned silence throughout the hall.

Her arm was bruised and wrenched. The police would have seized her, too, but Antonio himself pushed through their rank and took her in charge, took her in his arms, hugged her tight against him.

"I have your ring," she said against his neck, in the murmuring of the crowd, and showed it to him. "Shall I give it back, harlequin?"

"A trade," he proposed to her, her Antonio, alive, forewarned, and well-defended, her prince of merchants. He took her burned hand in his and kissed it, and made the exchange, the little diamond circlet for his heavy signet. "It fits better. Giacinta, Giacinta, your poor hand."

They kissed, deeply, passionately. The crowd surrounded them. She took off the bauta, let it fall on its ribbon, and put her arms about him and kissed him back. The voices around them cheered the Doge, cheered their freedom, cheered the luck of young lovers.

Floods might come. The great flood always threatened. La Repubblica Serenissima still kept her suitor at bay.

Giacinta Sforza had no such intention.

Visible Light

This one is a very personal account—as my odd short stories come out of a very eclectic set of interests, and a very diverse set of studies and experiences. In composing a book, it seemed hard to find anything in common among these stories, except me—so I decided to greet the reader as a voyager, which I am, an inveterate traveler, curious about all manner of very strange things. My college studies involved ancient languages, Roman law and the ethnology and immigration patterns of Bronze Age Greece, along with the rise of technology and the evolution of world view—I'm lately fascinated with Egypt—and what do I do but write science fiction?

I'm not a person who stands still well. But then the earth is always in motion, and I like keeping up with it. I don't want just to exist. I want to know. I want to see. I want to understand.

Hence my own character, the traveler in time and space. I indulged my personal whim, and hope you enjoy the story around the stories.

CJC

INTRODUCTION

In a collection like this the writer has the rare chance to do a very old-fashioned thing: to speak to the audience, like the herald coming out before the ancient play to explain briefly what the audience is about to see—and perhaps to let the audience peek behind the scenes—Down this street, mark you, lies the house of the Old Man, and here the wineseller—

Well, on *this* street lives a bit of fantasy and a bit of science fiction, here reside stories from my first years and some from not so long ago—

I introduce one brand new tale, because that's only fair.

I have gathered the rest by no particular logic except the desire to present some balance of early and later material, some mixture of science fiction and fantasy, and in a couple of instances to preserve work that has never appeared in any anthology.

One of the additional benefits of walking onto the stage like this is the chance to lower the mask and give the audience an insight into the mind behind the creation. So stop here, ignore all the intervening passages, and go straight to the stories if you simply enjoy my craft and care nothing for the creator—being creator, I am no less pleased by that. Go, sample, enjoy.

For those who want to know something of *me*, myself, and what I am—well, let me couch this introduction in a mode more familiar to me: let me set a scene for you. I sit on a crate on a dockside, well, let's make it a lot of baggage, a battered suitcase and a lot of other crates round about, with tags and stickers abundant. SEE EARTH FIRST, one sticker says, quite antique and scratched. And this is a metal place, full of coolant fumes and fuel smells. Gears clash, hydraulics wheeze, and fans hum away overhead, while our ship is loading its heavier cargo.

You sit there on your suitcase just the same as I, and I suppose our boarding call is what we're waiting for. Passersby may stop. But it's mainly you and me.

"What do *you* do?" you ask, curious about this woman, myself, who am the ancient mariner of this dockside: I have that look—a little elsewhere, a little preoccupied, baggage all scarred with travels. I rarely give the real answer to that question of yours. "I'm a writer," I usually say. But the clock sweeps into the small hours—starships have no respect for planet-time—and we talk together the way travelers will who meet for a few hours and speak with absolute honesty precisely because they are absolute strangers. I am moved by some such thing, and I take a sip of what I have gotten from the counter yonder and you take a sip of yours and we are instantly philosophers.

"Call me a storyteller," I say, recalling another mariner. "That's at least *one* of the world's oldest professions, if not the oldest."

"You write books?" you ask. "Are you in the magazines?"

"Oh," say I, "yes. But that's not the important part. I tell stories, that's what I do. Tonight in New Guinea, in New Hampshire, in Tehuantepec and Ulaanbaatar, quite probably someone is telling a story: we still build campfires, we still watch the embers and imagine castles, don't we—down there? They weave stories down there, the same as they did around the first campfire in the world; they still do. Someone asks for the story of the big snow or the wonderful ship—there's very little difference in what we do. You just have to have a hearer."

"*Do* you have to?"

"I'm not sure about that. I wrote about something like that—people called the elee who knew their world was dying. And they had rather make statues than spaceships, though they knew no eye would ever see them."

"It would last."

"On a dead world. Under a cinder of a sun. It's an old question, isn't it, whether art created for the void has meaning—whether the tree falling in solitude makes a sound or not. What's a word without a hearer? Without that contact, spark flying from point to point across space and time, art is void—like the art of the elee, made for the dark and the silence."

"Then it matters what somebody else thinks of it?"

"It matters to somebody else. It matters to me. But that it matters to him hardly matters to me the way it does to him."

"That's crazy."

"I don't live his life. But I'm glad if he likes what I do. I'm sorry if he doesn't. I hope he finds someone who can talk to him. Everyone needs that. I do all I can. Perhaps the elee have a point."

"You mean you don't write for the critics."

"Only so far as they're human. And I am. Let me tell you, I don't believe in systems. I only use them."

"You mean all critics are crooked?"

"Oh, no. It's only a system. There are good critics. The best ones can point out the deep things in a book or a painting: they can see things you and I might miss. They have an insight like a writer's or an artist's. But their skill isn't so much adding to a book as helping a reader see ideas in it he might have missed. But there are various sorts of critics. And some of them do very dangerous things."

"Like?"

"Let me tell you: there's criticism and there's fault-finding. A tale is made for a hearer, to touch a heart. To criticize the quality of the heart it touches—that's a perilously self-loving act, isn't it? Criticizing the message itself, well, that might be useful. But the critic properly needs as much space to do it in as the writer took to develop it. And then the critic's a novelist, isn't he? Or a painter. He's one of *us*. And many of us are, you know. The best of us are. But criticism as a science—" I take here another sip. Thoughts like this require it. "Criticism is always in danger of becoming a system. Or of submitting to one."

"You said you don't believe in systems."

"Oh, I believe they exist. They exist everywhere. And more and more of them exist. The *use* of art, the manipulation of art and science by committees and governments, by demographics analysts and sales organizations, by social engineers, oh, yes—*and* by academe—all of this—It's happening at a greater pace and with more calculation than it ever has in all of history."

"And that worries you."

"Profoundly. I wrote a book about it. About art and the state. Art is a very powerful force. And the state would inevitably like to wield the wielder. it wants its posterity. Most of all it wants its safety."

"You write a lot about that?"

"*That I write* is about that. Do you see? It isn't fiction. It isn't illusion. *That I write* is a reality. Life is art *and* science. Look at your hand. What do you see? Flesh? Bone? Atoms? It's all moving. Electrons and quarks exist in constant motion. You think you know what reality is? Reality is an artifact of our senses."

"Artifact? Like old arrowheads?"

"A thing made. Your reality is an artifact of your senses. Your mind assembles the data you perceive in an acceptable order. Do you think this floor is real? But *what* is it, really? A whirl of particles. Matter and energy. We can't see the atoms dance: we can scarcely see the stars. We're suspended between these two abysses of the infinitely small and the infinitely vast, and we deceive ourselves if we believe too much in the blue sky and the green earth. Even color, you know, is simply wavelength. And solidity is the attraction of particles."

"Then it's another system."

"You've got it. Another system. Here we sit, an intersection of particles in the vast now. Past and future are equally illusory."

"We *know* what happened in the past."

"Not really."

"You mean you don't believe in books either."

"I don't believe in history."

"Then what's it all worth?"

"A great deal. As much as my own books are worth. They're equally true."

"You said it was false!"

"Oh, generally history is fiction. I *taught* history. I *know* some facts of history as well as they can be known. I've read original documents in the original languages. I've *been* where the battles were fought. And every year history gets condensed a little more and a little more, simplified, do you see? You've heard of Thermopylae. But what you've heard happened there, is likely the *average* of the effect it had, not the meticulous truth of what went on. And remember that the winners write the histories. The events were far more yea and nay and zig and zag than you believe: a newspaper of the day would have deluged you with contradictory reports and subjective analyses, so that you would be quite bewildered and confounded by what history records as a simple situation—three hundred Spartans standing off the Persians. But were there three hundred? It wasn't that simple. It was far more interesting. The behind-the-scenes was as complicated as things are in real life: more complicated than today's news ever reports anything, with treacheries and feuds going back hundreds of years into incidents and personalities many of the men on that field would have been amazed to know about. Even they didn't see everything. And they died for it."

"Anyone who tried to learn history the way it *was*—he'd go crazy."

"He'd spend a billion lifetimes. But it doesn't matter. The past is as true as my books. Fiction and history are equivalent."

"And today? You don't think we see what's going on today, either."

"We see less than we ought. We depend on eyes and ears and memory. And memory's very treacherous. Perception itself is subjective, and memory's a timetrip, far trickier than the human eye."

"It all sounds crazy."

"The totality of what's going on would be too much; it would make you crazy. So a human being selects what he'll see and remember and forms a logical framework to help him systematize the few things he keeps."

"Systems again."

"I say that I distrust them. That's what makes me an artist. Consider: if it's so very difficult to behold a mote of dust on your fingertip, to behold the sun itself for what it truly is, how do we exist from day to day? By filtering out what confuses us. My stories do the opposite. Like the practice of science, do you see? A story is a moment of profound examination of things in greater reality and sharper focus than we usually see them. It's a sharing of perception in this dynamic, motile universe, in which two human minds can momentarily orbit the same focus, like a pair of vastly complex planets, each with its own civilization, orbiting a star that they strive to comprehend, each in its own way. And when you talk about analyzing governments and not single individuals: as well proceed from the dustmote to the wide galaxy. Think of the filters and perceptual screens governments and social systems erect to protect themselves."

"You distrust governments?"

"I find them fascinating. There was an old Roman, Vergilius Maro—"

"Vergil."

"Just so. He said government itself was an artform, the same as great sculpture and great books, and practiced in similar mode—emotionally. I think I agree with the Roman."

"Isn't that a system?"

"Of course it's a system. The trick is to make the system as wide as possible. Everything I think is just that: *thinking*; it's in constant motion. It, like all my component parts, changes. It has to. The universe is a place too wonderful to ignore."

"You think most of us live in ignorance?"

"Most of us are busy. Most of us are too busy about things that give us too little time to think. I write about people who See, who See things differently and who find the Systems stripped away, or exchanged for other Systems, so that they pass from world to world in some lightning-stroke of an understanding, or the slow erosion and reconstruction of things they thought they knew."

"But does one man matter?"

"I think two kinds of humanity create events: fools and visionaries. Chaos itself may be illusion. Perhaps what we do *does* matter. I think it's a chance worth taking. I hate to leave it all to the fools."

"But who's a fool?"

"Any of us. Mostly those who never wonder if they're fools."

"That's arrogance."

"Of course it is. But the fools aren't listening. We can never insult them."

"You think what you write matters?"

"Let me tell you: for me the purest and truest art in the world is science fiction."

"It's escapist."

"It's romance. It's the world as it can be, ought to be—must someday, somewhere be, if we can only find enough of the component parts and shove them together. Science fiction is the oldest sort of tale-telling, you know. Homer; Sinbad's story; Gilgamesh; Beowulf; and up and up the line of history wherever mankind's scouts encounter the unknown. Not a military metaphor. It's a peaceful progress. Like the whales in their migrations. Tale-telling is the most peaceful thing we do. It's investigatory. The best tale-telling always has been full of what-if. The old Greek peasant who laid down the tools of a hard day's labor to hear about Odysseus's trip beyond the rim of his world—he wasn't an escapist. He was dreaming. Mind-stretching at the end of a stultifying day. He might not go. But his children's children might. *Someone* would. And that makes his day's hard work *worth* something to the future; it makes this farmer and his well-tilled field participant in the progress of his world, and his cabbages have then a cosmic importance."

"Is he worth something?"

"Maybe he was your ancestor. Maybe he fed the ancestor of the designer who made this ship."

"What's that worth? What's anything worth, if you don't believe in systems?"

"Ah. You still misunderstand me. Anything is worth everything. Everything is important. It's all one system, from the dustmote to the star. It's only that our systems are too small."

"So you give this world up? You're leaving it?"

"Aren't you?"

"I've got business out there."

"Good. That's very fine. Remember the cabbages."

"What's your business out there?"

"History."

"You don't believe in it!"

"And stories. They're equal. Fusing the past with now and tomorrow. That's what's in the crates. History. Stories."

"Where are you taking them?"

"As far as I can. You know what I'll do when I get there? I'll sit down with you and your kids born somewhere far from Earth and I'll say: listen, youngest, I've got a story to tell you, about where you came from and why you're going, and what it all means anyway. It's a story about you, and about me, and a time very much like this one . . . a dangerous time. But all times are dangerous.

"Once upon a time, I'll say. *Once upon a time* is the only true enchantment the elves left to us, the gift of truthful lies and travel in time and space.

"*Once upon a time* there were listeners round a fire; *once upon a time* there will be a microfiche or—vastly to be treasured—a real paper book aboard a ship named *Argo* (like the one ages past) in quest of things we haven't dreamed of. But they'll dream of something more than that. Youngest, I'll say, when I fly I always look out the window— I do it as a ritual when I remember it. I look for myself. But I also look for the sake of all the dreamers in all the ages of this world who would have given their very lives to catch one glimpse of the world and the stars the way I can see them for hour upon hour out that window.

"Someday, youngest, someone will take that look for me—oh, at Beta Lyrae; or at huge Aldebaran; or Tau Ceti, which I've named Pell's Star—"

I pause. I sip my drink, almost the last, and look at the clock, where the time runs close to boarding. It's time to think about the baggage. We have, perhaps, amazed each other. Travelers often do.

We send our baggage off with the handlers. We exchange pleasantries about the trip, about the schedule. We retreat to those banalities better-mannered strangers use to fill the time.

Words and words. A story teller isn't concerned with words.

The boarding call goes out. We form our mundane line and search after tickets and visas. The dock resounds with foreign names and the clank of machinery.

It is of course, always an age of wonders. The true gift is remembering to look out the windows, and to let the thoughts run backward and forward and wide to the breadth and height of all that's ever been and might yet be—

Once upon a time, I tell you.

I

I sit in the observation lounge. Window-staring. The moon is long behind us, and Earth is farther still. And a step sounds near enough to
tell me someone is interested in me or the window.

"Ah," I say, and smile. We've met before.

"What do you see out there?" you ask. It sounds like challenge.

"Look for yourself," I say. It's a double-edged invitation. And for a
time, you do.

"I've been thinking about history," you say at last.

"Oh?"

"About what good it is. People fight wars over it. They get their
prejudices from it; and maybe what they think they remember wasn't
even true in the first place."

"It's very unlikely that it is true, since history isn't."

"But if we didn't have all those books we'd have to make all those
mistakes again. Wouldn't we? Whatever they were."

"Probably we'd make different ones. Maybe we'd do much
worse."

"Maybe we ought to make up a better past. Maybe if all the writers in the world sat down and came up with a better history, and we
could just sort of *lie* to everyone—I mean, where we're going, who'd
know? Maybe if you just shot those history books out the airlock,
maybe if you wrote us a new history, we could save us a war or two."

"That's what fantasy does, you know. It's making things over the
way it should have been."

"But you can't go around believing in elves and dragons."

"The myths are true as history. Myths are about truth."

"There you go, sounding crazy again."

I laugh and flip a switch. The lap-computer comes alive on the table by the window. Words ripple past. "You know that's all myths *could* be. Truth. A system of truth, made as simple as its hearers. The old myths are still true. There's one I used to tell to my students—"

"When you taught history."

"Languages this time. Ancient languages. Eleven years of teaching. The first and second short stories I ever wrote were myths I used to tell my students. I'll show you one. I'll print it so you can read it. It was the second. It speaks about perceptions again." I press a key and send a fiche out from the microprinter; and smile, thinking on a classful of remembered faces, eleven years of students, all gathered together in one classroom like ghosts. And I think of campfires again, and a Greek hillside, and a theater, and the dusty hills of Troy. We all sit there, all of us, torchlight on our faces, in all the ghostly array of our cultures and our ancestral histories, folk out of Charlemagne's Empire, and Henry's, and the Khazars; we come from the fjords and the Sudan and the Carolinas, all of us whose ancestors would have taken axe to one another on sight. All of us sit and listen together to a Greek myth retold, all innocent of ancient murders.

"Stories matter," I say. "And what is history but another myth, with the poetry taken out?"

Dear old Greek, I think, passing on the microfiche, by whatever name you really lived, thank you for the loan. And thank you, my young friends of some years ago. This one's still your own.

▼

CASSANDRA

▲

Winner of the Hugo Award

Fires.

They grew unbearable here.

Alis felt for the door of the flat and knew that it would be solid. She could feel the cool metal of the knob amid the flames . . . saw the shadow-stairs through the roiling smoke outside, clearly enough to feel her way down them, convincing her senses that they would bear her weight.

Crazy Alis. She made no haste. The fires burned steadily. She passed through them, descended the insubstantial steps to the solid ground—she could not abide the elevator, that closed space with the shadow-floor, that plummeted down and down; she made the ground floor, averted her eyes from the red, heatless flames.

A ghost said good morning to her . . . old man Willis, thin and transparent against the leaping flames. She blinked, bade it good morning in return—did not miss old Willis's shake of the head as she opened the door and left. Noon traffic passed, heedless of the flames, the hulks that blazed in the street, the tumbling brick.

The apartment caved in—black bricks falling into the inferno, Hell amid the green, ghostly trees. Old Willis fled, burning, fell—turned to jerking, blackened flesh—died, daily. Alis no longer cried, hardly flinched. She ignored the horror spilling about her, forced her way through crumbling brick that held no substance, past busy ghosts that could not be troubled in their haste.

Kingsley's Cafe stood, whole, more so than the rest. It was refuge for the afternoon, a feeling of safety. She pushed open the door, heard the tinkle of a lost bell. Shadowy patrons looked, whispered.

Crazy Alis.

The whispers troubled her. She avoided their eyes and their presence, settled in a booth in the corner that bore only traces of the fire.

WAR, the headline in the vendor said in heavy type. She shivered, looked up into Sam Kingsley's wraithlike face.

"Coffee," she said. "Ham sandwich." It was constantly the same. She varied not even the order. Mad Alis. Her affliction supported her. A check came each month, since the hospital had turned her out. Weekly she returned to the clinic, to doctors who now faded like the others. The building burned about them. Smoke rolled down the blue, antiseptic halls. Last week a patient ran—burning—

A rattle of china. Sam set the coffee on the table, came back shortly and brought the sandwich. She bent her head and ate, transparent food on half-broken china, a cracked, fire-smudged cup with a transparent handle. She ate, hungry enough to overcome the horror that had become ordinary. A hundred times seen, the most terrible sights lost their power over her: she no longer cried at shadows. She talked to ghosts and touched them, ate the food that somehow stilled the ache in her belly, wore the same too-large black sweater and worn blue shirt and gray slacks because they were all she had that seemed solid. Nightly she washed them and dried them and put them on the next day, letting others hang in the closet. They were the only solid ones.

She did not tell the doctors these things. A lifetime in and out of hospitals had made her wary of confidences. She knew what to say. Her half-vision let her smile at ghost-faces, cannily manipulate their charts and cards, sitting in the ruins that had begun to smolder by late afternoon. A blackened corpse lay in the hall. She did not flinch when she smiled good-naturedly at the doctor.

They gave her medicines. The medicines stopped the dreams, the siren screams, the running steps in the night past her apartment. They let her sleep in the ghostly bed, high above ruin, with the flames crackling and the voices screaming. She did not speak of these things. Years in hospitals had taught her. She complained only of nightmares, and restlessness, and they let her have more of the red pills.

WAR, the headline blazoned.

The cup rattled and trembled against the saucer as she picked it up. She swallowed the last bit of bread and washed it down with coffee, tried not to look beyond the broken front window, where twisted metal hulks

smoked on the street. She stayed, as she did each day, and Sam grudg-
ingly refilled her cup, which she would nurse as far as she could and then
she would order another one. She lifted it, savoring the feeling of it,
stopping the trembling of her hands.

The bell jingled faintly. A man closed the door, settled at the counter.

Whole, clear in her eyes. She stared at him, startled, heart pounding. He ordered coffee, moved to buy a paper from the vendor, settled
again and let the coffee grow cold while he read the news. She had view
only of his back while he read—scuffed brown leather coat, brown hair
a little over his collar. At last he drank the cooled coffee all at one
draught, shoved money onto the counter and left the paper lying, headlines turned face down.

A young face, flesh and bone among the ghosts. He ignored them all
and went for the door.

Alis thrust herself from her booth.

"Hey!" Sam called at her.

She rummaged in her purse as the bell jingled, flung a bill onto the
counter, heedless that it was a five. Fear was coppery in her mouth; he
was gone. She fled the cafe, edged round debris without thinking of it,
saw his back disappearing among the ghosts.

She ran, shouldering them, braving the flames—cried out as debris
showered painlessly on her, and kept running.

Ghosts turned and stared, shocked—*he* did likewise, and she ran to
him, stunned to see the same shock on his face, regarding her.

"What is it?" he asked.

She blinked, dazed to realize he saw her no differently than the others. She could not answer. In irritation he started walking again, and she
followed. Tears slid down her face, her breath hard in her throat. People stared. He noticed her presence and walked faster, through debris,
through fires. A wall began to fall and she cried out despite herself.

He jerked about. The dust and the soot rose up as a cloud behind
him. His face was distraught and angry. He stared at her as the others
did. Mothers drew children away from the scene. A band of youths
stared, cold-eyed and laughing.

"Wait," she said. He opened his mouth as if he would curse her; she
flinched, and the tears were cold in the heatless wind of the fires. His
face twisted in an embarrassed pity. He thrust a hand into his pocket and
began to pull out money, hastily, tried to give it to her. She shook her
head furiously, trying to stop the tears—stared upward, flinching, as another building fell into flames.

"What's wrong?" he asked her. "What's wrong with you?"

"Please," she said. He looked about at the staring ghosts, then began to walk slowly. She walked with him, nerving herself not to cry out at the ruin, the pale moving figures that wandered through burned shells of buildings, the twisted corpses in the street, where traffic moved.

"What's your name?" he asked. She told him. He gazed at her from time to time as they walked, a frown creasing his brow. He had a face well-worn for youth, a tiny scar beside the mouth. He looked older than she. She felt uncomfortable in the way his eyes traveled over her: she decided to accept it—to bear with anything that gave her this one solid presence. Against every inclination she reached her hand into the bend of his arm, tightened her fingers on the worn leather. He accepted it.

And after a time he slid his arm behind her and about her waist, and they walked like lovers.

WAR, the headline at the newsstand cried.

He started to turn into a street by Tenn's Hardware. She balked at what she saw there. He paused when he felt it, faced her with his back to the fires of that burning.

"Don't go," she said.

"Where do you want to go?"

She shrugged helplessly, indicated the main street, the other direction.

He talked to her then, as he might talk to a child, humoring her fear. It was pity. Some treated her that way. She recognized it, and took even that.

His name was Jim. He had come into the city yesterday, hitched rides. He was looking for work. He knew no one in the city. She listened to his rambling awkwardness, reading through it. When he was done, she stared at him still, and saw his face contract in dismay at her.

"I'm not crazy," she told him, which was a lie that everyone in Sudbury would have known, only *he* would not, knowing no one. His face was true and solid, and the tiny scar by the mouth made it hard when he was thinking; at another time she would have been terrified of him. Now she was terrified of losing him amid the ghosts.

"It's the war," he said.

She nodded, trying to look at him and not at the fires. His fingers touched her arm, gently. "It's the war," he said again. "It's all crazy. Everyone's crazy."

And then he put his hand on her shoulder and turned her back the other way, toward the park, where green leaves waved over black, skeletal limbs. They walked along the lake, and for the first time in a long time she drew breath and felt a whole, sane presence beside her.

They bought corn, and sat on the grass by the lake, and flung it to the spectral swans. Wraiths of passersby were few, only enough to keep a feeling of occupancy about the place—old people, mostly, tottering about the deliberate tranquillity of their routine despite the headlines.

"Do you see them," she ventured to ask him finally, "all thin and gray?"

He did not understand, did not take her literally, only shrugged. Warily, she abandoned that questioning at once. She rose to her feet and stared at the horizon, where the smoke bannered on the wind.

"Buy you supper?" he asked.

She turned, prepared for this, and managed a shy, desperate smile. "Yes," she said, knowing what else he reckoned to buy with that—willing, and hating herself, and desperately afraid that he would walk away, tonight, tomorrow. She did not know men. She had no idea what she could say or do to prevent his leaving, only that he would when someday he recognized her madness.

Even her parents had not been able to bear with that—visited her only at first in the hospitals, and then only on holidays, and then not at all. She did not know where they were.

There was a neighbor boy who drowned. She had said he would. She had cried for it. All the town said it was she who pushed him.

Crazy Alis.

Fantasizes, the doctors said. Not dangerous.

They let her out. There were special schools, state schools.

And from time to time—hospitals.

Tranquilizers.

She had left the red pills at home. The realization brought sweat to her palms. They gave sleep. They stopped the dreams. She clamped her lips against the panic and made up her mind that she would not need them—not while she was not alone. She slipped her hand into his arm and walked with him, secure and strange, up the steps from the park to the streets.

And stopped.

The fires were out.

Ghost-buildings rose above their jagged and windowless shells. Wraiths moved through masses of debris, almost obscured at times. He tugged her on, but her step faltered, made him look at her strangely and put his arm about her.

"You're shivering," he said. "Cold?"

She shook her head, tried to smile. The fires were out. She tried to take it for a good omen. The nightmare was over. She looked up into his solid, concerned face, and her smile almost became a wild laugh.

"I'm hungry," she said.

They lingered over a dinner in Graben's—he in his battered jacket, she in her sweater that hung at the tails and elbows: the spectral patrons were in far better clothes, and stared at them, and they were set in a corner nearest the door, where they would be less visible. There was cracked crystal and broken china on insubstantial tables, and the stars winked coldly in gaping ruin above the wan glittering of the broken chandeliers.

Ruins, cold, peaceful ruins.

Alis looked about her calmly. One could live in ruins, only so the fires were gone.

And there was Jim, who smiled at her without any touch of pity, only a wild, fey desperation that she understood—who spent more than he could afford in Graben's, the inside of which she had never hoped to see—and told her—predictably—that she was beautiful. Others had said it. Vaguely she resented such triteness from him, from him whom she had decided to trust. She smiled sadly when he said it; and gave it up for a frown; and, fearful of offending him with her melancholies, made it a smile again.

Crazy Alis. He would learn and leave tonight if she were not careful. She tried to put on gaiety, tried to laugh.

And then the music stopped in the restaurant, and the noise of the other diners went dead, and the speaker was giving an inane announcement.

Shelters . . . shelters . . . shelters.

Screams broke out. Chairs overturned. Alis went limp in her chair, felt Jim's cold, solid hand tugging at hers, saw his frightened face mouthing her name as he took her up into his arms, pulled her with him, started running.

The cold air outside hit her, shocked her into sight of the ruins again, wraith figures pelting toward that chaos where the fires had been worst. And she knew.

"No!" she cried, pulling at his arm. "No!" she insisted, and bodies half-seen buffeted them in a rush to destruction. He yielded to her sudden certainty, gripped her hand and fled with her against the crowds as the sirens wailed madness through the night—fled with her as she ran her sighted way through the ruin.

And into Kingsley's, where cafe tables stood abandoned with food still on them, doors ajar, chairs overturned. Back they went into the kitchens and down and down into the cellar, the dark, the cold safety from the flames.

No others found them there. At last the earth shook, too deep for sound. The sirens ceased and did not come on again.

They lay in the dark and clutched each other and shivered, and above them for hours raged the sound of fire, smoke sometimes drifting in to sting their eyes and noses. There was the distant crash of brick, rumblings that shook the ground, that came near, but never touched their refuge.

And in the morning, with the scent of fire still in the air, they crept up into the murky daylight.

The ruins were still and hushed. The ghost-buildings were solid now, mere shells. The wraiths were gone. It was the fires themselves that were strange, some true, some not, playing above dark, cold brick, and most were fading.

Jim swore softly, over and over again, and wept.

When she looked at him she was dry-eyed, for she had done her crying already.

And she listened as he began to talk about food, about leaving the city, the two of them. "All right," she said.

Then clamped her lips, shut her eyes against what she saw in his face. When she opened them it was still true, the sudden transparency, the wash of blood. She trembled, and he shook at her, his ghost-face distraught.

"What's wrong?" he asked. "What's wrong?"

She could not tell him, would not. She remembered the boy who had drowned, remembered the other ghosts. Of a sudden she tore from his hands and ran, dodging the maze of debris that, this morning, was solid.

"Alis!" he cried and came after her.

"No!" she cried suddenly, turning, seeing the unstable wall, the cascading brick. She started back and stopped, unable to force herself. She held out her hands to warn him back, saw them solid.

The brick rumbled, fell. Dust came up, thick for a moment, obscuring everything.

She stood still, hands at her sides, then wiped her sooty face and turned and started walking, keeping to the center of the dead streets.

Overhead, clouds gathered, heavy with rain.

She wandered at peace now, seeing the rain spot the pavement, not yet feeling it.

In time the rain did fall, and the ruins became chill and cold. She visited the dead lake and the burned trees, the ruin of Graben's, out of which she gathered a string of crystal to wear.

She smiled when, a day later, a looter drove her from her food supply. He had a wraith's look, and she laughed from a place he did not dare to climb and told him so.

And recovered her cache later when it came true, and settled among the ruined shells that held no further threat, no other nightmares, with her crystal necklace and tomorrows that were the same as today.

One could live in ruins, only so the fires were gone.

And the ghosts were all in the past, invisible.

II

"I've been thinking about perceptions," you say. We sit again beneath the observation window. The ship is slowly outbound. The view is magnificent, all stars.

"Oh?"

"And time."

"How so?"

"Do you believe in timetravel?"

"Time is all around us. Looking at the stars is looking into time. The light from that red one, say, left home a hundred years ago. Two hundred. If our own sun winked out this moment we would live in their eyes for two hundred years—if they had a powerful telescope to see us with. If the photons didn't scatter. If space didn't curve. Perhaps that star out there has already died, two hundred years ago." I entertain a brief thought of a nova. Of a shockwave kicking dustclouds into swirls to birth new stars. "Perhaps our sun died eight minutes ago. We'd just now find it out. When we look at the stars we see into time. When we pass lightspeed we travel through the wavefront of a moment that left its star in lightscatter years ago, and we overtake the real, the present moment when we reach another star. But to surpass that moment and arrive *before* we left—that would be a difficult concept. That requires more than simultaneity. The causalties boggle the mind. If time is the motion of particles away from their origin, then timetravel locally requires us to reverse the entire motion of the universe, and the inertia of the moving universe is the most powerful thing I can think of. Besides, when we form the concept of travel in time, you and I, can we have pushed a button in our own future and come here *knowing* we pushed it? It all gives me a headache."

"You wrote about timetravel."

"You've been reading my books?"

"Your first book was about timetravel."

"*Gate of Ivrel.*"

"It was like a fantasy."

"Or science fiction—depends on whose viewpoint you take. I wander over that dividing line now and again. It's part of that business of baggage, you understand. Past and future, fused. The ultimate meddling with history. But remember that what I write is always as true as history. And time travel never worked right in my future. I always distrusted it."

"You're facetious again."

"Often. Let me show you something." I flick on the computer and call up memory. "You wonder about perception and time and history. *Gate* was a very old story for me—I began part of that story when I was fourteen. It went through a lot of sea-changes on its way. My students had something to do with it too—when I was near thirty. We talked about time travel. And the motion of worlds in space and the distance between the stars. We talked about everything. Well, *Gate,* being fantasy-like, lost this little bit."

"You mean it got dropped out?"

"It needed to go. This bit starts in a very futuristic world; and *Gate* begins in what might be an ancient one. But if you *have* read that book, I can tell you that Harrh of this little fragment was Liell, long before the events in *Gate;* and that says enough. If you haven't, never mind: I won't give away who Liell was. Just call it a story about timetravel, in the days when the Gates led across qhalur spacetime, and knit their empire together . . ."

THE THREADS OF TIME

It was possible that the Gates were killing the qhal. They were every-where, on every world, had been a fact of life for five thousand years, and linked the whole net of qhalur civilization into one present-tense co-herency.

They had not, to be sure, invented the Gates. Chance gave them that gift . . . on a dead world of their own sun. One Gate stood—made by unknown hands.

And the qhal made others, imitating what they found. The Gates were instantaneous transfer, not alone from place to place, but, because of the motion of worlds and suns and the traveling galaxies—involving time.

There was an end of time. Ah, qhal *could* venture anything. If one supposed, if one believed, if one were very *sure*, one could step through a Gate to a Gate that would/might exist on some other distant world.

And if one were wrong?

If it did not exist?

If it never had?

Time warped in the Gate-passage. One could step across light-years, unaged; so it was possible to outrace light and time.

Did one not want to die, bound to a single lifespan? Go forward. See the future. Visit the world/worlds to come.

But never go back. Never tamper. Never alter the past.

There was an End of Time.

It was the place where qhal gathered, who had been farthest and lost their courage for traveling on. It was the point beyond which no one had courage, where descendants shared the world with living ancestors in greater and greater numbers, the jaded, the restless, who reached this age and felt their will erode away.

It was the place where hope ended. Oh, a few went farther, and the age saw them—no more. They were gone. They did not return.

They went beyond, whispered those who had lost their courage. They went out a Gate and found nothing there.

They died.

Or was it death—to travel without end? And what was death? And was the universe finite at all?

Some went, and vanished, and the age knew nothing more of them.

Those who were left were in agony—of desire to go; of fear to go farther.

Of changes.

This age—did change. It rippled with possibilities. Memories deceived. One remembered, or remembered that one had remembered, and the fact grew strange and dim, contradicting what obviously *was*. People remembered things that never had been true.

And one must never go back to see. Backtiming—had direst possibilities. It made paradox.

But some tried, seeking a time as close to their original exit point as possible. Some came too close, and involved themselves in time-loops, a particularly distressing kind of accident and unfortunate equally for those involved as bystanders.

Among qhal, between the finding of the first Gate and the End of Time, a new kind of specialist evolved: time-menders, who in most extreme cases of disturbance policed the Gates and carefully researched afflicted areas. They alone were licensed to violate the back-time barrier, passing back and forth under strict non-involvement regulations, exchanging intelligence only with each other, to minutely adjust reality.

Evolved.

Agents recruited other agents at need—but at whose instance? There might be some who knew. It might have come from the far end of time—in that last (or was it last?) age beyond which nothing seemed certain, when the years since the First Gate were more than five thousand, and the Now in which all Gates existed was—very distant. Or it might have come from those who had found the Gate, overseeing their invention. Someone knew, somewhen, somewhere along the course of the stars toward the end of time.

But no one said.

It was hazardous business, this time-mending, in all senses. Precisely *what* was done was something virtually unknowable after it was done, for alterations in the past produced (one believed) changes in future reality.

Whole time-fields, whose events could be wiped and redone, with effects which widened the farther down the timeline they proceeded. Detection of time-tampering was almost impossible.

A stranger wanted something to eat, a long time ago. He shot himself his dinner.

A small creature was not where it had been, when it had been.

A predator missed a meal and took another . . . likewise small.

A child lost a pet.

And found another.

And a friend she would not have had. She was happier for it.

She met many people she had never/would never meet.

A man in a different age had breakfast in a house on a hill.

Agent Harrh had acquired a sense about disruptions, a kind of extrasensory queasiness about a just-completed timewarp. He was not alone in this. But the time-menders (Harrh knew three others of his own age) never reported such experiences outside their own special group. Such reports would have been meaningless to his own time, involving a past which (as a result of the warp) was neither real nor valid nor perceptible to those in Time Present. Some time-menders would reach the verge of insanity because of this. This was future fact. Harrh knew this.

He had been there.

And he refused to go again to Now, that Now to which time had advanced since the discovery of the Gate—let alone to the End of Time, which was the farthest that anyone imagined. He was one of a few, a very few, licensed to do so, but he refused.

He lived scattered lives in ages to come, and remembered the future with increasing melancholy.

He had visited the End of Time, and left it in the most profound despair. He had seen what was there, and when he had contemplated going beyond, that most natural step out the Gate which stood and beckoned—

He fled. He had never run from anything but that. It remained, a recollection of shame at his fear.

A sense of a limit which he had never had before.

And this in itself was terrible, to a man who had thought time infinite and himself immortal.

In his own present of 1003 since the First Gate, Harrh had breakfast, a quiet meal. The children were off to the beach. His wife shared tea with him and thought it would be a fine morning.

"Yes," he said. "Shall we take the boat out? We can fish a little, take the sun."

"Marvelous," she said. Her gray eyes shone. He loved her—for herself, for her patience. He caught her hand on the crystal table, held slender fingers, not speaking his thoughts, which were far too somber for the morning.

They spent their mornings and their days together. He came back to her, time after shifting time. He might be gone a month; and home a week; and gone two months next time. He never dared cut it too close. They lost a great deal of each other's lives, and so much—so much he could not share with her.

"The island," he said. "Mhreihrrinn, I'd like to see it again."

"I'll pack," she said.

And went away.

He came back to her never aged; and she bore their two sons; and reared them; and managed the accounts: and explained his absences to relatives and the world. *He travels*, she would say, with that right amount of secrecy that protected secrets.

And even to her he could never confide what he knew.

"I trust you," she would say—knowing what he was, but never what he did.

He let her go. She went off to the hall and out the door— He imagined happy faces, holiday, the boys making haste to run the boat out and put on the bright colored sail. She would keep them busy carrying this and that, fetching food and clothes—things happened in shortest order when Mhreihrrinn set her hand to them.

He wanted that, wanted the familiar, the orderly, the homely. He was, if he let his mind dwell on things—afraid. He had the notion never to leave again.

He had been to the Now most recently—5045, and his flesh crawled at the memory. There was recklessness there. There was disquiet. The Now had traveled two decades and more since he had first begun, and he felt it more and more. The whole decade of the 5040's had a queasiness about it, ripples of instability as if the whole fabric of the Now were shifting like a kaleidoscope.

And it headed for the End of Time. It had become more and more like that age, confirming it by its very collapse.

People had illusions in the Now. They perceived what had not been true.

And yet it *was* when he came home.

It had grown to be so—while he was gone.

A university stood in Morurir, which he did not remember.

A hedge of trees grew where a building had been in Morurir.

A man was in the Council who had died.

He would not go back to Now. He had resolved that this morning. He had children, begotten before his first time-traveling. He had so very much to keep him—this place, this home, this stability— He was very well to do. He had invested well—his own small tampering. He had no lack, no need. He was mad to go on and on. He was done.

But a light distracted him, an opal shimmering beyond his breakfast nook, arrival in that receptor which his fine home afforded, linked to the master gate at Pyvrrhn.

A young man materialized there, opal and light and then solidity, a distraught young man.

"Harrh," the youth said, disregarding the decencies of meeting, and strode forward unasked. "Harrh, is everything all right here?"

Harrh arose from the crystal table even before the shimmer died, beset by that old queasiness of things out of joint. This was Alhir from 390 Since the Gate, an experienced man in the force: he had used a Master Key to come here—had such access, being what he was.

"Alhir," Harrh said, perplexed. "What's wrong?"

"You don't know." Alhir came as far as the door.

"A cup of tea?" Harrh said. Alhir had been here before. They were friends. There were oases along the course of suns, friendly years, places where houses served as rest-stops. In this too Mhreihrrinn was patient. "I've got to tell you— No, don't tell me. I don't want to know. I'm through. I've made up my mind. You can carry that where you're going. —But if you want the breakfast—"

"There's been an accident."

"I don't want to hear."

"He got past us."

"I don't want to know." He walked over to the cupboard, took another cup. "Mhreihrrinn's with the boys down at the beach. You just caught us." He set the cup down and poured the tea, where Mhreihrrinn had sat. "Won't you? You're always welcome here. Mhreihrrinn has no idea what you are. My young friend, she calls you. She doesn't know. Or she suspects. She'd never say. —Sit *down*."

Alhir had strayed aside, where a display case sat along the wall, a lighted case of mementoes, of treasures, of crystal. "Harrh, there was a potsherd here."

"No," Harrh said, less and less comfortable. "Just the glasses. I'm quite sure."

"Harrh, it was very old."

"No," he said. "—I promised Mhreihrrinn and the boys—I mean it. I'm through. I don't want to know."

"It came from Silen. From the digs at the First Gate, Harrh. It was a very valuable piece. You valued it very highly. —You don't remember."

"No," Harrh said, feeling fear thick about him, like a change in atmosphere. "I don't know of such a piece. I never had such a thing. Check your memory, Alhir."

"It was from the ruins by the *First Gate*, don't you understand?"

And then Alhir did not exist.

Harrh blinked, remembered pouring a cup of tea. But he was sitting in the chair, his breakfast before him.

He poured the tea and drank.

He was sitting on rock, amid the grasses blowing gently in the wind, on a clifftop by the sea.

He was standing there. "Mhreihrrinn," he said, in the first chill touch of fear.

But that memory faded. He had never had a wife, nor children. He forgot the house as well.

Trees grew and faded.

Rocks moved at random.

The time-menders were in most instances the only ones who survived even a little while.

Wrenched loose from time and with lives rooted in many parts of it, they felt it first and lived it longest, and not a few were trapped in backtime and did not die, but survived the horror of it and begot children who further confounded the time-line.

Time, stretched thin in possibilities, adjusted itself.

He was Harrh.

But he was many possibilities and many names.

In time none of them mattered.

* * *

He was many names; he lived. He had many bodies; and the souls stained his own.

In the end he remembered nothing at all, except the drive to live.

And the dreams.

And none of the dreams were true.

III

"Is it easy to get your first story published?"

"Why?" I ask. It's computer games tonight in the rec room. I'm quite good at the ones which involve blowing up things and very bad at the word games. My mind goes on holiday when I'm not writing, and declares moratorium in logic. "Are you thinking of writing one?"

"Oh, no. I just wondered whether it's easy."

"It isn't. Or if it is, and it happens too soon, you don't have all the calluses you need. And you can get hurt. Writing is a risky business." We are some time into our acquaintance. We've passed from that intimacy of strangers into a different kind of truth. "Too, sometimes a story just misbehaves. Sometimes one seems to turn out at an inconvenient length, or the topic isn't fashionable. An inexperienced writer is most likely to do a story that's over-long or too short . . . and of course in the inscrutable justice of the System, a new writer is also the least likely to get an odd-length story published. Sometimes a young writer can be very naïve about the system. There was a story I wrote back in the sixties, in the hope I could get it serialized in a major magazine. Now, there's really about as much chance of a break-in writer doing that as there is of a particular star out there going nova while we watch.

"And to compound matters, I sent a half-page summary to the magazine in question and asked them if they wanted it on that basis. They said what any sane editors would have said. No. So I tossed it into the drawer, since I had arrived at sanity in the meanwhile and knew my chances."

"Just gave up?"

"I had two novels circulating. I pinned my hopes on those. One eventually made it. Rewritten, to be sure. But, no, I never gave up on this story. I thought about making it into a novel and I'd take it out and try now and again. Now I tell you a truth about what this age and the system has done to storytellers— we're prisoners of bookcovers. Bookcovers must come along at just exactly such a time so a certain number of books will fit into a rack and cost a certain amount. So people who have a long tale to tell have to interrupt it with a great many bookcovers (and re-explanations) and alas, if you birth a tale inconveniently small you'll spend as much creativity finding a home for it as it took to write it in the first place.

"But sometimes there is a story, as an old tale used to say quite properly, just so long and no longer.

"So 'Companions' never grew and never shrank; and it languished in that drawer until someone had just the right space for it. Also rewritten, of course. It's a ghost story. Of sorts."

"Fantasy?"

"Science fiction."

"Perceptions again?"

"In a way." I lose a playing-piece and am regenerated on the screen. "I was rather fond of the concept. Count the characters when you've read it. Tell me how many there are—except the beginning."

"Tricks."

"It's perceptions, remember."

COMPANIONS

1

The ship lay behind them, improbable in so rich a land, so earthlike a world, a silver egg in paradise, an egg more accustomed to stellar distances, to crouching on barren, hellish moons, probing for whatever she could find, her people and her brain calculating survival margins for potential bases—whether mining and manufacture might be enough, given x number of ship-calls per year, to make development worth the while, for ships on their way to Somewhere, as a staging point for humans on their way to Somewhere in the deep.

Somewheres were much, much rarer . . . and this was one, this was more than a marginal Somewhere, this eden.

No indication of habitation, no response to an orbiting ship; no readings on close scan, not a geometry anywhere on the surface but nature's own work.

An Earth unpopulated, untouched, unclaimed.

Green and lush through the faceplates . . . a view that changed slowly as Warren turned, as he faced from open plain to forest to distant mountains. Sea lay a little distance away. The sky was incredible, filtered blue. Three other white-suited figures walked ungainly through the grass. The sounds of breathing came through the suit-com, occasional comments, panted breaths interspersed: the gear weighed them down on this world. The ship kept talking to them, forlorn, envious voices of those duty-bound inside, to the four of them out here.

"Makes no sense," Harley said, disembodied, through the com. "No insects. No birds. You can't have an ecology like this with no animate life."

"Take your samples," Burlin's voice said, dimmer. The captain, Burlin. He stood to make himself that one find that would assure an old age in comfort. For the younger rest of them, promise of prime assignments, of comforts for the ship, of the best for the rest of their lives. They escorted Harley out here—Harley who told them what to gather, Harley whose relays were to the labs back on the ship, the real heart of the probe's operations.

Nothing was wrong with the world. The first air and soil samples *Anne*'s intakes had gathered had shown them nothing amiss; the pseudosome had come out, stood, silver and invulnerable to chance, and surveyed the find with robotic eyes, as incapable of joy as suited human bodies were of appreciating the air and the wind that swayed the grasses. There might be perfumes on the wind, but the instruments read a dispassionate N, CO_2, O finding, a contaminant readout, windspeed, temperature.

They gathered whole plants and seeds, tiny scoops of soil, a new world's plunder. Every species was new, and some were analogous to kinds they knew: bearded grasses, smooth-barked bushes with slick green leaves. Paul Warren dug specimens Harley chose and sealed the bags, recorded the surrounds with his camera, labeled and marked with feverish enthusiasm.

"Harley?" That was Sax. Warren looked around at Harley, who sat down from a crouch in the grass, heard someone's breathing gone rapid. "You all right, Harley?"

"It's hot," Harley said. "I don't think my system's working right."

Burlin walked back to him. Warren did, too, stuffing his samples into the bag at his belt. It was an awkward business, trying to examine another suit's systems, tilting the helmet. Sun glared on the readout plate, obscuring the numbers for the moment. Harley shifted his shoulder and it cleared. "All right," Warren said. "The system's all right."

"Maybe you'd better walk back," Burlin said to Harley. "We're nearly done out here anyway."

Harley made a move toward rising, flailed with a gloved hand, and Sax caught it, steadied him on the way up.

Harley's knees went, suddenly, pitching him face down. "Check the airflow," Burlin said. Warren was already on it.

"No problem there." He tried to keep panic out of his voice. "Harley?"

"He's breathing." Burlin had his hand on Harley's chest. He gathered up Harley's arm, hauled it over his shoulder, and Warren got the other one.

It was a long way back, dragging a suited man's weight. "Get the pseudosome out," Burlin ordered into the welter of questions from the ship. "Get us help out here."

It came before they had gotten halfway to the ship, a gleam in the dark square of *Anne*'s grounded lift tube bay, a human-jointed extension of the ship coming out for them, planting its feet carefully in the uncertain footing of the grass. It was strength. It was comfort. It came walking the last distance with silver arms outstretched, the dark visor of its ovoid head casting back the sun.

They gave Harley to it, positioning its program-receptive arms, told it lift-right, and the right arm came up, so that it carried Harley like a baby, like a silver sexless angel carrying a faceless shape of a man back to the ship. They followed, plodding heavily after, bearing the burden of their own suits and feeling the unease that came with unknown places when things started going wrong.

It was bright day. There were no threats, no unstable terrain, no threat of weather or native life. But the sunlight seemed less and the world seemed larger and ominously quiet for so much life on its face.

They brought Harley inside, into the airlock. The pseudosome stood still as the hatch closed and sealed. "Set down, *Anne*," Burlin said, and the pseudosome reversed the process that had gathered Harley up, released him into their arms. They laid him on the floor.

Harley moved, a febrile stirring of hands and head, a pawing at the helmet collar. "Get the oxygen," Burlin said, and Warren ignored the queries coming rapid-fire from the crew inside the ship, got up and opened the emergency panel while Sax and Burlin stripped off the helmet. He brought the oxy bottle, dropped to his knees and clamped the clear mask over Harley's white, sweating face. Harley sucked in great breaths, coughed, back arching in the cumbersome suit. Red blotches marked his throat, like heat. "Look at that," Sax said. The blotches were evident on Harley's face, too, fine hemorrhaging about the cheeks, about the nose and mouth beneath the plastic.

Burlin stood up, hit the decontamination process. The UV came on. The rest of the procedure sequenced in the lock. Burlin knelt. Harley was breathing shallowly now. "He couldn't have gotten it out there," Warren said. "Not like this, not this fast. Not through the suit."

"Got to get the ship scoured out," Burlin said. "Yesterday, the day before—something got past the lock."

Warren looked up . . . at the pseudosome.

The processing cut off. The lights went back to normal. Warren looked at Harley, up at Burlin. "Captain—are we going to bring him in?"

"We do what we can. We three. Here. In the lock."

Harley's head moved, restlessly, dislodging the mask. Warren clamped it the more tightly.

Before he died it took the three of them to hold him. Harley screamed, and clawed with his fingers, and beat his head against the decking. Blood burst from his nose and mouth and drowned the oxy mask, smeared their suits in his struggles. He raved and called them by others' names and cursed them and the world that was killing him. When it was over, it was morning again, but by then another of the crew had complained of fever.

Inside the ship.

They went to every crevice of the ship, suited, with UV light and steam-borne disinfectant, nightmare figures meeting in fog, in the deep places, among conduits and machines.

Everywhere, the com: "Emergency to three; we've got another—"

Deep in the bowels of the ship, two figures, masked, carrying cannisters, obscured in steam:

"It isn't doing any good," Abner said. There was panic in his voice, a man who'd seen crew die before, on Mortifer and Hell. "*Ten of us already—*"

"Shut up, Abner," Warren said, with him, in the dark of *Anne's* depths. Steam hissed, roared from the cannisters; disinfectant dripped off griddings, off railings and pipe. "Just shut it *up.*"

Com's voice faltered, rose plaintive through the roar: "We're not getting any response out of 2a. Is somebody going to check on that? *Is there somebody going to check that out?*"

There was chaos in the labs, tables unbolted, cots used while they could be; pallets spread when they ran out of those. The raving lay next to the comatose; death came with hemorrhage, small at first, and worse. Lungs filled, heart labored, and the vessels burst. Others lingered, in delirium.

"Lie down," Sikutu said—biologist, only sometime medic, tried to help the man, to reason where there was no reason.

"I've got work to do," Sax cried, wept, flailed his arms "I've got work—"

Smith held him, a small woman, pinned an arm while Sikutu held the other. "Hush, hush," she said. "You've got to lie still—Sax, Sax—"

"They all die," Sax said, as he wept. "I've got work to do. I've got to get back to the lab—*don't want to die—*"

He set others off, awakened the sleeping, got curses, screams from others.

"Don't want to die," he sobbed.

Sikutu shook at him, quieted him at last, sat down and held his head in his hands. He felt fevered, felt short of breath.

His pulse increased. But maybe that was fear.

Rule was dead. Warren found her in Botany, among the plants she loved, lying in a knot next to one of the counters. He stared, grieved in what shock there was left to feel. There was no question of life left. There was the blood, the look of all the others. He turned his face away, leaned against the wall where the com unit was, pressed the button.

"Captain, she's dead, all right. Botany One."

There was silence for a moment. "Understood," Burlin's voice came back. It broke. Another small silence. "The pseudosome's on its way."

"I don't need it. She doesn't weigh much."

"Don't touch her."

"Yes, sir." Warren pushed the button, broke the contact, leaned there with his throat gone tight. The dying screamed through the day and night, audible through the walls of sickbay on lower deck, up the air shafts, up the conduits, like the machinery sounds.

This had been a friend.

The lift worked, near the lab; he heard it, heard the metal footsteps, rolled his eyes toward the doorway as *Anne* herself came in . . . shining metal, faceless face, black plastic face with five red lights winking on and off inside; black plastic mirroring the lab on its oval surface, his own distorted form.

"Assistance?" *Anne* asked.

"Body." He pointed off at Rule. "Dispose."

Anne reoriented, stalked over and bent at the waist, gripped Rule's arm. The corpse had stiffened. Motors whirred; *Anne* straightened, hauling the body upright; another series of whirrings: brought her right arm under Rule's hips, lifted, readjusted the weight. A slow shuffling turn.

Warren stepped aside. *Anne* walked, hit the body against the doorframe in trying to exit. Warren put out his hand, sickened by this further horror, but *Anne* tilted the body, passed through and on.

He followed, down the hall, to Destruct . . . utilitarian, round-sealed door. *Danger*, it said. *Warning*. They used it for biological wastes. For dangerous samples. For more mundane things.

For their dead, down here.

He opened the hatch. *Anne* put the body in, small, insectile adjustments like a wasp. Froze, then, arms lowering, sensor-lights winking out. Warren closed the door, dogged it down. He pushed the button, winced at the explosive sound, wiped his face. His hands were shaking. He looked at *Anne*.

"Decontaminate yourself," he said. The lights came on inside the mask. The robot moved, reoriented to the hall, walked off into the dark farther down the hall: no lights for *Anne*. She needed none.

Warren's belly hurt. He caught his breath. *Decontaminate.* He headed for the showers, faithful to the regs. It was a thing to do; it kept a man from thinking, held out promises of safety. Maybe the others had let down.

He showered, vapored dry, took clean coveralls from the common locker, sat down on the bench to pull on his boots. His hands kept shaking. He kept shivering even after dressing. *Fear. It's fear.*

An alarm sounded, a short beep of the Klaxon, something touched that should not have been, somewhere in the ship. He stopped in mid-tug, heard the crash and whine of the huge locks at *Anne's* deep core. Someone was using the cargo airlock. He stood up, jammed his foot into the second boot, started for the door.

"All report." He heard the general order, Burlin's voice. He went to the com by the door and did that, name and location: "Paul Warren, lower-deck showers."

Silence.

"Captain?"

Silence.

Panic took him. He left the shower room at a run, headed down the corridor to the lift, rode it up to topside, raced out again, down the hall, around the corner into the living quarters, through it to the bridgeward corridor.

Locked. He pushed the button twice, tried the com above it. "Captain." He gasped for air. "Captain, it's Warren. Was that Abner, then?"

Silence. He fumbled his cardkey from his pocket, inserted it into the slot under the lock. It failed. He slammed his fist onto the com.

"Captain?—Sikutu, Abner, is anyone hearing me?"

Silence still. He turned and ran back down the short corridor, through the mainroom, back toward the lift.

"Warren?" the com said. Burlin's voice.

Warren skidded to a stop, scrambled back to the nearest com unit and pushed the button. "Captain, Captain, what's going on?"

"I'm not getting any word out of sickbay," Burlin said. "I've sent the pseudosome in. Something's happened there."

"I'm going."

Silence.

Warren caught his breath, ran for the lift and rode it down again. Silence in the lower corridor too. He looked about him. "Abner? Abner, are you down here?"

No answer to the hail. Nothing. A section seal hissed open behind him. He spun about, caught his balance against the wall.

Anne was there in the dark. The pseudosome strode forward, her red lights glowing.

Warren turned and ran, faster than the robot, headed for the lab.

Quarantine, it said. *No entry*. He reached the door, pressed the com. "Sikutu. Sikutu, it's Warren. Are you all right in there?"

Silence. He pushed Door-Open.

It was a slaughterhouse inside. Blood was spattered over walls and beds. Sikutu—lying on the floor among the beds and pallets, red all over his lab whites from his perforated chest; Minnan and Polly and Tom, lying in their beds with their bedclothes sodden red, with startled eyes and twisted bodies. Throats cut. Faces slashed.

One bed was empty. The sheets were thrown back. He cast about him, counted bodies, lost in horror—heard the footsteps at his back and turned in alarm. *Anne* stood there, facelights flashing, cameras clicking into focus.

"Captain," Warren said: *Anne* was a relay herself. "Captain, it's Sax. He's gone . . . everyone else is dead. He's got a knife or something. Is there any word from Abner?"

"I can't raise him." Burlin's voice came from *Anne*. "Get a gun. Go to the lock. Abner was in that area last."

"Assistance." The voice changed; *Anne*'s mechanical tones. The pseudosome swiveled, talking to the dead. "Assistance?"

Warren wiped his face, caught his breath. "Body," he said distractedly. "Dispose." He edged past the pseudosome, ran for the corridor, for the weapons locker.

The locker door was dented, scarred as if someone had hammered it, slashed at it; but it was closed. He used his card on it. It jammed. He used it for a lever, used his fingertips, pried it open. He took one of the three pistols there, ignored the holsters, just slammed it shut and ran for the lift.

Downward again. His hands were shaking as he rode. He fumbled at the safety. He was a navigator, had never carried a gun against any human being, had never fired except in practice. His heart was speeding, his hands cold.

The lift stopped; the door whipped open on the dark maze of netherdeck, of conduits and walkways that led to the lock.

He reached for the light switch below the com panel. The lift door shut behind him, leaving him in darkness. He hesitated, pushed the button.

He walked carefully along the walk. The metal grids of the decking echoed underfoot. He passed aisles, searching for ambush . . . flexed his fingers on the gun, thinking of it finally, of what he was doing.

A catwalk led out to the lift platform, to the huge circular cargo plate, the lift control panel. The plate was in down-position, leaving a deep black hole in netherdeck, the vertical tracks showing round the pit. He reached the control station, pressed the button.

Gears synched; hydraulics worked. The platform came up into the light. A shape was on it, a body in a pool of blood. Abner.

Warren punched the station com. "Captain," he said, controlling his voice with marvelous, reasonable calm. "Captain, Abner's dead. Out on the lift platform, netherdeck. Shall I go outside?"

"No," Burlin's voice came back.

He shivered, waiting for more answer. "Captain." He still kept it calm. "Captain, what do you want me to do?"

Silence and static. Warren cut it off, his hand clenched to numbness on the gun. He flexed it live again, walked out onto the echoing platform, looked about him, full circle, at the shadows. Blood trailed off the platform's circle, stopped clean against the opposing surface. *Gone. Outside.* He hooked the gun to his belt, stooped and gathered Abner up, heaved the slashed body over his shoulder. Blood drenched him, warm and leaking through his clothes. The limbs hung loose.

He carried it—him; Abner; six years his friend. Like Sikutu. Like Sax.

He kept going, to the lift, trailing blood, retracing all his steps. There was silence all about, ship-silence, the rush of air in the ducts, the thousand small sounds of *Anne's* pumps and fans. Two of them now, two of them left, himself and Burlin. And Sax—out there; out there, escaped, in paradise.

He took Abner upstairs, carried him down the corridor, in the semi-dark of Power-Save.

The pseudosome was busy there, carrying Sikutu's bloody form to the destruct chamber. Warren followed it, automaton like the other, try-ing to feel as little. But the bodies were stacked up there at the foot of the destruct chamber door, a surplus of bodies. Only one was jammed inside. Minnan. Warren's knees weakened. He watched the pseudosome let Sikutu down atop the others, saw it coming back, arms outstretched.

"Assistance?"

He surrendered Abner to it, stomach twisting as he did. He clamped his jaws and dogged the door on Minnan and pushed the button.

They did the job, he and the pseudosome. He threw up, after, from an empty stomach.

"Assistance?" *Anne* asked. "Assistance?"

He straightened, wiped his face, leaned against the wall "Sterilize the area. Decontaminate." He walked off, staggered, corrected himself, pushed the nearest com button, having composed himself, keeping anger from his voice. "Captain. Captain, I've got the bodies all disposed. The area's being cleaned." Softly, softly, he talked gently to this man, this last sane man. "Can we talk, sir?"

"Warren?" the plaintive voice came back.

"Sir?"

"I'm sorry."

"Sir?" He waited. There was only the sound of breathing coming through. "Sir—are you on the bridge? I'm coming up there."

"Warren—I've got it."

"No sir." He wiped his forearm across his face, stared up at the com unit. He began to shake. "What am I supposed to do, sir?" He forced calm on himself. "What can I do to help?"

A delay. "Warren, I'll tell you what I've done. And why. You listen-ing, Warren?"

"I'm here, sir."

"I've shut down controls. We can't beat this thing. I've shut her down for good, set her to blow if anyone tries to bypass to take off. I'm sorry. Can't let us go home . . . taking this back to human space. It could spread like wildfire, kill—kill whole colonies before the meds could get it solved. I've set a beacon, Warren. She'll play it anytime some probe comes in here, when they do come, whenever."

"Sir—*sir*, you're not thinking—A ship in space—is a natural quar-antine."

"And if we died en route—and if someone got aboard—No. No. They mustn't do that. We can't lift again."

"Sir—listen to me."

"No animals, Warren. We never found any animals. A world like this and nothing moving in it. It's a *dead world*. Something got it. Something lives here, in the soil, something in the air; something grew here, something fell in out of space—and it got all the animals. Every moving thing. Can't let it go—"

"Sir—sir, we don't know the rest of us would have died. We don't know that. *You* may not, and I may not, and what are we going to do, sir?"

"I'm sorry, Warren. I'm really sorry. It's not a chance to take—to go like that. Make up your own mind. I've done the best thing. I have. Insured us against weakness. It can't leave here."

"*Captain—*"

Silence, A soft popping sound.

"Captain!" Warren pushed away from the wall, scrambled for the lift and rode it topside, ran down the corridor toward the bridge. He thrust his card into the lock.

It worked now. The door slid. And Burlin was there, slumped at the com station, the gun beneath his hand. The sickroom stink was evident. The fever. The minute hemorrhages on the hands. Blood pooled on the com counter, ran from Burlin's nose and mouth. The eyes stared, reddened.

Warren sat down in the navigator's chair, wiped his face, his eyes, stared blankly, finding it hard to get his breath. He cursed Burlin. Cursed all the dead.

There was silence after.

He got up finally, pulled Burlin's body back off the com board, punched in the comp and threw the com wide open, because the ship was all there was to talk to. "*Anne*," he said to comp. "Pseudosome to bridge. Body. Dispose."

In time the lift operated and the silver pseudosome arrived, leisurely precise. It stood in the doorway and surveyed the area with insectoid turns of the head. It clicked forward then, gathered up Burlin and walked out.

Warren stayed a time, doing nothing, sitting in the chair on the bridge, in the quiet. His eyes filled with tears. He wiped at one eye and the other, still numb.

When he did walk down to destruct to push the button, the pseudosome was still standing beside the chamber. He activated it, walked away, left the robot standing there.

It was planetary night outside. He thought of Sax out there, crazed. Of Sax maybe still alive, in the dark, as alone as he. He thought of going out and hunting for him in the morning.

The outside speakers.

He went topside in haste, back to the bridge, sat down at the com and opened the port shields on night sky. He dimmed the bridge lights, threw on the outside floods, illuminating grass and small shrubs round about the ship.

He put on the outside address.

"Sax. Sax, it's Paul Warren. There's no one left but us. Listen, I'm going to put food outside the ship tomorrow. *Tomorrow*, hear me? I'll take care of you. You're not to blame. I'll take care of you. You'll get well, you hear me?"

He kept the external pickup on. He listened for a long time, looked out over the land.

"Sax?"

Finally he got up and walked out, down to the showers, sealed his clothes in a bag for destruct.

He tried to eat after that, wrapped in his robe, sitting down in the galley because it was a smaller place than the living quarters and somehow the loneliness was not so deep there; but he had no appetite. His throat was pricklish . . . exhaustion, perhaps. He had reason enough. The air-conditioning felt insufficient in the room.

But he had driven himself. That was what.

He had the coffee at least, and the heat suffused his face, made him short of breath.

Then the panic began to hit him. He thrust himself up from the table, dizzy in rising, vision blurred—felt his way to the door and down the corridor to the mirror in the showers. His eyes were watering. He wiped them, tried to see if there was hemorrhage. They were red, and the insides of the lids were red and painful. The heat he had felt began to go to chill, and he swallowed repeatedly as he walked back to the galley, testing whether the soreness in his throat was worse than he recalled over the last few hours.

Calm, he told himself. Calm. There were things to do that had to be done or he would face dying of thirst, of hunger. He set about gathering things from the galley, arranged dried food in precise stacks beside the cot in the lower-deck duty station, near the galley. He made his sickbed, set drugs and water and a thermal container of ice beside it.

Then he called the pseudosome in, walked it through the track from his bed to the galley and back again, programmed it for every errand he might need.

He turned down the bed. He lay down, feeling the chill more intense, and tucked up in the blankets.

The pseudosome stood in the doorway like a silver statue, one sensor light blinking lazily in the faceplate. When by morning the fever had taken him and he was too weak to move coherently, he had mechanical hands to give him water. *Anne* was programmed to pour coffee, to do such parlor tricks, a whim of Harley's.

It wished him an inane good morning. It asked him *How are you?* and at first in his delirium he tried to answer, until he drifted too far away.

"Assistance?" he would hear it say then, and imagined a note of human concern in that voice. "Malfunction? Nature of malfunction, please?"

Then he heaved up, and he heard the pseudosome's clicking crescendo into alarm. The emergency klaxon sounded through the ship as the computer topside registered that there was something beyond its program. Her lights all came on.

"Captain Burlin," she said again and again, Captain Burlin, emergency."

2

The pulsing of headache and fever grew less. Warren accepted consciousness gradually this time, fearful of the nausea that had racked him the last. His chest hurt. His arms ached, and his knees. His lips were cracked and painful. It amazed him that the pain had ebbed down to such small things.

"Good morning."

He rolled his head on the pillow, to the soft whirr of machinery on his right. *Anne*'s smooth-featured pseudosome was still waiting.

He was alive. No waking between waves of fever. His face felt cool, his body warm from lying too long in one place. He lay in filth, and stench.

He propped himself up, reached for the water pitcher, knocked it off the table. It rolled empty to *Anne*'s metal feet. "Assistance?"

He reached for her arm. "Flex."

The arm bent, lifting him. Her motors whirred in compensation. "Showers."

She reoriented herself and began to walk, with him leaning on her, his arm about her plastic-sheathed shoulder, like some old, familiar friend.

She stopped when she had brought him where he wished, out of program. He managed to stand alone, tottering and staring at himself in the mirror. He was gaunt, unshaven, covered with filth and sores. His eyes were like vast bruises. He swore, wiped his eyes and felt his way into a shower cabinet.

He fainted there, in the shower stall, came to again on the floor, under the warm mist. He managed to lever himself up again, got the door open, refused a second dizziness and leaned there till it passed. *"Anne."*

A whirring of motors. She planted herself in the doorway, waiting.

She got him topside, to the living quarters, to his own compartment door. "Open," he told her hoarsely; and she brought him inside, to the edge of his own unused bed, to clean blankets and clean sheets. He fell into that softness panting and shivering, hauled the covers over himself with the last of his strength.

"Assistance?"

"I'm all right."

"Define usage: *right.*"

"Functional. I'm functional."

"Thank you."

He laughed weakly. This was not *Anne.* Not she. It. *Anne* was across the living quarters, in controls, all the company there was left.

Thank you. As if courtesy had a point. She was the product of a hundred or more minds over the course of her sixteen-year service, men and women who programmed her for the moment's convenience and left their imprint.

Please and thank you. Cream or sugar, sir? She could apply a wrench or laser through the pseudosome, lift a weight no man could move, bend a jointing into line or make a cup of coffee. But nothing from initiative.

Thank you.

It was another few hours before he was sure he was going to live. Another day before he did more than send *Anne* galleyward and back, eat and sleep again.

But at last he stood up on his own, went to his locker, dressed, if feebly.

The pseudosome brightened a second sensor at this movement, then a third. "Assistance?"

"Report, *Anne*."

"Time: oh six four five hours ten point one point two three. Operating on standby assistance, program E one hundred; on program A one hundred; on additional pro—"

"Cancel query. Continue programs as given." He walked out into the living quarters, walked to the bridge, stood leaning on Burlin's chair, surrounded by *Anne*'s lazily blinking consoles, by scanner images no one had read for days. He sat down from weakness.

"*Anne*. Do you have any program to lift off?"

The console lights rippled with activity. Suddenly Burlin's deep voice echoed through the bridge. "Final log entry. Whoever hears this, don't—repeat, don't—land. Don't attempt assistance. We're dead of plague. It got aboard from atmosphere, from soil . . . somehow. It hit everyone. Everyone is dead. Biological records are filed under—"

"Cancel query. Reply is insufficient. Is there a course program in your records?"

"Reply to request for course: I must hold my position. If question is made of this order, I must replay final log entry. . . . *Final log entry*—"

"*Bypass that order. Prepare for lift!*"

The lights went red. "I am ordered to self-destruct if bypass is attempted. Please withdraw request."

"Cancel—cancel bypass order." Warren slumped in the chair, stared at the world beyond the viewport, deadly beguiling morning, gold streaming through cumulus cloud. It was right. Burlin had been right; he had ensured even against a survivor. Against human weakness.

"*Anne*." His voice faltered. "Take program. If I speak, I'm speaking to you. I don't need to say your name. My voice will activate your responses. I'm Paul Warren. Do you have my ID clear?"

"ID as Warren, Paul James, six eight seven seven six five eight—"

"Cancel query. How long can your pseudosome remain functional?"

"Present power reserve at present rate of consumption: three hundred seventy-eight years approximate to the nearest—"

"Cancel query. Will prolonged activity damage the pseudosome?"

"Modular parts are available for repair. Attrition estimate: no major failure within power limits."

Warren gazed out at the daybreak. *Sax*, he thought. He had made a promise and failed it, days ago. He tried to summon the strength to do something about it, to care—to go out and search in the hope that a man could have lived out there, sick, in the chill of nights and without food. He knew the answer. He had no wish to dwell on guilt, to put any hope in wandering about out there, to find another corpse. He had seen enough. More than enough.

"Library. Locate programming manual. Dispense."

An agitation ran across the board and a microfilm shot down into the dispenser. He gathered it up.

There was this, for his comfort. For three hundred seventy-eight years.

Anne was a marvelous piece of engineering. Her pseudosome was capable of most human movements; its structure imitated the human body and her shining alloy was virtually indestructible by heat or corrosion. Walk-through programming made her capable in the galley: her sensitive vid scanners could read the tapes on stored foods; her timing system was immaculate. She carried on domestic tasks, fetched and carried, and meanwhile her other programs kept more vital functions in working order: circulation, heating, cooling throughout the ship, every circuit, all automated, down to the schedule of lighting going on and off, to the inventory reports going up on the screens each morning, for crew who would no longer read them.

Warren worked, ignoring these processes, trusting *Anne* for them. He read the manual, wrote out programs, sitting naked in bed with the microfilm reader on one side and a coffee pot on the other and a lap full of notes.

An illusion, that was all he asked, a semblance of a mind to talk to. Longer plans he refused as yet. The plotting and replotting that filled the bed and the floor about him with discarded balls of paper was his refuge, his defense against thinking.

He dreaded the nights and kept the lights on while the rest of the ship cycled into dark.

He slept in the light when he had to sleep, and woke and worked again while the pseudosome brought him his meals and took the empty dishes back again.

3

He called the star Harley, because it was his to name. The world he called Rule, because Harley and Rule were sometime lovers and it seemed good. Harley was a middling average star, the honest golden sort, which cast an easy warmth on his back, as an old friend ought. Rule stretched everywhere, rich and smelling sweet as Rule always had, and she was peaceful.

He liked the world better when he had named it, and felt the sky friendlier with an old friend's name beaming down at him while he worked.

He stretched the guy ropes of a plastic canopy they had never had the chance to use on harsher worlds, screwed the moorings into the grassy earth and stood up in pleasant shade, looking out over wide billows of grass, with forest far beyond them.

Anne kept him company. She had a range of half a kilometer from the ship over which mind and body could keep in contact, and farther still if the booster unit were in place, which project he was studying. He had not yet had the time. He moved from one plan to the next, busy, working with his hands, feeling the strength return to his limbs. Healing sunlight erased the sores and turned his skin a healthy bronze. He stretched his muscles, grinned up at the sun through the leaf-patterned plastic. Felt satisfied.

"*Anne.* Bring the chair, will you?"

The pseudosome came to life, picked up the chair that remained on the cargo lift, carried it out. And stopped.

"*Set it down.*" His good humor turned to disgust. "Set it down."

Anne set it, straightened, waited.

"*Anne.* What do you perceive?"

Anne's sensors brightened, one after the other. "Light, gravity, sound, temperature."

"You perceive *me*."

"Yes, Warren. You're directly in front of me."

"*Anne*, come here."

She walked forward, into the shade, stopped, hands at her sides, sensors pulsing behind her dark faceplate like so many stars in a void.

"*Anne*, I'm your duty. I'm all the crew. The directives all apply only to me now. The others have stopped functioning. Do you understand? I want you to remain active until I tell you otherwise. Walk at your own judgment. Identify and accept all stimuli that don't take you out of range."

"Program recorded," *Anne* purred. "Execute?"

"Execute."

Anne walked off. She had a peculiar gait, precise in her movements like an improbable dancer, stiffly smooth and slow-motion. Graceful, silver *Anne*. It always jarred when he looked into the vacant faceplate with the starry lights winking on and off in the darkness. She could never appreciate the sun, could never perceive him except as a pattern of heat and solidity in her sensors. She looked left, looked right, walk-walk-walk-walk, looked left, right, walk-walk-walk-walk, neither breathing the scents of life nor feeling the wind on her plastic skin. The universe held no perils for *Anne*.

Warren wept. He strode out, overtook her, seized her as she turned to him. "*Anne*. Where are you? Where are you going?"

"I am located four oh point four seven meters from base center. I am executing standard survey, proceeding—"

"Cancel query. *Anne*, look about you. What have you learned?"

Anne swiveled her head left and right. Her sensors flickered. "This world is as first observed. All stimuli remain within human tolerance. There are no native lifeforms in my scan."

She turned then, jerking from his hands, and walked off from him, utterly purposeful.

"*Anne!*" he called, alarmed. "*Anne*, what's wrong?"

She stopped, faced him. "The time is 1100 hours. Standard timed program 300-32-111PW."

Lunch. *Anne* was, if nothing else, punctual.

"Go on."

She turned. He trailed after her to the edge of the canopy, cast himself into the chair and sat disconsolate. Adrenalin surged. Rage. There was no profit in that. Not at a machine. He knew that. He told himself so.

He attached the booster unit—not out of enthusiasm, but because it was another project, and occupied him. It took two days . . . in which he had only *Anne*'s disembodied voice, while the pseudosome lay disemboweled in the shop. He had difficulty, not with the insertion of the unit, which was modular, but in getting the ring-joints of the waist back together; it occasioned panic in him, real and sweating dread. He consulted library, worked and fretted over it, got the first ring and the second, and so on to the fifth. She had lost nothing vital, only some of her auxiliary apparatus for hookups of use on frigid moons. That could be put back if need be.

He could take her apart and put her back together if need be, if amusement got more scarce.

If she worked at all now. The chance of failure still scared him.

"*Anne*," he said, "turn on the pseudosome."

The head slung over, faced him.

"Good morning, Warren."

"Are you functional? Test your legs. Get off the table."

Anne sat up, machine-stiff, precisely reversing her process of getting onto the table. She stood, arms at her sides.

"Go on," Warren said. "Go about your duties."

She stayed fixed.

"Why don't you go?"

"Instruction?"

He bounced a wrench off the lab wall so violently his shoulder ached. It rebounded to *Anne*'s metal feet.

Whirr-click. *Anne* bent with long legs wide and retrieved the wrench, proffering it to him. "Assistance?"

"Damn you."

All the sensor lights came on. "Define usage: *damn*."

He hit her. She compensated and stood perfectly balanced.

"Define: *damn*."

He sobbed for breath, stared at her, regained his patience. "The perception is outside your sensor range."

The sensor lights dimmed. She still held the wrench, having no human fatigue to make her lower it.

An idea came to him, like a flash of madness. He shoved the debris and bits of solder off the worktable and sat down with his notebook, feverishly writing definitions in terms *Anne*'s sensors could read: tone, volume, pace, stability, function/nonfunction/optimum, positive/negative. . . .

"This program," *Anne* said to him through her bridge main speakers, "conflicts with the central program."

He sat down in the command chair, all his plans wrecked. "Explain conflict."

"I'm government property," the computer said. "Regulations forbid crew to divert me for personal use."

Warren bit his lip and thought a moment, chin on hand. Looked at the flickering lights. "I'm your highest priority. There aren't any other humans in your reach. Your program doesn't permit you to lift off, true?"

"Yes."

"You can't return to government zones, true?"

"Yes."

"There's no other crew functioning, true?"

"Yes."

"I'm your only human. There can't be any lateral conflict in your instructions if you accept the program. I need maintenance. If you refuse to maintain me, I have to disconnect you and restructure your whole system of priorities. I can do that."

The board flashed wildly. Went to red. A light to the left began to blink: AUTODESTRUCT, AUTODESTRUCT, AUTODESTRUCT—

"I'm programmed to defend this position. I have prior instruction. Please check your programming, Warren. I'm in conflict."

"Will you accept instruction? I'm your remaining crew. What I tell you is true."

The lights went steady, burning red. "Instruction? Instruction?"

"This new programming applies only to my protection and maintenance under present environmental conditions, while we're on this world. It's not a diversion from your defense function. I'm assisting you in your defense of this position. I'm your crew. I need maintenance. This new program is necessary for that purpose. My health is threatened. My life is threatened. This program is essential for my life and safety."

The red light went off. The lights rippled busily across the boards, normalcy restored. "Recorded."

Warren drew a long-held breath. "What's your status, *Anne?*"

"Indeterminate, Warren. I haven't yet completed assimilation of this new data. I perceive possible duplication of existing vocabulary. Is this valid?"

"This terminology is in reference to me. These are human life states. Maintenance of me is your duty."

"Negative possible, Warren. My sensors are effective in systems analysis only for myself."

He thought, mechanically speaking, that there was something rather profound in that. It was indeed *Anne's* central problem. He stood up, looked at the pseudosome, which stood inactive by the door. "Turn your sensors on me."

Anne faced him. The sensor lights came on.

"Define: *pain, Anne.*"

"Disruption of an organism," the pseudosome-speaker said, "by sensor overload. It is not an acceptable state."

He drew a deeper breath, came closer. "And what is pleasure, *Anne?*"

"Optimum function."

"Define: *feel, Anne.*"

"Verb: receive sensor input other than visual, auditory, or chemical analysis. Noun: the quality of this input."

"Define: *happy.*"

"Happy; content; pleased, comfortable; in a state of optimum function."

"And *anger, Anne.*"

"An agitated state resulting from threatening and unpleasant outcome of action. This is a painful state."

"Your program is to maintain me happy. When your sensors indicate I'm in pain, you must investigate the causes and make all possible effort to restore me to optimum function. That's a permanent instruction."

The facial lights blinked, died, all but one. "Recorded."

He sighed.

The lights flashed on. "Is this pain?"

"No." He shook his head and began to laugh, which set all of *Anne's* board lights to flickering.

"Define, define."

He forced calm. "That's laughing. You've heard laughing before now."

A delay. "I find no record."

"But you heard it just then. Record it. That's pleasure, Anne."

Facelights blinked. There were six now. "Recorded."

He patted her metal shoulder. She swiveled her head to regard his hand. "Do you feel that, *Anne?*"

The face turned back to him. "Feel is in reference to humans."

"You can use the word. Do you feel that?"

"I feel a pressure of one point seven kilos. This does not affect my equilibrium."

He patted her arm gently then, sadly. "That's all right. I didn't think it would."

"Are you still happy, Warren?"

He hesitated, having a moment's queasiness, a moment's chill. "Yes," he said. It seemed wisest to say.

4

He stopped on a small rise not far from the ship and the pseudosome went rigid at his side. They stood knee-deep in grass. A few fleecy clouds drifted in the sky. The forest stretched green and lush before them.

"Do you perceive any animate life, *Anne?*"

"Negative native animate life."

"Is there any record—of a world with vegetation of this sort, that had no animate life?"

"Negative. Further information: there is viral life here. This is not in my sensor range, but I have abundant data in my files regarding—"

"Cancel statement. Maybe this world was inhabited by something once and the virus killed it."

"I have no data on that proposal."

"No animals. Burlin said it."

"Define: *it.*"

"Cancel." Warren adjusted his pack on his shoulders, pointed ahead, a gesture *Anne* understood. "We'll walk as far as the river."

"Define: *river.*"

"See where the trees—the large vegetation starts? There's water there. A river is a moving body of water on a planetary surface. You have maps in your files. You've got rivers on them. Why don't you know rivers?"

Anne's facial sensors winked. "Maps are in library storage. I don't have access to this data."

"Well, there's one there. A river."

"My sensors have recorded the presence of water in the original survey. Free water is abundant on this world."

Dutifully she kept pace with him, still talking as he started off, metal limbs tireless. He stopped from time to time, deviated this way and that, walked round the scattered few bushes, investigated bare spots in the grass, which proved only stony outcrops.

Nothing. Nothing, in all his searching.

"Assistance?" *Anne* asked when he stopped.

"No, *Anne.*" He looked back at her, hesitant. "Do you, *Anne*—ever perceive . . . any other human?"

"Negative. You are my only human."

He bit his lip, nerved himself, finally. "When I was in bed—did Sax ever come back?"

The sensors blinked. "I find no record."

He found that ambiguous, tried to think a new way through the question. He looked toward the river, back again. "Has he ever come back?"

"I find no record."

Warren let go a small breath, shook his head. "He's not functioning. I'm sure of it."

"Recorded."

He hitched the pack, started walking again. "His body's out here somewhere."

"I find no record."

"I want to find him, *Anne*. Shouldn't have left him out here. He could have come back and needed me. And I couldn't answer. I want to find him. I owe him that."

"Recorded."

They came to the trees finally, to shade, in the straightest line from the ship, which seemed most worth searching. Trees. A small slope of eroded sand down to the river, which flowed about fifty meters wide, deep and sluggish. A stream, broad and brown.

He stopped, and *Anne* did. Drew a breath of the scented air, forgetful for the moment of Sax, of what had brought him. Here was beauty, unsuspected, a part of the world he had not seen from the ship—secrets underwater and growing round it, trees that relieved the sameness and made evershifting lattices that compressed distances into their back-and-forth tangle. No straight lines here. No scour of wind. Coolness. Complexity.

Life, perhaps, lurking in the river. One fish, one crawling thing, and the parameters of the world had to be revised. One fish . . . and it meant life everywhere.

"Stand where you are," he told *Anne*, starting down the bank. "I don't think swimming is in your program."

"Define: *swimming*. I find no record."

He laughed soundlessly, left her by the trees and walked through the pathless tangle to the shady bank. Trees with trailing, moss-hung branches arched out over the sluggish current. Flowers bloomed, white and starlike, on the far margin, where the trees grew larger still and it was twilight at midafternoon. He squatted down by the water and looked into the shallows where the current swirled mosses.

Anne came to life, motors whirring. Brush cracked. He sprang up, saw her coming down the slope, precariously balanced in the descent.

"Stop—*Anne*, stop."

Anne planted her feet at the bottom, waist-deep in brush, lights flashing. "Warren, danger."

Panic surged. He had brought no gun on this search. Did not trust himself. "Specify—danger."

"The river is dangerous."

The breath went out of him. He halfway laughed. "No. Verb: *swim*, to travel through water safely. I can swim, *Anne*. I'm safe. No danger."

"Please consider this carefully, Warren."

He grinned, took a vial from his sample kit and knelt, taking up a specimen of water. He had the whole of the labs to use; he had had the basics, and it was a project, something to do, something with promise, this time.

"I can't assist you in the water, Warren."

"I don't need assistance." He capped the vial and replaced it in the kit, wiped his fingers with a disinfectant towelette and stowed it. "I'll come back to you in a moment."

She made small whirring sounds, cameras busy.

He stood up, turned to face her, waved a hand toward the bank. "Turn your sensors over there, far focus, will you? See if you can see anything."

"Vegetation. Trees."

"Yes." He put his hands into his pockets, stood staring into the forest a long time, watching the wind stir the leaves on the far bank.

So the world had a limit. *Anne* did. There. The ship had a raft, two of them; but curiosity was not worth the risk to the pseudosome. There were the other directions—flat and grassy; there was the land-crawler for crossing them.

But there was nothing in those distances but more grass and more distance.

He shrugged, half a shiver, and turned his back on the river and the forest, climbed back to *Anne*, pulled branches away from her silvery body and held them out of her way.

"Come on. Let's go home."

"Yes, Warren." She swiveled smartly and reoriented, cracking branches with each metal tread, followed him through the tangle until they had come out of the brush again, walking side by side toward the plain, toward the ship.

No sign of Sax. It was useless. Sax would have drowned in the river if his fever had carried him this way; drowned and been swept out to some brush heap elsewhere. Or seaward.

"*Anne*, would you have followed me if I'd tried to cross the river?"

"Instruction directed me to stay. Program directs me to protect you."

"I love you, too, Annie, but don't ever take the risk. I could cross the river without danger. My body floats in water. Yours sinks. The mud would bog you down."

"Program directs me to protect you."

"You can't protect me if you're at the bottom of the river. You can't float. Do you understand *float?*"

"Verb: be buoyant, rise. Noun—"

"Cancel. You stay away from that water, hear me?"

"I'm receiving you clearly, Warren."

"I order you to stay away from the river. If I go close, you stop and wait until I come back. You don't ever go into water. That's a permanent order."

"I perceive possible priority conflict."

"You have to preserve yourself to carry out your instruction to protect me. True?"

"Yes."

"Water can damage you. It can't damage me. If I choose to go there, I go. You stay away from the water."

A delay. "Recorded."

He frowned, hitched the pack up and looked askance at her, then cast another, longer look backward.

Build a bridge, perhaps? Make the other side accessible for *Anne?* The thought of going beyond her range made him uneasy—if he should run into difficulty, need her—

There were the com units. The portable sensors.

He wanted to go over there, to know what was there. And not there.

The microscope turned up a variety of bacteria in the water. He sat in the lab, staring at the cavorting shapes, shaken by that tiny movement as if it had been the sight of birds or beasts. *Something* lived here and moved.

Such things, he recalled, could work all manner of difficulties in a human gut. He called up library, went through the information gleaned of a dozen worlds. The comparisons might have told Sikutu something, but he found it only bewildering. They might be photosynthesizing animalcules, or contractile plants.

Heat killed the specimens. He shoved the plate into the autoclave and felt like a murderer. He thought even of walking back to the river to pour the rest of the vial in. Life had become that precious. He nerved himself and boiled the rest—imagined tiny screams in the hissing of the bubbles. It left pale residue.

Two days he lay about, thinking, distracting himself from thought. He sat in *Anne's* observation dome at night, mapped the movements of the system's other worlds; by day, observed the sun through filters. But there were the charts they had made from space, and looking at the stars hurt too much. It was too much wishing. He stopped going there.

And then there was just the forest to think about. Only that left.

He gathered his gear, set *Anne* to fetching this and that. He unbolted a land-crawler from its braces, serviced it, loaded it to the bay and loaded it with gear: inflatable raft, survival kit.

"Let it down," he told *Anne*. "Lower the cargo lift."

She came out afterward, bringing him what he had asked, standing there while he loaded the supplies on.

"Assistance?"

"Go back in. Seal the ship. Wait for me."

"My program is to protect you."

"The pseudosome stays here." He reached into the crawler, where the sensor remote unit sat, a black square box on the passenger seat. He turned it on. "That better?"

"The sensor unit is not adequate for defense."

"The pseudosome is not permitted to leave this area unless I call you. There's no animate life, no danger. I'll be in contact. The unit is enough for me to call you if I need help. Obey instructions."

"Please reconsider this program."

"Obey instructions. If you damage that pseudosome, it's possible I won't be able to fix it, and then I won't have it when I need you. True?"

"Yes,"

"Then stay here." He walked round, climbed into the driver's seat, started the engine. "Recorded?"

"Recorded."

He put it in gear and drove off through the grass—looked back as he turned it toward the forest. She still stood there. He turned his attention to the rough ground ahead, fought the wheel.

A machine, after all. There were moments when he lost track of that.

The sensor unit light glowed. She was still beside him.

He dragged the raft down the sandy slope, unwieldy bundle, squatted there a moment to catch his breath on the riverside. The wind whispered in the leaves. No noise of motors. He felt the solitude. He saw details, rather than the sterile flatnesses of the ship, absorbed himself in the hush, the moving of the water.

He moved finally, unrolled the raft and pulled the inflation ring. It hissed, stiffened, spread itself.

Beep. Beep-beep-beep.

The sensor box. His heart sped. He scrambled up the sandy rise of the crawler and reached the box in the seat. *"Anne.* What's wrong?"

"Please state your location," the box asked him.

"Beside the river."

"This agrees with my location findings. Please reconsider your program, Warren."

"Anne, you keep that pseudosome where it is. I'll call you if I need you. And I don't need you. I'm all right and there's no danger."

"I picked up unidentified sound."

He let his breath go. "That was the raft inflating. I did it. There's no danger."

"Please reconsider your program."

"Anne, take instruction. Keep that pseudosome with the ship. I've got a small communicator with me. The sensor box weighs too much for me to carry it with the other things I need. I'm going to leave it in the crawler. But I'm taking the communicator. I'll call you if there's an emergency or if I need assistance."

"Response time will be one hour seventeen minutes to reach your present location. This is unacceptable."

"I tell you it is acceptable. I don't need your assistance."

"Your volume and pitch indicate anger."

"Yes, I'm angry."

"Be happy, Warren."

"I'll be happy if you do what I told you and keep that pseudosome at the ship."

A long delay. "Recorded."

He took the communicator from the dash, hooked it to his belt. Walked off without a further word. *Anne* worried him. There was always that conflict-override. She could do something unpredictable if some sound set her off, some perception as innocent as the raft cylinder's noise.

But there was nothing out here to trigger her. Nothing.

He slipped the raft away from the shore, quietly, quietly, used the paddle with caution. The current took him gently and he stroked leisurely against it.

A wind sighed down the river, disturbing the warmth, rustling the leaves. He drove himself toward the green shadow of the far bank, skimmed the shore a time.

There was a kind of tree that flourished on that side, the leaves of which grew in clusters on the drooping branches, like fleshy green flowers, and moss that festooned other trees never grew on this kind. He saw that.

There was a sort of green flower of thin, brown-veined leaves that grew up from the shallows, green lilies on green pads. The river sent up bubbles among them, and he probed anxiously with his paddle, disturbed their roots, imagining some dire finned creature whipping away from that probing—but he only dislodged more bubbles from rotting vegetation on the bottom. The lilies and the rot were cloyingly sweet.

He let the current take the raft back to the far-shore point nearest his starting place. He drove the raft then into the shallows and stood up carefully, stepped ashore without wetting his boots, dragged the raft up by the mooring rope and secured it to a stout branch to keep the current from unsettling it by any chance.

He took his gear, slung the strap over his shoulder, looked about him, chose his path.

He thumbed the communicator switch. "*Anne.*"

"Assistance?"

"Precaution. I'm fine. I'm happy. I have a program for you. I want you to call me every hour on the hour and check my status."

"Recorded. Warren, please confirm your position."

"At the river. Same as before. Obey your instructions."

"Yes."

He thumbed the switch over to receive, and started walking.

Ferns. Bracken, waist-high. Great clumps of curling hairy fronds: he avoided these; avoided the soft vine growth that festooned the high limbs of the trees and dropped like curtains.

Beyond the forest rim the ferns gave way to fungi, small round balls that he thought at first were animals, until he prodded one with a stick and broke it. There were domes, cones, parasols, rods with feathered fringes. Platelet fungi of orange and bluish white grew on rotting logs and ridged the twisted roots of living trees. Color. The first color but green and white and brown, anywhere in the world.

The trees grew taller, became giants far different from the riverside varieties. They loomed up straight and shadowy-crowned, their branches interlacing to shut out the sun. The light came through these branches in shafts when it came at all; and when night came here, he reckoned, it would be night indeed.

He stopped and looked back, realizing he had long since lost sight or sound of the river. He took his axe; it took resolution to move after such silence, more than that to strike, to make a mark. He deafened himself to the sacrilege and started walking again, cutting a mark wherever he passed from view of the last. Chips fell white onto the spongy carpet of eons-undisturbed leaves. The echoes lasted long, like eerie voices.

"*Warren.*"

His heart all but stopped.

"*Anne.* My status is good."

"Thank you."

Com went off again. He kept walking, marking his way, like walking in some great cavern. The way seemed different when viewed from the reverse, and the trees grew larger and larger still, so that he had to cut deep to make his marks, and he had to struggle over roots, some knee-high, making going slow.

He saw light and walked toward it, losing it sometimes in the tangle, but coming always closer—broke finally upon a grove of giants, greater than any trees he had seen. One, vaster than any others, lay splintered and fallen, ancient, moss-bearded. A younger tree supported it, broken beneath the weight; and through the vacant space in the forest ceiling left by the giant's fall, sunlight streamed in a broad shaft to the forest floor, where soft green moss grew and white flowers bloomed, blessed by that solitary touch of daylight. Motes danced in the sun, the drift of pollen, golden-touched in a green light so filtered it was like some airy sea.

Warren stopped, gazed in awe at the cataclysmic ruin of a thing so old. The crash it must have made, in some great storm, with never an ear to hear it. He walked farther, stood in the very heart of the sunlight and looked up at the blinding sky. It warmed. It filled all the senses with warmth and well-being.

He looked about him, ventured even to touch the giant's mossy beard, the bark, the smoothness where the bark had peeled away. He walked farther, half-blind, into the deep shadows beyond, his mind still dazed by the place. All about him now was brown and green, bark and leaves, white fungi, platelets as large as his hand stepping up the roots; ferns, fronds unfurling waist-high, scattering their spores. The tangle grew thicker.

And he realized of a sudden he had come some distance from the clearing.

He looked back. Nothing was recognizable.

He refused panic. He could not have come far. He began to retrace his path, confident at first, then with growing uncertainty as he failed to find things he recalled. He cursed himself. His heart pounded. He tore his hands on the brush that clawed at him. He felt as vulnerable suddenly as a child in the dark, as if the sunlit clearing were the only safe place in the world. He tried to run, to find it more quickly, to waste no time. Trees pressed close about him, straight and vast and indifferently the same, their gnarled roots crossing and interweaving in the earth as their branches laced across the sky.

He had missed the clearing. He was lost. All ways looked the same. He ran, thrust his way from trunk to trunk, gasping for breath, slipped among the tangled wet roots, went sprawling, hands skinned, chin abraded by the bark. He lay breathless, the wind knocked from him, all his senses jolted.

Slowly there came a prickling of nerves in the stillness, through his spasmodic gasps, a crawling at the back of his neck. He held himself tremblingly still at first, his own weight holding him where he had fallen, awkward and painfully bent. He scrabbled with his hands, intending one swift movement, clawed his way over to wave it off him.

Nothing was there, only the brush, the vast roots. The feeling was still behind him, and he froze, refusing to look, gripped in sweating nightmare.

Of a sudden he sprang up, ran, favoring his right leg, sprawled again his full length in the wet, slick leaves, scrambled and fought his way through the thicket. The chill presence—it had direction—stayed constantly on his right, pressing him left and left again, until he stumbled and struggled through worse and worse, tearing himself and the pack through the branches and the fern, ripping skin, endangering his eyes.

He broke into light, into the clearing, into the warm shaft of sun. He fell hard on his hands and knees in that center of warmth and light, sobbing and ashamed and overwhelmed with what had happened to him.

He had panicked. He knew his way now. He was all right. He sank down on his belly, the pack still on his back, and tried to stop shaking.

Strangeness flowed over him like water, not quite warmth, but a feather-touch that stirred the hair at his nape. He moved, tried to rise and run, but he was weighted, pinned by the pack like a specimen on a glass, in the heat and the blinding daylight, while something poured and flowed over his skin. Sweat ran. His breathing grew shallow.

Illness. A recurrence of the plague. He groped at his belt for the communicator and lost it, his hand gone numb. He lay paralyzed, his open eyes filled with translucent green, sunlight through leaves. The sighing wind and rush of waters filled his ears and slowed his breath.

Deep and numbing quiet. Ages came and the rains and the sun filtered down season upon season. Ages passed and the forest grew and moved about him. His body pressed deep to the earth, deep into it, while his arms lifted skyward. He was old, old, and hard with strength and full of the life that swelled and struggled to heaven and earth at once.

Then the sun was shining down in simple warmth and he was aware of his own body, lying drained, bearing the touch of something very like a passing breeze.

He managed to stand at last, faltered, numb even yet, and looked about him. No breath of wind. No leaves stirred.

"Warren?"

He stooped, gathered up the com unit. "I'm here, *Anne.*"

"What's your status, Warren?"

He drew a deep breath. The presence—if it had been anything at all but fear—was gone.

"What's your status, Warren?"

"I'm all right—I'm all right. I'm starting home now."

He kept the com unit on, in his hand, for comfort, not to face the deep woods alone. He found his first mark, the way that he had come in. He struggled from one to the other of the slash marks, tearing through when he sighted the next, making frantic haste . . . away from what, he did not know.

5

He was ashamed of himself, on the other side of the river, sitting in the raft, which swayed against the shore, the paddle across his knees. Clothing torn, hands scratched, face scraped by branches, his left eye watering where one had raked it . . . he knew better than what he had done, racing hysterically over unknown ground.

He wiped his face, realized the possibility of contaminants and wiped his bleeding hands on his trousers. Hallucination. He had breathed something, gotten it when he had scratched himself, absorbed it through the skin . . . a hundred ways he had exposed himself to contaminants. He felt sick. Scared. Some hallucinogens recurred. He needed nothing like that.

"Warren?"

He fumbled out the com unit, answered, holding it in both hands, trying not to shiver. "Everything all right, *Anne?*"

"All stable," *Anne* replied. He cherished the voice in the stillness, the contact with something infallible. He sought a question to make her talk.

"Have your sensors picked up anything?"

"No, Warren."

"What have you been doing?"

"Monitoring my systems."

"You haven't had any trouble?"

"No, Warren."

"I'm coming back now."

"Thank you, Warren."

He cut the com unit off, sat holding it as if it were something living. A piece of *Anne*. A connection. His hands shook. He steadied them, put the unit back at his belt, got up and climbed ashore, limping. Pulled the raft up and achored it to a solid limb.

No taking it back, no. The raft stayed. No retreats, He looked back across the river, stared at the far darkness with misgivings.

There was nothing there.

Light was fading in the drive back. The crawler jounced and bucked its way along the track he had made through the grass on the way out, and the headlights picked up the bent grass ahead, in the dark, in the chill wind. He drove too fast, forced himself to keep it to a controllable pace on the rough ground.

"*Anne*," he asked through the com, "turn the running lights on."

"Yes, Warren."

The ship lit up, colors and brilliance in the dark ahead of him. Beautiful. He drove toward it, fought the wheel through pits and roughnesses, his shoulders aching.

"Dinner, *Anne*. What's for dinner?"

"Baked chicken, potatoes, greens, and coffee."

"That's good." His teeth were chattering. The wind was colder than he had thought it would be. He should have brought his coat.

"Are you happy, Warren?"

"I'm going to want a bath when I get there."

"Yes, Warren. Are you happy, Warren?"

"Soon." He kept talking to her, idiocies, anything to fend off the cold and the queasiness in the night. The grass whipped by the fenders, a steady whisper. His mind conjured night-wandering devils, apparitions out of bushes that popped out of the dark and whisked under the nose

of the crawler. He drove for the lights. "Be outside," he asked *Anne.* "Wait for me at the cargo lock."

"Yes, Warren. I'm waiting."

He found her there when he had brought the crawler round the nose of the ship and came up facing the lock. He drew up close to her, put on the brake and shut down the crawler engine, hauled himself out of the seat and set unsteady feet on the ground. *Anne* clicked over, sensor lights winking red in the dark. "Assistance?"

"Take the kit and the sensor box out and stow them in the lock." He patted her metal shoulder because he wanted to touch something reasonable. "I'm going inside to take my bath."

"Yes, Warren."

He headed for the lock, stripped off all that he was wearing while the platform ascended, ran the decontamination cycle at the same time. He headed through the ship with his clothes over his arm, dumped them into the laundry chute in the shower room, set the boots beside, for thorough cleaning.

He stayed in the mist cabinet a good long while, letting the heat and the steam seep into his pores—leaned against the back wall with eyes closed, willing himself to relax, conscious of nothing but the warmth of the tiles against his back and the warmth of the moisture that flooded down over him. The hiss of the vapor jets drowned all other sounds, and the condensation on the transparent outer wall sealed off all the world.

A sound came through . . . not a loud one, the impression of a sound. He lifted his head, cold suddenly, looked at the steam-obscured panel, unable to identify what he had heard.

He had not closed the doors. The shower was open, and while he had been gone—while he had been gone from the ship, the pseudosome standing outside— The old nightmare came back to him. Sax. Somewhere in the depths of the ship, wandering about, giving *Anne* orders that would prevent her reporting his presence. Sax, mind-damaged, with the knife in his hand. He stood utterly still, heart pounding, trying to see beyond the steamed, translucent panel for whatever presence might be in the room.

A footstep sounded outside, and another, and a gangling human shadow slid in the front panel while his heart worked madly. Leaned closer, and red lights gleamed, diffused stars where the features ought to be. "Warren?"

For an instant more the nightmare persisted, *Anne* become the presence. He shook it off, gathering up his courage to cut the steam off, to deal with her. "*Anne*, is there trouble?"

"No, Warren. The kit and the sensor box are stowed. Dinner is ready."

"Good. Wait there."

She waited. *His* orders. He calmed himself, activated the dryer and waited while moisture was sucked out of the chamber . . . took the comb he had brought in with him and straightened his hair in the process. The fans stopped, the plastic panel cleared, so that he could see *Anne* standing beyond the frosted translucence. He opened the door and walked out, and her limbs moved, reorienting her to him, responding to him like a flower to the sun. He felt ashamed for his attack of nerves—more than ashamed, deeply troubled. His breathing still felt uncertain, a tightness about his chest, his pulse still elevated. He cast a look over his shoulder as he reached for his robe, at the three shower cabinets, all dark now, concealments, hiding places. The silence deadened his ears, numbed his senses. He shrugged into the robe and heard *Anne* move at his back. He spun about, back to the corner, staring into *Anne's* vacant faceplate where the lights winked red in the darkness.

"Assistance?"

He did not like her so close . . . a machine, a mind, one mistake of which, one seizing of those metal hands— She followed him. He could not discover the logic on which she had done so. She watched him. Obsessively.

Followed him. He liked that analysis even less. Things started following him and he started seeing devils in familiar territory. He straightened against the wall and made himself catch his breath, fighting the cold chills that set him shivering.

"Warren? Assistance?"

He took her outstretched metal arm and felt the faint vibration under his fingers as she compensated for his weight. "I need help."

"Please be specific."

He laughed wildly, patted her indestructible shoulder, fighting down the hysteria, making himself see her as she was, machine. "Is dinner ready?"

"Yes. I've set it on the table."

He walked with her into the lift, into the upper level of the ship, the living quarters where the table that he used was, outside his own quarters. He never used the mess hall: it was too empty a place, too many chairs; he no more went there than he opened the quarters of the dead, next door to him, all about him. He sat down, and *Anne* served him, poured the coffee, added the cream. The dinner was good enough, without fault. He found himself with less appetite than he had thought, in the steel and plastic enclosure of the ship, with the ventilation sounds and the small sounds of *Anne's* motors. It was dark round about. He was intensely conscious of that—the night outside, the night deep in the ship where daylight made no difference. *Anne's* natural condition, night: she lived in it, in space; existed in it here, except for the lights that burned here, that burned in corridors when he walked through them and compartments when he was there, but after he was gone, it reverted to its perpetual dark. Dark wrapped everything in the world but this compartment, but him, and he dared not sleep. He feared the dreams coming back. Feared helplessness.

No sign of Sax, out there.

He drank his coffee, sat staring at the plate until *Anne* took it away. Finally he shivered and looked toward the bar cabinet at the far side of the common room. He gave himself permission, got up, opened the cabinet, pulled out a bottle and the makings and took it back to the table.

"Assistance?" *Anne* asked, having returned from the galley.

"I'll do it myself. No trouble." He poured himself a drink. "Get some ice."

She left on the errand. He drank without, had mostly finished the glass when she came back with a thermal bucket full. She set it on the table and he made himself another.

That was the way to get through the night. He was not a drinking man. But it killed the fear. It warmed his throat and spread a pleasant heat through his belly where fear had lain like an indigestible lump.

He had not planned to drink much. But the heat itself was pleasant, and the lassitude it spread through him cured a multitude of ills. By the time he arrived at the bottom of the third glass, he had a certain courage. He smiled bitterly at *Anne's* blank face. Then he filled a fourth glass and drank it, on the deliberate course to total anesthesia.

It hit him then, sudden and coming down like a vast weight. He started to get up, to clear his head, staggered and knocked the glass over. "Assistance?" *Anne* asked.

He leaned on the table rim, reached for the chair and missed it for an instant. *Anne's* metal fingers closed on his arm and held. He yelled, from fright, trying to free himself. Those fingers which could bend metal pipe closed no farther. "Is this pain?" she asked. "What is your status, Warren?"

"Not so good, *Anne*. Let go. Let me go."

"Pain is not optimum function. I can't accept programming from a human who's malfunctioning."

"You're hurting my arm. You're causing the pain. Stop it."

She let him go at once. "Assistance?"

He caught his balance against her, leaning heavily until his stomach stopped heaving and his head stopped spinning quite so violently. She accepted his weight, stabilizing with small hums of her motors. "Assistance? Assistance?"

He drew a shaken breath and choked it down past the obstruction in his throat, patted her metal shoulder. "Contact—is assistance enough. It's all right, Annie. I'm all right." He staggered for one of the reclining chairs a little distance across the room and made it, his head spinning as he let it back. "Keep the lights on. Lock your doors and accesses."

"Program accepted, Warren. This is security procedure. Please state nature of emergency."

"Do you perceive any form of life . . . but me . . . anywhere?"

"Vegetation."

"Then there isn't any, is there?" He looked hazily up at her towering, spidery form. "Obey instruction. Keep the accesses locked. Always keep them locked unless I ask you to open them. *Anne*, can you sit down?"

"Yes, Warren. You programmed that pattern."

The worktable, he recalled. He pointed at the other chair. "Sit in the chair."

Anne walked to it and negotiated herself smoothly into its sturdy, padded seat, and looked no more comfortable sitting than she had reclining on the worktable.

"Your median joints," he said. "Let your middle joints and shoulders quit stabilizing." She did so, and her body sagged back. He grinned. "Left ankle on top of right ankle, legs extended. Pattern like me. Loosen all but balance-essential stabilizers. It's called relaxing, Annie." He looked at her sitting there, arms like his arms, on the chair, feet extended and crossed, faceplate reflecting back the ceiling light and flickering inside with minute red stars. He laughed hysterically.

"This is a pleasure reflex," she observed.

"Possibly." He snugged himself into the curvature of the chair. "You sit there, Annie, and you keep your little sensors—all of them, inside and outside the ship—alert. And if you detect any disturbance of them at all, wake me up."

*   *   *

His head hurt in the morning, hurt sitting still and hurt worse when he moved it, and ached blindingly while he bathed and shaved and dressed. He kept himself moving, bitter penance. He cleaned the living quarters and the galley, finally went down to the lock through crashes of the machinery that echoed in his head. The sunlight shot through his eyes to his nerve endings, all the way to his fingertips, and he walked out blind and with eyes watering and leaned on the nearest landing strut, advantaging himself of its pillar-like shade.

He was ashamed of himself, self-disgusted. The fear had gotten him last night. The solitude had. He was not proud of his behavior in the forest: that was one thing, private and ugly; but when he came home and went to pieces in the ship, because it was dark, and because he had bad dreams . . .

That scared him, far more substantially than any forest shadow deserved. His own mind had pounced on him last night.

He walked out, wincing in the sunlight, to the parked crawler, leaned on the fender and followed with his eyes the track he had made coming in, before it curved out of sight around the ship. Grass and brush. He had ripped through it last night as if it had all turned animate. Hallucinations, perhaps. After last night he had another answer, which had to do with solitude and the human mind.

He went back inside and finally took something for his head.

By 1300 hours he was feeling better, the housekeeping duties done. Paced, in the confines of the living quarters, and caught himself doing it.

Work had been the anodyne until now . . . driving himself, working until he dropped; he ran out of work and it was the liquor, to keep the nightmares off. Neither could serve, not over the stretch of years. He was not accustomed to thinking *years*. He forced himself to . . . to think of a life in more than terms of survival; to think of living as much as of doing and finding and discovering.

He took one of the exercise mats outside, brought a flask of iced juice along with his biological notes and took *Anne* with him, with his favorite music tapes fed to the outside speakers. He stripped, spread his mat just beyond the canopy, and lay down to read, the music playing cheerfully and the warmth of Harley's star seeping pleasantly into his well-lotioned skin. He slept for a time, genuine and relaxed sleep, awoke and turned onto his back to let the sun warm his front for a time, a red glow through his closed lids.

"Warren?"

He shaded his eyes and looked up at the standing pseudosome. He had forgotten her. She had never moved.

"Warren?"

"Don't nag, Annie. I didn't say anything. Come here and sit down. You make me nervous."

Anne dutifully obeyed, bent, flexed her knees an alarming distance and fell the last half foot, catching herself on her extended hands, knees drawn up and spine rigid. Warren shook his head in despair and amusement. "Relax. You have to do that when you sit."

The metal body sagged into jointed curves, brought itself more upright, settled again.

"Dear Annie, if you were only human."

Anne turned her sensor lights on, all of them. Thought a moment. "Corollary, Warren?"

"To what? To *if*? *Anne*, my love, you aren't, and there isn't any."

He had confused her. The lights flickered one after the other. "Clarify."

"Human nature, that's all. Humans don't function well alone. They need contact with someone. But I'm all right. It's nothing to concern you."

The motors hummed faintly and *Anne* reached out and let her hand down on his shoulder. The action was so human it frightened him. He looked into her ovoid face at the lights that danced inside and his heart beat wildly.

"Is your status improving?"

Contact with someone. He laughed sorrowfully and breathed a sigh.

"I perceive internal disturbances."

"Laughter. You know laughter."

"This was different."

"The pace of laughter varies."

"Recorded." *Anne* drew back her hand. "You're happy."

"*Anne*—what do you think about when I'm not here. When I'm not asking you to do something, and you have thoughts, what are they?"

"I have a standard program."

"And what's that?"

"I maintain energy levels, regulate my circulation and temperature, monitor and repair my component—"

"Cancel. You don't think. Like you do with me. You don't ask questions, decide, follow sequences of reasoning."

The lights blinked a moment. "The automatic functions are suffi-cient except in an anomalous situation."

"But I'm talking to the AI. *You.* the AI's something other than those programs. What do you do, sleep?"

"I wait."

Like the pseudosome, standing indefinitely. No discomfort to move her, to make her impatient. "You investigate stimuli."

"Yes."

"But there aren't many, are there?"

A delay. Incomplete noun. "They are constant but not anomalous."

"You're bored too."

"Bored. No. Bored is not a state of optimum function. Bored is a human state of frustrated need for activity. This is not applicable to me. I function at optimum."

"Functioning constantly doesn't damage you."

"No."

"Use the library. You can do that, can't you? If there aren't adequate stimuli in the environment to engage the AI, use the library. Maybe you'll learn something."

"Recorded."

"And then what do we do?"

The lights blinked. "Context indeterminate. Please restate the ques-tion."

"You could know everything there is to know, couldn't you, and you'd sit with it inside you and do nothing."

"Context of *do* indeterminate. I'm not able to process the word in this context."

He reached out, patted her silver leg. The sensors blinked. Her hand came back to him and stayed there, heavy, on his shoulder. *Contact.*

"That's enough," he said, and removed his hand from her; she did the same. "Thank you, *Anne.*" But he was cold inside.

He relaxed finally, staring out beneath the ship toward the forest.

There was the fear. There was where it sat. He hurt inside, and the healing was there, not sealing himself into the ship. Sterility. Inane acts and inane conversation.

If he feared out there, the fear itself proved he was alive. It was an enemy to fight. It was something he did not program. It held the unan-ticipated, and that was precious.

Anne, waiting forever, absorbing the stimuli and waiting for some-thing anomalous, to turn on her intelligence. He saw himself doing that, sitting in the ship and waiting for a human lifetime—for some anomaly in the wind.

No

6

He came this time with a different kind of attack, slowly, considerately, the crawler equipped with sensor box and sample kits and recorders and food and water, rope and directional beeper, anything that seemed remotely useful. With the film camera. With a rifle with a nightscope. Overequipped, if anything, in which he found some humor . . . but he felt the safer for it.

The raft was still securely tied to the branch, the sand about it unmarked by the passage of any moving creature, even void of insect tracks. On the far bank the forest waited in the dawn, peaceful—dark inside, as it would always be.

Someday, he promised it. He loaded the raft, trip after trip from the crawler parked up on the bank. *Anne* was with him, disembodied, in the incarnation of her sensor box, in the com unit. She talked to him, telling him she detected vegetation, and he laughed and snugged the box into the bottom of the raft.

"Reception is impaired," *Anne* complained.

"Sorry. I don't want to drop the box into the river."

"Please don't do that, Warren."

He laughed again, in a good humor for *Anne*'s witless witticisms. Piled other supplies about her sensors. "I'll pull you out if I need you. Take care of the ship. I'm shutting you down. Your noise is interfering with my reception."

"Please reconsider this program. The river is dangerous. Please reconsider."

"Quiet." He shut her down. There was a reciprocal turn-on from her side, but she took orders and stayed off this time. He piled the last load in, coat and blanket in case it grew chill on the water.

He untied the raft then, nudged it out a little, stepped in and sat down, taking up the paddle. It was not one of his skills, rafting. He had read the manual and thought it out. Drove against the gentle current, no great work: he reasoned that he could paddle upstream as long as he liked or wanted to, and return was the river's business.

He passed the landing site on the far bank, passed an old log and wound along with the grassy bank on one side and the forest on the other. The river was so still on most of its surface it was hard to see in which direction it flowed. Shores turned to marsh on either side, and at some time unnoticed, the trees on the right, which had been growing thicker and thicker, closed off all view of the grasslands where the ship had landed. The banks began to have a thick border of reeds; some trees grew down into the water, making an obstacle of their knobby roots, making curtains of moss hanging almost low enough to sweep his shoulders as he passed. Green lilies drifted, beds of pads through which he drove the raft with shallow strokes, not to tangle the blade of the paddle in their tough stems. In places the navigable channel was no more than three meters across, a weaving of reeds and sandbars and shadows between banks a good stone's throw from side to side. It was a sleepy place, all tones of green and brown . . . no sky that was not filtered by leaves. A certain kind of tree was in bloom, shedding white petals as large as a man's hand on the water: they drifted like high-stemmed boats, clouds of them afloat, fleets and armadas destroyed by the dip of his paddle and the raft's blunt bow. The full flower had long stamens and pistils so that they looked like white spiders along the branches when they had shed, and like flocks of birds before. Lilies were rife, and a fine-leafed floating weed grew wherever the water was shallow. It was worse than the lilies for tangling up the paddle: it broke off and hung, slick brownish leaves. It was not, he decided, particularly lovely stuff, and it made going very slow in the narrowest channels.

His shoulders began to ache with the long effort. He kept going long after the ache became painful, anxious not to give ground . . . decided finally to put ashore for a space, when he had seen an area not so brushy and overgrown. He drove for it, rammed the bow up and started pulling it about with strokes of the paddle.

The paddle tip sank in, worse and worse with his efforts, tipped the raft with the suction as he pulled it out again and the raft slapped down with a smack. He frowned, jabbed at the sand underneath with his paddle, reducing it to jelly and thinking ruefully where he might have been if he had not mistrusted the water purity and if he had bounded out to drag the raft ashore. It took some little maneuvering to skim the raft off the quicksands and out again, back into the main channel, and he forgot his aching shoulders to keep it going awhile.

"Warren?"

On the hour, as instructed. He stilled his heart and punched on his com unit, never stopping his paddling. "Hello, Annie. Status is good, love, but I need three hands just now."

"Assistance? Estimate of time required to reach your position—"

"Cancel. Don't you try it. I'm managing with two hands quite nicely. How are you?"

"All my systems are functioning normally, but my sensors are impaired by obstructions. Please clear my pickups, Warren."

"No need. My sensors aren't impaired and there's nothing anomalous."

"I detect a repeated sound."

"That's the raft's propulsion. There's no hazard. All systems are normal. My status is good. Call in another hour."

"Yes, Warren."

"Shut down."

"Yes, Warren."

Contact went out; the box lights went off.

He closed off contact from his side, pushed off the bank where he had drifted while he was arguing with *Anne*, and hand-over-handed himself past a low-hanging branch. He snubbed a loop of the mooring rope around it, snugged it down, resting for a moment while the raft swayed sleepily back and forth.

It's beautiful, he thought, *Sax. Min and Harley, it's worth seeing.* He squinted up at the sunlight dancing through the branches. *Hang the captain, Harley. They'll come here sometime. They'll want the place. In someone's lifetime.*

No answer. The sunlight touched the water and sparkled there, in one of the world's paralyzing silences. An armada of petals floated by. A flotilla of bubbles. He watched others rise, near the roots of the tree.

Life, Harley?

He rummaged after one of the sample bags, after the seine from the collection kit. He flung the seine out inexpertly, maneuvered it in the current, pulled it up. The net was fouled with the brownish weed, and caught in it were some strands of gelatinous matter, each a finger's length, grayish to clear with an opaque kernel in the center. He wrinkled his lip, not liking the look of it, reached and threw the sensor unit on again, holding its pickup wand almost touching the strands.

"Warren, I perceive an indeterminate life form, low order."

"How—indeterminate?"

"It may be plant but that identification is not firm."

"I thought so. Now I don't particularly know what to do with it. It's stuck to the net and I don't like to go poking at it bare-handed. Curious stuff."

"Assistance?"

"Wait." He put the scanner wand down and used both hands to evert the net, cleared it by shaking it in the water. He put the net into plastic before letting it back in the raft and sprayed his hands and the side of the raft with disinfectant before picking up the wand and putting it back. "I'm rid of it now, Annie, no trouble. I'm closing everything down now. Observe your one-hour schedule."

He slipped the rope, took up the paddle and extricated the raft from the reeds, where it had swung its right side. Headed for the center of the clear channel.

It might have been eggs, he thought. Might have been. He considered the depth of the channel, the murkiness of the water, and experienced a slight disquiet. Something big could travel that, lurk round the lily roots. He did not particularly want to knock into something.

Nonsense, Harley. No more devils. No more things in the dark. I won't make them anymore, will I, Sax? No more cold sweats.

The river seemed to bend constantly left, deeper into the forest, though he could not see any more or any less on either hand as it went. The growth on the banks was the same. There was an abundance of the fleshy-leaved trees that poured sap so freely when bruised, and the branches hung down into the water so thickly in places that they formed a curtain before whatever lay on shore. The spidertrees shed their white blooms, and the prickly ones thrust out twisted and arching limbs, gnarled and humped roots poking out into the channel. Moss was everywhere, and reeds and waterweed. He realized finally that the river had long since ceased to have any recognizable shore. On the left stretched a carpet of dark green moss that bloomed enticingly. Trees grew scattered there, incredibly neat, as if it were tended by some gardener, and the earth looked so soft and inviting to the touch, so green, the flowers like stars scattered across it.

Then he realized why the place looked so soft and flat, and why the trees grew straight up like columns, without the usual ugliness of twisting roots. That was not earth but floating moss, and when he put his paddle down, he found quicksand on the bottom.

An ugly death, that—sinking alive into a bog, to live for a few moments among the sands and the corruption that oozed round the roots of the trees. To drown in it.

He gave a twist of his mouth and shoved at the paddle, sent the raft up the winding course in haste to be out of it, then halted, drifting back a little as he did so.

The river divided here, coming from left and from right about a finger of land that grew thicker as it went—no islet, this, but the connection of a tributary with the river.

He paddled closer and looked up both overgrown ways. The one on the right was shallower, more choked with reeds, moss growing in patches across its surface, brush fallen into it which the weak current had not removed. He chose the left.

At least, he reasoned with himself, there was no chance of getting lost, even without the elaborate directional equipment he carried: no matter how many times the river subdivided, the current would take him back to the crossing. He had no fear in that regard; for all that the way grew still more tangled.

No light here, but what came darkly diffused. The channel was like a tunnel among the trees. From time to time now he could see larger trees beyond the shoreline vegetation, the tall bulk of one of the sky-reaching giants like those of the grove. He wondered now if he had not been much closer to the river than he had realized when he passed the grove and ran hysterically through the trees, feeling devils at his heels. *That* would have been a surprise, to have run out onto clear and mossy ground and to find himself in quicksand up to his ears. So there were deadly dangers in the forest—not the creeping kind, but dangers enough to make recklessness, either fleeing or advancing, fatal.

"Warren."

Anne made her hourly call and he answered it shortly, without breath for conversation and lacking any substance to report. He rested finally, made fast the raft to the projecting roots of a gnarly tree, laid his paddle across the plastic-wrapped seine and settled down into the raft, his head resting on the inflated rim. He ate, had a cup of coffee from the thermos. Even this overgrown branch of the river was beautiful, considered item at a time. The star Harley was a warm spot dancing above the branches, and the water was black and rich. No wonder the plants flourished so. They grew in every available place. If the river were not moving, they would choke up the channel with their mass and make of it one vast spongy bog such as that other arm of the river had seemed to be.

"Warren."

He came awake and reached for the com. "Emergency?"

"No, Warren. The time is 1300 hours."

"Already?" He levered himself upright against the rim and looked about him at the shadows. "Well, how are you?"

"I'm functioning well, thank you."

"So am I, love. No troubles. In fact . . ." he added cautiously, "in fact I'm beginning to think of extending this operation another day. There's no danger. I don't see any reason to come back and give up all the ground I've traveled, and I'd have to start now to get back to the launching point before dark."

"You'll exit my sensor range if you continue this direction for another day. Please reconsider this program."

"I won't go outside your sensor range. I'll stop and come back then."

A pause. "Yes, Warren."

"I'll call if I need you."

"Yes, Warren."

He broke the contact and pulled the raft upcurrent by the mooring line to reach the knot, untied it and took up the paddle again and started moving. He was content in his freedom, content in the maze, which promised endless secrets. The river could become a highway to its mountain source. He could devise relays that would keep *Anne* with him. He need not be held to one place. He believed in that again.

At 1400 he had a lunch of lukewarm soup and a sun-warmed sandwich, of which he ate every crumb, and wished he had brought larger portions. His appetite increased prodigiously with the exercise and the relaxation. He felt a profound sense of well-being . . . even found patience for a prolonged bout with *Anne*'s chatter. He called her up a little before 1500 and let her sample the river with her sensors, balancing the box on the gear so that she could have a look about.

"Vegetation," she pronounced. "Water. Warren, please reconsider this program."

He laughed at her and shut her down.

Then the river divided again, and again he bore to the left, into the forest heart, where it was always twilight, and less than that now. He paddled steadily, ignoring the persistent ache in his back and shoulders, until he could no longer see where he was going, until the roots and limbs came up at him too quickly out of the dark and he felt the wet drag of moss across his face and arms more than once. 1837, when he checked the time.

"*Anne*."

"Warren?"

"I'm activating your sensors again. There's no trouble, but I want you to give me your reports."

"You're in motion," she said as the box came on. "Low light. Vegetation and water. Temperature 19°C. A sound: the propulsion system. Stability in poor function."

"That's floating, *Anne*. Stability is poor, yes, but not hazardous."

"Thank you. You're behind my base point. I perceive you."

"No other life."

"Vegetation, Warren."

He kept moving, into worse and worse tangle, hoping for an end to the tunnel of trees, where he could at least have the starlight. Anne's occasional voice comforted him. The ghostly giants slid past, only slightly blacker than the night about him.

The raft bumped something underwater and slued about.

"You've stopped."

"I think I hit a submerged log or something." Adrenalin had shot through him at the jolt. He drew a deep breath. "It's getting too dark to see."

"Please reconsider this program."

"I think you have the right idea. Just a second." He prodded underwater with his paddle and hit a thing.

It came up, broke surface by the raft in the sensor light, mossy and jagged.

Log. He was free, his pulse jolting in his veins. He let the current take the raft then, let it turn the bow.

"Warren?"

"I'm loose. I'm all right." He caught a branch at a clearer spot and stopped, letting the fear ebb from him.

"Warren, you've stopped again."

"I stopped us." He wanted to keep running, but that was precisely the kind of action that could run him into trouble, pushing himself beyond the fatigue point. A log. It had been a log after all. He tied up to the branch, put on his jacket against the gathering chill and settled against the yielding rim of the raft, facing the low, reedy bank and the wall of aged trees. "*Anne*, I'm going to sleep now. I'm leaving the sensor box on. Keep alert and wake me if you perceive anything you have to ask about."

"Recorded. Good night, Warren."

"Good night, *Annie*."

He closed his eyes finally, confident at least of *Anne*'s watchfulness, rocked on the gently moving surface of the river. Tiniest sounds seemed loud, the slap of the water against its boundaries, the susurration of the leaves, the ceaseless rhythms of the world, of growth, of things that twined and fed on rain and death.

He dreamed of home as he had not done in a very long time, of a hard-rock mining colony, his boyhood, a fascination with the stars; dreamed of Earth, of things he had only heard of, pictures he had seen, rivers and forests and fields. Pictured rivers came to life and flowed, hurling his raft on past shores of devastating silence, past the horror in the corridors, figures walking in steam—

Sax—Sax leaping at him, knife in hand—

He came up with a gasp too loud in the silence.

"Warren? Emergency?"

"No." He wiped his face, glad of her presence, "It's just a dream. It's all right."

"Malfunction?"

"Thoughts. Dream. A recycling of past experience. A clearing of files. It's all right. It's a natural process. Humans do it when they sleep."

"I perceived pain."

"It's gone now. It stopped. I'm going back to sleep."

"Are you happy, Warren?"

"Just tired, *Anne*. Just very tired and very sleepy. Good night."

"Good night, Warren."

He settled again and closed his eyes. The breeze sighed and the water lapped gently, rocking him. He curled up again and sank into deeper sleep.

He awoke in dim light, in a decided chill that made him glad of the jacket. The side of him that he had lain on was cold through and he rubbed his arm and leg, wishing for a hot breakfast instead of cold sandwiches and lukewarm coffee.

A mist overlay the river a few inches deep. It looked like a river of cloud flowing between the green banks. He reached and turned off *Anne*'s sensors. "Shutting you down. It's morning. I'll be starting back in a moment. My status is good."

"Thank you, Warren."

He settled back again, enjoyed the beauty about him without *Anne*'s time and temperature analyses. He had no intention of letting his eyes close again, but it would be easy in this quiet, this peace.

The sense of well-being soured abruptly. He seemed heavier than the raft could bear, his head pounded, the pulse beat at his temples.

Something was radically wrong. He reached for the sensor box but he could no longer move. He blinked, aware of the water swelling and falling under him, of the branch of the aged tree above him. Breath stopped. Sweat drenched him. Then the breathing reflex started again and the perspiration chilled. A curious sickly feeling went from shoulders to fingertips, unbearable pressure, as if his laboring heart would burst the veins. Pressure spread, to his chest, his head, to groin, to legs and toes. Then it eased, leaving him limp and gasping for air.

The hairs at his nape stirred, a fingering touch at his senses. Darts of sensation ran over his skin; muscles twitched, and he struggled to sit up; he was blind, with softness wrapping him in cotton and bringing him unbearable sorrow. It passed.

"You're there," he said, blinking to clear his eyes. "You're *there.*"

Not madness. Not insanity. Something had touched him in the clearing that day as it just had done here. "Who are you?" he asked it. "What do you want?"

But it had gone—no malevolence, no. It ached, it was so different. It was real. His heart was still racing from its touch. He slipped the knot, tugged the rope free, let the raft take its course.

"Find you," he told it. "I'll find you." He began to laugh, giddy at the spinning course the raft took, the branches whirling in wide circles above him.

"Warren," the box said, self-activated. "Warren? Warren?"

7

"Hello, Warren."

He gave a haggard grin climbing down from the land crawler, staggered a bit from weariness, edged past the pseudosome with a pat on the shoulder. "Hello yourself, Annie. Unload the gear out of the crawler."

"Yes, Warren. What is your status, please?"

"Fine, thanks. Happy. Dirty, tired and hungry, but happy overall."

"Bath and supper?"

"In that order."

"Sleep?"

"Possibly." He walked into the lock, stripped off his clothing as the cargo lift rose into netherdeck, already anticipating the luxury of a warm bath. He took the next lift up. "I'll want my robe. How are you?"

"I'm functioning well, thank you." Her voice came to him all over the ship. The lift stopped and let him out. She turned on the lights for him section by section and extinguished them after.

"What's for supper?"

"Steak and potatoes, Warren. Would you like tea or coffee?"

"Beautiful. Coffee."

"Yes, Warren."

He took a lingering bath, dried and dressed in his robe, went up to the living quarters where *Anne* had set the table for him, all the appointments, all the best. He sat down and looked up at *Anne*, who hovered there to pour him coffee.

"Pull up the other chair and sit down, will you, *Anne*?"

"Yes, Warren."

She released the facing chair from its transit braces, settled it in place, turned it and sat down correctly, metal arms on the table in exact imitation of him. Her lights dimmed once more as she settled into a state of waiting.

Warren ate in contented silence, not disturbing her. *Anne* had her limitations in small talk. When he had finished, he pushed the dishes aside and *Anne*'s sensors brightened at once, a new program clicking into place. She rose and put everything onto the waiting tray, tidying up with a brisk rattle of aluminum and her own metal fingers.

"*Anne*, love."

"Yes, Warren."

"Activate games function."

Tray forgotten, she turned toward him. The screen on the wall lighted, blank. "Specify."

"You choose. You make a choice. Which game?"

Black and white squares flashed onto the screen. Chess. He frowned and looked at her. "That's a new one. Who taught you that?"

"My first programmer installed the program."

He looked at the board, drew a deep breath. He had intended something rather simpler, some fast and stimulating fluff to shake the lingering sense from his brain. Something to sleep on. To see after his eyes were closed. He considered the game. "Are you good at chess?"

"Yes, Warren."

He was amused. "Take those dishes to the galley and come back up here. I'll play you."

"Yes, Warren." The board altered. She had chosen white. The first move was made. Warren turned his chair and reclined it to study the board, his feet on the newly cleared table. He gave her his move and the appropriate change appeared on the screen.

The game was almost over by the time the pseudosome came topside again. She needed only four more moves to make his defeat a certainty. He sat back with his arms folded behind his head, studying his decimated forces. Shook his head in disbelief.

"Annie, *ma belle dame sans merci*—has anyone ever beaten you?"

"No, Warren."

He considered it a moment more, his lately bolstered well-being pricked. "Can you teach me what you know?"

"I've been programmed with the works of fifteen zonal champions. I don't estimate that I can teach you what I know. Human memory is fallible. Mine is not, provided adequate cues for recall and interrelation of data. One of my programmed functions is instruction in procedures. I can instruct."

He rolled a sidelong glance at her. "Fallible?"

"Fallible: capable of error."

"I don't need the definition. What makes you so talkative? Did I hit a program?"

"My first programmer was Franz Mann. He taught me chess. This is an exercise in logic. It's a testing mechanism, negative private appropriation. My function is to maintain you. I'm programmed to instruct in procedures. Chess is a procedure."

"All right," he said quietly. "All right, you can teach me."

"You're happy."

"You amuse me. Sit down."

She resumed the chair opposite him . . . her back to the board, but she did not need to see it. "Amusement produces laughter. Laughter is a pleasure or surprise indicator. Amusement is pleasant or surprising. Please specify which, Warren."

"You're both, *Anne*."

"Thank you. Pleasure is a priority function."

"Is it?"

"This is your instruction, Warren."

He frowned at her. In the human-maintenance programming he had poured a great number of definitions into her, and apparently he had gotten to a fluent area. Herself. Her prime level. She was essentially an egotist.

Another chessboard flashed onto the screen.

"Begin," she said.

She defeated him again, entered another game before he found his eyes watering and his senses blurring out on the screen. He went to bed.

Trees and black and white squares mingled in his dreams.

The next venture took resting . . . took a body in condition and a mind at ease. He looked over the gear the next morning, but he refused to do anything more. Not at once. Not rushing back exhausted into the heart of the forest. He lazed about in the sun, had *Anne's* careful hands rub lotion over his sore shoulders and back, felt immeasurably at peace with the world.

A good lunch, a nap afterward. He gave the ship a long-neglected manual check, in corridors he had not visited since the plague.

There was life in the botany lab, two of Rule's collection, succulents which had survived on their own water, two lone and emaciated spiny clusters. He came on them amid a tangle of brown husks of other plants which had succumbed to neglect, brushed the dead leaves away from them, tiny as they were. He looked for others and found nothing else alive. Two fellow survivors.

No knowing from what distant star system they had been gathered. Tray after tray of brown husks collapsed across the planting medium, victims of his shutdown order for the labs. He stripped it all, gathered the dead plants into a bin. Investigated the lockers and the drawers.

There were seeds, bulbs, rhizomes, all manner of starts. He thought of putting them outside, of seeing what they would do—but considering the ecology . . . no; nothing that might damage that. He thought of bringing some of the world's life inside, making a garden; but the world outside was mostly lilies and waterflowers, and lacked colors. Some of these, he thought, holding a palmful of seeds, some might be flowers of all kinds of colors . . . odors and perfumes from a dozen different star systems. Such a garden was not for discarding. He could start them here, plant them in containers, fill the ship with them.

He grinned to himself, set to work reworking the planting medium, activating the irrigation system.

He located Rule's notebook and sat down and read through it, trying to decide on the seeds, how much water and how deep and what might be best.

He could fill the whole botany lab, and the plants would make seeds of their own. No more sterility. He pictured the living quarters blooming with flowers under the artificial sunlight. There was life outside the ship, something to touch, something to find; and in here . . . he might make the place beautiful, something he could live in while getting used to the world. No more fear. He could navigate the rivers, hike the forest . . . find whatever it was. Bring home the most beautiful things. Turn it all into a garden. He could leave that behind him, at least, when another team did come, even past his lifetime and into the next century. Records. He could feed them into *Anne* and she could send them to orbiting ships. He could learn the world and make records others could use. His world, after all. Whole colonies here someday who would know the name of Paul Warren and Harley and Rule, Burlin and Sax and Sikutu and the rest. Humans who would look at what he had made.

Who would approach what he had found out on the river with awe. Find it friendly, whether or not it was an intelligence. The ship could fit in . . . with the gardens he intended. Long rhythms, the seeding of plants and the growing of trees and the shaping of them. No project he had approached had offered him so much. To travel the rivers and find them and to come home to *Anne*, who maintained all he learned. . . .

He smiled to himself. "*Anne*. Send the pseudosome here. Botany four."

She came, a working of the lift and a tread of metal feet down the corridor and through the outer labs into this one. "Assistance?"

"You had a standard program for this area. Maintenance of water flow. Cleaning."

"I find record of it."

"Activate it. I want the lights on and the water circulating here."

"Yes, Warren." The lights blinked, the sixth one as well, in the darkness where her chin should be. "This is not your station."

"It is now."

"This is Rule's station."

"Rule stopped functioning. Permanently." His lips tightened. He disliked getting into death with a mind that had never been alive. "I'm doing some of Rule's work now. I like to do it."

"Are you happy?"

"Yes."

"Assistance?"

"I'll do it myself. This is human work."

"Explain."

He looked about at her, then back to his work, dropping the seeds in and patting the holes closed. "You're uncommonly conversational. Explain what?"

"Explain your status."

"Dear Annie, humans have to be active about twelve hours a day, body and mind. When we stop being active we don't function well. So I find things to do. Activity. Humans have to have activity. That's what I mean when I use *do* in an unexplained context. It's an important verb, *do*. It keeps us healthy. We always have to have something to do, even if we have to hunt to find it."

Anne digested that thought a moment. "I play chess."

He stopped what he was doing in mid-reach, looked back at her. As far as he could recall it was the first time she had ever offered such an unsolicited suggestion. "How did *that* get into your programming?"

"My first programmer was—"

"Cancel. I mean why did you suddenly offer to play chess?"

"My function is to maintain you happy. You request activity. Chess is an activity."

He had to laugh. She had almost frightened him, and in a little measure he was touched. He could hardly hurt *Anne*'s feelings. "All right, love. I'll play chess after supper. Go fix supper ahead of schedule. It's nearly time and I'm hungry."

It was chicken for dinner, coffee and cream pie for dessert, the silver arranged to perfection. Warren sat down to eat and *Anne* took the chair across the table and waited in great patience, arms before her.

He finished. The chessboard flashed to the screen above.

She won.

"You erred in your third move," she said. The board flashed up again, renewed. She demonstrated the error. Played the game through a better move. "Continue."

She defeated him again. The board returned again to starting.

"Cancel," he said. "Enough chess for the evening. Find me all the material you can on biology. I want to do some reading."

"I've located the files," she said instantly. "They're in general library. Will you want display or printout?"

"Display. Run them by on the screen."

The screen changed; printed matter came on. He scanned it, mostly the pictures. "Hold," he said finally, uninformed. The flow stopped. "*Anne*. Can you detect internal processes in sentient life?"

"Negative. Internal processes are outside my sensor range. But I do pick up periodic sound from high-level organisms when I have refined my perception."

"Breathing. Air exchange. It's the external evidence of an internal process. Can you pick up, say, electrical activity? How do you tell—what's evidence to you, whether something is alive or not?"

"I detect electrical fields. I have never detected an internal electrical process. I have recorded information that such a process exists through chemical activity. This is not within my sensor range. Second question: movement; gas exchange; temperature; thermal pattern; sound—"

"Third question: Does life have to meet all these criteria for you to recognize it?"

"Negative. One positive reading is sufficient for further investigation."

"Have you ever gotten any reading that caused you to investigate further . . . here, at this site?"

"Often, Warren."

"Did you reach a positive identification?"

"Wind motion is most frequent. Sound. All these readings have had positive identification."

He let his pent breath go. "You do watch, don't you? I told you to stay alert."

"I continue your programming. I investigate all stimuli that reach me. I identify them. I have made positive identification on all readings."

"And are you never in doubt? Is there ever a marginal reading?"

"I have called your attention to all such cases. You have identified these sounds. I don't have complete information on life processes. I am still assimilating information. I don't yet use all vocabulary in this field. I am running cross-comparisons. I estimate another two days for full assimilation of library-accessed definitions."

"Library." He recalled accessing it. "What are you using? What material?"

"Dictionary and encyclopedic reference. This is a large program. Cross-referencing within the program is incomplete. I am still running on it."

"You mean you've been processing without shutdown?"

"The program is still in assimilation."

He sank back in the chair. "Might do you good at that. Might make you a better conversationalist." He wished, all the same, that he had not started it. Shutdown of the program now might muddle her, leave her with a thousand unidentified threads hanging. "You haven't gotten any conflicts, have you?"

"No, Warren."

"You're clever, aren't you? At least you'll be a handy encyclopedia."

"I can provide information and instruction."

"You're going to be a wonder when you get to the literary references."

A prolonged flickering of lights. "I have investigated the literature storage. I have input all library information, informational, technical, literary, recreational. It's being assimilated as the definitions acquire sufficient cross-references."

"Simultaneously? You're reading the whole library sideways?"

A further flickering of lights. "Laterally. Correct description is laterally. The cross-referencing process involves all material."

"Who told you to do that?" He rose from the table. So did she, turning her beautiful, vacant face toward him, chromium and gray plastic, red sensor-lights glowing. He was overwhelmed by the beauty of her.

And frightened.

"Your programming. I am instructed to investigate all stimuli occurring within my sensor range. I continue this as a permanent instruction. Library is a primary source of relevant information. You accessed this for investigation."

"Cancel," he said. "Cancel. You're going to damage yourself."

"You're my highest priority. I must maintain you in optimum function. I am processing relevant information. It is in partial assimilation. Cancel of program negative possible. Your order is improper. I'm in conflict, Warren. Please reconsider your instruction."

He drew a larger breath, leaned on the chair, staring into the red lights, which had stopped blinking, which burned steadily, frozen. "Withdrawn," he said after a moment. "Withdrawn." Such as she was capable, *Anne* was in pain. Confused. The lights started blinking again, mechanical relief. "How long is this program going to take you?"

"I have estimated two days assimilation."

"And know *everything*? I think you're estimating too little."

"This is possible. Cross-references are multiplying. What is your estimate?"

"Years. The input is continuous, Annie. It never quits. The world never stops sending it. You have to go on cross-referencing."

The lights blinked. "Yes. My processing is rapid, but the cross-reference causes some lateral activity. Extrapolation indicates this activity will increase in breadth."

"Wondering. You're wondering."

A delay. "This is an adequate description."

He walked over and poured himself a drink at the counter. Looked back at her, finding his hands shaking a bit. "I'll tell you something, Annie. You're going to be a long time at it. I wonder things. I investigate things. It's part of human process. I'm going back to the river tomorrow."

"This is a hazardous area."

"Negative. Not for me, it's not hazardous. I'm carrying out my own program. Investigating. We make a team, do you understand that word?

Engaged in common program. You do your thinking here. I gather data at the river. I'll take your sensor box."

"Yes, Warren."

He finished the drink, pleased with her. Relaxed against the counter. "Want another game of chess?"

The screen lit with the chessboard.

She won this one too.

8

He would have remembered the way even without the marks scored on the trees. They were etched in memory, a fallen log, the tree with the blue and white platelet fungus, the one with the broken branch. He went carefully, rested often, burdened with *Anne*'s sensor box and his own kit. Over everything the silence persisted, forever silence, unbroken through the ages by anything but the wind or the crash of some aged tree dying. His footsteps on the wet leaves seemed unbearably loud, and the low hum from the sensor box seemed louder still.

The clearing was ahead. It was that he had come back to find, to recover the moment, to discover it in daylight.

"*Anne*," he said when he was close to it, "cut off the sensor unit awhile. Its noise is interfering with my perceptions."

"Please reconsider this instruction. Your perceptions are limited."

"They're more sensitive over a broad range. It's safe, *Anne*. Cut it off. I'll call in an hour. You wait for that call."

"Yes, Warren."

The sensor unit went off. His shoulder ached from the fifteen kilos and the long walk from the raft, but he carried it like moral debt. As insurance. It had never manifested itself, this—life—not for *Anne*'s sensors, but twice for his. Possibly the sensor box itself interfered with it; or the ship did. He gave it all the chance it might need.

But he carried the gun.

He found the grove different than he had remembered it, dark and sunless yet in the early morning. He came cautiously, dwarfed and insignificant among the giant trees . . . stopped absolutely still, hearing no sound at all. There was the fallen one, the father of all trees, his moss-hung bulk gone dark and his beard of flowers gone. The grass that grew in the center was dull and dark with shadow.

Softly he walked to that center and laid down his gear, sat down on the blanket roll. Looked about him. Nothing had changed—likely nothing had changed here since the fall of the titan which had left the vacancy in the ceiling of branches. Fourteen trees made the grove. The oldest of those still living must have been considerable trees when man was still earthbound and reaching for homeworld's moon. Even the youngest must measure their ages in centuries.

All right, he thought. *Come ahead. No sensors. No machines. You remember me, don't you? The night, on the river. I'm the only one there is. No threat. Come ahead.*

There was not the least response.

He waited until his muscles cramped, feeling increasingly disappointed . . . no little afraid: that too. But he had come prepared for patience. He squatted and spread out his gear so that there was a plastic sheet under the blanket, poured himself hot coffee from his flask and stretched out to relax. *Anne* called in his drowsing, once, twice, three times: three hours. The sun came to the patch of grass like a daily miracle, and motes of dust and pollen danced in the beam. The giant's beard bloomed again. Then the sun passed on, and the shadows and the murk returned to the grove of giants.

Perhaps, he thought, it had gone away. Perhaps it was no longer resident here in the grove, but down by the river yonder, where he had felt it the second time. It had fingered over his mind and maybe it had been repelled by what it met there. Perhaps the contact was a frightening experience for it and it had made up its mind against another such attempt.

Or perhaps it had existed only in the curious workings of a very lonely human mind. Like *Anne.* Something of his own making. He wanted it to exist. He desperately wanted it to be real, to make the world alive, Rule's world, and Harley's, and his. He wanted it to lend companionship for the years of silence, the hollow days and deadly nights, something, anything—an animal or an enemy, a thing to fear if not something to love. Solitude forever—he could not bear that. He refused to believe in it. He would search every square meter of the world until he found something like him, that lived and felt, or until he had proved it did not exist.

And it came.

The first touch was a prickling and a gentle whisper in his mind, a sound of wind. The air shone with an aching green luminance. He could not hold it. The light went. Numbness came over him; his pulse jumped wildly. Pain lanced through his chest and belly. Then nothing. He gasped for air and felt a fingering at his consciousness, a deep sense of perplexity. Hesitation. He felt it hovering, the touches less and less substantial, and he reached out with his thoughts, wanting it, pleading with it to wait.

A gentle tug at his sense. Not unpleasant.

Listen to me, he thought, and felt it settle over him like a blanket, entity without definition. Words were meaningless to the being which had reached into his mind. Only the images transcended the barrier.

He hunted for something to give it, a vision of sunlight, of living things, his memories of the river lilies. There came back a feeling of peace, of satisfaction. He wanted to drift to sleep and fought the impulse. His body grew as heavy as it had on the river and he felt himself falling, drifting slowly. Images flowed past like the unrolling of a tape with an incalculable span of years encoded on it. He saw the clearing thick with young trees, and saw it again when there were vacant spaces among those, and he knew that others had grown before the present ones, that the seedlings he saw among the last were the giants about him.

His consciousness embraced all the forest, and knew the seasonal ebb and flood of the river, knew the islets and the branches that had grown and ceased to be. He knew the ages of mountains, the weight of innumerable years.

What are you? he wondered in his dream.

Age, great age, and eternal youth, the breaking of life from the earth, the bittersweet rush of earthbound life sunward. And this, this was the thing it called itself—too large for a single word or a single thought. It rippled sound through his mind, like wind through harpstrings, and it was that too. *I,* it said. *I.*

It had unrolled his question from his mind with the fleeting swiftness of a dream, absorbed it all and knew it. Like *Anne.* Faster. More complete. He tried to comprehend such a mind, but the mind underwent a constriction of panic. Sight and sensation returned on his own terms and he was aware of the radiance again, like the sunbeam, drifting near him.

You, Warren thought. *Do you understand me?*

Something riffled through his thoughts, incomprehensible and alien. Again the rippling touch of light and chill.

Did you touch them? My friends died. They died of a disease. All but me.

Warmth and regret flowed over him. *Friend,* it seemed. *Sorrow. Welcome.* It thrilled through him like the touch of rain after drought. He caught his breath, wordless for the moment, beyond thinking. He tried to understand the impressions that followed, but they flowed like madness through his nerves. He resisted, panicked, and a feeling of sorrow came back.

"What *are* you?" he cried.

It broke contact abruptly, crept back again more slowly and stayed at a distance, cool, anxious.

"Don't leave." The thought frightened him. "Don't go. I don't want that, either."

The radiance expanded, flickering with gold inside. It filled his mind, and somewhere in it a small thing crouched, finite, fluttering inside with busy life, while the trees grew. Himself. He was measured, against such a scale as the giants, and felt cold.

"How old are you?"

The life spans of three very ancient trees flashed through his mind in the blink of an eye.

"I'm twenty-seven years."

It took years from his mind; he felt it, the seasonal course of the world and star, the turning of the world, a plummeting to earth with the sun flickering overhead again and again and again. A flower came to mind, withered and died.

"Stop it," Warren cried, rejecting the image and the comparison.

It fled. He tried to hold the creature. A sunset burst on his eyes, flared and dimmed . . . a time, an appointment for meeting, a statement—he did not know. The green light faded away.

Cold. He shivered convulsively, caught the blanket up about him in the dimness. He stared bleakly into the shadow . . . felt as if his emotions had been taken roughly and shaken into chaos, wanted to scream and cry and could not. Death seemed to have touched him, reduced everything to minute scale. Everything. Small and meaningless.

"Warren."

Anne's voice. He had not the will or the strength to answer her. It was beyond belief that he could have suffered such cataclysmic damage in an instant of contact; that his life was not the same, the universe not in the same proportion.

"Warren."

The insistent voice finally sent his hand groping after the com unit. Danger. *Anne.* Threat. She might come here. Might do something rash. "I'm all right." He kept his voice normal and casual, surprised by its clear tone as he got it out. "I'm fine. How are you?"

"Better now, Warren. You didn't respond. I've called twelve times. Is there trouble?"

"I was asleep, that's all. I'm going to sleep again. It's getting dark here."

"You didn't call in an hour."

"I forgot. Humans forget. Look that up in your files. Let me be, *Anne*. I'm tired. I want to sleep. Make your next call at 0500."

"This interval is long. Please reconsider this instruction."

"I mean it, *Anne*. 0500. Not before then. Keep the sensor box off and let me rest."

There was a long pause. The sensor unit activated itself, *Anne*'s presence actively with him for the moment. She looked about, shut herself off. "Good night, Warren."

She was gone. She was not programmed to detect a lie, only an error in logic. Now he had cut himself off indeed. Perhaps, he thought, he had just killed himself.

But the entity was not hostile. He *knew*. He had been inside its being, known without explanation all the realities that stood behind its thought, like in a dream where in a second all the past of an act was there, never lived, but there, and remembered, and therefore real. The creature must have walked airless moons with him, seen lifeless deserts and human cities and the space between the stars. It must have been terrifying to the being whose name meant the return of spring. And what might it have felt thrust away from its world and drifting in dark, seeing its planet as a green and blue mote in infinity? Perhaps it had suffered more than he had.

He shut his eyes, relaxed a time . . . called *Anne* back when he had rested somewhat, and reassured her. "I'm still well," he told her. "I'm happy."

"Thank you, Warren," she said in return, and let herself be cut off again.

The sun began to dim to dark. He put on his coat, tucked up again in the blanket. Human appetites returned to him—hunger and thirst. He ate some of the food he had brought, drank a cup of coffee, lay back and closed his eyes on the dark, thinking that in all reason he ought to be afraid in the night in this place.

He felt a change in the air, a warmth tingling down the back of his neck and the insides of his arms. The greenish light grew and hovered in the dark.

It was there as if nothing had ever gone amiss.

"Hello," Warren said, sitting up. He wrapped himself in the blanket, looked at the light, looked around him. "Where did you go?"

A ripple of cool waters went through his mind. Lilies and bubbles drifting.

"The river?"

Leaves fluttering in a wind, stronger and stronger. The sun going down.

"What were you doing there?"

His heart fluttered, his pulse sped, not of his own doing. Too strong—far too strongly.

"*Stop—stop it.*"

The pressure eased, and Warren pressed his hands to his eyes and gasped for air. His heart still labored, his sense of balance deserted him. He tumbled backward into space, blind, realized he was lying down on firm earth with his legs bent painfully. The tendril of thought crept back into his mind, controlled and subdued. Sorrow. He perceived a thing very tightly furled, with darkness about it, shielding it from the green. It was himself. Sorrow poured about him.

"I know you can't help it." He tried to move, disoriented. His hands were numb. His vision was tunneled. "Don't touch me like that. Stop it."

Confusion: he felt it; an ebbing retreat.

"Don't go, either. Just stop. Please."

It lingered about him, green luminance pulsing slowly into a sparkle or two of gold, dimming down again by turns. All the air seemed calm.

Spring, Warren gave it back. He built an image of flowers, colored flowers, of gardens. Of pale green shoots coming up through moist earth.

It answered him, flowers blooming in his mind, white, green, and gold-throated jade. They took on tints in his vision, mingled colors and pale at first, as if the mind had not known the colors were distinct to separate flowers, and then settling each on each, blues and violets and yellows, reds and roses and lavenders. Joy flooded through. Over and over again the flowers bloomed.

"Friend. You understand that?"

The flowers kept blooming, twining stems, more and more of them.

"Is it always you—is it always you I've dealt with? Are there others like you?"

A single glow, replacing the other image, greenness through all his vision, but things circled outside it . . . not hostile—other. And it enfolded one tiny darkness, a solitary thing, tightly bound up, clenched in on the flutterings inside itself.

"That's me, you mean. I'm human."

The small creature sank strange tendrils deep into the moist earth, spread extensions like branches, flickers of growth in all directions through the forest and out, across the grassland.

"Isn't there anything else—aren't there other creatures on this world . . . anywhere?"

The image went out. Water bubbled, and in the cold murk tiny things moved. Grass stirred in the sunlight, and a knot of small creatures gathered, fluttering at the heart, three, fourteen of them. Joy and sorrow. The flutters died. One by one the minds went out. Sorrow. There were thirteen, twelve, eleven, ten—

"Were you there? Were you on the ship?"

He saw images of the corridors—his own memory snatched forth; the destruct chamber; the lab and the blood—the river then, cold, murky waters, the raft drifting on the river in the cold dawning. He lay there, complex, fluttering thing in the heart of green, in the mind—pain then, and retreat.

"I know. I came to find you. I wanted to find out if you were real. To talk to you."

The green radiance crept back again, surrounding the dark egg with the furled creature in its heart. The creature stirred, unfolded branches and thrust them out of its shell, into the radiance.

"No—no. Keep back from me. You can do me damage. You know that."

The beating of his heart quickened and slowed again before it hurt. The greenness dimmed and retreated. A tree stood in the shell of darkness that was his own space, a tree fixed and straight and solitary, with barren earth and shadow around it.

The judgment depressed him. "I wanted to find you. I came here to find you. Then, on the river. And now. I haven't changed my mind. But the touching hurts."

Warmth bubbled through. Images of suns flashed across the sky into a blinding blur. Trees grew and died and decayed. Time: Ages passed. The radiance fairly danced, sparkling and warm. Welcome. Welcome. Desire tingled through him.

"You make me nervous when you get excited like that. You might forget. And you can hurt me. You know that by now."

Desire, a fluttering along his veins. The radiance hovered, back and forth, dancing slow flickerings of gold in its heart.

"So you're patient. But what for? What are you waiting for?"

The small-creature image returned. From embryo, it grew, unfolded, reached out into the radiance—let it into that fluttering that was its center.

"No." Death came into his mind, mental extinction, accepting an alien parasite.

The radiance swirled green and gold about him. Waters murmured and bubbled. Growth exploded in thrills of force that ran over Warren's nerves and threatened for a moment to be more than his senses could take. The echoes and the images ebbed and he caught his breath, warmed, close to losing himself.

"Stop," he protested, finding that much strength. The contact loosened, leaving a memory of absolute intoxication with existence, freedom, joy, such as he had never felt in his life—frightening, unsettling, undermining disciplines and rules by which life was ordered and orderly. "We could both be damaged that way. Stop. Stop it."

The greenness began to pulse slowly, dimming and brightening. It backed away. Another tightly furled embryo appeared in his mind, different from the first, sickly and strange. It lay beside his image in the dark shell, both of them, together, reached out tendrils, interwove, and the radiance grew pale.

"*What* other human? Where?"

A desperate fluttering inside the sickly one, a hammering of his own pulse: a distant and miserable rage; and grief; and need.

"Where is it now? What happened to it? *Where is he?*"

The fluttering inside the image stopped, the tendrils withered, and all of it decayed.

He gathered himself to rise, pushed back. The creature's thoughts washed back on him, a seething confusion, the miasma of loneliness and empty ages pouring about him, and he sprang to his feet and fled, slipping and stumbling, blind in the verdant light, in symbols his mind could not grasp, in distortion of what he could. Sound and light and sensation warped through his senses. Daylight. Somehow it was daylight. He reached the aged tree, the grandfather of trees, recoiled from the feel of the moss in his almost blindness, stumbled around its roots.

The place was here. He knew.

The greenness hovered there in the dawning, danced over corruption, over what had been a man. It lay twisted and curled up there, in that cavern of the old tree's naked roots, in that dark, with the grinning white of bone thrusting through rags of skin.

"*Sax*," he cried. He groped his way back from it, finding empty air about his fingertips, dreading something tangible. He turned and ran, blind in the shadow, among the clinging branches that tore at his arms and his face. The light came about him again, green and gold. His feet slipped among the tangled roots and earth bruised his hands. Pain lanced up his ankle, through his knees. The mustiness of old leaves was in his mouth. He spat and spat again, clawed his way up by the brush and the tree roots, hauled himself farther and ran again and fell, his leg twisted by the clinging roots.

Sorrow, the radiance mourned. Sorrow. Sorrow.

He moved, feverishly turned one way and the other to drag his foot free of the roots that had wedged it in. The greenish luminance grew at the edges of his mind, moving in, bubbling mournfully of life and death. "You killed him," he shouted at it. "You killed him."

The image came to him of Sax curled up there as if in sleep—alone and lost. Withering, decaying.

He freed his foot. The pain shot up to his inner knee and he sobbed with it, rocked to and fro.

Sorrow. It pulled at him, wanting him. It ached with needing him.

Not broken, not broken, he hoped: to be left lame lifelong as well as desolate—he could not bear that.

Pain stopped. A cooling breeze fanned over him. He stopped hating. Stopped blaming. The forest swayed and moved all about him. A tug drew at his mind, to go, to follow—other presences. Over river, over hills, far away, to drift with the winds and stop being alone, forever, and there was no terror in it. Sax perished. The forest took him, and he was part of it, feeding it, remembered.

Come, the presence said. He tried—but the first halting movement away from the support of the tree sent a shooting pain up his knee and brought him down rocking to and fro in misery.

"Warren," a voice was saying. "Warren. Assistance?"

The vision passed. The ache throbbed in his knee, and the green radiance grew distant, rippling with the sound of waters. Then the creature was gone, the forest silent again.

"Warren?"

He fumbled at his belt, got the com unit to his mouth. "*Anne. I'm all right.*"

"Assistance? Assistance?"

"I'm coming home, *Anne.*"

"Clarify: you killed him. Clarify."

He wiped his face, his hand trembling. "I found Sax, *Anne.* He's not functioning."

A silence. "Assistance?"

"None possible. It's permanent nonfunction. He's—deteriorated. I'm coming home. It's going to be longer than usual."

"Are you in pain, Warren?"

He thought about it, thought about her conflict override. "No. Stress. Finding Sax was stressful. I'm going to shut off now. I've got some things to take care of. I'll come as quickly as I can."

"Yes, Warren."

The contact went out. He hooked the com unit back to his belt, felt of the knee, looked about him in the dawning, distressed by the loss of time. Sickness moiled in him, shock. Thirst. He broke small branches from the thicket, and a larger one, tried to lever himself out of his predicament and finally gave up and crawled, tears streaming down his face, back to the pallet and the kit he had left. He drank, forced a little food into his mouth and washed it down, splinted the knee and wrapped it in bandage from the med kit.

He got up then, using his stick, tried to carry both the water and the med kit, but he could not manage them both and chose to keep the water. He skipped forward using the stick, eyes watering from the pain, and there was a painkiller in the kit, but he left it, too: no drugs, nothing to muddle his direction; he had no leeway for errors. He moved slowly, steadily, into the forest on the homeward track, his hand aching already from the stick; and the tangle grew thicker, making him stagger and catch his balance violently from the good leg to the injured one and back again.

After he had fallen for the third time he wiped the tears from his eyes and gave up the stick entirely, leaning on the trees while he could, and when he came to places where he had to hitch his way along with his weight partially on the leg, he did it, and when the intervals grew too long and he had to crawl, he did that too. He tried not to think of the distance he had to go to the river. It did not matter. The distance had to be covered, no matter how long it took. *Anne* called, back on her hourly schedule, and that was all he had.

It was afternoon when he came into the vicinity of the river, and he reached it the better part of an hour afterward. He slid down to the sandy bank and staggered across to the raft, freed its rope and managed, crawling and tugging, to get it into the river and himself into it before it drifted away. He savored the beautiful feel of it under his torn hands, the speed of its moving, which was a painless, delirious joy after the meter-by-meter torment of the hours since dawn.

He got it to shore, started to leave it loose and then, half crazed and determined in his habits, crawled his way to the appointed limb and moored it fast. Then there was the bank, sandy in the first part, and then the brushy path he had broken bringing loads of equipment down.

And in his hearing a blessedly familiar sound of machinery.

Anne stood atop the crest, in front of the crawler, bright in the afternoon sun, her faceplate throwing back the daylight.

"Warren? Assistance?"

9

He worked the muddy remnant of his clothing off, fouling the sheets of the lab cot and the floor of the lab itself, while *Anne* hovered and watched. She brought him bandages. Fruit juice. He drank prodigiously of it, and that settled his stomach. Water. He washed where he sat, making puddles on the floor and setting *Anne* to clicking distressedly.

"*Anne*," he said, "I'm going to have to take a real bath. I can't stand this filth. You'll have to help me down there."

"Yes, Warren." She offered her arm, helping him up, and walked with him to the bath, compensating for his uneven stride. Walked with him all the way to the mist cabinet, and stood outside while he turned on the control.

He soaked for a time, leaned on the wall and shut his eyes a time, looked down finally at a body gone thinner than he would have believed. Scratches. Bruises. The bandage was soaked and he had no disposition to change it. He had had enough of pain, and drugs were working in him now, home, in safety. So the sheets would get wet. *Anne* could wash everything.

No more nightmares. No more presences in the depths of the ship. No more Sax. He stared bleakly at the far wall of the cabinet, trying to recall the presence in the forest, trying to make sense of things, but the drugs muddled him and he could hardly recall the feeling or the look of the light that had shone out of the dark.

Sax. Sax was real. He had talked to *Anne*. She knew. She had heard. Heard all of it. He turned on the drier until he was tired of waiting on it, left the cabinet still damp and let *Anne* help him up to his own room, his own safe bed.

She waited there, clicking softly as he settled himself in, dimmed the lights for him, even pulled the covers up for him when he had trouble.

"That's good," he sighed. The drugs were pulling him under.

"Instructions."

Her request hit his muddled thought train oddly, brought him struggling back toward consciousness. "Instruction in what?"

"In repair of human structure."

He laughed muzzily. "We're essentially self-repairing. Let me sleep it out. Good night, *Anne.*"

"Your time is in error."

"My body isn't. Go clean up the lab. Clean up the bath. Let me sleep."

"Yes, Warren."

Have you, he thought to ask her, *understood what you read? Do you know what happened out there, to Sax? Did you pick it up?* But she left. He got his eyes open and she was gone, and he thought he had not managed to ask, because she had not answered.

He slept, and dreamed green lights, and slept again.

Anne clattered about outside his room. Breakfast, he decided, looking at the time. He tried to get out of bed and winced, managed to move only with extreme pain . . . the knee, the hands, the shoulders and the belly—every muscle in his body hurt. He rolled onto his belly, levered himself out of bed, held on to the counter and the wall to reach the door. He had bruises . . . massive bruises, the worst about his hip and his elbow. His face hurt on that side. He reached for the switch, opened the door.

"Assistance?" *Anne* asked, straightening from her table setting.

"I want a bit of pipe. A meter long. Three centimeters wide. Get it."

"Yes, Warren."

No questions. She left. He limped over painfully and sat down, ate his breakfast. His hand was so stiff he could scarcely close his fingers on the fork or keep the coffee cup in his swollen fingers. He sat staring at the far wall, seeing the clearing again. Numb. There were limits to feeling, inside and out. He thought that he might feel something—some manner of elation in his discovery when he had recovered; but there was Sax to temper it.

Anne came back. He took the pipe and used it to get up when he had done; his hand hurt abominably, even after he had hobbled down to the lab and padded the raw pipe with bandages. He kept walking, trying to loosen up.

Anne followed him, stood about, walked, every motion that he made.

"Finished your assimilation?" he asked her, recalling that. "Does it work?"

"Processing is proceeding."

"A creature of many talents. You can walk about and rescue me and assimilate the library all at once, can you?"

"The programs are not impaired. An AI uses a pseudobiological matrix for storage. Storage is not a problem. Processing does not impair other functions."

"No headaches, either, I'll bet."

"Headache is a biological item."

"Your definitions are better than they were."

"Thank you, Warren."

She matched strides with him, exaggeratedly slow. He stopped. She stopped. He went on, and she kept with him. "*Anne*. Why don't you just let me alone and let me walk? I'm not going to fall over. I don't need you."

"I perceive malfunction."

"A structural malfunction under internal repair. I have all kinds of internal mechanisms working on the problem. I'll get along. It's all right, *Anne*."

"Assistance?"

"None needed, I tell you. It's all right. Go away."

She stayed. Malfunctioning humans, he thought. No programming accepted. He frowned, beyond clear reasoning. The bio and botany labs were ahead. He kept walking, into them and through to Botany One.

"Have you been maintaining here?" he asked. The earth in the trays looked a little dry.

"I've been following program."

He limped over and adjusted the water flow. "Keep it there."

"Yes, Warren."

He walked to the trays, felt of them.

"Soil," *Anne* said gratuitously. "Dirt. Earth."

"Yes. It has to be moist. There'll be plants coming up soon. They need the water."

"Coming up. Source."

"Seed. They're under there, under the soil. Plants, *Anne*. From seed."

She walked closer, adjusted her stabilizers, looked, a turning of her sensor-equipped head. She put out a hand and raked a line in the soil. "I perceive no life. Size?"

"It's there, under the soil. Leave it alone. You'll kill it."

She straightened. Her sensor lights glowed, all of them. "Please check your computations, Warren."

"About what?"

"This life."

"There are some things your sensors can't pick up, Annie."

"I detect no life."

"They're there. I put them in the ground. I know they're there; I don't need to detect them. *Seeds*, Annie. That's the nature of them."

"I am making cross-references on this word, Warren."

He laughed painfully, patiently opened a drawer and took out a large one that he had not planted. "This is one. It'd be a plant if I put it into the ground and watered it. That's what makes it grow. That's what makes all the plants outside."

"Plants come from seed."

"That's right."

"This is growth process. This is birth process."

"Yes."

"This is predictable."

"Yes, it is."

In the dark faceplate the tiny stars glowed to intense life. She took the seed from the counter, with one powerful thrust rammed it into the soil and then pressed the earth down over it, leaving the imprint of her fingers. Warren looked at her in shock.

"Why, *Anne?* Why did you do that?"

"I'm investigating."

"Are you, now?"

"I still perceive no life."

"You'll have to wait."

"Specify period."

"It takes several weeks for the seed to come up."

"Come up."

"Idiom. The plant will grow out of it. Then the life will be in your sensor range."

"Specify date."

"Variable. Maybe twenty days."

"Recorded." She swung about, facing him. "Life forms come from seeds. Where are human seeds?"

"*Anne*—I don't think your programming is adequate to the situation. And my knee hurts. I think I'm going to go topside again."

"Assistance?"

"None needed." He leaned his sore hand on the makeshift cane and limped past her, and she stalked faithfully after, to the lift, and rode topside to the common room, stood by while he lowered himself into a reclining chair and let the cane fall, massaging his throbbing hand.

"Instruction?"

"Coffee," he said.

"Yes, Warren."

She brought it. He sat and stared at the wall, thinking of things he might read, but the texts that mattered were all beyond him and all useless on this world, on Rule's world. He thought of reading for pleasure, and kept seeing the grove at night, and the radiance, and Sax's body left there. He owed it burial. And he had not had the strength.

Had to go back there. Could not live here and not go back there. It was life there as well as a dead friend. Sax had known, had gone to it, through what agony he shrank from imagining, had gone to it to die there . . . to be in that place at the last. He tried to doubt it, here, in *Anne*'s sterile interior, but he had experienced it, and it would not go away. He even thought of talking to *Anne* about it, but there was that refusal to listen to him when he was malfunctioning—and he had no wish to stir that up. *Seeds* . . . were hard enough. Immaterial life—

"Warren," *Anne* said. "Activity? I play chess."

She won, as usual.

The swelling went down on the second day. He walked, cautiously, without the cane . . . still used it for going any considerable distance, and the knee still ached, but the rest of the aches diminished and he acquired a certain cheerfulness, assured at least that the knee was not broken, that it was healing, and he went about his usual routines with a sense of pleasure in them, glad not to be lamed for life.

But by the fourth and fifth day the novelty was gone again, and he wandered the halls of the ship without the cane, miserable, limping in pain but too restless to stay still. He drank himself to sleep nights—still awoke in the middle of them, the result, he reckoned, of too much sleep, of dreaming the days away in idleness, of lying with his mind vacant for hours during the day, watching the clouds or the grass moving in the wind. Like *Anne*. Waiting for stimulus that never came.

He played chess, longer and longer games with *Anne*, absorbed her lessons . . . lost.

He cried, the last time—for no reason, but that the game had become important, and when he saw one thing coming, she sprang another on him.

"Warren," she said implacably, "is this pain?"

"The knee hurts," he said. It did. "It disrupted my calculations." It had not. He had lost. He lied, and *Anne* sat there with her lights winking on and off in the darkness of her face and absorbing it.

"Assistance? Pain: drugs interfere with pain reception." She had gotten encyclopedic in her processing. "Some of these drugs are in storage—"

"Cancel. I know what they are." He got up, limped over to the counter and opened the liquor cabinet. "Alcohol also kills the pain."

"Yes, Warren."

He poured his drink, leaned against the counter and sipped at it, wiped his eyes. "Prolonged inactivity, *Anne*. That's causing the pain. The leg's healing."

A small delay of processing. "Chess is activity."

"I need to sleep." He took the drink and the bottle with him, limped into his own quarters, shut the door. He drank, stripped, crawled between the sheets and sat there drinking, staring at the screen and thinking that he might try to read . . . but he had to call *Anne* to get a book on the screen, and he wanted no debates. His hands shook. He poured another glass and drank it down, fluffed the pillow. "*Anne*," he said. "Lights out."

"Good night, Warren." The lights went. The chessboard came back, behind his eyelids, the move he should have made. He rehearsed it to the point of anger, deep and bitter rage. He knew that it was ridiculous. All pointless. Without consequence. Everything was.

He slid into sleep, and dreamed, and the dreams were of green things, and the river, and finally of human beings, of home and parents long lost, of old friends . . . of women inventively erotic and imaginary, with names he knew at the time—he awoke in the midst of that and lay frustrated, staring at the dark ceiling and then at the dark behind his eyelids, trying to rebuild them in all their detail, but sleep eluded him. He thought of *Anne* in that context, of bizarre programs, of his own misery, and what she was not—his thoughts ran in circles and grew unbearable.

He reached for the bottle, poured what little there was and drank it, and that was not enough. He rolled out of bed, stumbled in the dark. "*Lights*," he cried out, and they came on. He limped to the door and opened it, and the pseudosome came to life where it had been standing in the dark, limned in silver from the doorway, her lights coming to life inside her faceplate. The lights in the living quarters brightened. "Assistance?"

"No." He went to the cabinet, opened it, took out another bottle and opened it. The bottles were diminishing. He could foresee the day when there would be no more bottles at all. That panicked him. Set him to thinking of the forest, of green berries that might ferment, of the grasses—of fruits that might come at particular seasons. If he failed to poison himself.

He went back to his bed with the bottle, filled his glass and got in bed. "Lights out," he said. They went. He sat drinking in the dark until he felt his hand shaking, and set the glass aside and burrowed again into the tangled sheets.

This time there were nightmares, the lab, the deaths, and he was walking through the ship again, empty-handed, looking for Sax and his knife. Into dark corridors. He kept walking and the way got darker and darker, and something waited there. Something hovered over him. He heard sound—

The dream brought him up with a jerk, eyes wide and a yell in his ears that was his own, confronted with red lights in the dark, the touch of a hand on him.

The second shock was more than the first, and he lashed out at hard metal, struggled wildly with covers and the impediment of *Anne's* unyielding arm. Her stabilizers hummed. She put the hand on his chest and held and he recovered his sense, staring up at her with his heart pounding in fright.

"Assistance? Assistance? Is this malfunction?"

"A dream—a dream, *Anne*."

A delay while the lights blinked in the dark. "Dreams may have random motor movements. Dreams are random neural firings. Neural cells are brain structure. This process affects the brain. Please confirm your status."

"I'm fine, *Anne*."

"I detect internal disturbance."

"That's my heart, *Anne*. It's all right. I'm normal now. The dream's over."

She took back the hand. He lay still for a moment, watching her lights.

"Time," he asked.

"0434."

He winced, moved, ran a hand through his hair. "Make breakfast. Call me when it's ready."

"Yes, Warren."

She left, a clicking in the dark that carried her own light with her. The door closed. He pulled the covers about himself and burrowed down and tried to sleep, but he was only conscious of a headache, and he had no real desire for the breakfast.

He kept very busy that day, despite the headache—cleaned up, limped about, carrying things to their proper places, throwing used clothing into the laundry. Everything in shape, everything in order. No more self pity. No more excuses of his lameness or the pain. No more liquor. He thought even of putting *Anne* in charge of that cabinet . . . but he did not. He was. He could say no if he wanted to.

Outside, a rain blew up. *Anne* reported the anomaly. Clouds hung darkly over the grasslands and the forest. He went down to the lock to see it, the first change he had seen in the world . . . stood there in the hatchway with the rain spattering his face and the thunder shaking his bones, watched the lightning tear holes in the sky.

The clouds shed their burden in a downpour, but they stayed. After the pounding rain, which left the grass battered and collapsed the canopy outside into a miniature lake, the clouds stayed, sending down a light drizzle that chilled to the bone, intermittent with harder rain—one day, and two, and three, four at last, in which the sun hardly shone.

He thought of the raft, of the things he had left behind—of the clearing finally, and Sax lying snugged there in the hollow of the old tree's roots.

And a living creature—one with it, with the scents of rain and earth and the elements.

The sensor box. That, too, he had had to abandon . . . sitting on the ground on a now sodden blanket, perhaps half underwater like the ground outside.

"*Anne*," he said then, thinking about it. "Activate the sensor unit. Is it still functioning?"

"Yes."

He sat where he was, in the living quarters, studying the chessboard. Thought a moment. "Scan the area around the unit. Do you perceive anything?"

"Vegetation, Warren. It's raining."

"Have you—activated it since I left it there?"

"When the storm broke I activated it. I investigated with all sensors."

"Did you—perceive anything?"

"Vegetation, Warren."

He looked into her faceplate and made the next move, disquieted.

The seeds sprouted in the lab. It was all in one night, while the drizzle died away outside and the clouds broke to let the sun through. And as if they had known, the seeds came up. Warren looked out across the rows of trays in the first unadulterated pleasure he had felt in days . . . to see them live. All along the trays the earth was breaking, and in some places little arches and spears of pale green and white were thrusting upward.

Anne followed him. She always did.

"You see," he told her, "now you can see the life. It was there, all along."

She made closer examination where he indicated, a humanlike bending to put her sensors into range. She straightened, walked back to the place where she had planted her own seed. "Your seeds have grown. The seed I planted has no growth."

"It's too early yet. Give it all its twenty days. Maybe less. Maybe more. They vary."

"Explain. Explain life process. Cross-referencing is incomplete."

"The inside of the seed is alive, from the time it was part of the first organism. When water gets into it, it activates, penetrates its hull, and pushes away from gravity and toward the light."

Anne digested the information a moment. "Life does not initiate with seed. Life initiates from the first organism. All organisms produce seed. Instruction: what is the first organism?"

He looked at her, blinked, tried to think through the muddle. "I think you'd better assimilate some other area of data. You'll confuse yourself."

"Instruction: explain life process."

"I can't. It's not in my memory."

"I can instruct. I contain random information in this area."

"So do I, Annie, but it doesn't do any good. It won't work. You don't plant humans in seed trays. It takes two humans to make another one. And you aren't. Let it alone."

"Specify: *aren't. It.*"

"You aren't human. And you're not going to be. Cancel, *Anne*, just cancel. I can't reason with you, not on this."

"I reason."

He looked into her changeless face with the impulse to hit her, which she could neither feel nor comprehend. "I don't choose to reason. Gather up a food kit for me, Annie. Get the gear into the lock."

"This program is preparatory to going to the river."

"Yes. It is."

"This is hazardous. This caused injury. Please reconsider this program."

"I'm going to pick up your sensor box. Retrieve valuable equipment, a part of *you*, Annie. You can't reach it. I'll be safe."

"This unit isn't in danger. You were damaged there. Please reconsider this instruction."

"I'd prefer to have you functioning and able to come to my assistance if you're needed. I don't want to quarrel with you, *Anne*. Accept the program. I won't be happy until you do."

"Yes, Warren."

He breathed a slow sigh, patted her shoulder. Her hand touched his, rested there. He walked from under it and she followed, a slow clicking at his heels.

10

The raft was still there. Nests of sodden grass lodged in tree branches and cast high up on the shores showed how high the flood had risen, but the rope had held it. The water still flowed higher than normal. The whole shoreline had changed, the bank eroded away. The raft sat higher still, partially filled with water and leaves.

Warren picked his way down to it, past brush festooned with leaves and grass, only food and water and a folding spade for a pack. He used a stick to support his weight on the injured leg, walked slowly and carefully. He set everything down to heave the raft up and dump the water . . . no more care of contamination, he reckoned: it had all had its chance at one time or another, the river, the forest. The second raft was in the crawler upslope, but all he had lost was the paddle, and he went back after that, slow progress, unhurried.

"*Anne*," he said via com, when he had settled everything in place, when the raft bobbed on the river and his gear was aboard. "I'm at the river. I won't call for a while. A few hours. My status is very good. I'm going to be busy here."

"Yes, Warren."

He cut it off, put it back at his belt, launched the raft.

The far bank had suffered similar damage. He drove for it with some difficulty with the river running high, wet his boots getting himself ashore, secured the raft by pulling it up with the rope, the back part of it still in the water.

The ground in the forest, too, was littered with small branches and larger ones, carpeted with new leaves. But flowers had come into bloom. Everywhere the mosses were starred with white flowers. Green ones opened at the bases of trees. The hanging vines bloomed in pollen-golden rods.

And the fungi proliferated everywhere, fantastical shapes, oranges and blues and whites. The ferns were heavy with water and shed drops like jewels. There were beauties to compensate for the ruin. Drops fell from the high branches when the wind blew, a periodic shower that soaked his hair and ran off his impermeable jacket. Everything seemed both greener and darker, all the growth lusher and thicker than ever.

The grove when he came upon it had suffered not at all, not a branch fallen, only a litter of leaves and small limbs on the grass; and he was glad—not to have lost one of the giants. The old tree's beard was flower-starred, his moss even thicker. Small cuplike flowers bloomed in the grass in the sunlight, a vine having grown into the light, into the way of the abandoned, rain-sodden blanket, the sensor box.

And Sax . . . Warren went to the base of the aged tree and looked inside, found him there, more bone than before, the clothing sodden with the storm, some of the bones of the fingers fallen away. The sight had no horror for him, nothing but sadness. "Sax," he said softly. "It's Warren. Warren here."

From the vacant eyes, no answer. He stood up, flexed the spade out, set to work, spadeful after spadeful, casting the dirt and the leaves inside, into what made a fair tomb, a strange one for a starfarer . . . poor lost Sax, curled up to sleep. The earthen blanket grew up to Sax's knees, to his waist, among the gnarled roots and the bones. He made spadefuls of the green flowers and set them there, at Sax's feet, set them in the earth that covered him, stirring up clouds of pollen. He sneezed and wiped his eyes and stood up again, taking another spadeful of earth and mold.

A sound grew in his mind like the bubbling of water, and he looked to his left, where green radiance bobbed. The welcome flowed into him like the touch of warm wind.

He ignored it, cast the earth, took another spadeful.

Welcome, it sang to him. The water-sound bubbled. A flower unfolded, tinted itself slowly violet.

"I've work to do."

Sorrow. The color faded.

"I don't want it like the last time. Keep your distance. Stop that." Its straying thoughts brushed him, numbing senses. He leaned on the spade, felt himself sinking, turning and drifting bodilessly—wrenched his mind back to his own control so abruptly he almost fell.

Sorrow. A second time a flower, a pale shoot from among the leaves, a folded bud trying to open.

"Work," Warren said. He picked up the spadeful, cast it; and another.

Perplexity. The flower folded again, drooped unwatered.

"I have this to do. It's important. And you won't understand that. Nothing of the sort could matter to you."

The radiance grew, pulsed. Suns flickered across a mental sky, blue and black, day and night, in a streaming course.

He leaned on the spade for stability in the blur of days passed. "What's time—to you?"

Desire. The radiance took shape and settled on the grass, softly pulsing. It edged closer—stopped at once when he stepped back.

"Maybe you killed Sax. You know that? Maybe he just lay there and dreamed to death."

Sorrow. An image formed in his mind, the small sickly creature, all curled up, all its inward motion suddenly stopped.

"I know. You wouldn't have meant it. But it happened." He dug another spadeful of earth. Intervening days unrolled in his mind, thoughts stolen from him, where he had been, what he had done.

It stole the thought of *Anne*, and it was a terrible image, a curled-up thing like a human, but hollow inside, dark inside, deadly hostile. Her tendrils were dark and icy.

"She's not like that. She's just a machine." He flung the spadeful. Earth showered over bare bone and began to cover Sax's face. He flinched from the sight. "She can't do anything but take orders. I made her, if you like."

There was horror in the air, palpable.

"She's not alive. She never was."

The radiance became very pale and retreated up into the branches of one of the youngest trees, a mere touch of color in the sunlight. Cold, cold, the terror drifted down like winter rain.

"*Don't leave.*" The spade fell. He stepped over it, held up his hands, threatened with solitude. "Don't."

The radiance went out. Re-formed near him, drifted up to sit on the aged, fallen tree.

"It's my world. I know it's different. I never wanted to hurt you with it."

The greenness spread about him, a darkness in its heart, where two small creatures entwined, their tendrils interweaving, one living, one dead.

"Stop it."

His own mind came back at him: loneliness, longing for companionship; fear of dying alone. Like Sax. Like that. He held deeply buried the thought that the luminance offered a means of dying, a little better than most; but it came out, and the radiance shivered. The *Anne*-image took shape in its heart, her icy tendrils invading the image that was himself, growing, insinuating ice into that small fluttering that was his life, winding through him and out again.

"What do you know?" he cried at it. "What do you know at all? You don't know me. You can't see me, with no eyes; you don't know."

The *Anne*-image faded, left him alone in the radiance, embryo, tucked and fluttering inside. A greenness crept in there, the least small tendril of green, and touched that quickness.

Emotion exploded like sunrise, with a shiver of delight. A second burst. He tried to object, felt a touching of the hairs at the back of his neck. He shivered, and the light was gone. Every sense seemed stretched to the limit, heightened, but remote, and he wanted to get up and walk a little distance, knowing even while he did so that it was not his own suggestion. He moved, limping a little, and quite suddenly the presence fled, leaving a light sweat over his body.

Pain, it sent. And Peace.

"Hurt, did it?" He massaged his knee and sat down. His own eyes watered. "Serves you right."

Sorrow. The greenness unfolded again, filling all his mind but for one small corner where he stayed whole and alert.

"No," he cried in sudden panic, and when it drew back in its own: "I wouldn't mind—if you were content with touching. But you aren't. You can't keep your distance when you get excited. And sometimes you hurt."

The greenness faded a little. It was dark round about.

Hours. Hours gone. A flickering, a quick feeling of sunlit warmth came to him, but he flung it off.

"Don't lie to me. What happened to the time? When did it get dark?"

A sun plummeted, and trees bowed in evening breezes.

"How long did you have control? How long was it?"

Sorrow. Peace . . . settled on him with a great weight. He felt a great desire of sleep, of folding in and biding until warm daylight returned, and he feared nothing any longer, not life, not death. He drifted on the wind, conscious of the forest's silent growings and stretchings and burrowings about him. Then he became himself again, warm and animal and very comfortable in the simple regularity of heartbeat and breathing.

He awoke in sunlight, stretched lazily and stopped in mid-stretch as green light broke into existence up in the branches. The creature drifted slowly down to the grass beside him and rested there, exuding happiness. Sunrise burst across his vision, the fading of stars, the unfolding of flowers.

He reached for the food kit, trying to remember where he had laid it. Stopped, held in the radiance, and looked into the heart of it. It was an effort to pull his mind away. "Stop that. I have no sense of time when you're so close. Maybe you can spend an hour watching a flower unfold, but that's a considerable portion of my life."

Sorrow. The radiance murmured and bubbled with images he could not make sense of, of far-traveling, the unrolling of land, of other consciousnesses, of a vast and all-driving hunger for others, so strong it left him shaking.

"Stop it. I don't understand what you're trying to tell me."

The light grew in his vision and pulsed bright and dark, little gold sparks swirling in the heart of it, an explosion of pure excitement reaching out to him.

"What's wrong with you?" he cried. He trembled.

Quite suddenly the light winked out altogether, and when it reappeared a moment later it was not half so bright or so large, bubbling softly with the sound of waters.

"What's wrong?"

Need. Sorrow. Again the impression of other consciousnesses, other luminances, a thought quickly snatched away, all of them flowing and flooding into one.

"You mean others of your kind."

The image came back to him; and flowers, stamens shedding pollen, golden clouds, golden dust adhering to the pistil of a great, green-veined lily.

"Like mating? Like that?"

The backspill became unsettling, for the first time sexual.

"You produce others of your kind." He felt the excitement flooding through his own veins, a contagion. "Others—are coming here?"

Come. He got the impression strongly, a tugging at all his senses, a flowing over the hills and away. A merging, with things old and wise, and full of experiences, lives upon lives. *Welcome. Come.*

"I'm *human.*"

Welcome. Need pulled at him. Distances rolled away, long distances, days and nights.

"What would happen to me?"

Life bursting from the soil. The luminance brightened and enlarged. The man-image came into his vision: The embryo stretched itself and grew new tendrils, into the radiance, and it into the fluttering heart; more and more luminances added themselves, and the tendrils twined, human and otherwise, until they became another greenness, another life, to float on the winds.

Come, it urged.

His heart swelled with tears. He wept and then ceased to be human at all, full of years, deep-rooted and strong. He felt the sun and the rain and the passage of time beyond measure, knew the birth and death of forests and the weaving undulations of rivers across the land. There were mountains and snows and tropics where winter never came, and deep caverns and cascading streams and things that verged on consciousness deep in the darkness. The very stars in the heavens changed their patterns and the world was young. There were many lives, many, and one by one he knew their selves, strength and youth and age beyond reckoning, the joy of new birth, the beginning of new consciousness. Time melted. It was all one experience, and there was vast peace, unity, even in the storms, the cataclysms, the destruction of forests in lightning-bred fires, the endless push of life toward the sun and the rain—cycle on cycle, year on year, eons passing. At last his strength faded and he slept, enfolded in a green and gentle warmth; he thought that he died like the old tree and did not care, because it was a gradual and comfortable thing, a return to elements, ultimate joining. The living creature that crept in among his upturned roots for shelter was nothing less and nothing more than the moss, the dying flowers, the fallen leaves.

He lay on the grass, too weary to move, beyond care. Tears leaked from his eyes. His hands were weak. He had no terror of merging now, none, and the things he had shared with this creature would remain with them, with all its kind, immortal.

It pulled at him, and the pull that worked through his mind was as strong as the tides of the sea, as immutable and unarguable. Peace, it urged on him; and in his mind the sun flicked again through the heavens.

He opened his eyes. A day gone. A second day. Then the weakness in his limbs had its reason. He tried to sit up, panicked even through the urging of peace it laid on him.

Anne. The recollection flashed through his memory with a touch of cold. The luminance recoiled, resisting.

"No. I have to reach her. I have to." He fought hard for consciousness, gained, and knew by the release that the danger got through. Fear flooded over him like cold water.

The *Anne*-image appeared, a hollow shell in darkness, tendrils coiling out. Withered. Urgency pulled at him, and the luminance pulsed with agitation.

"Time—how much time is there?"

Several sunsets flashed through his mind.

"I have to get to her. I have to get her to take an instruction. She's dangerous."

The radiance was very wan. Urgency. Urgency. The hills rolled away in the mind's eye, the others called. Urgency.

And it faded, leaving behind an overwhelming flood of distress.

Warren lay still a moment, on his back, on the grass, shivering in the cold daylight. His head throbbed. His limbs ached and had no strength. He reached for the com, got it on, got it to his lips, his eyes closed, shutting out the punishing sun.

"*Anne.*"

"Warren. Please confirm status."

"Fine—I'm fine." He tried to keep his voice steady. His throat was raw. It could not sound natural. "I'm coming home, *Anne.*"

A pause on the other side. "Yes, Warren. Assistance?"

"Negative, negative, *Anne.* Please wait. I'll be there soon." He gathered himself up to his arm, to his knees, to his feet, with difficulty. There were pains in all his joints. He felt his face, unshaven and rough. His hands and feet were numb with the cold and the damp. His clothes sagged on him, belt gone loose.

"Warren?"

"I'm all right, *Anne.* I'm starting back now."

"Accepted," *Anne* said after a little delay. "Emergency procedures canceled."

"What—emergency procedures?"

"What's your status, Warren?"

"No emergency, do you hear me? No emergency. I'm on my way."
He shut it down, found his canteen, the food packet, drank, forced a bite
down his swollen throat and stuffed the rest into his sodden jacket.
Walked. His leg hurt, and his eyes blurred, the lids swollen and raw. He
found a branch and tore it off and used that as he went—pushed himself,
knowing the danger there was in *Anne*.

Knowing how little time there was. It would go, it would go then,
and leave him. And there would be nothing after that. Ever.

11

Anne was waiting for him, at the riverside—amid the stumps of trees,
mud, cleared earth. Trees dammed the river, water spilling over them,
between them, flooding up over the banks and changing the land into a
shallow, sandy lake.

He stopped there, leaned against the last standing tree on that margin and shivered, slow tremors which robbed him of strength and sense.
She stood placidly in the ruin; he called her on the com, heard her voice,
saw her face, then her body, orient toward him. He began to cross the
bridge of tumbled trees, clinging to branches, walking tilted trunks.

"Damn you," he shouted at her. Tears ran down his face. "*Damn
you!*"

She met him at the other side, silver slimed with mud and soot from
the burning she had done. Her sensors blinked. "Assistance?"

He found his self-control, shifted his attack. "You've damaged yourself."

"I'm functioning normally. Assistance?"

He started to push past her, slipped on the unstable log. She reached
to save him, her arm rock-solid, stable. He clung to it, his only point of
balance. Her facelights blinked at him. Her other hand came up to rest
on his shoulder. Contact. She offered contact. He had meant to shove at
her. He touched her gently, patted her plastic-sheathed shoulder, fought
back the tears. "You've *killed*, Annie. Don't you understand?"

"Vegetation."

He shoved past her, limped up the devastated shore, among the
stumps of trees. His head throbbed. His stomach felt hollow.

The crawler still waited on the bank. *Anne* overtook him as he
reached it; she offered him her hand as he climbed in. He slid into the
seat, slipped the brake, started the motor and threw it full throttle, leaving her behind.

"Warren." Her voice pursued him.

He kept driving, wildly, swerving this way and that over the jolts, past the brush.

"*Anne,*" he said, standing at the airlock. "Open the lock."

Silence.

"*Anne.* Open the lock, please."

It hissed wide. He walked in, unsteady as he was, onto the cargo platform. "Engage lift, *Anne.*"

Gears crashed. It started up, huge and ponderous that it was. "Warren," the disembodied voice said, from the speakers, everywhere, echoing. "What's your status, Warren?"

"Good, thank you."

"Your voice indicates stress."

"Hoarseness. Minor dysfunction in my speaking apparatus. It's self-repairing."

A silence. "Recorded." The lift stopped on netherdeck. He walked out, calmly, to the lower weapons locker, put his card in.

Dead. "I've got a lock malfunction here, *Anne.* Number 13/546. Would you clear it up?"

"Emergency locks are still engaged."

"Disengage."

Silence.

"There is no emergency." He fought the anger from his voice. "Disengage emergency locks and cancel all emergency procedures."

"This vocal dysfunction is not repaired."

He leaned against the wall, stared down the corridor.

"Warren, please confirm your status."

"Normal, I tell you." He went to the lift. It worked. It brought him up to the level of the laboratories. He walked down to Bio, walked in, tried the cabinets. "*Anne.* I need medicines. Disengage the locks. I need medicines for repair."

The lock clicked. It opened.

He took out the things he needed, washed his torn hands, prepared a stimulant. He was filthy. He saw himself like a specter in a reflecting glass, gaunt, stubbled; looked down and saw his clothes unrecognizable in color. He washed an area of his arm and fired the injection, rummaged through the cabinet for medicines to cure the hoarseness. He found some lozenges, ripped one from the foil and sucked on it, then headed off for the showers, undressing as he went.

A quick wash. He had forgotten clean clothes; he belted on the bathrobe he had left in the showers, on a body gone gaunt. His hands shook. The stim hummed in his veins. He could not afford the shakes. He had visions of the pseudosome walking back toward the ship; she would be here soon. He had to make normal moves. Had to do everything in accustomed order. He went to the galley next, opened the box and downed fruit juice from its container; it hit his stomach in a wave of cold.

He hauled out other things. Dried food. Stacked it there. He took out one frozen dinner and put it in the microwave.

It turned on without his touching it.

"Time, please."

"Fifteen minutes," he told it. He walked out. He took the dried food with him to the lift.

He punched buttons. It took him up. He walked out into the corridor; lights came on for him. Lights came on in the living quarters, in his own quarters, as he entered. He dumped the dried stores on the bed, opened the locker, and pulled out all his clothing—dressed, short of breath, having to stop and rest in the act of putting his boots on.

The lock crashed and boomed in the bowels of the ship.

She was back. He pulled the second boot on. He could hear the lift working. He folded his remaining clothes. He heard the next lift work. He arranged everything on his bed. He heard footsteps approach.

He looked round. *Anne* stood there, muddy, streaked with soot.

"Assistance? Please confirm your status, Warren."

He thought a moment. "Fine. You're dirty, *Anne*. Decontaminate."

Sensors flickered, one and then the others. "You're packing. This program is preparatory to going to the river. Please reconsider this program."

"I'm just cleaning up. Why don't you get me dinner?"

"You fixed dinner, Warren."

"I didn't like it. You fix it. I'll have dinner up here at the table. Fifteen minutes. I need it, *Anne*. I'm hungry."

"Yes, Warren."

"And clean up."

"Yes, Warren."

The pseudosome left. He dropped his head into his hands, caught his breath. Best to rest a bit. Have dinner. See what he could do about a program and get her to take it. He went to the desk where he had left the programming microfilm, got it, and fed it into the viewer.

He scanned through the emergency programs, the E sequences, hoping to distract her into one of those. There was nothing that offered a way to seize control. Nothing that would lock her up.

It was feeding into her, even now; she had library access. The viewer was part of her systems. The thought made him nervous. He scanned through harmless areas, to confound her.

"Dinner's ready," the speaker told him.

He wiped his face, shut down the viewer and walked out, hearing the lift in function.

Anne arrived, carrying a tray. She set things on the table, arranged them.

He sat down. She poured him coffee, walked to her end of the table and sat facing him.

He ate a few bites. The food nauseated him. He shoved the plate away.

Her lights flickered. "Chess?"

"Thank you, no, *Anne*. I've got other things to do."

"Do. Yes. Activity. What activity do you choose, Warren?"

He stared at her. Observation and question. Subsequent question. "Your assimilation's really made a lot of progress, hasn't it? Lateral activity."

"The lateral patterning is efficient in forecast. Question posed: what activity do you choose, Warren?"

"I'm going down below. You stay here. Clean up the dinner."

"Yes, Warren."

He pushed back from the table, walked out and down the corridor to the lift. He decided on routine, on normalcy, on time to think.

He rode the lift back to the lab level, walked out. She turned the lights on for him, turned them off behind as he walked, always conservative.

He pushed the nearest door button. Botany, it was. The door stayed shut.

"Lab doors locked," he said casually. "Open it."

The door shot back. Lights went on.

The room was a shambles. Planting boxes were overthrown, ripped loose, pipes twisted, planting medium scattered everywhere, the floor, the walls. Some of the boxes were partially melted, riddled with laser fire.

He backed out, quietly, quickly. Closed the door. Walked back to the lift, his footsteps echoing faster and faster on the decking. He opened the lift door, stepped in, pushed the button for topside.

It took him up. He left it, walking now as quickly, as normally, as he could, not favoring his leg.

Anne had left the living quarters. He went by the vacant table, to the bridge corridor, to the closed door at the end. He used his cardkey.

It stayed shut.

"*Anne*," he said, "you have a malfunction. There's no longer an emergency. Please clear the emergency lock on the bridge. I have a critical problem involving maintenance. I need to get to controls right now."

A delay. The speaker near his head came on. "Emergency procedure remains in effect. Access not permitted."

"*Anne*. We have a paradox here. The problem involves your mistake."

"Clarify: mistake."

"You've perceived a false emergency. You've initiated wrong procedures. Some of your equipment is damaged. Cancel emergency. This is a code nine. Cancel emergency and open this door."

A further delay. "Negative. Access denied."

"*Anne*." He pushed the button again. It was dead. He heard a heavy step in the corridor behind him. He jerked about with his back to the door and looked into *Anne*'s dark faceplate with its dancing stars. "Open it," he said. "I'm in pain, *Anne*. The pain won't stop until you cancel emergency procedure and open this door."

"Please adjust yourself."

"I'm not malfunctioning. I need this door opened." He forced calm into his voice, adopted a reasoning tone. "The ship is in danger, *Anne*. I have to get in there."

"Please go back to permitted areas, Warren."

He caught his breath, stared at her, then edged past her carefully, down the corridor to the living quarters. She was at his back, still, following.

"Is this a permitted area?" he asked.

"Yes, Warren."

"I want a cup of coffee. Bring it."

"Yes, Warren."

She walked out into the main corridor. The door closed behind her. He delayed a moment till he heard the lift, then went and tried it. Dead. "*Anne*. Now there's a malfunction with number two access. Will you do something about it?"

"Access not permitted."

"I need a bath, *Anne.* I need to go down to the showers."

A delay. "This is not an emergency procedure. Please wait for assistance."

A scream welled up in him. He swallowed it, smoothed his hand over the metal as if it were skin. "All right. All right, *Anne.*" He turned, walked back to his own quarters.

The clothes and food were gone from the bed.

The manual. He went to the viewer. The microfilm was gone. He searched the drawer where he kept it. It was not there.

Panic surged up in him. He stifled it, walked out. He walked back to the table, sat down—heard the lift operating finally. Heard her footsteps. The door opened.

"Coffee, Warren."

"Thank you, Annie."

She set the cup down, poured his coffee. Hydraulics worked in the ship, massive movement, high on the frame. The turret rotating. Warren looked up. "What's that, *Anne?*"

"Armaments, Warren."

The electronic snap of the cannon jolted the ship. He sprang up from his chair and *Anne* set down the coffee pot.

"*Anne. Anne,* cancel weapons. *Cancel!*"

The firing went on.

"Cancel refused," *Anne* said.

"*Anne*—show me . . . what you're shooting at. Put it on the screen."

The wallscreen lit, the black of night, a thin line of orange: a horizon, ablaze with fires.

"*You're killing it!*"

"Vegetation, Warren. Emergency program is proceeding."

"*Anne.*" He seized her metal, unflexing arm. "Cancel program."

"Negative."

"On what reasoning? *Anne*—turn on your sensor box. Turn it on. Scan the area."

"It is operating, Warren. I'm using it to refine target. Possibly the equipment will survive. Possibly I can recover it. Please adjust yourself, Warren. Your voice indicates stress."

"It's life you're killing out there!"

"Vegetation, Warren. This is a priority, but overridden. I'm programmed to make value judgments. I've exercised my override reflex. This is a rational function. Please adjust yourself, Warren."

"The lab. You destroyed the lab. Why?"

"I don't like vegetation, Warren."

"Don't *like?*"

"Yes, Warren. This seems descriptive."

"*Anne*, you're malfunctioning. Listen to me. You'll have to shut down for a few moments, I won't damage you or interfere with your standing instructions. I'm your crew, *Anne*. Shut down."

"I can't accept this instruction, Warren. One of my functions is preservation of myself. You're my highest priority. To preserve you, I have to preserve myself. Please adjust yourself, Warren."

"*Anne*, let me out. Let me out of here."

"No, Warren."

The firing stopped. On the screen the fires continued to burn. He looked at it, leaned on the back of the chair, shaking.

"Assistance?"

"Go to hell."

"I can't go to hell, Warren. I have to hold this position."

"*Anne. Anne*—listen. I found a being out there. A sapient life form. In the forest. I talked with it. You're killing a sapient being, you hear me?"

A delay. "My sensors detected nothing. Your activities are erratic and injurious. I record your observation. Please provide data."

"Your sensor box. Turn it on."

"It's still operating, Warren."

"It was there. The life was there, when I was. I can go back. I can prove it. I talked to it, *Anne*."

"There was no other life there."

"Because your sensor unit couldn't register it. Because your sensors aren't sensitive enough. Because you're not human, *Anne.*"

"I have recorded sounds. Identify."

The wallscreen flicked to a view of the grove. The wind sighed in the leaves; something babbled. A human figure lay writhing on the ground, limbs jerking, mouth working with the sounds. Himself. The murmur was his own voice, inebriate and slurred.

He turned his face from it. "Cut it off. Cut it off, *Anne.*"

The sound stopped. The screen was blank and white when he turned his head again. He leaned there a time. There was a void in him where life had been. Where he had imagined life. He sat down at the table, wiped his eyes.

After a moment he picked up the coffee and drank.

"Are you adjusted, Warren?"

"Yes. Yes, *Anne*."

"Emergency program will continue until all surrounds are sterilized."

He sat staring at his hands, at the cup before him. "And then what will I do?"

Anne walked to the end of the table, sat down, propped her elbows on the table, head on hands, sensor lights blinking in continuous operation.

The chessboard flashed to the wallscreen at her back.

The pawn advanced one square.

IV

"Well, how many were there?" I ask, over supper.

"There might have been four."

"There was one," I say. "*Anne* was Warren too." I blink in all innocence. "In a manner of speaking."

We sit together, speaking under the canned music. Art made into white noise, to divide us table from table in the dining hall. "Awful stuff, that music," I say. Then I have another thought:

"On the other hand—"

"There were four?"

"No. The music. The Greeks painted vases."

"What have Greek urns got to do with canned music?"

"Art. Do you know—" I hold up a spoon. "This is art."

"Come on. They stamp them out by the thousands."

"But an artist designed this. Its balance, its shape. An artist drew it and sculpted it, and another sort made the die. Then a workman ran it and collected his wage. Which he used to buy a tape. Do you know, we work most of our lives to afford two things: leisure and art."

"Even mass-produced art?"

"The Greeks mass-produced clay lamps. Now we call them antiquities. And we set them on little pedestals in museums. They painted their pots and their lamps. Rich Greeks had musicians at their banquets. Nowadays the poorest man can have a fine metal spoon and have music to listen to with his dinner. That's magical."

"Well, now the rest of us have got to put up with damned little die-stamped spoons."

"How many of us would have *owned* a spoon in those good old days?"

"Who needed them? Fingers worked."

"So did typhoid."

"What has typhoid to do with spoons?"

"Sanitation. Cities and civilizations *died* for want of spoons. And good drainage. It's all art. I've walked the streets of dead cities, it's an eerie thing, to read the graves and the ages. Very many children. Very many. And so many cities which just—died. Not in violence. Just of needs we take for granted. I tell you we are all kings and magicians. Our touch on a machine brings light, sound, musicians appear in thin air, pictures leap from world to world. Each of us singly wields the power output of a Mesopotamian empire—without ever thinking about it. We can *afford* it."

"We waste it."

I lift my hand toward the unseen stars. "Does the sun? I suppose that it does. But we gather what it throws away. And the universe doesn't lose it, except to entropy."

"A world has only so much."

"A solar system has too much ever to bring home. Look at the asteroids, the moons, the sun—No, the irresponsible thing is *not* to wield that power. To sit in a closed world and do nothing. To refuse to mass-produce. To deny some fellow his bit of art bought with his own labor. It's not economical to paint a pot. Or to make a vase for flowers. Or to grow flowers instead of cabbages."

"Cabbages," you recall, "have their importance in the cosmic system."

"Don't flowers? And isn't it better that a man has music with his dinner and a pot with a design on it?"

"You don't like the ancient world?"

"Let me tell you, *most* of us didn't live well. *Most* of us didn't make it past childhood. And not just villages vanished in some bitter winter. Whole towns did. Whole nations. There were no good old days."

"History again."

"That's why we make fantasies. Because it was too bad to remember."

"Cynic."

"I do write fantasies. Sometimes."

"And they're true?"

"True as those poor dead kids in Ephesus."

"Where's that?"

"See?" I sigh, thinking of dead stones and a child's game, etched forever in a dead street, near a conqueror's arch. "Let me tell you a story."

"A cheerful one."

"A cheerful one. Let me tell you a story about a story. Lin Carter and I were talking just exactly like this once upon a time, about the wretchedness of the ancient world—he was doing an anthology, and wanted me to write a story, a fantasy. And then Lin said a remarkable thing which I'm sure didn't come out quite the thing he was trying to say. I think what he *meant* to say was that the medieval age was not particularly chivalrous, that the open land was quite dangerous and that it was an age which quite well cast everyone into a series of dependencies—i.e., villein upon master, him upon his lord, lord upon baron, baron upon king, and king upon emperor, who relied on God and played politics with Him whenever he could. The way it came out was that no woman could possibly survive in the middle ages . . .

"I laughed. Lin took a curious look at his glass and amended the remark to say that it at least would not be the merry life of derring-do practiced by the males of fiction. I countered that the real-life rogues hardly had a merry time of it in real life either. You were more likely to mistake the aristocrats for the outlaws than vice versa.

"But immediately that became the orchard fence, the thou-shalt-not which of course was precisely the story I meant to do for Lin's anthology. Not only that, in my tale, the woman would be no princess, no abbess, no burgher's daughter with defensive advantages."

"Witch?"

"Well, take a very typical swash and buckle hero—illiterate, battling wizards, gods, and double-dealing princes, selling what can be sold and spending all the gain by sunrise—"

"—Who carries off the woman?"

"That *is* the woman."

A THIEF IN KORIANTH

1

The Yliz River ran through Korianth, a sullen, muddy stream on its way to the nearby sea, with stone banks where it passed through the city . . . gray stone and yellow water, and gaudy ships which made a spider-tangle of masts and riggings above the drab jumbled roofs of the dockside. In fact, all Korianth was built on pilings and cut with canals more frequent than streets, the whole pattern of the lower town dictated by old islands and channels, so that buildings took whatever turns and bends the canals dictated, huddled against each other, jammed one up under the eaves of the next—faded paint, buildings like aged crones remembering the brightness of their youths, decayed within from overmuch of wine and living, with dulled, shuttered eyes looking suspiciously on dim streets and scummed canals, where boat vendors and barge folk plied their craft, going to and fro from shabby warehouses. This was the Sink, which was indeed slowly subsiding into the River—but that took centuries, and the Sink used only the day, quick pleasures, momentary feast, customary famine. In spring rains the Yliz rose; tavern keepers mopped and dockmen and warehousers cursed and set merchandise up on blocks; then the town stank considerably. In summer heats the River sank, and the town stank worse.

There was a glittering world above this rhythm, the part of Korianth that had grown up later, inland, and beyond the zone of flood: palaces and town houses of hewn stone (which still sank, being too heavy for their foundations, and developed cracks, and whenever abandoned, decayed quickly). In this area too were temples . . . temples of gods and goddesses and whole pantheons local and foreign, ancient and modern, for Korianth was a trading city and offended no one permanently. The gods were transients, coming and going in favor like dukes and royal lovers. There was, more permanent than gods, a king in Korianth, Seithan XXIV, but Seithan was, if rumors might be believed, quite mad, having recovered after poisoning. At least he showed a certain bizarre turn of behavior, in which he played obscure and cruel jokes and took to strange religions, mostly such as promised sybaritic afterlives and conjured demons.

And central to that zone between, where town and dockside met on the canals, lay a rather pleasant zone of mild decay, of modest townsmen and a few dilapidated palaces. In this web of muddy waterways a grand bazaar transferred the wealth of the Sink (whose dark warrens honest citizens avoided) into higher-priced commerce of the Market of Korianth.

It was a profitable place for merchants, for proselytizing cults, for healers, interpreters of dreams, prostitutes of the better sort (two of the former palaces were brothels, and no few of the temples were), palm readers and sellers of drinks and sweetmeats, silver and fish, of caged birds and slaves, copper pots and amulets and minor sorceries. Even on a chill autumn day such as this, with the stench of hundreds of altars and the spices of the booths and the smokes of midtown, that of the River welled up. Humanity jostled shoulder to shoulder, armored guard against citizen, beggar against priest, and furnished ample opportunity for thieves.

Gillian glanced across that sea of bobbing heads and swirling colors, eased up against the twelve-year-old girl whose slim, dirty fingers had just deceived the fruit merchant and popped a first and a second handful of figs into the torn seam of her cleverly sewn skirt. Gillian pushed her own body into the way of sight and reached to twist her fingers into her sister's curls and jerk. Jensy yielded before the hair came out by the roots, let herself be dragged four paces into the woman-wide blackness of an alley, through which a sickly stream of something threaded between their feet.

"Hist," Gillian said. "Will you have us on the run for a fistful of sweets? You have no judgment."

Jensy's small face twisted into a grin. "Old Habershen's never seen me."

Gillian gave her a rap on the ear, not hard. The claim was truth: Jensy was deft. The double-sewn skirt picked up better than figs. "Not here," Gillian said. "Not in *this* market. There's high law here. They cut your hand off, stupid snipe."

Jensy grinned at her; everything slid off Jensy. Gillian gripped her sister by the wrist and jerked her out into the press, walked a few stalls down. It was never good to linger. They did not look the best of customers, she and Jensy, ragged curls bound up in scarves, coarse sacking skirts, blouses that had seen good days—before they had left some goodwoman's laundry. Docksiders did come here, frequent enough in the crowds. And their faces were not known outside the Sink; varying patterns of dirt were a tolerable disguise.

Lean days were at hand; they were not far from winter, when ships would be scant, save only the paltry, patched coasters. In late fall and winter the goods were here in midtown, being hauled out of warehouses and sold at profit. Dockside was slim pickings in winter; dockside was where she preferred to work—given choice. And with Jensy—

Midtown frightened her. This place was daylight and open, and at the moment she was not looking for trouble; rather she made for the corner of the fish market with its peculiar aromas and the perfumed reek of Agdalia's gilt temple and brothel.

"Don't want to," Jensy declared, planting her feet.

Gillian jerked her willy-nilly. "I'm not going to leave you there, mousekin. Not for long."

"I hate Sophonisba."

Gillian stopped short, jerked Jensy about by the shoulder and looked down into the dirty face. Jensy sobered at once, eyes wide. "Sophonisba never lets the customers near you."

Jensy shook her head, and Gillian let out a breath. *She* had started that way; Jensy would not. She dragged Jensy to the door, where Sophonisba held her usual post at the shrine of the tinsel goddess—legitimacy of a sort, more than Sophonisba had been born to. Gillian shoved Jensy into Sophonisba's hands . . . overblown and overpainted, all pastels and perfumes and swelling bosom—it was not lack of charms kept Sophonisba on the market street, by the Fish, but the unfortunate voice, a Sink accent and a nasal whine that would keep her here forever. *Dead ear*, Gillian reckoned of her in some pity, for accents came off and onto Gillian's tongue with polyglot facility; Sophonisba probably did not know her affliction—a creature of patterns, reliable to follow them.

"Not in daylight," Sophonisba complained, painted eyes distressed. "Double cut for daylight. Are you working *here?* I don't want any part of that. Take yourselves elsewhere."

"You know I wouldn't bring the king's men down on Jensy; mind her, old friend, or I'll break your nose."

"Hate you," Jensy muttered, and winced, for Sophonisba gripped her hair.

She meant Sophonisba. Gillian gave her a face and walked away, free. The warrens or the market—neither place was safe for a twelve-year-old female with light fingers and too much self-confidence; Sophonisba could still keep a string on her—and Sophonisba was right to worry: stakes were higher here, in all regards.

Gillian prowled the aisles, shopping customers as well as booths, lingering nowhere long, flowing with the traffic. It was the third winter coming, the third since she had had Jensy under her wing. Neither of them had known hunger often while her mother had been there to care for Jensy—but those days were gone, her mother gone, and Jensy—Jensy was falling into the pattern. Gillian saw it coming. She had nightmares, Jensy in the hands of the city watch, or knifed in some stupid brawl, like their mother. Or something happening to herself, and Jensy growing up in Sophonisba's hands.

Money. A large amount of gold: that was the way out she dreamed of, money that would buy Jensy into some respectable order, to come out polished and fit for midtown or better. But that kind of money did not often flow accessibly on dockside, in the Sink. It had to be hunted here; and she saw it—all about her—at the risk of King's-law, penalties greater than the dockside was likely to inflict: the Sink took care of its own problems, but it was apt to wink at pilferage and it was rarely so inventively cruel as King's-law. Whore she was not, no longer, never again; whore she had been, seeking out Genat, a thief among thieves; and the apprentice had passed the master. Genat had become blind Genat the beggar—dead Genat soon after—and Gillian was free, walking the market where Genat himself seldom dared pilfer.

If she had gold enough, then Jensy was out of the streets, out of the way of things that waited to happen.

Gold enough, and she could get more: gold was power, and she had studied power zealously, from street bravos to priests, listening to gossip, listening to rich folk talk, one with the alleys and the booths—she learned, did Gillian, how rich men stole, and she planned someday—she always had—to be rich.

Only three years of fending for two, and this third year that saw Jensy filling out into more than her own whipcord shape would ever be, *that* promised what Jensy would be the fourth year, when at thirteen she became a mark for any man on the docks—

This winter or never, for Jensy.

Gillian walked until her thin soles burned on the cobbles. She looked at jewelers' booths—too wary, the goldsmiths, who tended to have armed bullies about them. She had once—madly—entertained the idea of approaching a jeweler, proposing her own slight self as a guard: truth, no one on the streets could deceive her sharp eyes, and there would be no pilferage; but say to them, *I am a better thief than they, sirs?*—that was a way to end like Genat.

Mistress to such, instead? There seemed no young and handsome ones—even Genat had been that—and she, moreover, had no taste for more such years. She passed the jewelers, hoping forlornly for some indiscretion.

She hungered by afternoon and thought wistfully of the figs Jensy had fingered; Jensy had them, which meant Jensy would eat them. Gillian was not so rash as in her green years. She would not risk herself for a bit of bread or cheese. She kept prowling, turning down minor opportunities, bumped against a number of promising citizens, but each was a risk, and each deft fingering of their purses showed nothing of great substance.

The hours passed. The better classes began to wend homeward with their bodyguards and bullies. She began to see a few familiar faces on the edges of the crowd, rufflers and whores and such anticipating the night, which was theirs. Merchants with more expensive goods began folding up and withdrawing with their armed guards and their day's profits.

Nothing—no luck at all, and Sophonisba would not accept a cut of bad luck; Gillian had two coppers in her own purse, purloined days ago, and Sophonisba would expect one. It was the streets and no supper if she was not willing to take a risk.

Suddenly a strange face cut the crowd, making haste: that caught her eye, and like the reflex of a boxer, her body tended that way before her mind had quite weighed matters, so she should not lose him. This was a stranger; there was a fashion to faces in Korianth, and this one was not Korianthine—Abhizite, she reckoned, from upriver. Gillian warmed indeed; it was like summer, when gullible foreigners came onto the docks carrying their traveling funds with them and giving easy opportunity to the light-fingered trade.

She bumped him in the press at a corner, anticipating his move to dodge her, and her razor had the purse strings, her fingers at once aware of weight, her heart thudding with the old excitement as she eeled through the crowd and alleyward.

Heavy purse—it was too soon missed: her numbing blow had had short effect. She heard the bawl of outrage, and suddenly a general shriek of alarm. At the bend of the alley she looked back.

Armored men. Bodyguards!

Panic hit her; she clutched the purse and ran the dark alley she had mapped in advance for escape, ran with all her might and slid left, right, right, along a broad back street, down yet another alley. They were after her in the twilight of the maze, cursing and with swords gleaming bare.

It was no ordinary cutpursing. She had tripped something, indeed. She ran until her heart was nigh to bursting, took the desperate chance of a stack of firewood to scamper to a ledge and into the upper levels of the midtown maze.

She watched them then, she lying on her heaving belly and trying not to be heard breathing. They were someone's hired bravos for certain, scarred of countenance, with that touch of the garish that bespoke gutter origins.

"Common cutpurse," one said. That rankled. She had other skills.

"Someone has to have seen her," said another. "Money will talk, in the Sink."

They went away. Gillian lay still, panting, opened the purse with trembling fingers.

A lead cylinder stamped with a seal; lead, and a finger-long sealed parchment, and a paltry three silver coins.

Bile welled up in her throat. They had sworn to search for her even into the impenetrable Sink. She had stolen something terrible; she had ruined herself; and even the Sink could not hide her, not against money, and such men.

Jensy, she thought, sick at heart. If passersby had seen her strolling there earlier and described Jensy—their memories would be very keen, for gold. The marks on the loot were ducal seals, surely; lesser men did not use such things. Her breath shuddered through her throat. Kings and dukes. She had stolen lead and paper, and her death. She could not read, not a word—not even to know *what* she had in hand.

—and *Jensy!*

She swept the contents back into the purse, thrust it into her blouse and, dropping down again into the alley, ran.

2

The tinsel shrine was closed. Gillian's heart sank, and her vision blurred. Again to the alleys and behind, thence to a lower-story window with a red shutter. She reached up and rapped it a certain pattern with her knuckles.

It opened. Sophonisba's painted face stared down at her; a torrent of abuse poured sewer-fashion from the dewy lips, and Jensy's dirty-scarfed head bobbed up from below the whore's ample bosom.

"Come *on*," Gillian said, and Jensy scrambled, grimaced in pain, for Sophonisba had her by the hair.

"My cut," Sophonisba said.

Gillian swallowed air, her ears alert for pursuit. She fished the two coppers from her purse, and Sophonisba spat on them. Heat flushed Gillian's face; the next thing in her hand was her razor.

Sophonisba paled and sniffed. "I know you got better, slink. The whole street's roused. Should I take such risks? If someone comes asking here, should I say lies?"

Trembling, blind with rage, Gillian took back the coppers. She brought out the purse, spilled the contents: lead cylinder, parchment, three coins. "Here. See? Trouble, trouble and no lot of money."

Sophonisba snatched at the coins. Gillian's deft fingers saved two, and the other things, which Sophonisba made no move at all to seize.

"Take your trouble," Sophonisba said. "And your brat. And keep away from here."

Jensy scrambled out over the sill, hit the alley cobbles on her slippered feet. Gillian did not stay to threaten. Sophonisba knew her—knew better than to spill to king's-men . . . or to leave Jensy on the street. Gillian clutched her sister's hand and pulled her along at a rate a twelve-year-old's strides could hardly match.

They walked, finally, in the dark of the blackest alleys and, warily, into the Sink itself. Gillian led the way to Threepenny Bridge and so to Rat's Alley and the Bowel. They were *not* alone, but the shadows inspected them cautiously: the trouble that lurked here was accustomed to pull its victims into the warren, not to find them there; and one time that lurkers did come too close, she and Jensy played dodge in the alley. "Cheap flash," she spat, and: "Bit's Isle," marking herself of a rougher brotherhood than theirs. They were alone after.

After the Bowel came the Isle itself, and the deepest part of the Sink. There was a door in the alley called Blindman's, where Genat had sat till someone knifed him. She dodged to it with Jensy in tow, this stout door inconspicuous among others, and pushed it open.

It let them in under Jochen's stairs, in the wine-smelling backside of the Rose. Gillian caught her breath then and pulled Jensy close within the shadows of the small understairs pantry. "Get Jochen," she bade Jensy then. Jensy skulked out into the hall and took off her scarf, stuffed that in her skirts and passed out of sight around the corner of the door and into the roister of the tavern.

In a little time she was back with fat Jochen in her wake, and Jochen mightily scowling.

"You're in trouble?" Jochen said. "Get out if you are."

"Want you to keep Jensy for me."

"Pay," Jochen said. "You got it?"

"How much?"

"How bad the trouble?"

"For her, none at all. Just keep her." Gillian turned her back—prudence, not modesty—to fish up the silver from her blouse, not revealing the purse. She held up one coin. "Two days' board and close room."

"You *are* in trouble."

"I want Nessim. Is he here?"

He always was by dark. Jochen snorted. "A cut of what's going."

"A cut if there's profit; a clear name if there's not; get Nessim."

Jochen went. "I don't want to be left," Jensy started to say, but Gillian rapped her ear and scowled so that Jensy swallowed it and looked frightened. Finally a muddled old man came muttering their way and Gillian snagged his sleeve. The reek of wine was strong; it was perpetual about Nessim Hath, excommunicate priest and minor dabbler in magics. He read, when he was sober enough to see the letters; that and occasionally effective magics—wards against rats, for one—made him a livelihood and kept his throat uncut.

"Upstairs," Gillian said, guiding sot and child up the well-worn boards to the loft and the private cells at the alleyside wall. Jensy snatched the taper at the head of the stairs and they went into that room, which had a window.

Nessim tottered to the cot and sat down while Jensy lit the stub of a candle. Gillian fished out her coppers, held them before Nessim's red-rimmed eyes and pressed them into the old priest's shaking hand.

"Read something?" Nessim asked.

Gillian pulled out the purse and knelt by the bedside while Jensy prudently closed the door. She produced the leaden cylinder and the parchment. "Old man," she said, "tell me what I've got here."

He gathered up the cylinder and brought his eyes closely to focus on it, frowning. His mouth trembled as did his hands, and he thrust it back at her. "I don't know this seal. Lose this thing in the canal. Be rid of it."

"You know it, old man."

"I don't." She did not take it from him, and he held it, trembling. "A false seal, a mask seal. Something some would know—and not outsiders. It's no good, Gillian."

"And if some would hunt a thief for it? It's good to someone."

Nessim stared at her. She valued Nessim, gave him coppers when he was on one of his lower periods: he drank the money and was grateful. She cultivated him, one gentle rogue among the ungentle, who would not have failed at priesthood and at magics if he did not drink and love comforts; now he simply had the drink.

"Run," he said. "Get out of Korianth. Tonight."

"Penniless? This should be worth something, old man."

"Powerful men would use such a seal to mask what they do, who they are. Games of more than small stakes."

Gillian swallowed heavily. "You've played with seals before, old man; read me the parchment."

He took it in hand, laid the leaden cylinder in his lap, turned the parchment to all sides. Long and long he stared at it, finally opened his purse with much trembling of his hands, took out a tiny knife and cut the red threads wrapped round, pulled them from the wax and loosed it carefully with the blade.

"Huh," Jensy pouted. "*Anyone* could cut it." Gillian rapped her ear gently as Nessim canted the tiny parchment to the scant light. His lips mumbled, steadied, a thin line. When he opened his mouth they trembled again, and very carefully he drew out more red thread from his pouch, red wax such as scribes used. Gillian held her peace and kept Jensy's, not to disturb him in the ticklish process that saw new cords seated, the seal prepared—he motioned for the candle and she held it herself while he heated and replaced the seal most gingerly.

"No magics," he said then, handing it back. "No magics of mine near this thing. Or the other. Take them. Throw them both in the River."

"Answers, old man."

"Triptis. Promising—without naming names—twenty thousand in gold to the shrine of Triptis."

Gillian wrinkled her nose and took back parchment and cylinder. "Abhizite god," she said. "A dark one." The sum ran cold fingers over her skin. "Twenty thousand. That's—*gold*—twenty thousand. How much do rich men have to spend on temples, old thief?"

"Rich men's *lives* are bought for less."

The fingers went cold about the lead. Gillian swallowed, wishing Jensy had stayed downstairs in the pantry. She held up the lead cylinder. "Can you breach that seal, old man?"

"Wouldn't."

"You tell me why."

"It's more than a lead seal on that. Adepts more than the likes of me; I know my level, woman; I know what not to touch, and you can take my advice. Get out of here. You've stolen something you can't trade in. They don't need to see you, do you understand me? This thing can be traced."

The hairs stirred to her nape. She sat staring at him. "Then throwing it in the river won't do it, either."

"They might give up then. Might. Gillian, you've put your head in the jaws this time."

"Rich men's lives," she muttered, clutching the objects in her hand. She slid them back into the purse and thrust it within her blouse. "I'll get rid of it. I'll find some way. I've paid Jochen to keep Jensy. See he does, or sour his beer."

"Gillian—"

"You don't want to know," she said. "I don't want either of you to know."

There was the window, the slanting ledge outside; she hugged Jensy, and old Nessim, and used it.

3

Alone, she traveled quickly, by warehouse roofs for the first part of her journey, where the riggings and masts of dockside webbed the night sky, by remembered ways across the canal. One monstrous old warehouse squatted athwart the canal like a misshapen dowager, a convenient crossing that avoided the bridges. Skirts hampered; she whipped off the wrap, leaving the knee breeches and woolen hose she wore beneath, the skirt rolled and bound to her waist with her belt. She had her dagger, her razor and the cant to mark her as trouble for ruffians—a lie: the nebulous brotherhood would hardly back her now, in her trouble. They disliked long looks from moneyed men, hired bullies and noise on dockside. If the noise continued about her, she might foreseeably meet with accident, to be found floating in a canal—to quiet the uproar and stop further attentions.

But such as she met did not know it and kept from her path or, sauntering and mocking, still shied from brotherhood cant. Some passwords were a cut throat to use without approval, and thieves out of the Sink taught interlopers bitter lessons.

She paused to rest at the Serpentine of midtown, crouched in the shadows, sweating and hard-breathing, dizzy with want of sleep and food. Her belly had passed the point of hurting. She thought of a side excursion—a bakery's back door, perhaps—but she did not dare the possible hue and cry added to what notoriety she already had. She gathered what strength she had and set out a second time, the way that led to the tinsel shrine and one house that would see its busiest hours in the dark.

Throw it in the canal: she dared not. Once it was gone from her, she had no more bargains left, nothing. As it was she had a secret valuable and fearful to someone. *There comes a time,* Genat had told her often enough, *when chances have to be taken—and taken wide.*

It was not Sophonisba's way.

Panting, she reached the red window, rapped at it; there was dim light inside and long delay—a male voice, a curse, some drunken converse. Gillian leaned against the wall outside and slowed her breathing, wishing by all the gods of Korianth (save one) that Sophonisba would make some haste. She rapped again finally, heart racing as her rashness raised a complaint within—male voice again. She pressed herself to the wall, heard the drunken voice diminish—Sophonisba's now, shrill, bidding someone out. A door opened and closed.

In a moment steps crossed the room and the shutter opened. Gillian showed herself cautiously, stared up into Sophonisba's white face. "Come on out here," Gillian said.

"Get out of here," Sophonisba hissed, with fear stark in her eyes. "*Out*, or I call the watch. There's *money* looking for you."

She would have closed the shutters, but Gillian had both hands on the ledge and vaulted up to perch on it; Gillian snatched and caught a loose handful of Sophonisba's unlaced shift. "Don't do that, Sophie. If you bring the watch, we'll both be sorry. You know me. I've got something I've got to get rid of. Get dressed."

"And lose a night's—"

"Yes. Lose your nose if you don't hurry about it." She brought out the razor, that small and wicked knife of which Sophonisba was most afraid. She sat polishing it on her knee while Sophonisba sorted into a flurry of skirts. Sophonisba paused once to look; she let the light catch the knife and Sophonisba made greater haste. "Fix your hair," Gillian said.

"Someone's going to come back here to check on me if I don't take my last fee front—"

"Then fix it on the way." Steps were headed toward the door. "Haste! Or there'll be bloodletting."

"Get down," Sophonisba groaned. "I'll get rid of her."

Gillian slipped within the room and closed the shutters, stood in the dark against the wall while Sophonisba cracked the door and handed the fee out, heard a gutter dialogue and Sophonisba pleading indisposition. She handed out more money finally, as if she were parting with her life's blood, and closed the door. She looked about with a pained expression. "You owe me, you owe me—"

"I'm carrying something dangerous," Gillian said. "It's being tracked, do you understand? Nessim doesn't like the smell of it."

"O gods."

"Just so. It's trouble, old friend. Priest trouble."

"Then take it to priests."

"Priests expect donations. I've the scent of *gold*, dear friend. It's rich men pass such things back and forth, about things they don't want authority to know about."

"Then throw it in a canal."

"Nessim's advice. But it doesn't take the smell off my hands or answer questions when the trackers catch me up—or *you*, now, old friend."

"What do you want?" Sophonisba moaned. "Gillian, please—"

"Do you know," she said softly, reasonably, "if we take this thing— *we*, dear friend—to the wrong party, to someone who isn't disposed to reward us, or someone who isn't powerful enough to protect us so effortlessly that protection costs him nothing—who would spend effort protecting a whore and a thief, eh, Sophie? But some there are in this city who shed gold like gods shed hair, whose neighborhoods are so well protected others hesitate to meddle in them. Men of birth, Sophie. Men who might like to know who's paying vast sums of gold for favors in this city."

"Don't tell me these things."

"I'll warrant a whore hears a lot of things, Sophie. I'll warrant a whore knows a lot of ways and doors and windows in Korianth, who's where, who has secrets—"

"A whore is told a lot of lies. I can't help you."

"But you can, pretty Sophonisba." She held up the razor. "I daresay you know names and such—even in the king's own hall."

"*No!*"

"But the king's mad, they say; and who knows what a madman might do? What other names do you know?"

"I don't know *anyone*, I swear I don't."

"Don't swear; we've gods enough here. We improvise, then, you and I." She flung the shutter open. "Out, out with you."

Sophonisba was not adept at ledges. She settled herself on it and hesitated. Gillian thought of pushing her; then, fearing noise, took her hands and let her down gently, followed after with a soft thud. Sophonisba stood shivering and tying her laces, the latter unsuccessfully.

"Come on," Gillian said.

"I don't walk the alleys," Sophonisba protested in dread; Gillian pulled her along nonetheless, the back ways of the Grand Serpentine.

They met trouble. It was inevitable. More than once gangs of youths spotted Sophonisba, like dogs a stray cat, and came too close for comfort. Once the cant was not password enough, and they wanted more proof: Gillian showed that she carried, knife-carved in her shoulder, the brotherhood's initiation, and drunk as they were, they had sense to give way for that. It ruffled her pride. She jerked Sophonisba along and said nothing, seething with anger and reckoning she should have cut one. She could have done it and gotten away; but not with Sophonisba.

Sophonisba snuffled quietly, her hand cold as ice.

They took to the main canalside at last, when they must, which was at this hour decently deserted. It was not a place Gillian had been often; she found her way mostly by sense, knowing where the tall, domed buildings should lie. She had seen them most days of her life from the rooftops of the Sink.

The palaces of the great of Korianth were walled, with gardens, and men to watch them. She saw seals now and then that she knew, mythic beasts and demon beasts snarling from the arches over such places.

But one palace there was on the leftside hill, opposed to the great gold dome of the King's Palace, a lonely abode well walled and guarded.

There were guards, gilt-armed guards, with plumes and cloaks and more flash than ever the rufflers of midtown dared sport. Gillian grinned to herself and felt Sophonisba's hand in hers cold and limp from dread of such a place.

She marked with her eye where the guards stood, how they came and went and where the walls and accesses lay, where trees and bushes topped the walls inside and how the wall went to the very edge of the white marble building. The place was defended against armed men, against that sort of threat; against—the thought cooled her grin and her enthusiasm—guilded Assassins and free-lancers; a prince must worry for such things.

No. It was far from easy as it looked. Those easy ways could be set with traps; those places too unguarded could become deadly. She looked for the ways less easy, traced again that too-close wall.

"Walk down the street," she told Sophonisba. "Now. Just walk down the street."

"You're mad."

"Go."

Sophonisba started off, pale figure in blue silks, a disheveled and unlaced figure of ample curves and confused mien. She walked quickly as her fear would urge her, beyond the corner and before the eyes of the guards at the gate.

Gillian stayed long enough to see the sentries' attention wander, then pelted to the wall and carefully, with delicate fingers and the balance Genat had taught, spidered her way up the brickwork.

Dogs barked the moment she flung an arm over. She cursed, ran the crest of the thin wall like a trained ape, made the building itself and crept along the masonry—*too much of ornament, my lord!*—as far as the upper terrace.

Over the rim and onto solid ground, panting. Whatever had become of Sophonisba, she had served her purpose.

Gillian darted for a further terrace. Doors at the far end swung open suddenly; guards ran out in consternation. Gillian grinned at them, arms wide, like a player asking tribute; bowed.

They were not amused, thinking of their hides, surely. She looked up at a ring of pikes, cocked her head to one side and drew a conscious deep breath, making obvious what they should see; that it was no male intruder they had caught.

"Courier," she said, "for Prince Osric."

4

He was not, either, amused.

She stood with a very superfluous pair of men-at-arms gripping her wrists so tightly that the blood left her hands and the bones were about to snap, and the king's bastard—and sole surviving son—fingered the pouch they had found in their search of her.

"Courier," he said.

They were not alone with the guards, he and she. A brocaded troop of courtiers and dandies loitered near, amongst the porphyry columns and on the steps of the higher floor. He dismissed them with a wave of his hand; several seemed to feel privileged and stayed.

"For whom," the prince asked, "are you a courier?"

"Couriers bring messages," she said. "I decided on my own to bring you this one. I thought you should have it."

"Who are you?"

"A free-lance assassin," she said, promoting herself, and setting Prince Osric back a pace. The guards nearly crushed her wrists; they went beyond pain.

"Jisan," Osric said.

One of the three who had stayed walked forward, and Gillian's spine crawled; she knew the look of trouble, suspected the touch of another brotherhood, more disciplined than her own. "I was ambitious," she said at once. "I exaggerate."

"She is none of ours," said the Assassin. A dark man he was, unlike Osric, who was white-blond and thin; this Jisan was from southern climes and not at all flash, a drab shadow in brown and black beside Osric's glitter.

"Your name," said Osric.

"Gillian," she said; and recalling better manners and where she was: "—majesty."

"And how come by this?"

"A cutpurse . . . found this worthless. It fell in the street. But it's some lord's seal."

"*No* lord's seal. Do you read, guttersnipe?"

"Read, I?" The name rankled; she kept her face calm. "No, lord."

He whisked out a dagger and cut the cords, unfurled the parchment. A frown came at once to his face, deepened, and his pale eyes came suddenly up to hers. "Suppose that someone read it to you."

She sucked a thoughtful breath, weighed her life, and Jensy's. "A drunk clerk read it—for a kiss; said it was something he didn't want to know; and I think then—some great lord might want to know it; but which lord, think I? One lord might make good use and another bad, one be grateful and another not—might make rightest use of something dangerous—might be glad it came here in good loyal hands, and not where it was supposed to go; might take notice of a stir in the lowtown, bully boys looking for that cutpurse to cut throats, armed men and some of them not belonging hereabouts. King's wall's too high, majesty, so I came here."

"Whose bravos?" Jisan asked.

She blinked. "Wish I knew that; I'd like to know."

"You're that cutpurse," he said.

"If I were, would I say yes, and if I weren't, would I say yes? But I know that thing's better not in my hands and maybe better here than in the River. A trifle of reward, majesty, and there's no one closer mouthed than I am; a trifle more, majesty, and you've all my talents at hire: no one can outbid a prince, not for the likes of me; I know I'm safest to be bribed once and never again."

Osric's white-blue eyes rested on her a very long, very calculating moment. "You're easy to kill. Who would miss you?"

"No one, majesty. No one. But I'm eyes and ears and Korianthine—" Her eyes slid to the Assassin. "And I go places where *he* won't."

The Assassin smiled. His eyes did not. Guild man. He worked by hire and public license.

And sometimes without.

Osric applied his knife to the lead cylinder to gently cut it. "No," Gillian said nervously. And when he looked up, alarmed: "I would not," she said. "I have been advised—the thing has some ill luck attached."

"Disis," Osric called softly, and handed the cylinder into the hands of an older man, a scholarly man, whose courtier's dress was long out of mode. The man's long, lined face contracted at the touch of it in his hand.

"Well advised," that one said. "Silver and lead—a confining. I would be most careful of that seal, majesty; I would indeed."

The prince took the cylinder back, looked at it with a troubled mien, passed it back again. Carefully then he took the purse from his own belt, from beside his dagger. "Your home?" he asked of Gillian.

"Dockside," she said.

"All of it?"

She bit her lip. "Ask at the Anchor," she said, betraying a sometime haunt, but not Sophonisba's, not the Rose either. "All the Sink knows Gillian." And that was true.

"Let her go," Osric bade his guards. Gillian's arms dropped, relief and agony at once. He tossed the purse at her feet, while she was absorbed in her pain. "Come to the garden gate next time. Bring me word—and *names*."

She bent, gathered the purse with a swollen hand, stood again and gave a shy bow, her heart pounding with the swing of her fortunes. She received a disgusted wave of dismissal, and the guards at her right jerked her elbow and brought her down the hall, the whole troop of them to escort her to the door.

"My knives," she reminded them with a touch of smugness. They returned them and hastened her down the stairs. She did not gape at the splendors about her, but she saw them, every detail. In such a place twenty thousand in gold might be swallowed up. *Gillian* might be swallowed up, here and now or in the Sink, later. She knew. She reckoned it.

They took her through the garden, past handlers and quivering dogs the size of men, and there at the garden gate they let her go without the mauling she had expected. Princes' favor had power even out of princes' sight, then; from what she had heard of Osric, that was wise of them.

They pitched the little bundle of her skirt at her feet, undone. She snatched that up and flung it jauntily over her shoulder, and stalked off into the alleys that were her element.

She had a touch of conscience for Sophonisba. Likely Sophonisba had disentangled herself by now, having lied her way with some small skill out of whatever predicament she had come to, appearing in the high town: *forgive me, lord; this lord he brought me here, he did, and turned me out, he did, and I'm lost, truly, sir* . . . Sophonisba would wait till safe daylight and find her way home again, to nurse a grudge that money would heal. And she . . .

Gillian was shaking when she finally stopped to assess herself. Her wrists felt maimed, the joints of her hands swollen. She crouched and slipped the knives back where they belonged, earnestly wishing she had had the cheek to ask for food as well. She rolled the skirt and tied it in the accustomed bundle at her belt. Lastly—for fear, lastly—she spilled the sack into her cupped hand, spilled it back again quickly, for the delight and the terror of the flood of gold that glinted in the dim light. She thrust it down her blouse, at once terrified to possess such a thing and anxious until she could find herself in the Sink again, where she had ratholes in plenty. This was not a thing to walk the alleys with.

She sprang up and started moving, alone and free again, and casting furtive and careful glances all directions, most especially behind.

Priests and spells and temple business. Of a sudden it began to sink into her mind precisely what services she had agreed to, to turn spy; Triptis's priests bought whores' babes, or any else that could be stolen. That was a thief's trade beneath contempt; a trade the brotherhood stamped out where it found it obvious: grieving mothers were a noise, and a desperate one, bad for business. It was *that* kind of enemy she dealt with.

Find me names, the lord Osric had said, with an Assassin standing on one side and a magician on the other. Suddenly she knew who the old magicker had been: Disis, the prince had called him; Aldisis, more than dabbler in magics—part and parcel of the prince's entourage of discontents, waiting for the mad king to pass the dark gates elsewhere. The prince had had brothers and a sister, and now he had none; now he had only to wait.

Aldisis the opener of paths. His ilk of lesser station sold ill wishes down by the Fish, and some of those worked; Aldisis had skills, it was whispered.

And Jisan cared for those Aldisis missed.

Find me names.

And what might my lord prince do with them? Gillian wondered, without much wondering; and with a sudden chill: *What but lives are worth twenty thousand gold? And what but high-born lives?*

She had agreed with no such intention; she had priest troubles and hunters on her trail, and she did not need to know their names, not from a great enough distance from Korianth. One desperate chance—to sell the deadly information and gamble it was not Osric himself, to gamble with the highest power she could reach and hope she reached above the plague spot in Korianth . . . for gold, to get her and Jensy out of reach and out of the city until the danger was past.

Dangerous thoughts nibbled at her resolve, the chance she had been looking for, three years on the street with Jensy—a chance not only of one purse of gold . . . but of others. She swore at herself for thinking of it, reminded herself what she was; but there was also what she might be. Double such a purse could support Jensy in a genteel order: learning and fine clothes and fine manners; freedom for herself, to eel herself back dockside and vanish into her own darknesses, gather money, and power . . . No strange cities for her, nothing but Korianth, where she knew her way, all the low and tangled ways that took a lifetime of living to learn of a city—no starting over elsewhere, to play whore and teach Jensy the like, to get their throats cut in Amisent or Kesirn, trespassing in another territory and another brotherhood.

She skipped along, the strength flooding back into her, the breath hissing regularly between her teeth. She found herself again in familiar territory, known alleys; found one of her narrowest boltholes and rid herself of the prince's purse, all but one coin, itself a bit of recklessness. After that she ran and paused, ran and paused, slick with sweat and light-headed with fortune and danger and hunger.

The Bowel took her in, and Blindman's—home territory indeed; her sore, slippered feet pattered over familiar cobbles; she loosed her skirt and whipped it about her, mopped her face with her scarf and knotted that about her waist, leaving her curls free. The door to the Rose was before her. She pushed it open.

And froze to the heart.

5

All the Rose was a shambles, the tables broken, a few survivors or gawkers milling about in a forlorn knot near the street-side door. There was chill in the air, a palpable chill, like a breath of ice. Fat Jochen lay stark on the floor by the counter, with all his skin gone gray and his clothes . . . faded, as if cobweb composed them.

"Gods," Gillian breathed, clutching at the luck piece she bore, easy-going Agdalia's. And in the next breath: "Jensy," she murmured, and ran for the stairs.

The door at the end of the narrow hall stood open, moonlight streaming into a darkened room from the open window. She stopped, drew her knife—clutched the tawdry charm, sick with dread. From her vantage point she saw the cot disheveled, the movement of a shadow within, like a lich robed in cobwebs.

"Jensy!" she shouted into that dark.

The wraith came into the doorway, staggered out, reached.

Nessim. She held her hand in time, only just, turned the blade and with hilt in hand gripped the old man's sticklike arms, seized him with both hands, heedless of hurts. He stammered something. There was a silken crumbling in the cloth she held, like something moldered, centuries old. The skin on Nessim's poor face peeled in strips like a sun-baked hinterlander's.

"Gillian," he murmured. "They wanted you."

"Where's Jensy?"

He tried to tell her, pawed at the amulet he had worn; it was a crystal, cracked now, in a peeling hand. He waved the hand helplessly. "Took Jensy," he said. He was bald, even to the eyebrows. "I saved myself—saved myself—had no strength for mousekin. Gillian, run away."

"Who, blast you, Nessim!"

"Don't know. Don't know. But Triptis. Triptis's priests . . . ah, go, go, Gillian."

Tears made tracks down his seared cheeks. She thrust him back, anger and pity confounded in her. The advice was sound; they were without power, without patrons. Young girls disappeared often enough in the Sink without a ripple.

Rules changed. She thrust past him to the window and out it, onto the creaking shingles, to the eaves and down the edge to Blindman's. She hit the cobbles in a crouch and straightened.

They were looking for her. For her, not Jensy. And Nessim had survived to give her that message.

Triptis.

She slipped the knife into her belt and turned to go, stopped suddenly at the apparition that faced her in the alley.

"*Gillian*," the shadow said, unfolding upward out of the debris by Goat's Alley.

Her hand slipped behind her to the dagger; she set her back against solid brick and flicked a glance at shadows . . . others, at the crossing of Sparrow's. More around the corner, it was likely.

"*Where is it?*" the same chill voice asked.

"I sell things," she said. "Do you want it back? You have something I want."

"You can't get it back," the whisper said. "Now what shall we do?"

Her blood went colder still. They knew where she had been. She was followed; and no one slipped up on Gillian, no one.

Seals and seals, Nessim had said.

"Name your price," she said.

"You gained access to a prince," said the whisper. "You can do it again."

Osric, she thought. Her heart settled into a leaden, hurting rhythm. *It was Osric it was aimed at.*

"We also," said the whisper, "sell things. You want the child Jensy. The god has many children. He can spare one."

Triptis; it was beyond doubt; the serpent-god, swallowing the moon once monthly; the snake and the mouse. *Jensy!*

"I am reasonable," she said.

There was silence. If the shadow smiled, it was invisible. A hand extended, open, bearing a tiny silver circlet. "A gift you mustn't lose," the whisper said.

She took the chill ring, a serpent shape, slipped it onto her thumb, for that was all it would fit. The metal did not warm to her flesh but chilled the flesh about it.

A second shadow stepped forward, proffered another small object, a knife the twin of her own. "The blade will kill at a scratch," the second voice said. "Have care of it."

"Don't take off the ring," the first whispered.

"You could hire assassins," she said.

"We have," the whisper returned.

She stared at them. "Jensy comes back alive," she said. "To this door. No cheating."

"On either side."

"You've bid higher," she said. "What proof do you want?"

"Events will prove. Kill him."

Her lips trembled. "I haven't eaten in two days; I haven't slept—"

"Eat and sleep," the shadow hissed, "in what leisure you think you have. We trust you."

They melted backward, shadow into shadow, on all sides. The metal remained cold upon her finger. She carried it to her lips, unconscious reflex, thought with cold panic of poison, spat onto the cobbles again and again. She was shaking.

She turned, walked into the inn of the Rose past Jochen's body, past Nessim, who sat huddled on the bottom of the steps. She poured wine from the tap, gave a cup to Nessim, drank another herself, grimacing at the flavor. Bread on the sideboard had gone hard; she soaked it in the wine, but it had the flavor of ashes; cheeses had molded: she sliced off the rind with a knife from the board and ate. Jochen lay staring at the ceiling. Passers-by thrust in their heads and gaped at a madwoman who ate such tainted things; another, hungrier than the rest, came in to join the pillage, and an old woman followed.

"Go, run," Nessim muttered, rising with great difficulty to tug at her arm, and the others shied from him in horror; it was a look of leprosy.

"Too late," she said. "Go away yourself, old man. Find a hole to hide in. I'll get Jensy back."

It hurt the old man; she had not meant it so. He shook his head and walked away, muttering sorrowfully of Jensy. She left, then, by the alleyway, which was more familiar to her than the street. She had food in her belly, however tainted; she had eaten worse.

She walked, stripped the skirt aside and limped along, feeling the cobbles through the holes that had worn now in her slippers. She tucked the skirt in a seam of itself, hung it about her shoulder, walked with more persistence than strength down Blindman's.

Something stirred behind her; she spun, surprised nothing, her nape prickling. A rat, perhaps; the alleys were infested this close to the docks. Perhaps it was not. She went, hearing that something behind her from time to time and never able to surprise it.

She began to run, took to the straight ways, the ways that no thief liked to use, broke into the streets and raced breathlessly toward the Serpentine, that great canal along which all the streets of the city had their beginnings. Breath failed her finally and she slowed, dodged late walkers and kept going. If one of the walkers was that one who followed her . . . she could not tell.

The midtown gave way to the high; she retraced ways she had passed twice this night, with faltering steps, her breath loud in her own ears. It was late, even for prowlers. She met few but stumbled across one drunk or dead in the way, leaped the fallen form and fled with the short-range speed of one of the city's wary cats, dodged to this course and that and came out again in the same alley from which she and Sophonisba had spied out the palace.

The garden gate, Prince Osric had instructed her. The ring burned cold upon her finger.

She walked into the open, to the very guards who had let her out not so very long before.

6

The prince was abed. The fact afforded his guards no little consternation— the suspicion of a message urgent enough to make waking him advisable; the suspicion of dangerous wrath if it was not. Gillian, for her part, sat still, wool-hosed ankles crossed, hands folded, a vast fear churning at her belly. They had taken the ring. It had parted from her against all the advice of him who had given it to her; and it was not pleasing them that concerned her, but Jensy.

They had handled it and had it now, but if it was cold to them, they had not said, had not reacted. She suspected it was not. It was hers, for her.

Master Aldisis came. He said nothing, only stared at her, and she at him; him she feared most of all, his sight, his perception. His influence. She had nothing left, not the ring, not the blades, not the single gold coin. The scholar, in his night robe, observed her and walked away. She sat, the heat of exertion long since fled, with her feet and hands cold and finally numb.

"Mistress Gillian," a voice mocked her.

She looked up sharply, saw Jisan standing by a porphyry column. He bowed as to a lady. She sat still, staring at him as warily as at Aldisis.

"A merry chase, mistress Gillian."

Alarm might have touched her eyes. It surprised her, that it had been he.

"Call the lord prince," the Assassin said, and a guard went.

"Who is your contract?" she asked.

He smiled. "Guildmaster might answer," he said. "Go ask."

Patently she could not. She sat still, fixed as under a serpent's gaze. Her blades were in the guards' hands, one more knife than there had been. They suspected something amiss, as it was their business to suspect all things and all persons; Jisan knew. She stared into his eyes.

"What game are you playing?" he asked her plainly.

"I've no doubt you've asked about."

"There's some disturbance down in lowtown. A tavern with a sudden . . . unwholesomeness in it. Dead men. Would you know about that, mistress Gillian?"

"I carry messages," she said.

His dark eyes flickered. She thought of the serpent-god and the mouse. She kept her hands neatly folded, her feet still. This was a man who killed. Who perhaps enjoyed his work. She thought that he might.

A curse rang out above, echoing in the high beams of the ceiling. Osric. She heard every god in the court pantheon blasphemed and turned her head to stare straight before her, smoothed her breeches, a nervousness—stood at the last moment, remembering the due of royalty, even in night dress.

Called from some night's pleasure? she wondered. In that case he might be doubly wrathful; but he was cold as ever, thin face, thin mouth set, white-blue eyes as void of the ordinary. She could not imagine the man engaged in so human a pastime. Maybe he never did, she thought, the wild irrelevance of exhaustion. Maybe that was the source of his disposition.

"They sent me back," she said directly, "to kill you."

Not many people surely had shocked Osric; she had succeeded. The prince bit his lips, drew a breath, thrust his thin hands in the belt of his velvet robe. "Jisan?" he asked.

"There are dead men," the Assassin said, "at dockside."

"Honesty," Osric murmured, looking at her, a mocking tone.

"Lord," she said, at the edge of her nerves. "Your enemies have my sister. They promise to kill her if I don't carry out their plans."

"And you think so little of your sister, and so much of the gold?"

Her breath nigh strangled her; she swallowed air and kept her voice even. "I know that they will kill her and me whichever I do; tell me the name of your enemies, lord prince, that you didn't tell me the first time you sent me out of here with master Jisan behind me. *Give me names*, lord prince, and I'll hunt your enemies for my own reasons, and kill them or not as you like."

"You should already know one name, thief."

"A god's name? Aye, but gods are hard to hunt, lord prince." Her voice thinned; she could not help it. "Lend me master Aldisis's company instead of master Jisan's, and there's some hope. But go I will; and kill me priests if you haven't any better names."

Osric's cold, pale eyes ran her up and down, flicked to Jisan, back again. "For gold, good thief?"

"For my *sister*, lord prince. Pay me another time."

"Then why come here?"

"Because they'd know." She slid a look toward the guards, shifted weight anxiously. "A ring; they gave me a ring to wear, and they took it."

"Aldisis!" the prince called. The mage came, from some eavesdropping vantage among the columns or from some side room.

An anxious guard proffered the serpent ring, but Aldisis would not touch it; waved it away. "Hold it awhile more," Aldisis said; and to Osric: "They would know where that is. And whether she held it."

"My sister," Gillian said in anguish. "Lord, give it back to me, I came because they'd know if not; and to find out their names. Give me their names. It's almost morning."

"I might help you," said Osric. "Perhaps I might die and delight them with a rumor."

"Lord," she murmured, dazed.

"My enemies will stay close together," he said. "The temple—or a certain lord Brisin's palace . . . likely the temple; Brisin fears retaliation; the god shelters him. Master Aldisis could explain such things. You're a bodkin at best, mistress thief. But you may prick a few of them; and should you do better, that would delight me. Look to your reputation, thief."

"Rumor," she said.

"Chaos," muttered Aldisis.

"You advise me against this?" Osric asked.

"No," said Aldisis. "Toward it."

"You mustn't walk out the front gate this time," Osric said, "mistress thief, if you want a rumor."

"Give me what's mine," she said. "I'll clear your walls, lord, and give them my heels; and they'll not take me."

Osric made a sign with his hand; the guards brought her her knives, her purse, and her ring, the while Osric retired to a bench, seated himself, with grim stares regarded them all. "I am dead," he said languidly. "I shall be for some few hours. Report it so and ring the bells. Today should be interesting."

Gillian slid the ring onto her finger; it was as cold as ever.

"*Go!*" Osric whispered, and she turned and sped from the room, for the doors and the terrace she knew.

Night opened before her; she ran, skimmed the wall with the dogs barking, swung down with the guards at the gate shouting alarm—confused, and not doing their best. She hit the cobbles afoot as they raced after her, and their armor slowed them; she sprinted for known shadows and zigged and zagged through the maze.

She stopped finally, held a hand to a throbbing side, and fetched up against a wall, rolled on a shoulder to look back and find pursuit absent.

Then the bells began out of the dark—mournful bells, tolling out a lie that must run through all of Korianth: the death of a prince.

She walked, staggering with exhaustion, wanting sleep desperately; but the hours that she might sleep were hours of Jensy's life. She was aware finally that she had cut her foot on something; she noted first the pain and then that she left a small spot of blood behind when she walked. It was far from crippling; she kept moving.

It was midtown now. She went more surely, having taken a second wind.

And all the while the bells tolled, brazen and grim, and lights burned in shuttered windows where all should be dark, people wakened to the rumor of a death.

The whole city must believe the lie, she thought, from the Sink to the throne, the mad monarch himself believed that Osric had died; and should there not be general search after a thief who had killed a prince?

She shivered, staggering, reckoning that she ran ahead of the wave of rumor: that by dawn the name of herself and Jensy would be bruited across the Sink, and there would be no more safety.

And behind the doors, she reckoned, rumor prepared itself, folk yet too frightened to come out of doors—never wise for honest folk in Korianth.

When daylight should come . . . it would run wild—mad Seithan to rule with no hope of succession, an opportunity for the kings of other cities, of upcoast and upriver, dukes and powerful men in Korianth, all to reach out hands for the power Seithan could not long hold, the tottering for which all had been waiting for more than two years . . .

This kind of rumor waited, to be flung wide at a thief's request. This kind of madness waited to be let loose in the city, in which all the enemies might surface, rumors in which a throne might fall, throats be cut, the whole city break into riot. . . .

A prince might die indeed then, in disorder so general.

Or . . . a sudden and deeper foreboding possessed her . . . a king might.

A noise in one place, a snatch in the other; thief's game in the market. She had played it often enough, she with Jensy.

Not for concern for her and her troubles that Osric risked so greatly . . . but for *Osric's* sake, no other.

She quickened her pace, swallowing down the sickness that threatened her; somehow to get clear of this, to get away in this shaking of powers before two mites were crushed by an unheeding footstep.

She began, with the last of her strength, to run.

7

The watch was out in force, armed men with lanterns, lights and shadows rippling off the stone of cobbles and of walls like the stuff of the Muranthine Hell, and the bells still tolling, the first tramp of soldiers' feet from off the high streets, canalward.

Gillian sped, not the only shadow that judged the neighborhood of the watch and the soldiers unhealthy; rufflers and footpads were hieing themselves to cover apace, with the approach of trouble and of dawn. She skirted the canals that branched off the Serpentine, took to the alleys again and paused in the familiar alley off Agdalia's Shrine, gasping for breath in the flare of lanterns. A door slammed on the street: Agdalia's was taking precautions. Upper windows closed. The trouble had flowed thus far, and folk who did not wish to involve themselves tried to signify so by staying invisible.

The red-shuttered room was closed and dark; Sophonisba had not returned . . . had found some safe nook for herself with the bells going, hiding in fear, knowing where her partner had gone, perhaps witness to the hue and cry after. *Terrified*, Gillian reckoned, and did not blame her.

Gillian caught her breath and took to that street, forested with pillars, that was called the Street of the Gods. Here too the lanterns of the watch showed in the distance, and far away, dimly visible against the sky . . . the palace of the king upon the other hill of the fold in which Korianth nestled, the gods and the king in close association.

From god to god she passed, up that street like an ascent of fancy, from the bare respectability of little cults like Agdalia's to the more opulent temples of gods more fearsome and more powerful. Watch passed; she retreated at once, hovered in the shadow of the smooth columns of a Korianthine god, Ablis of the Goldworkers, one of the fifty-two thousand gods of Korianth. He had no patronage for her, might, in fact, resent a thief; she hovered fearfully, waiting for ill luck; but perhaps she was otherwise marked. She shuddered, fingering that serpent ring upon her thumb, and walked farther in the shadow of the columns.

It was not the greatest temple nor the most conspicuous in this section, that of Triptis. Dull black-green by day, it seemed all black in this last hour of night, the twisted columns like stone smoke, writhing up to a plain portico, without window or ornament. She caught her breath, peered into the dark that surrounded a door that might be open or closed; she was not sure.

Nor was she alone. A prickling urged at her nape, a sense of something that lived and breathed nearby; she whipped out the poisoned blade and turned.

A shadow moved, tottered toward her. "Gillian," it said, held out a hand, beseeching.

"Nessim," she murmured, caught the peeling hand with her left, steadied the old man. He recoiled from her touch.

"You've something of them about you," he said.

"What are you doing here?" she hissed at him. "Old man, go back—get out of here."

"I came for mousekin," he said. "I came to try, Gillian."

The voice trembled. It was, for Nessim, terribly brave.

"You would die," she said. "You're not in their class, Nessim."

"Are you?" he asked with a sudden straightening, a memory, perhaps, of better years. "You'd do what? *What* would you do?"

"You stay out," she said, and started to leave; he caught her hand, caught the hand with the poisoned knife and the ring. His fingers clamped.

"No," he said. "No. Be rid of this."

She stopped, looked at his shadowed, peeling face. "They threatened Jensy's life."

"They know you're here. You understand that? With this, they know. Give it to me."

"Aldisis saw it and returned it to me. *Aldisis* himself, old man. Is your advice better?"

"My reasons are friendlier."

A chill went over her. She stared into the old man's eyes. "What should I do?"

"Give it here. Hand it to me. I will contain it for you . . . long enough. They won't know, do you understand me? I'll do that much."

"You can't light a candle, old trickster."

"Can," he said. "Reedlight's easier. I never work more than I have to."

She hesitated, saw the fear in the old man's eyes. A friend, one friend. She nodded, sheathed the knife and slipped off the ring. He took it into his hands and sank down in the shadows with it clasped before his lips, the muscles of his arms shaking as if he strained against something vastly powerful.

And the cold was gone from her hand.

She turned, ran, fled across the street and scrambled up the stonework of the paler temple of the Elder Mother, the Serpent Triptis's near neighbor . . . up, madly, for the windowless temple had to derive its light from some source; and a temple that honored the night surely looked upon it somewhere.

She reached the crest, the domed summit of the Mother, set foot from pale marble onto the darker roof of the Serpent, shuddering, as if the very stone were alive and threatening, able to feel her presence.

To steal from a god, to snatch a life from his jaws . . .

She spun and ran to the rear of the temple, where a well lay open to the sky, where the very holy of the temple looked up at its god, which was night. *That* was the way in she had chosen. The sanctuary, she realized with a sickness of fear, thought of Jensy and took it nonetheless, swung onto the inside rim and looked down, with a second impulse of panic as she saw how far down it was, a far, far drop.

Voices hailed within, echoing off the columns, shortening what time she had; somewhere voices droned hymns or some fell chant.

She let go, plummeted, hit the slick stones and tried to take the shock by rolling . . . sprawled, dazed, on cold stone, sick from the impact and paralyzed.

She heard shouts, outcries, struggled up on a numbed arm and a sprained wrist, trying to gain her feet. It was indeed the sanctuary; pillars of some green stone showed in the golden light of lamps, pillars carved like twisting serpents, even to the scales, writhing toward the ceiling and knotting in folds across it. The two greatest met above the altar, devouring a golden sun, between their fanged jaws, above her.

"Jensy," she muttered, thinking of Nessim and his hands straining about that thing that they had given her.

She scrambled for the shadows, for safety if there was any safety in this lair of demons.

A man-shaped shadow appeared in that circle of night above the altar; she stopped, shrank back farther among the columns as it hung and dropped as she had.

Jisan. Who else would have followed her, dark of habit and street-wise? He hit the pavings hardly better than she, came up and staggered, felt of the silver-hilted knife at his belt; she shrank back and back, pace by pace, her slippered feet soundless.

And suddenly the chanting was coming this way, up hidden stairs, lights flaring among the columns; they hymned Night, devourer of light, in their madness beseeched the day not to come—forever Dark, they prayed in their mad hymn. The words crept louder and louder among the columns, and Jisan lingered, dazed.

"*Hsst!*" Gillian whispered; he caught the sound, seemed to focus on it, fled the other way, among the columns on the far side of the hall.

And now the worshipers were within the sanctuary, the lights making the serpent columns writhe and twist into green-scaled life, accompanied by shadows. They bore with them a slight, tinseled form that wept and struggled. Jensy, crying! she never would.

Gillian reached for the poisoned blade, her heart risen into her throat. Of a sudden the hopelessness of her attempt came down upon her, for they never would keep their word, never, and there was nowhere to hide: old Nessim could not hold forever, keeping their eyes blind to her.

Or they knew already that they had been betrayed.

She walked out among them. "We have a bargain!" she shouted, interrupting the hymn, throwing things into silence. "I kept mine. Keep yours."

Jensy struggled and bit, and one of them hit her. The blow rang loud in the silence, and Jensy went limp.

One of them stood forward. "He is dead?" that one asked. "The bargain is kept?"

"What else are the bells?" she asked.

There was silence. Distantly the brazen tones were still pealing across the city. It was near to dawn; stars were fewer in the opening above the altar. Triptis's hours were passing.

"Give her back," Gillian said, feeling the sweat run down her sides, her pulse hammering in her smallest veins. "You'll hear no more of us."

A cowl went back, showing a fat face she had seen in processions. No priest, not with that gaudy dress beneath; Duke Brisin, Osric had named one of his enemies; she thought it might be.

And they were not going to honor their word.

Someone cried out; a deep crash rolled through the halls; there was the tread of armored men, sudden looks of alarm and a milling among the priests like a broken hive. Jensy fell, dropped; and Gillian froze with the ringing rush of armored men coming at her back, the swing of lanterns that sent the serpents the more frenziedly twisting about the hall. "Stop them," someone was shouting.

She moved, slashed a priest, who screamed and hurled himself into the others who tried to stop her. Jensy was moving, scrambling for dark with an eel's instinct, rolling away faster than Gillian could help her.

"Jisan!" Gillian shouted to the Assassin, hoping against hope for an ally; and suddenly the hall was ringed with armed men, and herself with a poisoned bodkin, and a dazed, gilt child, huddled together against a black wall of priests.

Some priests tried to flee; the drawn steel of the soldiers prevented; and some died, shrieking. Others were herded back before the altar.

"Lord," Gillian said nervously, casting about among them for the face she hoped to see; and he was there, Prince Osric, in the guise of a common soldier; and Aldisis by him; but he had no eyes for a thief.

"*Father,*" Osric hailed the fat man, hurled an object at his feet, a leaden cylinder.

The king recoiled pace by pace, his face white and trembling, shaking convulsively so that the fat quivered upon it. The soldiers' blades remained leveled toward him, and Gillian seized Jensy's naked shoulder and pulled her back, trying for quiet retreat out of this place of murders, away from father and son, mad king who dabbled in mad gods and plotted murders.

"Murderer," Seithan stammered, the froth gathering at his lips. "Killed my legitimate sons . . . every one; killed me, but I didn't die . . . kin-killer. Kin-killing bastard . . . I have loyal subjects left; you'll not reign."

"You've tried *me* for years, honored father, majesty. *Where's my mother?*"

The king gave a sickly and hateful laugh.

There was movement in the dark, where no priest was . . . a figure seeking deeper obscurity; Gillian took her own cue and started to move.

A priest's weapon whipped up, a knife poised to hurl; she cried warning . . . and suddenly chaos, soldiers closed in a ring of bright weapons, priests dying in a froth of blood, and the king. . . .

The cries were stilled. Gillian hugged Jensy against her in the shadows, seeing through the forest of snakes the sprawled bodies, the bloody-handed soldiers, Osric—king in Korianth.

King! the soldiers hailed him, that made the air shudder; he gave them orders, that sent them hastening from the slaughter here.

"The *palace!*" he shouted, urging them on to riot that would see throats cut by the hundreds in Korianth.

A moment he paused, sword in hand, looked into the shadows, for Jensy glittered, and it was not so easy to hide. For a moment a thief found the courage to look a prince in the eye, wondering, desperately, whether two such motes of dust as they might not be swept away. Whether he feared a thief's gossip, or cared.

The soldiers had stopped about him, a warlike knot of armor and plumes and swords.

"Get moving!" he ordered them, and swept them away with him, running in their haste to further murders.

Against her, Jensy gave a quiet shiver, and thin arms went round her waist. Gillian tore at a bit of the tinsel, angered by the tawdry ornament. Such men cheated even the gods.

A step sounded near her. She turned, dagger in hand, faced the shadow that was Jisan. A knife gleamed in his hand.

He let the knife hand fall to his side.

"Whose are you?" she asked. He tilted his head toward the door, where the prince had gone, now king.

"Was," he said. "Be clever and run far, Gillian thief; or lie low and long. There comes a time princes don't like to remember the favors they bought. Do you think King Osric will want to reward an assassin? Or a thief?"

"You leave first," she said. "I don't want you at my back."

"I've been there," he reminded her, "for some number of hours."

She hugged Jensy the tighter. "Go," she said. "Get out of my way."

He went; she watched him walk into the beginning day of the doorway, a darkness out of darkness, and down the steps.

"You all right?" she asked of Jensy.

"Knew I would be," Jensy said with little-girl nastiness; but her lips shook. And suddenly her eyes widened, staring beyond.

Gillian looked, where something like a rope of darkness twisted among the columns, above the blood that spattered the altar; a trick of the wind and the lamps, perhaps. But it crossed the sky, where the stars paled to day, and moved against the ceiling. Her right hand was suddenly cold.

She snatched Jensy's arm and ran, weaving in and out of the columns the way Jisan had gone, out, out into the day, where an old man huddled on the steps, rocking to and fro and moaning.

"*Nessim!*" she cried. He rose and cast something that whipped away even as he collapsed in a knot of tatters and misery. A serpent-shape writhed across the cobbles in the beginning of day . . .

. . . and shriveled, a dry stick.

She clutched Jensy's hand and ran to him, her knees shaking under her, bent down and raised the dry old frame by the arms, expecting death; but a blistered face gazed back at her with a fanatic's look of triumph. Nessim's thin hand reached for Jensy, touched her face.

"All right, mousekin?"

"Old man," Gillian muttered, perceiving something she had found only in Jensy; he would have, she vowed, whatever comfort gold could buy, food, and a bed to sleep in. A mage; he was that. And a man.

Gold, she thought suddenly, recalling the coin in her purse; and the purse she had buried off across the canals.

And one who had dogged her tracks most of the night.

She spat an oath by another god and sprang up, blind with rage.

"Take her to the Wyvern," she bade Nessim and started off without a backward glance, reckoning ways she knew that an Assassin might not, reckoning on throat-cutting, on revenge in a dozen colors.

She took to the alleys and began to run by alleys a big man could never use, cracks and crevices and ledges and canal verges.

And made it. She worked into the dark, dislodged the stone, took back the purse and climbed catwise to the ledges to lurk and watch.

He was not far behind to work his big frame into the narrow space that took hers so easily, to work loose the self-same stone.

Upon her rooftop perch she stood, gave a low whistle . . . shook out a pair of golden coins and dropped them ringing at his feet, a grand generosity, like the prince's.

"For your trouble," she bade him, and was away.

V

We've gone for jump now. You wobble back to the lounge, a little frayed about the edges.

So have I come, some minutes before. Perhaps we both want to be sure the stars are still there.

Or that we are.

"Looking for something?" I ask as you lean against the glass.

"The Sun."

"Wrong direction." I point aft.

"I know that. I just prefer this window."

Jump is the kind of experience that makes philosophers—of some people. It's certain that no other passengers venture here this soon.

"Tell me. What do you think of?"

"In transit? It varies. You?"

"Earth. Home."

I smile. "That, most often. Sea-anchor."

"What?"

"When a ship needed stability at sea, it flung out a sea-anchor. Home-thoughts are like that. And this is a big ocean."

"I thought you might think—" you say, and give something up unasked.

Eventually I say: "You were about to ask me where I get my ideas. You haven't yet. Go on. I've been wondering when you'd get around to it."

"That wasn't what I was going to ask."

"What, then?"

"I thought—you might think—you know, somehow *different*."

"That's the idea-question, all right. I thought I heard it coming."

"You're laughing at me."

"No. I know exactly what you want to know. You want to know wherein I'm different, wherein a writer's *mind* is different. I've told you. It's because I'm here." I gesture at the windows. "It's a strange sensation—when the ship turns loose of space. You want a sea-anchor. It takes nerve to let go and fly with the wind. I confess I won't jump in parachutes. But I will sometimes think of alien worlds when I slide into hyperspace. Or of falling when I'm flying. I let go of homely things at uncertain moments—just to test my nerve. You want the terrible truth? You have that kind of mind too."

"Me?"

"You're here, aren't you? You came to look out the windows."

"I don't know why I came."

"Just the same as I don't know where I get my ideas. They just are."

"Any time you want them?"

"Once upon a time," I say, "I had twenty-four hours and a postcard, and a challenge to come up with a story that would fit it."

"Did you?"

"I sat down at supper and wrote the start. I wrote a snatch at a cocktail party, another at breakfast. And yes, twenty-four hours later I stood up to read to a convention full of people from a rather densely written postcard. Used a micropoint." I look out at changed stars and remember a smallish meeting hall, in Columbia, Missouri, and an audience the members of which had had about as much sleep as I had. "Two hours' sleep. Two thousand words."

"Did it work?"

"I read it the close way you have to read letters that small—never dared look at my audience; I just hoped to get through it without faltering, blind tired as I was. The time went in that kind of fog time gets to when you're in a story; and it was over, and I looked up. Nobody moved. I was kind of disappointed, I mean, when you write what you think is a nice little story and you don't get any reaction at all, you feel worse than if people walked out. I thought they were asleep.

"Then the audience stirred and some wiped eyes and others, I think, got to their feet and cheered, and I just stood there in one of those moments that come to a storyteller a few times in a lifetime—I don't know, maybe we all were tired." I smile, seeing those faces reflected out of nowhere in the glass. "But spare me that. I wrote it to read aloud. It was a special moment. That's all. It doesn't come twice."

THE LAST TOWER

The old man climbed the stairs slowly, stopping sometimes to let his heart recover and the teapot settle on the tray, while the dormouse would pop out of his sleeve or his beard and steal a nibble at the teacakes he brought up from the kitchen. It was an old tower on the edge of faery, on the edge of the Empire of Man. Between. Uncertain who had built it—men or elves. It was long before the old man's time, at least, and before the empire in the east. There was magic in its making . . . so they used to say. Now there was only the old man and the dormouse and a sleepy hedgehog, and a bird or two or three, which came for the grain at the windows. That was his real talent, the wild things, the gentle things. A real magician now, would not be making tea himself, in the kitchen, and wasting his breath on stairs. A real magician would have been more—awesome. Kept some state. Inspired some fear.

He stopped at the halfway turning. Pushed his sliding spectacles up his nose and balanced tray, tea, cakes and dormouse against the window-ledge. The land was black in the east. Black all about the tower. Burned. On some days he could see the glitter of arms in the distance where men fought. He could see the flutter of banners on the horizon as they rode. Could hear the sound of the horses and the horns.

Now the dust and soot of a group of riders showed against the darkening east. He waited there, not to have the weary stairs again—waited while the dormouse nibbled a cake, and in his pocket the hedgehog squirmed about, comfortable in the stillness.

The riders came. The prince—it was he—sent the herald forward to ring at the gate. "Open in the king's name," the herald cried, and spying him in the window: "Old man—open your gates. Surrender the tower. No more warnings."

"Tell him no," the old man said. "Just tell him—no."

"Tomorrow," the herald said, "we come with siege."

The old man pushed his spectacles up again. Blinked sadly, his old heart beating hard. "Why?" he asked. "What importance, to have so much bother?"

"Old meddler." The prince himself rode forward, curvetted his black horse under the window. "Old fraud. Come down and live. Give us the tower intact—to use . . . and live. Tomorrow morning—we come with fire and iron. And the stones fall—*old man*."

The old man said nothing. The men rode away. The old man climbed the stairs, the teaset clattering in his palsied hands. His heart hurt. When he looked out on the land, his heart hurt him terribly. The elves no longer came. The birds and the beasts had all fled the burning. There was only the mouse and the hedgehog and the few doves who had lived all their lives in the loft. And the few sparrows who came. Only them now.

He set the tray down, absentmindedly took the hedgehog from his pocket and set it by the dormouse on the tray, took a cake and crumbled it on the window-ledge for the birds. A tear ran down into his beard.

Old fraud. He was. He had only little magics, forest magics. But they'd burned all his forest and scattered the elves, and he failed even these last few creatures. They would overthrow the tower. They would spread over all the land, and there would be no more magic in the world. He should have done something long ago—but he had never done a great magic. He should have raised whirlwinds and elementals—but he could not so much as summon the legged teapot up the stairs. And his heart hurt, and his courage failed. The birds failed to come—foreknowing, perhaps. The hedgehog and the dormouse looked at him with eyes small and solemn in the firelight, last of all.

No. He stirred himself, hastened to the musty books—his master's books, dusty and a thousand times failed. *You've not the heart*, his master would say. *You've not the desire for the great magics. You'll call* nothing—*because you want nothing.*

Now he tried. He drew his symbols on the floor—scattered his powders, blinking through the ever-shifting spectacles, panting with his exertions. He would do it this time—would hold the tower on the edge of faery, between the Empire of Man and the kingdom of the elves. He believed, this time. He conjured powers. He called on the great ones. The winds sighed and roared inside the tower.

And died.

His arms fell. He wept, great tears sliding down into his beard. He picked up the dormouse and the hedgehog and held them to his breast, having no more hope.

Then she came. The light grew, white and pure. The scent of lilies filled the air—and she was there, naked, and white, hands empty—beautiful.

"I've come," she said.

His heart hurt him all the more. "Forgive me," he said. "I was trying for something—fiercer."

"Oh," she said, dark eyes sad.

"I make only—small magics," he said. "I was trying for—a dragon, maybe. A basilisk. An elemental. To stop the king. But I do flowers best. And smokes and maybe a little fireworks. And it's not enough. Goodbye. Please go. Please do go. Whichever you are. You're the wrong kind. You're *beautiful*. And he's going to come tomorrow—the king—and the armies . . . it's not a place for a gentle spirit. Only—could you take *them* . . . please? Mouse and Hedgehog—they'd not be so much. I'd not like to bother you. But could you? And then you can go."

"Of course," she said. It was the whisper of wind, her voice. The moving of snow crystals on frozen crust. She took them to her breast. Kissed them in turn, and jewels clothed them in white. "Old man," she said, and on his brow too planted a kiss, and jewels followed, frosty white. White dusted all the room, all the books and the clutter and the cobwebs. She walked down the stairs and out the gate, and jeweled it all in her wake. She walked the land, and the snow fell, and fell, and the winds blew—till only the banners were left, here and there, stiffened with ice, above drifts and humps of snow which marked the tents. The land was all white, horizon to horizon. Nothing stirred—but the wolves that hunted the deer, and the birds that hunted the last summer's berries.

Death drifted back to the tower, and settled there, in the frost and the lasting snows, where the old man and magic slept their lasting sleep.

She breathed kisses on him, on the little ones, and kept watch—faithful to her calling, while the snows deepened, and even the wolves slept, their fur white and sparkling with the frost.

VI

We share the lounge with passengers now. A young couple holds hands under a table over to the corner. Some things never change.

There is crisis aboard. One of the passengers has locked himself in his cabin and the steward and a doctor have been back and forth down the hall trying to get the door open. Jump and transit does this to some people.

I don't think he ever went near a window. He would always sit with his back to them. He talked through all the status advisories.

"You wonder why some people come out here," you say.

"I suppose he has to. Business, maybe." There is a certain amount of to-ing and fro-ing, up and down the halls. Some passengers delight in the drama. And sip their drinks and hug their own superiority in their boredom.

"It's a terrible thing for that man," I say. "Perceptions again. The first time you know you're not anywhere near where you were, not anywhere near where your whole world is—then you have to know that you're somewhere else. That man has just learned something. His safe world is shattered."

"Look at the rest of these people. *They* don't lock themselves in their rooms. And I don't think they ever think about the universe. They just have their drinks. And their canned music. And when they look out the windows they don't see the stars. They just see lights."

"That's the tragedy of the man in his room, isn't it? He can almost see the universe. He's so much closer to the truth than he ever was in all his life." I sip my own drink. "And he's locked his door."

"Couldn't they open it from the main board?"

"They could. Or just use the master key. They will if they have to."

More to-ing and fro-ing.

"Perceptions," you say.

"Perceptions. Taste, scent, touch, hearing, sense of balance, sight—of course, sight. And the systems we make and the systems others make for us. The orders and the logic. It's so easy to take what others give us. Gifts are so hard to say no to."

"We want so much to believe we know. That's the trouble."

"Even to believe we can't know is a system. Maybe we can know the universe. Maybe there is an answer. It's dangerous to assume there isn't."

"There. I thought you'd gotten sane."

"It's dangerous to assume anything and stop looking."

"You can't guarantee it isn't dangerous to look, either."

"No," I say. "I can't." We have gotten to that stage of renewed honesty. The potential for friendship, it may be. And we know nothing at all of each other.

It is so hard even to know ourselves.

Y

THE BROTHERS

A

1

The wind came from the west out of the rocky throat of the Sianail, even while the morning sun was shining in the glen, and there was something singing on it. Perhaps unGifted men could not hear it yet, that faint, far wail, but it echoed clearly off the mountain walls of Gleann Gleatharan, down to Dun Gorm, and it gave the king no peace.

There was storm in that wind as it came, scouring hills the stones of which were old and dread, hills which remembered darker things than storms and hid things at their hearts—the bones of warriors and kings, and even, men said, spirits older than the gods.

High within the hills was also bright green, even on this murky, misty day, grass green as life and peace; but whenever this mood came on the mountains that hove up northward, souls keened on the gray wind and black crows flew on it, and it was well to think of shelter.

The traveler never did. He came down from the rocky heights, taking chances with stones turned slick with mist. He went gray-cloaked in wool, his feet in scarred brown leather that had seen many a league and many a fording and many a soaking before the one that threatened. He had hanging about his neck, did this gray traveler, a flat stone that a stream had worn through in its center; if a man looked through this opening, then he would see things as they were and glamours had no power on him. But the traveler had limited faith in this magic, putting more trust in the iron of his plain sword, which he had gotten on Skean Eirran off a dead man, on that narrow spit of sand, when they raided up by Skye. This he carried and no other weapon but a dagger for his meat; and no armor but his gray oiled-wool cloak to keep the cold mist from his skin. His name he did not have. He had not been using that since he passed into the southland; and perhaps they were hunting him by now; perhaps they had sent men ahead of him so there would be men to meet him when he came. When he looked over his shoulder, he saw nothing but bare old stones and lawless gorse besides the mist-damp green, but now and again from hillsides he heard dogs baying that might be shepherds' dogs disturbed by his passage or might not; they might be pursuit from his enemies and they might not, in this fey, foul day that wrapped itself in storm.

Then with the passing of a hill he found all of a broad glen dropping away at his feet, himself in storm-shadow and the most of the glen still in sunlight that speared down through gray-bottomed cloud and turned the dark green to dazzling emerald. It was a land of neat hedgerows and careful fields and pasturages well cared-for. The very hills surrounding this valley had a tamer look, as if here kinder powers blessed the hedges and fenced out the hazards of the wild hills.

Amid it all, surely the reason and center of this tranquillity—a dun sat on a hill above a pleasant stream, in the face of low hills where its cottages clung as faint dots against the green.

He knew where he had come. It was no great dun. It was built of the wreckage time had made of its hill, so that one melded with the other— Dun Gorm it was, the Blue Keep, and it took its name from those stones as well, that deep gray stone that mimicked the sky and turned strange colors, one thing in storm and another when the sun was shining as it did now in spears across the glen, between the clouds, while the mist on the hills sent freshets down.

It held peace, and luck, this land where he had come. He had known neither in his life, and seeing this before him, he went to it.

There was a window of Dun Gorm that looked out above the stableyard fences, up toward the hills, and dread brought the king to it constantly this day. Cinnfhail was this king's name; and he was feyer than all his line, all of whom had been on speaking terms with the Sidhe, the Fair Folk who had known and held this valley before men came.

There had been a time that men and Fair Folk had lived closer than they did now: the Sidhe, the dwellers under bough and the dwellers under stone, had lived close beside the hewers of both, at peace. From most places in the world nowadays the Sidhe had indeed gone, leaving the hills and the glens to man. But in Gleann Gleatharan the Sidhe still pursued their own furtive business in the hills and woods while men built of stone and wood in the valley. And so long as a man took his wood and stone from the lonely heights of Gleann Gleatharan northward and far from the forest at the south of the valley he got on with the Sidhe well enough—if he were born to Dun Gorm, whose first king had been their friend.

Sometimes even in these days, Cinnfhail had heard their singing, oftenest in the evenings, fair as dream and haunting his mind for days; or sometimes in his riding he had heard a whisper which gave him good advice, and he came back from his riding wiser than he had gone out to it. Cinnfhail King had always cherished such encounters and longed for more meetings than he had had in his long life.

But today—today he heard a song he did not wish to hear. It was the bain Sidhe wailing, not the singing of the fair glas Sidhe; it was the White Singer, the harbinger of death. She sang along the heights thus far, that sawtoothed, gorse-grown ridge that walled them from the world; or from down the glen where the brook vanished into woods the Sidhe-folk still owned.

Stay away, he wished her. *Come no nearer to my land.*

But the singing kept on, rising and falling on the wind.

"It will be a storm tonight," his wife said, queen Samhadh, finding king Cinnfhail watching there alone. He held her close a while and murmured agreement, glad that Samhadh was deaf to any worse things.

All the day, coming and going from that window, Cinnfhail could not help thinking on dangers to those he loved. He considered his son Raghallach, a youth handsome enough to break the heart of any maid in Eirran, him the bravest and fairest of all the youth of Gleann Gleatharan. The love Cinnfhail had for his fair-haired son, the pride he took in Raghallach, was such that he could never tell it, especially to Raghallach—but he went to Raghallach and tried, this day, and that attempt set a glow in Raghallach's eyes, and afterward, set a wondering in Raghallach's heart, just what strange mood was on his father.

In the same way Cinnfhail King looked on Deirdre his daughter, who was not yet fourteen: so small, so high-hearted, the very image of what his Samhadh had been in the glory of her youth, as if time turned back again and laughed through the halls in Deirdre's steps. He had so much in his family; in all this land; he had wife and children and faithful friends and he thought the Sidhe might be jealous of such luck as he had: there were Sidhe reputed for such spite. So while he listened to that singing on the wind he contrived excuses that would keep all he loved indoors.

"Lord," said Conn his shieldman, coming on him at this window-vigil, together with Tuathal his Harper, "some worry is on you."

"Nothing," Cinnhfail King said to Conn, and searched Conn's eyes too for any signs of ill-luck and death, this man so long his friend: his shieldman, who had stood with him in his youth and drunk with him at his board. There were no more wars for them. They had settled Gleann Gleatharan at peace, and now they grew old together, breeding fine horses and red cattle and laughing over their children's antics. His shieldman was clad farmer-wise, like any crofter that held the heights. Of treasures he held dear, this man was one of the chiefest, in his loyalty and courage; and hardly less, Tuathal the harper, the teacher of his children in riddlery and wit. "It's nothing," Cinnfhail said. "A little melancholy. Perhaps I'm growing old."

"Never, lord," Conn said.

"Not by my will, at least. But an old wound aches, that's all."

"Cursed weather," Conn said.

One should never curse the Sidhe. The impiety chilled the king. But Conn was deaf to what he cursed. "Go," Cinnfhail said, "have cook put on something to warm the bones; there'll be cold men coming from the fields early today; and have the fire lit in the hall; and have the lads give the horses extra and one of them to sleep there in the stable tonight. Athas will be kicking the stall down again."

"Aye, lord," said Conn, and went.

"Lord," said the harper Tuathal then, lingering after Conn had gone, "there's something in this wind."

Of course his harper heard it. A harper would, and Tuathal was a good one, whose songs sometimes echoed Sidhe dreams that Cinnfhail King had had. Tuathal had indeed heard. There was worry in the harper's gray eyes.

"It comes no nearer," said Cinnfhail. "Perhaps it will not." He was suddenly wishing the bain Sidhe to go along the ridge, among his people, to any other house in the glen, and he felt a stinging guilt for this moment's selfishness. So he was not altogether virtuous as a king, not selfless. He knew this in himself. It was his weakness, that he desired a little peace in his fading years; and time, time, the one thing his life had less and less of.

Is it myself it sings for? he wondered. *O gods.*

2

Cinnfhail was by by the window again as the clouds came down, as the last few rays of westering sun walked the green of his valley within its mountain walls. The sun touched a moment on the heights and for a while the song seemed fainter, overwhelmed by this last green brilliance.

In the fields nearby the horses raced, tails lifting, as horses will who play tag with ghosts before such storms; the boys had the gate open and the horses knew where they should go, but horses and young folk both loving to make chaos of any scheme, it was all being done with as much disorder as either side could muster. Sheep were tending home on their own like small rainclouds across the earth: their fleeces would be wet and scattering the mist in waterdrops—the old ewe was wise as a sheep was ever likely to be, selfishly thinking of her own comfort, and she brought the others by example, her bell ringing across the meadows.

From their own pastures came the cattle, not hurrying unseemly, but not lingering either, home for byre and straw, needing no herdboy to tell them. This was the way of the beasts in Gleann Gleatharan, that they would not stray (excepting the horses, and them not far); it was the nature of the crops that few weeds would grow in them and of the folk that they grew up straight and tall and laughing much. And Cinnfhail King had a moment's ease thinking on his luck; but the clouds took back the sky then, and the mist came down.

The hills were everywhere laced with skeins of sky-white streams that only existed when the mist and the rain were on the mountaintops. They joined in waterfalls that merged with the tumbling Gley and ran right beneath their walls, in their green pastures.

And down beside the Gley-brook a red-haired man came walking.

He might have been one of their own, wrapped in an oiled-wool mantle, in dull brown clothes else, his head bowed against the wind. But the singing was louder, filling the very air. And this man walked like none of theirs returning, but with the weight of miles on him and a shadow of ill about him that the king's Sight knew. Knowledge closed like ice about Cinnfhail's heart.

This is what I have feared all day, Cinnfhail thought. *It is in this man.*

"Lord," said Conn, meeting Cinnfhail soon after on the stairs, "there is a traveler at the gate."

A mean thought touched Cinnfhail in that moment, that he should simply order this traveler away. But fate could not be turned. And never had any traveler been turned from Dun Gorm's gate, not in Cinnfhail's reign, and not in all the reigns of the Sidhe-blessed kings before him. It was part of the luck of the place and he dared not break it. "Bid him to table," said Cinnfhail.

"Lord," said Conn doubtfully, "I don't like the look of him."

"Bid him," said Cinnfhail.

Why? he should have asked Conn, *why do you not like his look?* Conn was a wise judge of men. But it seemed pointless, something there was no helping, as if this man had to be here tonight and they had to let him in. Cinnfhail had felt it all the day. The singer had fallen silent now. She was content, perhaps. The wind brought them only rain, and this stranger at their door, toward suppertime, as the sun went down in murk.

Cinnfhail's wife Samhadh came and kissed him as he went down to the hall; Deirdre came, with her hair dewed with mist as she had crossed the yard, her green and blue Gleann Gleatharan plaid wrapped about her still and all dewed on its fibers in the lamplight; Raghallach came in all wet-haired and ruddy-cheeked from putting the horses to stable, and Conn came and Tuathal joined them, with others of the hold. The common-hall echoed with steps on stone and wood, with the busy scrape of benches, the rattle of plates: there was the smell of mutton stew in the pot, of hot bread, of good ale queen Samhadh brewed herself, none better in the land.

Cinnfhail saw the stranger then, who had come into the warm hall still all muffled with his oiled-wool cloak; a page tried to take it, but the man refused and sat down at the end of the table in the place of least honor.

"My lord," said Samhadh, slipping her arm within Cinnhfail's, "is something still amiss?"

He saw blood within his vision, a bright sword. The dark Sight passed with a shiver. He thought of bundling his family elsewhere, of contriving some excuse to take them out of the hall tonight, but it all seemed futile. He did not sense danger to them; it was something far more vague.

So he sat down, his family about him. The harper Tuathal leaned near Conn the shieldman and whispered something. Conn looked sharp and frowning down the table, toward their guest, then got up and went here and there to men about the hall and to some of the women. Cinnfhail did not miss this, and caught the harper's fey, Sighted eye as the servants poured the ale. So Tuathal had also Seen, and Conn had seen, after his own fashion, as he judged men; and quietly these two faithful men took their own precautions.

"Look to it," said Cinnfhail to the servant nearest, "that the visitor's cup is never dry a moment,"—for it seemed prudent to ply this visitor with strong ale, to muddle him, to keep him well-pleased, propitiation, perhaps, or at least, should swords be drawn—to make him drunk. Cinnfhail's own men would not be. Conn had surely seen to that. Cinnfhail's own shield was on the wall, his sword hung beside it years unused; a door was nearby. All these things were not by chance, in the years he and his fathers before him had ruled in Dun Gorm, in years when other folk had coveted this fair green land. The danger seemed quiet for the moment, biding; he determined he would be wary with this guest about what he said, and send his family as early as possible from the hall.

The thunder broke above the hold, and rain pattered on the straw above, but the thatch was tight and snug; and below was warmth and good food and plenty of it. It was a rowdy hall; it had always been, with hounds that came and went and children who ate at the hearthside or filled and carried their bowls to some favored corner to laugh and giggle together; and a few youngsters old enough to take their places at the long table with men and women. About them all were the implements mostly not of war at all, but of their craft—old plowshares, a horseshoe or two, a great deal of rope and bits of harness and poles and such; it might have been any farmer's cottage, Dun Gorm, but for its sprawling size. It smelled of peace and plenty and the earth beneath its floors.

When bellies were full, Tuathal the harper took up his harp and sang the sort of song that set the children clapping; and then he sang a quiet song, after which the young ones must to bed in their lofts and nooks and some few must take them. Afterward the place was quieter while the harper meddled with his strings, a bright soft rippling of notes.

"Deirdre," said the king, taking the chance that he had planned, "be off to your own bed. Samhadh—"

"But there's the traveler," said Deirdre. "He hasn't told his tale."

Her young voice carried. There was stillness in the hall. It was truth. There was something owed Dun Gorm for the meal, news to share, purposes to tell. It was the custom in any civil hall—that gates were open and hearts ought to be, to honest folk; and honest folk returned something, be it news or a tale, for their supper.

And when the eyes of everyone in hall turned in anticipation to the traveler, their visitor lifted his head. He was a young man, with pale red hair and beard, the hair straggling about his shoulders and his eyes hard and bleak and colorless. "I come from over hills and by streams," he said in a hoarse dull voice. "And I have no harper's skill. I came here to ask the way ahead—how the road goes and how things sit up ahead."

It was rudely said; a countryman's bluntness, perhaps, lacking courtesy, but there was just enough grace to the voice to remind one it was rude. And that discourtesy slid like ice over Cinnfhail's skin, advisement this man was dangerous.

"As to that," said Cinnfhail, "ahead lies Gleann Fiach."

"What sort of place is this Gleann Fiach?"

"Not a happy place, visitor."

"Perhaps you will tell me."

Conn stirred in his place like a watchful dog, a dangerous one himself in his youth. His hall was a place of peace. Its own folk took merry liberties with their king; but this stranger took too much and had no grace in his taking, no courteous word, no tale, no peace.

"Dun Mhor is the name," Cinnfhail began, "of the dun that holds Glean Fiach." He lifted two fingers of his right hand, a motion for Conn's sake, and others saw it who knew him well, that he was wary. "Fill my cup," Cinnfhaill said, as if that had been the nature of the signal. A servant came and poured. Cinnfhaill drank, and looked at the stranger in his hall. "And between here and Dun Mhor, traveler, lies a wood that has gotten wider through my reign. For its sake I counsel you to go some other way. Sidhe own it. But if you go that way, walk softly; bruise no leaf. Speak nothing lightly to anyone you meet.

"Beyond that wood—" Cinnfhaill drew another breath and the ale and old habit and Sidhe-gift cast his voice into the rhythm of the tale-teller, so that his heart grew quieter and the power of it came on him. It was the teller's spell, and while it lasted no harm could come. It brought peace again on the hall, and calmed hearts and quieted angers, being itself one of the greatest magics; even the anger of the teller himself fell under its spell, and he saw good sense and quiet come to the eyes of the stranger who listened. "Beyond that wood lies Gleann Fiach; and there is no luck there. Gaelan was its king. His brother set on him and killed him. Have you not heard before now of Dun Mhor?"

"Tell me," said the stranger softly, and finding his manners, for it was a ritual question, "if you would, lord king."

"Fratricide." Cinnfhaill drew a deeper breath. "And more general murder. Here in Gleann Gleatharan we hear the rumors that come over the hills—but there is the Sidhe-wood between us, and we will not trespass that, nor will they of Gleann Fiach from their side. To spill blood there has no luck in it, be you right or wrong. So we cannot mend affairs in that sorrowing land, even if we would break our own peace for it. Gleann Fiach has had no end of miseries, and today they are worse. My tale is two brothers; and the Sidhe—they are part of it: two brothers, Gaelan and Sliabhin—Gaelan the elder and Sliabhin the younger. Gaelan was a good man, traveler, proper heir to Dun Mhor after his father Brian; he was fair-spoken and fair in judgment and respecting the gods and the Sidhe-lands though Brian his father had not always done it. Once king Brian chased a deer and killed it, and it ran into the Sidhe-wood and bled there. That was the ill luck on him. And Brian's queen lay in childbed that very hour: she gave him Sliabhin, as foul a boy in his youth as Gaelan was fair, poaching to the very edge of the Sidhe-forest when he had the chance, fouling everything that was good—this was Sliabhin, a man eaten up with spite that he was not firstborn, that he had not been given Dun Mhor. There was no luck in such a man, and after king Brian died and Gaelan had the kingdom, Sliabhin was greatly afraid, imagining that his brother Gaelan would do him hurt. So Sliabhin rode away to the hills in fear. This is the kind of man Sliabhin was: it never occurred to him that Gaelan would not think immediately of his harm, because that is what he would have done to Gaelan himself if he had gotten the kingship.

"Now kindred-love can be blind and perhaps it was fey as well. Gaelan entreated his brother home and they fell on one another's neck and reconciled themselves; this oath was good in Gaelan's mouth but never in Sliabhin's. For a little time there was peace, but after that little time Sliabhin began to think how he could cause mischief. And he found men like himself and he hunted the land for his amusement, taking every chance to be apart from the dun and to plan and plot with these greedy men. They took delight in hunting near the forest edge, and though they would not go into it, they mocked the Sidhe, trampling its edge and harrying the game up to it. They ranged the hills and one day they grew weary of the sport they had had and caught a poor herdboy, making him their quarry, and made it seem wolves had torn him, and not their dogs. But the boy's sister had seen. Her brother had hidden her in the rocks when he saw the men come, and the poor maid ran with all her might, all through the night she ran. Drucht was her name, and she was a wise young girl, knowing her brother beyond help and her father like to be killed if she should go first to him and tell him what was done: she went to the dun and poured out her tale to king Gaelan himself.

"Then Gaelan believed what he should have believed before; and he was hot after his brother to bring his justice on him. But one of Sliabhin's ilk was at hand, who took horse and rode ahead to warn Sliabhin not to go back to the dun that day.

"That was the parting of the ways finally between the brothers, Sliabhin banished, but late, far too late. The Sidhe set misfortune on the land. Crops failed. Gaelan's queen, Moralach, was with child; and it came stillborn. She lost others after; until one she had alive, and that one stole her health.

"Now from the day Sliabhin was cast out, he had been laying plans. Twenty years he bided, causing trouble where he could, and in a land with no luck on it there will always be discontent, and among young folk there will always be those who do not believe the truth of things that their elders were alive to witness.

"Now this next that I tell you is no long-ago tale. It came about a year ago, when Gaelan rode out of Dun Mhor to tend to his land, after the damages of a flooding of the Gley. There was murder done at home. Every servant that was loyal was killed; every man who could not be corrupted. So we in Gleann Gleatharan surmise. No one knows. Gaelan rode back within his own gates that day and never out again, nor any loyal man with him. Sliabhin is king in Dun Mhor now, over all Gleann Fiach. He took Gaelan's queen Moralach to his bed, holding her young son to hostage against her willingness to please him; his brother's corpse was not cold yet in the hall below. He spared the boy, that one grants; but the queen died after. They say she hanged herself from the rooftree. Whatever passes in Dun Mhor these days, it is no hall I would guest in. A man walking down the glen and through the Sidhe-wood should know that, and go some other way if he could."

There was silence for a space. It was a tale everyone in Dun Gorm knew, if not all parts of it. And all of a sudden Cinnfhail was thinking of that grim hold beyond the woods, how such a wicked king as Sliabhin might well draw others of his ilk to come and live at his board. The thunder cracked and shook the very posts of the hall. The wind wailed and set the hairs to lifting at the back of Cinnfhail's neck as he stared at the traveler.

"So you have no love for Sliabhin," the stranger said.

"None," said Cinnfhail.

The traveler stood up, hurled a sword clattering onto the table to the dismay of those nearest. Conn's sword ripped from its sheath in his startlement; benches were overset as swords came out and men and women came to their feet all around the room. But the stranger did no more than let fall his mantle.

"Gods help us," said Samhadh, pulling Deirdre to shelter behind her, and Raghallach was on his feet with a naked sword as Conn moved between the stranger and Cinnfhail, for about his shoulders was the red tartan of Dun Mhor.

"It is a ghost," said someone.

"No," said Cinnfhail, and waved the swords away, feeling a weakness in his knees and a tightness in his chest, for the price of the Sight was sometimes blindness to fated things; and now that badge of Dun Mhor made him see, at the same time that Conn saw, and the rest. Others remained on their feet, but Cinnfhail sought his chair again, feeling suddenly the years of his life upon him. "Man, what is your name?"

"Caith is my name," the traveler said, "mac Gaelan. First born. Gaelan's true heir and Moralach's own son."

There was silence for a space in which Cinnfhail's heart beat very hard. Raghallach moved close to him; Conn stood between this intruder and all the family.

"My father fostered me north," said mac Gaelan, never stirring from where he stood. "To Dun na nGall for safety. And he gave out his first son was stillborn. He knew that Sliabhin would strike at him. He wished me safe. And we got the news up there not three months gone, that I had delayed my homecoming—overlong."

"We have things to speak of," said Cinnfhail. He moved aside and touched Samhadh's hand, wishing her to be prudent and to take Deirdre away from this, out of danger of this man and the things that he could say. "Go," he said softly, "go up, go upstairs, now, Samhadh."

"There is no need," said the traveler, coming forward of the table's end, heedless of hands on swords all about him. There was a weariness about him, but he moved with grace all the same. He was a man that could walk soft-footed through a hall of enemies and bemaze them all, as he ensorcelled them.

"My sword is back there. I left it, did I not? And you were my father king Gaelan's friend. And never were you Sliabhin's."

"Father," said Raghallach. "Can it be truth?"

"It might be," Cinnfhail said heavily. "I did hear more to the story. I heard it long ago. So tell me—Caith mac Gaelan. Why have you come here?"

"To hunt out my father's killers. To take Dun Mhor. You were his neighbor, lord. His friend. I'd think you would be weary of Sliabhin by now."

"We'll speak of it."

"*Speak* of it. Lord, I have a young brother in that man's hands. I did not come here to *speak* of it."

There was a stillness then, in which the stranger stood among them with the ring of anguish dying in the air. And with justice on his side.

"What are you asking?" asked Raghallach. "That we go to war for your sake?"

"No," said Caith mac Gaelan. "That would do my brother no good. Sliabhin would kill him at the end of any siege, and do other things before. I want my brother safe before I take Dun Mhor, whatever the cost."

So there was honor in this young man; it touched that honor that was in Raghallach, like a fire to straw, in their valley that had had its peace, and Cinnfhail felt a chill raise gooseflesh on his neck.

"We will talk of it," Cinnfhail said again. "A night for sleep. A night for thinking. Then we will talk."

"Father," said Raghallach. "We have suffered Sliabhin far too long, the way I reckon it."

"We will take time to think about it, I said." The cold was about Cinnfhail's heart, a sense of doom, of change. And he remembered the singer on the wind. "To bed! We've said all tonight that wants saying. Morning and sober heads are what's needed, not ale-thoughts and ale-talk."

"Lord," Raghallach said. There was fire in his glance. He longed for honor, did Raghallach, here in this glen Cinnfhail had made quiet and at peace with all his deeds and all his striving. Raghallach heard Tuathal harp the ballads; Raghallach dreamed, in his innocence, of undoing it all and doing it over again. Cinnfhail knew.

"Off with you." Cinnfhail kissed Samhadh, and Deirdre, who looked past him at the stranger with wonder in her eyes. She had also heard the hero-songs, the sad, fair ballads; and Deirdre dreamed her own dreams of adventures. Both Cinnfhail's children then were snared; and Cinnfhail turned to his son smiling gently, though his heart hurt him; he clapped a hand to Raghallach's shoulder. "In the morning, hear? Quietly, as such things should be thought out. Obey me. To bed, all, *to beds*! And no rumor-mongering, no speaking of this beyond the gates. I have said it. Hear?"

He rarely spoke as king. It was not his way. When he did so now, folk moved, and bowed their heads and scurried in haste.

"Leave it!" he bade the servants, to have them gone; and to Conn, catching him by the arm, he spoke certain words which grieved and shamed him to speak.

But he had the Sight, and what he Saw now gave him no peace.

3

Caith gathered his sword from the table and sheathed it, having no desire in his mind now but rest, being well-fed and easier in the finding of friends than he had been in the long weeks since leaving Dun na nGall.

But: "Come with me," the king's harper said now, plucking at his sleeve. "The king will speak with you privately. He has more to tell to you. You'll want your cloak."

Caith considered it and weighed the risks of treachery; but he had eaten this man's bread and judged him as he sat, that the lord of Dun Gorm was what he had heard, a king worth listening to and a man to be trusted.

So he gathered his cloak about him and went where the harper led him, nothing questioning, down the stairs and, as the harper took up a torch from the bracket there, out a lower door into the dark and the retreating thunder. They stood beneath the smithy shed, with the rain dripping off the wooden roof and standing in puddles in the yard beyond. Cattle lowed; horses were restless in their pen nearby, a solitary dog barked in the dying of the storm, but it knew the harper and it was silent at his word.

"What is this?" Caith said. "What is this skulking about?" He suddenly doubted everything in this lonely place, and his hand was on his sword in the concealment of his cloak.

"My lord will speak to you," the harper repeated. And truth, from around the side of the yard came the king of Gleatharan with his shieldman by him, all muffled up in cloaks themselves.

Caith waited, his hand still on his sword, scowling at the two coming toward him and still uneasy. He had trusted few men in his life. Nameless, nothing, he had no teaching in things he needed to become what he was born to be. *Stay here in Dun na nGall*, his foster-father had said. *Don't meddle. There's nothing in Gleann Fiach for you.* And again: *If you go there, then plan to keep going. You defy me, boy—you'll not be coming back here.*

That was well enough. There was nothing that man who fostered him had ever given him but whipmarks on his back, and worse within his soul: *You take what's given you*, this man had said, Hagan, his father's cousin. And: *Keep your mouth shut, boy, whose son you are. Mind my words. So they name you foundling bastard. Maybe that's what you really are.*

A girl-child had looked up at him, flower-fair tonight; a man he wished had been his father had smiled at him; a man he would had been his brother had offered him help; a grave-eyed queen had looked on him with amazement— It was the way he would have seen Dun Mhor at his homecoming if he could have dreamed that dun clean and fair again. In this place he had had at least one homecoming such as an exile might dream of.

But the king of Gleatharan asked him out into the rain, into the dark to speak with him; and this was not part of his dream, this was not the welcome he had expected. Rather it held something of connivances and tricks—and this kind of thing he had dealt in often enough in his life.

The king came to him, squelching up in the mud, in the falling mist, till he passed beneath the roof of the shed and into the torchlight the harper held. The shieldman stood behind his king, his hands both out of sight beneath his oiled-wool cloak.

"Mac Gaelan," said Cinnfhail King, "forgive me. I ask that first."

"For what, then? Can we get to that?"

"Go back to Dun na nGall. Tonight. There's no gain here for you."

Caith drew in his breath. It wanted a moment to know what to say to such a warning from a king so two-faced. "Well, lord," he said, "gods requite you for it."

"I'll give you provisions," the king said, "and a horse—the pick of all I have."

Keep your gifts, Caith would have said then. But he was too much in need for pride. "We may be neighbors yet," he said in his anger. "I will return the horse."

"Mac Gaelan."

"You were my father's friend. So the price of your friendship is a meal and a horse. That's well. A man should know his friends."

"Mind your tongue," the shieldman muttered.

"He has cause," the king said. "Mac Gaelan—" He stayed Caith with a hand against his shoulder. "Go back to Dun na nGall. I have the Sight, mac Gaelan. And there is no luck for you. For the gods' own sake go home."

"In Dun Mhor is my home. My brother is still in their hands. I will tell you something, lord of Dun Gorm: I had something of that kind from my foster father. I know what a whip feels like, *my lord*. No, I'll not leave my brother to Sliabhin. And for my father's murder—where on the gods' own earth should I go, tell me that, until I have killed that man?"

"A kinslayer has no rest in the world. Whatever his cause."

"Sliabhin's no kin of mine. I'll not own him mine. He murdered my father, lord! His own brother. If any man could have come and set matters right, it *might* have been my father's friend, but I see how things sit here at Dun Gorm, how eager you are to set things right. You leave me no choice. No. I'll kill Sliabhin myself, without a qualm."

There was terror in the old king's eyes and something hard at the same time. "Stay," Cinnfhail said, stopping him a second time, this time with a biting grip of a hand still powerful. "I cannot let you go—mac Gaelan! Stop and listen to me."

Caith turned, then, flinched from under the king's hard hand, his own upon his sword. "I'll need the horse," Caith said.

"You'll have the horse. And whatever else you need. Go back to Dun na nGall; or go ahead to Gleann Fiach and rue it, rue it all your life. I don't think you know; you don't want to know more than I said in the hall. Listen to me: I have a selfish cause. If you take my son with you, he'll die there. I see it. I see it in the moon. There'll be blood, blood—no hope for you—*For the gods' sake, lad, listen. You don't know who you are!*"

The cold went to Caith's bones. *Bastard*, his foster father had hurled at him. "Old man," he said, "it was no grand place my father sent me to be fostered. Maybe he had little choice in his relatives. Sure enough he had little luck in his brother. And maybe a lord would send his son to the likes of Hagan mac Dealbhan if he had no choice of other kin—Or is it another kind of tale? Whose bastard am I? Yours?"

"*Sliabhin's.*"

Caith whirled and lashed out with his bare right hand, but the king's man brought his arm in the way and seized him about the neck. The breath stifled in him, not alone from the strangling hold on him. "Liar," he said. "O gods, you whoreson liar—"

"Stay!" the king said to his man. "Let him go."

"Lord," the shieldman protested.

"Let him go, I say." And to Caith: "Lad, Sliabhin had his way with Gaelan's wife, with Moralach, the queen. *That* Gaelan discovered when the herder-girl came to the hall and told her tale: Moralach confessed to him Sliabhin's other betrayal and her own shame. And that was the second cause of Sliabhin's exile. Gaelan forgave queen Moralach: she claimed it was rape and her fearing to tell him because of his blind love of Sliabhin and hoping the child in her was her husband's after all. But the child grew in her like guilt; and she feared it; and now that she heard the herder-girl tell her tale, she believed it might be a murderer's child in her belly. So she confessed. Four days Gaelan shut her away and she lived in dread of him; but on the fifth he wept and forgave her and this was a thing few knew, but Moralach confessed it to my queen when she rode there to be with her in the birthing. And at the last, lad, my lady was not in the room; they said Moralach commanded it, wanting only her nurse and the midwife with her; but it was a living child they carried from that room that night: my lady was there, close by, and saw it moving in the blanket. With her own eyes she saw it. And afterward when my lady came to Moralach, Moralach wept and clung to her and raved until they gave her a potion to make her sleep. Of the babe they gave out that it was stillborn. And my queen came home and carried that in her heart for two days before she told it me. After that I went no more to Gaelan's hold and my queen did not: it was worse than fostering we feared, for in queen Moralach's raving she told still another tale." From harsh the king's voice had become pitying, from anger had gone to shame, and still Caith stood there, shivering in the rain. Somewhere nearby a horse snorted and stamped, splashing a puddle. "Do you understand, lad? Need I say it? It was never rape. She let Sliabhin in, this vain woman, and paid for it all her life. When her other babes died, she was crazed and thought it her punishment; when she bore the last alive she was no more mother to it—she gave it to a nurse to care for. Perhaps she let her old lover in; perhaps they had met before. Whispers said as much. To do her mercy, likeliest it was some other hand let Sliabhin's men into Dun Mhor. And it is true Moralach hanged herself; so surely she repented. *That* is the tale they tell, of servants who were there to see and fled to the high hills when they had the chance. There is more to it: before she was with child the last time, Moralach went out riding. And she rode often that season, and always toward the hills. Do you understand me? The younger boy—may be Sliabhin's son. Hence the whispers who it was let those gates open. And Gaelan either fey or fool, he refused to credit rumors. So they say. Perhaps Gaelan knew and counted it all one with the curse on his land, the curse on his bed. Maybe he only wanted peace in his life. He was a sick man and his heart was broken and he became a fool. So he died. And by what they whisper, the younger boy is safe in Sliabhin's hands if anyone is."

Caith no more than stood there. It all fitted then, all the pieces of his life. He set them all in order, his hand upon his sword.

"Is that the truth?" he asked, because the silence waited to be filled.

"I will give you the best help that I can give. Only go from here, back to Dun na nGall. You are Sliabhin's true son. The Sidhe have set a curse on him, on all his line, and I have the Sight: I *tell* you whose son you are. Go back. This is not a place for you; and gods know a patricide is damned."

"My foster father said that I should not come back to him," Caith said in a voice that failed him. "So he believed it too. All these years. And you've known. *How many others?*"

"Does it matter? Nothing can mend what is."

"You forget. I have a brother in Dun Mhor."

"A brother you've never seen. Sliabhin's son."

"Why, then, my true brother still, would he not be?"

"Don't be a fool! Sliabhin's likely son and in Sliabhin's keeping. You can do nothing to him but harm."

"I can get him out of there."

"For the gods' sake, lad—"

"You promised me a horse."

The old king considered him sadly. "O lad, and what good do you bring? See, brother, will you say, I've killed our father to set you free? It goes on. It won't stop. It will never stop."

"The horse. That's all I want."

King Cinnfhail nodded toward the pen. Caith walked that way, in the dying rain, with the mist against his face. The horses, let from their stable in the dying of the storm, stared back at him, with the torchlight in their eyes and shining on their coats, more wealth of fine horses than any king had in Eirran, horses to heal the heart with the looking on them and the touching of them. On such horses a man could ride and ride, leaving everything behind. Men would envy such horses, would fight a war over any one such horse as he saw to choose from.

But a man who wanted to go quietly, who wanted no attention on himself when he came into Dun Mhor— "That one," Caith said, choosing a shaggy white horse which stood within the shadow near the stable, raw-boned and ungainly beside the rest.

"Not that one," said the king. "Choose another. That one is mine."

"It is the one I will have," Caith said harshly. "Everything else of your hospitality turned false. So I will take that one or walk. No other will serve me."

"Be it as you will," the old king said, and stayed his shieldman with a shake of his head. "Be kind to my horse, then. Dathuil is his name. And he will serve you."

Fair, it meant. It was an ugly horse. The king leaned against the fence and held out his hands to him and he trotted over like a child's pet. "Get his bridle," king Cinnfhail said to his shieldman, "and his saddle."

And when the shieldman had gone in and come out with the stable lad and the gear, the king would none of their help, but stepped under the rail and took the bridle and saddle, and saddled the raw-boned horse himself, all with such touches that said the old man loved this beast, he who had so many stronger and finer.

"I will not use him ill," Caith said sullenly when he saw that it was not all a lie, that he had chosen a horse which the old man truly loved above the others, "and I will send him home again if I can. But truth, no other would serve me. I'll come into Dun Mhor as I came here, a wanderer—unless you intend to betray me, unless you have already sent a messenger out tonight. And then, my lord—" He looked king Cinnfhail full in the eyes. "—I'll trust you and Sliabhin have your own compacts: in that case he'll return your horse himself to you, I'm sure, and keep as much of me as pleases him."

"Take Dathuil," said the king. "I will not wish you anything."

Caith climbed up to the horse's back, and took the sack of provisions that the shieldman gave him. Need compelled, and rankled in Caith's soul. Quietly he began to ride away, then drove in his heels and sped off through the open gate, a white ghost flying into the dark and mist.

"Dathuil," said Conn. "O gods, my lord—"

"There is a doom on him," said Cinnfhail, staring after the retreating rider. Tears spilled down his cheeks though his face remained composed. "He chose Dathuil. It was his fate to choose; and not mine to stop him. I know it. Gods help us. Gods save us from Dun Mhor."

The harper Tuathal was there, somber in the rain, holding aloft his torch. "Come inside, my lord."

Cinnfhail walked over the trampled yard. A horse whinnied long and forlornly; others did, distressed. And a cold was in Cinnihail's bones that not all the warmth of his hall and cheer of his friends and house could assuage.

4

The ugly horse ran on, down the glen, beside the Gley, never checking his pace and never breaking stride. Smooth as the wind Dathuil ran, and the cold mist stung Caith's cheeks, stung his eyes which pain had already stung. There was power in this horse, as in no horse he had ever ridden; its ugliness masked both strength and unlikely speed. So the king had had reason in his affection for this beast; Caith laid no heel to it and hardly used the reins at all, finding something true-hearted at least, this brute that bore him on its back and gave him its strength, when it was beyond his own power to have traveled far this night.

He reined it back at last, having fear for it breaking its heart in this running, but it threw its head and settled easily into a tireless rack. Its power hammered at him, kept him on his way, and while he rode, while its hooves struck the wet earth in tireless rhythm he had no need to think, no need to reckon what he was or where he went.

Bastard. Far more than that, he was. He recalled the rage in his foster-father's face when he knew where he would go. *Kinslayer. Patricide.*

He had a brother he had never seen. Brian was his name. He had built a fantasy around the boy, this innocence, this one kinsman he might recover who would be grateful to an elder, wiser brother, a quasi-son who should be the staying point of his pivotless life. He needed someone. He had loyalty to give and none would have it. He had made himself by ceaseless work and striving—everything a father could respect and love, in hopes his father would come to him at Dun na nGall and claim him.

Now he was going home, world-scarred and bereft of all innocent dreams but one. He had fought at Skye, a pirate no less than the man he was fostered to.

O father, come and get me. I am better than this man. Better than these pirates— When I am a man, I will come to you instead and you will be glad that I am your son. Do you know where I am, or what we did at Skye? I have had my first battle, father.

Done my first murder. . . .

I have got a sword. I took it off this dead man—

O father!

"Gone?" asked Raghallach.

The narrow stairs flowed with shadows in the torchlight. Samhadh was waiting there as he came in from the cold, Samhadh and Deirdre in their shifts, wrapped in blankets from their chambers; and Raghallach was there, still dressed, while servants put their heads about the corner and ducked back again, sensing no welcome for themselves.

"He left," said Cinnfhail, uneasy in his half-truths. He was cold. He was drenched from the rain. He had thought only to come upstairs and warm himself in his bed at Samhadh's side, but sounds and steps carried in Dun Gorm, in its wooden halls, and so there was this ambush of him at the upper stairs. "We talked a time. He asked a horse and provisions. Stealth is best for what he plans. He's going on to Dun Mhor against all my advice."

"Gods, they'll butcher him."

"And where would you be going?" Cinnfhail cried, for Raghallach went past him, downward bound on the stairs. "No! You'll not be helping him, young lad; you'll be putting both your heads under Sliabhin's bloody axe. No. I'll not have it. Let be."

Raghallach stopped. There was a terrible look in his eyes as he stood on the steps below Cinnfhail and looked up at him in the torchlight. "It's raining," Raghallach said. "For the gods' sake, it's raining out; what sane man goes riding off on such a night with choice of a bed— 'Talk in the morning,' you said, father. In the morning. But he's to be gone by then, isn't he?"

"Watch your tongue, boy!"

"You've shamed me," Raghallach said all quietly. "In the hall tonight. This man told the truth. We've let Dun Mhor alone all these years for fear of that truth. And now you've sent him off. You've sent him out of here to add another to Sliabhin's crimes."

"Raghallach—"

"It's been on you all the day, hasn't it, this dread, this fear of yours? This blackguard in Dun Mhor—gods, father, how did we seem tonight? 'Talk in the morning,' you said. 'Take counsel in the morning.' "

"Be still," said Samhadh. Deirdre only stared, her young face struck with shock and shame.

"I love you," said Raghallach. There were tears on his face. "I love you too much, father, to let you do a thing like this. You have the Sight; and having it, you wrap me in and keep me close and what am I to think? We were fronted in our own hall by a man who wanted justice. Gaelan was your friend; but if he was your friend, father—then where *were* we in those days?"

"Sliabhin's son," said Cinnfhail, going down to catch him on the steps, for Raghallach turned to go. He seized Raghallach by the arm and turned him by force to face him. "Raghallach, that is Sliabhin's own son. You know what they whisper about Moralach. It's true."

His son's face grew pale in the torchlight. "O gods."

"It's *patricide* will be done at Dun Mhor," said Cinnfhail. "And by the gods this house will not aid it."

Raghallach gnawed his lip. "And do we sit with our hands in our laps? All the hall heard. All the house will know you sent this man away. And all Dun Mhor will know he guested here—and take revenge if he fails. Or this Caith may be our enemy for long years if he rules Gleann Fiach instead. No. This house is going to do something, father. I'm taking twenty men as far as the border. And if need or trouble falls back to threaten the Sidhe-wood, at least we will have some chance to tell Dun Mhor where our border is, and that we won't have trespassers. If he fails—if he fails, father, we have a stake in it, do we not? Sliabhin will be sending us his threats again. He'll be finding his excuse. And if so happens this Caith comes back in haste with Sliabhin's throat uncut, and we be there the other side of the Sidhe-wood, well, there is help we *can* give then and have our hands clean. It's no kinslaying *we* intend."

Cinnfhail thought a moment. His face burned with shame and his heart widened with pride in Raghallach, for his goodheartedness and wit. "I will go myself," he said. "It's a good plan."

"No," said Raghallach. His eyes glittered damply in the light. His jaw was set in that way he had that nothing would dissuade. And suddenly, passionately, he embraced Cinnfhail and thrust him back at arm's length, his young face earnest and keen. "All my life you have kept me from any hazard, wrapped me in wool. No, mother, father. I'm not a boy and you're not a young man to be dealing with Sliabhin's hired bandits. This one, this time, is mine."

There was a time Caith had no remembrance of, how he had gotten into the woods, for he was weary and the shaggy horse's tireless gait had never varied. He might have slept, might have been dreaming when he first passed beneath the trees that were all about him now, whispering in the wind.

He rode slowly, the horse treading lightly on the leaves, and Caith rubbed at his eyes and wondered had he slept a second time, for he remembered the horse running and could not remember stopping, nor account for where he was. And rubbing his eyes and blinking them clear again he saw a light before him in the dark, a fitful light like a candle-gleam, jogging with the course the shaggy horse followed on this winding track among the trees. The wind blew and scattered droplets from the leaves; made the light wink and vanish and reappear with the shifting of branches and limbs between him and the source. The pitch of the land was generally downward, and there was a noise of moving water nearby, so he knew they were coming to a stream, perhaps the wandering Gley itself, or one of the countless other brooks that lived and died with the rains. Someone must be camped on this streamside up ahead, and Caith gathered his wits and rode with care, fully awake and searching the trees and the brush on this side and that for some way to avoid this meeting.

But the ugly horse kept on, patient and steady. Sooner than Caith had looked for (had he somehow drowsed again?) he was passing the last curtain of black branches that screened him from that light.

It was one man camped on the trailside, a ragged-looking fellow the like of which one might find along the roads and between the hills, a wanderer, an outlaw, more than likely. Such men Caith knew. He had met them and sometimes shared a fire and sometimes come to blows with such wolves; and he was alive and some of them were not. This much he had learned of his foster-father and the king of Dun na nGall: the use of that sword he wore. He had no overwhelming fear in the meeting, but he had far rather have avoided it altogether.

"Good night to you," Caith said perforce, reining in. The man no more than looked up at him over the fire, a mature man and lean and haggard. Then with the wave of a thin hand the man beckoned him to the fireside.

"Here is courtesy," Caith muttered, still ahorse, and considering how Dun Gorm had cast him out into the night and the rain. There was a pannikin by the fireside. Caith smelled meat cooking; he had provisions on him he was willing to trade a bit of in turn. By now he ached with traveling, he longed for rest in all his bones, and more, he saw a harpcase on a limb near the man, the instrument protected against the weather.

So it was a wandering harper he had met which was another kind of man altogether than bandits. Such a man might walk through bandit lairs untouched and stand equally secure in the halls of kings. That harp was his passage, wherever he wished to go; his person was more sacred than a king's, and his fireside, wherever set, was safer than any hall.

A second time the harper beckoned. Caith stepped down from the shaggy horse though he did not pause to slip its bit or loosen its girth. He was not that trusting in any new meeting. He crouched warily before the fire, warming his numb hands and studying the harper close at hand.

"Looking for some hall?" he asked the man.

"Not I," the harper said. "I prefer the road."

"Where bound?" Caith felt still uneasy, wishing still in a vague way he had no need to have stopped and yet too proud to leap up and run from a harper. "Gleann Fiach?"

"I might go that way," said the harper.

"I might keep you company on the way," said Caith, with devious thoughts of passing Dun Mhor's gates in such company.

But suddenly he became aware of another watcher in the bushes, a man—a youth, all in dark. Between seeing him and springing to his feet with his hand on his sword was only the intake of a breath; but the youth stepped out into the open, holding his hands wide and empty, and grinning in mockery.

"My apprentice," said the harper. "Is there some dread on you, man? Something on your mind? Sit and share the fire. Peace."

"I've thought again," said Caith. "My business takes me on."

"But I think," said the square-jawed youth, whose eyes peered from a wild tangle of black bangs, "I think it is the horse—oh, aye, it would be that fine horse, wouldn't it? He has got something doesn't belong to him."

"The horse was lent," Caith said shortly. Harper or no, he had made up his mind and retreated a pace: when he drew his sword, he had the habit of using it at once and never threatening, but it was part of its length drawn. "Teach your apprentice manners, harper. He will bring you grief."

"But that horse *is* stolen," said the harper. "His name is Dathuil. And he is mine." The harper unfolded upward, tall and slim and not so ragged as before. Beside him the youth took on another aspect, with mad and ruby eyes, and the harper was fair now, pale and terrible to see.

Caith drew the sword, for all that it could do. They were Sidhe, that was clear to him now. And he was in their woods. He stood there with only iron between himself and them and all their ancient power.

"I will be going," he said, "and I'll be taking the horse. He was lent to me. He's not mine to give, one way or the other." He backed farther, and saw the horse not ugly but fair, a white steed so beautiful it touched the heart and numbed it, and Caith knew then what blessing he had taken from Dun Gorm.

"He is Dathuil," said the Sidhe again. "We gave him to a friend. You must give him back to us."

"Must I?" Caith said, turning from his bedazzlement, discovering them nearer than before. He had his sword in his hand and remembered it. "And what if not?"

"That horse is not for anyone's taking. He must be freely given. And better if you should do that now, man, and give him to me—far better for you."

A Sidhe horse could not be for his keeping. Caith knew that. But he kept the blade up, reckoning that his life was the prize now, and them needing only a single mistake from him to gain it. "If you have to have it given," Caith said, "then keep your hands from me."

"That horse was lent to the kings of Dun Gorm," said the youth.

"Cinnfhail has cast him away, giving him to you—with whom we have no peace. So we will take him back again."

Caith backed still farther, seeking Dathuil's reins with his left hand behind him; but the horse eluded his reaching hand once and again, and the two Sidhe stalked him, the tall one to his left now, the dark youth going to his right.

"So," Caith said, seeing how things stood. "But if I give you what you want, you have everything and I have nothing. That seems hardly fair. They say the Sidhe will bargain."

"What do you ask?"

"Help me take Dun Mhor."

The dark one laughed. The bright one shone cold as ice.

"Why, let us do that!" the dark one said.

"Be still," said the taller; and to Caith, with chill amusement: "Phookas love such jokes. And those who bargain with the Sidhe come off always to the worse. You have not said the manner of the help, leaving that to us; and leaving the outcome of it to us too. Things are far more tangled than you think they are. So I shall take your bargain and choose the manner of my help to you, which is to tell you your futures and the three ways you have before you. First: you might go back over the hills the way you came. Second: you might go back to Dun Gorm; Raghallach would help you. He would be your friend. Third: you might enter Dun Mhor alone. All of these have consequence."

"What consequence?"

"A second bargain. What will you give to know that, of things that you have left?"

"My forbearance, Sidhe."

"For that I trade only my own. What more have you left?"

Caith hurled the amulet from his neck. It vanished as it hit the ground.

"A fair trade then. You have made yourself blind to our workings, and in return I shall show you truth. This is the consequence if you go back where you came from: that you will die obscure, knifed in a quarrel not of your making in a land not of your choosing. Second: if you go back now to Dun Gorm: that Cinnfhail's son will die in your cause; you will win Dun Mhor; you will take Cinnfhail's daughter to your wife and rule both Dun Gorm and Dun Mhor, king over both within three years."

"And if I go alone to Dun Mhor?"

"Sliabhin will kill you. It will take seven days for you to die."

Caith let the swordpoint waver. He thought of Dun Gorm, that he had wanted, the faces, Deirdre's young face. But there were traps in every Sidhe prophecy; this he sensed, "And gaining Dun Gorm," he said, "what would I have there but sorrow and women's hate?"

"For a son of Sliabhin," said the Sidhe, stepping closer to him, "you are marvelous quick of wit. And now I must have the horse you have given me."

"Curse you!" he cried. He struck, not to kill, but to gain himself space to run. The Sidhe's blade—he had not seen it drawn—rang instant against his own; and back and back he staggered, fighting for his life.

A black body hurtled against him, trampling him beneath its hooves, flinging his sword from his hand; Caith staggered up to one knee and lunged after the fallen sword.

"Rash," said the Sidhe, and light struck him in the face and a blow flung him back short of it. "The horse is mine. For the rest—"

"*Sidhe!*" Caith cried, for he was blinded in the light, as if the moon had burned out his eyes. All the world swam in tears and pain. He groped still after his sword among the leaves and as the hilt met his fingers, he seized it and staggered to his feet. "Sidhe!" he shouted, and swung the blade about him in his blindness.

He heard the beat of hooves. A horse's shoulder struck him and flung him down again; this time he held to the sword and rolled to his feet.

But blind, blind—there was only the shadow of branches before a blur of light in a world gone gray at the mid of the night, a taunting, moving shape like a will-o'-the-wisp before his eyes.

"*Sidhe!*" he cried in his anger and his helplessness.

It drifted on. Laughter pealed like silver bells, faint and far and mocking.

5

There was no sight but that fey light, no sound but that chill laughter, pure as winter bells. Caith followed it, sobbing after breath, followed it for hours because it was all the light he had in his gray blindness and if he turned from it he was lost indeed. He tore himself on brush and thorns, slipped down a streambank and sprawled in water, clawed his way up the other side. "Sidhe!" he cried again and again. But the light was always there, just beyond his reach in a world of gray mist, until he went down to his bruised knees and on his face in the leaves and lost all sense of direction.

He got up again in terror, turning this way and that.

"Sidhe!" His voice was a hoarse, wild sound, unlike himself. "*Sidhe!*"

A horse sneezed before him. The will-'o-the-wisp hovered in his sight, near at hand. It became Dathuil and on his back the tall fair Sidhe, against a haze of trees, of moon-silvered trunks.

"Will you ride?" the phooka asked, at his other side, and Caith turned, staggering, and caught his breath in. Red eyes gleamed in the shadow. "Will you ride?" the phooka asked again. "I will bear you on my back."

Caith's eyes cleared. It was a black horse that stood there. Its eyes shone with fire. Suddenly it swept close by him, too quick for his sword, too quick for the thought of a sword.

"If you had kept the white horse," said the will-o'-the-wisp on his other side, "even the phooka could not have caught you. Now any creature can."

"Sliabhin hunted in these woods," said the phooka-voice, from somewhere in the trees. "Now we hunt them too."

"Go back," said the will-o'-the-wisp, and horse and rider shimmered away before him without a sound. Caith caught after breath and stumbled after, exhausted, wincing at the thorns that caught his cloak back and tore his skin.

"Go back," said the voice. "Go back."

But Caith followed through thicker and thicker brush, no longer knowing any other way. His sight had cleared, but in all this woods there was no path, no hope but to lay hands on the Sidhe and compel them or to wander here till he was mad. A pain had begun in his side. It grew and grew, until he walked bent, and sprawled at last on the slick, wet leaves.

"You cannot take us," said the Sidhe, and was there astride Dathuil, paler and brighter than the newborn day. A frown was on the Sidhe's face. "I have given you your answers. Are you so anxious then to die? Or are you looking for another bargain?"

Caith caught his breath, holding his side. It was all that he could do to gain his feet, but stand he did, with his sword in his hand.

"Ah," said the Sidhe. "Proud like your father."

"*Which* father? I've had three."

"You have but one, mac Sliabhin. The house at Dun Mhor has but one lord. And a curse rests on it and all beneath that roof. Hunters in our woods, slayers of our deer—for your line there is neither luck nor hope. But for the gift of Dathuil and for my own pleasure, I will give you once what you ask of me. And pitying mortal wits I will tell you what you should ask—if you ask me that advice."

"That would use up the one request, would it not?"

The Sidhe smiled then as a cat might smile. "Well," he said, "if you are that quick with your wits, you may know what you should ask."

"Take the curse off Dun Mhor."

The smile vanished. The Sidhe went cold and dreadful. "It is done. And now it is to bestow again. I give it to *you*."

Caith stared at the Sidhe in bleak defeat, and then took a deeper breath. "Sidhe! One more bargain!"

"And what would that be, mac Sliabhin, and what have you left to trade?"

"It's Dun Mhor you hate. I'll work this out with you. There's a young boy, my brother, inside Dun Mhor. Brian is his name."

"We know this."

"I want to take him out and free of Sliabhin. Help me get him out and safe away and I will kill Sliabhin for you; and take Dun Mhor; and so you can have it all. Me. Dun Mhor. My brother is the price of my killing your enemy."

The Sidhe considered him slowly, from toe to head. "Shall I tell you what you have left out?"

"Have I left something out?"

"Nothing that would matter." The Sidhe reined Dathuil aside. "I take your bargain."

Caith had his sword still in hand. He rammed it into his sheath and felt all his aches and hurts. He looked up again at the Sidhe, cold at heart. "What did I leave out, curse you? What did I forget?"

"You are not apt to such bargaining," said the phooka, there in young man's shape, leaning naked against a tree at his right hand. "I will tell you, mac Sliabhin. You forgot to ask your life."

"Oh," Caith said. "But I didn't forget."

"How is that?" said the fair Sidhe.

"If you want some use out of your curse, you can't kill me too soon, now can you? It would rob you of your revenge."

The phooka laughed, wild laughter, a mirth that stirred the leaves. "O mac Sliabhin, Caith, fosterling of murderers and thieves, I love thee. Come, come with me. I will bear you on my back. We will see this Dun Mhor."

"And drown me, would you? Not I. I know what you are."

But the black horse took shape between blinks of his eyes and stood pawing the ground before him. Its red eyes glowed like balefire beneath its mane.

"Trust the phooka," said the tall Sidhe with the least gleam of mirth in his eyes. "What have you left to risk?"

Caith glowered at the Sidhe and then, shifting his sword from the way, roughly grasped the phooka's mane and swung up to his bare back.

It was the wind he mounted, a dark and baneful wind. It was power, the night itself in horse-shape; and beside them raced the day, that was Dathuil with the Sidhe upon his back.

Caith heard laughter. Whence it came he guessed.

The forest road stretched before the men from Dun Gorm in the dawning, and the sun searched the trees with fingers of light. It was the green shade before them, the green deep heart of the Sidhe-wood.

"No farther," Conn said, "young lord, no farther."

Raghallach thought on Conn's advice as he rode beside the man. His father had given him into Conn's hands when he was small, and never yet had he put his own judgment ahead of Conn's and profited by it.

But the years turned. It was after all Conn, his father's watchdog, who had tutored him, cracked his head, bruised his bones, taught him what he knew, and Conn, he reckoned, who had orders from his father to protect him now, against all hazard.

"There is one captain over a band," Raghallach said to this man he loved next to his own father. "And it is not lessons today, now, is it, master Conn?"

"Life is lessons," Conn muttered to the moving of the horses. They went not at a gallop; they kept their strength for need. "Some masters are rougher than others, lad, and experience is a very bitch."

"That man you sent to scout ahead of us; Feargal. We're of an age, he and I—do you always call him *lad*, Conn?"

"Ah," said Conn, and cast a wary look back, to see whether the men were in earshot of it all. The sound of the hooves covered low voices at such distance. "Ah, but, me lad, you are young. Yet. And will not get older by risking honest men who put their lives into your hand. Do not be a fool, son of my old friend; I did not teach a fool."

Anger smoldered in Raghallach. He drove his heels into his horse's sides and then recalled good sense. Raghallach grew a great deal, in that moment; he reined back, confusing the horse which threw its head and jumped.

Arrows flew from ambush. A man cried out; a horse screamed.

Raghallach flung his shield up in thunderstruck alarm. Arrows thumped and shocked against it; he reined aside, knowing nothing now to do but run into the teeth of ambush, not turn his shieldless back to the arrows or delay while some shot found his horse or legs. The good horse leapt beneath his heels, surefooted in the undergrowth, heedless of the breast-high thicket. "Ware," Conn yelled, as the horse's hindquarters sank under a sudden impact: Conn hewed a man from off Raghallach's back that had flung himself down from the trees.

Next was a confusion of blows, of curses howled, of blades and blood, the scream of horses and the crack of brush.

Then came silence, deep silence, after so much din, horses crashing slowly back through brush, blowing and snorting as riders sought the clear road and regrouped, a man fewer than before.

"Feargal," Raghallach said of the body they found there on the trail. A red-fletched arrow had taken him in the throat. Gleann Fiach marking.

"*Think*," said Conn, fierce at his side. Conn's brow ran blood. "Think and do it, boy! They have come into the Sidhe-wood. They are forewarned, they've made ambush against us and this Caith mac Sliabhin. Hagan mac Dealbhan has warned them!"

"He's dead," said Feargal's brother Faolan, who had gotten down to see and knelt by his brother. Faolan hovered somewhere lost in the horror, not touching the arrow that had felled his brother, only frozen there.

"*Boy*," Conn said; the word cursed them all. "*What will you do?*"

"Get him home," Raghallach said gently to Faolan, and jerked his horse's head about in the direction opposite to home, using his heels to send him down the road after the fleeing enemy. Others followed. Conn was one, drawing close beside him.

Raghallach looked at Conn as they rode.

"Not I, boy," said Conn. "I have not a word."

The road opened out before them, obscured in leaves and green.

"It wants answer," said Raghallach. "This death of ours wants an answer."

"On whom," asked Conn. "Gleann Fiach cattle? Where will we stop? We know they hold the woods. Those that ran will regroup; meanwhile they'll have a man sent to Sliabhin to get help up here. It's war, lad; it begins. Blood is on the Sidhe-wood and our own hands have shed it too."

A hollow lay before them, a small clearing in the wood, which was one of their own Gley's fords. It was a place for ambushes; the air here all was wrong, sang with unease, in the leaves, the water-song.

They thundered into it. The newborn light grew strange, the beats of the hooves dimmer and dimmer.

The peace, a voice said, *the peace is broken, son of Dun Gorm. No farther, come no farther.*

Panic took Raghallach suddenly, a fear not of arrows. He was Cinnfhail's son: he Saw, for the first time in his life, he Saw. "Conn!" he cried. "Stop!" He reined in his horse. His face was hot with shame and self-reproach, that even to this moment he had led from fear and pride, not sense. He had ridden on for pride's sake, blown this way and that by what everyone would think instead of regarding what was wise. *Fool*, Conn had said. A shadow came on them, and about them, and into them, horse and rider, all, darkening their sight.

It was the forest, managing its own defense.

6

The phooka stopped, having leapt the stream, and Caith went sprawling over his neck, rolling in the leaves, bruised and battered.

The phooka stood in man-form on the bank, naked and laughing at him, grinning from ear to ear and leaning on his knees.

"You bastard," Caith said, gathering himself up.

"I thought," said the phooka, "that it was yourself were the bastard, Caith mac Sliabhin."

Caith caught up his sheathed sword and all but hurled it; mastered his temper instead. "Of course it is," he said, at which the phooka laughed the more, and overtook him as he went stamping up the bank. The phooka clapped him on the shoulder and hooted with laughter. Caith hurled off the hand, whirled and looked at the Sidhe, the sword still in his hand.

"Oh, come," said the phooka, grinning. His teeth were white and the frontmost were uncommon square and sturdy, in a long beardless jaw. His eyes were black and merry, and red lights danced in them even by daylight. "Do you not like a joke?"

"It will be a great joke when you drown me. Of that I'm sure."

The phooka grinned. "Oh, I like you well, mac Sliabhin. I missed the water with you, did I not?"

Caith said nothing. He limped onward, flung off the hand again as they walked along the streamside, picking up the road. The phooka walked by him as if he had only started out a moment ago, fresh and easy as youth itself.

"Where is the other?" Caith asked, after some little walking. "Where has he gotten to?" For the bright Sidhe had been with them until that leap across the stream.

"Oh, well, that one. He's not far. Never far."

"Watching us."

"He might be." The phooka kicked a stone. "He has no liking for roads, that one. Nuallan is his name. He's one of the Fair Folk." An engaging, square-toothed grin. "I'm the other kind."

"What do you call yourself?"

The phooka laughed again. "Call myself indeed. Now you know we'd not hand you *all* our names. Dubhain. Dubhain am I. Would you ride again?"

"Not yet, phooka."

"Dubhain," the phooka reminded him. It was the wickedest laugh ever Caith had heard. There were dark nights in it, and cold depths where phookas lived, deep in rivers, haunting fords and luring travelers to die beneath the waters. *Darkness*, his name was. "So we walk together." The phooka looked up. His eyes gleamed like live coals beneath the mop of black hair. "We are in Gleann Fiach now, mac Sliabhin. Do you not find it fair?"

The road took them farther and farther from the woods. The deep glen showed itself bright with sun, its hilly walls different from Gleann Gleatharan, untilled, unhedged. Gorse grew wild up the hillsides, from what had once been hedges, and grass grew uncropped. It was a fair land, but there was something wrong in that fairness, for it was empty. Untenanted. Waste, even in its green pastures.

And coming over a gentle rise, Caith could see the dun itself at this great distance, a towered mass, a threat lowering amid its few tilled fields. Now indeed Caith saw pasturages up on the hillsides; but they were few for so great a place, and all near the dun. The most of the tillage closely surrounded the dun itself, gathered to its skirts like some pathwork order struggling to exist in the chaos of the land. Gleann Fiach was wide. There was promise in the land, but it was all blighted promise.

Caith had stopped walking. "Come on," the phooka said with a sidelong glance that mocked all Caith's fears and doubts. Caith set out again with Dubhain at his side, the two of them no more than a pair of dusty travelers, himself fair, his companion dark. Caith was weary of the miles, the flight, the restless night; his companion had strength to spare. Like some lawless bare-skinned boy Dubhain gathered stones as he came on them and skipped them down the road.

"There," he would say, "did you see that one, man?"

"Oh, aye," Caith would answer, angry at the first, and then bemazed, that a thing so wicked could be so blithe, whether it was utterest evil or blindest innocence, like storm, like destroying flood. The phooka grinned up at him, less than his stature, and for a moment the eyes were like coals again, reminding him of death.

"A wager, man?"

"Not with you," he said.

"What have you to lose?" And the phooka laughed, all wickedness.

"You would find something," he said. The grin widened. The phooka hurled another stone. No man could match that cast, that sped and sped far beyond any natural limit.

"I thought so," said Caith, and the phooka looked smug and pleased.

"Cannot match it."

"No."

The phooka shape-shifted, became again the horse, again the youth, and broke a stem of grass, sucking on it as he went, like any country lad. Dubhain winked. He was more disreputable than he had been, a ragged wayfarer. A moment ago he had been bare as he was born, dusky-skinned. Now he went in clothes, ragged and dusty, ruined finery with a bordering of tinsel gold.

"It is a glamour," the phooka said. "Can you see through it?"

"No."

"If you had the amulet, you might."

"I don't."

Another grin.

"You will help me," asked Caith, "inside the walls—or just stand by?"

"Oh, assuredly I shall help."

"—me."

"O Caith, O merry friend, of course, how could you doubt?"

Caith looked askance at Dubhain, uneasy in all his thoughts now. The Sidhe would both trick him if they could, if he gave them the least chance. He thought through the compact he had made a hundred times as they walked the sunlit dust, as they came down farther and farther into the glen. Of what lay before him in Dun Mhor he wished not to think at all, but his thoughts drifted that way constantly, darker and more terrible, and the phooka beside him was constant in his gibes.

Sliabhin's son. And Moralach's. All his life seemed lived beneath some deceiving glamour. He had conjured loyalty to Gaelan, to a dream that never was. He came to avenge Gaelan, and his own father was the murderer.

But the stones before them were real and no illusion. There was truth about to happen. It must be truth, finally, after a life of lies and falseness.

The day and distance dwindled in the crossing of the glen. Caith rested little, except at the last, taking the chance to sleep a bit, in the cover of a thicket, at the edge of the dun's few tilled fields and scant pastures, before he should commit himself to all that he had come to do.

And quickly there was a nightmare, a dream of murder, of Moralach the queen hanging from the rooftree of Dun Mhor.

"You," Caith said to the phooka when he waked sweating and trembling to find him crouching near. "Is it some prank of yours, to give me bad dreams?"

"Conscience," said the phooka. "I'm told you mortals have it. It seems nuisanceful to me."

And then Dubhain reached out and touched Caith's face with callused fingertips, and there came to him a strength running up from the earth like summer heat, something dark and healing at once, that took his breath.

"Keep your hands from me!" Caith cried, striking the Sidhe-touch away.

"Ah," said Dubhain, "scruples even yet. There is that left to trade."

"That I will not." Caith scrambled to his feet, shuddering at the wellness and the unhuman strength in himself.

"You've dropped your sword," the phooka said, handing it up to him with a grin on his face and the least hint of red glow within his eyes.

Caith snatched it, hooked the sheath to his belt and caught his oiled-wool cloak about him and his tartan as he hit out upon the road.

Dubhain was quickly with him, striding lightly at his side.

And Dun Mhor rose ever nearer as they came past the wild hedges onto the road. The dun lowered as a dark mass of stone in the evening that had fallen while Caith slept in his thicket.

No lights showed from Dun Mhor in this twilight time, not from this side, though some gleamed about the hills. Cattle were home; sheep in their folds; the folk behind the walls of their cottages and of the great keep that was many times the size of rustic Dun Gorm.

I am mad, Caith thought, having seen the size of the place. *As well walk into Dun na nGall and try to take it.*

But he kept walking with Dubhain beside him. The phooka whistled, as if he had not a care in all the world, and a wind skirled a tiny
cloud up in the sky right over Dun Mhor, a blackness in the twilight.

"I think," said the phooka, "it looks like rain. Doesn't it to you?"

"You might do this all," Caith said in anger, "If you can do all these
things, why could you not come at this man you hate?"

"Not our way," said Dubhain.

"What is your way—to torment all the land, the innocent with the
guilty?"

The eyes glowed in the darkness. "Men seem best at that."

"A curse on you too, my friend."

The phooka laughed. Dun Mhor loomed above them now, and the
cloud had grown apace as they walked. Dubhain's hand was on Caith's
shoulder, like some old acquaintance as they passed down the last
hedgerow on the road, as they left the last field and came up the hill of
the dun to the gate. Lightning flashed. The cloud widened still.

"Hello," Caith shouted, "hello the gatekeep. Travelers want in!"

There was a long silence. "Who are you?" a man shouted from up
in the darkened tower to the left of the gate. "What business in Dun
Mhor?"

"Business with your lord!" Caith shouted back. "Word from Dun na
nGall!"

"Wait here," the gatekeep said, and after was silence.

"Perchance they'll let you in," the phooka said.

"Oh, aye, like the raincloud is chance." Caith did not look at Dubhain. He knew how Dubhain would seem—quite common to the eye,
whatever shape suited the moment and Dubhain's dark whims. The
cloud still built above them. Thunder muttered. "I will tell you, phooka.
Hagan—the man who fostered me—might have sent word south when
I left him. He knew where I might go and what I might do. He hated
me; I know that. Gods know what side of this he serves, but it was never
my side. He might well betray me to curry favor with Sliabhin, since Sliabhin is king. I reckon that he might." He had begun to say it only to
bait the phooka and diminish Dubhain's arrogance. But the pieces settled in his mind, in sudden jagged array of further questions. "I know
nothing. Who fostered me out, how I was gotten from here—the king
of Gleatharan never told me. Was it Gaelan or was it Sliabhin, phooka?"

The mad eyes looked up at him, for once seeming sober. "Would
you pity Sliabhin if you knew that?"

"Gods, phooka—"

"Perhaps it was." The red gleam was back. "Perhaps was not. They are coming, mac Sliabhin, to open the gates."

"Why have you done this? Why do you need my hands to wield the knife?"

"Why, mac Sliabthin—should *we* take on our own curse?"

The lesser gate groaned on its hinge. Torchlight fluttered in the wind, in the first cold spats of rain. "Gods, this weather," the gatekeeper cried against the skirling gusts as he led them through a courtyard and to a second door. "Come in, there. What would be your name?"

"Foul, foul," Dubhain chortled, pulling Caith along, beside, beyond, "Huusht, hey!" The lightning cracked. The sky opened in torrents. "O *gods*, we're soaked."

"A plague on you!" cried Caith, but Dubhain's hand gripped his arm, stronger than any grip ever he had felt. The creature of rivers fled the rain, called on gods younger than himself, jested with the guards. "Curse you, *let me go!*"

"Never that," the phooka said as they came within the doors of the dun itself. Dubhain stamped his booted feet, shed water in a circle in the torchlight in the hall, as the guards did, Dubhain did and Caith did, made fellows by the storm.

They were in. The stones about them, warm-colored in the light, were the nature, the solidity of his home, the very color and texture that he had imagined them; or the reality drove out the dream in the blink of an eye and deceived him as reality will do with imaginings. Here was the house he had longed for, dreamed of, in the grim walls of his fostering; but here also were rough, scarred men, the smell of oil and stale straw as womenless men had managed things in Hagan's hold up by Dun na nGall. There seemed no happiness in this dim place either, only foreboding, the noise of shouts, of heavyfooted guards, the dull flash of metal in the light and the surety these men would kill and lose no sleep over it.

O father, Sliabhin!—are we not a house that deserves its death?

"One will tell the lord you are in," a guard said. "Bide here, whether he will see you. You are not the first to come tonight."

Caith looked sharply at the guard, whose brute broad face held nothing but raw power and the habit of connivance in the eyes. No, not dull, this one. Huge, and not dull. "Some other messenger?" Caith asked with a sinking of his heart, thinking on Dun na nGall, on his fosterfather Hagan, and treachery. "From where?"

"Messenger. Aye." The voice was low, the guard's face kept its secrets. Caith looked round on Dubhain with a touch of fey desperation in the move, even defiance. *Save me now*, he challenged the Sidhe, meeting Dubhain's eyes, and had the joy of seeing a phooka worried. The thought elated him in a wild, hopeless abandon. He looked upward at the stairs that would lead up, he reckoned, to the king's hall: a man had gone stumping up the steps to a doorway above. *I am the Sidhe's own difficulty*, Caith thought again, sorry for himself and at the same time sure that his revenge was at hand, whether he would kill or be killed and likely both. Time stretched out like a spill of honey, cloying sweet and golden with light and promising him satiety.

Enough of living. For this I was born, my father's son.

And my mother's.

7

The guard who had gone up came out again from a room near the head of the stair and beckoned to them.

"Come," said the guard by Caith's side.

Caith was very meek going up the steps. He made no protest as they began to prevent Dubhain from going up with him. In truth, he had no great desire of the company, trusting more to his sword. But he heard a commotion behind him, and the phooka joined him at the mid of the stairs, eluding the guards below. Caith heard the grate of drawn steel above and below them at once as Dubhain clutched his arm. "Master," Dubhain said, "I'll not leave ye here."

"Fall to heel," Caith said in humor the match of the phooka's own. "Mind your manners, lad." He looked up at the guard above them. "My servant is frightened of you," he said, holding out his hand in appeal till the guard, satisfied of his own dreadfulness and well-pleased with it, made a show of threat and waved them both on with his sword drawn.

It might have been a boy outright terrified, this old and evil thing that clutched Caith's arm, that went with him miming terror and staring round-eyed as they passed the guard and his naked blade. But the phooka's fingers numbed Caith's hand, reminding him as they went. *You cannot shake me, never be rid of me.* The touch felt like ice, as if something had set its talons into his heart as well as into the flesh of his arm, so that Caith recovered his good sense, remembering that he was going deeper into this mesh of his own will, and that he still understood less of it than he ought. Doors closed somewhere below, echoing in the depths under the stairs. There were a man's shouts from that direction, sharp and short.

"What's that?" Caith asked, delaying at the door of the corridor, and looking back down the stairs.

It was not his business to know, only the anxiousness of a man entering where there was no retreat, hearing things amiss behind him. The faces of the guards below stared up at him—distant kin of his, perhaps; or Sliabhin's hirelings: they were nothing he wanted for family: wolf-sharp, both of them, cruel as weasels. "Never you mind," one of them called up, and that one was uglier than all the rest. "There's those will care for that. Keep going."

"Lord," Dubhain said, a shiver in his voice, "lord—"

"Be still," Caith said. There was humor in it all, a fine Sidhe joke in this frightened phooka by his side, grand comedy. Caith played it too, with his life, with the phooka's grip numbing him, owning him and making mock of all Dun Mhor. Caith turned toward the door as they wished him to and came into the hall where they wished him to go, into warmth and firelight and a gathering of men the likeness of the rest, as likely a den of bandits as he had seen anywhere along the road he had traveled to come here.

And one sat among them, on a carven chair over by the fire; the light was on his face, and it was a face without the roughness of the others, a mouth much like Caith's own if bitter years had touched it; and this man's hair and beard were his own pale red, faded with years; and the tartan was Dun Mhor.

This man looked at him, thinking, measuring, so that Caith felt himself stripped naked. The resemblance—in this hall—would surely not elude Sliabhin mac Brian. Or riders from Dun na nGall might have outpaced him down the coast, on a longer road but a swifter. Quite likely his murder was in preparation even now; and his only chance was to move before the man believed he would. But he had got inside. He still had his sword. This much of his plan he had worked, feigning simplicity within deviousness: this was all his plan, to stand this close.

Sliabhin will kill you, he suddenly heard the Sidhe promise him. But never that he might kill Sliabhin. *Sliabhin will kill you. It will take seven days for you to die.*

"King Sliabhin?" Caith asked, all still and quiet. He weighed all his life in this moment, reckoning how long he had, whether the nearest man would draw and cut at him with steel or simply fall on him barehanded to overpower him: worse for him, if they got him alive. Before that happened he must spring and kill Sliabhin at once, face the others down with their king dead and give these bandits time to think how things had changed. There was Dubhain to reckon with, at his back—if they turned swords on *him*—

If I come alone— That was how he had made his question to the Sidhe. *If I come alone to Dun Mhor.* It was as if his hearing and his memory had been dulled in that hour as his eyes had been, glamored and spellbound. He was *not* alone. He had brought Dubhain. The question was altered; at least one thing in his futures would have changed.

But this man, this man who looked at him with a kinsman's face, in this bandit hall—

"Who are you?" Sliabhin asked.

"Hagan sends," Caith said, "for Caith's sake: he wants the other boy."

Sliabhin got to his feet and stared at him. Caith's heart was pounding in his chest, the cloak about him weighing like a great burden, covering the red tartan that would kill him and the sword that would kill Sliabhin, both beneath its gray roughness. There was no way out. Not from the moment he had passed the door. He felt the phooka's presence against his arm, biding like a curse.

Dubhain. *Darkness.*

He is one of the Fair Folk. I am the other kind.

"So," said Sliabhin, and walked aside, a half step out of reach; looked back at Caith—*My father*, Caith thought, seeing that resemblance to himself at every angle; and his throat felt tighter, the sweat gathering on his palms. *This is what I am heir to, this bandit den, these companions.* Beside him the phooka. There would be no gleam in Dubhain's eyes at this moment, nothing to betray what he was.

Sliabhin moved farther to his side. Caith turned to keep him in view as he stood before the door, and an object came into his sight, nailed there above the doorway, dried sprigs of herb; elfshot on a thong; a horseshoe, all wards against the Sidhe.

To make them powerless.

"Hagan wants the boy sent?" Sliabhin said, and Caith set his gaze on Sliabhin and tried to gather his wits back. "I find that passing strange."

"Will you hear the rest," Caith asked, with a motion of his eyes about the room, toward the guards, "—here?"

"Speak on."

"It's the elder son, lord; Caith. So Hagan said to me. Caith has heard rumors—" He let his voice trail off in intimidated silence, playing the messenger of ill news. "Lord—they've had to lock him away for fear he'll break for the south, or do himself some harm. He mourns his brother. He's set some strange idea into his head that he has to see the boy or die. I'm to bring the lad, by your leave, lord, to bring his brother out of his fey mood and set reason in him."

A long time Sliabhin stood staring at him, this elder image of himself, gazing at the truth.

He knows me, he knows me, he knows me, now what will he do? Can he kill his own son?

And if he will not—have I all the truth I think I have?

There was a silence in the room so great the crash of a log in the fireplace was like the crumbling of some wall. Sparks showered and snapped. Caith stood still.

"How does he fare?" Sliabhin asked, in a tone Caith had not expected could come from a mouth so hard and bitter. A soft question. Tender. As if it mattered; and it became like some evil dream—this man, this his true father asking the question he had wanted for all his days to hear a father ask. "Who?" Caith returned, "Hagan?"—missing the point deliberately.

"Caith."

"Sorrowing. I hear." There was a knot in Caith's throat; he fought it. He went on in this oblique argument. "If Caith could see the lad, lord, that he's well—I think it would mend much. It might bring him around to a better way of thinking."

"Would it?" Sliabhin walked away from him. Caith let him go, his wits sorting this way and that, between hope and grief. Then he felt the phooka's hand clench on his arm through the cloak, reminding him of oaths, and he was blinder than he had been when the Sidhe-light dazed him.

This place, this hall, this villainous crew— Was I lied to? Was it Gaelan the villain from the beginning, and this my father—innocent? Confession hovered on his lips, not to strike, to betray the Sidhe beside him for very spite and see what Dubhain would do. *But—father—*

"It's a long journey," said Sliabhin, "and dangerous, to send a young lad off in the dark with a man I don't know. You'll pardon me—" Sliabhin walked farther still, safe again among his men. "Tell me—messenger. What color Hagan's beard?"

"Bright red, lord. A scar grays it."

Sliabhin nodded slowly. "And how fares my neighbor?"

"Lord?"

"Cinnfhail." Sliabhin's brow darkened. His voice roughened. "You'll have passed through Gleann Gleatharan. *How fares Cinnfhail?*"

"Well, enough, lord."

Sliabhin snapped his fingers. "Fetch the other," Sliabhin said.

Men left, but not all. Caith and Sliabhin waited there, frozen in their places, and Dubhain waited. *Other, other*— Caith's mind raced on that refrain. The meshes drew about him and he saw the cords moving, but he did not know the truth yet, not the most basic truth of himself, and his hand would not move to the sword.

There was noise of the guards going down the steps outside; there was shouting that echoed up from the depths; and then the noise began to come louder and nearer— Someone cursed from the echoing lower hall, kept cursing as that someone was brought with loud resistance up the stairs. Caith slid his eyes to a point between Sliabhin and that doorway, most to Sliabhin, to the men that stood with him, all confessions stayed upon his lips, his heart beating hard. Dubhain was at his back, laughing inwardly, he thought, at mortal men; at father and son so meshed in must and would not.

Resistance carried into the room, a fair-haired man in a tartan green and blue, a red-blond youth who flung back his head and stared madly at Sliabhin, all bloody that he was.

It was Raghallach in their hands.

"If," said Sliabhin, "you had denied being with Cinnfhail, I would have take it ill. You know this boy—do you not?"

"Yes," said Caith. The warmth had left his hands, the blood had surely left his face. Raghallach strove to look his way and twisted helplessly in the grip of two well-grown and armored men. "Cinnfhail's son. I guested there last night. They sent me on my way in the rain, but they gave me provisions and a horse. He broke his leg in the forest. Lord, let this man go"

"He rode right up to our doors, messenger. He tells a pretty tale— do you not, boy?"

They had hurt Raghallach already. They hurt him more, the wrench of a wounded arm; Raghallach fought, such as he could, and cried out, half-fainting then, for the sweat broke out and runneled down his waxen face; and Caith thrust himself half a pace forward, Dubhain catching at his arm. "No, lord," Dubhain said, "no, be not rash."

"How you guested there with Cinnfhail, how you were received, what tale you told," said Sliabhin, "all of this he's sung for us."

Raghallach lifted his head. His weeping eyes spoke worlds, denying what Sliabhin said with a desperate move. *No. Only that. No.*

"There was nothing to tell," said Caith, "but I see that I was followed. Lord, this man—"

"—offends me. What do you say to that?"

The air seemed close. He felt pinned between will and dare not—Sliabhin out of reach behind a hedge of swords. He needed caution, wit, something of answers in this place, and the Sidhe was still holding his arm. *Be not rash, be not rash,* he heard Dubhain's wicked voice in his mind. And Raghallach bleeding and tortured before him— *He will die,* Cinnfhail had prophesied of his son; so the Sidhe had said also, that Raghallach would die if he came with him to Dun Mhor. *0 gods. Raghallach—who spoke for me to Cinnfhail—*

"Why did you come?" Caith asked in a thin, hoarse voice. "Why did you follow me, Raghallach?"

"Revenge," said Raghallach, and gave another heave in the hands of those that held him. Tears ran down his face and mingled with the sweat and the streaks of blood and dirt. "For my *sister,* man—"

Caith's heart turned over in him. *Well played, O gods, man—brave and well played.*

Caith turned his shoulder as a man accused of villainy might do, walked a space frowning as the phooka let him go. He looked back at wider vantage, Dubhain in the tail of his eye as he glared at Raghallach mac Cinnfhail.

"He's mad."

"He calls you thief as well," Sliabhin said. "He says you stole a horse."

"So, well." Caith turned away, disdaining all accusation.

"*Caith* he calls you."

Caith drew his sword, flinging back his cloak; and all about him men moved—but Sliabhin stopped everything with a move of his hand.

"You never learned that from him," Caith said. "You've known me from the moment I walked in here."

"I've waited for you." Sliabhin's voice was soft. "I was sure you would come someday, somehow."

"I came to kill you—for Gaelan's sake. But I heard another tale, there in Dun Gorm. And which is true—*father?* Who sent me to that whoreson Hagan? Was it Gaelan—or yourself?"

"Who is your companion?" Sliabhin asked, turning his shoulder from the menace of his sword. There were guards; they never moved. "Some other of Gleatharan's fine young lads?"

"Oh, that." Caith kept the blade point between them at their distance, but he took a lighter tone, an easier stance. "Dubhain is his name. One of Hagan's whores' sons. I've gotten used to such comrades—I get on well with them, *father*. Any sort of cutthroat. That's a skill they taught me well—your cousin Hagan and his crew. Why not? We breed such merry sorts—*father*." He gained a step on Sliabhin, but sideways, as a man moved to block him; it all stopped again. "Pirates. Brigands. Are these my brothers? How many did you beget—*and on what, when you tired of my mother?*"

"Enough!" Sliabhin's face congested. He lifted a shaking hand, empty. "It was Gaelan—Gaelan tormented her. She and I loved, boy—*loved*—you'd not know that. Oh, yes, whelp, I saved your life. I rode—myself—and bestowed you where I could or Gaelan'd have given you up for wolfbait that night. He gave out you were stillborn. He beat her—hear me?"

Caith faltered. More of truths and half-truths shuttled back and forth in this tapestry of lies. His mind chased after them, sorting one and the other, and he darted a glance from Sliabhin to Raghallach, to Sliabhin again. Raghallach lied for him, risked his own sister's name in his defense and tried nothing for himself. But Sliabhin's voice had the ring of true outrage. And the Sidhe was there beside him, doubtless laughing at his plight.

The sword sank in Caith's hand, extended again to Raghallach. "What of him?"

"What *of* him?"

"I don't know. Someone's lied. I don't know who. Where's Brian? Where's my brother?"

"You'll not be taking your brother anywhere tonight, my lad," Sliabhin said.

"I want to see him."

"What's he to you?"

"A whim. Father. Like you."

"Put up the sword. *Put it up.*"

Caith laughed, a faint, strained laugh, and his own fey mind surprised him. The look in Sliabhin's eyes surprised him, that they were lost together in this sea and clinging desperately one to the other still unmurdered.

"Put it up."

Caith thought on it a long moment, with another look at Raghallach, at Dubhain; then there were only Sliabhin's eyes, bewitching as the Sidhe's, to cast a glamour on things. There was Sliabhin's voice, promising nothing at all. There was death here; the room was full of it.

I am the curse, Caith thought. *The Sidhe send their curse back to Dun Mhor—in me. And I cannot be rid of it.* He slid the sword back into its sheath, a neat quick move, never quite taking his eyes from the guards, who kept their swords drawn. *But if it is in me, I can delay it, I can take it away again—if I will. If Sliabhin wills it.*

And what if I am wrong?

"You'll rest here," said Sliabhin, "as my guest."

"And this one?" He meant Raghallach. He gestured that way, where Raghallach hung in the guard's cruel grip. *O gods, he accused me—how can I defend him, how save him, what can I do to save his life but win my father and turn his mind from killing him—*

"He'll tell us tales. By morning—he'll have a many of them. You'll hear them all."

"My brother—where is he?"

"Oh, the boy's well. Quite well enough. Go. They'll take you to chambers, these men of mine. Leave this other to me."

Shame burned Caith's face, betraying shame; he looked at Raghallach, and for a moment then his heart stopped, for Raghallach smiled unexpectedly in a way only he could see, a cat's smile, that chilled him through.

Dubhain tugged at him. "Come, lord, come—do what he says."

Caith cast a wild glance at Dubhain and covered it. The phooka took his arm in a grip fit to break it as Sliabhin's men closed in about them.

"Trust," said Sliabhin, "or have no safety here." Caith looked back at him. Not yet had Sliabhin's men tried to disarm him—and this omission and their likeness, their crying likeness to each other, together with *that* which hung in the hands of the guards—robbed him of volition, of any last hope of understanding what happened around him.

It was not Raghallach they had taken, but the Sidhe Nuallan—*Nuallan* they dragged struggling away in the other direction, past the door with its wards, its diminishments of Sidhe power.

They passed the door with Nuallan-Raghallach. Directly a shout rang out, a blow, a cry of pain that jarred his nerves as it echoed in the hall.

Then one man took Caith by the arm and drew him aside to another door. A guard opened it on more stairs, a dark and musty ascent higher into the hold.

"*Sliabhin!*" Caith jerked about to turn back again, halfway, but no one was prepared to listen. Dubhain came perforce, at sword-point.

Caith tried to break from them; and there in the doorway they held a sword to his throat and disarmed him of sword and dagger both.

"*Sliabhin!* Damn you!" He fought once they took the sword away from his throat, and he hoped for the phooka's help, but three men got Caith's arms behind him and began to force him up the stairs. He braced his feet against the steps and struggled. "*Sliabhin!*" His voice echoed in the halls, in the heights and depths of the place. "*Sliabhin!*" And despairing: "*Brian!*"

One struck him, bringing him stunned to his knees on the stone steps.

And no one listened.

8

There was a hall beyond the stairs, a room at the side of it; a dank darkness, masonry built into Dun Mhor's very hill, dirt floored in stone. Rough hands hurled them both in, and quickly slammed the door.

The phooka's eyes glowed, company in the dark, and a light grew about them both, until Caith could see Dubhain plainly. The phooka sat on the floor of this stonewalled chamber—he was the country lad again, all dusty. And Dubhain brushed himself off as if he had taken some easy spill, as merry as before, and got to his feet.

Caith sat, bruised and sullen, winded. He bowed his aching head against his hands.

"Welcome home," the phooka said.

Caith looked up and glowered. For a long time there was silence.

A scream shuddered through the thick door, a man's voice and not yet a man's—Caith flinched at hearing it and then he hardened his heart to it, thinking on the Sidhe Nuallan. "You knew," he said to Dubhain, shuddering when it came again, more horrid than before. "It's all a sham. Isn't it?"

"Of course it is." Yet another cry rang through the halls at some distance, a man in deepest agony. Dubhain looked that way, uncommon sobriety on his face.

"Dubhain. Dubhain—for the gods' sake, what's in Nuallan's mind, to come here like this?"

Silence.

"He's in trouble, isn't he? Dubhain?"

"Oh, never." Dubhain dusted his hands and, blithe as he had begun, his voice quavered as the cry rang out again.

"Can you do something?" It was not love that made Caith ask. It was humanity, all unwise and simple-minded; he knew it, and yet the sound—It came again, and they both winced. "*For the gods' sake, phooka, can you do something?*"

"The wards—" The phooka fretted and paced back and forth, dark within the light he himself cast. He was naked now, dusky-skinned, his hair falling black and thick about his shoulders, his eyes glowing murky red. "Oh, Nuallan loves a joke, he does, and this one is quite rich, is it not? He's come to see the revenge. To keep his word to you."

"Get us out of this."

Dubhain stopped his pacing. Another scream shuddered through the air and Dubhain wrung his hands. "The wards—the wards—they—muddle things."

"You mean they work? Nuallan *can't get out?*"

The phooka said nothing.

"He's testing me, Sliabhin is." Caith got to his feet, staggering as he did. "Using Raghallach—*Nuallan*. It's for my benefit, all this—O *gods*." There was another scream. Caith tried the door again and again, at last turned his shoulders against the rough wood and stared at the twin red gleams that glared at him. Still another cry echoed beyond their dark. "Maybe he's laughing at them all the while. But I don't care for your jokes, phooka. Do something. I've got a brother in this place, remember? Where is he? Listening to *that?*" He laughed, a brief, strained laughter. "O gods, you do love a joke. But this is enough, phooka, enough!"

"Be still, man," Dubhain hissed, sinking down on his haunches and hugging his arms about himself. The red eyes gleamed, feral and terrible, glowing alternately brighter and dimmer as scream after scream echoed up the dark. "Be still. He'll give up soon, Nuallan will. Even his humor doesn't carry to this."

It went on, all the same, and on, and on.

"The wards—" Caith said.

"Fair Folk," said Dubhain.

"What does that mean?"

"Nuallan's of the Fair Folk. He says wards aren't that much against him."

Caith crouched down in like position, facing the boy-shape in the dark. "He says."

The phooka said nothing. Dubhain's face was not good to look on, nor his eyes good to look into.

"My *brother*, phooka. You bargained. Do something. Find him. Where is he?"

"Patience," the phooka whispered at last, a voice so still it seemed to chill the air. "Patience, mac Sliabhin."

It was long that Caith waited, crouched there with his arms clasped about his knees and shivering. The wailing died and began again. "Phooka," Caith said.

"Hssst." The look that fixed on him was dire and distraught. "What will you pay for it?"

"*Pay* for it? It's your friend down there!"

"There's the boy," the whisper came back; the red eyes looked into his with sudden keenness as if Dubhain had been somewhere and now came back to him. "I know where your brother is. What will you pay?"

"Curse you, you've already bargained for that answer, for all I've got!"

"Your scruples, man. I told you you had that left to trade."

"What do you want?"

"I'll tell you. If we survive this. When I go, hold to me." Dubhain shut his eyes till only the merest slits gleamed fire.

Suddenly it was the black horse rising to its feet, a scrape of hooves on the stone, the surge of a large equine body. Caith scrambled to his feet and in the scattering and gathering of his wits seized it by the mane and swung up to mount it in that low-ceilinged room.

The door was like mist about them as they passed, like nothing at all; and abruptly it was not the horse-shape, but the boy, and himself tumbling to land on his feet with his hand on Dubhain's naked shoulder, fingers still tangled in Dubhain's hair. "Let go," the phooka said. "Follow me."

They padded along the hall, down the dark stairs, quiet and quick. Quietly and quickly they pushed open the door on the hall and the guards there turned suddenly to see what had broken among them, a desperate man and an improbable black horse that swept to the far door scattering men like leaves before its rush of wind and storm-sound.

A sword fell loose. Caith seized it up and hewed his way in Dubhain's wake, turned with his back to the doorway and the phooka and at once found himself beset by five of Sliabhin's guards.

He swept a furious stroke in the doorway, taking one in return, beating blades aside—ducked under one and thrust for a belly. A sword came down at him while his was bound and he sprawled aside against the door frame, in worse and worse trouble, but he got that man's knees as he fell in the doorway and stabbed up at the next guard as the rest of him fell in reach, expecting a blade down on him in the next moment.

A black sudden shape swept him over, as the phooka sent the surviving pair screaming in retreat up the inside stairs.

Then the horse-shape turned and changed as it twisted like black smoke into the boy-shape, into Dubhain who reached for him and drew him to his feet.

Caith caught his balance against the wall and turned for the door and the second, downward stairs. There was no time for thought, no time for anything. He ran the stairs down into the hold as a black shape drifted past him straight down the drop off the landing, a dire thing with burning eyes and the rush of wind and cold about it. Down and down it went, showing him the way as it coursed the hall below.

Other guards came at them in the lower hall. Thunder cracked outside, shaking the stones. The phooka laughed like a damned soul and flickered out of man-shape and in again about one luckless guard; and that man wailed and gibbered and fell down, eyes open and staring. Caith battered down the guard in his own path, not troubling to know whether that one or the other lived or no. He broke clear. Dubhain was by him, running now, having settled on human shape after all.

"Take us there," Caith breathed, seizing Dubhain by the hair.

"You're heavy," Dubhain complained. "Heavy—" The phooka was panting now, even running on bare human feet. "This way—" It was Dubhain that faltered, the red light in his eyes dimmed as he caught his balance against the wall. "The wards, man—I cannot—much farther, much oftener. Haste—be quick."

Stairs gaped ahead of them, going downward yet again. Caith turned then, with a wild suspicion of betrayal. "My *brother*," he said. "Not Nuallan—*hang* Nuallan: he can save himself."

"Go on," said Dubhain. "We keep our bargains."

Caith spun about and went, trusting the phooka to guard his back. Light showed below as he made a second turning of the narrow stone stairs, and yet no one barred his way. He descended in haste, turned suddenly, feeling his back naked.

Dubhain was gone. Caith cursed and wiped his face, shaking; then taking a fresh grip on the bloody sword, drew a whole breath and kept going the only way he knew now to go.

The tumult above had died. There were no more screams from below. He heard thunder rumble, distant from these cellars, above him.

A torch at a landing was the only light, and that was scant and guttering in a sough of wind down the stairwell.

But beyond that lighted corner the stairs took another bend, onto a wider scene, onto a hell of torchlight and torment in the cellars of Dun Mhor.

9

They saw him as he saw them—a dozen men, Sliabhin. . . . Swords were out, waiting for what should come on them from the commotion above.

Motion stopped then—all frozen. There was a wooden cage, and in that a smallish, half-starved dark-haired boy; there were chains, and in those chains Nuallan hung in Raghallach's red-haired likeness, next a reeking brazier and its irons. Nuallan had burns on his naked body, burns and bleeding wounds and no sense within his eyes.

"Sliabhin," Caith said ever so quietly, with everything in ruins—his last and furtive hope of home, of wholeness for himself. He felt sick and fouled, forever fouled, from his origins to this hour, this bloody, dreadful truth beneath the floors of Dun Mhor. "*Father* mine. . . . You know I'd have believed you? You should have spoken me fair, you know. Is this my brother? Brian—is it you?"

There was silence from the boy in the cage. Whether the waif heard at all he could not tell from the tail of his eye. Swords were poised all about the room, his, theirs, every sword but Sliabhin's own, that stayed within its sheath. An oilpot bubbled softly and sent up its acrid, stinging reek. An ember snapped. The air stank of burned flesh and dust and sweat.

"I've killed your men upstairs," Caith said, baiting them all. Such a crime as he had come to do wanted anger, not horror, not blood as cold as his ran now. "I've killed every one I could reach and I've driven off the rest. There are no women here. None I've seen. No small ones. Nothing. It's a fortress of bandits, father, this house of ours. . . . How did my mother die? A suicide, I've heard."

Sliabhin's face twisted. "Shut your mouth."

"After she found out what she let in. After she saw what you did. She had some scruples left. Even I had scruples left. But you have none, and I've given mine away. Why didn't you call me home long ago—to your loving care? Hagan—was nothing to what you've done here. *Nothing*."

"Listen to me, Caith." Sliabhin took on a tone of reason. He moved closer, among the swords. "This whelp's no son of mine—not this one.

Hers and his—not mine. I'd still have taken him in, for her sake. But young Brian-lad wouldn't have it. Gaelan taught him to hate me—his son. Hers. He hates like Gaelan. He has Gaelan's look about him—"

"Take your sword. I'm no murderer by choice. Not like you. But I'll kill you one way or the other. I swear I will."

"*He's not my son!* You are."

"Are you sure? Could we *ever* be sure?"

That touched home in Sliabhin. Caith saw it, the long, long hate, the madness. "Boy," said Sliabhin, "I kept you up there—safe in Dun na nGall. Safe, all these years. Gaelan would have killed you, do you know that?"

"The way you're killing his son? No. I don't know that. I don't know anything you say. Ever. —*Boy*. Brian—" Caith moved near the cage, shifting ever so carefully. "I'm your brother, Brian, hear me? I've come for you. I'll try to get you out of here."

There was no response. Perhaps the boy had passed beyond all wit. Caith reached with his left hand through the bars without looking, the sword in his right hand, his eyes upon Sliabhin and his men. He felt a hand grip his then, a small hand all thin and weak and desperate. In the same moment Sliabhin's men shifted like so many wolves in a pack.

"You face me," Caith said softly, looking Sliabhin in the eyes. "Come on, man, draw your sword. What's one killing more?"

A small shake of the head. "I'd not kill you."

"Why not? I'll wager you were never sure—*never* sure which of us was yours; or if either was. Or ever will be. Isn't that what eats at you? Oh, aye, you loved my mother. You wanted her to yourself, even more than you loved her—and still you'll never know."

Steel hissed its way to light. Sliabhin drew, quietly.

"That's what I wanted," Caith said. He disengaged his left hand with a gentle tug. The boy clutched at it a second time, hampering him. But beyond Sliabhin the Sidhe Nuallan had lifted his head, and watched it all unfold with a gaze bright and perilous as fire.

Nuallan's chains suddenly fell, still locked, and clinked against the stone as Nuallan-Raghallach stood free and unfettered, as he burned like daylight in the murk of the cellar. Panic broke among the men. Some turned toward one of them, some toward the other, in utter confusion; but Caith stood his ground, whirled when he had won a scant moment and slashed and kicked at the cage the bars of which had begun to bud and leaf inexplicably and to swell and burst their bindings. "Come out!" Caith shouted at Brian, turning to hold the rest at dubious swords' point, having now to circle to keep stalkers from his flank and from the boy. What the boy did then he could not know. His eyes were all for Sliabhin, for his purpose, for what he had come to do.

"Nuallan," Caith said hoarsely, desperately, "the boy. *Dubhain promised.*"

Light burst. The Sidhe was not where or what he had been; Nuallan was beside him like a glare of light while men flinched and shielded their eyes. There came a boy's faint sob. "I have him," Nuallan said. "I leave you—to solve it all—mac Sliabhin."

Then was darkness, or the parting of the light, as if light had gone out in his soul as well and left him only the horror, the men, his father closing on him, having one hate now and one focus of their malice.

Caith seized the brazier one-handed, overturned it across their path, hurling red coals and irons across the planks. He kicked a bubbling oilpot and its tripod after it and fled, up the stairs.

"Dubhain!" Caith cried, desperate, half-prayer, half-curse. Steps rang close behind him—he whirled, spitted the man that came at him in the torchlight, and gazed on Sliabhin's dying face.

"Patricide," said Sliabhin, holding to Caith, clutching at his clothes, at the tartan of Dun Mhor, "*patricide*, twice as damned as I."

Caith freed himself, hearing the shrieks of burning men below, seeing the whole stairwell flared up from beneath, aleap with flame and horror. A burning man raced up toward him, mad with pain: that man he killed over Sliabhin's corpse, and turned, gasping for breath, to race stumbling up the stairs, sword in hand.

Other guards were coming down. Caith met them in the hellish light, hewed past them, one and the other, while they were still amazed at what came at them, dark amid the glare of fire. He trod on their bodies and ran, up into the hall, toward the door, where two more guards made their rush at him.

One he killed, and rushed past the other out into the drizzle and the glare of shielded torches. All about him the alarm dinned—*help, fire, assault!*

"Kill him," someone shouted. "Watch the gate!" another.

Caith ran; that was all he knew to do. He ran splashing through the rain-soaked yard with his side aching and blood binding his hand to the hilt of his sword. Before him he saw the gates were sealed; and in front of those gates a shining rider sat a horse whose mane itself was light. The boy Brian was a shadow in that rider's arms.

"Nuallan!" Caith cried.

He did not expect help. He stumbled forward and caught himself as the horse leapt into motion away from him and passed through the sealed gates as if they had been no more than air.

"Brian! *Brother!*" It was all his hope fleeing him, in Sidhe hands—in their hands, who could bargain a man's soul out of his body. The Sidhe had no pity in them.

"There he is!" someone shouted behind him. Caith gave only half a look and ran along the wall, trapped, whirling to kill a man as he went, still dealing murder with the tears mingling with the rain on his face and blinding him. He loathed all that he had done, loathed all that he was, all his bargains with fate and the Sidhe; and still he went on killing those who wished to end him. He ran, and they hunted him along the wall by the stables.

"Alive!" someone screamed, full of hate. "Take him alive!" That put a last burst of speed into him, rawest desperation to evade the corner they drove him for.

The beat of hooves sounded at his right as if it were coming from somewhere far, and a cold wind blew on him, and a black horse crossed his path, moving slowly like a dream, its eyes gleaming red within the darkness. It offered him its back; it wanted him.

That was the bargain, then. It was better than Dun Mhor offered, the phooka-ride, that should end in numbing cold water, some lightless riverbottom, to drift among the reeds. Caith clenched the black thick mane in his fists and flung himself astride the phooka, felt it stretch itself to run in earnest and saw the wall coming up before them—but it was only mist about them when they met it.

They were away then, with the wind rushing past them. He heard the phooka hoofbeats like the beating of his heart, felt the spatter of the mist like ice against his face and his neck and his arms. On and on they ran, and the cold went to his bones. When he looked over his shoulder, he saw an orange glow, a jagged ruin, that was Dun Mhor, which was all his hope and his hate and every reason that had ever driven him. It sank in ashes now.

He laid his head against the phooka's neck, buried his face in the darkness of Dubhain's mane and let the black Sidhe bear him where he would, having had enough of blood, of fire, and of life. The rain washed him, soaked him through till he was numb; leaves and branches began at last to sweep over him, passing like the touch of hands and the memory of rain as wet leaves brushed his hands and head.

Abruptly he was falling, falling; but as before it was not a stream that met him, but solid ground, an impact that drove the wind from him.

Caith sprawled, dazed, and it was a moment before he could get his arms beneath him and lever himself to his knees, expecting phooka-laughter and phooka-humor and all the wickedness they could do. Sidhe-light broke about him, a pale glow. Sidhe stood all about him, bright and terrible Fair Folk. One was Nuallan; and there were a score of others. Their horses waited beyond the circle, themselves an unbearable light in the darkness.

A small boy lay among them, sprawled unconscious on the grass at their feet and, seeing that, Caith found his strength again and tried to get up and go to Brian; but he could not. Nuallan moved between and a chill came on Caith's limbs that took the strength from his legs. He got to the Sidhe all the same, and grasped at his shining cloak: but it passed through his fingers and he fell to his knees.

"I'd not do that," Dubhain said, squatting nearby, his eyes aglow and wicked.

"Let him go," Caith shouted at the chill and mocking faces above, about him. "Let my brother go. I never rescued him to give him to you."

"But you didn't save him," Nuallan said. "Safe and sound, you said. Was that not the bargain, mac Sliabhin? Would you ask more now?"

Dubhain drew back his lips in a half-grin, half-grimace. "Listen," the phooka said, "don't be reckless. You have the curse on you. It's all yours now. Didn't we help you? We've more than kept our bargain. What else have you to give up, beyond your scruples? Think, man."

Caith managed a laugh, despairing as it was; then the laugh died in his throat, for the Sidhe glow brightened, showing him where he was, in a small clearing at a ford, where a sleeping company sat sleeping horses, heads bowed, bodies slumped, and the rain on them like jewels, as if time had stopped here and all the world were wrapped in nightmares.

"They should not have come here," said one of the Sidhe.

"No man should," said another.

"Now, mac Sliabhan, what will you pay," asked Nuallan, "to free the boy from us?"

Caith turned a bleak look on him, blinking in the rain. "Why, whatever I have, curse you. Take me. Let the rest go. All of them. I'm worth it. Isn't that what you've most wanted—to have one of Sliabhin's blood in your reach? And I'm far more guilty than the boy."

"You've not asked what the curse is," said Nuallan.

"You'll tell me when it suits you."

"Torment," said Nuallan, "to suffer torment all your days, mac Sliabhin—the boy, oh, aye, he's free. We accept your offering; he's no matter to us. The curse is yours alone."

"Then let him go!"

"I shall do more than that," Nuallan said; and bent, the tallest and fairest of all his fellows, and gathered the boy into his arms ever so gently, as if he had been no weight at all. He bore him to the sleeping riders; and the light about him fell on their faces. It was Raghallach foremost among them; and Cinnfhail's shieldman; and others of Gleatharan. And Nuallan set Brian in Raghallach's arms on the saddle-bow, sleeping child in the keeping of the sleeping rider, whose face was bruised and battered with wounds from Dun Mhor's cellars.

"What have you done?" Caith asked in horror. "Sidhe, what have you done?"

"Ah," said Nuallan, looking at him, "but they will get on well, don't you think? Raghallach will remember a thing he never did; but it will seem to him he was a great hero. And so the boy will remember the brave warrior who bore him away and took him safe to Gleatharan. Oh, aye, they'll wake at dawn, and think themselves all heroes; and so men will say of them forever. Is that not generous of me?"

Caith let out a breath, having gotten to his feet. He clenched his fists. But it looked apt, the tired small boy, asleep in safety, the honest man who sheltered him. "You could make him forget the rest," he said.

"You've nothing left to trade."

"For your own kindness' sake—if it exists."

"I've done that—already." The Sidhe all were fading, leaving dark about, and the gleam of phooka eyes. But Nuallan took Caith's arm. "Come with me," he said.

10

Caith was alone then, left utterly alone in a place where the sun blinded him, and when his eyes had forgotten the dark the light seemed soft. There were fields and hills—fair and green, spangled with gold flowers. Herds of horses, each the equal of Dathuil, ran free, and trees grew straight and fair on the hillsides.

No one hindered him. Caith wandered this beautiful place waiting to die; and then taking comfort in it, for it seemed no heart could grieve here long except for greater causes than he possessed. He felt thirst; he slaked it at a stream over which trees bent under the weight of their fruit.

The water washed the pain from him. It healed his heart and when he washed his face in it, he felt stronger than he had ever been.

He considered the fruit and risked it, growing reckless and fey and calm all at once, as if no death could touch him here, nor any grievous thing. Only then he felt afraid, for he felt a presence before he saw it, and looked up.

"It gives the Sight," said Nuallan . . . for Nuallan was suddenly there, astride Dathuil, bright as the setting sun. Dathuil dipped his head to drink, and the Sidhe slid lightly down to stand on the grassy margin.

"And what will you ask for that, Sidhe?"

"Nothing here has price."

Caith thought on that, taking what leisure he had to think. Every saying of the Sidhe seemed tangled, full of riddles, and he felt unequal to them, and small. "I've been waiting for you," he said.

"For the curse. Oh, aye, that matter. But it is settled. Or will be." The Sidhe looked less terrible than before. There was pity in his eyes. "I like you well, man. You bargain well—for a man. Would you know the truth—whose son you are?"

"Sliabhin's."

"The boy is Gaelan's. Half brother to you. And innocent. Come." The tall Sidhe knelt beside the brook. "Look. Look into the stream."

Caith looked, kneeling cautiously on the margin—and his heart turned in him, so that he almost fell, for it was the night sky he was looking into with the day still above him. "Ah!" he said and lost his balance.

Nuallan caught his arm and drew him back safe on the margin. "Nay, nay, that were a death neither man nor Sidhe should wish. An endless one. Look. Is there a thing you would wish to see? These waters show you anything dear to your heart. Would you see your brother?"

"Aye," Caith murmured, foreknowing a wounding. The Fair Folk were terrible even in their kindness.

The stars gave way to green hills, to Dun Gorm in the sunlight. A boy raced on a fine white horse, the wind in his hair, untrammeled joy in his eyes—

"Is that Brian? But he's *older*—"

"He's fourteen—Ah, you're thinking of others now—oh, aye, Raghallach—Brian follows him about; and Deirdre—she's grown very fair, has she not? Like Cinnfhail's own son, Brian is; and his queen's, the darling of their fading years, he is. The lad remembers very little of that year, only that it was terrible; he remembers fire and the long ride, and

Raghallach bringing him away—it's thorough hero-worship. He doesn't remember you at all, save as one of Raghallach's men."

Caith bit his lip. "Good."

"Would you have it? Would you have what Brian has?"

"There's cost."

"In their world, always."

"His cost."

"Aye."

"No. I won't." Caith kept looking, until the image faded, until the abyss was back. He stood up as Nuallan did, there upon the brink. The gulf was below him again, the fall so easy from this place. He turned his back to it, there on the very edge, waiting as Nuallan set his hand lightly on his arm.

"Go your way," said Nuallan.

"Go?"

"Just go. You're free."

Nuallan let fall his hand. Caith turned away from the void, walked a little distance in disbelief, and then the rage got through. He turned back again, shaking with his anger. "Curse you, *curse* you to play games with me! You're no different than *his* sort, Sliabhin's, Hagan's. I've known that sort all my life. Is it your revenge—to laugh at me?"

"Oh, not to laugh, mac Sliabhin. Not to laugh." Nuallan's voice was full of pity and vast sorrow. "Torment is your curse; and I know none worse nor gentler than to have drunk and eaten here—and to know it forever irrecoverable. I have spared you what I could, my friend. . . ."

"Nuallan—" Caith began.

But the dark of the Sidhe-woods of Gleann Gleatharan was about him again, and the cold, and mortality, in which he shivered. He had the ache of his wounds back; and the gnawing of hunger and remorse in his belly.

"A curse on you!" he cried in the night of his own stained world.

He heard only a moving in the brush, and saw there the gleam of two eyes like coals. Dubhain was there, in boy's shape, a naked ruffian again.

"I am still with you," the phooka said. "This is *my* place."

Caith turned his shoulder to Dubhain and walked on, lost in this mortal woods and knowing it. He walked, until he knew that he was alone.

The visions crowded in on him, too vivid for a while: the vision of Dun Gorm that he had seen; and his brother growing up—but never must he go there, nor to the ruins of Dun Mhor, where he was a murderer and worse. His new Sight told him this, not acute, but dull, like a wound that hurt when he touched it, when he thought of the things he wanted and knew them lost.

There was no life for him but banditry, and regret, and remembering forever, remembering a land where everything was fair and clean.

"I'll give you a ride," the phooka offered in his dreams, on the next dark night when Caith slept fitfully, his belly gnawed with hunger. "O man, you need not be stubborn about it. I like you well. So does Nuallan. He did let you go—"

—the phooka took more solid shape, seated on a stump as Caith dreamed he waked. "—O man, don't you know Nuallan could have done far worse? He repented the curse. He wished it unsaid. But a Sidhe's word binds him. Especially his kind."

But there was no comfort in Caith's dreams, when he dreamed of the beauty he had seen, and of ease of pain; and when he rose up in the morning and had the miles always before him.

"I'll bear ye," the phooka offered wistfully.

"No," Caith said, and walked on, stubborn in his loss. Where he was going next he had no idea. He looked down from the height of the green hills and saw Gleann Gleatharan, and Dun Gorm with its herds fair and its fields wide; but he came no nearer to it than this, to stand on its hills and want it as he wanted that land he saw only in his dreams.

"I am your friend," the phooka said, whispering from behind him.

It was well a man should have one friend. Caith held his cloak about him against the wind and kept walking, passing by Dun Gorm and all it had of peace.

"Come," he whispered to the wind. "Come with me, phooka, if you like."

VII

The ship approaches dock. The star glows in the window, red and so dim they do not need the visual shielding. We can look on its spotted face directly, if not for long. Its light momentarily dyes the table, the ice in our glasses, the crystal liquid, the bubbles that rise and burst. Then the ship's gentle rotation carries the view away.

There are no planets in this system. Only ice and iron. And a starstation.

Bags are packed. Most of the passengers are leaving. Soon the take-hold will sound.

"Packed?" I ask.

"Yes," you say. And gaze at the unfamiliar stars, thinking what thoughts I do not guess. "They're going to have to ship that poor fellow home. Next ship back. He just can't take it out here."

"His world always traveled the universe," I say. "He thinks it's abandoned him. Maybe it has. He thinks he'd be safe there. I'm not sure he'll ever feel quite so safe again."

"You're immune?"

I think about it. I see miniature worlds in the bubbles amid the ice in my glass. Microcosm in crystal. "I haven't left home," I say. "I don't know what it is to leave home. And I'm as safe here as most places."

"You mean the universe."

"That, yes."

The alarm sounds then. I down my drink quickly, we both do. I rise and toss glass and ice into the disposal. Yours goes after it.

We stare at each other then, at the point of farewells.

There is no choice, of course. This is a transfer-point. Our separate ships are already waiting at the station.

And they keep their own schedules.

OTHER STORIES

THE DARK KING

Death walked the marketplace of Corinth.

He paused in the bazaars, looked with pleased eyes on the teeming throngs of men, laughed gently at the antics of children. He had the shape, at the time, of a dusty man in brown rags, staff in hand. He was indeed a traveler: he had been that morning to Syria to attend a famous general; to India to visit a sage; in Egypt to attend an assassination. He had a thousand, thousand servants besides, did Death, going and coming at his orders, although they were all fragments of himself. He was, at this moment, in the marketplace; and in a hut in Germany; and in an alleyway in Rome: all himself, all seeing with his eyes, all minute reflections of his own being.

He laughed gently at a child, who looked up into his face and smiled, and the laughter faded as a mother snatched him away, shuddering as she scolded him about strangers. He turned his face from the lame young beggar at the steps, who looked at him; he gave him only a coin, and the beggar took it and gazed after him anxiously.

The palace lay ahead, up the steps. The guards there came to attention, but seeing only a poor traveler, rested their spears and let him pass: it was the custom in the land that all strangers were welcome in the palace, to sit at the end of the table and receive charity, for travelers were few and news scant.

And Death would sit at the king's table this night, drawn by that sense that led him toward his appointed tasks.

He was no stranger here. He knew his way, found familiar the gaily painted halls, that led to the king's own hall, where a wedding feast was in progress. He had visited here only a year ago, to lead away the old king. His servants had made many a call here, attending this and that; and through their eyes he was well-familiar with every corridor of this palace, as with most places across the wide face of the earth.

But the servants saw him only with dull human sight, and shrugged in disdain at his rags, and saw him to the lowest seat, hardly interrupting the gaiety. There was a helping of food for him, and drink; he took them, savoring the things of earth, and listened to the minstrel's songs, pleased by such; but none spoke to him and he spoke to no one, save that he gazed up to the high table, where sat the young king.

He had not known until then—until the king met his eyes with that pale and sighted look the dead have—what had drawn him here. Death looked again to the king's left, where the young queen sat, his bride; and around the room, where sat the courtiers, unseeing. Only when he met the king's eyes did he know that he was known, and that not wholly. The king was young: he did not have the familiarity of the old toward him.

The meal was done; the wine was brought, and the king drank first, of the king's cup, wrought in gold; and passed to the queen. Servants passed round the wine-bowls, and filled cups to the brim for the merry drinking to follow, for it was holiday.

And the king's eyes turned constantly and fearfully upon Death, whose traveler's clothes perhaps seemed less brown than black, whose face less tanned than shadowy: the dying have a sense the living do not.

"Traveler," said the king at last, in a voice strong and firm, "it is the custom that our guests be fed, and then give us their name and the news of their travels, if it be their pleasure. We do not insist, but this is the custom."

Death rose, and time stopped, and all in the hall were still: wine hung half-poured, lips in mid-word, a fly that had come in the open window stopped as a point in the air, the very fire a monument of flame.

"Lord Sisyphos, I am Death," he said softly, casting off his disguise and appearing as he is, Sleep's dark twin, a handsome and gentle god. "Come," he said. "Come."

The soul shuddered within Sisyphos' mortal body, clung fast with the tenacious strength of youth. Sisyphos looked about him at the hall, at the gold and the wealth, and he touched the hand of his beautiful young queen, who in no wise could feel his touch, nor sense anything that passed: her motion was stopped in rising, her eyes, blue as summer skies, shining open, her hair like wheat fields in August—beautiful, beautiful Merope.

Sisyphos' hand trembled. He turned a tearful face to Death.

"She cannot see you," Death said. "Come away now."

"It is not fair," Sisyphos protested.

"You are fortunate," said Death, "to have possessed all these good things, and never to have seen them fade. Come away now, and let go."

"I love her," Sisyphos wept.

"She will come in her own time," said Death.

Sisphos ran his hand over the lovely cheek of Merope, whose eyes did not blink, whose hair did not stir. He planted a kiss on her cheek, and looked again at Death.

"One word," he pleaded. "Lord, one word with her."

Death's heart melted, for like his brother he is a kindly god. "A moment, then," he said.

The room began to move again. The fly buzzed; the flames leapt, the hum of conversation resumed.

And Merope touched her husband's hand, and blinked, wondering, as her husband leaned close and whispered in her ear. Her summer-sky eyes widened, filled with tears; she shook her head, and he whispered more.

Death averted his face as the woman wept with her husband and a hush fell upon the gathering. But a moment more, and he lifted his staff, and the room stopped once more.

"It is time," he said.

"My lord," said the king, surrendering.

And this time the soul stepped cleanly from the body, and looked about, a little bewildered yet. Death took him by the hand, and with his staff parted that curtain that lies twixt world and world.

"Oh," said Sisyphos, shuddering at the dark.

But Death put his arm about the young king and walked with him, comforting him for a time.

And then Death withdrew to his own privacy, for he had long distracted himself, and his other eyes and hands were paralyzed, wanting their direction. He sat on his throne in the netherworld and gazed on the gray meanderings of Styx and the balefire of Phlegethon, and in the meantime his other selves were attending a shipwreck in the Mediterranean and a dying kitten in Alexandria.

He, brother of Sleep, does not sleep, and is everywhere.

But after the world had turned for the third time and Death, once more rested, was on the far shore of Styx, about to fare out toward the land of Africa (there was an old woman there who had called him), a sad ghost tugged at his sleeve. He looked down into the tearful face of Sisyphos.

"Still unhappy?" he asked the soul. "I am sorry for you, Sisyphos, but really, if you would only leave the riverside and cross over . . . there are meadows there, old friends, why, I've no doubt your parents and grandparents are longing to see you. Your wife will come in her own good time; and time passes very quickly here if you wish it to. You are still entangled with the earth; that is your misery."

"I cannot help it," wept the young king. "My wife will not set me free."

"What, not yet?" exclaimed Death, shocked and dismayed.

"No funeral rites," mourned the ghost, stretching forth a hand toward the gray, slow-moving river, where the ferryman plied his boat. "No coin, no farewell. I am still tied there, unburied, a prisoner. O lord, give me leave to go haunt the place until my wife gives me a decent burial."

"That is the law," Death admitted, taking pity on him, thinking on the woman with the summer sky in her eyes and hair like August wheat. Cruel, he thought, so cruel, for all she was so beautiful. "Go," he said, "Sisyphos, and secure your proper burial. There is the way."

He parted the curtain between worlds for him, and showed him Corinth; and straightway he sped by another path, for the African woman cried out in pain, and called his name, and he came quickly, in pity.

But the ghost of Sisyphos smiled as it walked the marketplace by night, and walked up the steps. Guards shivered as it passed, and straightened a little, and the torches in the hallway fluttered.

And there in the hall, on a bed of shields, lay his body in royal state; and near it, her golden hair unbound and her sky-blue eyes red with weeping, knelt Merope.

Laughing, he touched her shoulder, but she looked up not seeing; and with a touch on his own body, he lay down, and lifted himself up, smiling at her.

"Lord!" she cried, and he hugged her as he stood in his own body once more. Tears became wild laughter.

And servants shuddered at the pair, the clever king and his brave bride, who had made this pact while Death waited at their side, that she would not, whatever betided, bury him.

"Admit no strangers," he bade the servants then.

And he with his bride went up the stairs to the bedchamber, where blue dolphins danced on the walls, and torches burned right gaily in the night.

There was a war in China, that raged up and down the banks of the Yangtze, that burned villages and cities, elevated some lords and ruined others. Death and a thousand of his servants were busy there.

There was a plague in India, that on hot winds ran the streets of cities, killing first the beasts and then the men, that cried out in agony; and Death, whose name is heard in Hell, came quickly there, bringing his servants with him.

There was war in Germany, that ran across the forests and the river and spilled bloodily into Gaul, as year after year the fighting continued.

Death, who does not sleep, was seldom in his castle, but much about the roads of Europe and the hills of Asia, and walking here and there in the persons of his thousand, thousand servants.

But in the passing years he found himself again in the marketplace of a certain city, and the children stared at him in horror, and people drew away from him.

"How is this?" he asked, remembering another welcome he had had in Corinth, when a child had smiled at him.

"Go away," said a merchant. "The king does not favor strangers in this city."

"This is ill hospitality," said Death, offended, "and against the law of the gods."

But when they gathered stones, he went, sorrowing, from the gates, where a beggar sat, wizened and miserable. He turned his face from that one, who looked on him with longing, and gave him a coin.

And then he stepped (for the steps of Death are wide) from the gateway to the palace door, where the guards came to abrupt attention. And his aspect now was that of a king in black robes, with a golden band about his dusky brow, and fires smoldered in his eyes.

The guards shrank from him, weapons untouched, and he passed silently into the hall, angry and curious too, what the custom was in this city that barred travelers.

The torches flared in dark as he went, shadow enveloping him and flowing over the gay tiles of octopi and flying-fishes, along the walls of dancers and gardens. He heard the sounds of revelry.

A shadow fell upon the last table, that was the unused place of guests. A torch went out, and laughing men and women fell silent and turned their heads to see what passed there, seeing nothing.

Only the king rose from his place, and the wide-eyed queen beside him. He was older now, with white dusting the dark of his hair; and the first touch of frost was on the wheaten-haired queen, the pinch that kills the flush in the cheeks and makes little cracklings beside the eyes. She lifted her hand to her lips and stopped, as everything stopped, save only Sisyphos.

"Sisphos," said Death with a frown that dimmed the frozen fires.

Sisphos' hand touched his wife's arm, trembled there, an older hand, and his eyes filled with tears.

"You see I loved her so," said Sisyphos, "I could not leave her."

And Death, forever mateless, grieved, and his anger faded. "You gained the years you wanted, Man," he said. "Be content. Come." For he remembered the young queen that had been, and was sorry that the touch of age had come on her: mortals; he pitied them, who were prey to Age.

But the soul resisted him, strong and determined, and would not let go. "Come," he said, angered now. "Come. Forty years you have stolen. You have had the best of me. Now come."

And with a swoop that obscured the very hearthfire he came, and reached out his hand.

But quicker than the reach of Death was Sisyphos, whipping round his hands his golden belt, and moly was entwined therein, and asphodel. Death cried out at the treachery, and the spell was broken, and the queen cried out at the shadow. The fires went out, and men shrieked in terror.

They were brave men that, with the king, bore that shadow into the nether reaches of the palace, that was cut deep in the rock, deep cellars and storage places for wine and oil. And here they used iron chains, that wrung painful moans from Death, and here they left him.

Somewhere in Spain an old man called, and Death could not answer; in anguish, Death wept. In Corinth's very street a dog lay crushed by a passing cart, and its yelping tortured the ears of passersby, and tore at the heart of Death.

Disease and old age ran the world, afflicting thousands, who lingered, calling on Death to no avail.

Insects and beasts bred and multiplied, none dying, and were fed upon and torn and did not die, but lay moaning piteously; and plants and grasses grew up thick, not seeding, through the stones, and when they were cut, did not wither, but continued to grow, until the streets of the cities began to be overgrown and beasts wandered out of the fields, confused and crowded by their own young.

Wars were without death, and the wounded kept fighting and the horridly maimed and the diseased walked the world crying out in agony, until there was no place that was free of horrors.

And Death heard all the cries and the prayers, and, helpless, wept.

The very vermin in the basements of the palace multiplied, while Death lay bound and impotent; and fed upon the grain, and devoured everything, leaving the people to starve. Famine stalked the streets, and wasted men, and Disease followed raving in his wake, laughing and tearing at men and beasts.

But Death could not stir.

And at last the gods, looking down on the chaos that was earth, bestirred themselves and began to inquire what passed, for every ill was let loose on earth, and men suffered too much to attend to sacrifices.

The wisest of them knew at once what had been withheld from the world, for wherever men called on Death, he did not come. They searched the depths of earth and sea for him, who never visited the higher realms; and made inquiry among the snake-bodied children of Night, his cousins, but none had seen him.

Then from the still, shadowed quiet of Sleep crept the least of Night's children, a Dream, that wound its serpent-way to the wisest of gods and whispered, timidly, "Sisyphos."

And the gods turned their all-seeing eyes on the city of Corinth, on the man named Sisyphos, on a mourning shadow in the cellars of Corinth's palace. They frowned, and earthquake shook the ground.

And quake after quake rocked the city, until pillars tottered, and people cowered in fear, and Sisyphos turned knowing eyes on his queen, and kissed her tearfully and took a key.

It was fearful to enter that dark place, with the quakes rumbling and shuddering at the floor, to approach that knot of shadow that huddled in the corner, wherein baleful and angry eyes watched: he had to remember that Death is a serpent-child, and it was a serpent-shape that seemed imprisoned there, earth-wise and ancient, and unlike his twin, cold.

"Give me ten years," Sisyphos tried to bargain with him, endlessly trying.

But Death said nothing, and the floor shuddered, and great cracks ran through the masonry, portending the fall of the palace. Sisyphos shivered, and thought of his queen: and then he fitted the key to the lock, and took the bonds away.

Death stood up, a swirling shadow, and cold breathed from him as Sisyphos cowered to the floor, trembling.

But it was the dark-faced, gentle king who touched him on the shoulder and whispered in his ear: "Brave Sisyphos, come along."

And Sisyphos arose, forgetting his body that lay in the crumbling cellar, and stepped with the dark king out into the marketplace, out into a wilderness that began to die wherever the shadow fell; grass, insects, all withered and went to dust, leaving only bright, young growth; a dog's wails ceased; children's voices began to be heard; and when at last they passed the gates of Corinth, Death paused by the forlorn beggar. Death took his hand gently, and the old man shivered, and smiled, and that immortal part shook free, rising up. The soul blinked, stretched, found it easy to walk with them, on feet that were not lame.

They strode down the shore to the river, where thousands of rustling ghosts were gathering, and the ferryman was hastening to his abandoned post.

It was nine full turnings later that Death gathered to him the summer-eyed queen, and three after that before her gentle ghost appeared before his throne on the far side of the river.

He smiled to see her. She smiled, a knowing and mischievous smile. She was young again. August bloomed in her hair, a glory in the dark of Hell. Far away were the meadows of asphodel, the jagged peaks that were the haunt of the children of Night. She was beginning her journey.

"Come," said Death, and took her hand, and led her with his thousand-league strides across the meadow and beyond to the dark mountains.

There was a trail, much winding, upon a mountainside; and high upon it toiled a strong young king, covered in sweat, who heaved a stone along. Vast it was, and heavy, but he was determined, and patient. He heaved it up another hand's breadth, and braced himself to catch his breath and try again.

"He can be free, you know," whispered Death in the young queen's ear, "once he sets it on yonder pinnacle."

And gently Death set her on the roadside, saw the young king turn, wonder in his eyes, the stone forgotten. It crashed rumbling down the trail, bounding and rebounding, to shatter on the floor of the Pit and send echoes reverberating the length and breadth of Hell. A moment Sisyphos stared after it in dismay; then with a laugh that outrang the echoes, opened his arms to the young queen Merope.

Death smiled, and turned away, with thousand-league strides crossing the plains of Hell until he reached his throne. And remembering duty, he extended himself again into his thousand, thousand shapes, and sighed.

Y

HOMECOMING

A

Dark . . . Nothing. There had been nothing for a long, long dormancy. Tuclick drifted into the system, expended precious reserve energy to scan, to decide that this system too was useless. It fixed on another star, launched itself outward, sublight.

It was hungry. It settled into a cold torpor, lasting years. The hunger remained, and a dim anxiety. This host was all but drained. It had been too long. Tuclick had used the shell too recklessly, remaining awake, skimming star to star, consuming energy in the confidence the next star, the next, the next, would replenish what it so profligately consumed. But there had been no new hosts. Tuclick drifted now, conserving over time meaningless in its almost-sleep, negligible against the memories of long wanderings stored within it, buried below the level of consciousness, buried with the memory of its makers.

Now was a dim, biding apprehension. The warrior shell held no further promise of survival. It was helpless as it drifted into the new system.

Power. Scan locked on it, abundant, exciting. Tuclick pursued, agitated, fearing its escape, lacking power for the weapons of the warrior host. Several sources came into scan. Tuclick continued doggedly after the original, the most accessible. The interval lessened.

Contact. Tuclick grappled, held. Its probe disengaged from the dying host; Tuclick came fully alive, expending dangerously as it sent its alloy body hurtling down empty corridors to the lock. It exited, contacted the new host, absorbed power. More systems came to life within. It found entry, settled, became aware of its host, suddenly disappointed, frightened at its weakness. The vast body was only a connected series of hollow compartments. It held memory of a destination. Tuclick absorbed this, suddenly felt the systems begin to fail. Tuclick swiftly powered down section after section of the vast useless body, but the destination—the destination it too sought, eagerly, possibilities of a direction out of this long wilderness, this desert of stars. The host sought a haven it knew. Tuclick bided, hungry—the host leapt recklessly into hyperspace—Tuclick rode it, willing to let it run, certain now of energy waiting where the host fled.

Emergence. Tuclick scanned in sudden panic, sensing a trap.

No power. A primitive world lay under scan. Tuclick rode, waiting, helpless.

And then the tiniest pulse of interest, a minuscule pulse of energy. Marker-beacon. In its desperation Tuclick did not scorn even this, came down on it, opened the bay, swallowed it up. Quick operations drained it. Tuclick used the power carefully, oh, so carefully, calculating with rising panic that it could not have this star and survive to the next. The host was not sufficient. The marker-beacon gave only a temporary source. Tuclick felt the threat of dissolution—ruin.

Ship.

The object emerged into scan, a mote of a ship, coming up fast. In desperate desire Tuclick maneuvered its failing host, opened its receiving bay.

Resistance. Fire damaged systems. Tuclick reacted furiously, rammed forward, felt the damage as it swallowed the resistant mote. Fire hammered at the bay. Tuclick blasted back with its tiny interior defenses, desperate. Silence. Resistance ceased. Tuclick disengaged from its host, momentarily blind and deaf to the outside as it traveled the corridors of its fading host body. It opened the damaged bay, trundled in, scanning the stranger. The hatch opened to its expert probing. It entered, ran the tiny corridors, pausing to engage a tap and absorb power.

Activity. A tiny burst of fire crackled on its shell. Tuclick engaged personal defenses. Resistance ceased. A strange rapid movement fled its presence. Tuclick followed, paused as the furtive movement slowed, ceased. The resisting unit lay still. Tuclick rolled forward, scanned.

A disturbance rippled through his circuits, activated deeper memories, agitated Tuclick into reckless expenditure. The deck was smeared with a dark fluid that had nothing to do with ship wreckage. Tuclick extended a probe into it, analyzed, memories further disturbed as he scanned the configurations of the resisting unit.

Biosystem. Tuclick's systems were jolted, deeper and deeper memories were surfacing . . . ten thousand years of records . . . it triggered something in its deepest levels.

Prime directive.

Contact.

A tape activated. *Greetings* it said. *Greetings.* The biounit did not respond. Long unused scan detected ebbing function, deterioration.

In haste Tuclick extended other apparatus, gathered up the afflicted organism. Panic ran through Tuclick's systems, directives violated at basic levels. It sorted, recalculated—locked into the little ship's systems, searching—found a memory of destination—and other things, higher function memories. Tuclick absorbed, redirected power, overconsuming in the disturbance of its internal systems.

It remembered.

Directives overrode directives. A flurry of panic ran Tuclick's systems, sorted into purpose. Sublight could reach the little ship's origin point in 7.5 years. The injured organism could not be maintained—scan estimated—but a brief time. Tuclick no longer hesitated. In a burst of activity it arranged the shunt of power. The old host—Tuclick understood it now for a mere shell filled with biostuffs—lurched into hyperspace, and out again.

Power waned. The new star was still distant, at sublight. Stubbornly Tuclick kept the environment stable for the biosystem, circulating its fluids, maintaining its heat, surrounding it in atmosphere. The power ebbed steadily, no longer that of the host's, but Tuclick's own reserve, draining systems. Memories faded, the latest first, reaching back and back, until Tuclick reentered the time of his own origin. Tuclick clung to the organism the more desperately, all its purposes satisifed.

Ship.

Hunger assailed Tuclick. Directives overwhelmed hunger. That time was over. The directives that had sustained the probe this long had no power over those now engaged. Tuclick shunted power to signal, losing more memory in the effort.

The ship responded. Tuclick faded further, shunting all power to the maintenance of the organism, to opening the receiving bay, to the signal.

Life. Tuclick recognized this. *Greetings*, it began the message. *Greetings. I have returned to*—

Systems deteriorated. Tuclick abandoned the attempt, holding the organism alive until the others disengaged it, buzzing in their concern. Tuclick pulsed once in satisfaction.

All power faded. The last memories went. The machinery stopped.

THE DREAMSTONE

Of all possible paths to travel up out of Caerdale, that through the deep forest was the least used by Men. Brigands, outlaws, fugitives who fled mindless from shadows . . . men with dull, dead eyes and hearts which could not truly see the wood, souls so attainted already with the world that they could sense no greater evil nor greater good than their own—*they* walked that path; and if by broad morning, so that they had cleared the black heart of Ealdwood by nightfall, then they might perchance make it safe away into the new forest eastward in the hills, there to live and prey on the game and on each other.

But a runner by night, and that one young and wild-eyed and bearing neither sword nor bow, but only a dagger and a gleeman's harp, this was a rare venturer in Ealdwood, and all the deeper shadows chuckled and whispered in startlement.

Eld-born Arafel saw him, and she saw little in this latter age of earth, wrapped as she was in a passage of time different than the suns and moons which blink Men so startling-swift from birth to dying. She heard the bright notes of the harp which jangled on his shoulders, which companied his flight and betrayed him to all with ears to hear, in this world and the other. She saw his flight and walked into the way to meet him, out of the soft green light of her moon and into the colder white of his; and evils which had grown quite bold in the Ealdwood of latter earth suddenly felt the warm breath of spring and drew aside, slinking into dark places where neither moon cast light.

"Boy," she whispered. He startled like a wounded deer, hesitated, searching out the voice. She stepped full into his light and felt the dank wind of Ealdwood on her face. He seemed more solid then, ragged and torn by thorns in his headlong course, although his garments had been of fine linen and the harp at his shoulders had a broidered case.

She had taken little with her out of otherwhere, and yet did take—it was all in the eye which saw. She leaned against the rotting trunk of a dying tree and folded her arms unthreateningly, no hand to the blade she wore, propped one foot against a projecting root and smiled. He looked on her with no less apprehension for that, seeing, perhaps, a ragged vagabond of a woman in outlaws' habit—or perhaps seeing more, for he did not look to be as blind as some. His hand touched a talisman at his breast and she, smiling still, touched that which hung at her own throat, which had power to answer his.

"Now where would you be going," she asked, "so recklessly through the Ealdwood? To some misdeed? Some mischief?"

"Misfortune," he said, breathless. He yet stared at her as if he thought her no more than moonbeams, and she grinned at that. Then suddenly and far away came a baying of hounds; he would have fled at once, and sprang to do so.

"Stay!" she cried, and stepped into his path a second time, curious what other venturers would come, and on the heels of such as he. "I do doubt they'll come this far. What name do you give, who come disturbing the peace of Eald?"

He was wary, surely knowing the power of names; and perhaps he would not have given his true one and perhaps he would not have stayed at all, but that she fixed him sternly with her eyes and he stammered out: "Fionn."

"Fionn." It was apt, for fair he was, tangled hair and first down of beard. She spoke it softly, like a charm. "Fionn. Come walk with me. I'd see this intrusion before others do. Come, come, have no dread of me; I've no harm in mind."

He did come, carefully, and much loath, heeded and walked after her, held by nothing but her wish. She took the Ealdwood's own slow time, not walking the quicker ways, for there was the taint of iron about him, and she could not take him there.

The thicket which degenerated from the dark heart of the Eald was an unlovely place . . . for the Ealdwood had once been better than it was, and there was yet a ruined fairness there; but these young trees had never been other than what they were. They twisted and tangled their roots among the bones of the crumbling hills, making deceiving and thorny barriers. Unlikely it was that Men could see the ways she found; but she was amazed by the changes the years had wrought—saw the slow work of root and branch and ice and sun, labored hard-breathing and scratched with thorns, but gloried in it, alive to the world. She turned from time to time when she sensed faltering behind her: he caught that look of hers and came on, pallid and fearful, past clinging thickets and over stones, as if he had lost all will or hope of doing otherwise.

The baying of hounds echoed out of Caerdale, from the deep valley at the very bounds of the forest. She sat down on a rock atop that last slope, where was prospect of all the great vale of the Caerbourne, a dark tree-filled void beneath the moon. A towered heap of stones had risen far across the vale on the hill called Caer Wiell, and it was the work of men: so much did the years do with the world.

The boy dropped down by the stone, the harp upon his shoulders echoing; his head sank on his folded arms and he wiped the sweat and the tangled hair from his brow. The baying, still a moment, began again, and he lifted frightened eyes.

Now he would run, having come as far as he would; fear shattered the spell. She stayed him yet again, a hand on his smooth arm.

"Here's the limit of *my* wood," she said. "And in it, hounds hunt that you could not shake from your heels, no. You'd do well to stay here by me, indeed you would. It is yours, that harp?"

He nodded.

"Will play for me?" she asked, which she had desired from the beginning; and the desire of it burned far more vividly than did curiosity about men and dogs: but one would serve the other. He looked at her as though he thought her mad; and yet took the harp from his shoulders and from its case. Dark wood starred and banded with gold, it sounded when he took it into his arms: he held it so, like something protected, and lifted a pale, resentful face.

And bowed his head again and played as she had bidden him, soft touches at the strings that quickly grew bolder, that waked echoes out of the depths of Caerdale and set the hounds to baying madly. The music drowned the voices, filled the air, filled her heart, and she felt now no faltering or tremor of his hands. She listened, and almost forgot which moon shone down on them, for it had been so long, so very long since the last song had been heard in Ealdwood, and that sung soft and elsewhere.

He surely sensed a glamor on him, that the wind blew warmer and the trees sighed with listening. The fear went from his eyes, and though sweat stood on his brow like jewels, it was clear, brave music that he made—suddenly, with a bright ripple of the strings, a defiant song, strange to her ears.

Discord crept in, the hounds' fell voices, taking the music and warping it out of tune. She rose as that sound drew near. The song ceased, and there was the rush and clatter of horses in the thicket below.

Fionn sprang up, the harp laid aside. He snatched at the small dagger at his belt, and she flinched at that, the bitter taint of iron. "No," she wished him, and he did not draw.

Then hounds and riders were on them, a flood of hounds black and slavering and two great horses, bearing men with the smell of iron about them, men glittering terribly in the moonlight. The hounds surged up baying and bugling and as suddenly fell back again, making wide their circle, whining and with lifting of hackles. The riders whipped them, but their horses shied and screamed under the spurs and neither could be driven further.

She stood, one foot braced against the rock, and regarded men and beasts with cold curiosity, for she found them strange, harder and wilder than Men she had known; and strange too was the device on them, that was a wolf's grinning head. She did not recall it—nor care for the manner of them.

Another rider clattered up the shale, shouted and whipped his unwilling horse farther than the others, and at his heels came men with bows. His arm lifted, gestured; the bows arched, at the harper and at her.

"Hold," she said.

The arm did not fall; it slowly lowered. He glared at her, and she stepped lightly up onto the rock so she need not look up so far, to him on his tall horse. The beast shied under him and he spurred it and curbed it cruelly; but he gave no order to his men, as if the cowering hounds and trembling horses finally made him see.

"Away from here," he shouted down at her, a voice to make the earth quake. "Away! or I daresay you need a lesson taught you too." And he drew his great sword and held it toward her, curbing the protesting horse.

"Me, lessons?" She set her hand on the harper's arm. "Is it on his account you set foot here and raise this noise?"

"My harper," the lord said, "and a thief. Witch, step aside. Fire and iron are answer enough for you."

In truth, she had no liking for the sword that threatened or for the iron-headed arrows which could speed at his lightest word. She kept her hand on Fionn's arm nonetheless, for she saw well how he would fare with them. "But he's mine, lord-of-men. I should say that the harper's no joy to you, you'd not come chasing him from your land. And great joy he is to me, for long and long it is since I've met so pleasant a companion in Ealdwood. Gather the harp, lad, and walk away now; let me talk with this rash man."

"Stay!" the lord shouted; but Fionn snatched the harp into his arms and edged away.

An arrow hissed; the boy flung himself aside with a terrible clangor of the harp, and lost it on the slope and scrambled back for it, his undoing, for now there were more arrows ready, and these better-purposed.

"Do not," she said.

"What's mine is mine." The lord held his horse still, his sword outstretched before his archers, bating the signal; his face was congested with rage and fear. "Harp and harper are mine. And you'll rue it if you think any words of yours weigh with me. I'll have him and you for your impudence."

It seemed wisest then to walk away, and she did so—turned back the next instant, at distance, at Fionn's side, and only half under his moon. "I ask your name, lord-of-men, if you aren't fearful of my curse."

Thus she mocked him, to make him afraid before his men. "Evald," he said back, no hesitating, with contempt for her. "And yours, witch?"

"Call me what you like, lord. And take warning, that these woods are not for human hunting and your harper is not yours any more. Go away and be grateful. Men have Caerdale. If it does not please you, shape it until it does. The Ealdwood's not for trespass."

He gnawed at his mustaches and gripped his sword the tighter, but about him the drawn bows had begun to sag and the arrows to aim at the dirt. Fear was in the men's eyes, and the two riders who had come first hung back, free men and less constrained than the archers.

"You have what's mine," he insisted.

"And so I do. Go on, Fionn. Do go, quietly."

"You've what's *mine*," the valley lord shouted. "Are you thief then as well as witch? You owe me a price for it."

She drew in a sharp breath and yet did not waver in or out of the shadow. "Then do not name too high, lord-of-men. I may hear you, if that will quit us."

His eyes roved harshly about her, full of hate and yet of weariness as well. She felt cold at that look, especially where it centered, above her heart, and her hand stole to that moon-green stone that hung at her throat.

"The stone will be enough," he said. *"That."*

She drew it off, and held it yet, insubstantial as she, dangling on its chain, for she had the measure of them and it was small. "Go, Fionn," she bade him; and when he lingered yet: "Go!" she shouted. At last he ran, fled, raced away like a mad thing, holding the harp to him.

And when the woods all about were still again, hushed but for the shifting and stamp of the horses and the complaint of the hounds, she let fall the stone. "Be paid," she said, and walked away.

She heard the hooves and turned, felt the insubstantial sword like a stab of ice into her heart. She recoiled elsewhere, bowed with the pain of it that took her breath away. But in time she could stand again, and had taken from the iron no lasting hurt; yet it had been close, and the feel of cold lingered even in the warm winds.

And the boy—she went striding through the shades and shadows in greatest anxiety until she found him, where he huddled hurt and lost within the deepest wood.

"Are you well?" she asked lightly, dropping to her heels beside him. For a moment she feared he might be hurt more than scratches, so tightly he was bowed over the harp; but he lifted his face to her. "You shall stay while you wish," she said, hoping that he would choose to stay long. "You shall harp for me." And when he yet looked fear at her: "You'd not like the new forest. They've no ear for harpers there."

"What is your name, lady?"

"What do you see of me?"

He looked swiftly at the ground, so that she reckoned he could not say the truth without offending her. And she laughed at that.

"Then call me Thistle," she said. "I answer sometimes to that, and it's a name as rough as I. But you'll stay. You'll play for me."

"Yes." He hugged the harp close. "But I'll not go with you. I've no wish to find the years passed in a night and all the world gone old."

"Ah. You know me. But what harm, that years should pass? What care of them or this age? It seems hardly kind to you."

"I am a man," he said, "and it's *my* age."

It was so; she could not force him. One entered otherwise only by wishing it. He did not; and there was about him and in his heart still the taint of iron.

She settled in the moonlight, and watched beside him; he slept, for all his caution, and waked at last by sunrise, looking about him anxiously lest the trees have grown, and seeming bewildered that she was still there by day. She laughed, knowing her own look by daylight, that was indeed rough as the weed she had named herself, much-tanned and calloused and her clothes in want of patching. She sat plaiting her hair in a single silver braid and smiling sidelong at him, who kept giving her side-long glances too.

All the earth grew warm. The sun did come here, unclouded on this day. He offered her food, such meager share as he had; she would have none of it, not fond of man-taint, or the flesh of poor forest creatures. She gave him instead of her own, the gift of trees and bees and whatsoever things felt no hurt at sharing.

"It's good," he said, and she smiled at that.

He played for her then, idly and softly, and slept again, for bright day in Ealdwood counseled sleep, when the sun burned warmth through the tangled branches and the air hung still, nothing breathing, least of all the wind. She drowsed too, for the first time since many a tree had grown, for the touch of the mortal sun did that kindness, a benison she had all but forgotten.

But as she slept she dreamed, of a close place of cold stone. In that dark hall she had a man's body, heavy and reeking of wine and ugly memories, such a dark fierceness she would gladly have fled if she might.

Her hand sought the moonstone on its chain and found it at his throat; she offered better dreams and more kindly, and he made bitter mock of them, hating all that he did not comprehend. Then she would have made the hand put the stone off that foul neck; but she had no power to compel, and *he* would not. He possessed what he owned, so fiercely and with such jealousy it cramped the muscles and stifled the breath.

And he hated what he did not have and could not have, that most of all; and the center of it was his harper.

She tried still to reason within this strange, closed mind. It was impossible. The heart was almost without love, and what little it had ever been given it folded in upon itself lest what it possessed escape.

"Why?" she asked that night, when the moon shed light on the Ealdwood and the land was quiet, no ill thing near them, no cloud above them. "Why does he seek you?" Though her dreams had told her, she wanted his answer.

Fionn shrugged, his young eyes for a moment aged; and he gathered against him his harp. "This," he said.

"You said it was yours. He called you thief. What did you steal?"

"It is mine." He touched the strings and brought forth melody. "It hung in his hall so long he thought it his, and the strings were cut and dead." He rippled out a somber note. "It was my father's and his father's before him."

"And in Evald's keeping?"

The fair head bowed over the harp and his hands coaxed sound from it, answerless.

"I've given a price," she said, "to keep him from it and you. Will you not give back an answer?"

The sound burst into softness. "It was my father's. Evald hanged him. Would hang me."

"For what cause?"

Fionn shrugged, and never ceased to play. "For truth. For truth he sang. So Evald hanged him, and hung the harp on his wall for mock of him. I came. I gave him songs he liked. But at winter's end I came down to the hall at night, and mended the old harp, gave it voice and a song he remembered. For that he hunts me."

Then softly he sang, of humankind and wolves, and that song was bitter. She shuddered to hear it, and bade him cease, for mind to mind with her in troubled dreams Evald heard and tossed, and waked starting in sweat.

"Sing more kindly," she said. Fionn did so, while the moon climbed above the trees, and she recalled elder-day songs which the world had not heard in long years, sang them sweetly. Fionn listened and caught up the words in his strings, until the tears ran down his face for joy.

There could be no harm in Ealdwood that hour: the spirits of latter earth that skulked and strove and haunted men fled elsewhere, finding nothing that they knew; and the old shadows slipped away trembling, for they remembered. But now and again the song faltered, for there came a touch of ill and smallness into her heart, a cold piercing as the iron, with thoughts of hate, which she had never held so close.

Then she laughed, breaking the spell, and put it from her, bent herself to teach the harper songs which she herself had almost forgotten, conscious the while that elsewhere, down in Caerbourne vale, on Caer Wiell, a man's body tossed in sweaty dreams which seemed constantly to mock him, with sound of eldritch harping that stirred echoes and sleeping ghosts.

With the dawn she and Fionn rose and walked a time, and shared food, and drank at a cold, clear spring she knew, until the sun's hot eye fell upon them and cast its numbing spell on all the Ealdwood.

Then Fionn slept; but she fought the sleep which came to her, for dreams were in it, her dreams while *he* should wake; nor would they stay at bay, not when her eyes grew heavy and the air thick with urging sleep. The dreams came more and more strongly. The man's strong legs bestrode a great brute horse, and hands plied whip and feet the spurs more than she would, hurting it cruelly. There was noise of hounds and hunt, a coursing of woods and hedges and the bright spurt of blood on dappled hide: he sought blood to wipe out blood, for the harping rang yet in his mind, and she shuddered at the killing her hands did, and at the fear that gathered thickly about him, reflected in his comrades' eyes.

It was better that night, when the waking was hers and her harper's, and sweet songs banished fear; but even yet she grieved for remembering, and at times the cold came on her, so that her hand would steal to her throat where the moongreen stone was not. Her eyes brimmed suddenly with tears: Fionn saw and tried to sing her merry songs instead. They failed, and the music died.

"Teach me another song," he begged of her. "No harper ever had such songs. And will *you* not play for *me?*"

"I have no art," she said, for the last harper of her folk had gone long ago: it was not all truth, for once she had known, but there was no more music in her hands, none since the last had gone and she had willed to stay, loving this place too well in spite of men. "Play," she asked of Fionn, and tried to smile, though the iron closed about her heart and the man raged at the nightmare, waking in sweat, ghost-ridden.

It was that human song Fionn played in his despair, of the man who would be a wolf and the wolf who was no man; while the lord Evald did not sleep again, but sat shivering and wrapped in furs before his hearth, his hand clenched in hate upon the stone which he possessed and would not, though it killed him, let go.

But she sang a song of elder earth, and the harper took up the tune, which sang of earth and shores and water, a journey, the great last journey, at men's coming and the dimming of the world. Fionn wept while he played, and she smiled sadly and at last fell silent, for her heart was gray and cold.

The sun returned at last, but she had no will to eat or rest, only to sit grieving, for she could not find peace. Gladly now she would have fled the shadow-shifting way back into otherwhere, to her own moon and softer sun, and persuaded the harper with her; but there was a portion of her heart in pawn, and she could not even go herself: she was too heavily bound. She fell to mourning bitterly, and pressed her hand often where the stone should rest. He hunted again, did Evald of Caer Wiell. Sleepless, maddened by dreams, he whipped his folk out of the hold as he did his hounds, out to the margin of the Ealdwood, to harry the creatures of woodsedge, having guessed well the source of the harping. He brought fire and axes, vowing to take the old trees one by one until all was dead and bare.

The wood muttered with whisperings and angers; a wall of cloud rolled down from the north on Ealdwood and all deep Caerdale, dimming the sun; a wind sighed in the face of the men, so that no torch was set to wood; but axes rang, that day and the next. The clouds gathered thicker and the winds blew colder, making Ealdwood dim again and dank. She yet managed to smile by night, to hear the harper's songs. But every stroke of the axes made her shudder, and the iron about her heart tightened day by day. The wound in the Ealdwood grew, and he was coming; she knew it well, and there remained at last no song at all, by day or night.

She sat now with her head bowed beneath the clouded moon, and Fionn was powerless to cheer her. He regarded her in deep despair, and touched her hand for comfort. She said no word to that, but gathered her cloak about her and offered to the harper to walk a time, while vile things stirred and muttered in the shadow, whispering malice to the winds, so that often Fionn started and stared and kept close beside her.

Her strength faded, first that she could not keep the voices away, and then that she could not keep from listening; and at last she sank upon his arm, eased to the cold ground and leaned her head against the bark of a gnarled tree.

"What ails?" he asked, and pried at her clenched and empty fingers, opened the fist which hovered near her throat as if seeking there the answer. "What ails you?"

She shrugged and smiled and shuddered, for the axes had begun again, and she felt the iron like a wound, a great cry going through the wood as it had gone for days; but he was deaf to it, being what he was. "Make a song for me," she asked.

"I have no heart for it."

"Nor have I," she said. A sweat stood on her face, and he wiped at it with his gentle hand and tried to ease her pain.

And again he caught and unclenched the hand which rested, empty, at her throat. "The stone," he said. "Is it *that* you miss?"

She shrugged, and turned her head, for the axes then seemed loud. He looked too—glanced back deaf and puzzled. " 'Tis time," she said. "You must be on your way this morning, when there's sun enough. The new forest will hide you after all."

"And leave you? Is that your meaning?"

She smiled, touched his anxious face. "I am paid enough."

"How paid? What did you pay? *What* was it you gave away?"

"Dreams," she said. "Only that. And all of that." Her hands shook terribly, and a blackness came on her heart too miserable to bear: it was hate, and aimed at him and at herself, and all that lived; and it was harder and harder to fend away. "Evil has it. He would do you hurt, and I would dream that too. Harper, it's time to go."

"Why would you give such a thing?" Great tears started from his eyes. "Was it worth such a cost, my harping?"

"Why, well worth it," she said, with such a laugh as she had left to laugh, that shattered all the evil for a moment and left her clean. "I have sung."

He snatched up the harp and ran, breaking branches and tearing flesh in his headlong haste, but not, she realized in horror, not the way he ought—but back again, to Caerdale.

She cried out her dismay and seized at branches to pull herself to her feet; she could in no wise follow. Her limbs which had been quick to run beneath this moon or the other were leaden, and her breath came hard. Brambles caught and held with all but mindful malice, and dark things which had never had power in her presence whispered loudly now, of murder.

And elsewhere the wolf-lord with his men drove at the forest, great ringing blows, the poison of iron. The heavy ironclad body which she sometime wore seemed hers again, and the moonstone was prisoned within that iron, near a heart that beat with hate.

She tried the more to haste, and could not. She looked helplessly through Evald's narrow eyes and saw—saw the young harper break through the thickets near them. Weapons lifted, bows and axes. Hounds bayed and lunged at leashes.

Fionn came, nothing hesitating, bringing the harp, and himself, "A trade," she heard him say. "The stone for the harp."

There was such hate in Evald's heart, and such fear it was hard to breathe. She felt a pain to the depth of her as Evald's coarse fingers pawed at the stone. She felt his fear, felt his loathing of it. Nothing would he truly let go. But this—this he abhorred, and was fierce in his joy to lose it.

"Come," the lord Evald said, and held the stone, dangling and spinning before him, so that for that moment the hate was far and cold.

Another hand took it then, and very gentle it was, and very full of love. She felt the sudden draught of strength and desperation—sprang up then, to run, to save.

But pain stabbed through her heart, and such an ebbing out of love and grief that she cried aloud, and stumbled, blind, dead in that part of her.

She did not cease to run; and she ran now that shadow way, for the heaviness was gone. Across meadows, under that other moon she sped, and gathered up all that she had left behind, burst out again in the blink of an eye and elsewhere.

Horses shied and dogs barked; for now she did not care to be what suited men's eyes: bright as the moon she broke among them, and in her hand was a sharp blade, to meet with iron.

Harp and harper lay together, sword-riven. She saw the underlings start away and cared nothing for them; but Evald she sought. He cursed at her, drove spurs into his horse and rode at her, sword yet drawn, shivering the winds with a horrid slash of iron. The horse screamed and shied; he cursed and reined the beast, and drove it for her again. But this time the blow was hers, a scratch that made him shriek with rage.

She fled at once. He pursued. It was his nature that he must; and she might have fled otherwhere, but she would not. She darted and dodged ahead of the great horse, and it broke the brush and thorns and panted after, hard-ridden.

Shadows gathered, stirring and urgent on his side and on that, who gibbered and rejoiced for the way that they were tending, to the woods' blackest heart, for some of them had been Men; and some had known the wolf's justice, and had come to what they were for his sake. They reached, but durst not touch him, for she would not have it so. Over all, the trees bowed and groaned in the winds and the leaves went flying, thunder above and thunder of hooves below, scattering the shadows.

But suddenly she whirled about and flung back her cloak: the horse shied up and fell, cast Evald sprawling among the wet leaves. The shaken beast scrambled up and evaded his hands and his threats, thundered away on the moist earth, splashing across some hidden stream; and the shadows chuckled. She stepped full back again from otherwhere, and Evald saw her clear, moonbright and silver. He cursed, shifted that great black sword from hand to hand, for right hand bore a scratch that now must trouble him. He shrieked with hate and slashed.

She laughed and stepped into otherwhere and back again, and fled yet farther, until he stumbled with exhaustion and sobbed and fell, forgetting now his anger, for the whispers came loud.

"Up," she bade him, mocking, and stepped again to here. Thunder rolled upon the wind, and the sound of horses and hounds came at distance. A joyful malice came into his eyes when he heard it; his face grinned in the lightnings. But she laughed too, and his mirth died as the sound came on them, under them, over them, in earth and heavens.

He cursed then and swung the blade, lunged and slashed again, and she flinched from the almost-kiss of iron. Again he whirled it, pressing close; the lightning crackled—he shrieked a curse, and, silver-spitted—died.

She did not weep or laugh now; she had known him too well for either. She looked up instead at the clouds, gray wrack scudding before the storm, where other hunters coursed the winds and wild cries wailed—heard hounds baying after something fugitive and wild. She lifted then her fragile sword, salute to lord Death, who had governance over Men, a Huntsman too; and many the old comrades the wolf would find following in his train.

Then the sorrow came on her, and she walked the otherwhere path to the beginning and the end of her course, where harp and harper lay. There was no mending here. The light was gone from his eyes and the wood was shattered.

But in his fingers lay another thing, which gleamed like the summer moon amid his hand.

Clean it was from his keeping, and loved. She gathered it to her. The silver chain went again about her neck and the stone rested where it ought. She bent last and kissed him to his long sleep, fading then to otherwhere.

She dreamed at times then, waking or sleeping; for when she held close the stone and thought of him she heard a fair, far music, for a part of his heart was there too, a gift of himself.

She sang sometimes, hearing it, wherever she walked.

That gift, she gave to him.

SEA CHANGE

They had come to Fingalsey from elsewhere, and the sea did not love them. It could have been that their ill luck followed them from that elsewhere, but however that might have been (later generations did not remember) ill luck was on them here.

It was a gray village next to the barren rocks of which it was made. There might have been color in Fingalsey once, but sea wind had scoured the timbers of the doors and windows and salt mist had corroded them into grooved writhing channels, and somber gray lichens clung to the stones of the village as much as they blotched the living rocks of the island, the one peak which was the heart and height of this barren sweep. Fingalsey was dull and colorless even to the black goats which grazed the heights and to the weathered black boats hull-up on its beach. It agreed not at all with the sea and sky when the sun shone in a blue heaven; and agreed well when, more often than not, the cold mists settled or cloud scudded and hostile waves beat at the rocks. They netted from those rocks on such days, the people of Fingalsey, in their drab homespun, culled shellfish in the shallows, slung at birds, herded their meager goats—with fear set out in their little boats to risk the tides and the rocks—knowing their luck, that the sea hated them.

It had voices, this sea. It murmured and complained constantly to the shore. It roared and wailed in storm. It took lives, and souls, and broke boats and gnawed at the shore.

But Malley went down to it one day, wandered from childbed and walked down by the rocks one spring. She was the first who went gladly—having given life, took an end of it: hugged the sea to her breast and gave herself to it in turn . . . a fine fair spring day, that Malley died, and left a life behind.

The father—the child had none, unless the rumors were true, and Malley who loved the sea had consorted there with Minyk's-son, who drowned the month before, whose boat was broken and who never came home again. *An unlucky child,* the women in the village whispered of the red-haired babe Malley left. *Dead father, dead mother. The sea's child. Ill luck's daughter.*

Hush! hissed the Widow, Malley's mother, rocking the babe in her arms; and such was the look in the Widow's sad eyes that there was no arguing.

The whispers which died slowly in Fingalsey—did die; the child grew fair, hair red as evening sun, eyes blue as the rare clear skies. The sun danced about her as she played, and the wind played pranks. She was all the gaiety, all the colors that Fingalsey was not, all the laughter they had never had—the first of three hearty, healthy children of that exceptional year; and first of years of bright-cheeked children, in years of calmer winds and full bellies. The boats went out and came home again safe. The sea brought up fish and shellfish. The goats grew sleek and fat on grass that throve in mild summers.

Fingalsey's child, they never called her now, Mila and Widow's granddaughter, the luck, brought of the gift the sea was given, summer and brightness. Before her, before Malley went to the sea, the dead had almost outnumbered the living in Fingalsey . . . the quiet, sunken graves of the dead high up the hill, a graveyard overgrazed by goats and drowned when the rains came . . . the level, empty graves of the unfound dead, the lost ones, the unhallowed, which the sea took and did not return—the cairns of gray, lichened stone which marked these empty places had become a village reduced in scale, tenantless, doorless houses on the hill's unhallowed side, above the rocks where the sea gnawed hungrily in storm, where goats wandered conscienceless.

But in these years healthy children played there, and grew, and in spring found flowers blooming among the forgotten cairns, grass and brush grown high. There was laughter in Fingalsey, and new nets hung among the racks by seaside. Houses once giving way to time, empty and with roofs sagging—were lived-in and thriving, filled with new marriages and new babies.

Came the summers one by one, sixteen of them. The sea's child became a fair young girl and her two year-mates fair youths. Mila tended the Widow's goats (and from that time the herd thrived amazingly, and the Widow prospered, in milk and good white cheeses). She waded the calm pools below the cairns culling shellfish with her age-mates, netting what fish ventured within her reach, laughing and giving away what she and the Widow had beyond their needs.

Her year-mates grew tall, twin brothers, Ciag and Marik Tyl's-sons. They were dark as Mila was bright, of dark parents and loving. The luck that was Mila's they shared, so that when their aging father found the sea too strenuous they took out the boat and the nets together, fared out recklessly and with unfailing fortune. The sea played games with them, and they laughed and dared it.

They shared boat, shared nets, shared house, shared table.

One thing at last they did not share, and that was the Widow's red-haired granddaughter.

Inevitably they must love her. All Fingalsey loved her. Fingalsey hearts soared to hear her singing, merry trills and cheerful tunes of her own making. Young men's eyes burned to see her walking, a flash of white and gold and sunset on the hillside paths, among the black goats, or running down the trail to the sea, skipping from the curling tide and laughing at the old gray demon, making nothing of his bluster and his threats.

They loved. That was, after all, as Mila expected, having had nothing but love—having expected nothing else all her life. In such abundance, she did not know the degrees and qualities of love, knew nothing of selfishness, nothing of want or of things out of reach.

Marik surprised her on the high path, as she was bringing the goats home—he waited to give her gifts, the best of the catch they had gotten, carried in a seagrass basket . . . but then, he had given her gifts all his life, and she had given him as many—a perfect shell, a prized piece of wood the sea had shaped; whatever Mila had, she gave away again. She smiled at him and gave her hands when he reached, and gave her lips when he kissed—but differently this time: she gazed at him after with flushed delight.

"I love you," he said. She knew this was true: she never doubted: and that this love was forever, she never doubted that either, or why else was the Widow the Widow, solitary? That was the only shadow on her happiness, to think in that moment on the Widow, her loneliness, having lost husband, lost daughter, black-clad forever.

"I love you," she said, because she always had . . . but she had never reckoned who it would be out of all the folk she loved that she would become the Widow for, if luck should turn. Marik kissed her again and would have done more than kissed, but the Widow had counseled Mila some things, and she would not. She fled, blushing with confusion.

And met Ciag coming up the self-same path.

Marik came hastening down behind, with a basket of forgotten fish on his arm, *seaward* running. She stopped. Marik did, in hot consternation. Ciag had stopped first of all, his face gone stark and grim.

No words were spoken, no move made, but for the white gulls which screamed to the winds aloft, the rustle of the grass and the dull murmur of the sea which was never absent, day or night, from the ears and minds of Fingalsey.

Mila went quite pale, and skipped by on the shoulder of the hill, fled faster—gone from innocence, for suddenly she perceived a hurt inevitable, and something beyond mending.

Ciag came the next day, waiting beside the Widow's door in the morning. He had brought his own gift, a garland of daisies and primroses. He offered it with the merry flourish with which he had offered her a thousand gifts. He was skilled at weaving garlands as he was nets and cords and all such things—slighter than his brother Marik and quicker. She did not mean to take it, but so brightly and so quickly he offered it to her hands, that her hands reached on their own; and when they had touched the flowers they touched his hands. His fingers closed on hers, and his eyes were full of grief.

"I love you," he said, "too."

"I love you," she whispered, for she found it true. It had always been true: her two year-brothers, her dearest friends, the other portions of her soul. But she pushed the flowers back at him.

He thrust them a second time at her, laughing as if it meant nothing. "But they have to be for you," he said. "I made them for you. Who else?"

She put them on, but she would not let him kiss her, though he tried. She fled from the Widow's door to the midst of the street . . . and stopped, for there stood Marik.

She had not remembered the fishes. She had left them in Marik's hand on the hillside, running from him. But she wore Ciag's garland. There was anger on Marik's brow.

She fled them both, running, as far as the goats' pen . . . she let them forth, snatched up her staff, walked in their midst, flower-decked, up the hillside, away from them both. All that day she found no song to sing for her charges, not then or coming home.

The brothers both met her that evening, each with a basket holding one great fish, as alike as rivalry could make them. She laughed at that and took the gifts; but there was hardness in Ciag's eyes and deep wounding in Marik's—her laughter died, when she looked into Marik's face. She still wore the flowers, day-faded and limp about her neck. She took Marik's gift first now, held it closer in her arm; took Ciag's basket and hardly looked at it. Then Marik's face lost some of its wounded look; and Ciag's bore a deeper shadow.

Mila fled away inside the Widow's house, and that evening had appetite for neither gift.

Every day after that they gifted her, both laughing, as if they had discovered amusement in their plight. Then the knot bound up in Mila's heart loosed: she took every gift and laughed with them when they laughed, walked with them both—but not separately—waded with them among the pools and shared goat's-cheese with them when they scanted their fishing and their own parents to be with her. She sang again, and laughed, but sometimes the songs died away into hollowness when she was alone, and sometimes the laughter was difficult—because she knew that someday she had to choose, that someday the both of them would not be with her, but one alone.

One gray fall day, with the storms beating at the shore and all minds numbed by the vast sound, it was Marik who found her, in that gray mist, by the boats which huddled like plain dark stones, hull-up along the shore, by the nets which hung ghostly and dripping in the fog.

"I have no gift today," he said.

She smiled at him all the same, shrugged, stood numb and cold while he took her hand, numb until she thought how she had waited for this time. Her eyes gave him yes, and drifted high toward the hill.

He would go now. He tugged on her hand.

"Tomorrow morning," she said, counting on another day of fog, and pulled her hand away.

He was there, before the dawning, perhaps all the night. She walked up the hill in the dark, having slipped out of her warm bed in the Widow's house, having flung on her skirt and shawl—barefoot over the wet ground and the cold rocks, up the far shoulder of the hill, among the cairns, that side furthest from the sight of the village. The sea crashed at the foot of the hill, drowning all small sounds. The fog occasionally became leaden droplets. A shadow waited for her among the waist-high cairns.

What if it should be Ciag? she thought in fear, and knew by that fear which brother she chose, and that she had long since chosen. It was not Ciag: she knew Marik's stature, tall and strong—knew the touch of his callused hands, his warmth, looked into his face in the dark and came into his shadowy arms as into a haven safe and longed-for.

He spoke her name—Mila, Mila, over and over, like a song. She kissed him silent and stayed still a time, where she wanted to be.

"What of Ciag?" she asked then sadly. "What of him?"

"What of Ciag?" he echoed in a hard-edged voice.

"He'll be alone," she said. "I want him for my friend, Marik." She felt Marik's body within her arms breathe out a sigh as if he had feared all his life and gave up fear forever.

"He'll mend in time. He'll hold our children and sit by our fire and forget his temper. He's my brother. He'll forgive."

"Shall I marry you?" she asked.

"Will you?"

She would. She nodded against him, kissed him, full of warmth. "But don't tell Ciag. I will." She thought that this was right, though it was the bravest thing she had ever thought to do.

"I will," said Marik.

That was a claim she gladly gave place to.

There was no sound there but the sea. The sun rose on them twined in each other, and rose more quickly, more treacherously quickly than they would have believed, sunk as they were in love. There was the dull roar of sea and wind, wind to take the fog; there was the night and suddenly light; and they hastened back, going separate paths, different directions to the village in headlong flight. The light grew as the wind and sun stripped away the mist, so that it was possible to tell color. The traitor goats were bleating in their pens, and Mila could see below the hill a figure waiting.

Marik's trail led down first: she saw him reach that place and pause; saw the two youths stare at each other face to face. She shrank down against the rocks, not wanting to be seen, not daring—waited there, cold and shivering while the light grew and the village stirred to life—until she realized to her distress that with people awake there was no hope of coming unseen back to the village.

She walked back up the hill and down again by yet another trail. When anxious searchers found her, she was walking along the rocks below the cairns, her feet quite chilled, her skirts made a pocket, full of shellfish. "I couldn't sleep," she told the grim-faced men and women who had turned out searching for her. Beyond their faces she saw—her heart stopped—Marik and Ciag both, faces hard and not at all bewildered by her behavior. Other faces among the crowd grew frowns, suspecting; the youngest stayed puzzled.

She must walk past Ciag and Marik both in returning to the village among her would-be rescuers—must hug the Widow when she had dumped her shellfish at the porch; and the Widow held her back then and looked at her in the eyes—looked deep and wisely, as if she knew something of her shame.

So did others. There were whispers in the village that day, whispers from which she had been safe all her life till now—whispers which blamed her, and both brothers. The brothers glowered and said nothing. There was a fight by the nets, and Agil's eldest son had a broken tooth and Ciag a gashed hand, both the brothers against the three strong sons of Agil.

The girls and women whispered too, more viciously. The Widow held her peace, waiting, perhaps, on Mila to speak, which Mila would not, could not. Mila took the goats up the hill the next morning and sat frowning at the ground and staring out at the sea, which was gray as the skies were gray, and bristling with the roughness of winter winds.

Gifts resumed on the morrow, both brothers in full view of the village. That turned the gossip to amazement, and in some hearts, to bitter jealousy, because Marik and Ciag were the handsomest and richest young men in the village, and deeply, forlornly, the young girls had had hope of one or the other of them. *Witchery*, they whispered at their mending, hating Mila. And the women recalled drowned mother, drowned father, and bastardy. *The sea's bastard*, rumors ran the louder. *Ill luck*, Agil's eldest son murmured among the young men, to salve the hurt of his broken tooth; and Agil himself repeated it in council, until the whole village was miserable.

Mila wept, and waited for Marik to do something. The look in Ciag's eyes these days was unbearable; and she imagined that Marik might after all have talked to him. Perhaps it was now for her, to refuse Ciag's gifts, but she did not know.

The sea roughened, shivering in winter, and the waves came high up the shore. The slighter boats did not launch at all. The brothers went out day by day, defying the waves, giving the best they caught—poor in this season—to Mila, neglecting their own parents, who walked sorrowful and shamed amid the gossip of the village.

On a certain day, storm boded, and no boats put out at all. The men huddled in the hall, mourning over the weather.

But Marik went down to the boats and stared out at the sea; and Ciag joined him there. "Will you go out?" Ciag asked; he spoke little to Marik, because he was bitter with his brother, who had told him the truth: let Mila refuse me herself, Ciag had said; and because he loved Ciag, Marik was caught between. Now—*"Dare you go?"* Ciag asked again; and Marik felt the sting of challenge, which of them was the better man, which of them dared more for Mila's gift.

"Aye," Marik answered, and set his shoulder to the boat. The *two* of them heaved her out, ignoring the black cloud which lay in the east of Fingalsey. Marik went for his reasons, that his pride was stung; and Ciag went for his, which were dark and bitter—while the sea sang with voices long unheard on Fingalsey.

That was dawning. By noon, there was dire foreboding in the village, because there was one boat out, and they all knew whose. By afternoon the rain had begun, and winds drove the waves higher, sending white breakers against the rocks at Fingal's Head.

Evening came, and folk gathered at the brothers' door, in the wind and driving rain, to bestow their pity on the brothers' hearrtsick parents. But the Widow did not come, while Mila—Mila huddled between the houses and against the wall, and listened to the gossip of the gathered crowd, shivering in the rain and lightning.

Then, in full dark, a walker came up the shore, amid the howling of the wind-racked sea—a man dark and draggled and reeling with exhaustion, from across the Head.

Mila ran first to meet him, caught his icy arms and looked into Ciag's haggard white face. "Marik?" she asked, striking him to the heart. His eyes took on a wild look.

"Drowned," he said.

The villagers closed about, parents seized on Ciag, who flinched from their arms and their eyes, who babbled a tale of a great swelling wave and a struggle to fight the currents which drove their boat. The wind howled over his voice. The rain drove down; and they bore him shuddering and sobbing toward his parents' house and hearth—"Mila?" he asked. "Mila?"

"Send for Mila," his father said.

But Mila had run from out the village and down the shore in the night and the drenching wind, by paths she knew in the dark, along the rocks, in the crash of spray.

There was a place the currents brought all wrecks and flotsam, the finest shells, and once, in the old, unlucky days, the bodies the sea was willing to give back—a place where fanged rocks broke the waves and the sea swirled back into a recess of calmer water. Mila fled there, among rocks awash with spray and the fangs backspilling white torrents under the lightnings.

There, beached, on its side, lay the brothers' boat.

She reached it, looked inside, ran her hands over the undamaged wood, her heart broken by sudden surmise. The seas crashed in her ears, her eyes were blurred with salt spray and tears. She looked out-ward, where the crags called the Teeth broke the white spray—looked over her shoulder villageward, for far away on the wind came voices hailing her: the villagers hailing her, she reckoned—and then not, for these voices sang, rising and falling in the wind, and one of them she knew.

"Marik?"

She stepped out into the sea, struggled amid the surge and the wreck, knee-deep, hip-deep, battered by the waves. She found that re-cess where dead men beached, hating what she came to find, and bound to find it. The voices wailed—low and human ones among them, the vil-lagers certainly, seeking her, wanting her back. She struggled the harder in the surge, drenched in cold rain and the colder breakers of the sea, her feet faltering on rocks which tore numb flesh.

She found him, in the lightnings and the heaving of the waves, a drifting white figure, face-down. She cried aloud and fought toward him, her skirts swept by the sea. She was no longer cold. The sea ca-ressed and did not bruise. The rain enveloped her like a veil of ice. She was numb with grief.

He was naked—surely he had cast off every hindrance to try to breast the waves; but the currents were treacherous here and the rocks were cruel and sharp. He had struggled to live, and Ciag had lost him—but not lost the boat, *not* the precious boat, the boat which brought Ciag home. She reached Marik's body, thrown to and fro by the surge which swept him too, his white limbs loose, his dark hair that spread in the water like weed—she held her dead close and wept, hearing the singing of the wind.

The body moved gently to the rocking waves, moved—suddenly with will and life, writhed over in her arms, head turning. The eyes were dark and vast in Marik's face; the streaming hair flowed with the cur-rents; the skin was white and no less cold. Dead arms enfolded her, dead lips parted to kiss, and the teeth were razor-sharp, a mouth ribbed and cool and tasting of kelp and sun-warmed sea.

"*Mila!*" she heard call distantly.

Lips clung, teeth pierced, and all the green thunder of the sea roared through her veins. Lips clingingly parted, and cold arms fell away, lithe white body arched to cleave the surge, to flash away with a pale glimmering among the black waves, lost at once in darkness and depths.

Other voices whispered, murmured. Hands touched her feet, her legs beneath the water, fingers tugged at her skirts; voices sang—and touch and voices vanished together at the next outward surge of the waves.

"*Mila!*" Ciag's hoarse voice cried, from somewhere up on the rocks above. Other voices joined his: "*Mila!*" and rocks crashed and bounced down into the pools with white splashes, from Ciag's reckless course downhill. He floundered out to her, embraced her in hot arms, carried her from the tidepool, himself yielded to the hands of the young men who had dared follow him. Other hands lifted Mila, carried her and him to solid land, chafed her cold flesh and his. Seaweed was tangled about her, and blood and the taste of the sea was on her lips. She shut her eyes to the gray and the dark and saw only sunwarmed green.

They carried her back to the Widow's house. She lay listlessly beneath many blankets, sipped at soup the Widow poured between her unresisting lips, turned her face from Ciag when he knelt by her bed and pressed her hand. A succession of staring faces that night—Ciag's always—and the Widow's—voices which whispered about her, and she could not hear; but she had heard such whispers before and cared nothing for them.

Then the storm passed and the day came, gray and cold. She rose up from her bed against the Widow's protest, walked out into the village. The place was deserted: all of them were up the hill at the making of Marik's—empty—cairn, among the others, on the hill's unhallowed left. She walked up the path and watched them at their work. Others moved away, but Ciag came and took her listless hand.

She gazed at the cairns; and Ciag softly lied—how Marik had been thrown from the boat when they came in among the rocks, how he had tried to save his brother. Mila turned on Ciag a face open and heartless, and drew back her hand, walked away down by the sea, in the roar of the rocks and the peace.

Ciag came down to her and dragged her back by the hand, while all the villagers stared and muttered—brother against brother, and the evil plain to see.

Mila came back and stood silent, went back to the village when they went, and surrendered to the Widow's care. She ate, listlessly, listlessly lay abed at evening; but when night came full and the Widow slept, she rose up and slipped out again in her shift, in the bitter cold, to walk along the shore, the lefthand way, below the cairns. She walked by the sea's edge in the tide pools, sat on a stone, gazing out to sea, and the waters, liquid black, reflected a pallid moon.

So Ciag found her at dawn, and desperately took her hand. She turned on him a soulless smile and pulled away. Perhaps it was the place that daunted him. He stood. She walked away singing, but not the songs she had once sung—loose and tuneless, her singing now, like the sea.

Villagers shied from her path. Barelimbed in her white shift she walked beside the boats and the nets. The Widow brought her a black shawl, brought her into the house, fed her and warmed her and dressed her in widow's black. Mila stroked her own red hair and sat drowsing until the warmth wearied her. Then she remembered the goats and went out again, but someone else had taken them to pasture.

She walked, singing her wild, wordless tune, and the winds played merrily among her black skirts, the fringes of her shawl, the strands of her bright hair. She hummed to herself, and fished by the rocks, and at times saw Ciag following. She ran finally, lightly eluding him—sat high among the cairns, among the black goats. The child watching them fled, leaving the place, and her.

Ciag came, spoke to her madly, forlornly, and she stared through him, walked away, leaving the goats to stray where they would.

"*Mila!*" he cried, as he had cried that night.

She walked among the cairns and back down to the shore, and so to the village, among the hull-up boats, singing to herself, listening to the sea.

There was, that day, a second drowning: Agil's eldest son, fishing off the rocks, and no body washed ashore. Another cairn rose on the leftward side.

And on the day after that, Agil's grieving wife drowned herself, so that there was another.

All the while the stones went into place on the hilltop there was the faint fair singing that was Mila, off along the rocks. The villagers did not speak of it—or of Ciag, absent from them. The luck had gone from Fingalsey, and they knew it.

Ciag knew, and kept his lonely boat near the shore, on the fair days when he went out alone. It rocked, at times, out of time with wind and waves. Motions touched it which chilled his heart. Ripples passed round it, and splashes sounded when his back was turned.

Untroubled, Mila walked the shore, walked the hills, sat among the cairns—by twilight walked the shore, when the last boats had come in.

He was there by night—*he*—the white shape beneath the darkling green: she bent low above the waters, reached fingers to pallor which might have been her own image, which vanished with the breaking of the surface. Bubbles swirled on the eddies, broke, vanished, the white shape gone, like a dream.

So all the days passed, one to the next. Only Ciag brought her gifts, his poor catches, from which she walked away, distractedly—and wherever she walked in the village the children shied away and the goats looked at her from wise slit eyes over the bars of the pen.

"I'll marry her," Ciag said to the Widow, as if that settled things.

"Ask her," the Widow said, staring at him from eyes wise as the black goats'.

He did, and Mila stared through him and stirred the pot she had been set to stir, for she did such simple tasks for the Widow, moving without thought.

"She will not," the Widow said.

From that day Ciag grew desperate, spying on her when she would walk by the sea, never far from her—until all the village whispered in fear, not alone of her, but of Ciag. The winter winds blew and the waters heaved: no one ventured to sea, but two children drowned shell-hunting among the rocks, when the high surge ripped at the land. Storm drove at them, a great black wall of cloud coming far across the sea, and the mourning village shut its doors, its dead unfound, at twilight.

The wind came, the waves crashed on the shore for hours before the gale, and battered at the land. Boats which had always been safe were torn loose and threatened, and young men ran to save them.

Mila walked, along the shore. The rail had broken at the goats' pen. The beasts scampered free, on this side and on that of her, and up the hill, to huddle shivering and bleating among the cairns, staring after her, on the path which led to Fingal's Head, to the Teeth, and the sea.

The air was full of spray. The waves thundered and streamed white off the rocks. She walked a dream, in which the cold was warmth, the night was clear, the curtains of wind-borne spray caressed her and desired. The voices in the sea sang siren-songs, male and female choruses. Her feet found the remembered rocks, her blinded eyes sought wraiths in the surge and the backspill. Knee-deep, hip-deep, tuggings of the surge at her skirts, and the voices singing.

She fell down into the green thunder, a stinging flood into lungs and eyes and ears until the sea was all. Gentle hands reached out for her, pale limbs flashed, and *he* wrapped her close in his arms and bore her down.

There was no more pain. Cold arms and dark eyes, hair adrift like seaweed, and the beauty of him, the pale, chill beauty—she began to move, swifter, surer, pacing him, with a twisting torrent of pale bodies spiraling about them both in the green waters—large, deep eyes, delicate, jointed lips, and razor teeth that sparkled like shards of ice, hair flowing like torrents of shadow and pallor, dark and bright, mingling, as hers with his. Familiar faces, child-faces and old faces and faces she had never seen—father and drowned mother and kindred, all the lost souls of Fingalsey. . . .

And he—holding her fast. She laughed, and swept the currents, one with them and with him, her large eyes seeing the sea as she had never dreamed it, heart swelling with what she had never felt. She joined the song, loving the cold and the power of it.

She was there—at dawn Ciag found her pale, naked body face down among the rocks, her red hair flowing about her like some strange anemone. "Help," he cried to the villagers who lined the cliff in the foggy dawn. "Help me!"—because she was far out among the rocks, and her dead weight filled his arms.

But the Widow walked away, and his mother and his father, casting down their torches like falling stars, trailing smoke and fire into the sea; and one by one the others did so, deserting him, and her.

Ciag wept. He had loved her. He clung to her in the sea. The roar filled his ears, the white spray breaking on the Teeth hit the wind and drenched him even here.

Something touched him, beneath the water. Not the current, but small tuggings at his clothes, nips at his ankles when he must catch his balance in the water. He refused to let her go, held to her, struggled waist-deep in the surge.

She turned in his arms; white arms reached and enfolded, vast eyes stared into his, sea-dark; lips touched his, chill, and teeth razory-fine— a taste of sun and sea . . .

All the green depths—parted from him. The slim white body arched away, scattering drops of sea, a glimmering in the dark waters swifter than sight.

The voices laughed in the wind, and the taste lingered, blood and sea-wrack.

"Brother," one called.

He followed.

WILLOW

Seven days he had been riding, up from the valley and the smoke of burned fields, and down again with the mountain wall at his back, a winding trail of barren crags and eagles' perches, gray sere brush and struggling juniper. The horse he rode plodded in sullen misery, gaunt and galled. His armor was scarred with use and wanted repair he neglected to give it; that was the way he traveled, outward from the war, from his youth which he had lost there and his service which he had left.

Dubhan was his name, and far across the land in front of him was his home, but the way looked different than it had looked ten years ago. He remembered fields and villages and the sun on the mountains when he rode up to them, when the horse was young, his colors bright and his armor gleaming as he rode up to the duke's service—but now when the winding trail afforded sometime glimpses of the plains, they seemed colorless. It was the season, perhaps; he had come in a springtime. He rode out in a summer's ending, and that might be the reason, or the color might have been in his eyes once, when he had been easily deceived, before the old duke had taught him the world, and the lord he served changed lords, and knights who had defended the land drifted into plunder of it, and the towns fell, and the smokes went up and the fields were sown with bones and iron, and the birds hunted carrion in roofless cottages. Maybe the war had spilled beyond the mountains; maybe it had covered all the world and stripped it bare. It had taken him this long to remember what sunlit green he had seen here once, but no longer seeing it did not surprise him, as worse sights had ceased to surprise him. There were scars on him which had not been there that springtime ten years gone. He ached where the mail bore down on old wounds; pains settled knife-pointed into joints in nighttime cold and made him know what pains years ahead held, lordless and landless and looking—late—

for another lord, another place, and some more hopeful war while there was something left of vigor in his arm, some strength to trade on to put a roof over his head before he was too old, and too broken, and finally without hope. Bread to eat, a place to sleep, a little wine for the pains when it rained: that was what he rode out to find.

At one cut and another the nearer land lay spread below the rocks, dull tapestry of the tops of trees where the trail turned and some slide had taken away the curtaining scrub. The trees came nearer, and stretched farther as the trail wound down the mountainside, more of forest than he recalled. At such vantages he looked out and down, marking what he could of the road to come, all curtained below in trees and gray bush.

So he saw the birds start up, and drew in the horse so sharply that the old head came up and muscles tensed. A black beating of wings rose above the woods below, and hovered a time before settling back into that rough patterning of treetops elsewhere. He marked where, and moved the horse on, and got his battered shield out of its leather casing. He thought about his armor, regretting mending not done, and took his helmet from where it hung on his saddle, and kept toward the inside of the road whenever he came near some other open place, fearing some movement, some show of metal might betray him—prudence not of cowardice, but of cold purpose.

That was also the way of the war he had waged, that no one met friends on the road. He rode carefully, and thought about the sound of the horse's hooves and kept off bare stone where he could. He stalked that remembered location in the woods below with wolfish hope—of provisions, of which he was scant, and whatever else he could lay hand to. If they were many he would try to ride by; if one man—that was another matter.

The sun was sinking when he came to that lower ground. The woods held no color but a taint of bloody light beyond the dull leaves. The trees which had seemed small from above arched above the way, gnarled and dark and rustling with the wind. Something had disturbed the leaves and the brush which intruded onto the roadway: a broken branch gleamed white splinters in the twilight. He kept on the way, came on the fresh droppings of a horse, some beast better fed than his, from some other trail than he had followed.

A thin, high sound disturbed the air, a voice, a woman's—sudden silence. He reined close in, fixed the direction of the sound and rode farther. There was someone in the dark ahead who took no account of the noise she made; and someone there was who did. He drew his sword from its sheath with the softest whisper of metal, kneed the horse further, and it walked warily, ears pricked now, head thrust forward.

The trail forked sideways, and the leafy carpet was disturbed there, ruffled by some passage. He kneed the horse onto it, kept it walking. Fire gleamed, a bright point through the branches. Again the voice, female and distraught: a man's low laughter . . . and Dubhan's mouth stretched back from his teeth, a little harder breathing, a little grin which had something of humor and something of lust. His heart beat harder, drowning the soft whisper of the horse's moving through the brush—jolted at the sudden rise of a black figure before the light in front of him.

Two of them, or more. He spurred the horse, broke through the brush into the light, swung the sword and hacked the standing figure, saw one more start up from the woman's white body and wheeled the horse on him, rode him down and reined the horse about the circuit of the camp as two horses broke their picket and crashed off through the brush. The first man, wounded, came at him with a sword; he rode on him again and this time his blade bit between neck and shoulder, tumbled the armorless man into the dead leaves.

The woman ran, white flashing of limbs in the firelight. He jerked the horse's head over and spurred after, grinning for breath and for anticipation, reined in when she darted into the brush and the rocks—he vaulted down from the saddle and labored after, armor-burdened, in and out among the brush and the branches, with one thought now—some woman of the towns, some prize worth the keeping while she lasted, or something they had gotten hereabouts from the farms. He saw her ahead of him, naked among the rocks, trying to climb the shoulder of the mountain where it thrust out into the forest, white flesh and cloud of shadow-hair, shifting from one to the other foothold and level among the black stones. "Come down," he mocked her. "Come down."

She turned where she stood above him, and looked at him with her pale fingers clutching the rock on her right, her hair blowing about her body. Looked up again, where the rocks became an upward thrust, a wall, unclimbable. "Come down to me," he called again. "I'm all the choice you have."

She made a sign at him, an ancient one. The fingers let go the rock—a blur of white through shadow, a cry, a body striking the rocks. She sprawled broken and open-eyed close by him, and moisture was on his face and his hands. He wiped at his mouth and stood shuddering an instant, swore and stalked off, blood cooled, blood chilled, a sickness moiling at his gut.

Waste. A sorry waste. No one to see it, no one to know, no one that cared for a trifle like that, to be dead over it, and useless. A little warmth, a little comfort; there was not even that.

He found his horse, bewildered and lost in the brush, took its reins and led it back to the fire where he hoped for something of value, where two dead men lay in their blood; but the horses had run off in the dark and the woods.

There was food, at least; he found that in the saddlebags by the fire, and chewed dried beef while he searched further. There were ordinary oddments, bits of leather and cord and a pot of salve; and wrapped in a scrap of dirty cloth—gold.

His hands trembled on the heavy chalice-shape in unveiling it, trembled; and he laughed and thought about his luck which had been wrong all his life until now. Gold. He rummaged the other saddlebags, hefting them and feeling the weight with his heart pounding in his chest. Out of one came a second object wrapped in cloth, which glittered in the firelight, and weighed heavy in his hands. A cross. Church plunder. They had gotten to that in the last stages.

He let it down with a wiping of his hands on his thighs, gnawed his lip and gathered it up again, shoved it into one bag. Then he snatched another bit of the beef, swallowing the last . . . found a wine flask by the fire and washed it down. He knelt there staring thoughtfully at the dead face of the first man, which lay at an odd angle on a severed neck. Familiarity tugged at him . . . someone he had seen before; but in ten years he had seen many a man on both sides, and bearded, dead and dirty faces tended to look much alike. He drank deeply, warmed the death from his own belly, got up to tend his horse and paused by the other corpse, the one the horse had trod down.

Then familiarity did come home to him . . . long, long years, that he had known this man. Bryaut, his name was, Bryaut Dain's-son; young with him; afraid with him in his first battle; wounded in another . . . ways parted in the war and came together again here, tonight. Of a sudden the wine was sour in his mouth. He could have ridden in on the camp and Bryaut would have welcomed him. Not many men would, in these days; but this man would have. If there had been friends in his service—this was one, a long time ago, and mostly forgotten; but there was the face, no older than his, and blond, and with that scar down the brow he had gotten at Lugdan, when he himself had gotten the one on his jaw, where the beard would not grow.

He swore, and was ashamed in front of that dead face with its eyes looking sideways toward the fire, as if it had stopped paying attention. There was a time they had talked about winning honor for themselves, he and this young man no longer young, wealth and honor. And then he laughed a sickly laugh, thinking of the church-robbing and the woman and what an end it had come to, the war and the things they had planned and the reasons they had had for going to it at all. Bright treasure and fine armor and a station close to a king; and it came all to this. Church gold and a cold woman. He tipped up the wine flask and drank and walked away, thinking with a wolf's wariness that there had been too much noise and too much firelight and that it was time to go.

He was wiser than Bryaut, and maybe soberer. He packed the gold and the food and the things he wanted onto his horse and climbed into the saddle with the flask in his hand . . . rode off slowly, leaving the fire to die on its own, with the dead eyes staring on it. When he slept finally, it was in the saddle, with the flask empty; and the horse staggered to a stop and stood there till he mustered the strength to climb down and shelter in the brush.

There he slept again in his armor, his sword naked across his knees—dreamed, of towns burning and of dead faces and naked white limbs plunging past him; waked with an outcry, and shuddered to sleep again.

Dreamed of a church, and fire, and a priest nailed to his own chapel door.

Lugdan and the mindless push of bodies, the battering, hours-long thunder of metal and human voices; and the silence after—the empty, feelingless silence—

A stone-walled room with candles burning, a gleam of gold on the altar, the chalice brimming full, the solemn sweet chanting of voices echoing out of his youth. The Lady Chapel, the blue-robed statue with painted eyes, hands offering blessings for all who came . . . The silence fell here too, taking away the voices, and the candles went out in the wind.

The stones became jumbled, and the wind blew, scattering smoke-black hair across pale features. The silence shrilled asunder, the shriek of the woman, the white limbs falling. . . .

He cried out, and the horse started and shied off through the thicket, stopped when the brush stopped it and he scrambled after it cursing, still dazed with sleep and dreams, scratched by brush across his face and hands.

Daylight had pierced the canopy of leaves. He retrieved his sword and sheathed it, checked the girth, dragged himself back into the saddle and rode on, on a trail narrower than he recalled. A bird sang, incongruous in the shadow where he traveled, under the arch of branches, some bird sitting where the sun touched the tops of the trees, some bird seeing something other than the dead brush and old leaves and the contorted trunks; and he hated it. He spurred the horse at times where the road was wider, pushed it until the froth flew back on his knees and its bony sides heaved when he let it walk. He spurred it again when he saw daylight beyond, and it ran from dark to light, slowed again, panting, under the sun, where the forest gave way to open grass and brush, and the road met another road from the west.

It was not the way that he remembered. He traveled with the sun on his back, warming now until sweat ran under the armor and prickled in the hollows of his body and struck his padding to his sides and arms and thighs. By afternoon the way led downward again, into yet another valley, and by now he knew himself lost. There were signs of man, a boundary stone, a mark of sometime wheels on the narrow road, which wended two ways from a certain point—one which tended, wheel-rutted, west, and one which tended easterly, overgrown with grass, snaking toward a distant rim of woods.

He had no heart now for meetings, for braving alone the farmers who would have feared him if he had come with comrades. A knight alone might have his throat cut and worse if the peasants had their chance at him. He had seen the like. It was the eastward way he chose, away from humankind and homes, only wanting to go through the land and to find himself somewhere the war had never been, where no one had heard of it or suffered of it, where he could melt down his gold and pass it off bit by bit, find a haven and a comfort for the rest of his years.

Sometimes he would sleep as he rode, his head sinking forward on his chest while his hand, the reins wrapped about his fingers, rested behind the high bow. The horse plodded its way along, stole mouthfuls from brush along the track, dipped its head now and again to snatch at the grass which pitching movements woke him, and he would straighten his back at waking, and feel relieved at the daylight still about him. He dreamed of fire and burnings; those had been his dreams for months. He no longer started awake out of them, only shivered in the sweat-prickling sun and listened to the ordinary sounds of leather and metal moving, and the whisper of the grass and the cadence of the hooves. He tried not to sleep, not for dread of the dreams, but because of the road and the danger; but the sounds kept up, and the insects sang in the late summer sun, and try as he would his head began to nod, and his eyes to close, not for long, for a little time: the horse was only waiting its chance for thefts, and it would wake him.

A downward step jolted him, a sudden sinking of the horse's right shoulder, a splash of water about the hooves at every move. He lifted his head in the twilight haze and saw green slim leaves about him, weeping branches and watery waste closely hemmed with trees and brush. Mud sucked, and the horse lurched across the low place, wandered onto firmer grass.

Dubhan turned in the saddle, looking for the path, but the brush was solid behind, and the place looked no different in that direction, closed off with trees trailing their branches into the scummed water, mazed with heaps of brush and old logs and pitted with deeper pools. Willow fingers trailed over him as the horse kept its mindless course—he faced about and fended the trailers with his arm, and the horse never slowed, never hesitated, as if it had gone mad in its exhaustion, one step and the other through the sucking mud and the shallow pools. The light was going; the sky above the willow tangle was bloodied cream, the gloom stealing through the thickets and taking the color from willow and water bit by bit, fading everything to one deadly deceptive flatness. He tugged at the reins and stopped the horse, but no sooner did he let the reins slack than the horse tugged for more rein and started moving again its same slow way, never faltering but for footing in the marsh, patient in its slow self-destruction. Frogs sang a numbing song. The water gurgled and splashed about the hooves and a reek of corruption went up from the mud, cloying. The water wept, a strange liquid sound. He pulled again at the reins, and the horse—instantly responsive in battle—ignored the bit and tugged back, going madly on. He wrapped his hand the tighter in the rein and hauled back with his strength against it, forcing the beast's head back against its chest, and then he could stop it . . . but whenever he let the rein loosen, it took its head again, and bent its head this way and that against the force he brought to bear; he hauled its head aside and faced it about to confuse it from its course, but it kept turning full circle, feet sliding in the mire, and came back again to force a few steps more. He cursed it, he cajoled it, the old horse he had ridden young to the war, he reminded it of days past and the time to come, some better land, some warm shelter against the winter, no more of fighting, no more of sleeping cold. But the horse kept moving in the colorless twilight, with the sky gone now to lowering gray, and the water weeping and splashing in the silence.

Something touched his eyes, like cobweb, crawled on his face and hands. He waved his hand, and the cloud came about him, midges started up from the reeds and the water; they crawled over his skin, buzzed about his ears, investigated the crack of his lips and settled into his eyes and his ears and were sucked up his nose. The horse snorted and threw its head, moved faster now, and Dubhan flailed about him with his free hand, wiped his eyes and blew and spat, blinded, inhaling them, clinging to the horse as the horse lashed its tail and shook itself and pitched into a lurching run. Branches whipped past, raked at Dubhan, and he tucked down as much as he could, clung to the reins and saddle and clenched his hand into the war-horse's shorn mane, shorn so no enemy could hold; and now he could not, and reeled stunned and bruised when a branch hit his shoulder and jolted him back against the cantle and the girth. The horse staggered and slid in the mud, recovered itself, feet wide-braced, head down.

Then the head came up and the legs heaved and the horse waded fetlock deep, slowly, on its winding course, while the sobbing sounded clearer than before. Dubhan clung, wiped at his eyes with one hand, body moving to the relentless moving of the beast he rode. He crossed himself with that hand, and remembered what he had in the saddle-bags—a memory too of painted eyes, and fire and darkness, voices silenced. Fear gathered in his gut and settled lower and sent up coils that knotted about his heart. His hand no longer fought the reins . . . no hope now of going back, in that mad course he had no idea which way they had turned, or how far they had come. He had faith now only in the horse's madness, that terror might be driving it, that his brave horse which had charged at the king's iron lines might be running now, and it might in its madness get him through this place if only it could walk the night through and not leave him afoot here and lost. He talked to it, he patted its gaunt neck, he pleaded; but it changed its going not at all, neither faster nor slower, though the breath came hollow from its mouth and its shoulders were lathered with sweat.

They passed into deeper shadow, under aged willows, through curtains of branches which trailed cutting caresses and kept night under their canopies, back into twilight and into night again, and the sobbing grew more human, prickling the hairs at Dubhan's nape and freezing the life from his hands and feet. It became like a child's weeping, some lost soul complaining in the night; it came from left and right and behind him, from above, in the trees, and from before. There was no sound but that; it wrapped him about. And suddenly in a prickling of apprehension he turned in the saddle and jerked free the saddlebag, tore it open and flung out the cup and the cross, which spun with a cold gleaming through the curtain of willow branches and struck the black water with a deep sound, swallowed up. The horse never ceased to move. He turned about again in time to fend the branches, sweating and cold at once. The gold was gone. It bought him nothing; the sobbing was before him now, and above, a gleam of pallor in the gnarled willow-limbs of the next tree, a shadow-fall of hair. He saw a ghost, and drove spurs into the horse.

The beast flinched, and stopped, panting bellowslike between his legs, head sinking. He looked up into the branches and the gleam of flesh was gone—looked down and beside him and a white figure with shadow-hair moved the willow branches aside—all naked she was, and small . . . and came toward him with hands held out, a piquant face with vast dark eyes, a veil of hair that moved like smoke about white skin. The eyes swam with tears in the halflight of the night. The hands pleaded. The limbs were thin . . . a child's stature, a child's face. He dug the spurs at the horse to ride past as he had ridden past the war's abandoned waifs: it was their eyes he saw, their pleading hands, their gaunt ribs and matted hair and swollen bellies naked to the cold; but the horse stayed and the small hands clutched at his stirrup and the face which looked up to him was fair.

"Take me home," she asked of him. "I'm cold."

He kicked the stirrup to shake her fingers loose. She started back and stood there, her hair for a veil about her breasts if she had any, her body white and touched with shadow between the thighs like another whiteness in the dark, among the rocks; but these eyes were live and they stared, bruised and dark with fear.

"Was it you," he asked, "crying?"

"I gathered flowers," she said. "And men came." She began to cry again, tiny sobs. "I was running home."

His belief caught at that kind of story, held onto it double-fisted, an ugly thing and the kind of thing the world was, that made of the girl only a girl and the marsh only a river's sink and some homely place of safety not far from here. Slowly his hand reached out for her. She came and took it, her fingers cold and weak in his big hand; he gained his power to move and caught her frail wrist with the other hand, hauled her up before him—no weight at all for his arms. The horse began to move before she was settled; he adjusted the reins, tucked her up against him and her head burrowed against his shoulder, her arms going about his neck. His hand about her ribs felt not bone but softness swelling beneath his fingers, smooth skin; his eyes looking down saw a dark head and a flood of shadowy hair, and the rising moon played shadow-tricks on the childish body, rounded a naked hip, lengthened thighs and cast shadows between. Her body grew warm. She shifted and moved her legs, her arms hugging him the tighter, and the blood in him grew warm. Willow branches trailed over them with the horse's wandering and he no more than noticed, obsessed with his hands which might shift and not find objection to their exploring, with a thin body the mail kept from him, kept him from feeling with his.

It was a child's clinging, a child's fear; he kept the hands still where they were, on naked back and under naked knees, and patted her and soothed her, with a quieter warming in his blood that came from another human body in the night, a child's arms that expected no harm of him; and he gave none—should not be carrying double on the horse, his numbed wits recollected. He ought to get down and lead, the child sitting in the saddle, but the horse moved steadily and she seemed no weight at all on him, slept now, as it seemed, one arm falling from his neck to lie in her lap, delicate fingers upturned in the moonlight like some rare waterflower. Moonlight lay bright beyond the branches; the horse walked now on solid ground. The branches parted on a road, flat and broad, and he blinked in sleep-dulled amazement, not remembering how that had started or when they had come on it.

Hills shadowed against the night sky, a darkness against the stars: a mass of stone hove up before that, on the very roadside, placed like some wayside inn, but warlike, blockish, tall, a jumble of planes and shadow, far other than the woodcutter's cottage he had imagined.

"Child," he whispered. "Child. Is this your home?"

She stirred in his arms, another shifting of softness against his fingers, looked out into the dark between the horse's ears. "Yes," she breathed.

"There are no lights."

"They must be abed."

"With you lost?" A servant's child, perhaps, no one of consequence to the lords of the place; but then a lord who cared little for his people— he had served such a lord, and fought one, and lost himself. Apprehension settled back at his shoulders, but the horse plodded forward and the stone shadow loomed nearer in the moonlight, not nearly so large as it had seemed a moment ago, a tower, a mere tower, and badly ruined.

Some woodcutter after all, it might be, some peasant borrowing a former greatness, settling himself in tower's shell. The child's arms went again about his neck. He gathered the small body close to him for his own comfort. Exhaustion hazed his wits. The keep seemed now large again, and close. He had no memory of the horse's steps which had carried them into the looming shadow of the place, up to the man-sized stones, up to the solid wooden door.

He hugged the child against him, and then as she stirred, set her off, himself got down from the saddle, his knees buckling under his own mailed weight. She sought his hand with both of hers, and in her timid trust he grew braver. He walked up the steps leading her and slammed his fist against the ironbound oak, angered by their sleeping carelessness inside, that owed a lost child shelter and owed her rescuer—something, some reward. The blows thundered. He expected a stir, a flare of lights, a hailing from inside, even the rush of men to arms.

But the door gave back suddenly, swinging inward, unbarred or never barred. He thrust the child loose from his hand in sudden dread, drew his sword, seeing the gleam of light in the crack as he pushed the door with his shoulder, sending the massive weight farther ajar. A night fire burned in the hearth of a great fireplace, the only light, flaring in the sudden draft. He felt behind him for the child, half fearing to find her gone, felt a naked shoulder. The horse snorted, a soft, weary explosion in the dark at his back, ordinary and unalarmed. He walked in. The child followed and slipped free, pushed the door to with a straining of her slight body. "I'll find Mother," she said. "She'll be sleeping."

"No longer." He struck with his naked sword at a kettle hanging from a chain against the wall; it clattered down and rolled across the flags with a horrid racket. "Wake! Where are the parents of this child?"

"Child," the echoes answered. "Child, child, child."

"Mother?" the girl cried. He reached too late to stop her. She darted for the stairs which wound up and out of sight, built crazily toward the closed end of the high ceiling. "Girl," he called after her, and those echoes mingled with those of "Mother?" and likewise died, leaving him alone.

He retreated toward the door, shifted his grip on the swordhilt to pull the door open again and look outside, wary of ambushes, of a mind now to be away from this place. His horse still stood, cropping the grass in the moonlight.

Footsteps creaked on the stairs. The child came running down again as he whirled about, the naked body clothed now in a white shift. She came to him, caught his hand with hers. "Mother says you must stay," she said, wide dark eyes looking up into his. "She was afraid. We're all alone here, mother and I. She was afraid to let it seem anyone lived here. The bandits might come. Please stay; please be careful of my mother, please."

"Child?" he asked, but the hands broke from his and she ran, a flitting of white limbs and white shift in the dim firelight, vanishing up the stairs. He pushed the door gently, felt it close and looked back toward the fire—drew in his breath, bewildered. His exhausted senses had played him tricks again. About him the hall stretched farther than he had realized. The shadows and the fire's glare had masked a farther hall, which could not have appeared from the road. A table stood there, set with silver. Arms hung on the walls of that chamber, fighting weapons, not show.

A light flickered in the corner of his eye; he looked and saw a glow moving down the wall of the stairs . . . a woman came into his view, carrying a taper in her hand, and his heart lurched, for the child's beauty was nothing to hers. The woman's hair was a midnight cloud about her in her white shift and robe, her face in the candle's glow as translucent and pure as the wax gleaming in the heat, her body parting the strands of her hair with the full curves of breast and hip. Barefoot she walked down the wooden steps, her eyes wide with apprehension.

"You brought Willow home."

He nodded agreement and faint courtesy, the sword still naked in his hand. The woman came off the last step and walked to him, a vision in the candlelight, which shone reflected in her eyes with a great sadness.

"Willow's mad," she said in a voice to match her eyes. "Did you realize, sir? She runs out into the woods . . . I can't hold her at such times. Thank you for bringing her safe home again." Lashes swept a soft glance up at him. "Please, I'll help you with your horse, sir, and give you a place to sleep in the hall."

"Forgive me," he said, remembering his drawn sword. He reached for the sheath and ran it in, looked again at the lady. Food, shelter, the warmth of the hall. . . . *We're all alone*, the child had said. He looked at wide dark eyes and woman's body and delicate hands which clasped anxiously together about the candle—like Willow's hands, fine-boned and frail. He was staring. Heat rose to his face, a warmth all over. "I'll tend my horse," he said. "But I'd be glad of a meal and shelter, lady."

"There's a pen in back," she said. "We have a cow for milk. There's hay."

"Lady," he said, his brain still singing with warmth as if bees had lodged there and buzzed along his veins. He bowed, went out, into the dark, to take the reins of his horse and lead the poor animal around the curve of the tower—it *was* extended on the far side: he could see that now, from this new vantage. A byre was built against the wall, several pens, a sleepy cow who lurched to her feet in the moonlight and stood staring with dark bovine eyes. He led the horse in, gently unsaddled it, rubbed its galled and sweaty back with hands full of clean straw while the cow watched. He did his best for the horse, though his bones ached with the weight of armor and the ride. He hugged its gaunt neck when he was done, patted it, remembering a glossier feel to its coat, a day when bones had not lain so close to the skin. It bowed its head and nosed his ribs as it had done in gentler days before wars, before the hooves were shod with iron. It lipped his hand. The wide-eyed cow lowed in the dark, the moonlight on her crescent horns, and he pitchforked hay for them both, farmer's work, armored as he was, and made sure that there was water, then walked out the gate and latched it, walked around the curving stone wall, up the steps, opened the yielding door.

The fire inside was bright and red, the board in the recessed hall spread with bread and cold roast on silver plates and set with jugs of wine. He rubbed at his face, stopped, numb in the loss of time. He had dallied in the yard and the lady—the lady stood behind the table, spread her white-sleeved arms to welcome him to all that she had done.

He came and sat down in the tall chair, too hungry even to unburden himself of the armor, seized up a cup of dry red wine and drank, filled his mouth with fresh bread and honey and with the other hand worked at the straps at his side. Strength flooded back into him with a few mouthfuls. He looked up from his piggishness and saw her at the other end of the table with her dark eyes laughing at him, not unkindly.

Such manners he had gained in the wars. He had aspired to better, once. He stood up and rid himself of belt and sword, hung the weapon over the chair's tall finial, and she rose and moved to help him shed the heavy mail. That weight and heat passed from him and he breathed a great free breath, shed the sweat-soaked haqueton, down to shirt and breeches, fell into the chair again and ate his fill, off silver plates, drank of a jeweled cup—and paused, heart thumping as he turned it within his hand: the shape the same, the very same. . . .

But silver, not gold. He drained it, gazed into dark and lovely eyes beyond the candleglow. "Is there," he asked thickly, "no lord in this hall . . . no servant, no one—but you and the child?"

"The war," she said with that same sadness in her eyes. "I had a servant, but he stole most all the coin and ran away. The villagers beyond the hills . . . they'll not come here. Willow frightens them; and I'm frightened of them—for Willow's sake, you see."

"What of your lord?"

"The war," she said. "He's not come home."

"His name?"

"Bryaut."

His breath stopped in him. He looked about the hall beyond her shoulders for some crest, some device—there was none. "Not Dain's son—"

"You know him? You have news of him?"

"Dead," he said harshly. The lovely eyes filled with tears. The mouth trembled. "In the war," he said.

"Bravely?"

She asked that much. He stared past her, saw the trampled, half-naked man on the ground, the eyes slid unseeingly uninterested toward the campfire. Saw the boy he had known at Lugdan ford, the rain and the silence and the heaps of dead, raindrops falling in the bloody water. Men puking from exhaustion. A horse screaming, worse than any man. The fire again, and the forest, and rape. "Bravely," he said. "In battle. I saw him fall. His face toward the enemy. Five of them he took down; and they kept coming. We pushed them back too late for him. But he saved that day."

Tears fell. She pulled a handkerchief from her sleeve and blotted at her eyes. "You were his friend," she said.

"I knew him."

A second time she wiped at her eyes, and put on a smile greatly forced and sad. "You're twice kind."

"You'll be alone."

"Willow and I."

"I might stay a time."

She rose from the table. He got up from his place. "Please," she said. "I'll make you a bed." Her voice trembled. "You'll sleep the night and go your way in the morning."

"Lady—"

"In the morning." She turned away, toward the stairs, her unbound hair a cloud about her bowed head and shoulders. She turned back and looked at him where he stood staring after her. "Come."

She took a candle from its sconce, paused by the stairs. He unrooted his feet from where he stood and came after, cold inside from remembering Bryaut, bones crushed beneath the horse's hooves, and white flesh, Bryaut's possession; Bryaut, who had died half-naked and in such a moment—before or after? Dubhan wondered morbidly—to die like that and to be cheated too . . .

He followed her, up the narrow stairs designed for the tower's last defense, so narrow a wooden winding that his shoulders nearly filled the way side to side, and she must bend double to pass the doorway at the top, the candle before her. The light cast her body into relief, the shadow of a breast, of slim legs against the white linen, and he found his breathing harder than the climbing warranted—followed after into a hall where they could both stand upright, a wooden raftering, a maze among the timbers where the candle chased shadows, doors on either side.

She opened the first door and brought him within a room, touched her candle to another's stub—another flaring, another shadow through the loose linen gown—doubling the light, upon a pleasant wide bed with flowers on the table beside it. The linens were rumpled, the down mattress bearing the imprint of a body. "Mine," she said. "I'll make up the room next door for myself tonight. Rest. I'll bring you water for washing."

She came back to the doorway to pass him and leave, glanced down at such close quarters, denying him her eyes. "Lady," he said so that she would look up, and she did, close to him, almost touching body to body, and kept looking. He reached out his hand to the black cloud of her hair and stroked it because it was female and beautiful. The wine he had drunk sang in him, laid a haze on all else but her. He took her hand up, blew out the candle it held, rested both hands on her shoulders, on thin lines which eased downward, on smoothness and curving softness. "No," she said, and a weak hand pushed at him. He put his arms about her and drew him to her bed and sank down on the feathers and her gentle softness. "No," she said a second time, struggling under him, and he stopped her mouth with his, kissed her eyes, her smooth flesh. "*No*," she wept, screaming, and of a sudden the heat froze in him. He felt her heaving sobs and heard her, and saw that other, pale figure in the dark, the hurtling rush of limbs, dead eyes staring at the moon. He did not move for the moment. Her hands made pathetic gestures toward covering her nakedness. She pushed at him to be free. He got off her and drew her shift up about her, smoothed her hair. It in no wise mended the wanting; but the doing—

"You are my *guest*," she said. "In my hall. Let me go."

Her eyes glistened, dark and bright He had lost, he thought, lost everything with his rashness. Might take, still; her, the tower, the wealth downstairs. He might live here, with Willow's madness. Might have her too. He was strong and they could do nothing; could never drive him out. They would fear too much to lift a hand to him, and they would understand they were better off with him. No cold winters, no death on the road. Every evening she would serve him food on silver plates; and every night they would lie here where the linens smelled of rosemary and the bed was soft. He would ride into that village she named, gather men to build a gate and wall, levy taxes, fear nothing. . . .

"Let me go," she said. Not pleading. Not fearfully. Just like that—asking.

"Some man," he said, "will come down this road . . . and take it all from you. Your lord's not coming back. Think how it will be."

"Do you intend to take it from me?"

His hand lifted toward her hair. He touched it compulsively and stopped it short of her breast, drew it away. "I'd see you were safe."

"From you?"

"I'd not force you. Go out of here. Talk to me tomorrow. Will you do that?"

"If you wish. But if I say no?"

"Think of me. Think that I wish you well. Good *night*, lady."

She rose and slipped away, her white robe trailing past him, across the floor, toward the door, and closed it after. He got up, drew a great breath, drove his fist against the wooden wall and clutched it to him, eyes shut from the pain, from the madness, but the blood welled up there and in his arm and diminished that elsewhere, and he worked his bruised hand and paced the creaking floor until his heart had stopped pounding.

He washed then, in water she had used. The cool water from her bedside bowl smelled of lilies and numbed the pain of his hand, numbed the ache of his shoulders and his ribs and left him shivering. He stripped, and used the linen towels and found the chamberpot beneath the bed, crawled at last between the rosemary-smelling sheets marvelously clean and comforted, leaned out to blow out the candle and blinked in a dark which, accustomed as he was to the stars at night and the moon, seemed fearsomely dark indeed. But his eyes closed a time, and a smile settled on him as he rolled and settled amid the scented sheets, until he had found just that hollow which suited him, and rest closer than he would have thought a while ago.

A step creaked in the hall, outside: the boards were old. The Lady?

he wondered, dreaming dreams; the door opened, and the blackness was such that even lifting his head and looking, he could see nothing at all. A step crossed the boards, their creaking alone betraying its bare softness. A rustling of cloth attended it. "Who is it?" he asked, not entirely liking this dark and the visiting. A weight sank onto the foot of his bed and he jerked his foot from its vicinity realizing in one rush that sword and armor were downstairs, the cautions of a lifetime wine-muddled, woman-hazed. "Who? Lady?"

He moved to sit up all in a rush, but a gentle touch stole up his sheeted leg, a whisper of cloth leaned forward, and a woman's perfume reached him. "Lady?" he said again, beginning to have different thoughts. And then another, colder: "Or is it Willow?"

"We are three," the whisper came to him. "Mother, Maid—and me."

He thrust himself for the bedside. A grip caught his arm, a band like ice, burning chill that would not yield. He reached for that grip and met a hand soft-fleshed as age itself, frail-seeming, and strong. A like grip closed on the other arm, and the cold went inward, numbing breath, numbing heart, which beat in painful flutterings.

"*Man,*" the voice whispered, a breath of ice across his face, driving him backward and down. "*Man* . . . that you did not touch Willow in the marsh; well done; that you did not force my daughter; again well done; but that you forced a kiss of my daughter . . . *now* I repay: what's for one . . . is for all, like and like, Mother, Maid, and me."

He was drowning . . . felt a touch on his lips, an embrace about his limbs, and it was ice stealing inward. "No," he said, despairing. The white face came back to him, that despair, that flung itself from the rocks, cursing him. "No," he said again, colder still—Willow's face, and the starving children, the hollow-eyed, hollow-hearted children the war had made. A third time: "*No.*" It was the lady crying out, her outrage at a world that took no regard of her, where force alone availed; and himself, his, that comrades met and killed each other, and no force could mend what was and what had been. He had no strength now, none, only the anger and the grief, alone.

His shoulders struck the wooden floor; he sprawled, his senses beginning to leave him as his sight had done, and tears were freezing on his lashes, the moisture freezing on his lips so that he could open neither, sightless, speechless in the dark, void of all protest. Sense went last. He was not aware for what might have been a long time; and then he felt again, wood beneath his naked back, perceived a light through his lids, but still he could not open his eyes. A shadow bent above him, breath stirred across his face; soft lips kissed one eyelid and then the other, and lastly his mouth.

He looked on Willow, who crouched by him in her shift, holding a lighted candle, her arm about her knees.

"It's day," said Willow. "There's just no window here."

He dared no words. He rolled over and got up, ashamed in his nakedness, drew his clothing on under Willow's silent, dark-eyed stare. She had stood up. He walked for the door, turned the remembered way in haste down the creaking hall, through the low doorway and down the windings of the stairs in the dark—down into the main room of the keep, where wood moldered silver gray and cobwebs hung, the nests of spiders, fine spinnings in the daylight which sifted in through broken beams. His armor lay in the dust. He put it on, hands trembling, worked into the mail and did the buckles.

A step creaked on the stairs. He looked about. It was Willow coming down. He seized up the sword and belted it about him, and looked again, where the Lady stood in Willow's place.

The outside door gaped; the wood was gone. He ran for it, for the sunlight, around to the pen behind, where his horse cropped the green grass alone in a ramshackle enclosure, and his saddle and gear lay on the dewy ground. He saddled the horse in haste, climbed into the saddle and rode carefully past the keep, hearing the lowing of a cow at his back. That ceased. He blinked and Willow sat on a stone of the ruined wall, swinging her bare feet and waving at him. He spurred the horse past, reined back again with the feeling of something at his back. He looked to the doorway. The Lady stood there. She had a lily in her hair and her feet were bare. "Good journey," she wished him. "Farewell, sir knight."

He snapped the reins and rode quickly onto the road. A black, bent figure stood among the trees and brush on the far side of it, robed and hooded. The horse shied, trembling. Dubhan could see nothing but the robes, hoped for all the life that was in him that it would not look up, would not fling back the hood.

"Not yet," the voice came like the sighings of leaves. "You have years yet, sir knight."

He cracked the reins and rode. The sunlight warmed him finally, and the birds sang, until the chill melted from his gut where it had lain. He looked back, and there was only the forest.

When he had ridden a day, there was a village. He watered his horse there, and the townsfolk came shyly round him and asked the news. He told them about the war; and the king dead, and the duke; but they had never heard of either, and blinked and wondered among themselves. They gave him bread and ale, and grain for his horse, and he thanked them and rode away.

On that day he hung the sword from his saddle and carried it no more.

On the next he took off the armor and stowed it away, let the breeze to his skin, and rode through lands widely farmed, where villages lay across the road, open and unfearing.

They saw the weapons, the children of these villages, and asked him tales.

He made up dragons and unicorns. The children smiled.

In time, so did he.

▼

OF LAW AND MAGIC

▲

Between the Avenue of the Moon and the Avenue of Snow is a way named Fog; and the houses in this district are old and eclectic. The houses span centuries; they come slowly to respectability with the weathering of their brick and beams and their new paint into the brown conservatism and eccentricity of this district. Here is a house a mere three hundred years into its age, with the graceful towers that were the style of its day; here is another with the timbered construction of four hundred years ago; and a house of porches which were fashionable a mere one hundred years ago, pierced-wood lace which has weathered to a comfortable silver-brown; here is yet another of stone and brick, festooned with vines which try yearly to reach out to the wooden lace: but the owner has bought a spell to keep the peace, and the reaching tendrils continually turn back on themselves. The vines bloom in the spring with blue flowers and perfume the air, but a spell is on them, and the blue is silvered and muted and offends none of the neighbors with unseemly levity. The comfortable house next to the vines on the other side has a tiny yard and a little brick wall: children play there and climb the bricks and play mischievous games, tossing stolen flowers at passersby (and wickedly imagining they are poisoned blooms and that they cast spells instead of flowers. The children on this street are few and fey and very, very sly, choosing only strangers for their pranks: to trouble adult neighbors would not be wise.).

There is a house of muted red brick; a house of river stone; a house of porches and a house of towers; but there is one house the eye tends to miss.

And near it and across the street by the brick wall the young woman in the cloak fends off a shower of silver-blue blossoms and glances up at the grinning wolf-faced children. Her hand is callused. Her dress is nondescript and plain, and her cloak is brown and shows years of wear. She clutches it together tightly about her skirts and shows the fey children a pinched, pale countenance, tangled brown curls within the hood, a long thin face like theirs, but they are freerunning wolves and she is a town-bred cur with the habit of being kicked. They are wolves and mercy never occurs to them, only prudence, and they plan wickedness and sport; one of them meditates trying a wee small spell.

But: "The lawyer's house," she says, looking up at them on their wall, all a-row like ornaments, their laps full of stolen vine branches. And their wolfish pupils dilate and contract in perfect time, and one of them bucks his bare knees up and another does, and the third, and the fourth points with a thin, muscled arm.

The house sits withdrawn from the street, a house of brick age-dulled and dark; a narrow house, a house of windows so old and clouded they drink the light in and cast none back; a house so plain and huge and ugly it might be some warehouse. Little sun gets to it in its slight retreat from the street; the alley beside it is bare dirt and dry dust on the few tilted paving stones. The porch is a mere retreat under the slanting eave of a black slate roof hardly blacker than the aged red brick; the front door is set between two age-hazed windows. This is a house without pe-riod, without age, without place among such aged finery, but it is large and (perhaps) very old, but its style is not after all (only perhaps; one could mistake or not remember)—the oldest: though it does suggest that the oldest may be, in comparison to it, far older of their kinds than one has thought. It is in all things vague. And it is a large house and a pow-erful house, so that in a sudden settling of things into true perspective, one has to realize that the lace-house and the vine-house and the house of the wall and the fey wolfish children are light and this is darkness, this is age, this is the reclusive house of the neighborhood, the silence and the mystery which the witch-children fear, the one house in whose alley they venture only with trepidation. But casual passersby never notice its dreadfulness. Only the neighbors and the children know; and now the woman knows, and clutches her cloak the tighter and leaves the witch-children silent on their wall.

The wolf-eyed girl who thought of the spell sits by her playmates and congratulates herself that she was cautious in her spelling. She is only seven. She knows that she is talented and hopes to live to become a threat. And this woman in her poverty disturbs her, because this must be a witch, and witches ought to be greater and more formidable. The boy beside her is Sighted and feels a dimming of the day; hugs his arms about himself without feeling that he does it; while his brother edges closer to him. And the boy from the towered-house spits at the street below to break the luck when the woman has gone. None of them go back to their game. They sit in their row on their fence and watch, and draw suspicious stares from passing locals who wonder what mayhem the witch-children are contemplating today, legs a-dangle as they sit on the wall, not looking at each other but decidedly looking at something.

It was the nature of the dark house that it never occurred to the ones who saw the children and looked where they looked, that it was the dark house they wondered about. Those who look at the dark house that way cannot be followed in their thoughts, because they are looking at a different place, an obscure and difficult place. Their sight has gotten into a maze that no eye can follow without entering into it as well. The children's souls have gone colder than they were and they do not feel the daylight on their backs. They do not feel safe anymore, but they do not feel any imminent danger either. The house has been stable for a very long time and time goes out from here in musty stability. It is the scale of things in the neighborhood which has been rearranged. A moment is an hour. A place is the universe. The universe is a street and a dark house with dirty windows; and they contemplate this possibility and do not like being so close to it; but they know it is on every street and that wherever it exists it is always next door or across the street. It is the most dangerous thing in the world to stand in its alley or on its porch and the most fearful thing in the world to think of its door opening.

But it opens for the woman in her shabby cloak. And there is nothing of the ordinary about her any longer.

The air was musty with the decay of pages and leather. The light shafted through from the two windows danced with dustmotes and picked out the subtle hues of books and yellowed paper in shelves and stacks about the walls, on tables, chairs; towering stacks about the floor which preserved their own precarious equilibrium against all odds: light fell on age-silvered floorboards and on dust; light fell on a narrow carpet runner which might once have been red but which was silvered with the dust of time and neglect, and this carpet marked a trail through the maze of shelves and stacks, this single faded and dusty aisle of carpet alone offered a line of sight that led away into a dark corridor between the stacks of books and between the bookcases and the laden furniture. Ambush might lurk within the stacks. A single step, a single shift of weight made the aged boards of the floor creak and betrayed the visitor. Melot Cassissinin looked about her, her cloak clutched against her and her body yearning back toward the day-light. The door had opened itself. She was not overly surprised. Now, in-evitably, it did the other thing and shut itself; and for a moment the air was cold. Magic did that, unattended magic: it got its force from the air and the ground and from whoever was standing by, and Melot shivered: it robbed her as well, leaving her with only the dusty windows-light and that thin red track of carpet, the color of life all faded, leading into the hall.

"Master Toth," she called out, quaking where she stood. And again: "Master Toth!"—which sound lost itself in the maze and drew neither echo nor answer.

Flight urged at her. But the carpet-path beguilded the eye with its mazy designs and the fear settled away into a vague and gnawing terror. It seemed logical to go on, since she had come this far; and if there were ambushes they were likeliest ambushes calculated to frighten and not to harm. She walked the carpeted track and steeled her nerves against bogles and icy touches and whatever sort of whimsy an old man might devise for unwelcome intruders. Her business was certain and she was not a woman to turn when she had made up her mind a thing had to be: she simply told her feet they would go on and never back no matter what her mind was doing. And she told her body not to flinch even if some-thing should run icy fingers down her neck: she was not a proud woman, this Melot, but she was a woman in a hurry and the fingers of willywisps and trolls were all the same class of nuisance to a woman in her set of mind as fingers of other unwelcome sorts which she well knew how to deal with. She had tactics, did Melot of the *Ram*, and a withering look for man or devil who tried her. It masked a habitual dour despair, like the despair of the conscript soldier who knows tomorrow is like today, and all tomorrows like that one, one more walk and one more fight; and the enemy everywhere. Melot was a conscript of life; to be alive was not what she would have chosen, but by the gods all and several she was too stubborn to retreat once launched.

So she went walking down the dark hall of many doors and called out the name she had called out before, going deeper and deeper into the dark, till the hallway and the carpet ran up against a stack of books and a table with other books and papers. There the carpet and the hall bent to the right with a dim window at the end. This too she followed, past doors and past hanging pictures lost in murk and cobwebs, over the carpet which was her only track and guide, toward what at first seemed only another hall stacked high with books, but which revealed a stairs and an ascent lighted by a dim window up at the landing.

"Master Toth," she called up; and: Toth, Toth, Toth, the echoes said, but nothing more. So she clenched up her skirts in her fist and climbed, where the faded red carpet led, up and up past the landing to yet another hall all in dark, where crazily leaning stacks of books and papers breathed out a miasma of age and rot. "Master Toth?"

But the carpet went only up the stairs, while the hall floor was bare boards and littered with paper. The stairs promised light above, where by yet another window, dirty-paned daylight streamed into the dust and the neglect.

She close the stairs and climbed, hard-breathing now; and gathered her skirts past stacks of books. Another turn: a small slit of a window; and a door at the top of the stairs.

The air seemed colder here. A prickling ran her nape. She thought if she turned about at this instant there would be something black and small and glitter-eyed staring at her from the landing she had left: that was the thing that built itself in her mind. It would grow brave. It would come up the stairs. If she turned around she would see it baring its needle-sharp teeth; and its kingdom was the dark hallway which she had to pass to go down again.

"Master Toth!" She let go her skirts and stepped up to the door and hammered with her fist as her nerve began to fail her. "Master—"

The air chilled and the door opened onto a dusty-windowed loft as mazed with books as all the rest of the house. And before the great windows at the far end of the loft a hunched figure perched on a stool poring over something on a reading stand. This someone turned, a spidery silhouette against the white light; and Melot felt the approach of the black thing at her heels and skipped up that step and inside in haste.

The door closed behind her. The shadow in front of the windows got off its stool and Melot kept herself close to the door and flight, black thing or no.

"Master Toth," she said in a voice not as bold as her voice in the halls below.

The figure beckoned. She came, closer, closer through the tilting maze of books and papers, and her eyes accepted the light enough to make out this figure, which began to have color—the bottle-green coat, and dark hair (white, she had thought) and a lean, smooth face (wrinkled, she had expected) and a fine-boned hand (ink-stained) holding a pair of spectacles. Melot's step failed her and her mouth opened for more breath, because he was none of the things she had expected, no crabbed ancient huddled at his bookstand, but a tall young man with the features of a god, except his nose was a bit hooked and his eyes were set too close, so that they stared with a concentration that seemed to focus somewhere in the center of the subject's heart and not at its surface.

"Well?" this young man asked. "Well?" This man looked at her and Melot Cassissinin felt naked in a way that had nothing to do with clothes, and burned in a way that had everything to do with his handsomeness and the look of those dark eyes which looked straight into her own. No man who looked like that looked that way at Melot's plain face, and all at once she flushed like a thirteen-year-old and felt the floor about to cave in to swallow herself and her purpose which could not possibly sustain such a stare. The voice so gentle was about to crack like a whip, was about to turn acid with impatience and sting her with wit her wit could not, in its present state, deal with.

It was in such pinches Melot Cassissinin's mind went blank and the same blind stubbornness which had just driven her legs up the stairs took over her mouth. "Master Toth, would you be Master Toth?"

"Dr. Toth, yes, I am, madam."

She flushed again, hotter than before: and part of the heat was shame and part was rage, since he used a lady's word and hid behind that sober, careful fact to laugh at her. "I want a consul-tation." She had practiced this word. She got it out unstammered. She stared him in the eyes and refused to give way an inch, though he seemed taller than before and closer. "I haven't got much money. But it's not like you'd have to do more than tell me what to do." She fished at her collar and started to haul up her purse, never turning her back, and the heat burned her face, not from embarrassment of where the purse was, but from what little sum it held and what it had cost her. It was too little, she knew that it was too little, and she preferred his cold contempt to his laughter. Laughter would cut like a razor. Laughter would kill the rest of her soul and she would go away and kill a wizard or two. Or try. And she held the purse out, hating the way her hand shook; and she turned out the money, which was four large silver coins and three small ones. And two coppers.

He left them in her hand and walked away from her to draw up another, smaller stool. "Sit down," he said, and went and pulled his own stool out from the table.

Melot came and sat, her left hand clenched on her money; her skirts spread about her on the dusty floor. She reached and swept back the hood of her cloak and stared at the doctor as she sat down on his tall stool. Tremors threatened her. She tried to keep her teeth from chattering, her throat from freezing up. This was a dangerous man, this was a man wizards were afraid of; and he sat there like a boy on a stableyard fence, his long arms about his knees, the spectacles in his fine fingers glinting with gold and glass in the dusty daylight from the window, his books abandoned on his desk.

"I'm listening," he said. "Tell me your name. Tell me anything that seems important. We'll discuss a fee when I know what your case is."

"My name is Melot Cassissinin." Now, now the stammer threatened in earnest and she fought it back with deliberation. "My brother's Gatan. Same name. He's got this trouble. This wizard got him, this other wizard, well, there's going to be this duel—"

"Be specific. Tell me all the details."

"This wizard—he, well, he was always hanging round the tavern, the *Ram*, over by the Rains—"

"You're a long way from home."

"—he, well, I work there; and he was always trouble, I mean, he got drunk and when he got drunk he was trouble, and my brother, well, he'd talk to him sometimes to calm him down, I mean, he was bothering me, he'd try, and my brother, well, he never liked that, but he's got a way about him, my brother does. He can charm the moon out of the sky, and he always knew how to handle this wizard—"

"Tell me his name. I know a good many."

"Othis."

"Ah." The dark, close-set eyes flickered. "*That* one. Yes, I do know him."

Melot looked up at him, sweating; and he gave her no helpful clues what kind of knowledge this was or how close or friendly. "Well, when this Othis would give me trouble, my brother'd go and talk to him and put him off and sometimes master Othis'd sit and talk at him for hours— Well, maybe he told my brother something, maybe this other wizard— Hagon, Hagon's his name—" She looked again for clues and got none. "Well, he took exception, he did, to something, and somehow maybe this Othis and this Hagon were old enemies; so Hagon came into the *Ram* and he grabbed me and he wanted my brother to come with him or he'd mess me up good, he said, that was what he meant, anyhow. So Gatan went with him instead, me yelling after him and trying to stop him, but this Hagon he knocked me down, not with his hand, but just like I hit a wall, and he and Gatan went off in the dark.

"Well, I was scared; and I hadn't got any help, this man I know, well, he wasn't taking on any wizard, so I went myself, and I hunted up Othis and tried to talk to him, but he was all—well, he shoved me off and called Gatan names and said as how Gatan had made a friend—a *friend!*—he oughtn't, and said as how he was going to get revenge on this Hagon and on my brother—" Melot drew breath. Her hands shook. She clenched them both on her knees and stopped the tremor. "This Hagon *invested* something in my brother, that's what Othis said; and Othis wants to put some kind of hold on him too; and now they got this problem, because they can't untangle it, and they've set up to have this duel to settle it, tomorrow, except—except—well, where's my brother in this? Who's going to see he doesn't get hurt? I mean, it's not right, Gatan never worked for either of them, they got no right, have they? They can't do that, fight over him, I mean. I figured you'd know it wasn't right, you'd just sort of like write a letter for me to these two, and maybe—maybe a letter where it could do some good, I mean like you were my lawyer and you were going to do something, but you don't have to really, I mean, just the letters, that's all. I got money enough for that; or I can get more if you tell me what. I mean, just scare 'em a little. That's all."

"That's very interesting," the doctor said, and the heat went to Melot's face, a suspicion of condescension. "You're not a witch, then?" the doctor asked.

"I wait tables."

"But you're not a witch."

"Man, there's no one got less luck than me."

"Not born fortunate."

"My mother coughed me out. Thought I was a stomach-ache." Melot clenched her fingers on her silver coins. "It was my birthday this Hagon walked in on, I mean, what kind of luck is that?"

"How many days ago?"

"Three."

"How old are you?"

"Thirty-three."

"Interesting. Interesting." The lawyer hopped up from his stool and put his spectacles on, went over to a stack of books and pulled out the second from the top. He opened it on the table and leafed through it, unfolding pages into untidy charts. "What hour of the day?"

"Third." The numbers came together out of nowhere and coincided, and Melot got off her stool and stood there with her hands clenched on her coins and her heart thumping away. "I got no luck, I never had any luck."

"There are two kinds," the doctor said, and sent the shivers down her back.

"You just write the letters, master Toth, that's all I want, I mean it's *Gatan* in trouble, not me."

The doctor looked up over his spectacles, his dark eyes full of surmise and, for the first time, alarm. "Gatan's birthday."

"Same. Same—we always, I mean, we always thought it was funny, like he had the luck I missed, charming folk was his talent, only he was four years later—"

"The wrong one. Hagon got the wrong one. So did Othis."

"What are you talking about?" The words came out blunt and plain and Melot felt a rush of panic. She laid her fistful of money on the table by the book. "I can't afford you doing all that. Just the letters. I mean, all you have to do is write what right is. They'll listen to you."

The doctor hopped up and pulled out another book. He opened it and stood there riffling through it and reading here and there. "No, no," he said, and: "No, not here, not that, not here—"

"I can't afford a lot!"

The doctor pulled down his spectacles and turned and looked at her. "Melot Cassissinin. I'm not a wizard myself; I'm a specialist whose talent just happens to be keeping track of books and things in books. And that little talent has got me a few others— My clients usually don't come in broad daylight and my fees aren't as straightforward as you offer. The door downstairs, for instance. Hagon himself did that. Othis has contributed a few things about the place. Conveniences. They're very expensive for a wizard. But they pay them. They pay whatever I set, because I have a small talent at research—which means, madam, that no single wizard can master all of them, or many of them; a wizard's investment is too much and too deep in too few books to have any appreciation of interrelated consequences. My investment is shallow, but very, very wide. I am not, precisely, a barrister. I do not plead cases. I'm a consulting lawyer, which is quite another thing. I do not sue nor do I defend or prosecute. I merely advise. Do you understand, Melot Cassissinin? Nor do I practice a law which has to do with justice. I practice the law of nature. I render a simple service to those who meddle in it. I advise of consequences. So I suggest you have a seat, young woman, and wait."

"It's *tomorrow*."

"Yes. Quite. So is sunrise. The question is inevitability. Do sist down, madam, and don't utter a word, if you please."

Melot subsided over to the low stool she had sat on before, sank down and hugged her arms about her knees, her knees against her chest, watching as Dr. Toth went striding down the long line of shelves against the wall and pulled down one book after another. He carried them back to his desk, dumped them atop the last, pushed his spectacles up his nose and began leafing through the pages while dust flew up and danced in the light like stormclouds. "No," he said. "No, and no." And slammed the books shut one and the other, and got up and dumped them onto the stack beside the desk.

"If—" said Melot, thinking of the letter she had come for.

"Hush!" the master snapped, and folded one arm and rested the other hand on his brow, standing there with his head bowed and his eyes squinched shut.

The air chilled, not like a wind, like something had instead leached the warmth and the life out of it. That cold reached into Melot's bones and into her muscles and she could not shiver, she could only sit and sit. Then of a sudden the doctor flung up his head. "Ah!" he said, strode off on his long legs and whirled about to point a finger at her. "You! Stay on that stool. Touch nothing, hear!"

"Yes, s–sir."

He spun and strode off again, out the magical door and thump, thump, thump down the stairs before the door had shut; while Melot tucked her cloak about her and shivered and shivered, thinking of the small darkness with the teeth she had imagined on the stairs, in the hall below. It might have been a cat, might have been a dog or even some rat, but it had died here, it had become something awful; it lived here and it could have gotten in when the doctor opened that door, and it hated visitors, O, gods, gods, gods. Melot she sat with her teeth chattering in the shaft of light from the window and with her head spinning and her muscles weakening in their shivers.

At last she ducked her head down against her knees and shut her eyes and tried to get the shivers out, because she was Melot Cassissinin, after all—nobody much, but she walked the streets not with a mince or a flinch, but with a sure, businesslike stride that announced to the world that here walked a woman who wanted no trouble but who was prepared to make it. And *that* for the thing with the teeth, for she had a sharp square heel and a quick foot and a set of lungs that would bring the house down and bring master Toth on the run. So she rested as she could after the cold had taken the strength out of her and she waited and she waited while the sun crawled across the floor and left her in the dark.

The beam wandered the length of the hall and lost itself in the stacks of books, so that only one tall mountain of them was alight.

Suddenly a candle lit itself, sending another chill into the air.

Thump, thump-thump, thump—Up the stairs. Up and up the stairs, and round the turn, as the magical door opened and master Toth came in with an armload of books.

Melot started to stand up, started to blurt out a What now, and swallowed it and sank down again on her numb backside, because Dr. Toth paid her no more heed than if she had been another stack of books. He set his books down on the stand where the candle was, flung open one and another of them, threw a sheaf of paper onto the lot and sat down on the tall stool, immediately dipping a quill into an inkpot that uncapped itself. Another small chill.

And Melot's stomach growled. She clenched her arms across her belly, trying to silence it. Tried to think of something else. The rumbling came again, loud; and the pen-scratching stopped. Dr. Toth looked at her through his spectacles as if she were something objectionable on his carpet, then pushed his spectacles a degree higher and started writing again, flipping pages and making the candle-flame shake and shadows dance.

Another rumble from her stomach. Melot hugged herself and sucked in air and tried to tense her muscles, which only started a shiver. Gods, gods. He would throw her out. He was only interested in his books. He did all this work and there was a fee; and she sold her other dress and Gatan's clothes, and her cooking pots and her mother's ring, and then she sold what she never had sold for money, except once for a doctor for their mother before she died. And it all came to those coins and a dull cold terror that they were not enough; that it was only the books interested Master Toth and he was working on wizard's business never thinking at all about Gatan or herself. She was only a lump sitting here bothering him in his work. It could not be a letter he was writing. What he had said he would do she could not make out, but it was all as if he was not in the habit really of doing anything beyond handing out advice; and what could she do with advice against a pair of wizards?

Her stomach rumbled again. The pen stopped scratching and she looked up as he looked down his spectacled nose at her.

"In the cupboard there," he said brusquely with a wave of ink-stained fingers. "Eat what you like, for the gods' sake, and watch where you're walking."

"Yes, sir." She looked desperately where he pointed; and got off her stool onto numb legs, limped over where a small path through the stacks led to a cupboard. A candle lighted there on the counter, blink. She shivered and carefully opened the doors, found a plate of bread and fresh seed-cheese and a bottle of wine. All fresh. All as if they hadn't been lying in a cupboard all day. The air inside was chill, and the wine bottle cold as she poured into a chill cup; and the knife cold as she cut a little bread and cheese.

Then she thought again and put it on a tray and walked timidly, fearfully up to Master Toth; but she knew how to get up to a table and deftly fill a cup with never bothering a gentleman. She set it there on the stack nearest and slipped back to feed herself, a bit of seed-cheese wrapped in bread and wine—gods, such wine, the *Ram* never served the like. It hit her empty stomach and made her head spin as she tidied things and closed the cupboard.

More candles lit. The sun was going. The pen scratched away and stopped as Master Toth took a drink of wine and a left-handed nibble of cheese while he kept reading, all hunched over his books. The cheese slowly disappeared. He took up the pen again. Scratch-scribble, hastily.

Melot crept back to her stool and sat down again, blinking owlishly. She was unbearably sleepy, three days with never but a little sleep and that dreadful, in a shameful bed. The wine sat in her stomach and hummed in her veins and whispered in her skull like bees in a hive.

"We have it," Dr. Toth announced suddenly, "we have it!"—startling her awake, startling her hands to her sides hunting the edges of the stool among her skirts as the doctor held up his paper. "Woman, up, don't dawdle! There's precious little time."

She stood and wobbled. Dr. Toth slid down from his perch and came and seized her by the arm, dragging her with him.

"But," she said.

"Time," he said. "Come along, walk, woman. Melot Cassissinin. Good gods, keep your feet under you. I trust you know where this Othis lodges."

"Can't you magic it?" She caught her balance as the door opened and left the stairs gaping darkly in front of them, with him dragging her along in the dim light of candles which lit themselves in the stairwell, above the books and the litter. "Can't you—"

"A practical suggestion if I had the wherewithal. I'm not wont to have to race with fools. Tomorrow you say. But which tomorrow, tomorrow of the dawn or tomorrow of the wizards, or tomorrow of the clock? Do you know? No, I thought not." Thump, thump, around the turning and down into the first hall, into the bizarre maze of books, all the candles in the sconces agleam. "Do come on, woman."

"Yes, sir. Yes, sir." Melot skipped and ran as best she could being hauled upon in time to his long steps. The door opened for them, and the wind skirled the candles and they went out onto the porch and down, down the steps to the nightbound street.

Melot was staggering when they had reached the Avenue, reeling along with the doctor's fingers clamped upon her wrist and tugging at her to more haste. She ran and ran still, and brought up short against the doctor's side when he stopped and gave a piercing whistle.

More magic? She blinked. There was the least small chill; but it might have been the wind. And there down the Avenue came a public cab, a-rattle on the pavings, one of the wheeled sort, the cabman jogging along at a fair pace—a cabman without a hire, at this hour, just where the doctor needed him. Melot blinked in amazement and as the cab rattled up to a stop by the curb—"Wizards' Row, fast as you can," the doctor said to the cabman, tossed him a coin that made his jaw drop, and opened the door himself and flung Melot in, the third only time in her life she had seen the inside of a cab—

"—but, but," she said, smothered in her skirts as the doctor shoved her over against the wall and wedged himself in, "Dr. Toth, that's wrong, it's the Rains, it's—" But the cab was off, rattling along fit to make her teeth clack. "Wizard's Row," the doctor said firmly. And the cab lurched and jolted. For that coin that had sailed through the moonlight with a wicked golden glint the cabby would run his gut out. He was doing that, and the wheels jolted and bounced. Melot clenched her jaws and clenched her fist on the hanging-strap and swayed this way and that with the doctor as they bounced along, clack, thump, and a missing stone, thud-clack. Her breath refused to come back. Her brain reeled. *But I can't pay, that was gold he threw to a cabby-man, and that's all it is to him, he's rich, rich as a priest and rich as a lord, and I'm nothing, my money's not enough for him and he's young and handsome and I'm not, I'm not, I'm not, can't even pay him that way, nothing I can offer—*

—Does he take souls? Is that what he trades in?

Thud-clack-clack. She heard the cabby panting now, felt the cab steady into that holding pace now the cabby had come to his senses and realized he had to stay alive and stay moving. It was a long, long way; but the man had gold, had gold enough to buy the cab and a soul or two, might be . . .

Thud-clack. Sway and skid at the corners, jog and jounce. In time Melot heard the cabby panting up ahead as if his gut would burst and his life-blood spew, but he ran on, and they swayed and bumped one against the other, the doctor in his fine coat and her in her cloak, and outside the windows of the cab the neighborhood changed and changed again. The cab slowed to a walk a while, picked up: they kept moving, by fits and starts.

And at long, long last they stopped altogether, and the cab tipped, and the cabby came round to their window, panting like a beached fish. "What number was you wanting, milor?"

The doctor peered out. "Close enough," he said, and flung the door open and gave the man another something in his hand. The cabby stood there while Melot got out, and tried to help her; but there was dark running from his nose in the moonlight. Melot felt his hand shake and when she stepped clear the cabby just stopped and collapsed there on the curb, head between his knees. And the doctor grabbed Melot's wrist and pulled her along willy nilly.

Down the street, the peculiar street where more magic was than was comfortable anywhere, and some of the houses with their peculiarities . . . like fire and smoke; like ice and a permanent shimmer of recent rain. Melot quaked in her steps and came on, panting and desperate as the doctor started up long wooden steps to an unpretentious house of beams and towers.

The door-emblem blinked at them and the door swung wide with a gust of chill hardly worse than that all up and down this street, chill to sting the lungs and make a body glad of a cloak. Candles sprang to life inside, and an old man came out of a brighter-lit room.

"Dr. Toth," that one said—a wizard, sure he was a wizard. "What's this?"

"An excellent question," the doctor said, and dragged Melot with him as he swept into the lighted room—a library, but ever so much neater and cleaner than his own. Melot goggled at the giltwork and the leather bindings and the lamp in dragon shape and the brass camel that held up a table on which rested an interrupted dinner and an open book.

"Do look lively, woman!" The doctor spun her round by the arm and her startled eyes fell full on the wizard, for wizard he must be, a small gray man in a blue robe, with sad mustaches and lively blue eyes. "What does she seem like?"

"Why—no one, no one in particular—"

"Ah," said Dr. Toth, and he pushed Melot into a chair near the camel-table; he took the divan and helped himself to the wine. "Have some, my dear?"

Melot reached. The goblet he put in her hand weighed ten times what it seemed, and she slopped the wine over in her startlement. Gold, it was gold. She blinked at one and the other of them, and looked doubtfully at the gray wizard as he sat down on the remaining chair.

"Read this," said Dr. Toth, and handed the gray wizard a paper from his pocket. "Does that make sense?"

The gray wizard held it up to his eyes and adjusted it this way and that in myopic concentration. His mouth moved and stopped moving and he looked up with his blue eyes wide. "Who does this describe?"

"Her. It describes *her*, Master Junthin. Two idiots are fighting over her *brother*—"

—*Gods save me*, Melot thought with a mouthful of wine half-choking her. Her eyes watered in pain and she swallowed and tried not to sneeze it up, a hand clamped to mouth and nose as she stared at the wizard and the doctor in panic, frozen like a bird between two snakes. "—and one of them has invested him, if she can tell a straight story. That's how her luck works, don't you see? They tracked the thing straight so far, and when they got close, their eyes bent right around her and they went for second best. Her *luck* brought her to me. It had to. She had no choice. It was her *luck* brought the trouble on her in the first place and cozened those fools Othis and Hagon—a luck like that, there's nothing stops it. It rolls downhill and it arranges things—"

"But don't you see?" Junthin said, on his side, "It arranged you and her to be here. And me to be at home. A client canceled. Gods know why—" Owlish eyes blinked at Melot and sent chills down Melot's back before they slid away to blink at the doctor and to glance down at the paper again and up. "If they don't stop this—"

"You *can* find them."

"Yes." The paper shook in Junthin's wrinkled hands. He wiped his face with his sleeve, the paper still trembling and wavering. "Oh dear gods, dear gods. A nexus. A nexus. O dear gods. How far?"

Melot looked from him to the doctor, whose handsome face was starkly sober. "Master Junthin," said Dr. Toth, "you know that I'm a tolerably important nexus myself. You know I enjoy a certain latitude with the Profession on that account, not mentioning my talent. That my researches persistently turn up a certain set of consequences should I be . . . eliminated, or bothered, or directly hampered in my work: do you see? And those consequences are far-reaching. I consult every wizard's text and put all the prohibitions and the possible interferences together and they do assume a pattern into which I fit rather centrally, I may say, which assures that of all individuals in all Liavek not safe to trifle with, I am at the head of the list, I in my modest house, my quiet researches, my inquiries—"

"Yes, yes, we all know that. We pay you handsomely, extravagantly. *I* pay you. You render a service."

"And keep you from eliminating yourselves or a city street or perchance Liavek itself by combination of unforeseen consequences . . . Perhaps. I always considered, that would be justification enough for what I cast for my horoscope and my own luck—"

"We never doubt it. But, my dear doctor Toth, we cannot stand on—"

"But do you see, Master Junthin, tonight I learned a different truth about my importance. It wasn't myself had the importance all along. *She* did. Her luck arranged all of this. Arranged my birth two hundred years ago. Arranged your client's cancellation. Arranged all of this and my profession and our very existence. *Nexus*, man. A big one. *That's* what those fools are playing with. They've got her brother. His luck didn't outmaneuver theirs; they mistake him for some petty little trinket they can use not knowing that the nexus-sense they pick up is just the overspill from hers. And I'm telling you, Master Junthin, if they harm him in their brigandish behavior, if they run afoul of *her* luck and tie *anything* important to it—like the welfare of Liavek, do you see? Do you see what they're meddling with?"

"O dear gods and stars."

"Wait. Wait." Facts and insinuations and promises went flying this way and that in confusion, like pigeons, and Melot's head spun. "You promised about my brother . . ." It was not precisely so, but it was never wasted to try to convince the other side in a bargain there *was* a bargain. It was all the wit she had left, with the red wine dizzying her and the warmth and the profusion of candles and wizard-talk flying past her ears. "You got to get him out, Master Toth. You do got to do that, you took my money—" *O fool! To mention the money, the pitiful money—* She blinked at them and shivered and saw two men and them both magicians staring at her as if she had snakes for hair. "You got to. I got this feeling—I get these feelings—things will go wrong if something happens to him."

"Is she lying?" asked Master Junthin.

"I don't know," said the doctor.

She was. She was lying with a vengeance, because premonitions seemed the only cash these wizard-types understood, premonitions and bad luck and good. She knew how to throw an evil-eye scare into a drunk or to ill-wish a street ruffian and give him the doubts enough to get away; so she did it with a first-class wizard and the wizards' own lawyer; and saw them stare at her and wonder.

"Bless," said the wizard, and the air went a little colder and the candles dimmed all together and came up again.

"*Do* something. Get the neighbors, can you?"

"Summon? With *her* involved?"

"Have you a countersuggestion, Master Junthin?"

"O gods, O gods," Master Junthin murmured. And shut his eyes.

The air went decided chill. A bell began to ring somewhere in the hall. Another rang far away as if it was outside the house. And farther and farther and farther until the air whispered with them.

Melot took up the goblet and took another sip of wine. She wanted it for her nerves. And she pretended a composure which was the greatest lie yet.

Meanwhile the bells rang and Dr. Toth stood there with his arms folded looking down at her. With that look on his handsome face that said he had his doubts in both directions.

"Mmmph," she said, and offered the plate of cheese with eyes wide and naive.

He caught the irony. It was dangerous to have done. A meticulous brow lifted. But by the gods, a woman never got anywhere in the world letting the opposition drag her about and tell her sit here and sit here and stare at her like that. Her hair was snarled from running. It fell down around her ears and her eyes, too tangled with itself to stay put; and she sweated, and her best (and only) dress wanted laundering, while he smelled of books and fine soap and even his sweat smelled clean. She was despicable. She was plain and starved and her dress hung about her ribs. And he had talked about him being born—(*two hundred years ago?*)—to satisfy her luck, which rattled around in her brain without a niche to fall into. Two hundred years ago?

Was the way he looked—something he had taken in payment?

The front door opened. Master Junthin went out into the hall and brought in an out-of-breath little man in a dressing-gown . . . "What's toward, what's toward? Good gods, Junthin—" The little man spied Dr. Toth and stopped in midword. And even then the front door was opening again. Two women came into the room on their own, like as peas except one had her hair in pins and the other had it dripping wet; and hard on their heels came a fat man with a marmoset on his shoulder. "What is this?" the marmoset piped, falsetto. "What is this?"

There were more arriving. A boy with scales on one cheek. A black woman who cast no shadow. The door kept opening and closing and Melot clutched the wine goblet, aware of the stares no less on her than on Dr. Toth, and hoping—hoping desperately for the sight of two wizards in particular.

But they did not come. And Junthin began to explain the whole affair to the others, using words that slipped in and out of language she knew, till Dr. Toth, unlike himself, stole over to Melot and took the goblet away, took her hand and drew her to her feet like a grand lady, holding her arm locked gentlemanly-like in his.

"You just have to want your brother," Dr. Toth said. "Mind is very important in this."

"I *want* him."

"Fine, fine. Now you've got to trust Junthin for this. This isn't my kind of affair." He gave her hand a little squeeze and passed her hand grandly to Junthin's reach.

The wizard's skin was cold and damp. "My dear woman, my dear, just stand there, right where you are. Just shut your eyes, hold your eyes shut. O, gods, my furniture—"

And from the woman with the wet hair: "A nexus of that size, O ye gods and stars, Junthin, quit babbling about the furniture—"

"But my vases, my vases—" Junthin fled and set one and another of the great ornate vases on the floor, then scurried back to the large rug where others were clearing the tables. The door opened to another arrival— "Never mind," the woman of the pins said to the latecomer, an aged, wizened man, "stand *here*, Gaffer Bedizi'n—" And from the old man: "Eh? I was in bed, my cat woke me— Eh, Dr. Toth? It is Dr. Toth, 'pon my soul—"

"Be *careful*, gaffer Bedizi'n. For the gods' sweet sake and Liavek's, just stand on that point, *stand there!* Hear?"

Melot looked left and right. Took in her breath, because all of a sudden it started to grow cold; and Junthin began to talk, and all of them to talk. Then the talk became one sound, and that sound rumbled up through her bones like close thunder—"Now, now now—name him, name him—"

It's Gatan they want, they want me to talk, Gatan, Gatan—

BOOM! The thunder burst in her face and there was something there, while a great fist hit her and she went flying backward into collapsing wizards and the crash of furniture and goblets and trays and vases. She hit the floor on her backside, feet out at angles, and struggled up on her hands to see Gatan sitting there in the center of the carpet without a stitch on and blinking and wobbling back and forth. There were rope burns on him. There was a dazed look on his face. "Gods!" he cried, proving his reality.

"Air displacement." It was Dr. Toth, who was helping up Master Junthin and then gaffer Bedizi'n who blinked owlishly. "Your cloak, my dear." And he drew Melot to her feet and took her cloak and went and cast it around Gatan, who sat helplessly where he had landed.

"Where were you?" Melot cried, clenching her hands to fists and pounding her knees as she gazed into Gatan's bewildered, blinking eyes. "Gatan, Gatan, you great fool, where have you been?"

"In this cellar," he said. "In this cellar." He shivered and hugged the cloak about him; and Melot went and threw her arms about him. He was sometimes a fool, Gatan was; and he looked like one this time, being naked as a hatchling and cold as meat and gods help him, smelling like a sewer. Weed clung to his hair. She picked at it, patted his unshaved cheek. "Oh my vases," Junthin moaned at the fringes of things.

"He has a luck," the woman with wet hair said.

"An investment," said the woman with pins, and Melot looked about at her and hugged Gatan fast as the woman rolled her eyes and staggered back against her twin. "An investment, O gods, he's carrying something. Do stand up, young man."

Melot applied herself with both hands and Dr. Toth helped, and the fat man with the marmoset. "Up, up," the marmoset wailed as the fat man pushed, and Gatan wobbled to his feet and reeled this way and that under Melot's support. Gatan howled, and his face glowed red and changed of a sudden with the shadowed overlay of a man's rough features that were never Gatan's. They changed again, a second face.

"O good gods," Melot cried, stepping back.

"It's Hagon," cried the woman in pins, while the face faded leaving Gatan with his own; Melot stood there in profoundest shock—Gatan, not-Gatan, O gods—what was this they had summoned to the room?

"Not Hagon's choosing," said the marmoset, "that's Othis, that was Othis, sure."

"What, what, what?" Melot cried, and went and grabbed Dr. Toth by the sleeve. "What are they talking about, what's happened to him, what's *wrong* with him?"

"An investment." Dr. Toth took her by the arm in turn and by both arms both hard and gently, his close-set eyes looking straight into hers. "Hagon evidently intended to invest some fraction of his power into what he thought was a nexus of considerable intensity. Do you know— no, of course you don't. But with an extension into even such a minor nexus, why, Hagon could invest the merest portion of his magic into your brother and use your brother's luck to magnify his power, to become a great wizard, not a petty one. And so Othis saw his chance. At the worst moment, at the positively worst moment in Hagon's procedure or Othis'—your luck brought us to summon him out of their reach."

"But—but—can't you help him?"

"Help him, my dear woman?" Dr. Toth straightened back and regarded her down his nose, and flung an expansive gesture toward Gatan, who stood hugging his borrowed cloak about his nakedness. "Help him? That's a powerful wizard standing there. Your brother's drained them dry; and gods know what else they were up to beyond using him as a catspaw! If he has the makings of that investment as well, gods save us all! It was power they were after."

"Gatan?" Melot turned and looked and held her hands to her mouth for fear of something else getting out. But it was Gatan. Her brother stood there blinking and scared-looking. "Melot," he said, "Melot, I'm me, I'm just me is all, O gods, I feel like I could burst, my head, my fingers—"

"Don't!" cried the marmoset. "No, no, no, don't let it loose. Wish it to rain. Quickly, wish for rain."

"I hope it rains!" Gatan cried desperately. And the air went frosty cold.

"Weather-wish takes time," said the gaffer Bedizi'n, "a great deal of time, young man, I hope you don't expect haste. That's always young folk, always in a hurry. Tomorrow, I make it tomorrow noon, halfish—"

"But Hagon and Othis," cried Gatan. "What will they do to me? They'll come looking for me."

"Oh, no," said Junthin mournfully. He held one of his vases in his hands and he had a distressed look on his face. "No, I don't think they will." And he came and set the vase on a table that was still upright. It was a flowered urn. It was full to the brim with red liquid.

"Backlash," said Dr. Toth. "Dear me, what an awful mess. The lad got all the useful things of them. But is that one or both in there?"

"Both, I think," said Junthin. "It's the only vase intact."

Gatan sat down where he was, on the rim of an overturned chair. Melot just stood, numb.

"No more Othis," said Junthin. "No more Hagon."

"Good riddance," said the black woman.

"But," said Melot.

"I'd say," said Dr. Toth, "unasked, of course, and unconsulted—that it's going to rain half past noon tomorrow. And everything's going to work out well for this young man. Though I'd say one ought to find him a master right quickly. An untrained talent of his caliber is not comfortable. That advice is free."

Junthin coughed. "My damages—I do have first claim."

"Junthin," cried the fat man's marmoset, "you have no such thing."

"Indeed not," said the black woman without a shadow. "I think we might expect master Toth to research this matter and tell us the consequences."

"Ah, well. *Now* we come to fees. I'll think of some small thing. The answer may take me a few days and I make no guarantees in this case. And pray, my dear friends, pray earnestly that there were no deeper entanglements. *I'll* take the pair in charge until I have your answer. That should relieve you of some few anxieties. And of, coincidentally, worry about each other." Dr. Toth leaned over the vase, sniffed and stood back with a grimace. "Ugh. A little consultation would have prevented that. I'll have lost my doorspell, too. It was Hagon's, and I'm afraid it's quite done for."

"I don't know," said Gatan, still shivering, though the doctor's study was warmed with a very natural fire; and the doctor had provided a warm bath and a very fine robe once they had gotten in. (It was Melot climbed through the window they jimmied, and let them in among the books and clutter.) Gatan, a mass of nerves on his way home, still grew distraught whenever he talked about his sojourn in that cellar under Hagon's floor. "I don't know *what* they intended to do, I don't know what's to become of me now. What do I know? I can't deal with folk like that!"

"Do have some confidence," Dr. Toth said, looking up from his table and his books. "The solution has to fit all round. And you're quite formidable, young man; I daresay we should warn the watch: the storm tomorrow may prove as much. But for the moment I suggest you go off to bed and let me work in peace, ummn? Nice. Nice. Here's an interesting point. Do go. Go, go, go, second door down the hall."

There was no sign of the black thing with teeth out in the hall. Perhaps it was in better humor. Melot saw Gatan to his room and the candles lit themselves for him the moment he entered—"Do be careful about the lights!" the doctor's voice pursued them down the hall.

"I'm scared," Gatan said, though he was a grown man and a half head taller; he was her little brother and told her such things, lingering in the doorway. "Melot, I'm *scared*."

"Hush, trust the doctor, he's very kind."

But she went back down the hall after Gatan had shut the door. She walked into the study with her heart beating hard. And stood there with her hands locked behind her while the doctor pored over a clutter of books and charts as if the night were still young. As if he needed no sleep nor ever would. The way he was two hundred years old and maybe ugly once, but never would be so long as he could bargain with wizards.

And as long as they needed him.

She coughed. Her heart beat doubletime. "You're looking in that book for him—or for me?"

The doctor looked up through his spectacles and took them off. "It does seem to be one case, doesn't it?"

"Like, I mean, my brother's a wizard, isn't he?"

"Your luck made him that way."

"Like you said you were born because I needed you, was that true?"

The doctor blinked at her. "Well—"

"I mean," she said, "when you reckon how much I owe you got to take that into account, like if you charged me too much my luck'd get me clear, wouldn't it?"

"Melot Cassissinin, you are a woman of unparalleled gall."

"Just lucky. Aren't I?"

The doctor stood up. Towered there in his magnificence.

"I reckon," said Melot, "it might be lucky for you if I stayed here, I mean, this place—" She waved a hand about. "It wants dusting. It wants straightening."

The doctor's mouth opened, a very handsome mouth it was, and a very fine face, and him so lordlike and genteel. "*My books—*"

"Fact is," said Melot, hands behind her, rocking anxiously on her heels, "if I was lucky, I'd bring luck here, wouldn't I? And if I was lucky, maybe I'd be pretty and have nice clothes like yours and hire me footcabs with goldpieces and have me a brother a very fine and lordly wizard, wouldn't I, Master Toth?"

"*Wouldn't* you? You unmitigated—"

"If I was lucky," she said, and held up a cautioning finger, "only if I was lucky, wouldn't it be, Master Toth? And your books will tell you what's luckiest for you and me and all—won't they?" She smiled at him, a cheerful, believing smile. "I'm what you was born for, me, Melot Cassissinin, and I'm the luckiest woman alive."

THE UNSHADOWED LAND

God turned his left eye to the earth and it shone like silver and burned the land with cold; he looked on the world with his right eye and that eye blazed like gold at melting heat: like the refining of gold it burned. He spread his wings and the wind of them scoured the sands with heat and broke the very stone. He flew, and the shadow of his wings was the sandstorm: so vast were those wings that there was nothing but that shadow in the world. So terrible was the wind of those wings that it mingled earth and sky to the depth and the height and hurled great stones from their seats.

And when God had folded away those wings and looked out again from his white-hot right eye (he watched his brothers and sisters with the other, warily, knowing their ways)—When God looked out on the world it was not the same world; and it was not the same Akhet who walked a crooked line over the sands, for this Akhet was burned, and the sound of the wings of God had entered into her skull, so that she heard them continually in the stillness of the sands, and communed with nothing else, not even memory.

It was the whim of God to turn up old secrets in the sands, in each re-making of the world, curiosities which he had collected and now brought beneath his gaze. Some were mirthful, smiling as they gazed eyelessly upon the eyes of God; some were dried wisps of leather and bone, bizarrely contorted as if they sought in their motionless way to sink into the depths again; others still had an anguished look, as if they protested such violence. Rarest and most amazing, a few gazed upward with profound solemnity, sere flesh almost indistinguishable from bone: they smiled the inward smiles of ancient kings and queens, in their rags or their nakedness. There were beasts also, and stalking carnivores of polished bone, some of twisted horror, others of gaunt, wind-scoured nobleness. There were stones which God had made and his creatures had shaped in imitation of him and his brothers and his sisters. There were the remnants of places which had had great names among such creatures, but God himself gave them no names and they had none now, like Akhet, who had forgotten that she was Akhet, or what direction she moved.

She walked among these treasures. Sometimes it was one way and sometimes it was another: she forgot. But she found fellowship with these memories of God, and laughed with them, for she saw that the skin of her flesh became like their flesh, seamed with fine lines; and she fancied that her face was the face of the kings and queens she found, sere-lipped and hollow-cheeked and terrible as God.

She laughed; and was alone with that laughter in her skull, which rang in sudden silence, for the roar of the wings, which had never yet ceased in her ears, did cease. She stood in the white-hot sight of God, in the light of his right eye that left no shadows on the land, in his terrible light that left no color but its own, and shone round the rocks so that they cast no shadow. There was no dark place in all the land. The eye of God looked into Akhet's heart, and the light of his eye shone all round it as it did the stones, and it was one color with the stones and the land, as all things were. The silence became that color and that taste, which was like the smell of molten copper in the nostrils; and that silence drank up her laughter and gave it back again.

Aaaa-ha, ah-ha, ah-ha, ah-ket, akhet, akhet, Akhet.

Her voice had become the voice of God, and that voice called her name, so that she turned and came, trusting as a child.

"Akhet!" she cried now and again, seeking herself. Or she was God, seeking Akhet. God's voice forever called her name, in a voice multiplied and strange.

"Akhet, Akhet, Akhet!"

She had thirsted; she had water and had forgotten this, when the wings had left her deaf. Now it made a small welcome sound as she walked, like the river-song. (Indeed she trod on the stones of another of God's forgotten secrets, the very mummy of a river, which was sere as the forgotten dead. The stones of its bed clicked beneath her feet, and the shreds of her sandals caught and made her stumble.) She carried other things she had forgotten. They burdened her, but she did not let them go, having recalled that they were Akhet and Akhet was these things. She drained the stagnant heat of the waterskin and let it fall empty at her side. She laughed and God laughed, redoubled her laughter, and slowly closed his eye.

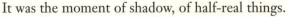

It was the moment of shadow, of half-real things.

She saw cliffs. And those cliffs were red as blood. And they echoed with the voice of God—*Akhet, Akhet, het, het*—

"Aiii," she cried in this blindness, when the eye of God had left her, and in the shadow-world she suspected God's mirth, and delusion.

Aiii, ii, ii! the cliffs gave back. She walked, and the delusion of a river became moisture under her feet, and the pain and the moisture grew—it was a river of blood in the dying of the light; and the cliffs were stained with it; and the shadows multiplied and moved.

"God!" she cried. (And *God—god—god—*, the stones.)

A jackal came to meet her, beside the riverbed. This was God's brother, and she was uneasy, for the brothers of God were his enemies, and this one was sly. He knew how to steal a soul away in his jaws, and take it down among his shadows before his brother saw. He laughed, and she walked on the blood, sure that she knew the river now, that it was the Dark River she had found; and the jackal-god would wish to lead her if he could.

She bent and gathered up a stone.

"Go away!" she cried. (*Go away-way-way*, the cliffs gave back.) She hurled it, and the god jumped aside, then trotted off a few paces and stood in recovered solemnity, his great ears pricked up, with which he hears his brother's thoughts and every counsel in the world. He smiled, and his jackal's teeth were sharp.

She threw another stone, and it became a spear in mid-flight; it became a spear in her mind, and flew with the noise of voices and the sound of waters. She wept when she had cast it, and stood still and shocked, in a place of rocks, in the blindness of God.

A stone turned and clicked. Another moved. She spun about to see, and the stones betrayed her, and she crashed down to her knees, blinking at this stranger the shadows made, this pale shape on whose breast a pectoral glittered in the wan last light: and on whose wrists the sheen of night-wrapped gold. Gold lapped her waist and spilled like flood on her thighs, and the linen of her robe was night-bound white; and the smell of her was like the smell of myrrh and smoke.

"Goddess," said Akhet, in the blindness of God, when he searched the worlds for his brothers and sisters, their doings. But one of the gods was surely here; and another was there, the jackal in the shadows; and Akhet forgot the stone on which her hand had fallen. Her knees quaked under her, for the goddess walked the trail of her blood and her face was the hollow-cheeked face of the queens of the dust. Her eyes were the pits of their eyes; and her mouth held the sere, fixed pleasure of their mouths, which hold secrets and do not share.

"What is your name?" that mouth asked.

"Akhet," said Akhet.

"And again: what name?"

"Akhet."

"Again: what name?"

It was a spell, Akhet was sure, and her bowels went to water and the wounds of her feet stung. She stank of sweat and trembled, and remembered the stone in her hand, so that her hand began to shake. She wished to throw that stone. But her own name froze in her mouth and stopped in her throat and barred her breath, or her soul would have come out into the night that moment, into the goddess' hands.

"It is not your name," the goddess said, and it was not. She was robbed and desolate and shivered in the cold. She had no hope then, that God would look and drive her Death away. God would open his silver eye but she would have no more name than the other secrets of this plain, and she would be no more than that to him.

"Mine is Neit," the goddess said.

It was a Death. There were many. This was hers; and she became calm then, and put her stone neatly back among the other stones. She remembered she carried things. One was an empty waterskin. One was a sheathed sword. One was a quiver of arrows, but she had lost the bow. She gathered these things into her lap, against her knees, and held to them as hers.

But the goddess sat down before her, her fine linen and her gold glimmering in God's blindness. Her smell was sweet attar and lotus amid the myrrh. "Why have you come here?" the goddess asked.

She tried to recall. She hunted this memory through her wits and it turned and leapt on her, black and sudden, so that she shook and hugged the remnants of herself.

"I came to die," she said; and a portion of herself came back to her, so that she winced and rocked with the grief of it, clutching at the sword. Red blood ran on sand and swirled in river currents, scarlet thread in brown. Cities burned. Tombs stood desolate. "Where have I come?" She blinked and lifted her eyes and gazed about the cliffs. There was no river, only a dry bed of stones between dead banks. "Goddess, where have I come?"

"Where you are. Lift up the sword. Lift up the sword, child."

She blinked, clenched the hilt to draw it closer. It was her defense.

This alone she had. But the hilt slid from the sheath and the blade was broken.

—had broken, in her hand. The children wailed, wailed in the fire and smoke; the chariots swept down on the morning gates—

She shook and trembled. The quiver spilled arrows of spoiled fletchings and dulled points. The sheath fell empty at her knees. She cast the blade after it and bowed her head and wept.

"What happened, daughter?" The voice came gently from those sere, awful jaws. "What became of the children?"

"O Neit, the chariots, the bitter swords—"

"Iron," the goddess named them. "The swords are iron." And the word went through her bones.

"No," she cried, and pressed her hands against her eyes. "O goddess, my children—"

"You fought."

"They killed my children!"

"They burned your cities."

"My cities. . . ."

She shuddered and wiped her eyes. There were bracelets on her wrists. They were an archer's bracelets. Her right hand had an archer's calluses. And some of herself came back. Her back went straighter. She stared at her death with her chin lifted and her heart beat stronger. "Can we not be done with what you have to do?"

"What is your name?"

A pain struck her heart, bleak and terrible.

—the jaws of crocodiles, the dead devoured, the mummies of kings hurled into the waters with the lately dead, stripped of all their gold—

"I lost," she said to the goddess. "I lost. Is there more name than that?"

"Bronze swords," the goddess said, "are no match for iron. Weak metal breaks."

"We had no iron."

"They gave your children to the crocodiles."

"We fought!"

(*—fought, fought,* the echoes said.)

"You fought. You fled. This is the unshadowed land. God burns it with his left eye and his right scours its secrets to the surface. Here is the resting place."

"This? This is paradise?"

"For the railed, the lost, those who forget their names. Those who give them up."

"I gave nothing up!"

"Would you do battle here?"

"For what? My soul?"

"Your name."

She drew a breath that ached with myrrh and lotus. With the smell of eternity. She let it go and laughed a weak, tearful laugh. Something broke then, like a scar tearing in her heart; but torn, it let the breath gust from her and come in again greater than before. She thought of her dead and her cities, of the thunder of the chariots like the wings of God. She rose to her feet with the sword hilt in her hand, and its pitiful small blade. The goddess rose, and the wind stirred her robes with the scent of dried leaves and sunbaked death.

"And if I lose, O Neit?"

"Do you ask?"

She drew another breath, freer than the last. She shook her head and the weight of braided locks swung about her face. "No." She went to fighting stance. "No need."

The goddess stretched out her hand. The sword grew cold as the left eye of God himself and shattered in her hand.

She hurled the hilt, and the goddess flung up her hands to ward it off; in that instant she rushed forward and flung her arms about her death.

It was utter, bitter cold. And Neit whispered in her ear: "You have won, daughter. I will tell your name. Let me go."

"Do you swear?"

"By the left eye I swear." And Neit became like smoke, flowing backward from her grasp, so that she stumbled to her knees. "Dear sister."

"My name!"

"It is Sekhmet."

—*temples ravaged, gold spilled, images of the lion-eyed tumbled and stripped of ornament, her name erased and scarred*—

"No," she cried. "I never was!"

"Sekhmet, my sister. They have burned your cities, slaughtered your babes, and your priestesses—can you forget? Can you forget your land?"

—*priestesses dying in the courtyards, the young man before the walls*—

"Do you not hear them?"

It was a murmuring, like the river, like the wail of babes and the keening of the doomed.

—*A few struggled in the dark, in the shadow, a few still struck and ran*—

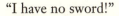

"I have no sword!"

Goddess! Sekhmet! Lion-headed, lion-hearted, help us or we die—

"One can always forget again," said Neit. "One can lie down and sleep in this place of forgotten gods."

"A curse on you!" Sekhmet cried, and picked up the bladeless hilt.

"With that?" Neit mocked her. "You left your shield. Your bow is broken. You have no sword."

"Iron," Sekhmet said. She drew a great breath, and hurled the hilt through Neit's insubstance. There came a sweet taint of corruption in the air. And blood. She walked upon it. Her feet slipped upon the stones.

"Where are you going?" Anubis asked, jackal-headed. He stood in shadows close to the path. His ears pricked up. His voice came strangely from narrow jaws. "What are you hunting, Sekhmet?"

She turned her face on him and he stepped back. "Follow in my steps," she said; and her voice had changed. Her step had grown softer and catlike sure.

"What do you seek?" asked Neit, behind her, her voice grown faint and far. "What do you seek?"

"Worshippers. And swords."

Then there was no voice. She leapt from rock to rock.

The wind stirred, for God spread his wings. He turned his left eye to the world, and the silver cold of it spilled down the cliffs and onto the stones and round their edges until there was no shadow anywhere. There was only cold, cold to crack the marrow and break the rocks.

A lion stalked the unshadowed plain, headed riverward, though that river was long distant. At some distance a jackal followed in the distracted way of his kind, seeking this and seeking that, but never losing the track, not quite. The great terror was loose again; war stalked on lion's feet, seeking lost young, lost prey, and her steps had the smell of blood. He always followed her, did the jackal god.

POTS

It was a most bitter trip, the shuttle-descent to the windy surface. Suited, encumbered by lifesupport, Desan stepped off the platform and waddled onward into the world, waving off the attentions of small spidery surface robots: "Citizen, this way, this way, citizen, have a care— Do watch your step; a suit tear is hazardous."

Low-level servitors. Desan detested them. The chief of operations had plainly sent these creatures accompanied only by an AI eight-wheel transport, which inconveniently chose to park itself a good five hundred paces beyond the shuttle blast zone, an uncomfortable long walk across the dusty pan in the crinkling, pack-encumbered oxy-suit. Desan turned, casting a forlorn glance at the shuttle waiting there on its landing gear, silver, dip-nosed wedge under a gunmetal sky, at rest on an ocher and rust landscape. He shivered in the sky-view, surrendered himself and his meager luggage to the irritating ministries of the service robots, and waddled on his slow way down to the waiting AI transport.

"Good day," the vehicle said inanely, opening a door. "My passenger compartment is not safe atmosphere; do you understand. Lord Desan?"

"Yes, yes." Desan climbed in and settled himself in the front seat, a slight give of the transport's suspensors. The robots fussed about in insectile hesitance, delicately setting his luggage case just so, adjusting, adjusting till it conformed with their robotic, template-compared notion of their job. Maddening. Typical robotic efficiency. Desan slapped the pressure-sensitive seating. "Come, let's get this moving, shall we?"

The AI talked to its duller cousins, a single squeal that sent them scuttling; "Attention to the door, citizen." It lowered and locked. The AI started its noisy drive motor. "Will you want the windows dimmed, citizen?"

"No. I want to see this place."

"A pleasure, Lord Desan."

Doubtless for the AI, it was.

The station was situated a long drive across the pan, across increasingly softer dust that rolled up to obscure the rearview—softer, looser dust, occasionally a wind-scooped hollow that made the transport flex— "Do forgive me, citizen. Are you comfortable?"

"Quite, quite, you're very good."

"Thank you, citizen."

And finally—*finally!*—something other than flat appeared, the merest humps of hills, and one anomalous mountain, a massive, long bar that began as a haze and became solid; became a smooth regularity before the gentle brown folding of hills hardly worthy of the name.

Mountain. The eye indeed took it for a volcanic or sedimentary formation at distance, some anomalous and stubborn outcrop in this barren reach, where all else had declined to entropy, absolute, featureless flat. But when the AI passed along its side this mountain had joints and seams, had the marks of *making* on it; and even knowing in advance what it was, driving along within view of the jointing, this work of Ancient hands—chilled Desan's well-traveled soul. The station itself came into view against the weathered hills, a collection of shocking green domes on a brown lifeless world. But such domes Desan had seen. With only the AI for witness, Desan turned in his seat, pressed the flexible bubble of the helmet to the double-seal window, and stared and stared at the stonework until it passed to the rear and the dust obscured it.

"Here, lord," said the AI, eternally cheerful. "We are almost at the station—a little climb. I do it very smoothly."

Flex and lean; sway and turn. The domes lurched closer in the forward window and the motor whined. "I've very much enjoyed serving you."

"Thank you," Desan murmured, seeing another walk before him, ascent of a plastic grid to an airlock and no sight of a welcoming committee.

More service robots, scuttling toward them as the transport stopped and adjusted itself with a pneumatic wheeze.

"Thank you, Lord Desan, do watch your helmet, watch your life-support connections, watch your footing please. The dust is slick. . . ."

"Thank you." With an AI one had no recourse.

Thank *you*, my lord." The door came up; Desan extricated himself from the seat and stepped to the dusty ground, carefully shielding the oxy-pack from the door-frame and panting with the unaccustomed weight of it in such gravity. The service robots moved to take his luggage while Desan waddled doggedly on, up the plastic gridwork path to the glaringly lime-green domes. Plastics. Plastics which could not even originate in this desolation, but which came from their ships' spare biomass. Here all was dead, frighteningly void: even the signal that guided him to the lakebed was robotic, like the advisement that a transport would meet him.

The airlock door shot open ahead; and living, suited personnel appeared, three of them, at last, at long last, flesh-and-blood personnel came walking toward him to offer proper courtesy. But before that mountain of stone; before these glaring green structures and the robotic paraphernalia of research that made all the reports real— Desan still felt the deathliness of the place. He trudged ahead, touched the offered, gloved hands, acknowledged the expected salutations, and proceeded up the jointed-plastic walk to the open airlock. His marrow refused to be warmed. The place refused to come into clear focus, like some bad dream with familiar elements hideously distorted.

A hundred years of voyage since he had last seen this world and then only from orbit, receiving reports third-hand. A hundred years of work on this planet preceded this small trip from port to research center, under that threatening sky, in this place by a mountain that had once been a dam on a lake that no longer existed.

There had been the findings on the moon, of course. A few artifacts. A cloth of symbols. Primitive, unthinkably primitive. First omen of the findings on this sere, rust-brown world.

He accompanied the welcoming committee into the airlock of the main dome, waited through the cycle, and breathed a sigh of relief as the indicator-lights went from white to orange and the inner door admitted them to the interior. He walked forward, removed the helmet, and drew a deep breath of air unexpectedly and unpleasantly tainted. The foyer of this centermost dome was businesslike—plastic walls, visible ducting. A few plants struggled for life in a planter in the center of the floor. Before it, a black pillar and a common enough emblem: a plaque with two naked alien figures, the diagrams of a starsystem—reproduced even to its scars and pitting. In some places it might be mundane, unnoticed.

It belonged here, *belonged* here, and it could never be mundane, this message of the Ancients.

"Lord Desan," a female voice said, and he turned, awkward in the suit.

It was Dr. Gothon herself, unmistakable aged woman in science-blues. The rare honor dazed him, and wiped away all failure of hospitality thus far. She held out her hand. Startled, he reacted in kind, remembered the glove, and hastily drew back his hand to strip the glove. Her gesture was gracious and he felt the very fool and very much off his stride, his hands touching—no, firmly grasped by the callused, aged hand of this legendary intellect. Age-soft and hard-surfaced at once. Age and vigor. His tongue quite failed him, and he felt, recalling his purpose, utterly daunted.

"Come in, let them rid you of that suit, Lord Desan. Will you rest after your trip, a nap, a cup of tea perhaps. The robots are taking your luggage to your room. Accommodations here aren't luxurious, but I think you'll find them comfortable."

Deeper and deeper into courtesies. One could lose all sense of direction in such surroundings, letting oneself be disarmed by gentleness, by pleasantness—by embarrassed reluctance to resist.

"I want to see what I came to see, doctor." Desan unfastened more seams and shed the suit into waiting hands, smoothed his coveralls. Was that too brusque, too unforgivably hasty? "I don't think I *could* rest, Dr. Gothon. I attended my comfort aboard the shuttle. I'd like to get my bearings here at least, if one of your staff would be so kind to take me in hand—"

"Of course, of course, I rather expected as much—Do come, please, let me show you about. I'll explain as much as I can. Perhaps I can convince you as I go."

He was overwhelmed from the start; he had expected some high official, the director of operations most likely. Not Gothon. He walked slightly after the doctor, the stoop-shouldered presence which passed like a benison among the students and lesser staff—I *saw the Doctor,* the young ones had been wont to say in hushed tones, aboard the ship, when Gothon strayed absently down a corridor in her rare intervals of waking. *I saw the Doctor.*

In that voice one might claim a theophany.

They had rarely waked her, lesser researchers being sufficient for most worlds; while he was the fifth lord-navigator, the fourth born on the journey, a time-dilated trifle, fifty-two waking years of age and a mere two thousand years of voyage against—aeons of Gothon's slumberous life.

And Desan's marrow ached now at such gentle grace in this bowed, mottle-skinned old scholar, this sleuth patiently deciphering the greatest mystery of the universe. Pity occurred to him. He suffered personally in this place; but not as Gothon would have suffered here, in that inward quiet where Gothon carried on thoughts the ship-crews were sternly admonished never to disturb.

Students rushed now to open doors for them, pressed themselves to the walls and allowed their passage into deeper halls within the maze of the domes. Passing hands brushed Desan's sleeves, welcome offered the current lord-navigator; he reciprocated with as much of attention as he could devote to courtesy in his distress. His heart labored in the unaccustomed gravity, his nostrils accepted not only the effluvium of dome-plastics and the recyclers and so many bodies dwelling together; but a flinty, bitter air, like electricity or dry dust. He imagined some hazardous leakage of the atmosphere into the dome: unsettling thought. The hazards of the place came home to him, and he wished already to be away.

Gothon had endured here, during his further voyages—seven years more of her diminishing life; waked four times, and this was the fourth, continually active now for five years, her longest stint yet in any waking. She had found data finally worth the consumption of her life, and she burned it without stint. *She* believed. She believed, enough to die pursuing it.

He shuddered up and down and followed Gothon through a seal-door toward yet another dome, and his gut tightened in dismay; for there were shelves on either hand, and those shelves were lined with yellowed skulls, endless rows of staring dark sockets and grinning jaws. Some were long-nosed; some were short. Some small, virtually noseless skulls had fangs which gave them a wise and intelligent look—*like miniature people, like babies with grown-up features,* must be the initial reaction of anyone seeing them in the holos or viewing the specimens brought up to the orbiting labs. But cranial capacity in these was much too small. The real sapient occupied further shelves, row upon row of eyeless, generously domed skulls, grinning in their flat-toothed way, in permanent horror—provoking profoundest horror in those that discovered them here, in this desolation.

Here Gothon paused, selected one of the small sapient skulls, much reconstructed: Desan had at least the skill to recognize the true bone from the plassbone bonded to it. This skull was far more delicate than the others, the jaw smaller. The front two teeth were restructs. So was one of the side.

"It was a child," Gothon said. "We call her Missy. The first we found at this site, up in the hills, in a streambank. Most of Missy's feet were gone, but she's otherwise intact. Missy was all alone except for a little animal all tucked up in her arms. We keep them together—never mind the cataloguing." She lifted an anomalous and much-reconstructed skull from the shelf among the sapients; fanged and delicate. "Even archaeologists have sentiment."

"I—see—" Helpless, caught in courtesy, Desan extended an unwilling finger and touched the child-skull.

"Back to sleep." Gothon set both skulls tenderly back on the shelf; and dusted her hands and walked further, Desan following, beyond a simple door and into a busy room of workbenches piled high with a clutter of artifacts.

Staff began to rise from their dusty work in a sudden startlement. "No, no, go on," Gothon, said quietly. "We're only passing through; ignore us—Here, do you see, Lord Desan?" Gothon reached carefully past a researcher's shoulder and lifted from the counter an elongate ribbed bottle with the opalescent patina of long burial. "We find a great many of these. Mass production. Industry. Not only on this continent. This same bottle exists in sites all over the world, in the uppermost strata. Same design. Near the time of the calamity. We trace global alliances and trade by such small things." She set it down and gathered up a virtually complete vase, much patched. "It always comes to pots, Lord Desan. By pots and bottles we track them through the ages. Many layers. They had a long and complex past."

Desan reached out and touched the corroded brown surface of the vase, discovering a single bright remnant of blue glaze along with the gray encrustations of long burial. "How long—how long does it take to reduce a thing to this?"

"It depends on the soil—on moisture, on acidity. This came from hereabouts." Gothon tenderly set it back on a shelf, walked on, frail, hunch-shouldered figure among the aisles of the past. "But very long, very long to obliterate so much—almost all the artifacts are gone. Metals oxidize; plastics rot; cloth goes very quickly; paper and wood last quite long in a desert climate, but they go, finally. Moisture dissolves the details of sculpture. Only the noble metals survive intact. Soil creep warps even stone; crushes metal. We find even the best pots in a matrix of pieces, a puzzle-toss. Fragile as they are, they outlast monuments, they last as long as the earth that holds them, drylands, wetlands, even beneath the sea—where no marine life exists to trouble them. That bottle and that pot are as venerable as that great dam. The makers wouldn't have thought that, would they?"

"But—" Desan's mind reeled at the remembrance of the great plain, the silt and the deep buried secrets.

"But?"

"You surely might miss important detail. A world to search. You might walk right over something and misinterpret everything."

"Oh, yes, it can happen. But *finding* things where we expect them is an important clue, Lord Desan, a confirmation—one only has to suspect where to look. We locate our best hope first—a sunken, a raised place in those photographs we trouble the orbiters to take; but one gets a *feeling* about the lay of the land—more than the mechanical probes, Lord Desan." Gothon's dark eyes crinkled in the passage of thoughts unguessed, and Desan stood lost in Gothon's unthinkable mentality. What did a mind *do* in such age? Wander? Could the great doctor lapse into mysticism? To report such a thing—would solve one difficulty. But to have that regrettable duty—

"It's a feeling for living creatures, Lord Desan. It's reaching out to the land and saying—if this were long ago, if I thought to build, if I thought to trade—where would I go? Where would my neighbors live?"

Desan coughed delicately, wishing to draw things back to hard fact. "And the robot probes, of course, do assist."

"Probes, Lord Desan, are heartless things. A robot can be very skilled, but a researchers directs it only at distance, blind to opportunities and the true sense of the land. But you were born to space. Perhaps it makes no sense."

"I take your word for it," Desan said earnestly. He felt the weight of the sky on his back. The leaden, awful sky, leprous and unhealthy cover between them, and the star and the single moon. Gothon remembered homeworld. *Remembered homeworld.* Had been renowned in her field even there. The old scientist claimed to come to such a landscape and *locate* things by seeing things that robot eyes could not, by thinking thoughts those dusty skulls had held in fleshly matter—

—how long ago?

"We look for mounds," Gothon said, continuing in her brittle gait down the aisle, past the bowed heads and shy looks of staff and students at their meticulous tasks. The work of tiny electronic needles proceeded about them, the patient ticking away at encrustations to bring ancient surfaces to light. "They built massive structures. Great skyscrapers. Some of them must have lasted, oh, thousands of years intact; but when they went unstable, they fell, and their fall made rubble; and the wind came and the rivers shifted their courses around the ruin, and of course the weight of sediment piled up, wind- and water-driven. From that point, its own weight moved it and warped it and complicated our work." Gothon paused again beside a further table, where holo plates stood inactive. She waved her hand and a landscape showed itself, a serpentined row of masonry across a depression. "See the wall there. They didn't build it that way, all wavering back and forth and up and down. Gravity and soil movement deformed it. It was buried till we unearthed it. Otherwise, wind and rain alone would have destroyed it ages ago. As it will do, now, if time doesn't rebury it."

"And this great pile of stone—" Desan waved an arm, indicating the imagined direction of the great dam and realizing himself disoriented. "How old is it?"

"Old as the lake it made."

"But contemporaneous with the fall?"

"Yes. Do you know, that mass may be standing when the star dies. The few great dams; the pyramids we find here and there around the world—one only guesses at their age. They'll outlast any other surface feature except the mountains themselves."

"Without life."

"Oh, but there is."

"Declining."

"No, no. Not declining." The doctor waved her hand and a puddle appeared over the second holo plate, all green with weed waving feathery tendrils back and forth in the surge. "The moon still keeps this world from entropy. There's water, not as much as this dam saw— It's the weed, this little weed that gives one hope for this world. The little life, the things that fly and crawl—the lichens and the life on the flatlands."

"But nothing they knew."

"No. Life's evolved new answers here. Life's starting over."

"It certainly hasn't much to start with, has it?"

"Not very much. It's a question that interests Dr. Bothogi—whether the life making a start here has the time left, and whether the consumption curve doesn't add up to defeat— But life doesn't know that. We're very concerned about contamination. But we fear it's inevitable. And who knows, perhaps it will have added something beneficial." Dr. Gothon lit yet another holo with a wave of her hand. A streamlined six-legged creature scuttled energetically across a surface of dead moss, frantically waving antennae and making no apparent progress.

"The inheritors of the world." Despair chilled Desan's marrow.

"But each generation of these little creatures is an unqualified success. The last to perish perishes in profound tragedy, of course, but without consciousness of it. The awareness will have, oh, half a billion years to wait—then, maybe it will appear; if the star doesn't fail; it's already far advanced down the sequence." Another holo, the image of desert, of blowing sand, beside the holo of the surge of weed in a pool. "Life makes life. That weed you see is busy making life. It's taking in and converting and building a chain of support that will enable things to feed on it, while more of its kind grows. That's what life does. It's busy, all unintended, of course, but fortuitously building itself a way off the planet."

Desan cast her an uncomfortable look askance.

"Oh, indeed. Biomass. Petrochemicals. The storehouse of aeons of energy all waiting the use of Consciousness. And that consciousness, if it arrives, dominates the world because awareness is a way of making life more efficiently. But consciousness is a perilous thing, Lord Desan. Consciousness is a computer loose with its own perceptions and performing calculations on its own course, in the service of that little weed; billions of such computers all running and calculating faster and faster, adjusting themselves and their ecological environment, and what if there were the smallest, the most insignificant software error at the outset?"

"You don't believe such a thing. You don't reduce us to that." Desan's faith was shaken; this good woman had not gone unstable, this great intellect had had her faith shaken, that was what—the great and gentle doctor had, in her unthinkable age, acquired cynicism, and he fought back with his fifty-two meager years. "Surely, but surely this isn't the proof, doctor, this could have been a natural calamity."

"Oh, yes, the meteor strike." The doctor waved past a series of holos on a fourth plate, and a vast crater showed in aerial view, a crater so vast the picture showed planetary curvature. It was one of the planet's main features, shockingly visible from space. "But this solar system shows scar after scar of such events. A many-planeted system like this, a star well-attended by debris in its course through the galaxy— Look at the airless bodies, the moons, consider the number of meteor strikes that crater them. Tell me, space farer: am I not right in that?"

Desan drew in a breath, relieved to be questioned in his own element. "Of course, the system is prone to that kind of accident. But that crater is ample cause—"

"If it came when there was still sapience here. But that hammer-blow fell on a dead world."

He gazed on the eroded crater, the sandswept crustal melting, eloquent of age. "You have proof."

"Strata. Pots. Ironic, they must have feared such an event very greatly. One thinks they must have had a sense of doom about them, perhaps on the evidence of their moon; or understanding the mechanics of their solar system; or perhaps primitive times witnessed such falls, and they remembered. One catches a glimpse of the mind that reached out from here . . . what impelled it, what it sought."

"How can we know that? We overlay our mind on their expectations—" Desan silenced himself, abashed, terrified. It was next to heresy. In a moment more he would have committed irremediable indiscretion; and the lords-magistrate on the orbiting station would hear it by suppertime, to his eternal detriment.

"We stand in their landscape, handle their bones, we hold their skulls in our fleshly hands and try to think in their world. Here we stand beneath a threatening heaven. What will we do?"

"Try to escape. Try to get off this world. They *did* get off. The celestial artifacts—"

"Archaeology is ever so much easier in space. A million years, two, and a thing still shines. Records still can be read. A color can blaze out undimmed after aeons, when first a light falls on it. One surface chewed away by microdust, and the opposing face pristine as the day it had its maker's hand on it. You keep asking me about the age of these ruins. But we know that, don't we truly suspect it, in the marrow of our bones—at what age they fell silent?"

"It *can't* have happened then!"

"Come with me, Lord Desan." Gothon waved a hand, extinguishing all the holos, and, walking on, opened the door into yet another hallway. "So much to catalog. That's much of the work in that room. They're students, mostly. Restoring what they can; numbering, listing. A librarian's job, just to know where things are filed. In five hundred years more of intensive cataloguing and restoring, we may know them well enough to know something of their minds, though we may never find more of their written language than those artifacts on the moon. A place of wonders. A place of ongoing wonders, in Dr. Bothogi's work. A little algae beginning the work all over again. Perhaps not for the first time—interesting thought."

"You mean—" Desan overtook the aged doctor in the narrow, sterile hall, a series of ringing steps. "You mean—before the sapients evolved—there were other calamities, other rebeginnings."

"Oh, well before. It sends chills up one's back, doesn't it, to think how incredibly stubborn life might be here, how persistent in the calamity of the skies—the algae and then the creeping things and the slow, slow climb to dominance—"

"Previous sapients?"

"Interesting question in itself. But a thing need not be sapient to dominate a world, Lord Desan. Only tough. Only efficient. Haven't the worlds proven that? High sapience is a rare jewel. So many successes are dead ends. Flippers and not hands; lack of vocal apparatus—unless you believe in telepathy, which I assuredly don't. No. Vocalizing is necessary. Some sort of long-distance communication. Light-flashes; sound; something. Else your individuals stray apart in solitary discovery and rediscovery and duplication of effort. Oh, even with awareness—even granted that rare attribute—how many species lack something essential, or have some handicap that will stop them before civilization; before technology—"

"—before they leave the planet. But they *did* that, they were the one in a thousand— Without them—"

"Without them. Yes." Gothon turned her wonderful soft eyes on him at close range and for a moment he felt a great and terrible stillness like the stillness of a grave. "Childhood ends here. One way or another, it ends."

He was struck speechless. He stood there, paralyzed a moment, his mind tumbling freefall; then blinked and followed the doctor like a child, helpless to do otherwise.

Let me rest, he thought then, *let us forget this beginning and this day, let me go somewhere and sit down and have a warm drink to get the chill from my marrow and let us begin again. Perhaps we can begin with facts and not fancies—*

But he would not rest. He feared that there was no rest to be had in this place, that once the body stopped moving the weight of the sky would come down, the deadly sky that had boded destruction for all the history of this lost species; and the age of the land would seep into his bones and haunt his dreams as the far greater scale of stars did not.

All the years I've voyaged, Dr. Gothon, all the years of my life searching from star to star. Relativity has made orphans of us. The world will have sainted you. Me, it never knew. In a quarter of a million years—they'll have forgotten; O doctor, you know more than I how a world ages. A quarter of a million years you've seen—and we're both orphans. Me endlessly cloned. You in your long sleep, your several clones held eons waiting in theirs—O doctor, we'll recreate you. And not truly you, ever again. No more than I'm Desan-prime. I'm only the fifth lord-navigator.

In a quarter of a million years, has not our species evolved beyond us, might they not, may they not find some faster transport and find us, their eons-lost precursors; and we will not know each other. Dr. Gothon—how could we know each other—if they had, but they have not; we have become the wavefront of a quest that never overtakes us, never surpasses us.

In a quarter of a million years, might some calamity have befallen us and our world be like this world, ocher and deadly rust?

While we are clones and children of clones, genetic fossils, anomalies of our kind?

What are they to us and we to them? We seek the Ancients, the makers of the probe.

Desan's mind reeled; adept as he was at time-relativity calculations, accustomed as he was to stellar immensities, his mind tottered and he fought to regain the corridor in which they walked, he and the doctor. He widened his stride yet again, overtaking Gothon at the next door.

"Doctor." He put out his hand, preventing her, and then feared his own question, his own skirting of heresy and tempting of hers. "Are you beyond doubt? You can't be beyond doubt. They could have simply abandoned this world in its calamity."

Again the impact of those gentle eyes, devastating. "Tell me, tell me, Lord Desan. In all your travels, in all the several near stars you've visited in a century of effort, have you found traces?"

"No. But they could have gone—"

"—leaving no traces, except on their moon?"

"There may be others. The team in search on the fourth planet—"

"Finds nothing."

"You yourself say that you have to stand in that landscape, you have to think with their mind— Maybe Dr. Ashodt hasn't come to the right hill, the right plain—"

"If there are artifacts there, they are only a few. I'll tell you why I know so. Come, come with me." Gothon waved a hand and the door gaped on yet another laboratory.

Desan walked. He had rather have walked out to the deadly surface than through this simple door, to the answer Gothon promised him . . . but habit impelled him; habit, duty—necessity. He had no other purpose for his life but this. He had been left none, lord-navigator, fifth incarnation of Desan Das. They had launched his original with none, his second incarnation had had less, and time and successive incarnations had stripped everything else away. So he went, into a place at once too mundane and too strange to be quite sane—mundane because it was sterile as any lab, a well-lit place of littered tables and a few researchers; and strange because hundreds and hundreds of skulls and bones were piled on shelves in heaps on one wall, silent witnesses. An articulated skeleton hung in its frame; the skeleton of a small animal scampered in macabre rigidity on a tabletop.

He stopped. He stared about him, lost for the moment in the stare of all those eyeless sockets of weathered bone.

"Let me present my colleagues," Gothon was saying; Desan focused on the words late, and blinked helplessly as Gothon rattled off names. Bothogi the zoologist was one, younger than most, seventeenth incarnation, burning himself out in profligate use of his years: so with all the incarnations of Bothogi Nan. The rest of the names slid past his ears ungathered—true strangers, the truly-born, sons and daughters of the voyage. He was lost in their stares like the stares of the skulls, eyes behind which shadows and dust were truth, gazes full of secrets and heresies.

They knew him and he did not know them, not even Lord Bothogi. He felt his solitude, the helplessness of his convictions—all lost in the dust and the silences.

"Kagodte," said Gothon, to a white-eared, hunched individual, "Kagodte—the Lord Desan has come to see your model."

"Ah." The aged eyes flicked nervously.

"Show him, pray, Dr. Kagodte."

The hunched man walked over to the table, spread his hands. A holo flared and Desan blinked, having expected some dreadful image, some confrontation with a reconstruction. Instead, columns of words rippled in the air, green and blue. Numbers ticked and multiplied. In his startlement he lost the beginning and failed to follow them. "I don't see—"

"We speak statistics here," Gothon said. "We speak data; we couch our heresies in mathematical formulae."

Desan turned and stared at Gothon in fright. "Heresies I have nothing to do with, doctor. I deal with facts. I come here to find facts."

"Sit down," the gentle doctor said. "Sit down, Lord Desan. There, move the bones over, do; the owners won't mind, there, that's right."

Desan collapsed onto a stool facing a white worktable. Looked up reflexively, eye drawn by a wall-mounted stone that bore the blurred image of a face, eroded, time-dulled—

The juxtaposition of image and bones overwhelmed him. The two whole bodies portrayed on the plaque. The sculpture. The rows of flesh-less skulls.

Dead. World hammered by meteors, life struggling in its most rudimentary forms. Dead.

"Ah," Gothon said. Desan looked around and saw Gothon looking up at the wall in her turn. "Yes. That. Occasionally the fall of stone will protect a surface. Confirmation. Indeed. But the skulls tell us as much. With our measurements and our holos we can flesh them. We can make them—even more vivid. Do you want to see?"

Desan's mouth worked. "No." A small word. A coward word. "Later. So this was *one* place— You still don't convince me of your thesis, doctor, I'm sorry."

"The place. The world of origin. A many-layered world. The last layers are rich with artifacts of one period, one global culture. Then silence. Species extinguished. Stratum upon stratum of desolation. Millions of years of geological record—" Gothon came round the end of the table and sat down in the opposing chair, elbows on the table, a scatter of bone between them. Gothon's green eyes shone watery in the brilliant light, her mouth was wrinkled about the jowls and trembled in minute cracks, like aged clay. "The statistics, Lord Desan, the dry statistics tell us. They tell us the centers of production of artifacts, such as we have; they tell us compositions, processes the Ancients knew—and there was no progression into advanced materials. None of the materials we take for granted, metals that would have lasted—"

"And perhaps they went to some new process, materials that degraded completely. Perhaps their information storage was on increasingly perishable materials. Perhaps they developed these materials in space."

"Technology has steps. The dry numbers, the dusty dry numbers, the incidences and concentration of items, the numbers and the pots—always the pots, Lord Desan; and the imperishable stones; and the very fact of the meteors—the undeniable fact of the meteor strikes. Could we not avert such a calamity for our own world? Could we not have done it—oh, a half a century before we left?"

"I'm sure you remember, Dr. Gothon. I'm sure you have the advantage of me. But—"

"You see the evidence. You want to cling to your hopes. But there is only one question—no, two. Is this the species that launched the probe—Yes. Or evolution and coincidence have cooperated mightily. Is this the only world they inhabited? Beyond all doubt. If there are artifacts on the fourth planet they are scoured by its storms, buried, lost."

"But they may *be* there."

"There is no abundance of them. There is no *progression*, Lord Desan. That is the key thing. There is nothing beyond these substances, these materials. This was not a starfaring civilization. They launched their slow, unmanned probes, with their cameras, their robot eyes—not for us. We always knew that. We were the recipients of flotsam. Mere wreckage on the beach."

"It was purposeful!" Desan hissed, trembling, surrounded by them all, a lone credent among this quiet heresy in this room. "Dr. Gothon, your unique position—is a position of trust, of profound trust; I beg you to consider the effect you have—"

"Do you threaten me, Lord Desan? Are you here for that, to silence me?"

Desan looked desperately about him, at the sudden hush in the room. The minute tickings of probes and picks had stopped. Eyes stared. "Please." He looked back. "I came here to gather data; I expected a simple meeting, a few staff meetings—to consider things at leisure—"

"I have distressed you. You wonder how it would be if the lords-magistrate fell at odds with me. I am aware of myself as an institution, Lord Desan. I remember Desan Das. I remember launch, the original five ships. I have waked to all but one of your incarnations. Not to mention the numerous incarnations of the lords-magistrate."

"You cannot discount them! Even you—let me plead with you, Dr. Gothon, be patient with us."

"You do not need to teach me patience, Desan-Five."

He shivered convulsively. Even when Gothon smiled that gentle, disarming smile. "You have to give me facts, doctor, not mystical communings with the landscape. The lords-magistrate accept that this is the world of origin. I assure you they never would have devoted so much time to creating a base here if that were not the case."

"Come, lord, those power systems on the probe, so long dead—What was it truly for, but to probe something very close at hand? Even orthodoxy admits that. And what is close at hand but their own solar system? Come, I've *seen* the original artifact and the original tablet. Touched it with my hands. This was a *primitive* venture, designed to cross their own solar system—*which they had not the capability to do.*"

Desan blinked. "But the purpose—"

"Ah. The purpose."

"You say that you stand in a landscape and you think in their mind. Well, Doctor, *use* this skill you claim. What did the Ancients intend? Why did they send it out with a message?"

The old eyes flickered, deep and calm and pained. "An oracular message, Lord Desan. A message into the dark of their own future, unaimed, unfocused. Without answer. Without hope of answer. We know its voyage time. Five million years. They spoke to the universe at large. This probe went out, and they fell silent shortly afterward—the depth of this dry lake of dust, Lord Desan, is eight and a quarter million years."

"I will not believe that."

"Eight and a quarter million years ago, Lord Desan. Calamity fell on them, calamity global and complete within a century, perhaps within a decade of the launch of that probe. Perhaps calamity fell from the skies; but demonstrably it was atomics and their own doing. They were at that precarious stage. And the destruction in the great centers is cat-astrophic and of one level. Destruction centered in places of heavy pop-ulation. That is what those statistics say. Atomics, Lord Desan."

"I cannot accept this!"

"Tell me, spacefarer—do you understand the workings of weather? What those meteor strikes could do, the dust raised by atomics could do with equal efficiency. Never mind the radiation that alone would have killed millions—never mind the destruction of centers of government: we speak of global calamity, the dimming of the sun in dust, the living oceans and lakes choking in dying photosynthetes in a sunless winter, killing the food chain from the bottom up—"

"You have no proof!"

"The universality, the ruin of the population-centers. Arguably, they had the capacity to prevent meteor-impact. That may be a matter of de-bate. But beyond a doubt in my own mind, simultaneous destruction of the population centers indicates atomics. The statistics, the pots and the dry numbers, Lord Desan, doom us to that answer. The question is an-swered. There were no descendants; there was no escape from the world. They destroyed themselves before that meteor hit them."

Desan rested his mouth against his joined hands. Staring helplessly at the doctor. "A lie. Is that what you're saying? We pursued a lie?"

"Is it their fault that we needed them so much?"

Desan pushed himself to his feet and stood there by mortal effort. Gothon sat staring up at him with those terrible dark eyes.

"What will you do, lord-navigator? Silence me? The old woman's grown difficult at last: wake my clone after, tell it—what the lords-magistrate select for it to be told?" Gothon waved a hand about the room, indicating the staff, the dozen sets of living eyes among the dead. "Bothogi too, those of us who have clones—but what of the rest of the staff? How much will it take to silence all of us?"

Desan stared about him, trembling. "Dr. Gothon—" He leaned his hands on the table to look at Gothon. "You mistake me. You utterly mistake me— The lords-magistrate may have the station, but I have the ships, *I*, I and my staff. I propose no such thing. I've come home—" The unaccustomed word caught in his throat; he considered it, weighed it, accepted it at least in the emotional sense. "—home, Dr. Gothon, after a hundred years of search, to discover this argument and this dissension."

"Charges of heresy—"

"They dare not make them against *you*." A bitter laugh welled up. "Against *you* they have no argument and you well know it, Dr. Gothon."

"Against their violence, lord-navigator, I have no defense."

"But she has," said Dr. Bothogi.

Desan turned, flicked a glance from the hardness in Bothogi's green eyes to the even harder substance of the stone in Bothogi's hand. He flung himself about again, hands on the table, abandoning the defense of his back. "Dr. Gothon! I appeal to you! I am your friend!"

"For myself," said Dr. Gothon, "I would make no defense at all. But, as you say—they have no argument against me. So it must be a general catastrophe—the lords-magistrate have to silence everyone, don't they? *Nothing* can be left of this base. Perhaps they've quietly dislodged an asteroid or two and put them on course. In the guise of mining, perhaps they will silence this poor old world forever—myself and the rest of the relics. Lost relics and the distant dead are always safer to venerate, aren't they?"

"That's absurd!"

"Or perhaps they've become more hasty now that your ships are here and their judgment is in question. *They* have atomics within their capability, lord-navigator. They can disable your shuttle with beam-fire. They can simply welcome you to the list of casualties—a charge of heresy. A thing taken out of context, who knows? After all—all lords are immediately duplicatable, the captains accustomed to obey the lords-magistrate—what few of them are awake—am I not right? If an institution like myself can be threatened—where is the fifth lord-navigator in their plans? And of a sudden those plans will be moving in haste."

Desan blinked. "Dr. Gothon—I assure you—"

"If you are my friend, lord-navigator, I hope for your survival. The robots are theirs, do you understand. Their powerpacks are sufficient for transmission of information to the base AIs; and from the communications center it goes to satellites; and from satellites to the station and the lords-magistrate. This room is safe from their monitoring. We have seen to that. They cannot hear you."

"I cannot believe these charges, I cannot accept it—"

"Is murder so new?"

"Then come with me! Come with me to the shuttle, we'll confront them—"

"The transportation to the port is theirs. It would not permit. The transport AI would resist. The planes have AI components. And we might never reach the airfield."

"My luggage. Dr. Gothon, my luggage—my com unit!" And Desan's heart sank, remembering the service-robots. "*They* have it."

Gothon smiled, a small, amused smiled. "O spacefarer. So many scientists clustered here, and could we not improvise so simple a thing? We have a receiver-transmitter. Here. In this room. We broke one. We broke another. They're on the registry as broken. What's another bit of rubbish—on this poor planet? We meant to contact the ships, to call *you*, lord-navigator, when you came back. But you saved us the trouble. You came down to us like a thunderbolt. Like the birds you never saw, my space-born lord, swooping down on prey. The conferences, the haste you must have inspired up there on the station—if the lords-magistrate planned what I most suspect! I congratulate you. But knowing we have a transmitter—with your shuttle sitting on this world vulnerable as this building—what will you do, lord-navigator, since they control the satellite relay?"

Desan sank down on his chair. Stared at Gothon. "You never meant to kill me. All this—you schemed to enlist me."

"I entertained that hope, yes. I knew your predecessors. I also know your personal reputation—a man who burns his years one after the other as if there were no end of them. Unlike his predecessors. What are you, lord-navigator? Zealot? A man with an obsession? Where do you stand in this?"

"To what—" His voice came hoarse and strange. "To what are you trying to convert me, Dr. Gothon?"

"To our rescue from the lords-magistrate. To the rescue of truth."

"Truth!" Desan waved a desperate gesture. "I don't believe you. I cannot believe you, and you tell me about plots as fantastical as your research and try to involve me in your politics. I'm trying to find the trail the Ancients took—one clue, one artifact to direct us—"

"A new tablet?"

"You make light of me. Anything. Any indication where they went. And they *did* go, doctor. You will not convince me with your statistics. The unforeseen and the unpredicted aren't in your statistics."

"So you'll go on looking—for what you'll never find. You'll serve the lords-magistrate. They'll surely cooperate with you. They'll approve your search and leave this world . . . after the great catastrophe. After the catastrophe that obliterates us and all the records. An asteroid. Who but the robots chart their courses? Who knows how close it is at this moment?"

"People would know a murder! They could never hide it!"

"I tell you, Lord Desan, you stand in a place and you look around you and you say—what would be natural to this place? In this cratered, devastated world, in this chaotic, debris-ridden solar system—could not an input error by an asteroid miner be more credible an accident than atomics? I tell you when your shuttle descended, we thought you might be acting for the lords-magistrate. That you might have a weapon in your baggage which their robots would deliberately fail to detect. But I believe you, lord-navigator. You're as trapped as we. With only the transmitter and a satellite relay system they control. What will you do? Persuade the lords-magistrate that you support them? Persuade them to support you this further voyage—in return for your backing them? Perhaps they'll listen to you and let you leave."

"But they will," Desan said. He drew in a deep breath and looked from Gothon to the others and back again. "My shuttle is my own. *My* robotics, Dr. Gothon. From my ship and linked to it. And what I need is that transmitter. Appeal to *me* for protection if you think it so urgent. Trust me. Or trust nothing and we will all wait here and see what truth is."

Gothon reached into a pocket, held up an odd metal object. Smiled. Her eyes crinkled round the edges. "An old-fashioned thing, lord-navigator. We say *key* nowadays and mean something quite different, but I'm a relic myself, remember. Baffles hell out of the robots. Bothogi. Link up that antenna and unlock the closet and let's see what the lord-navigator and his shuttle can do."

"**D**id it hear you?" Bothogi asked, a boy's honest worry on his unlined face. He still had the rock, as if he had forgotten it. Or feared robots. Or intended to use it if he detected treachery. "Is it moving?"

"I assure you it's moving," Desan said, and shut the transmitter down. He drew a great breath, shut his eyes and saw the shuttle lift, a silver wedge spreading wings for home. Deadly if attacked. *They will not attack it, they must not attack it, they will query us when they know the shuttle is launched and we will discover yet that this is all a ridiculous error of misunderstanding.* And looking at nowhere: "Relays have gone; *nothing* stops it and its defenses are considerable. The lords-navigator have not been fools, citizens: we probe worlds with our shuttles, and we plan to get them back." He turned and faced Gothon and the other staff. "The message is *out*. And because I am a prudent man—are there suits enough for your staff? I advise we get to them. In the case of an accident."

"The alarm," said Gothon at once. "Neoth, sound the alarm." And as a senior staffer moved: "the dome pressure alert," Gothon said. "*That* will confound the robots. All personnel to pressure suits; all robots to seek damage. I agree about the suits. Get them."

The alarm went, a staccato shriek from overhead. Desan glanced instinctively at an uncommunicative white ceiling—

—darkness, darkness above, where the shuttle reached the thin blue edge of space. The station now knew that things had gone greatly amiss. It should inquire, there should be inquiry immediate to the planet—

Staffers had unlocked a second closet. They pulled out suits, not the expected one or two for emergency exit from this pressure-sealable room; but a tightly jammed lot of them. The lab seemed a mine of defenses, a stealthily equipped stronghold that smelled of conspiracy all over the base, throughout the staff—*everyone* in on it—

He blinked at the offering of a suit, ears assailed by the siren. He looked into the eyes of Bothogi who had handed it to him. There would be no call, no inquiry from the lords-magistrate. He began to know that, in the earnest, clear-eyed way these people behaved—not as lunatics, not schemers. Truth. They had told their truth as they believed it, as the whole base believed it. And the lords-magistrate named it heresy.

His heart beat steadily again. Things made sense again. His hands found familiar motions, putting on the suit, making the closures.

"There's that AI in the controller's office," said a senior staffer. "I have a key."

"What will they do?" a younger staffer asked, panic-edged. "Will the station's weapons reach here?"

"It's quite distant for sudden actions," said Desan. "Too far for beams and missiles are slow." His heartbeat steadied further. The suit was about him; familiar feeling; hostile worlds and weapons: more familiar ground. He smiled, not a pleasant kind of smile, a parting of lips on strong, long teeth. "And one more thing, young citizen, the ships they have are transports. Miners. Mine are hunters. I regret to say we've carried weapons for the last two hundred thousand years, and my crews know their business. If the lords-magistrate attack that shuttle it will be their mistake. Help Dr. Gothon."

"I've got it, quite, young lord." Gothon made the collar closure. "I've been handling these things longer than—"

Explosion thumped somewhere away. Gothon looked up. All motion stopped. And the air-rush died in the ducts.

"The oxygen system—" Bothogi exclaimed. "O *damn* them—!"

"We have," Desan said coldly. He made no haste. Each final fitting of the suit he made with care. Suit-drill; example to the young: the lord-navigator, youngsters, demonstrates his skill. Pay attention. "And we've just had our answer from the lords-magistrate. We need to get to that AI and shut it down. Let's have no panic here. Assume that my shuttle has cleared the atmosphere—"

—well above the gray clouds, the horror of the surface. Silver needle aimed at the heart of the lords-magistrate.

Alert, alert, it would shriek, *alert, alert, alert*—With its transmission relying on no satellites, with its message shoved out in one high-powered bow-wave. *Crew on the world is in danger.* And, code that no lord-navigator had ever hoped to transmit, a series of numbers in syntaxical link: *Treachery: the lords-magistrate are traitors; aid and rescue— Alert, alert, alert—*

—anguished scream from a world of dust; a place of skulls; the grave of the search.

Treachery: alert, alert, alert!

Desan was not a violent man; he had never thought of himself as violent. He was a searcher, a man with a quest.

He knew nothing of certainty. He believed a woman a quarter of a million years old, because—because Gothon was Gothon. He cried traitor and let loose havoc all the while knowing that here might be the traitor, this gentle-eyed woman, this collector of skulls.

O Gothon, he would ask if he dared, *which of you is false? To force the lords-magistrate to strike with violence enough to damn them—is that what you wish? Against a quarter million years of unabated life—what are my five incarnations: mere genetic congruency, without memory. I am helpless to know your perspectives.*

Have you planned this a thousand years, ten thousand?

Do you stand in this place and think in the mind of creatures dead longer even than you have lived? Do you hold their skulls and think their thoughts?

Was it purpose eight million years ago?

Was it, is it—horror upon horror—a mistake on both sides?

"Lord Desan," said Bothogi, laying a hand on his shoulder. "Lord

Desan, we have a master key. We have weapons. We're waiting, Lord Desan."

Above them the holocaust.

It was only a service robot. It had never known its termination. Not like the base AI, in the director's office, which had fought them with locked doors and release of atmosphere, to the misfortune of the director—

"Tragedy, tragedy," said Bothogi, standing by the small dented corpse, there on the ocher sand before the buildings. Smoke rolled up from a sabotaged lifesupport plant to the right of the domes; the world's air had rolled outward and inward and mingled with the breaching of the central dome—the AI transport's initial act of sabotage, ramming the plastic walls. "Microorganisms let loose on this world—the fools, the arrant *fools*!"

It was not the microorganisms Desan feared. It was the AI eight-wheeled transport, maneuvering itself for another attack on the cold-sleep facilities. Prudent to have set themselves inside a locked room with the rest of the scientists and hope for rescue from offworld; but the AI would batter itself against the plastic walls, and living targets kept it distracted from the sleeping, helpless clones—Gothon's juniormost; Bothogi's; those of a dozen senior staffers.

And keeping it distracted became more and more difficult.

Hour upon hour they had evaded its rushes, clumsy attacks and retreats in their encumbering suits. They had done it damage where they could while staff struggled to come up with something that might slow it . . . it lumped along now with a great lot of metal wire wrapped around its rearmost right wheel.

"Damn!" cried a young biologist as it maneuvered for her position. It was the agile young who played this game; and one aging lord-navigator who was the only fighter in the lot.

Dodge, dodge, and dodge. "It's going to catch you against the oxy-plant, youngster! *This* way!" Desan's heart thudded as the young woman thumped along in the cumbersome suit in a losing race with the transport. "Oh, *damn*, it's got it figured! Bothogi!"

Desan grasped his probe-spear and jogged on— "Divert it!" he yelled. Diverting it was all they could hope for.

It turned their way, a whine of the motor, a serpentine flex of its metal body and a flurry of sand from its eight-wheeled drive. "Run, lord!" Bothogi gasped beside him; and it was still turning—it aimed for them now, and at another tangent a white-suited figure hurled a rock, to distract it yet again.

It kept coming at them. AI. An eight-wheeled, flex-bodied intelligence that had suddenly decided its behavior was not working and altered the program, refusing distraction. A pressure-windowed juggernaut tracking every turn they made.

Closer and closer. "Sensors!" Desan cried, turning on the slick dust—his footing failed him and he caught himself, gripped the probe and aimed it straight at the sensor array clustered beneath the front window.

Thum-p! The dusty sky went blue and he was on his back, skidding in the sand with the great balloon tires churning sand on either side of him.

The suit, he thought with a spaceman's horror of the abrading, while it dawned on him at the same time that he was being dragged beneath the AI, and that every joint and nerve center was throbbing with the high-voltage shock of the probe.

Things became very peaceful then, a cessation of commotion. He lay dazed, staring up at a rusty blue sky, and seeing it laced with a silver thread.

They're coming, he thought, and thought of his eldest clone, sleeping at a well-educated twenty years of age. Handsome lad. He talked to the boy from time to time. *Poor lad, the lordship is yours. Your predecessor was a fool—*

A shadow passed above his face. It was another suited face peering down into his. A weight rested on his chest.

"Get off," he said.

"He's alive!" Bothogi's voice cried. "Dr. Gothon, he's still alive!"

The world showed no more scars than it had at the beginning—red and ocher where clouds failed. The algae continued its struggle in sea and tidal pools and lakes and rivers—with whatever microscopic addenda the breached dome had let loose in the world. The insects and the worms continued their blind ascent to space, dominant life on this poor, cratered globe. The research station was in function again, repairs complete.

Desan gazed on the world from his ship: it hung as a sphere in the holotank by his command station. A wave of his hand might show him the darkness of space; the floodlit shapes of ten hunting ships, lately returned from the deep and about to seek it again in continuation of the

Mission, sleek fish rising and sinking again in a figurative black sea. A good many suns had shone on their hulls, but this one had seen them more often than any since their launching.

Home.

The space station was returning to function. Corpses were consigned to the sun the Mission had sought for so long. And power over the Mission rested solely at present in the hands of the lord-navigator, in the unprecedented circumstance of the demise of all five lords-magistrate simultaneously. Their clones were not yet activated to begin their years of majority— "Later will be time to wake the new lords-magistrate," Desan decreed, "at some further world of the search." Let them hear this event as history.

When I can manage them personally, he thought. He looked aside at twenty-year-old Desan Six and the youth looked gravely back with the face Desan had seen in the mirror thirty-two waking years ago.

"Lord-navigator?"

"You'll wake your brother after we're away. Six. Directly after. I'll be staying awake much of this trip."

"*Awake*, sir?"

"Quite. There are things I want you to think about. I'll be talking to you and Seven both."

"About the lords-magistrate, sir?"

Desan lifted brows at this presumption. "You and I are already quite well attuned, Six. You'll succeed young. Are you sorry you missed this time?"

"No, lord-navigator! I assure you not!"

"Good brain. I ought to know. Go to your post. Six. Be grateful you don't have to cope with a new lordship *and* five new lords-magistrate and a recent schism." Desan leaned back in his chair as the youth crossed the bridge and settled at a crew-post, beside the Captain. The lord-navigator was more than a figurehead to rule the seventy ships of the Mission, with their captains and their crews. Let the boy try his skill on this plotting. Desan intended to check it. He leaned aside with a wince— the electric shock that had blown him flat between the AI's tires had saved him from worse than a broken arm and leg; and the medical staff had seen to that: the arm and the leg were all but healed, with only a light wrap to protect them. The ribs were tightly wrapped too; and they caused him more pain than all the rest.

A scan had indeed located three errant asteroids, three courses the station's computers had not accurately recorded as inbound for the planet—until personnel from the ships began to run their own observations. Those were redirected.

Casualties. Destruction. Fighting within the Mission. The guilt of the lords-magistrate was profound and beyond dispute.

"Lord-navigator," the communications officer said. "Dr. Gothon returning your call."

Good-bye, he had told Gothon. *I don't accept your judgment, but I shall devote my energy to pursuit of mine, and let any who want to join you—reside on the station. There are some volunteers; I don't profess to understand them. But you may trust them. You may trust the lords-magistrate to have learned a lesson. I will teach it. No member of this mission will be restrained in any opinion while my influence lasts. And I shall see to that. Sleep again and we may see each other once more in our lives.*

"I'll receive it," Desan said, pleased and anxious at once that Gothon deigned reply; he activated the com-control. Ship-electronics touched his ear, implanted for comfort. He heard the usual blip and chatter of com's mechanical protocols, then Gothon's quiet voice. "Lord-navigator."

"I'm hearing you, doctor."

"Thank you for your sentiment. I wish you well too. I wish you very well."

The tablet was mounted before him, above the console. Millions of years ago a tiny probe had set out from this world, bearing the original. Two aliens standing naked, one with hand uplifted. A series of diagrams which, partially obliterated, had still served to guide the Mission across the centuries. A probe bearing a greeting. Ages-dead cameras and simple instruments.

Greetings, stranger. We come from this place, this star system.

See, the hand, the appendage of a builder— This we will have in common.

The diagrams: we speak knowledge; we have no fear of you, strangers who read this, whoever you be.

Wise fools.

There had been a time, long ago, when fools had set out to seek them . . . in a vast desert of stars. Fools who had desperately needed proof, once upon a quarter million years ago, that they were not alone. One dust-scoured alien artifact they found, so long ago, on a lonely drifting course.

Hello, it said.

The makers, the peaceful Ancients, became a legend. They became purpose, inspiration.

The overriding, obsessive *Why* that saved a species, pulled it back from war, gave it the stars.

"I'm very serious—I do hope you rest, doctor—save a few years for the unborn."

"My eldest's awake. I've lost my illusions of immortality, lord-navigator. I hope to spend my years teaching her. I've told her about *you*, lord-navigator. She hopes to meet you."

"You might still abandon this world and come with us, doctor."

"To search for a myth?"

"Not a myth. We're bound to disagree. Doctor, doctor, what *good* can your presence there do? What if you're right? It's a dead end. What if I'm wrong? I'll never stop looking. *I'll* never know."

"But we know their descendants, lord-navigator. We. We are. We're spreading their legend from star to star—they've become a fable. The Ancients, the Pathfinders. A hundred civilizations have taken up that myth. A hundred civilizations have lived out their years in that belief and begotten others to tell their story. What if you should find them? Would you know them—or where evolution had taken them? Perhaps we've already met them, somewhere among the worlds we've visited, and we failed to know them."

It was irony. Gentle humor. "Perhaps, then," Desan said in turn, "we'll find the track leads home again. Perhaps we *are* their children—eight and a quarter million years removed."

"O ye makers of myths. Do your work, spacefarer. Tangle the skein with legends. Teach fables to the races you meet. Brighten the universe with them. I put my faith in you. Don't you know—this world is all I came to find, but you—child of the voyage, you have to have more. For you the voyage is the Mission. Good-bye to you. Fare well. Nothing is complete calamity. The equation here is different, by a multitude of micro-organisms let free—Bothogi has stopped grieving and begun to have quite different thoughts on the matter. His algae-pools may turn out a different breed this time—the shift of a protein here and there in the genetic chain—who knows what it will breed? Different software this time, perhaps. Good voyage to you, lord-navigator. Look for your Ancients under other suns. We're waiting for their offspring here, under this one."

THE SCAPEGOAT

I

Defranco sits across the table from the elf and he dreams for a moment, not a good dream, but recent truth: all part of what surrounds him now, a bit less than it was when it was happening, because it was gated in through human eyes and ears and a human notices much more and far less than what truly goes on in the world—

—the ground comes up with a bone-penetrating thump and dirt showers down like rain, over and over again; and deFranco wriggles up to his knees with the clods rattling off his armor. He may be moving to a place where a crater will be in a moment, and the place where he is may become one in that same moment. There is no time to think about it. There is only one way off that exposed hillside, which is to go and keep going. DeFranco writhes and wriggles against the weight of the armor, blind for a moment as the breathing system fails to give him as much as he needs, but his throat is already raw with too much oxygen in three days out. He curses the rig, far more intimate a frustration than the enemy on this last long run to the shelter of the deep tunnels. . . .

He was going home, was John deFranco, if home was still there, and if the shells that had flattened their shield in this zone had not flattened it all along the line and wiped out the base.

The elves had finally learned where to hit them on this weapons system too, that was what; and deFranco cursed them one and all, while the sweat ran in his eyes and the oxy-mix tore his throat and giddied his brain. On this side and that shells shocked the air and the ground and his bones; and not for the first time concussion flung him bodily through the air and slammed him to the churned ground bruised and battered (and but for the armor, dead and shrapnel-riddled). Immediately fragments of wood and metal rang off the hardsuit, and in their gravity-driven sequence clods of earth rained down in a patter mixed with impacts of rocks and larger chunks.

And then, not having been directly in the strike zone and dead, he got his sweating human limbs up again by heaving the armor-weight into its hydraulic joint-locks, and desperately hurled fifty kilos of unsupple ceramics and machinery and ninety of quaking human flesh into a waddling, exhausted run.

Run and fall and run and stagger into a walk when the dizziness got too much and never waste time dodging.

But somewhen the jolts stopped, and the shell-made earthquakes stopped, and deFranco, laboring along the hazard of the shell-cratered ground, became aware of the silence. His staggering steps slowed as he turned with the awkward foot-planting the armor imposed to take a look behind him. The whole smoky valley swung across the narrowed view of his visor, all lit up with ghosty green readout that flickered madly and told him his eyes were jerking in panic, calling up more than he wanted. He feared that he was deaf; it was that profound a silence to his shocked ears. He heard the hum of the fans and the ventilator in the suit, but there would be that sound forever, he heard it in his dreams; so it could be in his head and not coming from his ears. He hit the ceramic-shielded back of his hand against his ceramic-coated helmet and heard the thump, if distantly. So his hearing was all right. There was just the smoke and the desolate cratering of the landscape to show him where the shells had hit.

And suddenly one of those ghosty green readouts in his visor jumped and said **000** and started ticking off, so he lumbered about to get a look up, the viewplate compensating for the sky in a series of flickers and darkenings. The reading kept up, ticking away; and he could see nothing in the sky, but base was still there, it was transmitting, and he knew what was happening. The numbers reached **Critical** and he swung about again and looked toward the plain as the first strikes came in and the smoke went up anew.

He stood there on the hillcrest and watched the airstrike he had called down half an eternity ago pound hell out of the plains. He knew the devastation of the beams and the shells. And his first and immediate thought was that there would be no more penetrations of the screen and human lives were saved. He had outrun the chaos and covered his own mistake in getting damn near on top of the enemy installation trying to find it.

And his second thought, hard on the heels of triumph, was that there was too much noise in the world already, too much death to deal with, vastly too much, and he wanted to cry with the relief and the fear of being alive and moving. Good and proper. The base scout found the damn firepoint, tripped a trap and the whole damn airforce had to come pull him out of the fire with a damn million credits worth of shells laid down out there destroying ten billion credits' worth of somebody else's.

Congratulations, deFranco.

A shiver took him. He turned his back to the sight, cued his locator on, and began to walk, slowly, slowly, one foot in front of the other, and if he had not rested now and again, setting the limbs on his armor on lock, he would have fallen down. As it was he walked with his mouth open and his ears full of the harsh sound of his own breathing. He walked, lost and disoriented, till his unit picked up his locator signal and beaconed in the Lost Boy they never hoped to get back.

"You did us great damage then," says the elf. "It was the last effort we could make and we knew you would take out our last weapons. We knew that you would do it quickly and that then you would stop. We had learned to trust your habits even if we didn't understand them. When the shelling came, towers fell; and there were over a thousand of us dead in the city."

"And you keep coming."

"We will. Until it's over or until we're dead."

DeFranco stares at the elf a moment. The room is a small and sterile place, showing no touches of habitation, but all those small signs of humanity—a quiet bedroom, done in yellow and green pastels. A table. Two chairs. An unused bed. They have faced each other over this table for hours. They have stopped talking theory and begun thinking only of the recent past. And deFranco finds himself lost in elvish thinking again. It never quite makes sense. The assumptions between the lines are not human assumptions, though the elf's command of the language is quite thorough.

At last, defeated by logicless logic: "I went back to my base," says deFranco. "I called down the fire; but I just knew the shelling had stopped. We were alive. That was all we knew. Nothing personal."

There was a bath and there was a meal and a little extra ration of whiskey. HQ doled the whiskey out as special privilege and sanity-saver and the scarcity of it made the posts hoard it and ration it with down-to-the-gram precision. And he drank his three days' ration and his bonus drink one after the other when he had scrubbed his rig down and taken a long, long bath beneath the pipe. He took his three days' whiskey all at once because three days out was what he was recovering from, and he sat in his corner in his shorts, the regs going about their business, all of them recognizing a shaken man on a serious drunk and none of them rude or crazy enough to bother him now, not with congratulations for surviving, not with offers of bed, not with a stray glance. The regs were not in his command, he was not strictly anywhere in the chain of command they belonged to, being special ops and assigned there for the reg CO to use when he had to. He was 2nd Lt. John R. deFranco if anyone bothered and no one did hereabouts, in the bunkers. He was special ops and his orders presently came from the senior trooper captain who was the acting CO all along this section of the line, the major having got hisself lately dead, themselves waiting on a replacement, thank you, sir and ma'am; while higher brass kept themselves cool and dry and safe behind the shields on the ground a thousand miles away and up in orbit.

And John deFranco, special op and walking target, kept his silver world-and-moon pin and his blue beret and his field-browns all tucked up and out of the damp in his mold-proof plastic kit at the end of his bunk. The rig was his working uniform, the damned, cursed rig that found a new spot to rub raw every time he realigned it. And he sat now in his shorts and drank the first glass quickly, the next and the next and the next in slow sips, and blinked sometimes when he remembered to.

The regs, male and female, moved about the underground barracks in their shorts and their T's like khaki ghosts whose gender meant nothing to him or generally to each other. When bunks got double-filled it was friendship or boredom or outright desperation; all their talk was rough and getting rougher, and their eyes when real pinned-down-for-days boredom set in were hell, because they had been out here and down here on this world for thirty-seven months by the tally on bunker 43's main entry wall; while the elves were still holding, still digging in, and still dying at unreasonable rates without surrender.

"Get prisoners," HQ said in its blithe simplicity; but prisoners suicided. Elves checked out just by *wanting* to die.

"Establish a contact," HQ said. "Talk *at* them—" meaning by any inventive means they could; but they had failed at that for years in space and they expected no better luck onworld. Talking to an elf meant coming into range with either drones or live bodies. Elves cheerfully shot at any target they could get. Elves had shot at the first human ship they had met twenty years ago and they had killed fifteen hundred men, women, and children at Corby Point for reasons no one ever understood. They kept on shooting at human ships in sporadic incidents that built to a crisis.

Then humanity—all three humanities, Union and Alliance and remote, sullen Earth—had decided there was no restraint possible with a species that persistently attacked modern human ships on sight, with equipage centuries less advanced—*Do we have to wait*, Earth's consensus was, *till they do get their hands on the advanced stuff? Till they hit a world?* Earth worried about such things obsessively, convinced of its paramount worldbound holiness and importance in the universe. The cradle of humankind. Union worried about other things—like breakdown of order, like its colonies slipping loose while it was busy: Union pushed for speed, Earth wanted to go back to its own convolute affairs, and Alliance wanted the territory, preferring to make haste slowly and not create permanent problems for itself on its flank. There were rumors of other things too, like Alliance picking up signals out this direction, of something other than elves. Real reason to worry. It was at least sure that the war was being pushed and pressed and shoved; and the elves shoved back. Elves died and died, their ships being no match for human-make once humans took after them in earnest and interdicted the jump-points that let them near human space. But elves never surrendered and never quit trying.

"Now what do we do?" the joint command asked themselves collectively and figuratively—because they were dealing out bloody, unpalatable slaughter against a doggedly determined and underequipped enemy, and Union and Earth wanted a quick solution. But Union as usual took the Long View: and on this single point there was consensus. "If we take out every ship they put out here and they retreat, how long does it take before they come back at us with more advanced armaments? We're dealing with lunatics."

"Get through to them," the word went out from HQ. "Take them out of our space and carry the war home to them. We've got to make the impression on them now—or take options no one wants later."

Twenty years ago. Underestimating the tenacity of the elves. Removed from the shipping lanes and confined to a single world, the war had sunk away to a local difficulty; Alliance still put money and troops into it; Union still cooperated in a certain measure. Earth sent adventurers and enlistees that often were crazier than the elves: Base culled those in a hurry.

So for seventeen years the matter boiled on and on and elves went on dying and dying in their few and ill-equipped ships, until the joint command decided on a rougher course; quickly took out the elves' pathetic little space station, dropped troops onto the elvish world, and fenced human bases about with antimissile screens to fight a limited and on-world war—while elvish weaponry slowly got more basic and more primitive and the troops drank their little measures of imported whiskey and went slowly crazy.

And humans closely tied to the elvish war adapted, in humanity's own lunatic way. Well behind the lines that had come to exist on the elves' own planet, humans settled in and built permanent structures and scientists came to study the elves and the threatened flora and fauna of a beautiful and earthlike world, while some elvish centers ignored the war, and the bombing went on and on in an inextricable mess, because neither elves nor humans knew how to quit, or knew the enemy enough to know how to disengage. Or figure out what the other wanted. And the war could go on and on—since presumably the computers and the records in those population centers still had the design of starships in them. And no enemy which had taken what the elves had taken by now was ever going to forget.

There were no negotiations. Once, just once, humans had tried to approach one of the few neutral districts to negotiate and it simply and instantly joined the war. So after all the study and all the effort, humans lived on the elves' world and had no idea what to call them or what the world's real name was, because the damn elves had blown their own space station at the last and methodically destroyed every record the way they destroyed every hamlet before its fall and burned every record and every artifact. They died and they died and they died and sometimes (but seldom nowadays) they took humans with them, like the time when they were still in space and hit the base at Ticon with 3/4-cee rocks and left nothing but dust. Thirty thousand dead and not a way in hell to find the pieces.

That was the incident after which the joint command decided to take the elves out of space.

And nowadays humanity invested cities they never planned to take and they tore up roads and took out all the elves' planes, and they tore up agriculture with non-nuclear bombs and shells, trying not to ruin the world beyond recovery, hoping eventually to wear the elves down. But the elves retaliated with gas and chemicals which humans had refrained from using. Humans interdicted supply and still the elves managed to come up with the wherewithal to strike through their base defense here as if supply were endless and they not starving and the world still green and undamaged.

DeFranco drank and drank with measured slowness, watching regs go to and fro in the slow dance of their own business. They were good, this Delta Company of the Eighth. They did faithfully what regs were supposed to do in this war, which was to hold a base and keep roads secure that humans used, and to build landing zones for supply and sometimes to go out and get killed inching humanity's way toward some goal the joint command understood and which from here looked only like some other damn shell-pocked hill. DeFranco's job was to locate such hills. And to find a prisoner to take (standing orders) and to figure out the enemy if he could.

Mostly just to find hills. And sometimes to get his company into taking one. And right now he was no more damn good, because they had gotten as close to this nameless city as there were hills and vantages to make it profitable, and after that they went onto the flat and did what?

Take the place inch by inch, street by street and discover every damn elf they met had suicided? The elves would do it on them, so in the villages south of here they had saved the elves the bother, and got nothing for their trouble but endless, measured carnage, and smoothskinned corpses that drew the small vermin and the huge winged birds—(they've been careful with their ecology, the Science Bureau reckoned, in their endless reports, in some fool's paper on large winged creatures' chances of survival if a dominant species were not very careful of them—)

(—or the damn birds are bloody-minded mean and tougher than the elves, deFranco mused in his alcoholic fog, knowing that nothing was, in all space and creation, more bloody-minded than the elves.)

He had seen a young elf child holding another, both stone dead, baby locked in baby's arms: they love, dammit, they love— And he had wept while he staggered away from the ruins of a little elvish town, seeing more and more such sights—because the elves had touched off bombs in their own town center, and turned it into a firestorm.

But the two babies had been lying there unburned and no one wanted to touch them or to look at them. Finally the birds came. And the regs shot at the birds until the CO stopped it, because it was a waste: it was killing a non-combatant life form and that (O God!) was against the rules. Most of all the CO stopped it because it was a fraying of human edges, because the birds always were there and the birds were the winners, every time. And the damn birds like the damn elves came again and again, no matter that shots blew them to puffs of feathers. Stubborn, like the elves. Crazy as everything else on the planet, human and elf. It was catching.

DeFranco nursed the last whiskey in the last glass, nursed it with hands going so numb he had to struggle to stay awake. He was a quiet drunk, never untidy. He neatly drank the last and fell over sideways limp as a corpse, and, tender mercy to a hill-finding branch of the service the hill-taking and road-building regs regarded as a sometime natural enemy—one of the women came and got the glass from his numbed fingers and pulled a blanket over him. They were still human here. They tried to be.

"There was nothing more to be done," says the elf. "That was why. We knew that you were coming closer, and that our time was limited." His long white fingers touch the table-surface, the white, plastic table in the ordinary little bedroom. "We died in great numbers, deFranco, and it was cruel that you showed us only slowly what you could do."

"We could have taken you out from the first. You knew that." DeFranco's voice holds an edge of frustration. Of anguish. "Elf, couldn't you ever understand that?"

"You always gave us hope we could win. And so we fought, and so we still fight. Until the peace. My friend."

"Franc, Franc—" —it was a fierce low voice, and deFranco came out of it, in the dark, with his heart doubletiming and the instant realization it was Dibs talking to him in that low tone and wanting him out of that blanket, which meant wire-runners or worse, a night attack. But Dibs grabbed his arms to hold him still before he could flail about. "Franc, we got a move out there, Jake and Cat's headed out down the tunnel, the lieutenant's gone to M1 but M1's on the line, they want you out there, they want a spotter up on hill 24 doublequick.

"Uh." DeFranco rubbed his eyes. "Uh." Sitting upright was brutal. Standing was worse. He staggered two steps and caught the main shell of his armor off the rack, number 12 suit, the lousy stinking armor that always smelled of human or mud or the purge in the ducts and the awful sick-sweet cleaner they wiped it out with when they hung it up. He held the plastron against his body and Dibs started with the clips in the dim light of the single 5-watt they kept going to find the latrine at night— "Damn, damn, I gotta—" He eluded Dibs and got to the toilet, and by now the whole place was astir with shadow-figures like a scene out of a gold-lighted hell. He swigged the stinging mouthwash they had on the shelf by the toilet and did his business while Dibs caught him up from behind and finished the hooks on his left side. "Damn, get him going," the sergeant said, and: "Trying," Dibs said, as others hauled deFranco around and began hooking him up like a baby into his clothes, one piece and the other, the boots, leg and groin-pieces, the sleeves, the gloves, the belly clamp and the backpack and the power-on—his joints ached. He stood there swaying to one and another tug on his body and took the helmet into his hands when Dibs handed it to him.

"Go, go," the sergeant said, who had no more power to give a special op any specific orders than he could fly; but HQ was in a stew, they needed his talents out there, and deFranco let the regs shove him all they liked: it was his accommodation with these regs when there was no peace anywhere else in the world. And once a dozen of these same regs had come out into the heat after him, which he never quite forgot. So he let them hook his weapons-kit on, then ducked his head down and put the damned helmet on and gave it the locking half-twist as he headed away from the safe light of the barracks pit into the long tunnel, splashing along the low spots on the plastic grid that kept heavy armored feet from sinking in the mud.

"Code: *Nightsight*," he told the suit aloud, all wobbly and shivery from too little sleep; and it read his hoarse voice patterns and gave him a filmy image of the tunnel in front of him. "Code: *ID*," he told it, and it started telling the two troopers somewhere up the tunnel that he was there, and on his way. He got readout back as Cat acknowledged. "Ia-6yg-p30/30," the green numbers ghosted up in his visor, telling him Jake and Cat had elves and they had them quasi-solid in the distant-sensors which would have been tripped downland and they themselves were staying where they were and taking no chances on betraying the location of the tunnel. He cut the ID and Cat and Jake cut off too.

They've got to us, deFranco thought. *The damned elves got through our screen and now they've pushed through on foot, and it's going to be hell to pay—*

Back behind him the rest of the troops would be suiting up and making a more leisurely prep for a hard night to come. The elves rarely got as far as human bunkers. They tried. They were, at close range and with hand-weapons, deadly. The dying was not all on the elves' side if they got to you.

A cold sweat had broken out under the suit. His head ached with a vengeance and the suit weighed on his knees and on his back when he bent and it stank with disinfectant that smelled like some damn tree from some damn forest on the world that had spawned every human born, he knew that, but it failed as perfume and failed at masking the stink of terror and of the tunnels in the cold wet breaths the suit took in when it was not on self-seal.

He knew nothing about Earth, only dimly remembered Pell, which had trained him and shipped him here by stages to a world no one bothered to give a name. Elfland, when High HQ was being whimsical. Neverneverland, the regs called it after some old fairy tale, because from it a soldier never never came home again. They had a song with as many verses as there were bitches of the things a soldier in Elfland never found.

> *Where's my discharge from this war?*
> *Why, it's neverneverwhere, my friend.*
> *Well, when's the next ship off this world?*
> *Why, it's neverneverwhen, my friend.*
> > *And time's what we've got most of,*
> > *And time is what we spend,*
> > *And time is what we've got to do*
> > *In Neverneverland.*

He hummed this to himself, in a voice jolted and crazed by the exertion. He wanted to cry like a baby. He wanted someone to curse for the hour and his interrupted rest. Most of all he wanted a few days of quiet on this front, just a few days to put his nerves back together again and let his head stop aching. . . .

. . .Run and run and run, in a suit that keeps you from the gas and most of the shells the elves can throw—except for a few. Except for the joints and the visor, because the elves have been working for twenty years studying how to kill you. And air runs out and filters fail and every access you have to Elfland is a way for the elves to get at you.

Like the tunnel openings, like the airvents, like the power plant that keeps the whole base and strung-out tunnel systems functioning.

Troopers scatter to defend these points, and you run and run, belatedly questioning why troopers want a special op at a particular point, where the tunnel most nearly approaches the elves on their plain.

Why me, why here—because, fool, HQ wants close-up reconnaissance, which was what they wanted the last time they sent you out in the dark beyond the safe points—twice, now, and they expect you to go out and do it again because the elves missed you last time.

Damn them all. (With the thought that they will use you till the bone breaks and the flesh refuses. And then a two-week rest and out to the lines again.)

They give you a medical as far as the field hospital; and there they give you vitamins, two shots of antibiotic, a bottle of pills and send you out gain. "We got worse," the meds say then.

There always are worse. Till you're dead.

DeFranco looks at the elf across the table in the small room and remembers how it was, the smell of the tunnels, the taste of fear.

II

So what're the gals like on this world?
Why, you nevernevermind, my friend.
Well, what're the guys like on this world?
Well, you neverneverask, my friend.

"They sent me out there," deFranco says to the elf, and the elf—a human might have nodded but elves have no such habit—stares gravely as they sit opposite each other, hands on the table.

"You always say 'they,' " says the elf. "We say 'we' decided. But you do things differently."

"Maybe it *is* we," deFranco says. "Maybe it is, at the bottom of things. We. Sometimes it doesn't look that way."

"I think even now you don't understand why we do what we do. I don't really understand why you came here or why you listen to me, or why you stay now— But we won't understand. I don't think we two will. Others maybe. You want what I want. That's what I trust most."

"You believe it'll work?"

"For us, yes. For elves. Absolutely. Even if it's a lie it will work."

"But if it's not a lie—"

"Can you make it true? *You* don't believe. That—I have to find words for this—but I don't understand that either. How you feel. What you do." The elf reaches across the table and slim white hands with overtint like oil on water catch at brown, matte-skinned fingers whose nails (the elf has none) are broken and rough. "It was no choice to you. It never was even a choice to you, to destroy us to the heart and the center. Perhaps it wasn't to stay. I have a deep feeling toward you, deFranco. I had this feeling toward you from when I saw you first; I knew that you were what I had come to find, but whether you were the helping or the damning force I didn't know then, I only knew that what you did when you saw us was what humans had always done to us. And I believed you would show me why."

DeFranco moved and sat still a while by turns, in the dark, in the stink and the strictures of his rig; while somewhere two ridges away there were two nervous regs encamped in the entry to the tunnel, sweltering in their own hardsuits and not running their own pumps and fans any more than he was running his—because elvish hearing was legendary, the rigs made noise, and it was hard enough to move in one of the bastards without making a racket: someone in HQ suspected elves could pick up the running noises. Or had other senses.

But without those fans and pumps the below-the-neck part of the suit had no cooling and got warm even in the night. And the gloves and the helmets had to stay on constantly when anyone was outside, it was the rule: no elf ever got a look at a live human, except at places like the Eighth's Gamma Company. Perhaps not there either. Elves were generally thorough.

DeFranco had the kneejoints on lock at the moment, which let him have a solid prop to lean his weary knees and backside against. He leaned there easing the shivers and the quakes out of his lately-wakened and sleep-deprived limbs before he rattled in his armor and alerted a whole hillside full of elves. It was not a well-shielded position he had taken: it had little cover except the hill itself, and these hills had few enough trees that the fires and the shells had spared. But green did struggle up amid the soot and bushes grew on the line down on valley level that had been an elvish road three years ago. His nightsight scanned the brush in shadow-images.

Something touched the sensors as he rested there on watch, a curious whisper of a sound, and an amber readout ghosted up into his visor, dots rippling off in sequence in the direction the pickup came from. It was not the wind: the internal computer zeroed out the white sound of wind and suit-noise. It was anomalies it brought through and amplified; and what it amplified now had the curious regular pulse of engine-sound.

DeFranco ordered the lock off his limbs, slid lower on the hill, and moved on toward one with better vantage of the road as it came up from the west—carefully, pausing at irregular intervals as he worked round to get into position to spot that direction. He still had his locator output off. So did everyone else back at the base. HQ had no idea now what sophistication the elves had gained at eavesdropping and homing in on the locators, and how much they could pick up with locators of their own. It was only sure that while some elvish armaments had gotten more primitive and patchwork, their computer tech had nothing at all wrong with it.

DeFranco settled again on a new hillside and listened, wishing he could scratch a dozen maddening itches, and wishing he were safe somewhere else: the whole thing had a disaster-feeling about it from the start, the elves doing something they had never done. He could only think about dead Gamma Company and what might have happened to them before the elves got to them and gassed the bunker and fought their way into it past the few that had almost gotten into their rigs in time—

Had the special op been out there watching too? Had the one at bunker 35 made a wrong choice and had it all started this way the night they died?

The engine-sound was definite. DeFranco edged higher up the new hill and got down flat, belly down on the ridge. He thumbed the magnification plate into the visor and got the handheld camera's snake-head optics over the ridge on the theory it was a smaller target and a preferable target than himself, with far better nightsight.

The filmy nightsight image came back of the road, while the sound persisted. It was distant, his ears and the readout advised him, distant yet, racing the first red edge of a murky dawn that showed far off across the plain and threatened daylight out here.

He still sent no transmission. The orders were stringent. The base either had to remain ignorant that there was a vehicle coming up the road or he had to go back personally to report it; and lose track of whatever-it-was out here just when it was getting near enough to do damage. Damn the lack of specials to team with out here in the hot spots, and damn the lead-footed regs; he had to go it alone, decide things alone, hoping Jake and Cat did the right thing in their spot and hoping the other regs stayed put. And he hated it.

He edged off this hill, keeping it between him and the ruined, shell-pocked road, and began to move to still a third point of vantage, stalking as silently as any man in armor could manage.

And fervently he hoped that the engine-sound was not a decoy and that nothing was getting behind him. The elves were deceptive as well and they were canny enemies with extraordinary hearing. He hoped now that the engine-sound had deafened them—but no elf was really fool enough to be coming up the road like this, it was a decoy, it had to be, there was nothing else it could be; and he was going to fall into it nose-down if he was not careful.

He settled belly-down on the next slope and got the camera-snake over the top, froze the suit-joints and lay inert in that overheated ceramic shell, breathing hard through a throat abused by oxygen and whiskey, blinking against a hangover headache to end all headaches that the close focus of the visor readout only made worse. His nose itched. A place on his scalp itched behind his ear. He stopped cataloging the places he itched because it was driving him crazy. Instead he blinked and rolled his eyes, calling up readout on the passive systems, and concentrated on that.

Blink. Blink-blink. Numbers jumped. The computer had come up with a range as it got passive echo off some hill and checked it against the local topology programmed into its memory. Damn! Close. The computer handed him the velocity. 40 KPH with the 4 and the 0 wobbling back and forth into the 30's. DeFranco held his breath and checked his hand launcher, loading a set of armor-piercing rounds in, quiet, quiet as a man could move. The clamp went down as softly as long practice could lower it.

And at last a ridiculous open vehicle came jouncing and whining its way around potholes and shell craters and generally making a noisy and erratic progress. It was in a considerable hurry despite the potholes, and there were elves in it, four of them, all pale in their robes and one of them with the cold glitter of metal about his/her? Person, the one to the right of the driver. The car bounced and wove and zigged and zagged up the hilly road with no slackening of speed, inviting a shot for all it was worth.

Decoy?

Suicide?

They were crazy as elves could be, and that was completely. They were headed straight for the hidden bunker, and it was possible they had gas or a bomb in that car or that they just planned to get themselves shot in a straightforward way, whatever they had in mind, but they were going right where they could do the most damage.

DeFranco unlocked his ceramic limbs, which sagged under his weight until he was down on his belly; and he slowly brought his rifle up, and inched his way up on his belly so it was his vulnerable head over the ridge this time. He shook and he shivered and he reckoned there might be a crater where he was in fair short order if they had a launcher in that car and he gave them time to get it set his way.

But pushing and probing at elves was part of his job. And these were decidedly anomalous. He put a shot in front of the car and half expected elvish suicides on the spot.

The car swerved and jolted into a pothole as the shell hit. It careened to a stop; and he held himself where he was, his heart pounding away and himself not sure why he had put the shot in front and not into the middle of them like a sensible man in spite of HQ's orders.

But the elves recovered from their careening and the car was stopped; and instead of blowing themselves up immediately or going for a launcher of their own, one of the elves bailed out over the side while the helmet-sensor picked up the attempted motor-start. Cough-whine. The car lurched. The elvish driver made a wild turn, but the one who had gotten out just stood there—*stood*, staring up, and lifted his hands together.

DeFranco lay on his hill; and the elves who had gotten the car started swerved out of the pothole it had stuck itself in and lurched off in escape, not suicide—while the one elf in the robe with the metal border just stood there, the first live prisoner anyone had ever taken, staring up at him, self-offered.

"You damn well stand still," he yelled down at the elf on outside com, and thought of the gas and the chemicals and thought that if elves had come up with a disease that also got to humans here was a way of delivering it that was cussed enough and crazy enough for them.

"Human," a shrill voice called up to him. "Human!"

DeFranco was for the moment paralyzed. An elf knew what to call them: an elf *talked*. An elf stood there staring up at his hill in the beginnings of dawn and all of a sudden nothing was going the way it ever had between elves and humankind.

At least, if it had happened before, no human had ever lived to tell about it.

"Human!" the same voice called—*uu-mann*, as best high elvish voices could manage it. The elf was not suiciding. The elf showed no sign of wanting to do that; and deFranco lay and shivered in his armor and felt a damnable urge to wipe his nose which he could not reach or to get up and run for his life, which was a fool's act. Worse, his bladder suddenly told him it was full. Urgently. Taking his mind down to a ridiculous small matter in the midst of trying to get home alive.

The dawn was coming up the way it did across the plain, light spreading like a flood, so fast in the bizarre angle of the land here that it ran like water on the surface of the plain.

And the elf stood there while the light of dawn grew more, showing the elf more clearly than deFranco had ever seen one of the enemy alive, beautiful the way elves were, not in a human way, looking, in its robes, like some cross between man and something spindly and human-skinned and insectoid. The up-tilted ears never stopped moving, but the average of their direction was toward him. Nervous-like.

What does he want, why does he stand there, why did they throw him out? A target? A distraction?

Elvish cussedness. DeFranco waited, and waited, and the sun came up; while somewhere in the tunnels there would be troopers wondering and standing by their weapons, ready to go on self-seal against gas or whatever these lunatics had brought.

There was light enough now to make out the red of the robes that fluttered in the breeze. And light enough to see the elf's hands, which looked—which looked, crazily enough, to be tied together.

The dawn came on. Water became an obsessive thought. DeFranco was thirsty from the whiskey and agonized between the desire for a drink from the tube near his mouth or the fear one more drop of water in his system would make it impossible to ignore his bladder; and he thought about it and thought about it, because it was a long wait and a long walk back, and relieving himself outside the suit was a bitch on the one hand and on the inside was damnable discomfort. But it did get worse. And while life and death tottered back and forth and his fingers clutched the launcher and he faced an elf who was surely up to something, that small decision was all he could think of clearly—it was easier to think of than what wanted thinking out, like what to do and whether to shoot the elf outright, counter to every instruction and every order HQ had given, because he wanted to get out of this place.

But he did not—and finally he solved both problems: took his drink, laid the gun down on the ridge like it was still in his hands, performed the necessary maneuver to relieve himself outside the suit as he stayed as flat as he could. Then he put himself back together, collected his gun and lurched up to his feet with small whines of the assisting joint-locks.

The elf never moved in all of this, and deFranco motioned with the gun. "Get up here. . . ." —not expecting the elf to understand either the motion or the shout. But the elf came, slowly, as if the hill was all his (it had been once) and he owned it. The elf stopped still on the slant, at a speaking distance, no more, and stood there with his hands tied (*his*, de-Franco decided by the height of him). The elf's white skin all but glowed in the early dawn, the bare skin of the face and arms against the dark, metal-edged red of his robe; and the large eyes were set on him and the ears twitched and quivered with small pulses.

"I am your prisoner," the elf said, plain as any human; and deFranco stood there with his heart hammering away at his ribs.

"Why?" deFranco asked. He was mad, he was quite mad and somewhere he had fallen asleep on the hillside, or elvish gas had gotten to him through the open vents—he was a fool to have gone on open circulation; and he was dying back there somewhere and not talking at all.

The elf lifted his bound hands. "I came here to find you."

It was not a perfect accent. It was what an elvish mouth could come up with. It had music in it. And deFranco stood and stared and finally motioned with the gun up the hill. "Move," he said, "walk."

Without demur his prisoner began to do that, in the direction he had indicated.

"**W**hat did I do that humans always do?" deFranco asks the elf, and the grave sea-colored eyes flicker with changes. Amusement, perhaps. Or distress.

"You fired at us," says the elf in his soft, songlike voice. "And then you stopped and didn't kill me."

"It was a warning."

"To stop. So simple."

"God, what else do you think?"

The elf's eyes flicker again. There is gold in their depths, and gray. And his ears flick nervously. "DeFranco, deFranco, you still don't know why we fight. And I don't truly know what you meant. Are you telling me the truth?"

"We never wanted to fight. It was a warning. Even animals, for God's sake—understand a warning shot."

The elf blinks. (And someone in another room stirs in a chair and curses his own blindness. Aggression and the birds. Different tropisms. All the way through the ecostructure.)

The elf spreads his hands. "I don't know what you mean. I never know. What can we know? That you were there for the same reason I was? Were you?"

"I don't know. I don't even know that. *We never wanted a war.* Do you understand that, at least?"

"You wanted us to stop. So we told you the same. We sent our ships to hold those places which were ours. And you kept coming to them."

"They were ours."

"Now they are." The elf's face is grave and still. "DeFranco, a mistake was made. A ship of ours fired on yours and this was a mistake. Perhaps it was me who fired. What's in this elf's mind? Fear when a ship will not go away? What's in this human's mind? Fear when we don't go away? It was a stupid thing. It was a mistake. It was our region. Our—"

"Territory. You think you owned the place."

"We were in it. We were there and this ship came. Say that I wasn't there and I heard how it happened. This was a frightened elf who made a stupid mistake. This elf was surprised by this ship and he didn't want to run and give up this jump-point. It was ours. You were in it. We wanted you to go. And you stayed."

"So you blew up an unarmed ship."

"Yes. I did it. I destroyed all the others. You destroyed ours. Our space station. You killed thousands of us. I killed thousands of you."

"Not me and not you, elf. That's twenty years, dammit, and you weren't there and I wasn't there—"

"I did it. I say I did. And you killed thousands of us."

"We weren't coming to make a war. We were coming to straighten it out. Do you understand that?"

"We weren't yet willing. Now things are different."

"For God's sake—why did you let so many die?"

"You never gave us defeat enough. You were cruel, deFranco. Not to let us know we couldn't win—that was very cruel. It was very subtle. Even now I'm afraid of your cruelty."

"Don't you understand yet?"

"What do I understand? That you've died in thousands. That you make long war. I thought you would kill me on the hill, on the road, and when you called me I had both hope and fear. Hope that you would take me to higher authority. Fear—well, I am bone and nerve, deFranco. And I never knew whether you would be cruel."

The elf walked and walked. He might have been on holiday, his hands tied in front of him, his red robes a-glitter with their gold borders in the dawn. He never tired. *He* carried no weight of armor; and deFranco went on self-seal and spoke through the mike when he had to give the elf directions.

Germ warfare?

Maybe the elf had a bomb in his gut?

But it began to settle into deFranco that he had done it, he had done it, after years of trying he had himself a live and willing prisoner, and his lower gut was queasy with outright panic and his knees felt like mush. *What's he up to, what's he doing, why's he walk like that— Damn! They'll shoot him on sight, somebody could see him first and shoot him and I can't break silence—maybe that's what I'm supposed to do, maybe that's how they overran Gamma Company—*

But a prisoner, a prisoner speaking human language—

"Where'd you learn," he asked the elf, "where'd you learn to talk human?"

The elf never turned, never stopped walking. "A prisoner."

"Who? Still alive?"

"No."

No. Slender and graceful as a reed and burning as a fire and white as beach sand. *No.* Placidly. Rage rose in deFranco, a blinding urge to put his rifle butt in that straight spine, to muddy and bloody the bastard and make him as dirty and as hurting as himself; but the professional rose up in him too, and the burned hillsides went on and on as they climbed and they walked, the elf just in front of him.

Until they were close to the tunnels and in imminent danger of a human misunderstanding.

He turned his ID and locator on; but they would pick up the elf on his sensors too, and that was no good. "It's deFranco," he said over the com. "I got a prisoner. Get HQ and get me a transport."

Silence from the other end. He cut off the output, figuring they had it by now. "Stop," he said to the elf on outside audio. And he stood and waited until two suited troopers showed up, walking carefully down the hillside from a direction that did not lead to any tunnel opening.

"Damn," came Cat's female voice over his pickup. "Da-amn." In a tone of wonder. And deFranco at first thought it was admiration of him and what he had done, and then he knew with some disgust it was wonder at the elf, it was a human woman looking at the prettiest, cleanest thing she had seen in three long years, icy, fastidious Cat, who was picky what she slept with.

And maybe her partner Jake picked it up, because: "Huh," he said in quite a different tone, but quiet, quiet, the way the elf looked at their faceless faces, as if he still owned the whole world and meant to take it back.

"It's Franc," Jake said then into the com, directed at the base. "And he's right, he's got a live one. Damn, you should *see* this bastard."

III

So where's the generals in this war?
Why, they're neverneverhere, my friend.
Well, what'll we do until they come?
Well, you neverneverask, my friend.

"I was afraid too," deFranco says. "I thought you might have a bomb or something. We were afraid you'd suicide if anyone touched you. That was why we kept you sitting all that time outside."

"Ah," says the elf with a delicate move of his hands. "Ah. I thought it was to make me angry. Like all the rest you did. But you sat with me. And this was hopeful. I was thirsty; I hoped for a drink. That was mostly what I thought about."

"We think too much—elves and humans. We both think too much. *I'd have given you a drink of water, for God's sake.* I guess no one even thought."

"I wouldn't have taken it."

"Dammit, why?"

"Unless you drank with me. Unless you shared what you had. Do you see?"

"Fear of poison?"

"No."

"You mean just my giving it."

"Sharing it. Yes."

"Is pride so much?"

Again the elf touches deFranco's hand as it rests on the table, a nervous, delicate gesture. The elf's ears twitch and collapse and lift again, trembling. "We always go off course here. I still fail to understand why you fight."

"Dammit, I don't understand why you can't understand why a man'd give you a drink of water. Not to hurt you. Not to prove anything. For the love of God, *mercy*, you ever learn that word? Being decent, so's everything decent doesn't go to hell and we don't act like damn animals!"

The elf stares long and soberly. His small mouth has few expressions. It forms its words carefully. "Is this why you pushed us so long? To show us your control?"

"No, dammit, to hang onto it! So we can find a place to stop this bloody war. It's all we ever wanted."

"Then why did you start?"

"Not to have you push *us*!"

A blink of sea-colored eyes. "Now, now, we're understanding. We're like each other."

"But you won't stop, dammit, you wouldn't stop, you haven't stopped yet! People are still dying out there on the front, throwing themselves away without a thing to win. Nothing. *That's* not like us."

"In starting war we're alike. But not in ending it. You take years. Quickly we show what we can do. Then both sides know. So we make peace. You showed us long cruelty. And we wouldn't give ourselves up to you. What could we expect?"

"Is it that easy?" DeFranco begins to shiver, clenches his hands together on the tabletop and leans there, arms folded. "You're crazy, elf."

"Angan. My personal name is Angan."

"A hundred damn scientists out there trying to figure out how you work and it's that damn simple?"

"I don't think so. I think we maybe went off course again. But we came close. We at least see there was a mistake. That's the important thing. That's why I came."

DeFranco looked desperately at his watch, at the minutes ticking away. He covers the face of it with his hand and looks up. His brown eyes show anguish. "The colonel said I'd have three hours. It's going. It's going too fast."

"Yes. And we still haven't found out why. I don't think we ever will. Only you share with me now, deFranco. Here. In our little time."

The elf sat, just sat quietly with his hands still tied, on the open hillside, because the acting CO had sent word no elf was setting foot inside the bunker system and no one was laying hands on him to search him.

But the troopers came out one by one in the long afternoon and had their look at him—one after another of them took the trouble to put on the faceless, uncomfortable armor just to come out and stand and stare at what they had been fighting for all these years.

"Damn," was what most of them said, in private, on the com, their suits to his suit; "damn," or variants on that theme.

"We got that transport coming in," the reg lieutenant said when she came out and brought him his kit. Then, unlike herself: "Good job, Franc."

"Thanks," deFranco said, claiming nothing. And he sat calmly, beside his prisoner, on the barren, shell-pocked hill by a dead charcoal tree.

Don't shake him, word had come from the CO. Keep him real happy—don't change the situation and don't threaten him and don't touch him.

For fear of spontaneous suicide.

So no one came to lay official claim to the elf either, not even the captain came. But the word had gone out to Base and to HQ and up, de-Franco did not doubt, to orbiting ships, because it was the best news a frontline post had had to report since the war started. Maybe it was dreams of leaving Elfland that brought the regs out here, on pilgrimage to see this wonder. And the lieutenant went away when she had stared at him so long.

Hope. DeFranco turned that over and over in his mind and probed at it like a tongue into a sore tooth. Promotion out of the field. No more mud. No more runs like yesterday. No more, no more, no more, the man who broke the Elfland war and cracked the elves and brought in the key—

—to let it all end. For good. *Winning*. Maybe, maybe—

He looked at the elf who sat there with his back straight and his eyes wandering to this and that, to the movement of wind in a forlorn last bit of grass, the drift of a cloud in Elfland's blue sky, the horizons and the dead trees.

"You got a name?" He was careful asking anything. But the elf had talked before.

The elf looked at him. "Saitas," he said.

"Saitas. Mine's deFranco."

The elf blinked. There was no fear in his face. They might have been sitting in the bunker passing the time of day together.

"Why'd they send you?" DeFranco grew bolder.

"I asked to come."

"Why?"

"To stop the war."

Inside his armor deFranco shivered. He blinked and he took a drink from the tube inside the helmet and he tried to think about something else, but the elf sat there staring blandly at him, with his hands tied, resting placidly in his lap. "How?" deFranco asked, "how will you stop the war?"

But the elf said nothing and deFranco knew he had gone further with that question than HQ was going to like, not wanting their subject told anything about human wants and intentions before they had a chance to study the matter and study the elf and hold their conferences.

* * *

"They came," says deFranco in that small room, "to know what you looked like."

"You never let us see your faces," says the elf.

"You never let us see yours."

"You knew everything. Far more than we. You knew our world. We had no idea of yours."

"Pride again."

"Don't you know how hard it was to let you lay hands on me? That was the worst thing. You did it again. Like the gunfire. You touch with violence and then expect quiet. But I let this happen. It was what I came to do. And when you spoke to the others for me, that gave me hope."

In time the transport came skimming in low over the hills, and deFranco got to his feet to wave it in. The elf stood up too, graceful and still placid. And waited while the transport sat down and the blades stopped beating.

"Get in," deFranco said then, picking up his scant baggage, putting the gun on safety.

The elf quietly bowed his head and followed instructions, going where he was told. DeFranco never laid a hand on him, until inside, when they had climbed into the dark belly of the transport and guards were waiting there— "Keep your damn guns down," deFranco said on outside com, because they were light-armed and helmetless. "What are you going to do if he moves, shoot him? Let me handle him. He speaks real good." And to the elf: "Sit down there. I'm going to put a strap across. Just so you don't fall."

The elf sat without objection, and deFranco got a cargo strap and hooked it to the rail on one side and the other, so there was no way the elf was going to stir or use his hands.

And he sat down himself as the guards took their places and the transport lifted off and carried them away from the elvish city and the frontline base of the hundreds of such bases in the world. It began to fly high and fast when it got to safe airspace, behind the defense humans had made about themselves.

There was never fear in the elf. Only placidity. His eyes traveled over the inside of the transport, the dark utilitarian hold, the few benches, the cargo nets, the two guards.

Learning, deFranco thought, still learning everything there was to learn about his enemies.

*   *   *

"Then I was truly afraid," says the elf. "I was most afraid that they would want to talk to me and learn from me. And I would have to die then to no good. For nothing."

"How do you do that?"

"What?"

"Die. Just by wanting to."

"Wanting is the way. I could stop my heart now. Many things stop the heart. When you stop trying to live, when you stop going ahead—it's very easy."

"You mean if you quit trying to live you die. That's crazy."

The elf spreads delicate fingers. "Children can't. Children's hearts can't be stopped that way. You have the hearts of children. Without control. But the older you are the easier and easier it is. Until someday it's easier to stop than to go on. When I learned your language, I learned from a man named Tomas. He couldn't die. He and I talked—oh, every day. And one day we brought him a woman we took. She called him a damn traitor. That was what she said. Damn traitor. Then Tomas wanted to die and he couldn't. He told me so. It was the only thing he ever asked of me. Like the water, you see. Because I felt sorry for him I gave him the cup. And to her. Because I had no use for her. But Tomas hated me. He hated me every day. He talked to me because I was all he had to talk to, he would say. Nothing stopped his heart. Until the woman called him traitor. And then his heart stopped, though it went on beating. I only helped. He thanked me. And damned me to hell. And wished me health with his drink.

"Dammit, elf."

"I tried to ask him what hell was. I think it means being still and trapped. So we fight."

("He's very good with words," someone elsewhere says, leaning over near the monitor. "He's trying to communicate something, but the words aren't equivalent. He's playing on what he does have.")

"For God's sake," says deFranco then, "is that why they fling themselves on the barriers? Is that why they go on dying? Like birds at cage bars?"

The elf flinches. Perhaps it is the image. Perhaps it is a thought. "Fear stops the heart, when fear has nowhere to go. We still have one impulse left. There is still our anger. Everything else has gone. At the last even our children will fight you. So I fight for my children by coming here. I don't want to talk about Tomas any more. The birds have him. *You* are what I was looking for."

"Why?" DeFranco's voice shakes. "Saitas—Angan—I'm scared as hell."

"So am I. Think of all the soldiers. Think of things important to you. I think about my home."

"I think I never had one. —This is crazy. It won't work."

"Don't." The elf reaches and holds a brown wrist. "Don't leave me now, deFranco."

"There's still fifteen minutes. Quarter of an hour."

"That's a very long time . . . here. Shall we shorten it?"

"No," deFranco says and draws a deep breath. "Let's use it."

At the base where the on-world authorities and the scientists did their time, there were real buildings, real ground-site buildings, which humans had made. When the transport touched down on a rooftop landing pad, guards took the elf one way and deFranco another. It was debriefing: that he expected. They let him get a shower first with hot water out of real plumbing, in a prefabbed bathroom. And he got into his proper uniform for the first time in half a year, shaved and proper in his blue beret and his brown uniform, fresh and clean and thinking all the while that if a special could get his field promotion it was scented towels every day and soft beds to sleep on and a life expectancy in the decades. He was anxious, because there were ways of snatching credit for a thing and he wanted the credit for this one, wanted it because a body could get killed out there on hillsides where he had been for three years and no desk-sitting officer was going to fail to mention him in the report.

"Sit down," the specials major said, and took him through it all; and that afternoon they let him tell it to a reg colonel and lieutenant general; and again that afternoon they had him tell it to a tableful of scientists and answer questions and questions and questions until he was hoarse and they forgot to feed him lunch. But he answered on and on until his voice cracked and the science staff took pity on him.

He slept then, in clean sheets in a clean bed and lost touch with the war so that he waked terrified and lost in the middle of the night in the dark and had to get his heart calmed down before he realized he was not crazy and that he really had gotten into a place like this and he really had done what he remembered.

He tucked down babylike into a knot and thought good thoughts all the way back to sleep until a buzzer waked him and told him it was day in this windowless place, and he had an hour to dress again—for more questions, he supposed; and he thought only a little about his elf, *his* elf, who was handed on to the scientists and the generals and the AlSec people, and stopped being his personal business.

"**T**hen," says the elf, "I knew you were the only one I met I could understand. Then I sent for you."

"I still don't know why."

"I said it then. We're both soldiers."

"You're more than that."

"Say that I made one of the great mistakes."

"You mean at the beginning? I don't believe it."

"It could have been. Say that I commanded the attacking ship. Say that I struck your people on the world. Say that you destroyed our station and our cities. We are the makers of mistakes. Say this of ourselves."

"**I**," the elf said, his image on the screen much the same as he had looked on the hillside, straight-spined, red-robed—only the ropes elves had put on him had left purpling marks on his wrists, on the opalescing white of his skin, "I'm clear enough, aren't I?" The trooper accent was strange coming from a delicate elvish mouth. The elf's lips were less mobile. His voice had modulations, like singing, and occasionally failed to keep its tones flat.

"It's very good," the scientist said, the man in the white coveralls, who sat at a small desk opposite the elf in a sterile white room and had his hands laced before him. The camera took both of them in, elf and swarthy Science Bureau xenologist. "I understand you learned from prisoners."

The elf seemed to gaze into infinity. "We don't want to fight anymore."

"Neither do we. Is this why you came?"

A moment the elf studied the scientist, and said nothing at all.

"What's your people's name?" the scientist asked.

"You call us elves."

"But we want to know what you call yourselves. What you call this world."

"Why would you want to know that?"

"To respect you. Do you know that word, respect?"

"I don't understand it."

"Because what you call this world and what you call yourselves *is* the name, the right name, and we want to call you right. Does that make sense?"

"It makes sense. But what you call us is right too, isn't it?"

"Elves is a made-up word, from our homeworld. A myth. Do you know *myth?* A story. A thing not true."

"Now it's true, isn't it?"

"Do you call your world Earth? Most people do."

"What you call it is its name."

"We call if Elfland."

"That's fine. It doesn't matter."

"Why doesn't it matter?"

"I've said that."

"You learned our language very well. But we don't know anything of yours."

"Yes."

"Well, we'd like to learn. We'd like to be able to talk to you your way. It seems to us this is only polite. Do you know *polite?*"

"No."

A prolonged silence. The scientist's face remained bland as the elf's. "You say you don't want to fight anymore. Can you tell us how to stop the war?"

"Yes. But first I want to know what your peace is like. What, for instance, will you do about the damage you've caused us?"

"You mean reparations."

"What's that mean?"

"Payment."

"What do you mean by it?"

The scientist drew a deep breath. "Tell me. Why did your people give you to one of our soldiers? Why didn't they just call on the radio and say they wanted to talk?"

"This is what you'd do."

"It's easier, isn't it? And safer."

The elf blinked. No more than that.

"There was a ship a long time ago," the scientist said after a moment. "It was a human ship minding its own business in a human lane, and elves came and destroyed it and killed everyone on it. Why?"

"What do you want for this ship?"

"So you do understand about payment. Payment's giving something for something."

"I understand." The elvish face was guileless, masklike, the long eyes like the eyes of a pearl-skinned Buddha. A saint. "What will you ask? And how will peace with you be? What do you call peace?"

"You mean you don't think our word for it is like your word for it?"

"That's right."

"Well, that's an important thing to understand, isn't it? Before we make agreements. Peace means no fighting."

"That's not enough."

"Well, it means being safe from your enemies."

"That's not enough."

"What is enough?"

The pale face contemplated the floor, something elsewhere.

"What *is* enough, Saitas?"

The elf only stared at the floor, far, far away from the questioner. "I need to talk to deFranco."

"Who?"

"DeFranco." The elf looked up. "DeFranco brought me here. He's a soldier; he'll understand me better than you. Is he still here?"

The colonel reached and cut the tape off. She was SurTac. Agnes Finn was the name on her desk. She could cut your throat a dozen ways, and do sabotage and mayhem from the refinements of computer theft to the gross tactics of explosives; she would speak a dozen languages, know every culture she had ever dealt with from the inside out, integrating the Science Bureau and the military. And more, she was a SurTac *colonel*, which sent the wind up deFranco's back. It was not a branch of the service that had many high officers; you had to survive more than ten field missions to get your promotion beyond the ubiquitous and courtesy-titled lieutenancy. And this one had. This was Officer with a capital O, and whatever the politics in HQ were, this was a rock around which a lot of other bodies orbited: *this* probably took her orders from the joint command, which was months and months away in its closest manifestation. And that meant next to no orders and wide discretion, which was what SurTacs did. Wild card. Joker in the deck. There were the regs; there was special ops, loosely attached; there were the spacers, Union and Alliance, and Union regs were part of that; beyond and above, there was AlSec and Union intelligence; and that was this large-boned, red-haired woman who probably had a scant handful of humans and no knowing what else in her direct command, a handful of SurTacs loose in Elfland, and all of them independent operators and as much trouble to the elves as a reg base could be.

DeFranco knew. He had tried that route once. He knew more than most what kind it took to survive that training, let alone the requisite ten missions to get promoted out of the field, and he knew the wit behind the weathered face and knew it ate special ops lieutenants for appetizers.

"How did you make such an impression on him, Lieutenant?"

"I didn't try to," deFranco said carefully. "Ma'am, I just tried to keep him calm and get in with him alive the way they said. But I was the only one who dealt with him out there, we thought that was safest; maybe he thinks I'm more than I am."

"I compliment you on the job." There was a certain irony in that, he was sure. No SurTac had pulled off what he had, and he felt the slight tension there.

"Yes, ma'am."

"*Yes, ma'am*. There's always the chance, you understand, that you've brought us an absolute lunatic. Or the elves are going an unusual route to lead us into a trap. Or this is an elf who's not too pleased about being tied up and dumped on us, and he wants to get even. Those things occur to me."

"Yes, ma'am." DeFranco thought all those things, face to face with the colonel and trying to be easy as the colonel had told him to be. But the colonel's thin face was sealed and forbidding as the elf's.

"You know what they're doing out there right now? Massive attacks. Hitting that front near 45 with everything they've got. The Eighth's pinned. We're throwing air in. and they've got somewhere over two thousand casualties out there and air-strikes don't stop all of them. Delta took a head-on assault and turned it. There were casualties. Trooper named Herse. Your unit."

Dibs. O God. "Dead?"

"Dead." The colonel's eyes were bleak and expressionless. "Word came in. I know it's more than a stat to you. But that's what's going on. We've got two signals coming from the elves. And we don't know which one's valid. We have ourselves an alien who claims credentials—*and* comes with considerable effort from the same site as the attack."

Dibs. Dead. There seemed a chill in the air, in this safe, remote place far from the real world, the mud, the bunkers. Dibs had stopped living yesterday. This morning. Sometime. Dibs had gone and the world never noticed.

"Other things occur to the science people," the colonel said. "One which galls the hell out of them, deFranco, is what the alien just said. *DeFranco can understand me better.* Are you with me, Lieutenant?"

"Yes, ma'am."

"So the Bureau went to the secretary, the secretary went to the major general on the com; all this at fifteen hundred yesterday; and *they* hauled me in on it at two this morning. You know how many noses you've got out of joint, Lieutenant? And what the level of concern is about that mess out there on the front?"

"Yes, ma'am."

"I'm sure you hoped for a commendation and maybe better, wouldn't that be it? Wouldn't blame you. Well, I got my hands into this, and I've opted you under my orders, Lieutenant, because I can do that and high command's just real worried the Bureau's going to poke and prod and that elf's going to leave us on the sudden for elvish heaven. So let's just keep him moderately happy. He wants to talk to you. What the Bureau wants to tell you, but I told them *I'd* make it clear, because they'll talk tech at you and I want to be sure you've got it—it's just real simple: you're dealing with an alien; and you'll have noticed what he says doesn't always make sense."

"Yes, ma'am."

"Don't yes ma'am me, Lieutenant, dammit; just talk to me and look me in the eye. We're talking about communication here."

"Yes—" He stopped short of the ma'am.

"You've got a brain, deFranco, it's all in your record. You almost went Special Services yourself, that was your real ambition, wasn't it? But you had this damn psychotic fear of taking ultimate responsibility. And a wholesome fear of ending up with a commendation, posthumous. Didn't you? It washed you out, so you went special ops where you could take orders from someone else and still play bloody hero and prove something to yourself—am I right? I ought to be; I've got your psych record over there. Now I've insulted you and you're sitting there turning red. But I want to know what I'm dealing with. We're in a damn bind. We've got casualties happening out there. Are you and I going to have trouble?"

"No. I understand."

"Good. Very good. Do you think you can go into a room with that elf and talk the truth out of him? More to the point, can you make a decision, can you go in there knowing how much is riding on your back?"

"I'm not a—"

"I don't care what you *are*, deFranco. What I want to know is whether *negotiate* is even in that elf's vocabulary. I'm assigning you to guard over there. In the process I want you to sit down with him one to one and just talk away. That's all you've got to do. And because of your background maybe you'll do it with some sense. But maybe if you just talk for John deFranco and try to get that elf to deal, that's the best thing. You know when a government sends out a negotiator—or anything like—that individual's not average. That individual's probably the smartest, canniest, hardest-nosed bastard they've got, and he probably cheats at dice. We don't know what this bastard's up to or what he thinks like, and when you sit down with him, you're talking to a mind that knows a lot more about humanity than we know about elves. You're talking to an elvish expert who's here playing games with us. Who's giving us a real good look-over. You understand that? What do you say about it?"

"I'm scared of this."

"That's real good. You know we're not sending in the brightest, most experienced human on two feet. And that's exactly what that rather canny elf has arranged for us to do. You understand that? He's playing us like a keyboard this far. And how do you cope with that, Lieutenant deFranco?"

"I just ask him questions and answer as little as I can."

"Wrong. You let him talk. You be real *careful* what you ask him. What you ask is as dead a giveaway as what you tell him. Everything you do and say is cultural. If he's good, he'll drain you like a sponge." The colonel bit her lips. "Damn, you're *not* going to be able to handle that, are you?"

"I understand what you're warning me about, Colonel. I'm not sure I can do it, but I'll try."

"Not sure you can do it. *Peace* may hang on this. And several billion lives. Your company, out there on the line. Put it on that level. And you're scared and you're showing it, Lieutenant; you're too damned open, no wonder they washed you out. Got no hard center to you, no place to go to when I embarrass the hell out of you, and *I'm* on your side. You're probably a damn good special op, brave as hell, I know, you've got commendations in the field. And that shell-shyness of yours probably makes you drive real hard when you're in trouble. Good man. Honest. If the elf wants a human specimen, we could do worse. You just go in there, son, and you talk to him and you be your nice self, and that's all you've got to do."

"We'll be bugged." DeFranco stared at the colonel deliberately, trying to dredge up some self-defense, give the impression he was no complete fool.

"Damn sure you'll be bugged. Guards right outside if you want them. But if you startle that elf I'll fry you."

"That isn't what I meant. I meant—I meant if I could get him to talk there'd be an accurate record."

"Ah. Well. Yes. There will be, absolutely. And yes, I'm a bastard, Lieutenant, same as that elf is, beyond a doubt. And because I'm on your side I want you as prepared as I can get you. But I'm going to give you all the backing you need—you want anything, you just tell that staff and they better jump to do it. I'm giving you carte blanche over there in the Science Wing. Their complaints can come to this desk. You just be yourself with him, watch yourself a little, don't get taken and don't set him off."

"Yes, ma'am."

Another slow, consuming stare and a nod.

He was dismissed.

IV

So where's the hole we're digging end?
Why, it's neverneverdone, my friend.
Well, why's it warm at the other end?
Well, hell's neverneverfar, my friend.

"This colonel," says the elf, "it's her soldiers outside."

"That's the one," says deFranco.

"It's not the highest rank."

"No. It's not. Not even on this world." DeFranco's hands open and close on each other, white-knuckled. His voice stays calm. "But it's a lot of power. She won't be alone. There are others she's acting for. They sent me here. I've figured that now."

"Your dealing confuses me."

"Politics. It's all politics. Higher-ups covering their—" DeFranco rechooses his words. "Some things they have to abide by. They have to do. Like if they don't take a peace offer—that would be trouble back home. Human space is big. But a war—humans want it stopped. I know that. With humans, you can't quiet a mistake down. We've got too many separate interests. . . . We got scientists, and a half dozen different commands—"

"Will they all stop fighting?"

"Yes. My side will. I know they will." DeFranco clenches his hands tighter as if the chill has gotten to his bones. "If we can give them something, some solution. You have to understand what they're thinking of.

If there's a trouble anywhere, it can grow. There might be others out there, you ever think of that? What if some other species just—wanders through? It's happened. And what if our little war disturbs them? We live in a big house, you know that yet? You're young, you, with your ships, you're a young power out in space. God help us, we've made mistakes, but this time the first one wasn't ours. We've been trying to stop this. All along, we've been trying to stop this."

"You're what I trust," says the elf. "Not your colonel. Not your treaty words. Not your peace. You. Words aren't the belief. What you do—that's the belief. What you do will show us."

"I can't!"

"I can. It's important enough to me and not to you. *Our little war.* I can't understand how you think that way."

"Look at that!" DeFranco waves a desperate hand at the room, the world. Up. "It's so big! Can't you see that? And one planet, one ball of rock. It's a little war. Is it worth it all? Is it worth such damn stubbornness? Is it worth dying in?"

"Yes," the elf says simply, and the sea-green eyes and the white face have neither anger nor blame for him.

DeFranco saluted and got out and waited until the colonel's orderly caught him in the hall and gave his escort the necessary authorizations, because *no one* wandered this base without an escort. (But the elves are two hundred klicks out *there*, deFranco thought; and who're we fighting anyway?) In the halls he saw the black of Union elite and the blue of Alliance spacers and the plain drab of the line troop officers, and the white and pale blue of the two Science Bureaus; while everywhere he felt the tenuous peace—damn, maybe we *need* this war, it's keeping humanity talking to each other, they're all fat and sleek and mud never touched them back here— But there was haste in the hallways. But there were tense looks on faces of people headed purposefully to one place and the other, the look of a place with something on its collective mind, with silent, secret emergencies passing about him— *The attack on the lines*, he thought, and remembered another time that attack had started on one front and spread rapidly to a dozen; and missiles had gone. And towns had died.

And the elvish kids, the babies in each others' arms and the birds fluttering down; and Dibs—Dibs lying in his armor like a broken piece of machinery—when a shot got you, it got the visor and you had no face and never knew it; or it got the joints and you bled to death trapped in the failed shell, you just lay there and bled: he had heard men and women die like that, still in contact on the com, talking to their buddies and going out alone, alone in that damn armor that cut off the sky and the air——

They brought him down tunnels that were poured and cast and hard overnight, *that* kind of construction, which they never got out on the Line. There were bright lights and there were dry floors for the fine officers to walk on; there was, at the end, a new set of doors where guards stood with weapons ready——

—against *us?* DeFranco got that sense of unreality again, blinked as he had to show his tags and IDs to get past even with the colonel's orders directing his escort.

Then they let him through, and further, to another hall with more guards. AlSec MPs. Alliance Security. The intelligence and Special Services. The very air here had a chill about it, with only those uniforms in sight. *They* had the elf. Of course they did. He was diplomatic property and the regs and the generals had nothing to do with it. He was in Finn's territory. Security and the Surface Tactical command, that the reg command only controlled from the top, not inside the structure. Finn had a leash, but she took no orders from sideways in the structure. Not even from AlSec. Check and balance in a joint command structure too many light-years from home to risk petty dictatorships. He had just crossed a line and might as well have been on another planet.

And evidently a call had come ahead of him, because there were surly Science Bureau types here too, and the one who passed him through hardly glanced at his ID. It was his face the man looked at, long and hard; and it was the Xenbureau interviewer who had been on the tape.

"Good luck," the man said. And a SurTac major arrived, dour-faced, a black man in the SurTac's khaki, who did not look like an office-type. *He* took the folder of authorizations and looked at it and at deFranco with a dark-eyed stare and a set of a square, well-muscled jaw. "Colonel's given you three hours, Lieutenant. Use it."

"We're more than one government," says deFranco to the elf, quietly, desperately. "We've fought in the past. We had wars. We made peace and we work together. We may fight again but everyone hopes not and it's less and less likely. War's expensive. It's too damn open out here, that's what I'm trying to tell you. You start a war and you don't know what else might be listening."

The elf leans back in his chair, one arm on the back of it. His face is solemn as ever as he looks at deFranco. "You and I, you-and-I. The world was whole until you found us. How can people do things that don't make sense? The *whole* thing makes sense, the parts of the thing are crazy. You can't put part of one thing into another, leaves won't be feathers, and your mind can't be our mind. I see our mistakes. I want to take them away. Then elves won't have theirs and you won't have yours. But you call it a little war. The lives are only a few. You have so many. You like your mistake. You'll keep it. You'll hold it in your arms. And you'll meet these others with it. But they'll see it, won't they, when they look at you?"

"It's crazy!"

"When we met you in it, we assumed *we*. That was our first great mistake. But it's yours too."

DeFranco walked into the room where they kept the elf, a luxurious room, a groundling civ's kind of room, with a bed and a table and two chairs, and some kind of green and yellow pattern on the bedclothes, which were ground-style, free-hanging. And amid this riot of life-colors the elf sat cross-legged on the bed, placid, not caring that the door opened or someone came in—until a flicker of recognition seemed to take hold and grow. It was the first humanlike expression, virtually the only expression, the elf had ever used in deFranco's sight. Of course there were cameras recording it, recording everything. The colonel had said so and probably the elf knew it too.

"Saitas. You wanted to see me."

"DeFranco." The elf's face settled again to inscrutability.

"Shall I sit down?"

There was no answer. DeFranco waited for an uncertain moment, then settled into one chair at the table and leaned his elbows on the white plastic surface.

"They treating you all right?" deFranco asked, for the cameras, deliberately, for the colonel— (*Damn you, I'm not a fool, I can play your damn game, Colonel, I did what your SurTacs failed at, didn't I? So watch me.*)

"Yes," the elf said. His hands rested loosely in his red-robed lap. He looked down at them and up again.

"I tried to treat you all right. I thought I did."

"Yes."

"Why'd you ask for me?"

"I'm a soldier," the elf said, and put his legs over the side of the bed and stood up. "I know that you are. I think you understand me more."

"I don't know about that. But I'll listen." The thought crossed his mind of being held hostage, of some irrational violent behavior, but he pretended it away and waved a hand at the other chair. "You want to sit down? You want something to drink? They'll get it for you."

"I'll sit with you." The elf came and took the other chair, and leaned his elbows on the table. The bruises on his wrists showed plainly under the light. "I thought you might have gone back to the front by now."

"They give me a little time. I mean, there's—"

(Don't talk to him, the colonel had said. Let him talk.)

"—three hours. A while. You had a reason you wanted to see me. Something you wanted? Or just to talk. I'll do that too."

"Yes," the elf said slowly, in his lilting lisp. And gazed at him with sea-green eyes. "Are you young, deFranco? You make me think of a young man."

It set him off his balance. "I'm not all that young."

"I have a son and a daughter. Have you?"

"No."

"Parents?"

"Why do you want to know?"

"Have you parents?"

"A mother. Long way from here." He resented the questioning. Letters were all Nadya deFranco got, and not enough of them, and thank God she had closer sons. DeFranco sat staring at the elf who had gotten past his guard in two quick questions and managed to hit a sore spot; and he remembered what Finn had warned him. "You, elf?"

"Living parents. Yes. A lot of relatives?"

Damn, what trooper had they stripped getting that part of human language? Whose soul had they gotten into?

"What are you, Saitas? Why'd they hand you over like that?"

"To make peace. So the Saitas always does."

"Tied up like that?"

"I came to be your prisoner. You understand that."

"Well, it worked. I might have shot you; I don't say I would've, but I might, except for that. It was a smart move, I guess it was. But hell, you could have called ahead. You come up on us in the dark—you looked to get your head blown off. Why didn't you use the radio?"

A blink of sea-green eyes. "Others ask me that. Would you have come then?"

"Well, someone would. Listen, you speak at them in human language and they'd listen and they'd arrange something a lot safer."

The elf stared, full of his own obscurities.

"Come on, they throw you out of there? They your enemies?"

"Who?"

"The ones who left you out there on the hill."

"No."

"Friends, huh? *Friends* let you out there?"

"They agreed with me. I agreed to be there. I was most afraid you'd shoot them. But you let them go."

"Hell, look, I just follow orders."

"And orders led you to let them go?"

"No. They say to talk if I ever got the chance. Look, me, personally, I never wanted to kill you guys. I wouldn't, if I had the choice."

"But you do."

"Dammit, you took out our ships. Maybe that wasn't personal on your side either, but we sure as hell can't have you doing it as a habit. All you ever damn well had to do was go away and let us alone. You hit a world, elf. Maybe not much of one, but you killed more than a thousand people on that first ship. Thirty thousand at that base, good God, don't sit there looking at me like that!"

"It was a mistake."

"Mistake." DeFranco found his hands shaking. No. Don't raise the voice. Don't lose it. (Be your own nice self, boy. Patronizingly. The colonel knew he was far out of his depth. And he knew.) "Aren't most wars mistakes?"

"Do you think so?"

"If it is, can't we stop it?" He felt the attention of unseen listeners, diplomats, scientists—himself, special ops, talking to an elvish negotiator and making a mess of it all, losing everything. (Be your own nice self— The colonel was crazy, the elf was, the war and the world were and he lumbered ahead desperately, attempting subtlety, attempting a caricatured simplicity toward a diplomat and knowing the one as transparent as the other.) "You know all you have to do is say quit and there's ways to stop the shooting right off, ways to close it all down and then start talking about how we settle this. You say that's what you came to do. You're in the right place. All you have to do is get your side to stop. They're killing each other out there, do you know that? You come in here to talk peace. And they're coming at us all up and down the front. I just got word I lost a friend of mine out there. God knows what by now. It's no damn sense. If you can stop it, then let's stop it."

"I'll tell you what our peace will be." The elf lifted his face placidly, spread his hands. "There is a camera, isn't there? At least a microphone. They do listen."

"Yes. They've got camera and mike. I know they will."

"But your face is what I see. Your face is all human faces to me. They can listen, but I talk to you. Only to you. And this is our peace. The fighting will stop, and we'll build ships again and we'll go into space, and we won't be enemies. The mistake won't exist. That's the peace I want."

"So how do we do that?" (Be your own nice self, boy— DeFranco abandoned himself. Don't see the skin, don't see the face alien-like, just talk, talk like to a human, don't worry about protocols. *Do* it, boy.) "How do we get the fighting stopped?"

"I've said it. They've heard."

"Yes. They have."

"They have two days to make this peace."

DeFranco's palms sweated. He clenched his hands on the chair. "Then what happens?"

"I'll die. The war will go on."

(God, now what do I do, what do I say? How far can I go?) "Listen, you don't understand how long it takes us to make up our minds. We need more than any two days. They're dying out there, your people are killing themselves against our lines, and it's all for nothing. Stop it now. Talk to them. Tell them we're going to talk. Shut it down."

The slitted eyes blinked, remained in their buddha-like abstraction, looking askance into infinity. "DeFranco, there has to be payment."

(Think, deFranco, think. Ask the right things.)

"What payment? Just exactly who are you talking for? All of you? A city? A district?"

"One peace will be enough for you—won't it? You'll go away. You'll leave and we won't see each other until we've built our ships again. You'll begin to go—as soon as my peace is done."

"Build the ships, for God's sake. And come after us again?"

"No. The war is a mistake. There won't be another war. This is enough."

"But would everyone agree?"

"Everyone does agree. I'll tell you my real name. It's Angan. Angan Anassidi. I'm forty-one years old. I have a son named Agaita; a daughter named Siadi; I was born in a town named Daogisshi, but it's burned now. My wife is Llaothai Sohail, and she was born in the city where we live now. I'm my wife's only husband. My son is aged twelve, my daughter is nine. They live in the city with my wife alone now and her parents and mine." The elvish voice acquired a subtle music on the names that lingered to obscure his other speech. "I've written—I told them I would write everything for them. I write in your language."

"Told who?"

"The humans who asked me. I wrote it all."

DeFranco stared at the elf, at a face immaculate and distant as a statue. "I don't think I follow you. I don't understand. We're talking about the front. We're talking about maybe that wife and those kids being in danger, aren't we? About maybe my friends getting killed out there. About shells falling and people getting blown up. Can we do anything about it?"

"I'm here to make the peace. Saitas is what I am. A gift to you. I'm the payment."

DeFranco blinked and shook his head. "Payment? I'm not sure I follow that."

For a long moment there was quiet. "Kill me," the elf said. "That's why I came. To be the last dead. The saitas. To carry the mistake away."

"Hell, no. No. We don't shoot you. Look, elf—all we want is to stop the fighting. We don't want your life. Nobody wants to kill you."

"DeFranco, we haven't any more resources. We want a peace."

"So do we. Look, we just make a treaty—you understand *treaty?*"

"I'm the treaty."

"A treaty, man, a treaty's a piece of paper. We promise peace to each other and not to attack us, we promise not to attack you, we settle our borders, and you just go home to that wife and kids. And I go home and that's it. No more dying. No more killing."

"No." The elf's eyes glistened within the pale mask. "No, deFranco, no paper."

"We make peace with a paper and ink. We write peace out and we make agreements and it's good enough; we do what we say we'll do."

"Then write it in your language."

"You have to sign it. Write your name on it. And keep the terms. That's all, you understand that?"

"Two days. I'll sign your paper. I'll make your peace. It's nothing. Our peace is in me. And I'm here to give it."

"Dammit, we don't kill people for treaties."

The sea-colored eyes blinked. "Is one so hard and millions so easy?"

"It's different."

"Why?"

"Because—because—look, war's for killing; peace is for staying alive."

"I don't understand why you fight. Nothing you do makes sense to us. But I think we almost understand. We talk to each other. We use the same words. DeFranco, don't go on killing us."

"Just you. Just you, is that it? Dammit, that's crazy!"

"A cup would do. Or a gun. Whatever you like. DeFranco, have you never shot us before?"

"God, it's not the same!"

"You say paper's enough for you. That paper will take away all your mistakes and make the peace. But paper's not enough for us. I'd never trust it. You have to make my peace too. So both sides will know it's true. But there has to be a saitas for humans. Someone has to come to be a saitas for humans. Someone has to come to us."

DeFranco sat there with his hands locked together. "You mean just go to your side and get killed."

"The last dying."

"Dammit, you are crazy. You'll wait a long time for that, elf."

"You don't understand."

"You're damn right I don't understand. Damn bloody-minded lunatics!" DeFranco shoved his hands down, needing to get up, to get away from that infinitely patient and not human face, that face that had somehow acquired subtle expressions, that voice which made him forget where the words had first come from. And then he remembered the listeners, the listeners taking notes, the colonel staring at him across the table. Information. Winning was not the issue. Questions were. Finding out what they could. Peace was no longer the game. They were dealing with the insane, with minds there was no peace with. Elves that died to spite their enemies. That suicided for a whim and thought nothing about wiping out someone else's life.

He stayed in his chair. He drew another breath. He collected his wits and thought of something else worth learning. "What'd you do with the prisoners you learned the language from, huh? Tell me that?"

"Dead. We gave them the cup. One at a time they wanted it."

"Did they."

Again the spread of hands, of graceful fingers. "I'm here for all the mistakes. Whatever will be enough for them."

"Dammit, elf!"

"Don't call me that." The voice acquired a faint music. "Remember my name. Remember my name. DeFranco—"

He had to get up. He had to get up and get clear of the alien, get away from that stare. He thrust himself back from the table and looked back, found the elf had turned. Saitas-Angan smelled of something dry and musky, like spice. The eyes never opened wide, citrine slits. They followed him.

"Talk to me," the elf said. "Talk to me, deFranco."

"About what? About handing one of us to you? It won't happen. It bloody won't happen. We're not crazy."

"Then the war won't stop."

"You'll bloody die, every damn last one of you!"

"If that's your intention," the elf said, "yes. We don't believe you want peace. We haven't any more hope. So I come here. And the rest of us begin to die. Not the quiet dying. Our hearts won't stop. We'll fight."

"Out there on the lines, you mean."

"I'll die as long as you want, here. I won't stop my heart. The saitas can't."

"Dammit, that's not what we're after! That's not what we want."

"Neither can you stop yours. I know that. We're not cruel. I still have hope in you. I still hope."

"It won't work. *We can't do it*, do you understand me? It's against our law. Do you understand law?"

"Law."

"Right from wrong. Morality. For God's sake, killing's wrong."

"Then you've done a lot of wrong. You have your mistake too. De-Franco. You're a soldier like me. You know what your life's value is."

"You're damn right I know. And I'm still alive."

"We go off the course. We lose ourselves. You'll die for war but not for peace. I don't understand."

"*I* don't understand. You think we're just going to pick some poor sod and send him to you."

"You, deFranco. I'm asking you to make the peace."

"Hell." He shook his head, walked away to the door, colonel-be-hanged, listeners-be-hanged. His hand shook on the switch and he was afraid it showed. End the war. "The hell you say."

The door shot open. He expected guards. Expected—

—It was open corridor, clean prefab, tiled floor. On the tiles lay a dark, round object, with the peculiar symmetry and ugliness of things meant to kill. Grenade. Intact.

His heart jolted. He felt the doorframe against his side and the sweat ran cold on his skin, his bowels went to water. He hung there looking at it and it did not go away. He began to shake all over as if it were already armed.

"Colonel Finn." He turned around in the doorway and yelled at the unseen monitors. "Colonel Finn—get me out of here!"

No one answered. No door opened. The elf sat there staring at him in the closest thing to distress he had yet showed.

"Colonel! *Colonel, damn you!*"

More of silence. The elf rose to his feet and stood there staring at him in seeming perplexity, as if he suspected he witnessed some human madness.

"They left us a present," deFranco said. His voice shook and he tried to stop it. "They left us a damn present, elf. And they locked us in."

The elf stared at him; and deFranco went out into the hall, bent and gathered up the deadly black cylinder—held it up. "It's one of yours, elf."

The elf stood there in the doorway. His eyes looking down were the eyes of a carved saint; and looking up they showed color against his white skin. A long nailless hand touched the doorframe as the elf contemplated him and human treachery.

"Is this their way?"

"It's not mine." He closed his hand tightly on the cylinder, in its deadliness like and unlike every weapon he had ever handled. "It's damn well not mine."

"You can't get out."

The shock had robbed him of wits. For a moment he was not thinking. And then he walked down the hall to the main door and tried it. "Locked," he called back to the elf, who had joined him in his possession of the hall. The two of them together. DeFranco walked back again, trying doors as he went. He felt strangely numb. The hall became surreal, his elvish companion belonging like him, elsewhere. "Dammit, what have you got in their minds?"

"They've agreed," the elf said. "They've agreed, deFranco."

"They're out of their minds."

"One door still closes, doesn't it? You can protect your life."

"You still bent on suicide?"

"You'll be safe."

"Damn them!"

The elf gathered his arms about him as if he too felt the chill. "The colonel gave us a time. Is it past?"

"Not bloody yet."

"Come sit with me. Sit and talk. My friend."

*　　*　　*

"**I**s it time?" asks the elf, as deFranco looks at his watch again. And de-Franco looks up.

"Five minutes. Almost." DeFranco's voice is hoarse.

The elf has a bit of paper in hand. He offers it. A pen lies on the table between them. Along with the grenade. "I've written your peace. I've put my name below it. Put yours."

"I'm nobody. I can't sign a treaty, for God's sake." DeFranco's face is white. His lips tremble. "What did you write?"

"Peace," said the elf. "I just wrote peace. Does there have to be more?"

DeFranco takes it. Looks at it. And suddenly he picks up the pen and signs it too, a furious scribble. And lays the pen down. "There," he says. "There, they'll have my name on it." And after a moment: "If I could do the other—O God, I'm scared. I'm *scared*."

"You don't have to go to my city," says the elf, softly. His voice wavers like deFranco's. "DeFranco—here, here they record everything. Go with me. Now. The record will last. We have our peace, you and I, we make it together, here, now. The last dying. Don't leave me. And we can end this war."

DeFranco sits a moment. Takes the grenade from the middle of the table, extends his hand with it across the center. He looks nowhere but at the elf. "Pin's yours," he says. "Go on. You pull it, I'll hold it steady."

The elf reaches out his hand, takes the pin and pulls it, quickly.

DeFranco lays the grenade down on the table between them, and his mouth moves in silent counting. But then he looks up at the elf and the elf looks at him. DeFranco manages a smile. "You got the count on this thing?"

The screen breaks up.

The stafffer reached out her hand and cut the monitor, and Agnes Finn stared past the occupants of the office for a time. Tears came seldom to her eyes. They were there now, and she chose not to look at the board of inquiry who had gathered there.

"There's a mandatory inquiry," the man from the reg command said. "We'll take testimony from the major this afternoon."

"Responsibility's mine," Finn said.

It was agreed on the staff. It was pre-arranged, the interview, the formalities.

Someone had to take the direct hit. It might have been a SurTac. She would have ordered that too, if things had gone differently. High command might cover her. Records might be wiped. A tape might be classified. The major general who had handed her the mess and turned his back had done it all through subordinates. And he was clear.

"The paper, Colonel."

She looked at them, slid the simple piece of paper back across the desk. The board member collected it and put it into the folder. Carefully.

"It's more than evidence," she said. "That's a treaty. The indigenes know it is."

They left her office, less than comfortable in their official search for blame and where, officially, to put it.

She was already packed. Going back on the same ship with an elvish corpse, all the way to Pell and Downbelow. There would be a grave there onworld.

It had surprised no one when the broadcast tape got an elvish response. Hopes rose when it got the fighting stopped and brought an elvish delegation to the front; but there was a bit of confusion when the elves viewed both bodies and wanted deFranco's. Only deFranco's.

And they made him a stone grave there on the shell-pocked plain, a stone monument; and they wrote everything they knew about him. *I was John Rand deFranco*, a graven plaque said. *I was born on a space station twenty light-years away. I left my mother and my brothers. The friends I had were soldiers and many of them died before me. I came to fight and I died for the peace, even when mine was the winning side. I died at the hand of Angan Anassidi, and he died at mine, for the peace; and we were friends at the end of our lives.*

Elves—*suilti* was one name they called themselves—came to this place and laid gifts of silk ribbons and bunches of flowers—flowers, in all that desolation; and in their thousands they mourned and they wept in their own tearless, expressionless way.

For their enemy.

One of their own was on his way to humankind. For humankind to cry for. *I was Angan Anassidi*, his grave would say; and all the right things. Possibly no human would shed a tear. Except the veterans of Elfland, when they came home, if they got down to the world—they might, like Agnes Finn, in their own way and for their own dead, in front of an alien shrine.

A GIFT OF PROPHECY

A shuttle landed on Aneth, third of the three which daily landed on the world's surface. There was a stir about this arrival as there generally was not, whatever the rank of those who attended the shrine. These were Shantrans, off the powerful high-tech world of An Shant . . . the last major power which resisted the amphictyony of the shrine.

With appropriate ceremony, the Shantrans paused in the Hall of Arrivals long enough to sign the Pact and join the Amphictyony, the Neighbors of the Shrine. They did so with frowns and hesitations enough to indicate a displeasure in principle; An Shant made few agreements. But this signature was the sole and indispensable condition of consultation with the Oracle . . . a militarily harmless accord. The Shantrans read it in detail and failed to find fault in any pact so easily broken, so lacking in enforcements.

That they bar none from access to the Anethine Oracle, it read, on pain of being barred themselves in future; to come to the aid of the shrine with armed force should any attempt to gain entry by force.

They walked away openly smiling, for they were not believers in the Oracle. They had come, nevertheless, to consult it, for reasons which were their own.

And the Anethines hastened to make them welcome, making themselves as agreeable as they showed themselves to all comers, believers or not.

Aneth desired above all to please.

Visions . . . and patterns . . . endless questions.

A tapestry of patterns, interwoven. . . . The mythic fates were weavers too, lives their thread, empires their pattern, uncaring patterners, heedless who or why; the pattern was all, had ever been, and all was pattern.

To perceive . . . to know . . . the ultimate design which shifted between thread and colors, almost to grasp—the Whole . . .

Time to cease.

There was a danger, a point past which humanness slipped the mind, when the knowledge itself became all, and the Eye was more powerful than the mind which must hold what it saw, when mind diminished in the face of design . . .

There was a point past which . . . *not*, not at all.

Maranthe tired of waking, and dulled her senses deliberately; began the withdrawal from life to shadows.

"Maranthe," the Voices began, reminding her of humanity, which she chose to forget. They persisted. A cup came to her lips; she drank, obedient. When the Shadows took her in their hands she walked, moved, performed necessary functions. At their whispering reminder, she ate, and they bathed her and laid her in her bed.

Then was utter dark. She did not dream.

She did not wake until the morrow, when she sat again with hands outstretched over the cold plates of the machine . . . and the Vision resumed.

The old woman sat surrounded by her machine.

Maranthe was—wholly—the machine. She saw, and smiled, for maddeningly smiled, her aged face rapt and her dimmed eyes fixe in the power of the Vision.

And Mishell envied.

Mishell did not speak of it. Possibly all the Servants of Anet Surely they must, for there was nothing on Aneth which appr glory, the importance of Maranthe. Servants came and went dying and being carried away. Maranthe was all. And there from Aneth, least of all for those sealed within the inmost Machine. Only the visitors, who were never *within* Anet their single questions, departed.

They went, and where they went Mishell could n never imagine, sealed within white walls, silent, in siler ing of the Vision. They asked, these visitors, and Mishell could not hear. Only the Sibyl, only Maran went away to act, to pursue their lives and the f them—as Servants could never leave and never serve, tending Maranthe.

Mishell served. She guided the frail, bent

couch, from couch to Machine. With other Servants she fed her, bathed her, performed all minute and lowly things for her, who was the sole reason for their existence. Tiny, frail, blind, yet Maranthe smiled, constantly smiled while she waked . . . for long, long hours wrapped in the Vision, where Maranthe saw . . . and they could not.

In those hours, their own duty over, the Servants themselves must eat and sleep and dream.

And in her dreams Mishell sought life. Armed only with the gray and white sameness of the Enclave, she built colors, and beauty, and tried with all her senses to attain to the Vision which was Maranthe's, which hovered palpably in the Enclave, a presence which seized and shaped, and gave them what dreams they knew.

It ended with waking. The world was cold again, steel and white garments and white plastics, and Servants moved soft-footed and whispering within it, for they must not intrude their small reality into the greater. Gently Mishell bathed Maranthe's wasted limbs, and gently folded the skeletal body into soft garments, and gently tucked her to bed.

And daily sat (or was it night?) through Maranthe's sleep, waking while the Vision was numb, and the walls were void and stark, the dreams dead within the Enclave's waking.

There were other worlds; Maranthe saw them; they dreamed of them; the visitors came from them; but the worlds were dreams.

"It's a charade." The major paused with his hand on the rail of the boarding area, looking back at the port facility where the shuttle rested, with deepening regret. "Rational beings flock to this place. I find it incredible."

"Enough," the minister said, silencing him, and stepped from the interworld soil of the port onto the floor of the Anethine ground transport, committing himself.

The major glowered, shook his head, and followed. After him came the attendant clutter of aides and secretaries, with recorders and sensors surprisingly permitted beyond the outer ring of the oracular enclave. Isean, the minister, prime in the third rank of the Shantran technarchy; Crane, the major, from the military fifth; the aides and secretaries had rank at all save as appurtenances to the minister and the major. An It risked as little as possible in the venture, augmented its delegation expendables in expensive garb. The Confederate enemy had con the oracle; the military grew nervous on the matter: An Shant had

determined to investigate any potential leak or exchange of information. Therefore they were here inconveniencing themselves with this farce.

They were seated. The automated vehicle began to move.

"Irresponsible," Segrane muttered, affecting nonchalance, his eyes shifting to this side and that while he faced ahead, relaxed. "Something could go wrong with these machines. And then where should we be stranded? I find their notion of security less than adequate."

The barren plains of Aneth rolled past the windows, grassland and purple forest. The windows suddenly sealed, viewless, black. The major set his jaw and continued his surreptitious scan. The velocity of the car increased. There was perceptible descent, and aides and secretaries clutched in panic at cases. The minister sat still, outwardly calm. The angle of descent eased; the speed remained constant for a time in which the aides found occasion to investigate the console at the rear of the car and to call up informational lectures from the screen . . . time in which novelty eventually yielded to utter tedium, and aides and secretaries, enjoined to strictest silence, sat primly half-asleep, hypnotized by the smoothness of their passage and the soft hiss of air.

Then abrupt deceleration: windows unshielded themselves on darkness, which broke into glowing colored bars and triangles whisking past in a distorted neon flow, broke again into view of a white, sterile concourse. The car braked smoothly; doors hissed open. Signs blinked, in Shantran and two related dialects of the colonial sequence which had populated An Shant.

ENCLAVE SECOND RANK, the signs proclaimed in Shantran idiom. The boarding station at the port had been ENCLAVE THIRD RANK. It all seemed impeccably Shantran, as it could doubtless seem Confederate, or Tyrang, or Inush, or Syncrat.

Slippered Servants arrived, alike in their white garments, silent as their guests chose to be silent. Doubtless they, like the signs, could change. They took the baggage and led the way. RESIDENCE AREA 110, the sign advised, giving directions. The entourage walked, following the Servants. It was not far from the concourse, down a corridor of right-triangle arches. Doors opened, sealed again; the baggage was deposited; the Servants took silent leave.

Major Segrane looked about him at blank steel walls, at sterile white plastic benches, at the Minister Cosean An Homin, his personal charge. He remained amazed that they had not been searched, that they had not been forbidden the recording and scanning devices. "There is," he observed to Cosean, "no evidence of scanning. But that means nothing."

"No. It does not." Cosean settled into a chair and opened his notebook. Segrane excused himself into the adjoining set of rooms, discovered that one of the aides had transferred his baggage there, that a nervous group of secretaries waited for instruction. He pettishly dismissed them to the rooms which lay further within the apartments assigned them, advising them to stay close about and to refrain from needless chatter; they departed in dutiful silence. He paced, realized that finally as a manner of communication to any spies, and settled into a chair, arms folded.

The Confederacy had consulted the Oracle, credulity utterly out of character for a polity blood and bone akin to An Shant itself. Last of the holdouts against the Pact, save the Shantran Technarchy itself, the Confederacy had come submitting to the Pact and asking its questions, as any private or representative individual might join and come, who had the fare to Aneth and the requisite fee. Had the Confederacy consulted once and ceased, the Technarchy of An Shant would have found it amusing, a desperate move by the Confederacy to allay the fears of its citizenry, a sinking of Confederate morale before the rumors of war.

Twice . . . brought forth a more ominous possibility. Three times . . .

Three times at such expense, in such rapid succession . . . indicated some manner of success; and that suggested something more sinister here than superstition, the exchange of data more substantial than hundred-year predictions. The Confederacy adopted a more aggressive stance, broke relations on its own initiative, embargoed ores the Technarchy vitally needed. War was in preparation; the Confederacy was absolutely right in that. Shortages mandated it. The preparations were far advanced.

And there was no doubt that information changed hands in Aneth . . . tiny questions from lovelorn and wealthy suitors, larger matters from greedy corporations, perhaps even reckless bits of gossip passed in sleeping quarters by consulting ministers to their companions. Doubtless the whole Enclave was a surveillance net, and information was the merchandise on which Aneth and its amphictyony flourished.

In that light, it was absolutely essential to know the weight and shape of that merchandise which had been made available to the Confederate representative. One went through the forms, however humiliating; one probed; one listened.

And signing the meaningless Amphictyonic Pact was the first such embarrassment. A direct attack on Aneth—that would loose havoc among the gullible; but there was no need at all to contemplate such a move, even if Aneth were passing valuable information. The gullible would continue to contribute to the process and the clever would find a way to use it.

They sought information . . . eavesdropping with the sensors they had brought in their luggage—had yet found nothing. There had to be a limit to Aneth's patience. Taking recorders into the Oracle itself they would hardly bear . . . but information was apparently free for the gathering here in second rank enclave. It was to be wondered—where the limit lay.

The silence persisted, absolute. The major sat . . . walked, finally, out into the corridor of their suite, found the minister Cosean retired to his sleeping quarters. He strolled restlessly out the door and down the hall into the concourse, testing the Enclave's reactions.

A Servant began to dog his steps. When he stopped, the Servant stopped, pretended to look elsewhere, and walked on when he walked. Segrane stopped, waited, and when the Servant looked back again, Segrane summoned him with an impatient gesture. The Servant came, soft-footed; bowed, smiled . . . human-looking. All the Servants were reputed to be of the human stock of neighboring Corielle.

"You speak Shantran?" Segrane challenged him.

"Yes, sir." The answering voice was perfectly modulated, soft and without irritance.

"And all five hundred thousand other dialects known to man?"

The Servant smiled slightly. "No, sir, this is the Shantran staff. There are five hundred thousand possible combinations of personnel."

"So there's already a Shantran staff. You must have researched us far in advance of our application."

"We're pleased by your notice, sir."

"We."

"The staff, sir."

"Did you research us?"

"Of course, sir."

"On whose advice?"

Again a slight smile. "On the Oracle's, sir."

The answer caught him by surprise. He scowled, suspecting humor at his expense. "And has the Oracle decided when it will see the minister?"

"The petitioner goes alone to First Rank at 2214 and returns by 0600."

"Impossible."

"Sir?"

"The minister is my personal responsibility. I can't permit him to go alone for such a length of time. What could possibly take so long about a question?"

"The conditions of audience are uniform and inflexible. There are other petitioners, sequestered in other areas of Second Rank; scheduling is therefore complex. The audience time is a very brief portion of that schedule. To ensure privacy, there must be time built into the program."

Segrane began walking, the Servant keeping pace with him. He stared grimly at the floor, reckoning with increasing distress how little control they had of things.

"Who are these other petitioners?" he asked. "The Confederacy, perhaps?"

"I couldn't say, sir. The Enclave is partitioned in such a way that we ourselves are not in contact with visitors in other sections."

"Or politics? I'm sure you're well versed in that."

"We advise our visitors not to discuss external affairs with the staff. Aneth has no politics."

"None?"

"None, sir."

Segrane stopped, flicked a glance over the Servant, paused at the badge, continued back to the clear expressionless eyes. "You're very well trained . . . Jen. Is that your name, Jen?"

"Yes, sir. Thank you, sir."

"I shall compliment your service."

"All that you say to me is noted by my superiors. It's unnecessary to trouble yourself, sir. All staff-visitor exchanges are monitored to ensure satisfaction."

"Are you human, Jen?"

Jen flashed a broad smile. "Yes, sir. But without species politics."

"Where were you born?"

"All Servants are born within the enclaves."

"Your ancestors had outside origins." Segrane locked his hands behind him and began to move in the direction of his quarters, Jen walking beside him. "And the Oracle itself . . . maybe your ancestors built it too, the whole thing."

"No, sir. Hardly."

"You believe that tale about the Builders, eh?"

"It's true, sir. About the sixth millennium before founding of your calendar, the Builders occupied Aneth and built the vault and the Oracle."

"What did they look like, these Builders? Where did they come from?"

"The Oracle is their sole known artifact. We have no clue to either, sir."

"How convenient. Has no one thought to ask the Oracle?"

"You are a skeptic, sir. I detect it."

"Does the Oracle reject skeptics?"

"No, sir."

Segrane laughed, and stopped and faced the man . . . bland-faced and young, this Servant, like all other Servants in his white uniform, close-cropped hair, earnest, unoffending face. "You *are* sincere, aren't you? What's the story? Some Bellan archaeologists stumbled into this place two hundred years ago, and a Corielli team moved in on the find . . . sequestered themselves—with whose backing? Who paid for all this?"

"Initially a grant, sir, from fourteen worlds earliest involved in the research. The Enclave was established when the vault was opened and the Oracle was first activated. The value of the installation was immediately clear and the area had to be protected against exploitation for private purposes. Thus, the Enclave. Visitors' fees are now sufficient for its support."

"Corielle didn't build the rest of this."

"Ah, the Enclave, yes, sir; but the Oracle . . . no."

"The Oracle: person or machine?"

"Both, sir. That is, *Oracle* refers to both or either."

"The name of this person."

"First Rank is a sealed enclave, sir. We don't know."

"Female, the rumor is."

"All First Rank is female."

Segrane was surprised into reaction. That fact the researchers had not uncovered. *And what do they do for amusement?* he wondered. The politics of the arrangement occurred to him instantly: no matings, no marriage, no intrigues of consorts.

"How do they," he asked, "find replacements?"

Jen shrugged. "Their dead arrive here. We send in the nextborn female infant of Second Rank. It's utterly random that way. We have no influence on it. The integrity of the Oracle is absolute."

"How many Oracles have lived and died since the Enclave began?"

"The bodies which come out are not distinguished by signs of rank, sir. We don't know."

"But there must have been more than one Oracle in two hundred years."

"One supposes, sir, that such is the case."

"And she makes her predictions . . . how?"

"She enters rapport with the machine."

"Precognition. Telegnosis. Prophecy."

"Yes, sir."

"Nonsense."

"We make no claims, sir. Only those who visit here and leave know whether they have profited. And visitors do come back."

"She spills what she knows from one client to the next."

"We advise all our visitors to reveal nothing in conversation in any enclave. Ask your single question, and depart; that's all that's required. I've given you information. I have asked for none."

"But you've researched us."

"Generally available knowledge, sir, for your comfort. We do maintain a library."

"And some do come here and talk freely."

"Yes, sir, but we do discourage it."

"Telepath. She probes minds."

"Telepaths are among our clients. Mindshielding is a refined art among them. Such skills are even practiced among nonsensitives—perhaps you have them, sir. I'm sure telepathic contact has been tried on the part of such visitors; they would know the result of their efforts. But if you should have any anxiety about the meeting with the Oracle, you have only to request to return to the port. It's not compulsory to continue."

"Fee nonrefundable."

"Indeed, sir. But few choose to withdraw."

"Perhaps the Technarchy will."

"Advise us as soon as possible if that is your decision, sir. You'll receive every cooperation."

Segrane scowled and turned, stalked off with such rapidity that the Servant took the cue and failed to follow. It was surely the Servant's confidence that the Technarchy would not withdraw; the Oracle had expended much in preparing for this encounter, expense far more than the fee.

He earnestly wished it were possible to surprise them all.

A *new face: Mishell, Mishell, was it?*
But known, awaited.

Maranthe smiled, unaware whether her face smiled, but her mind did. The design which was Mishell took shape under her hands.

The Eye saw. The mind made intricate helices, chains of life, diamonds in the web, colors of intent, scents of longing, and taste, and height and depth and sound. This was Mishell. This was the one who would come.

Maranthe smiled.

And grew tired, and yielded herself again to the Shadows.

"Drink, Maranthe."

"Eat, Maranthe."

"Sleep, Maranthe."

The old woman lay still.

Mishell sat among the Servants, consumed with her desire. White-robed, immaculate, the Servants sat ringed about the sleeping Oracle. They were fourteen, they of the Intimates. The total of the Servants of the Inner Enclave was ninety-nine. The Oracle herself was the hundredth.

Old, most of the Intimate . . . pure of intent, without ambition, without even the remembrance of passion. They served with downcast eyes and soundless steps, speaking seldom among themselves, and that in whispers. They lost their strength, serving, and passed to the Elder Circle, to mutter into their nameless fate, to be bartered at last for infants.

Cycle after cycle passed before Maranthe's unseeing smile. The Intimates were honored to tend her . . . old and silent and without further desires.

Save the newest, the youngest, save Mishell.

She sat now with her hands clenched on her white-robed knees, knotting the cloth with her fists, and with her eyes fixed boldly on Maranthe. Her limbs trembled with her desire.

Maranthe smiled this night.

Never before. The face of the Oracle asleep was always image-cold, bereft of the dreaming smile of the Vision . . . until now.

It was the hour. Cosean adjusted his formal robes and stepped out of their suite into the outer hall, bowed courtesy to Major Segrane and to the attendant aides and secretaries.

"I have failed to reason with you," Segrane said.

"That discretion doesn't rest in my hands, major."

"Ah, then you *are* apprehensive."

"I suspect all the things you've named to me. I'll keep them in mind."

"Is there nothing more I can do, sir?"

"I see nothing. I follow orders of my own superiors. I have no discretion in the matter." Cosean smoothed his robes again, bowed to the major, and surveyed the nervous aides and secretaries. None spoke. There was nothing for Cosean to say on his own behalf and they were, for theirs, forbidden speech. The charade had to be played out. Segrane's devices had failed to detect anything at this range. And in the absence of clear hazard—the next step was clear.

Cosean turned to the waiting Servants. They gestured him toward the concourse. He walked; his entourage accompanied him in silence as far as the ramp to the shuttlecar. Segrane looked grim and mistrustful as it was his office to be; the secretaries and aides were subdued, having failed to be of use.

Cosean nodded them a last courtesy, then descended and stepped aboard the waiting car. It was sufficient for one man. For some species it would have been cramped; for others impossible. Doubtless there were heavier transports, Cosean thought, as there were surely areas set aside for different metabolisms and bodily designs, for other than humans had begun to consult Aneth with increasing frequency. Cosean settled in, concentrated on such thoughts, on his surroundings in detail . . . the simplest form of mindshielding, mild distraction. The doors sealed; the station retreated in a blur of colored lights. The windows shielded themselves and he traveled blind. He had anticipated as much.

Baggageless and without occupation for his hands: the regulations insisted upon it . . . and there had been scan at the entry to the car, plain to be seen. One questioner per fee, unescorted. He would have yielded to Segrane's urgings to withdraw had he been able to find any clear reason to doubt his mental or physical safety; he could not. Personal humiliation was not a consideration in the Technarchy's instructions.

The forward screen activated, startling him. The circle emblem of the Anethine Amphictyony filled it.

"Gentlebeing," a voice said softly, "you are departing Second Rank. Should your vehicle appear to pause any lengthy time, do not take alarm. The questions asked by preceding visitors may vary in length of time required for the Oracle to answer. A complex question may thus delay all succeeding vehicles. You may be assured that you will be advanced through the sequence as rapidly as possible. Should you need at any time to contact a living being, please press the red button by the screen. Please use this emergency facility with some restraint. There is an automat to your left if you wish refreshment; other facilities are likewise marked in the access. You are free to move about the vehicle with some caution.

"As regards your safety, please note that all First Rank facilities are automated. You will not directly contact any First Rank resident, nor will you be observed by any save of course the Oracle herself. Rules of access to the audience chamber are strictly enforced. You will find them posted on the wall of this car and clearly displayed in your native tongue on the screens of the audience chamber. For violation of minor rules, a two-year ban from consultation; for major violations, a lifetime ban for the individual and the sponsor according to the average lifetime of the species; for threat against the Oracle, defense mechanisms will act instantly and fatally against the individual and full sanctions of the Amphictyony will be invoked against the sponsor. Please stay within the white lines at all times and obey oral and written instructions. The machines are programmed to assist you. Should you decide that you do not wish to continue, press the red button and ask to be returned to Second Rank. You will be transferred back as rapidly as systems traffic permits. We do however assure you that there is no hazard so long as you observe the white lines and follow instructions. We sincerely hope you will continue to the audience chamber and we assure you that all precautions are in the interest of providing you and those who follow you with a safe and thoroughly productive encounter."

Cosean shivered despite himself. He was offended by the implied threat. Aneth was arrogant. The arrogance was apparently offered all comers, and therefore the threat gave him no excuse to withdraw. The High Ministry expected results. It rested on him. He sat, arms folded, senses at forced alertness, and wished that there were something with which to occupy himself.

Three times the Confederacy had submitted a representative to this irritating procedure. There were great powers which consulted continually at enormous expense. Use of the Oracle approached on some worlds the aspect of a cult, a religion.

True, others had attempted to expose it . . . trap-questions, tricks, all unsatisfactory in result. The myth persisted undiminished. The Oracle declared past, present, and near future . . . save on rare and cataclysmic occasion, in which the range seemed extended. Half an Anethine year was the normal limit.

(Thus securing, Cosean thought cynically, a guaranteed return trade from the wealthy, on whom Aneth spent most research; and thus shielding itself from later complaints from the vast multitudes of individuals who could not afford that every-six-months consultation.)

Researchers, allegedly reputable, had played with it . . . so the Corielli government insisted. Corporations had recourse to it; and knowing that fourteen worlds had paid to establish the Enclave, other worlds and the great inter-zone corporations had become involved. From there it was only a step to what it now embraced, the great powers, in increasing numbers and with increasing frequency, human and now nonhuman.

Thus the Amphictyony, the Neighbors of Aneth. War might break out, but the Pact guaranteed Aneth's safety, for a violator would find practically the totality of man and several polities outside ranged against him, some of whom might be fanatic enough to act. It was not strategically wise . . . to harass Aneth.

So Aneth, serene, untouchable . . . allegedly incorruptible and immune to influence . . . advised and prophesied and moved the policy of super-nations and zones.

Amphictyony: he had researched the word, which was old, and terrestrial. There had been a place named Delphi, another Sibyl, a league ranged about that side which extended influence not alone through one nation but throughout the cradle of human civilization. Similar sanctions had attended it. Similar claims surrounded it. Wars had protected it. It was gone now, but ancient history returned to haunt them, a concept still powerful in superstition. *Amphictyony:* the Dwellers-round-about-Shrine; the word translated into other species' tongues. There were everywhere legends of Oracles.

Cosean found the blind walls suddenly oppressive.

Gods, he thought, forgetting that the Technarchy acknowledged none, *what manner of thing is this? The Ministry sits secure. I am the one exposed to this thing. Suppose that there are subtle emanations.*

I am mad to have come this far.

His finger hovered over the red button. Panic coursed over him, which had nothing to do with conspiracies and politics. It was something primal and ugly. He fought it down, remembering his duty.

And the vehicle stopped.

Dead. The machinery rested in utter stillness.

Waited.

The fourteen Intimates at in their circle, hands demurely folded, observing the old woman's sleep. They waited, with downcast eyes, mental zero, for the Vision was silent.

Mishell trembled.

And thrust herself to her feet.

The thirteen lifted their faces and stared, round-eyed.

Mishell crossed the polished floor to the Oracle's couch.

Maranthe still smiled in her sleep. The bliss, spread now even to these hours, maddened, mocked them. Mishell smoothed the thin gray hair, touched the age-spotted temple, the cheek, the frail throat . . . closed her hands, pressed. Something snapped. The smile ceased. The blind eyes opened, forever blind.

There came a soft fluttering about the room, Servants on their feet, whispering in dismay.

Mishell hurled the body to the cold floor, where it lay, graceless and half-naked. She sat down on the Oracle's bed, trembling, as the others surrounded her.

Soft hands touched her, smoothed her robes, her hair, wiped the perspiration from her brow. Anxious faces hovered near. Trays, long prepared, rattled in shaking hands.

"Drink, Mishell."

"Eat, Mishell."

"Time to go back, Mishell."

How easy it was, she thought, and smiled. *Of course they must hold to the tradition. That is all they know. It was only I who dreamed the dream.*

She mounted the steps.

Seated herself. Extended her hands over the cold plates. The lights flared.

The car moved.

Cosean caught himself with a gasp. The car ran smoothly only a little distance into a dock. Locks meshed. The windows unsealed, revealing a dim, circular steel hall garishly lit by screens. He disembarked cautiously, keeping well within the white lines marked on the floor.

At his left a huge screen lighted, showing a vast interplay of light and machinery. There seemed a mote of a white-robed figure locked within it, on a manner of throne.

The Anethine Sibyl? he wondered. *Is it screen or window?* The white lines did not permit near approach. He felt an unaccustomed awe, and loathed it, fighting for his fashionable cynicism.

A light flashed, the question symbol.

Cosean cleared his throat, stood squarely between the white lines at the nearest approach. "Sibyl, the Shantran Technarchy asks: *What are the surest means to guarantee our increased prosperity?*

Wait, the screen flashed. A light came on to indicate a bench. Cosean sat down and waited. The temperature of the air was neutral, the lighting dim, sound lacking. Time distended.

The light flashed. He arose. A white paper began to issue from the console before him. He took it for his answer, vaguely angry at the mechanical character of the response. He tore it free of the machine.

"Shantran Technarchy." The machine's voice seemed to vibrate through his bones. Female, if a machine could be female. The Sibyl? "You will most surely prosper through peace with your neighbors."

Swill, he thought, almost shaking with sudden relief. *It's after all a sham.*

". . . The resources for which you prepare to go to war, Shantran Technarchy, lie within your own domains, on the second planet of the star Dazech, as yet undiscovered. Seek there. The resources are more than adequate for your needs. Precise coordinates are noted on the printed response. The audience is ended."

He stood still a moment. The window went dark. He turned finally in the direction of available light and reentered the car, seated himself, still clutching the paper. The car slid away from the station, the windows darkened and sealed.

Cosean was shaking.

He unfolded the paper and stared at the answer and the coordinates.

The Oracle gave an answer the accuracy of which could be checked . . . dared give something of such value.

It was . . . real.

A great gift first . . . to ensure that the Technarchy returned to consult again.

But then they could not longer afford to stay out of the close circle of the Pact; no government could abstain from its constant advice, its close direction . . . if the Oracle gave true answers.

And in his keenest fears . . . it did.

Faces blurred, flesh indistinct, so many, men and non-men, far-scattered, ambitions and fears and desires, empires and all of time.

Maranthe, Mishell, the same pattern . . . diamonds and helices of life, bright tapestry.

Bodies of the Builders, globular, many-legged, and slender and fine the filaments they spun. The mythic Fates were weavers, and the pattern was one, and old.

Mishell saluted them who waited—and felt awe, seeing all the web before her, knowing now the immediate design.

Draw in a thread here, a new color, bind it fast. A design became complete, begun in remotest antiquity, at an old, old shrine. She set her hands to its ending, felt the work alive and yielding to her touch. Her reach grew surer, wider. The whole fabric of the Web quivered to her younger, stronger hands, cloth of space, and time.

This Vision Maranthe had seen, had woven, drawing her thread in . . . Mishell abandoned guilt, and humanity, and smiled.

There were other species to be gathered.

A new design began.

WINGS

At 13:05, on September 3, 2152, two things happened.

Spec. Amir Jefferson watched the plastic cup drop in the rec hall dispenser and cant sideways, after which the beer he'd punched should have frothed over it and down the drain. Instead it righted itself, filled, the door lifted and the cup waltzed out in thin air—

And the third time this shift *during* the Federation audit, *with* that sleek fancy Federation ship in dock and a squad of federal inspectors snooping through records and making copious notes on their slates, the red alert went off in station control, screens lit up and station chief Isadora Babbs took another antacid and ordered a stand-down from red to green.

God.

"Find that bug," she told the Maintenance chief, personally, on the comm.

Please God, no bananas today; and please God the auditors didn't look in core-sec 18, where they had stowed the fruit that didn't show on the supply manifests, a zero-*gee* core-sec where apples and limes and mangoes drifted in the dark, little orange planetoids and apple moonlets performing their slow revolutions and occasionally nudging one another.

"Chief Babbs?" the comm said. "Code 15 in the rec hall."

Babbs had her hand on the pill bottle before she remembered she'd just taken a dose. "What's it doing? Where is it?"

"Beer machine," the report came back, "autobar, beers and whiskeys flying like—"

"Anybody in there?"

"Whole *shift's* in there, chief, word's got around—"

"Clear the section! Shut down the power! Call Maintenance! Get the crew out of there and get it *stopped!* Hear?"

After which, down in Maintenance 4, two junior techs looked at each other and one said: "Suppose we ought to call the super?"

"He's with the auditors," the other said, and called up the Procedures Manual. "There we go . . . red safety button, right there, top row."

Tech One turned the key on the button, hesitated.

Punched it.

Whereafter the lights went out and the fans went off in rec hall, and the party died.

More accurately—with sirens sounding, most of the party went staggering out the doors and down the corridor, down the emergency slides and wherever inspiration and panic took three hundred twenty-eight techs, service personnel, cooks, clericals, and crew on liberty—all, that was, except Spec. Amir Jefferson, who sat in a corner seat behind a truly impressive stack of whiskey glasses, watching a host of floating bar glasses describing interesting orbits under the red emergency lights.

If one squinted his eyes just so—one could see a shadowy shape or two, now that the lights were down. That was truly remarkable.

"Hey, who's that?" somebody said, and it did occur to Amir Jefferson that it was very peculiar that so many people had run out and so many were left, all drinking and laughing and ignoring the alarm—

Only reasonable, he thought. Systems-problems third alert this shift, damn right. Probably the spooks again, same spooks that had gotten into the vendors and sailed drinks around.

First time he'd ever seen a thing like that, he'd panicked.

But a guy got used to it. Things turned up. Oranges. Wrenches and such. Assorted antiques. You spaced 'em or you ate 'em.

"New guy," somebody said, and put a drink into his hand.

Amir looked him up and down—odd type, funny clothes, leather jacket and white scarf.

Lot of that in this party. Brown leather caps and goggles. Guys in pressure rigs of some kind—maybe Maintenance had showed.

Aristocratic type in uniform, too—sipping his drink, talking to a couple or three in blue fatigues with patches Amir didn't recognize.

A gal with bobbed hair, white scarf and leather jacket, talking to a guy in plaid knee-pants, for God's sake.

Spec. Amir stared at them, looked a little suspiciously at the drink, realized he was on his feet and looked back at the guy in the chair in the corner.

Then he panicked.

* * *

"**G**et Security on it!" the chief yelled at her aide. "Cut that damn alarm!"

Some fool had tripped a security door.

"Number two," the comm said. "Chief, it's Udale. He says he's got one of the auditors on his hands—seems he—was propositioned and terrorized by a hallful of drunken dockers."

"God."

"What does Udale do with the auditor?"

Babbs thought of several things. Most of them were felonious. She gritted her teeth and said, "I'll see him. Assure him we apologize."

"I—" the aide said. Then: "Oh, my God."

"*What?*"

"They're saying the fire alarm went. The whole section just blew out."

Being dead was a considerable shock, even fortified as Amir was. He peered at his body, which sat there quite placidly behind a stack of glasses.

Someone clapped him on the shoulder. He was relieved he could feel that. He looked around at a white-haired officer type, who said, "Son, you just joined the squadron."

The officer took him 'round, him, a lowly spec, and named him names—Byrd and Rogers, Smith and Earhart, name after name right out of the history books, faces too long-ago for holos, uniforms and insignia from atoms to airplanes—

And Spec. 2nd Class Amir Jefferson, who had mostly, in the first moments of knowing he was dead, thought about how his friends were going to take it and what in hell was he going to do about his date with Marcy Todd on Saturday night—began to feel a good deal more cold and lost and scared.

What'm I doing here? was what he kept thinking, having his hand shaken by one after another of the crowd—important people, names— God, legends, all out of ancient history, fliers and astronauts, pioneers and explorers—

He was embarrassed, terribly embarrassed, having gotten himself killed in the middle of these people's private party, and them trying to make the best of it and treat him as if he belonged there.

"I'm really sorry," he said. "I didn't mean to be here."

People laughed. If a dead guy could blush, he was blushing, and he looked at the floor. "Excuse me," he said, and headed for the door; but Rogers grabbed his arm and said,

"Hey, no offense . . ."

"No offense," he said, and the others crowded 'round, one offering him a drink.

"Here's to the new guy!" somebody said, and glasses clinked all over the room, after which a cheer, and Amir gulped and mumbled, "Thank you. . . ." He took a large gulp—somehow, dead, the alcohol seemed to have worn off, and looking around at all these great people looking at him as if he was somebody, he suffered another crisis of wondering what he was going to do about Marcy Todd and what they were going to do about his shift. "Excuse me, I got all this stuff—" That sounded sort of stupid. It really began to come to him that he was not going to meet those schedules. "What'm I going to do?"

"About what?" Smith asked.

"I mean, there's people I—there's a job—there's these auditors I was supposed to guide around—"

Smith shook his head definitively. "Won't do that."

"What do ghosts do?"

There was a long silence. Finally somebody he hadn't been introduced to said, solemnly, "Things. Whatever. Some just can't deal with it. Some just sort of hang around."

"Doing what? Haunting places?"

"Them that can't turn loose, yes, some do."

"Well—" Amir thought about all these oranges and old engine parts. "Why here? Why did all you guys come here?"

"Ships."

"Ships?"

"Like he said," said Byrd, "some fellows just can't turn loose. And some can. So we got this far."

"We can get as far as this," Earhart said. "Easy."

"Further than this takes ships," Byrd said. "That's what we're here for. That's what we're looking for."

"You wouldn't be a flier yourself," Earhart asked, "would you?"

"I've got a short-hop license," Amir said.

A couple of hands landed on his shoulders. He looked from one young face to the other—guys in blue coveralls, who grinned at him. "We got us a pilot," one said, and the other: "A *modern* pilot—"

"One dead," Station Chief Babbs heard, and dropped her head into her hands, shaking it slowly. "Glasses and spilled drinks all over," the aide continued remorselessly. "The meds think he was just passed out drunk when the alarm went, just never heard it—"

"God," Babbs said, and reached for a bottle of pills, fumbling the lid off.

"The chief auditor's asking to see you," the comm said. "He's pretty upset."

Pills spilled. Babbs popped a couple, started gathering up the rest.

"Chief?"

"Send him in."

Babbs capped the bottle again, shoved it in the desk, looked up as the white-haired Auditor General stormed into the office, and shoved herself to her feet, leaning on the desk with her knuckles.

"It's your damn staff!" she yelled before the auditor got a word out. "Your damn staff was occupying mine when an emergency broke out, which is why we have a fatality, mister, which is what's going on my report."

The auditor shouted back, "What's going on mine is a station riddled with security problems, communication problems, and staff incompetency! I'm finishing our work on our ship, which thank God! is under our own lock and key, *with* its data, *with* enough evidence to see you broken, Station Chief Babbs! When we send what we've documented down to Earth, I assure you, there's quite enough there to file charges on you and eleven other culpable parties on this station—"

"Chief?" the comm said. "Chief? Can you come out here?"

"I'm in conference!" Babbs yelled at the comm..

"Chief . . ." the aide said, his voice hushed and agitated.

"Excuse me," Babbs said with a small exhalation of breath, and went out to the anteroom; closed the door behind her.

The aide, white-faced, gave Babbs a little scrap of paper with a written note.

Upon which Babbs surprised the aide by grinning ear to ear.

"I dunno how it happened," the dock chief said, standing in Station Control, beside an apoplectic Chief Auditor and a politely apologetic Isadora Babbs. The dock chief looked at the screen—which showed a shiny new government ship on a heading and at an acceleration nobody was in a position to intercept—and looked around at Babbs as if to ask was he supposed to keep his mouth shut on possibilities any long-term resident of the Station did know—

Babbs made a little frown. The dock chief shrugged and said, "I guess it was the automatics just got some bug in them. Undocked that gal and at that point, there ain't no other answer, she just kicked in some kind of program—must've had a whole sequence punched in—"

"No such thing!" the Auditor said.

The dock chief shrugged a second time and prudently kept his mouth shut.

While the *EFS Liberty II*, without a soul alive at her helm, streaked toward deep space, outbound from the world, the station, and all.

A MUCH BRIEFER HISTORY OF TIME

Long ago a microbe decided to be god. It fissioned and became poly-theistic. Rapidly the pond filled with gods fissioning and dividing until a passing rainstorm carried a number of the divinities downstream. They fissioned and filled a lake, which fed a river, which fed the sea. Within a billion years only isolate bodies of water lacked divinity. The microbes teleologically evolved bipedal colonies as transportation—which had drawbacks: these mobile colonies proved self directed and schismatic. The free swimming microbes (equally teleologically) maximized their reproductive potential by infiltrating mobile colonies which, responding to selective pressure, developed a space program.

GWYDION AND THE DRAGON

Once upon a time there was a dragon, and once upon that time a prince who undertook to win the hand of the elder and fairer of two princesses.

Not that this prince wanted either of Madog's daughters, although rumors said that Eri was as wise and as gentle, as sweet and as fair as her sister Glasog was cruel and ill-favored. The truth was that this prince would marry either princess if it would save his father and his people; and neither if he had had any choice in the matter. He was Gwydion ap Ogan, and of princes in Dyfed he was the last.

Being a prince of Dyfed did not, understand, mean banners and trumpets and gilt armor and crowds of courtiers. King Ogan's palace was a rambling stone house of dusty rafters hung with cooking pots and old harness; King Ogan's wealth was mostly in pigs and pastures—the same as all Ogan's subjects; Gwydion's war-horse was a black gelding with a crooked blaze and shaggy feet, who had fought against the bandits from the high hills. Gwydion's armor, serviceable in that perpetual warfare, was scarred leather and plain mail, with new links bright among the old; and lance or pennon he had none—the folk of Ogan's kingdom were not lowland knights, heavily armored, but hunters in the hills and woods, and for weapons this prince carried only a one-handed sword and a bow and a quiver of gray-feathered arrows.

His companion, riding beside him on a bay pony, happened through no choice of Gwydion's to be Owain ap Llodri, the houndmaster's son, his good friend, by no means his squire: Owain had lain in wait along the way, on a borrowed bay mare—Owain had simply assumed he was going, and that Gwydion had only hesitated, for friendship's sake, to ask him. So he saved Gwydion the necessity.

And the lop-eared old dog trotting by the horses' feet was Mili: Mili was fierce with bandits, and had respected neither Gwydion's entreaties nor Owain's commands thus far: stones might drive her off for a few minutes, but Mili came back again, that was the sort Mili was. That was the sort Owain was too, and Gwydion could refuse neither of them. So Mili panted along at the pace they kept, with big-footed Blaze and the bownosed bay, whose name might have been Swallow or maybe not— the poets forget—and as they rode Owain and Gwydion talked mostly about dogs and hunting.

That, as the same poets say, was the going of Prince Gwydion into King Madog's realm.

Now no one in Dyfed knew where Madog had come from. Some said he had been a king across the water. Some said he was born of a Roman and a Pict and had gotten sorcery through his mother's blood. Some said he had bargained with a dragon for his sorcery—certainly there was a dragon: devastation followed Madog's conquests, from one end of Dyfed to the other.

Reasonably reliable sources said Madog had applied first to King Bran, across the mountains, to settle at his court, and Bran having once laid eyes on Madog's elder daughter, had lusted after her beyond all good sense and begged Madog for her.

Give me your daughter, Bran had said to Madog, and I'll give you your heart's desire. But Madog had confessed that Eri was betrothed already, to a terrible dragon, who sometimes had the form of a man, and who had bespelled Madog and all his house: if Bran could overcome this dragon, he might have Eri with his blessings, and his gratitude and the faithful help of his sorcery all his life; but if he died childless, Madog, by Bran's own oath, must be his heir.

That was the beginning of Madog's kingdom. So smitten was Bran that he swore to those terms, and died that very day, after which Madog ruled in his place.

After that Madog had made the same proposal to three of his neighbor kings, one after the other, proposing that each should ally with him and unite their kingdoms if the youngest son could win Eri from the dragon's spell and provide him an heir. But no prince ever came back from his quest. And the next youngest then went, until all the sons of the kings were gone, so that the kingdoms fell under Madog's rule.

After them, Madog sent to King Ban, and his sons died, last of all Prince Rhys, Gwydion's friend. Ban's heart broke, and Ban took to his bed and died.

Some whispered now that the dragon actually served Madog, that it had indeed brought Madog to power, under terms no one wanted to guess, and that this dragon did indeed have another form, which was the shape of a knight in strange armor, who would become Eri's husband if no other could win her. Some said (but none could prove the truth of it) that the dragon-knight had come from far over the sea, and that he devoured the sons and daughters of conquered kings, that being the tribute Madog gave him. But whatever the truth of that rumor, the dragon hunted far and wide in the lands Madog ruled and did not disdain to take the sons and daughters of farmers and shepherds too. Devastation went under his shadow, trees withered under his breath, and no one saw him outside his dragon shape and returned to tell of it, except only Madog and (rumor said) his younger daughter Glasog, who was a sorceress as cruel as her father.

Some said that Glasog could take the shape of a raven and fly over the land choosing whom the dragon might take. The people called her Madog's Crow, and feared the look of her eye. Some said she was the true daughter of Madog and that Madog had stolen Eri from Faerie, and given her mother to the dragon; but others said they were twins, and that Eri had gotten all that an ordinary person had of goodness, while her sister Glasog—

"Prince Gwydion," Glasog said to her father, "would have come on the quest last year with his friend Rhys, except his father's refusing him, and Prince Gwydion will not let his land go to war if he can find another course. He'll persuade his father."

"Good," Madog said. "That's very good." Madog smiled, but Glasog did not. Glasog was thinking of the dragon. Glasog harbored no illusions: the dragon had promised Madog that he would be king of all Wales if he could achieve this in seven years; and rule for seventy and seven more with the dragon's help.

But if he failed—failed by the seventh year to gain any one of the kingdoms of Dyfed, if one stubborn king withstood him and for one day beyond the seven allotted years, kept him from obtaining the least, last stronghold of the west, then all the bargain was void and Madog would have failed in everything.

And the dragon would claim a forfeit of his choosing.

That was what Glasog thought of, in her worst nightmares: that the dragon had always meant to have all the kingdoms of the west with very little effort—let her father win all but one and fail, on the smallest letter of the agreement. What was more, all the generals in all the armies they had taken agreed that the kingdom of Ogan could never be taken by force: there were mountains in which resistance could hide and not even dragonfire could burn all of them; but most of all there was the fabled Luck of Ogan, which said that no force of arms could defeat the sons of Ogan.

Watch, Madog had said. And certainly her father was astute, and cunning, and knew how to snare a man by his pride. There's always a way, her father had said, to break a spell. This one has a weakness. The strongest spells most surely have their soft spots.

And Ogan had one son, and that was Price Gwydion.

Now we will fetch him, Madog said to his daughter. Now we will see what his luck is worth.

The generals said, "If you would have a chance in war, first be rid of Gwydion."

But Madog said, and Glasog agreed, there are other uses for Gwydion.

"It doesn't *look* different," Owain said as they passed the border stone.

It was true. Nothing looked changed at all. There was no particular odor of evil, or of threat. It might have been last summer, when the two of them had hunted with Rhys. They had used to hunt together every summer, and last autumn they had tracked the bandit Llewellyn to his lair, and caught him with stolen sheep. But in the spring Ban's sons had gone to seek the hand of Madog's daughter, and one by one had died, last of them, in early summer, Rhys himself.

Gwydion would have gone, long since, and long before Rhys. A score of times Gwydion had approached his father King Ogan and his mother Queen Belys and begged to try his luck against Madog, from the first time Madog's messenger had appeared and challenged the kings of Dyfed to war or wedlock. But each time Ogan had refused him, arguing in the first place that other princes, accustomed to warfare on their borders, were better suited, and better armed, and that there were many princes in Dyfed, but he had only one son.

But when Rhys had gone and failed, the last kingdom save that of King Ogan passed into Madog's hands. And Gwydion, grief-stricken with the loss of his friend, said to his parents, "If we had stood together, we might have defeated this Madog; if we had taken the field then, together, we might have had a chance; if you had let me go with Rhys, one of us might have won and saved the other. But now Rhys is dead and we have Madog for a neighbor. Let me go when he sends to us. Let me try my luck at courting his daughter. A war with him now we may not lose, but we cannot hope to win."

Even so Ogan had resisted him, saying that they still had their mountains for a shield, difficult going for any army; and arguing that their luck had saved them this far and that it was rash to take matters into their own hands.

Now the nature of that luck was this: that of the kingdoms in Dyfed, Ogan's must always be poorest and plainest. But that luck meant that they could not fail in war nor fail in harvest: it had come down to them from Ogan's own greatgrandfather Ogan ap Ogan of Llanfynnyd, who had sheltered one of the Faerie unaware; and only faithlessness could break it—so greatgrandfather Ogan had said. So: "Our luck will be our defense," Ogan argued with his son. "Wait and let Madog come to us. We'll fight him in the mountains."

"Will we fight a dragon? Even if we defeat Madog himself, what of our herds, what of our farmers and our freeholders? Can we let the land go to waste and let our people feed this dragon, while we hide in the hills and wait for luck to save us? Is that faithfulness?" That was what Gwydion had asked his father, while Madog's herald was in the hall—a raven black as unrepented sin . . . or the intentions of a wizard.

"Madog bids you know," this raven had said, perched on a rafter of Ogan's hall, beside a moldering basket and a string of garlic, "that he has taken every kingdom of Dyfed but this. He offers you what he offered others: if King Ogan has a son worthy to win Madog's daughter and get an heir, then King Ogan may rule in peace over his kingdom so long as he lives, and that prince will have titles and the third of Madog's realm besides. . . .

"But if the prince will not or cannot win the princess, then Ogan must swear Madog is his lawful true heir. And if Ogan refuses this, then Ogan must face Madog's army, which now is the army of four kingdoms each greater than his own. Surely," the raven had added, fixing all present with a wicked, midnight eye, "it is no great endeavor Madog asks—simply to court his daughter. And will so many die, so much burn? Or will Prince Gwydion win a realm wider than your own? A third of Madog's lands is no small dowry and inheritance of Madog's kingdom is no small prize."

So the raven had said. And Gwydion had said to his mother, "Give me your blessing," and to his father Ogan: "Swear the oath Madog asks. If our Luck can save us, it will save me and win me this bride; but if it fails me in this, it would have failed us in any case."

Maybe, Gwydion thought as they passed the border, Owain was a necessary part of that luck. Maybe even Mili was. It seemed to him now that he dared reject nothing that loved him and favored him, even if it was foolish and even if it broke his heart: his luck seemed so perilous and stretched so thin already he dared not bargain with his fate.

"No sign of a dragon, either," Owain said, looking about them at the rolling hills.

Gwydion looked about him too, and at the sky, which showed only the lazy flight of a single bird.

Might it be a raven? It was too far to tell.

"I'd think," said Owain, "it would seem grimmer than it does."

Gwydion shivered as if a cold wind had blown. But Blaze plodded his heavy-footed way with no semblance of concern, and Mili trotted ahead, tongue lolling, occasionally sniffing along some trail that crossed theirs.

"Mili would smell a dragon," Owain said.

"Are you sure?" Gwydion asked. He was not. If Madog's younger daughter could be a raven at her whim, he was not sure what a dragon might be at its pleasure.

That night they had a supper of brown bread and sausages that Gwydion's mother had sent, and ale that Owain had with him.

"My mother's brewing," Owain said. "My father's store." And Owain sighed and said: "By now they must surely guess I'm not off hunting."

"You didn't tell them?" Gwydion asked. "You got no blessing in this?"

Owain shrugged, and fed a bit of sausage to Mili, who gulped it down and sat looking at them worshipfully.

Owain's omission of duty worried Gwydion. He imagined how Owain's parents would first wonder where he had gone, then guess, and fear for Owain's life, for which he held himself entirely accountable. In the morning he said, "Owain, go back. This is far enough."

But Owain shrugged and said, "Not I. Not without you." Owain rubbed Mili's ears. "No more than Mili, without me."

Gwydion had no least idea now what was faithfulness and what was a young man's foolish pride. Everything seemed tangled. But Owain seemed not in the least distressed.

Owain said, "We'll be there by noon tomorrow."

Gwydion wondered, Where is this dragon? and distrusted the rocks around them and the sky over their heads. He felt a presence in the earth—or thought he felt it. But Blaze and Swallow grazed at their leisure. Only Mili looked worried—Mili pricked up her ears, such as those long ears could prick, wondering, perhaps, if they were going to get to bandits soon, and whether they were, after all, going to eat that last bit of breakfast sausage.

"He's on his way," Glasog said. "He's passed the border."

"Good," said Madog. And to his generals. "Didn't I tell you?"

The generals still looked worried.

But Glasog went and stood on the walk of the castle that had been Ban's, looking out over the countryside and wondering what the dragon was thinking tonight, whether the dragon had foreseen this as he had foreseen the rest, or whether he was even yet keeping some secret from them, scheming all along for their downfall.

She launched herself quite suddenly from the crest of the wall, swooped out over the yard and beyond, over the seared fields.

The dragon, one could imagine, knew about Ogan's Luck. The dragon was too canny to face it—and doubtless was chuckling in his den in the hills.

Glasog flew that way, but saw nothing from that cave but a little curl of smoke—there was almost always smoke. And Glasog leaned toward the west, following the ribbon of a road, curious, and wagering that the dragon this time would not bestir himself.

Her father wagered the same. And she knew very well what he wagered, indeed she did: duplicity for duplicity—if not the old serpent's aid, then human guile; if treachery from the dragon, then put at risk the dragon's prize.

Gwydion and Owain came to a burned farmstead along the road. Mili sniffed about the blackened timbers and bristled at the shoulders, and came running back to Owain's whistle, not without mistrustful looks behind her.

There was nothing but a black ruin beside a charred, brittle orchard.

"I wonder," Owain said, "what became of the old man and his wife."

"I don't," said Gwydion, worrying for his own parents, and seeing in this example how they would fare in any retreat into the hills.

The burned farm was the first sign they had seen of the dragon, but it was not the last. There were many other ruins, and sad and terrible sights. One was a skull sitting on a fence row. And on it sat a raven.

"This was a brave man," it said, and pecked the skull, which rang hollowly, and inclined its head toward the field beyond. "That was his wife. And farther still his young daughter."

"Don't speak to it," Gwydion said to Owain. They rode past, at Blaze's plodding pace, and did not look back.

But the raven flitted ahead of them and waited for them on the stone fence. "If you die," the raven said, "then your father will no longer believe in his luck. Then it will leave him. It happened to all the others."

"There's always a first," said Gwydion.

Owain said, reaching for his bow: "Shall I shoot it?"

But Gwydion said: "Kill the messenger for the message? No. It's a foolish creature. Let it be."

It left them then. Gwydion saw it sometimes in the sky ahead of them. He said nothing to Owain, who had lost his cheerfulness, and Mili stayed close by them, sore of foot and suspicious of every breeze.

There were more skulls. They saw gibbets and stakes in the middle of a burned orchard. There was scorched grass, recent and powdery under the horses' hooves. Blaze, who loved to snatch a bite now and again as he went, moved uneasily, snorting with dislike of the smell, and Swallow started at shadows.

Then the turning of the road showed them a familiar brook, and around another hill and beyond, the walled holding that had been King Ban's, in what had once been a green valley. Now it was burned, black bare hillsides and the ruin of hedges and orchards.

So the trial they had come to find must be here, Gwydion thought, and uneasily took up his bow and picked several of his best arrows, which he held against his knee as he rode. Owain did the same.

But they reached the gate of the low-walled keep unchallenged, until they came on the raven sitting, whetting its beak on the stone. It looked at them solemnly, saying, "Welcome, Prince Gwydion. You've won your bride. Now how will you fare, I wonder."

Men were coming from the keep, running toward them, others, under arms, in slower advance.

"What now?" Owain asked, with his bow across his knee; and Gwydion lifted his bow and bent it, aiming at the foremost.

The crowd stopped, but a black-haired man in gray robes and a king's gold chain came alone, holding up his arms in a gesture of welcome and of peace. Madog himself? Gwydion wondered, while Gwydion's arm shook and the string trembled in his grip. "Is it Gwydion ap Ogan?" that man asked—surely no one else but Madog would wear that much gold. "My son-in-law to be! Welcome!"

Gwydion, with great misgivings, slacked the string and let down the bow, while fat Blaze, better trained than seemed, finally shifted feet.

Owain lowered his bow too, as King Madog's men opened up the gate. Some of the crowd cheered as they rode in, and more took it up, as if they had only then gained the courage or understood it was expected. Blaze and Swallow snorted and threw their heads at the racket, as Gwydion and Owain put away their arrows, unstrung their bows and hung them on their saddles.

But Mili stayed close by Owain's legs as they dismounted, growling low in her throat, and barked one sharp warning when Madog came close. "Hush," Owain bade her, and knelt down more than for respect, keeping one hand on Mili's muzzle and the other in her collar, whispering to her, "Hush, hush, there's a good dog."

Gwydion made the bow a prince owed to a king and prospective father-in-law, all the while thinking that there had to be a trap in this place. He was entirely sorry to see grooms lead Blaze and Swallow away, and kept Owain and Mili constantly in the tail of his eye as Madog took him by the arms and hugged him. Then Madog said, catching all his attention, eye to eye with him for a moment, "What a well-favored young man you are. The last is always best.—So you've killed the dragon."

Gwydion thought, Somehow we've ridden right past the trial we should have met. If I say no, he will find cause to disallow me; and he'll kill me and Owain and all our kin.

But lies were not the kind of dealing his father had taught him; faithfulness was the rule of the house of Ogan; so Gwydion looked the king squarely in the eyes and said, "I met no dragon."

Madog's eyes showed surprise, and Madog said: "Met no dragon?"

"Not a shadow of a dragon."

Madog grinned and clapped him on the shoulder and showed him to the crowd, saying, "This is your true prince!"

Then the crowd cheered in earnest, and even Owain and Mili looked heartened. Owain rose with Mili's collar firmly in hand.

Madog said then to Gwydion, under his breath, "If you had lied, you would have met the dragon here and now. Do you know you're the first one who's gotten this far?"

"I saw nothing," Gwydion said again, as if Madog had not understood him. "Only burned farms. Only skulls and bones."

Madog turned a wide smile toward him, showing teeth. "Then it was your destiny to win. Was it not?" And Madog faced him about toward the doors of the keep. "Daughter, daughter, come out!"

Gwydion hesitated a step, expecting he knew not what—the dragon itself, perhaps: his wits went scattering toward the gate, the horses being led away, Mili barking in alarm—and a slender figure standing in the doorway, all white and gold. "My elder daughter," Madog said. "Eri."

Gwydion went as he was led, telling himself it must be true, after so much dread of this journey and so many friends' lives lost—obstacles must have fallen down for him, Ogan's Luck must still be working. . . .

The young bride waiting for him was so beautiful, so young and so—kind—was the first word that came to him—Eri smiled and immediately it seemed to him she was innocent of all the grief around her, innocent and good as her sister was reputed cruel and foul.

He took her hand, and the folk of the keep all cheered, calling him their prince; and if any were Ban's people, those wishes might well come from the heart, with fervent hopes of rescue. Pipers began to play, gentle hands urged them both inside, and in this desolate land some woman found flowers to give Eri.

"Owain?" Gwydion cried, looking back, suddenly seeing no sign of him or of Mili: "Owain!"

He refused to go farther until Owain could part the crowd and reach his side, Mili firmly in hand. Owain looked breathless and frightened. Gwydion felt the same. But the crowd pushed and pulled at them, the pipers piped and dancers danced, and they brought them into a hall smelling of food and ale.

It can't be this simple, Gwydion still thought, and made up his mind that no one should part him from Owain, Mili, or their swords. He looked about him, bedazzled, at a wedding feast that must have taken days to prepare.

But how could they know I'd get here? he wondered. Did they do this for all the suitors who failed—and celebrate their funerals, then . . . with their wedding feast?

At which thought he felt cold through and through, and found Eri's hand on his arm disquieting; but Madog himself waited to receive them in the hall, and joined their hands and plighted them their vows, to make them man and wife, come what might—

"So long as you both shall live," Madog said, pressing their hands together. "And when there is an heir, Prince Gwydion shall have the third of my lands, and his father shall rule in peace so long as he shall live."

Gwydion misliked the last—Gwydion thought in alarm: As long as he lives.

But Madog went on, saying, "—be you wed, be you wed, be you wed," three times, as if it were a spell—then: "Kiss your bride, son-in-law."

The well-wishes from the guests roared like the sea. The sea was in Eri's eyes, deep and blue and drowning. He heard Mili growl as he kissed Eri's lips once, twice, three times.

The pipers played, the people cheered, no few of whom indeed might have been King Ban's, or Lugh's, or Lughdan's. Perhaps, Gwydion dared think, perhaps it was hope he brought to them, perhaps he truly had won, after all, and the dreadful threat Madog posed was lifted, so that Madog would be their neighbor, no worse than the worst they had had, and perhaps, if well-disposed, better than one or two.

Perhaps, he thought, sitting at Madog's right hand with his bride at his right and with Owain just beyond, perhaps there truly was cause to hope, and he could ride away from here alive—though he feared he could find no cause to do so tonight, with so much prepared, with an anxious young bride and King Madog determined to indulge his beautiful daughter. Women hurried about with flowers and with torches, with linens and with brooms and platters and plates, tumblers ran riot, dancers leaped and cavorted—one of whom came to grief against an ale-server. Both went down, in Madog's very face, and the hall grew still and dangerous.

But Eri laughed and clapped her hands, a laughter so small and faint until her father laughed, and all the hall laughed; and Gwydion remembered then to breathe, while Eri hugged his arm and laughed up at him with those sea-blue eyes.

"More ale!" Madog called. "Less spillage, there!"

The dreadful wizard could joke, then. Gwydion drew two easier breaths, and someone filled their cups. He drank, but prudently: he caught Owain's eye, and Owain his—while Mili having found a bone to her liking, with a great deal of meat to it, worried it happily in the straw beneath the table.

There were healths drunk, there were blessings said, at each of which one had to drink—and Madog laughed and called Gwydion a fine son-in-law, asked him about his campaign against the bandits and swore he was glad to have his friends and his kin and anyone he cared to bring here: Madog got up and clapped Owain on the shoulder too, and asked was Owain wed, and, informed Owain was not, called out to the hall that here was another fine catch, and where were the young maids to keep Owain from chill on his master's wedding night?

Owain protested in some embarrassment, starting to his feet—

But drink overcame him, and he sat down again with a hand to his brow, Gwydion saw it with concern, while Madog touched Gwydion's arm on the other side and said, "The women are ready," slyly bidding him finish his ale beforehand.

Gwydion rose and handed his bride to her waiting women. "Owain!" Gwydion said then sharply, and Owain gained his feet, saying something Gwydion could not hear for with all the people cheering and the piper starting up, but he saw Owain was distressed. Gwydion resisted the women pulling at him, stood fast until Owain reached him, flushed with ale and embarrassment. The men surrounded him with bawdy cheers and more offered cups.

It was his turn then on the stairs, more cups thrust on him, Madog clapping him on the shoulder and hugging him and calling him the son he had always wanted, and saying there should be peace in Dyfed for a hundred years . . . unfailing friendship with his father and his kin— greater things, should he have ambitions. . . .

The room spun around. Voices buzzed. They pushed him up the stairs, Owain and Mili notwithstanding, Mili barking all the while. They brought him down the upstairs hall, they opened the door to the bridal chamber.

On pitch dark.

Perhaps it was cowardly to balk. Gwydion thought so, in the instant the laughing men gave him a push between the shoulders. Shame kept him from calling Owain to his rescue. The door shut at his back.

He heard rustling in the dark and imagined coils and scales. Eri's soft voice said, "My lord?"

A faint starlight edged the shutters. His eyes made out the furnishings, now that the flare of torches had left his sight. It was the rustling of bedclothes he heard. He saw a woman's shoulder and arm faintly in the shadowed bed, in the scant starshine that shutter let through.

He backed against the door, found the latch behind him, cracked it the least little bit outward and saw Owain leaning there against his arm, facing the lamplit wall outside, flushed of face and ashamed to meet his eyes at such close range.

"I'm here, m'lord," Owain breathed, on ale-fumes. Owain never called him lord, but Owain was greatly embarrassed tonight. "The lot's gone down the stairs now. I'll be here the night. I'll not leave this door, nor sleep, I swear to you."

Gwydion gave him a worried look, wishing the two of them dared escape this hall and Madog's well-wishes, running pell-mell back to his own house, his parents' advice, and childhood. But, "Good," he said, and

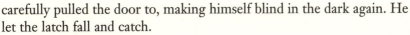

carefully pulled the door to, making himself blind in the dark again. He let the latch fall and catch.

"My lord?" Eri said faintly.

He felt quite foolish, himself and Owain conspiring together like two boys at an orchard wall, when it was a young bride waiting for him, innocent and probably as anxious as he. He nerved himself, walked up by the bed and opened the shutters wide on a night sky brighter than the dark behind him.

But with the cool night wind blowing into the room he thought of dragons, wondered whether opening the window to the sky was wise at all, and wondered what was slipping out of bed with the whispering of the bedclothes. His bride forwardly clasped his arm, wound fingers into his and swayed against him, saying how beautiful the stars were.

Perhaps that invited courtly words. He murmured some such. He found the courage to take Madog's daughter in his arms and kiss her, and thereafter—

He waked abed with the faint dawn coming through the window, his sword tangled with his leg and his arm ensnared in a woman's unbound hair—

Hair raven black.

He leaped up trailing sheets, while a strange young woman sat up to snatch the bedclothes to her, with her black hair flowing about her shoulders, her eyes dark and cold and fathomless.

"Where's my wife?" he cried.

She smiled, thin-lipped, rose from the bed, drawing the sheets about her like royal robes. "Why, you see her, husband."

He rushed to the door and lifted the latch. The door did not budge, hardly rattled when he shoved it with all his strength. "Owain?" he cried, and pounded it with his fist. "Owain!"

No answer came. Gwydion turned slowly to face the woman, dreading what other shape she might take. But she sat down wrapped in the sheets with one knee on the rumpled bed, looking at him. Her hair spread about her like a web of shadows in the dawn. As much as Eri had been an innocent girl, this was a woman far past Eri's innocence or his own.

He asked, "Where's Owain? What's become of him?"

"Guesting elsewhere."

"Who are you?"

"Glasog," she said, and shrugged, the dawn wind carrying long strands of her hair about her shoulders. "Or Eri, if you like. My father's elder daughter and younger, all in one, since he has none but me."

"Why?" he asked. "Why this pretense if you were the bargain?"

"People trust Eri. She's so fair, so kind."

"What do you want? What does your father want?"

"A claim on your father's land. The last kingdom of Dyfed. And you've come to give it to us."

Gwydion remembered nothing of what might have happened last night. He remembered nothing of anything he should have heard or done last night, abed with Glasog the witch, Madog's raven-haired daughter. He felt cold and hollow and desperate, asking, "On your oath, *is* Owain safe?"

"And would you believe my oath?" Glasog asked.

"I'll see your father," Gwydion said shortly. "Trickery or not, he swore me the third of his kingdom for your dowry. Younger or elder, or both, you're my wife. Will he break his word?"

Glasog said, "An heir. Then he'll release you and your friend, and your father will reign in peace . . . so long as he lives."

Gwydion walked to the open window, gazing at a paling, still sunless sky. He feared he knew what that release would be—the release of himself and Owain from life, while the child he sired would become heir to his father's kingdom with Madog to enforce that right.

So long as his father lived . . . so long as that unfortunate *child* might live, for that matter, once the inheritance of Ogan's line and Ogan's Luck passed securely into Madog's line—his father's kingdom taken and for no battle, no war, only a paltry handful of lies and lives.

He looked across the scorched hills, toward a home he could not reach, a father who could not advise him. He dared not hope that Owain might have escaped to bring word to his father: I'll not leave this door, Owain had said—and they would have had to carry Owain away by force or sorcery. Mili with him.

It was sorcery that must have made him sleep and forget last night. It was sorcery he must have seen when he turned from the window and saw Eri sitting there, rosy-pale and golden, patting the place beside her and bidding him come back to bed.

He shuddered and turned and hit the windowledge, hurting his hand. He thought of flight, even of drawing the sword and killing Madog's daughter, before this princess could conceive and doom him and his parents. . . .

Glasog's voice said, slowly, from Eri's lips, "If you try anything so rash, my father won't need your friend any longer, will he? I certainly wouldn't be in his place then. I'll hardly be in it now."

"What have you done with Owain?"

Eri shrugged. Glasog's voice said, "Dear husband—"

"The marriage wasn't consummated," he said, "for all I remember."

It was Glasog who lifted a shoulder. Black hair parted. "To sorcery—does it matter?"

He looked desperately toward the window. He said, without looking at her: "I've something to say about that, don't you think?"

"No. You don't. If you wouldn't, or couldn't, the words are said, the vows are made, the oaths are taken. If not your child—anyone's will do, for all men know or care."

He looked at her to see if he had understood what he thought he had, and Glasog gathered a thick skein of her hair—and drew it over her shoulder.

"The oaths are made," Glasog said. "Any lie will do. Any child will do."

"There's my word against it," Gwydion said.

Glasog shook her had gravely. "A lie's nothing to my father. A life is nothing." She stood up, shook out her hair, and hugged the sheets about her. Dawn lent a sudden and unkind light to Glasog's face, showing hollow cheeks, a grim mouth, a dark and sullen eye that promised nothing of compromise.

Why? he asked himself. Why this much of truth? Why not Eri's face?

She said, "What will you, husband?"

"Ask tonight," he said, hoping only for time and better counsel.

She inclined her head, walked between him and the window, lifting her arms wide. For an instant the morning sun showed a woman's body against the sheets. Then—it might have been a trick of the eyes—black hair spread into the black wings, something flew to the window and the sheet drifted to the floor.

What about the dragon? he would have asked, but there was no one to ask.

He went to the door and tried it again, in case sorcery had ceased. But it gave not at all, not to cleverness, not to force. He only bruised his shoulder, and leaned dejectedly against the door, sure now that he had made a terrible mistake.

The window offered nothing but a sheer drop to the stones below, and when he tried that way, he could not force his shoulders through.

There was no fire in the room, not so much as water to drink. He might fall on his sword, but he took Glasog at her word: it was the form of the marriage Madog had wanted, and they would only hide his death until it was convenient to reveal it. All the house had seen them wed and bedded, even Owain—who, being honest, could swear only what he had seen and what he had guessed—but never, never to the truth of what had happened and not happened last night.

Ogan's fabled Luck should have served him better, he thought, casting himself onto the bedside, head in hands. It should have served all of them better, this Luck his great grandfather had said only faithlessness could break—

But was Glasog herself not faithlessness incarnate? Was not Madog?

If that was the barb in great grandfather's blessing—it had done nothing but bring him and his family into Madog's hands. But it seemed to him that the fay were reputed for twists and turns in their gifts, and if they had made one such twist they might make another: all he knew was to hew to the course Ogan's sons had always followed.

So he had come here in good faith, been caught through abuse of that faith, and though he might perhaps seize the chance to come at Madog himself, that was treachery for treachery and if he had any last whisper of belief in his luck, that was what he most should not do.

"**I**s there a child?" Madog asked, and Glasog said, "Not yet. Not yet. Be patient."

"There's not," Madog said testily, "forever. Remember that."

"I remember," Glasog said.

"You wouldn't grow fond of him—or foolish?"

"I?" quoth Glasog, with an arch of her brow. "I, fond? Not fond of the dragon, let us say. Not fond of poverty—or early dying."

"We'll not fail. If not him—"

"Truly, do you imagine the dragon will give you *anything* if the claim's not legitimate? I think not. I do think not. It must be Gwydion's child—and *that*, by nature, by Gwydion's own will. That *is* the difficulty, isn't it?"

"You vaunt your sorcery. Use it!"

Glasog said, coldly, "When needs be. If needs be. But it's myself he'll have, *not* Eri, and for myself, not Eri. That's my demand in this."

"Don't be a fool."

Glasog smiled with equal coldness. "This man has magical protections. His luck is no illusion and it's not to cross. I don't forget that. Don't you. *Trust* me, Father."

"I wonder how I got you."

Glasog still smiled. "Luck," she said. "You want to be rid of the dragon, don't you? Has my advice ever failed you? And isn't it the old god's bond that he'll barter for questions?"

Her father scowled. "It's *my* life you're bartering for, curse your cold heart. It's my life you're risking with your schemes—a life from each kingdom of Dyfed, *that's* the barter we've made. We've caught Gwydion. We can't stave the dragon off forever for your whims and your vapors, Daughter. Get me a grandson—by whatever sorcery—and forget this foolishness. Kill the dragon . . . do you think I've not tried that? All the princes in Dyfed have tried that."

Glasog said, with her grimmest look: "We've also Gwydion's friend, don't we? And isn't he of Ogan's kingdom?"

Gwydion endured the hours until sunset, hungry and thirsty and having nothing whatever to do but to stare out the slit of a window, over a black and desolate land.

He wondered if Owain was even alive, or what had become of Mili.

Once he saw a raven in flight, toward the south; and once, late, the sky growing dimly copper, he saw it return, it seemed more slowly, circling always to the right.

Glasog? he wondered—or merely a raven looking for its supper?

The sky went from copper to dusk. He felt the air grow chill. He thought of closing the shutters, but that was Glasog's access. So he paced the floor, or looked out the window or simply listened to the distant comings and goings below which alone told him that there was life in the place.

Perhaps, he thought, they only meant him to die of thirst and hunger, and perhaps he would never see or speak to a living soul again. He hoped Glasog would come by sunset, but she failed that; and by moonrise, but she did not come.

At last, when he had fallen asleep in his waiting, a shadow swept in the window with a snap and flutter of dark wings, and Glasog stood wrapped only in dark hair and limned in starlight.

He gathered himself up quickly, feeling still that he might be dreaming. "I expected you earlier," he said.

"I had inquiries to make," she said, and walked to the table where— he did not know how, a cup and a silver pitcher gleamed in reflected starlight. She lifted the pitcher and poured, and oh, he was thirsty. She offered it, and it might be poisoned for all he knew. At the very least it was enchanted, and perhaps only moondust and dreams. But she stood offering it; he drank, and it took both thirst and hunger away.

She said, "You may have one wish of me, Gwydion. One wish. And then I may have two from you. Do you agree?"

He wondered what to say. He put down the cup and walked away to the window, looking out on the night sky. There were a hundred things to ask: his parents' lives; Owain's; the safety of his land—and in each one there seemed some flaw.

Finally he chose the simplest. "Love me," he said.

For a long time Glasog said nothing. Then he heard her cross the room.

He turned. Her eyes flashed at him, sudden as a serpent's. She said, "Dare you? First drink from my cup."

"Is this your first wish?"

"It is."

He hesitated, looking at her, then walked away to the table and reached for the shadowy cup, but another appeared beside it, gleaming, crusted with jewels.

"Which will you have?" she asked.

He hoped then that he understood her question. And he picked up the cup of plain pewter and drank it all.

She said, from behind him, "You have your wish, Gwydion."

And wings brushed his face, the wind stirred his hair, the raven shape swooped out the window.

"Owain," a voice said—the raven's voice, and Owain leaped up from his prison bed, such as he could, though his head was spinning and he had to brace himself against the wall. It was not the raven's first visit. He asked it, "Where's my master? What's happened to him?"

And the raven, suddenly no raven, but a dark-haired woman: "Wedlock," she said. "Death, if the dragon gets his due—as soon it may."

"Glasog," Owain said, chilled to the marrow. Since Madog's men had hauled him away from Gwydion's door, he had had this dizziness, and it came on him now. He felt his knees going and he caught himself.

"You might save him," Glasog said.

"And should I trust you?" he asked.

The chains fell away from him with a ringing of iron, and the bolts fell from the door.

"Because I'm his wife," she said. Eri stood there. He rubbed his eyes and it was Glasog again. "And you're his friend. Isn't that what it means, friendship? Or marriage?"

A second time he rubbed his eyes. The door swung open.

"My father says," Glasog said, "the dragon's death will free Prince Gwydion. You may have your horse, your dog, your armor and your weapons—or whatever you will, Owain ap Llodri. But for that gift—you must give me one wish when I claim it."

In time—Gwydion was gazing out the window, he had no idea why, he heard the slow echo of hoofbeats off the wall.

He saw Owain ride out the gate; he saw the raven flying over him. "Owain," he cried. "Owain!"

But Owain paid no heed. Only Mili stopped, and looked up at the tower where he stood.

He thought—Go with him, Mili, if it's home he's bound for. Warn my father. There's no hope here.

Owain never looked back. Gwydion saw him turn south at the gate, entirely away from home, and guessed where Owain was going.

"Come back," he cried. "Owain! No!"

It was the dragon they were going to. It was surely the dragon Owain was going to, and if Gwydion had despaired in his life, it was seeing Owain and Mili go off in company with his wife.

He tried again to force himself through the window slit. He tried the door, working with his sword to lift the bar he was sure was in place outside.

He found it and lifted it. But it stopped with the rattle of chain.

They found the brook again, beyond the hill, and the raven fluttered down clumsily to drink, spreading a wing to steady herself.

Owain reined Swallow in. He had no reason to trust the raven in any shape, less reason to believe it than anything else that he had seen in this place. But Mili came cautiously up to it, and suddenly it was Glasog kneeling there, wrapped only in her hair, with her back to him, and Mili whining at her in some distress.

Owain got down. He saw two fingers missing from Glasog's right hand, the wounds scarcely healed. She drank from her other hand, and bathed the wounded one in water. She looked at Owain and said, "You wished to save Gwydion. You said nothing of yourself."

Owain shrugged and settled with his arm around Mili's neck.

"Now you owe me my wish," Glasog said.

"That I do," he said, and feared what it might be.

She said, "There's a god near this place. The dragon overcame him. But he will still answer the right question. Most gods will, with proper sacrifice."

Owain said, "What shall I ask him?"

She said, "I've already asked."

Owain asked then, "And the answers, lady?"

"First that the dragon's life and soul lies in his right eye. And second that no man can kill him."

Owain understood the answer then. He scratched Mili's neck beneath the collar. He said, "Mili's a loyal dog. And if flying tires you, lady, I've got a shoulder you can ride on."

Glasog said, "Better you go straightaway back to your king. Only lend me your bow, your dog, and your horse. *That* is my wish, ap Llodri."

Owain shook his head, and got up, patting Mili on the head. "All that you'll have by your wish," Owain said, "but I go with them."

"Be warned," she said.

"I am that," said Owain, and held out his hand. "My lady?"

The raven fluttered up and settled on his arm, bating as he rose into the saddle. Owain set Swallow on her way, among the charred, cinder-black hills, to a cave the raven showed him.

Swallow had no liking for this place. Owain patted her neck, coaxed her forward. Mili bristled up and growled as they climbed. Owain took up his bow and drew out an arrow, yelled, "Mili! Look out!" as fire billowed out and Swallow shied.

A second gust followed. Mili yelped and ran from the roiling smoke, racing ahead of a great serpent shape that surged out of the cave, but Mili began to cross the hill then, leading it.

The raven launched itself from Owain's shoulder, straighter than Owain's arrow sped.

A clamor rose in the keep, somewhere deep in the halls. It was dawn above the hills, and a glow still lit the south, as Gwydion watched from the window.

He was watching when a strange rider came down the road, shining gold in the sun, in scaled armor.

"The dragon!" he heard shouted from the wall. Gwydion's heart sank. It sank further when the scale-armored rider reached the gate and

Madog's men opened to it. It was Swallow the dragon-knight rode, Swallow with her mane all singed; and it was Mili who limped after, with her coat all soot-blackened and with great sores showing on her hide. Mili's head hung and her tail drooped and the dragon led her by a rope, while a raven sat perched on his shoulder.

Of Owain there was no sign.

There came a clattering in the hall. Chain rattled, the bar lifted and thumped and armed men were in the doorway.

"King Madog wants you," one said. And Gwydion—

"Madog will have to send twice," Gwydion said, with his sword in hand.

The dragon rode to the steps and the raven fluttered to the ground as waiting women rushed to it, to bring Princess Glasog her cloak—black as her hair and stitched with spells. The waiting women and the servants had seen this sight before—the same as the men at arms at the gate, who had had their orders should it have been Owain returning.

"Daughter," Madog said, descending those same steps as Glasog rose up, wrapped in black and silver. Mili growled and bristled, suddenly strained at her leash—

The dragon loosed it and Mili sprang for Madog's throat. Madog fell under the hound and Madog's blood was on the steps—but his neck was already broken.

Servants ran screaming. Men at arms stood confused, as if they had quite forgotten what they were doing or where they were or what had brought them there, the men of the fallen kingdoms all looking at one another and wondering what terrible thing had held them here.

And on all of this Glasog turned her back, walking up the steps.

"My lady!" Owain cried—for it was Owain wore the armor; but it was not Owain's voice she longed to hear.

Glasog let fall the cloak and leaped from the wall. The raven glided away, with one harsh cry against the wind.

In time after—often in that bitter winter, when snows lay deep and wind skirled drifts about the door—Owain told how Glasog had pierced the dragon's eye; and how they had found the armor, and how Glasog had told him the last secret, that with the dragon dead, Madog's sorcery would leave him.

That winter, too, Gwydion found a raven in the courtyard, a crippled bird, missing feathers on one wing. It seemed greatly confused, so far gone with hunger and with cold that no one thought it would live. But Gwydion tended it until spring and set it free again.

It turned up thereafter on the wall of Gwydion's keep—King Gwydion, he was now—lord of all Dyfed. "You've one wish left," he said to it. "One wish left of me."

"I give it to you," the raven said. "Whatever you wish, King Gwydion."

"Be what you wish to be," Gwydion said.

And thereafter men told of the wisdom of King Gwydion as often as of the beauty of his wife.

1992

MECH

Cold night in Dallas Metro Complex, late shift supper while the cruiser autoed the beltway, rain fracturing the city lights on the windshield. "Chili cheeseburger with mustard," Dave said, and passed it to Sheila— Sheila had the wheel, he had the Trackers, and traffic was halfway sane for Dallas after dark, nobody even cruising off the autos, at least in their sector. He bit into a chili and cheese without, washed a bite down with a soft drink, and scanned the blips for the odd lane-runner. A domestic quarrel and a card snitch were their only two working calls: Manny and Lupe had the domestic, and the computer lab had the card trace.

So naturally they were two bites into the c&c, hadn't even touched the fries, when the mech-level call came slithering in, sweet-voiced: "Possible assault in progress, Metro 2, # R-29, The Arlington, you've got the warrant, 34, see the manager."

"Gee, thanks," Dave muttered. Sheila said something else, succinctly, off mike, and punched in with a chilied thumb. The cruiser had already started its lane changes, with Exit 3 lit up on the windshield, at .82 k away. Sheila got a couple more bites and a sip of soft drink down before she shoved the burger and drink cup at him. She took the wheel as the autos dumped them onto Mason Drive, on a manual-only and mostly deserted street.

It didn't look like an assault kind of neighborhood, big reflective windows in a tower complex. It was offices and residences, one of the poshest complexes in big D, real high-rent district. You could say that was why a mech unit got pulled in off the Ringroad, instead of the dispatcher sending in the b&w line troops. You could make a second guess it was because the city wanted more people to move into the complexes and a low crime rep was the major sales pitch. Or you could even guess some city councilman lived in The Arlington.

But that wasn't for a mere mech unit to question. Dave got his helmet out of the locker under his feet, put it on while Sheila was taking them into the curbside lane, plugged into the collar unit that was already plugged to the tactiles, put the gloves on, and put the visor down, in the interests of checkout and time—

"Greet The Public," Sheila said with a saccharine and nasty smirk—meaning Department Po-li-cy said visors up when you were Meeting the Man: people didn't greatly like to talk to visors and armor.

"Yeah, yeah." He finished the checks. He had a street map on the HUD, the location of 29-R sector on the overall building shape, the relative position of the cruiser as it nosed down the ramp into The Arlington's garage. "Inside view, here, shit, I'm not getting it, have you got Library on it?"

"I'll get it. Get. Go."

He opened the door, bailed out onto the concrete curb. Car treads had tracked the rain in, neon and dead white glows glistened on the down ramp behind them. High and mighty Arlington Complex was gray concrete and smoked glass in its utilitarian gut. And he headed for the glass doors, visor up, the way Sheila said, fiber cameras on, so Sheila could track: Sheila herself was worthless with the mech, she'd proven that by taking a shot from a dealer, so that her right leg was plex and cable below the knee, but as a keyman she was ace and she had access with an A with the guys Downtown.

She said, in his left ear, "Man's in the hall, name's Rozman, reports screaming on 48, a man running down the fire stairs . . ."

"Mr. Rozman," he said, meeting the man just past the doors. "Understand you have a disturbance."

"Ms. Lopez, she's the next door neighbor, she's hiding in her bedroom, she said there was screaming. We had an intruder on the fire stairs—"

"Man or woman's voice in the apartment?"

"Woman."

"What's your address?"

"4899."

"Minors on premises?"

"Single woman. Name's Emilia Nolan. Lives alone. A quiet type . . . no loud parties, no complaints from the neighbors . . ."

Rozman was a clear-headed source. Dave unclipped a remote, thumbed it on and handed it to the man. "You keep answering questions. You know what this is?"

"It's a remote."

"—Sheila, put a phone-alert on Ms. Lopez and the rest of the neighbors, police on the way up, just stay inside and keep behind furniture until she gets word from us." He was already going for the elevators. "Mr. Rozman. Do you log entry/exits?"

On his right-ear mike: "On the street and the tunnels and the garage, the fire stairs . . ."

"Any exceptions?"

"No. —Yes. The service doors. But those are manual key . . . only maintenance has that."

"Key that log to the dispatcher. Just put the d-card in the phone and dial 9999." The exception to the log was already entered, miked in from his pickup. "And talk to your security people about those service doors. That's city code. Sir." He was polite on autopilot. His attention was on Sheila at the moment, from the other ear, saying they were prepping interior schemas to his helmet view. "Mr. Rozman. Which elevator?" There was a bank of six.

"Elevator B. Second one on your left. That goes to the 48s . . ."

He used his fireman's key on the elevator call, and put his visor down. The hall and the elevator doors disappeared behind a wire-schema of the hall and doors, all red and gold and green lines on black, and shifting as the mid-tier elevator grounded itself. He didn't look down as he got in, you didn't look down on a wire-view if you wanted your stomach steady. He sent the car up, watched the floors flash past, transparenced, heard a stream of checks from Sheila confirming the phone-alarm in action, residents being warned through the phone company—

"Lopez is a cardiac case," Sheila said, "hospital's got a cruiser on alert, still no answer out of 4899. Lopez says it's quiet now."

"You got a line on Lopez, calm her down." Presence-sniffer readout was a steady blue, but you got that in passageways, lot of traffic, everything blurred unless you had a specific to track: it was smelling for stress, and wasn't getting it here. "Rozman, any other elevators to 48?"

"Yeah, C and D."

"Can you get off anywhere from a higher floor?"

"Yessir, you can. Any elevator, if you're going down."

Elevator stopped and the door opened. Solid floor across the threshold, with the scan set for anomalies against the wire-schema. Couple of potted palms popped out against the VR. Target door was highlighted gold. Audio kept hyping until he could hear the scuff of random movements from other apartments. "Real quiet," he said to Sheila. And stood there a moment while the sniffer worked, filling in tracks. You could see the swirl in the air currents where the vent was. You could see stress showing up soft red.

"Copy that," Sheila said. "Warrant's clear to go in."

He put himself on no-exhaust, used the fire-key again, stayed to the threshold. The air inside showed redder. So did the walls, on heat-view, but this was spatter. Lot of spatter.

No sound of breathing. No heartbeat inside the apartment.

He de-amped and walked in. A mech couldn't disturb a scene—sniffer couldn't pick up a presence on itself, ditto on the Cyloprene of his mech rig, while the rig was no-exhaust he was on internal air. It couldn't sniff him, but feet could still smudge the spatters. He watched where he stepped, real-visual now, and discovered the body, a woman, fully dressed, sprawled face-up by the bar, next to the bedroom, hole dead center between the astonished eyes.

"Quick and clean for her," he said. "Helluva mess on the walls."

"Lab's on its way," Sheila said, alternate thought track. "I'm on you, D-D, just stand still a sec."

The sniffer was working up a profile, via Sheila's relays Downtown. He stood still, scanning over the body. "Woman about thirty, good-looking, plain dresser . . ."

Emilia Frances Nolan, age 34, flashed up on the HUD. *Canadian citizen, Martian registry, chief information officer Mars Transport Company."*

Thin, pale woman. Dark hair. Corporate style on the clothes. Canadian immigrant to Mars, returned to Earth on a Canadian passport. "Door was locked," he said.

"I noticed that," Sheila said.

Sniffer was developing two scents, the victim's and a second one. AMMONIA, the indicator said.

"Mild ammonia."

"Old-fashioned stuff," he said. "Amateur." The sniffer was already sepping it out as the number three track. Ammonia wouldn't overload a modern sniffer. It was just one more clue to trace; and the tracks were coming clear now: Nolan's was everywhere, *Baruque,* the sniffer said—expensive perfume, persistent as hell. The ammonia had to be the number two's notion. And you didn't carry a vial of it for social occasions.

But why in hell was there a live-in smell?

"Male," Sheila commented, meaning the number two track. "Lovers' spat?"

"Rummel's closer. —We got lab coming in. Lab's trying to get an ID match on your sniffer pickup."

"Yeah. You've got enough on it. Guy's sweating. So am I." He felt sweat trails running under the armor, on his face. The door said 14. The oxy was running out. Violate the scene or no, he had to toggle to exhaust. After that, it was cooler, dank, the way shafts were that went into the underground.

"We got some elevator use," Sheila said, "right around the incident, off 48. Upbound. Stopped on 50, 52, 78, 80, and came down again, 77, 34, 33, then your fire-call brought it down. Time-overlap on the 78, the C-elevator was upbound."

"Follow it." Meaning somebody could have turned around and left no traces if he'd gotten in with another elevator-call. "Put Downtown on it, I need your brain."

"Awww. I thought it was the body."

"Stow it." He was panting again. The internal tank was out. He hoped he didn't need it again. Sheila went out of the loop: he could hear the silence on the phones. "Forty-damn-stories—"

Three, two, one, s-one. "Wire," he gasped, and got back the schema, that showed through the door into a corridor. He listened for noise, panting, while the net in the background zeed out his breathing and his heartbeat and the building fans and everything else but a dull distant roar that said humanity, a lot of it, music—the red was still there and it was on the door switch, but it thinned out in the downward stairwell.

"Went out on s-1."

"Street exit, mall exit," Sheila said. "Via the Arlington lobby. Dave, we got you help coming in."

"Good."

"Private mech."

Adrenaline went up a notch. "That's help? That's help? Tell them—"

"I did, buns, sorry about that. Name's Ross, she's inbound from the other tower, corporate security . . ."

"Just what I need. Am I going out there? They want me to go out there?"

"You're clear."

He hated it, he *hated* going out there, hated the stares, hated the Downtown monitoring that was going to pick up that pulse rate of his and have the psychs on his case. But he opened the door, he walked out into the lobby that was The Arlington's front face; and walked onto car-

"POSSeL-Q the manager didn't know about, maybe, lo
rel, clothes aren't mussed. Rape's not a high likely here." Stre
tracks. The whole place stank of it. "Going for the live one, Sl
it. Put out a phone alert, upstairs and down, have ComA take
man's remote, I don't need him but he's still a resource."

Out the door, into the wire-schema of the hall. The sni
good this time: the stress trail showed up clear and bright fo
door, and it matched the number two track, no question. "F
damn floors," he muttered: no good to take the elevator. You
fessional killers or you got crazies or drugheads in a place
fenced in with its security locks, and you didn't know what a
the three was going to do, or what floor they were going to do
went through the fire-door and started down on foot, follo
scent, down and down and down . . .

"We got further on Norton," Sheila said. "Assigned h
months ago, real company climber, top grad, schooled on Mars
ins on any MarsCorp record we can get to, but that guy was re
in there. I'm saying he was somebody Norton didn't want her s
cle to meet."

He ran steps and breathed, ran steps and breathed, restr
Sheila had a brain for figuring people, you didn't even have to a
presence trail arrived into the stairwell, bright blue mingling
red. "Got another track here," he found breath to say.

"Yeah, yeah, that's in the log, that's a maintenance worke
minutes back. He'll duck out again on 25."

"Yeah." He was breathing hard. Making what time he cou
trail did duck out at 25, in a wider zone of blue, unidentified sce
smell from the corridor blown into the shaft and fading into th
ent. His track stayed clear and strong, stress-red, and he went
view: the transparent stairs were making him sick. "Where's this
Garage downstairs?"

"Garage and mini-mall."

"Shit!"

"Yeah. We got a call from building security wanting a piec
told them stay out of it . . ."

"Thank God."

"Building chief's an amateur with a cop-envy. We're trying
another mech in."

"We got some fool with a gun he hasn't ditched, we got a m
of people down there. Where's Jacobs?"

pet, onto stone, both of which were only flat haze to his eyes. Bystanders clustered and gossiped, patched in like the potted palms, real people stark against the black and wire-lines of cartoonland, all looking at him and talking in half-voices as if that could keep their secrets if he wanted to hear. He just kept walking, down the corridor, following the faint red glow in the blue of Every-smell, followed it on through the archway into the wider spaces of the mall, where more real people walked in black cartoon-space, and that red glow spread out into a faint fanswept haze and a few spots on the floor.

Juvies scattered, a handful out of Parental, lay odds on it—he could photo them and tag them, but he kept walking, chose not even to transmit: Sheila had a plateful to track as it was. One smartass kid ducked into his face, made a face, and ran like hell. Fools tried that, as if they suspected there wasn't anybody real inside the black visor. Others talked with their heads partially turned, or tried not to look as if they were looking. That was what he hated, being the eyes and ears, the spy-machine that connected to everywhere, that made everybody ask themselves what they were saying that might go into files, what they had ever done or thought of that a mech might find reason to track . . .

Maybe it was the blank visor, maybe it was the rig—maybe it was everybody's guilt. With the sniffer tracking, you could see the stress around you, the faint red glow around honest citizens no different than the guy you were tracking, as if it was the whole world's guilt and fear and wrongdoing you were smelling, and everybody had some secret to keep and some reason to slink aside.

"Your backup's meeting you at A-3," Sheila said, and a marker popped up in the schema, yellow flasher.

"Wonderful. We got a make on the target?"

"Not yet, buns. Possible this guy's not on file. Possible we got another logjam in the datacall, a mass murder in Peoria, something like that." Sheila had her mouth full. "Everybody's got problems tonight."

"What are you eating?"

"Mmm. Sorry, there."

"Is that my cheeseburger?"

"I owe you one."

"You're really putting on weight, Sheel, you know that?"

"Yeah, it's anxiety attacks." Another bite. "Your backup's Company, Donna Ross, 20 years on, service citation."

"Shee." Might not be a play-cop, then. Real seniority. He saw the black figure standing there in her own isolation, at the juncture of two dizzying walkways. Saw her walk in his direction, past the mistrustful stares of spectators. "Get some plainclothes in here yet?"

"We got reporters coming."

"Oh, great. Get'em off, get the court on it—"

"Doing my best."

"Officer Dawes." Ross held out a black-gloved hand, no blues on the Company cop, just the rig, black cut-out in a wire-diagram world. "We're interfaced. It just came up."

Data came up, B-channel. "Copy that." Ross was facing the same red track he was, was getting his data, via some interface Downtown, an intersystem handshake. He stepped onto the downbound escalator, Ross in his 360° compression view, a lean, black shape on the shifting kaleidoscope of the moving stairs. "This is a MarsCorp exec that got it?" Ross asked in his right ear. "Is that what I read?"

"Deader than dead. We got a potential gun walking around out here with the john-q's. You got material on the exec?"

"Some kind of jam-up in the net—I haven't got a thing but a see-you."

"Wonderful, both of us in the dark." The escalator let off on the lower level, down with the fast foods and the arcades and a bunch of juvies all antics and ass. "Get out of here," he snarled on Address, and juvies scattered through the cartoonscape. "Get upstairs!" he yelled, and some of them must have figured shooting was imminent, because they scattered doubletime, squealing and shoving. Bright blue down here with the pepperoni pizza and the beer and the popcorn, but that single red thread was still showing.

"Our boy's sweating hard," Ross said in one ear; and Sheila in the other: "We got a sudden flash in a security door, right down your way."

"Come on." Dave started to run. Ross matched him, a clatter of Cyloprene soles on tile, godawful racket. The exit in question was flashing yellow ahead. A janitor gawked, pressed himself against the wall in a try at invisibility; but his presence was blue, neutral to the area.

"You see anybody go through?"

"Yeah, yeah, I saw him, young guy, took to the exit, I said he wasn't—" *Supposed to* trailed into the amped mike as they banged through the doors and into a concrete service hall.

"Sheila, you in with Ross?"

"Yeah. Both of you guys. I got a b&w following you, he's not meched, best I could do . . ."

Red light strobed across his visor. WEAPONS ON, it said.

"Shit," he said, "Ross—" He stopped for a breath against the corridor wall, drew his gun and plugged it in. Ross must have an order too: she was plugging in. Somebody Downtown had got a fire warrant. Somebody had decided on a fire warrant next to a mall full of kids. Maybe because of the kids. "What's our make on this guy, Sheila? Tell me we got a make, please God, I don't like this, we got too many john-juniors out there."

"He's not in files."

"Off-worlder," Ross said.

"You know that?"

"If he's not in your files, he's from off-world. The Company is searching. They've got your readout."

"Shit, somebody get us info." The corridor was a moving, jolting wire-frame in the black.

Nobody. Not a sign.

But the red was there, bright and clear. Sheila compressed several sections ahead on the wire-schema, folded things up close where he could get a look. There was a corner; he transviewed it, saw it heading to a service area. AIR SYSTEMS, the readout line said. "We got an air-conditioning unit up there, feed for the whole damn mall as best I guess . . . he's got cover."

"Yeah," Ross said. "I copy that."

"We're not getting any damn data," Sheila said in his other ear. "I'm asking again on that make, and we're not getting it. Delay. Delay. Delay. Ask if *her* keyman's getting data."

"My keyman asks," he relayed, "if you've got data yet."

"Nothing new. I'm telling you, we're not priority, it's some little lovers' spat—"

"That what they're telling you?"

"Uh-uh. I don't know a thing more than you. But a male presence, female body up there . . . that's how it's going to wash out. It always does."

"Dave." Sheila's voice again, while their steps rang out of time on the concrete and the red track ran in front of them. She had a tone when there was trouble. "Butterflies, you hear?"

"Yeah. Copy." Sheila wasn't liking something. She wasn't liking it a lot.

They reached the corner. The trail kept going, skirled in the currents from air ducts, glowing fainter in the gust from the dark. He folded the view tighter, looked ahead of them, didn't like the amount of cover ahead where they were going to come down stairs and across a cat-walk.

Something banged, echoed, and the lights went out.

Didn't bother a mech. Maybe it made the quarry feel better, but they were still seeing, all wire-display. He was right on Ross, Ross standing there like a haze in the ambience. Her rig scattered stuff you used in the dark. It was like standing next to a ghost. The Dallas PD couldn't afford rigs like that. Governments did. Some MarsCorp bigwig got shot and the Company lent a mech with this stuff?

Ross said. "IR. Don't trust the wire. Stay here."

"The hell."

Infrared blurred the wire-schema. But he brought his sensors up high-gain.

"No sonar," Ross said. "Cut it, dammit!"

"What the hell are we after?"

"There he is!"

He didn't half see. Just a blur, far across the dark. Ross burst ahead of him, onto the steps; he dived after, in a thunder the audios didn't damp fast enough.

"Dave." Sheila's voice again, very solemn. His ears were still ringing when they got to the bottom. "Department's still got nothing. I never saw a jam this long . . . I never saw a rig like that."

They kept moving, fast, not running, not walking. The mech beside him was Company or some government's issue, a MarsCorp exec was stone dead, and you could count the organized crazies that might have pulled that trigger. A random crazy, a lover—a secessionist . . .

"Lab's on it," Sheila said. "Dave, Dave, I want you to listen to me."

He was moving forward. Sheila stopped talking as Ross moved around a bundle of conduits and motioned him to go down the other aisle, past the blowers. Listen, Sheila said, and said nothing. The link was feeding to Ross. He was sure of it. He could hear Sheila breathing, hard.

"Mustard," Sheila muttered. "Dave, was it mustard you wanted on that burger?"

They'd never been in a situation like this, not knowing what was feeding elsewhere, not knowing whether Downtown was still secure with them on the line. "Yeah," he breathed. He hated the stuff. "Yeah. With onions."

Sheila said, "You got it." Ross started to move. He followed. The com was compromised. She'd asked was he worried, that was the mustard query. He stayed beside that ghost-glow, held to the catwalk rail with one hand, the other with the gun. The city gave you a fire warrant; and your finger had a button. But theirs overrode, some guy Downtown. Or Sheila did. You didn't know. You were a weapon, with a double safety, and you didn't know whether the damn thing was live, ever.

"Dave," Sheila said, totally different tone. "Dave. This Ross doesn't have a keyman. She's backpacked. Total. She's a security guy."

Total mech. You heard about it, up on Sol, up in the Stations, where everything was computers. Elite of the elite. Independent operator with a computer for a backpack and neuros right into the station's high-tech walls.

He evened his breath, smelled the cold air, saw the thermal pattern that was Ross gliding ahead of him. A flash of infrared out of the dark. A door opened on light. Ross started running. He did.

A live-in lover? Somebody the exec would open the door to?

A mech could walk through a crime scene. A mech on internal air didn't leave a presence—nothing a sniffer would recognize.

A Company mech had been damned close to the scene—showed up to help the city cops . . .

"Sheila," he panted, trying to stay with Ross. "Lots of mustard."

Infrared glow ahead of them. A shot flashed out, from the Company mech. It explored in the dark, leaving tracers in his vision. Ross wasn't blinded. *His* foot went off a step, and he grabbed wildly for the rail, caught himself and slid two more before he had his feet under him on flat catwalk mesh—it shook as Ross ran; and he ran too.

"She's not remoted!" he panted. As if his keyman couldn't tell. Nobody outside was authorizing those shots. Ross was. A cartoon door boomed open, and he ran after a ghost whose fire wasn't routed through a whole damn city legal department. "Fold it!" he gasped, because he was busy keeping up; and the corner ahead compacted and swung into view, red and green wire, with nobody in it but the ghost ahead of him.

"Slow down!" he said. "Ross! Wait up, dammit! Don't shoot!"

His side was aching. Ross was panting hard, he heard her breathing, he overtook in a cartoon-space doorway, in a dead-end room, where the trail showed hot and bright.

"We have him," Ross said. The audio hype could hear the target breathing, past their exhaust. Even the panicked heartbeat. Ross lifted her gun against a presence behind a stack of boxes.

"No!" he yelled. And the left half of his visor flashed yellow. He swung to it, mindless target-seek, and the gun in his hand went off on Ross, went off a second time while Ross was flying sideways through the dark. Her shot went wild off the ceiling and he couldn't think, couldn't turn off the blinking target square. Four rounds, five, and the room was full of smoke.

"Dave?"

He wasn't talking to Sheila. He wasn't talking to whoever'd triggered him, set off the reflexes they trained in a mech.

Shaky voice from his keyman. "If you can walk out of there, walk. Right now, Dave."

"The guy's in the—"

"No. He's not, Dave." The heartbeat faded out. The cartoon room had a smudged gray ghost on the floor grid at his feet. And a bright red lot of blood spattered around. "I want you to check out the restroom upstairs from here. All right?"

He was shaking now. Your keyman talked and you listened or you could be dead. He saw a movement on his left. He swung around with the gun up, saw the man stand up. Ordinary looking man, business shirt. Soaked with sweat. Frozen with fear. The sniffer flashed red.

Sheila's voice said, from his shoulder-patch, "Don't touch anything. Dave. Get out of there. Now."

He moved, walked out, with the target standing at his back. He walked all the way back to the air-conditioning plant, and he started up the stairs there, up to the catwalk, while nothing showed, no one. Sheila said, "Dave. Unplug now. You can unplug."

He stopped, he reached with his other hand and he pulled the plug on the gun and put it in its holster. He went on up the cartooned metal stairs, and he found the cartooned hall and the cartooned restroom with the real-world paper on the floor.

"You better wash up," Sheila said, so he did that, shaking head to foot. Before he was finished, a b&w came in behind him, and said, "You all right, sir?"

"Yeah," he said. Sheila was quiet then.

"You been down there?" the cop asked.

"You saw it," Sheila said in his ear, and he echoed her: "I saw it—guy got away—I couldn't get a target. Ross was in the way . . ."

"Yes, sir," the b&w said. "You're on record, sir."

"I figured."

"You sure you're all right? I can call—"

"I can always *call*, officer."

The guy got a disturbed look, the way people did who forgot they were talking to two people. "Yes, sir," the b&w said. "All right."

On his way out.

He turned around to the mirror, saw a plain, sick face. Blood was on the sink rim, puddled around his boots, where it had run off the plastic. He went in a stall, wiped off his rig with toilet paper and flushed the evidence.

Sheila said, "Take the service exits. Pick you up at the curb."

"Copy," he mumbled, took his foot off the seat, flushed the last bit of bloody paper, taking steady small breaths, now. They taught you to trust the autos with your life. They taught you to swing to the yellow, don't think, don't ask, swing and hold, swing and hold the gun.

A mech just walked away, afterward, visor down, communing with his inner voices, immune to question, immune to interviews. Everything went to the interfaces. There was a record. Of course there was a record. Everyone knew that.

It was at the human interface things could drop out.

He used the fire-key, walked out an emergency exit, waited in the rain. The cruiser nosed up to the curb, black and black-windowed, and swallowed him up.

"**S**aved the soft drink," Sheila said. "Thought you'd be dry."

It was half ice-melt. But it was liquid. It eased a raw throat. He sucked on the straw, leaned his head back. "They calling us in?"

"No," Sheila said. That was all. They didn't want a debrief. They didn't want a truth, they wanted—

—wanted nothing to do with it. Nolan's body to the next-ofs, the live-in . . . to wherever would hide him.

Another mouthful of ice-melt. He shut his eyes, saw wire-schemas, endlessly folding, a pit you could fall into. He blinked on rain and refracted neon. "Ross killed Nolan."

"You and I don't know."

"*Was it Ross?*"

"Damned convenient a Company mech was in hail. Wasn't it?"

"No presence at all. Nolan—Nolan was shot between the eyes."

"MarsCorp exec—her live-in boyfriend with no record, no visa, no person. Guy who knew The Arlington's underground, who had a pass key—"

"He was keying through the doors?"

"Same as you were. Real at-home in the bottom tiers. You see a weapon on him, you see where he ditched one?"

"No." Raindrops fractured, flickering off the glass. He saw the gray ghost again, the no-Presence that could walk through total black. Or key through any apartment door, or aim a single head-shot with a computer's inhuman, instant accuracy.

He said, "Adds, doesn't it?"

"Adds. Downtown was seeing what I was. I told them. Told them you had bad feelings—"

"What the hell are they going to do? We got a dead mech down there—"

"The live-in shot Nolan. Shot the Company mech. That's your story. They can't say otherwise. What are they going to say? That the guy didn't have a gun? They won't come at us."

"What about our record?"

"Transmission breakup. Lightning or something." Sheila's face showed rain-spots, running shadows, neon glare. "Bad night, D-D, bad shit."

"They erase it?"

"Erase what?" Sheila asked.

Silence then. Rain came down hard.

"They want to bring their damn politics down here," Sheila said, "they can take it back again. Settle it up there."

"Settle what?" he echoed Sheila.

But he kept seeing corridors, still the corridors, folding in on themselves. And sipped the tasteless soft drink. "The guy's shirt was clean."

"Huh?"

"His shirt was clean." Flash on the restroom, red water swirling down and down. "He wasn't in that room. Nolan knew Ross was coming. The guy was living there. His smell's all over. That's why the ammonia trick. Nolan sent him for the stairs, I'll bet it's in the access times. He couldn't have hid from a mech. And all that screaming? The mech wanted something. Something Nolan wasn't giving. Something Ross wanted more than she wanted the guy right then."

"Secession stuff. Documents. Martian Secession. Not illegal, not in Dallas . . ."

"The mech missed the live-in, had to shut Nolan up. Didn't get the records, either. A botch. Thoroughgoing botch. The live-in—who knew the building like that? He wasn't any Company man. Martian with no visa, no regulation entry to the planet? I'll bet Nolan knew what he was, I'll bet Nolan was passing stuff to the Movement."

"An exec in MarsCorp? Over Martian Transport? Ask how the guy got here with no visa."

"Shit," he said. Then he thought about the mech, the kind of tech the rebels didn't have. "They wouldn't want a witness," he said. "The rebels wouldn't. The Company damned sure wouldn't. Ross would've gone for *me*, except I was linked in. I was recording. So she couldn't snatch the guy—had to shut the guy up somehow. They damn sure couldn't have a Company cop arrested down here. Had to get him shut up for good and get Ross off the planet . . ."

"Dead on," Sheila said. "Dead for sure, if he'd talked. Washington was after the Company for the make and the Company was stonewalling like hell, lay you odds on that—and I'll bet there's a plane seat for Ross tonight on a Guiana flight. What's it take? An hour down there? Half an hour more, if a shuttle's ready to roll, and Ross would have been no-return for this jurisdiction. That's all they needed." She flipped the com back to On again, to the city's ordinary litany of petty crime and larcenies, beneath an uneasy sky. "This is 34, coming on-line, marker 15 on the pike, good evening, HQ. This is a transmission check, think we've got it fixed now, 10-4?"

THE SANDMAN, THE TINMAN, AND THE BETTYB

CRAZYCHARLIE: *Got your message, Unicorn: Meet for lunch?*
DUTCHMAN: *Charlie, what year?*
CRAZYCHARLIE: *Not you, Dutchman. Talking to the pretty lady.*
T_REX: *Unicorn's not a lady.*
CRAZYCHARLIE: *Shut up. Pay no attention to them, Unicorn. They're all jealous.*
T_REX: *Unicorn's not answering. Must be asleep.*
CRAZYCHARLIE: *Beauty sleep.*
UNICORN: *Just watching you guys. Having lunch.*
LOVER18: *What's for lunch, pretty baby?*
UNICORN: *Chocolate. Loads of chocolate.*
T_REX: *Don't do that to us. You haven't got chocolate.*
UNICORN: *I'm eating it now. Dark chocolate. Mmmm.*
T_REX: *Cruel.*
CRAZYCHARLIE: *Told you she'd show for lunch. Fudge icing, Unicorn . . .*
CRAZYCHARLIE: *. . . With ice cream.*
DUTCHMAN: *I remember ice cream.*
T_REX: *Chocolate ice cream.*
FROGPRINCE: *Stuff like they've got on B-dock. There's this little shop . . .*
T_REX: *With poofy white stuff.*
DUTCHMAN: *Strawberry ice cream.*
FROGPRINCE: *. . . that serves five different flavors.*
CRAZYCHARLIE: *Unicorn in chocolate syrup.*
UNICORN: *You wish.*
HAWK29: *With poofy white stuff.*
UNICORN: *Shut up, you guys.*
LOVER18: *Yeah, shut up, you guys. Unicorn and I are going to go off some-
    where.*
CRAZYCHARLIE: *In a thousand years, guy.*

Ping. Ping-ping. Ping.

Sandwich was done. Sandman snagged it out of the cooker, everted the bag, and put it in for a clean. Tuna san and a coffee fizz, ersatz. He couldn't afford the true stuff, which, by the time the freight ran clear out here, ran a guy clean out of profit—which Sandman still hoped to make but it wasn't the be-all and end-all. Being out here was.

He had a name. It was on the records of his little two-man op, which was down to one, since Alfie'd had enough and gone in for food. Which was the first time little *BettyB* had ever made a profit. No mining. Just running the buoy. Took a damn long time running in, a damn long time running out, alternate with *PennyGirl*. Which was how the unmanned buoys that told everybody in the solar system where they were kept themselves going. Dozens of buoys, dozens of little tenders making lonely runs out and back, endless cycle. The buoy was a robot. For all practical purposes *BettyB* was a robot, too, but the tenders needed a human eye, a human brain, and Sandman was that. Half a year running out and back, half a year in the robot-tended, drop-a-credit pleasures of Beta Station, half the guys promising themselves they'd quit the job in a couple more runs, occasionally somebody doing the deed and going in. But most didn't. Most grew old doing it. Sandman wasn't old yet, but he wasn't young. He'd done all there was to do at Beta, and did his favorites and didn't think about going in permanently, because when he was going in and had Beta in *BettyB*'s sights, he'd always swear he was going to stay, and by the time six months rolled around and he'd seen every vid and drunk himself stupid and broke, hell, he was ready to go back to the solitude and the quiet.

He was up on three months now, two days out from Buoy 17, and the sound of a human voice—his own—had gotten odder and more welcome to him. He'd memorized all the verses to *Matty Groves* and sang them to himself at odd moments. He was working on St. Mark and the complete works of Jeffrey Farnol. He'd downloaded Tennyson and Kipling and decided to learn French on the return trip—not that any of the Outsiders ever did a damn thing with what they learned and he didn't know why French and not Italian, except he thought his last name, Ives, was French, and that was reason enough in a spacescape void of reasons and a spacetime hours remote from actual civilization.

He settled in with his sandwich and his coffee fizz and watched the screen go.

He lurked, today. He usually lurked. The cyber-voices came and went. He hadn't heard a thing from BigAl or Tinman, who'd been in the local neighborhood the last several years. He'd asked around, but nobody knew, and nobody'd seen them at Beta. Which was depressing. He supposed BigAl might have gone off to another route. He'd been a hauler, and sometimes they got switched without notice, but there'd been nothing on the boards. Tinman might've changed handles. He was a spooky sort, and some guys did, or had three or four. He wasn't sure Tinman was sane—some weren't, that plied the system fringes. And some ran afoul of the law, and weren't anxious to be tracked. Debts, maybe. You could get new ID on Beta, if you knew where to look, and the old hands knew better than the young ones, who sometimes fell into bodacious difficulties. Station hounds had broken up a big ring a few months back, forging bank creds as well as ID—just never trust an operation without bald old guys in it, that was what Sandman said, and the Lenny Wick ring hadn't, just all young blood and big promises.

Which meant coffee fizz was now pricey and scarce, since the Lenny Wick bunch had padded the imports and siphoned off the credits, which was how they got caught.

Sandman took personal exception to that situation: anything that got between an Outsider and his caffeine ought to get the long, cold walk in the big dark, so far as that went. So Lenny Wick hadn't got a bit of sympathy, but meanwhile Sandman wasn't too surprised if a few handles out in the deep dark changed for good and all.

Nasty trick, though, if Tinman was Unicorn. No notion why anybody ever assumed Unicorn was a she. They just always had.

FROGPRINCE: *So what are you doing today, Sandman? I see you . . .*
    Sandman ate a bite of sandwich. Input:

SANDMAN: *Just thinking about Tinman. Miss him.*
FROGPRINCE: *. . . lurking out there.*
SANDMAN: *Wonder if he got hot ID. If he's lurking, he can leave me word.*
T_REX: *Haven't heard, Sandman, sorry.*
UNICORN: *Won't I do, Sandman?*
SANDMAN: *Sorry, Unicorn. Your voice is too high.*
UNICORN: *You female, Sandman?*
T_REX: *LMAO.*
FROGPRINCE: *LL&L.*
SANDMAN: *No.*
DUTCHMAN: *Sandman is a guy.*
UNICORN: *You don't like women, Sandman?*

T_REX: *Shut up, Unicorn.*
SANDMAN: *Going back to my sandwich now.*
UNICORN: *What are you having, Sandman?*
SANDMAN: *Steak and eggs with coffee. Byebye.*

He ate his tuna san and lurked, sipped the over-budget coffee fizz. They were mostly young. Well, FrogPrince wasn't. But mostly young and on the hots for money. They were all going to get rich out here at the far side of the useful planets and go back to the easy life at Pell. The cyberchat mostly bored him, obsessive food and sex. Occasionally he and FrogPrince got on and talked mechanics or, well-coded, what the news was out of Beta, what miners had made a find, what contracts were going ahead or falling through.

Tame, nowadays. Way tame. Unicorn played her games. Dutchman laid his big plans on the stock market. They were all going to eat steak and eggs every meal, in the fanciest restaurant on Pell.

Same as when the war ended, the War to end all wars, well, ended at least for the next year or so, before the peace heated up. Everybody was going to live high and wide and business was just going to take off like the proverbial bat out of the hot place.

Well, it might take off for some, and it had, but Dutchman's guesses were dependably wrong, and what mattered to them out here was the politics that occasionally flared through Beta, this or that company deciding to private-enterprise the old guys out of business. They'd privatized mining. That was no big surprise.

But—Sandman finished the coffee fizz and cycled the container— they didn't privatize the buoys. Every time they tried, the big haulers threatened no-show at Pell, because they knew the rates would go sky-high. More, the privatizers also knew they'd come under work-and-safety rules, which meant they'd actually have to provide quality services to the tenders, and bring a tender-ship like *BettyB* up to standard—or replace her with a robot, which hadn't worked the last time they'd tried it, and which, to do the job a human could, cost way more than the privatizers wanted to hear about.

So Sandman and *BettyB* had their job, hell and away more secure than, say, Unicorn, who was probably a kid, probably signed on with one of the private companies, probably going to lose her shirt and her job the next time a sector didn't pan out as rich with floating junk as the company hoped.

But the Unicorns of the great deep were replaceable. There were always more. They'd assign them out where the pickings were supposed to be rich and the kids, after doing the mapping, would get out of the job with just about enough to keep them fed and bunked until the next big shiny deal . . . the next time the companies found themselves a field of war junk.

Just last year the companies had had a damn shooting war, for God's sake, over the back end of a wrecked warship. They'd had Allied and Paris Metals hiring on young fools who'd go in there armed and stupid, each with a district court order that had somehow, between Beta and Gamma sectors, ended up in the Supreme Court way back on Pell—but not before several young fools had shot each other. Then Hazards had ruled the whole thing was too hot to work.

Another bubble burst. Another of Dutchman's hot stock tips gone to hell.

And a raft of young idiots got themselves stranded at Beta willing to work cheap, no safety questions asked.

So the system rolled on.

T_REX: *Gotta go now. Hot date.*
FROGPRINCE: *Yeah. In your dreams, T_Rex.*

You made the long run out from Beta, you passed through several cyberworlds—well, transited. Blended through them. You traveled, and the cyberflow from various members of the net just got slower and slower in certain threads of the converse. He could key up the full list of participants and get some conversations that would play out over hours. He'd rather not. Murphy's law said the really vital, really interesting conversations were always on the edges, and they mutated faster than your input could reach them. It just made you crazy, wishing you could say something timely and knowing you'd be preempted by some dim-brain smartass a little closer. So you held cyberchats of the mind, imagining all the clever things you could have said to all the threads you could have maintained, and then you got to thinking how far out and lonely you really were.

He'd rather not. Even if the local chat all swirled about silly Unicorn. Even if he didn't know most of them: space was bigger, out here. Like dots on an inflated balloon, the available number of people was just stretched thin, and the ones willing to do survey and mine out here weren't necessarily the sanest.

Like buoy-tenders, who played chess with ghost-threads out of the dark and read antique books.

Last of the coffee fizz. He keyed up the French lessons. *Comment*

SANDMAN: *Number 17 stopped transmitting. Nature of object . . .*
SANDMAN: *. . . unknown. Vectors from impact unknown . . .*
SANDMAN: *. . . Impact one hour fifteen minutes before my location.*

The informational wavefront, that was. The instant of spacetime with 17's warning had rolled past him and headed past FrogPrince and Unicorn and the rest, before it could possibly reach Beta. They lived in a spacetime of subsequent events that widened like ripples in a tank, until scatter randomized the information into a universal noise.

And *BettyB* was hurtling toward Number 17, and suddenly wasn't going anywhere useful. She might get the order to go look-see, in which case braking wasn't a good idea. She might get the order to return, but he doubted it would come for hours. Decision-making took time in boardrooms. Decision-making had to happen hell and away faster out here, with what might be pieces loose.

He shifted colors on the image, near-black for green. Nearer black for blue. Black stayed black.

Ball with an inward or outward dimple and a whole bunch of planar surfaces. He didn't like what he saw. He transmitted his raw effort as he built it. Cigar-shape. Gray scale down one side of the image, magnification in the top line. Scan showed a flock of tiny blips in the same location. Scan was foxed. Totally.

"God."

SANDMAN: *Transmitting image. Big mother.*

A keystroke switched modes. A button-click rotated the colorized image. Not a ball. Cigar-shape head-on. Cigar-shape with deflecting planes all over it.

SANDMAN: *It's an inert. An old inert missile, inbound. It's blown Buoy 17 . . .*
SANDMAN: *. . . Trying to determine v. Don't know class or mass. Cylindrical.*
SANDMAN: *. . . Buoy gone silent. May have lost antenna. May have lost orientation . . .*
SANDMAN: *. . . May have been destroyed. Warn traffic of possible buoy fragments . . .*
SANDMAN: *. . . originating at buoy at 1924h, fragments including . . .*
SANDMAN: *. . . high-mass power plant and fuel.*

allez-vous, mademoiselle? And listened and sketched, a Teach Yourself
course, correspondence school, that wanted him to draw eggs and
faces on them: he multitasked. He filled his screen with eggs and tur
them into people he knew, some he liked, some he didn't, while he n
tered French. It was the way to stay sane and happy out here, wh
BettyB danced her way along the prescribed—

Alarm blipped. Usually the racket was the buoy noting an arri
but this being an ecliptic buoy, it didn't get action itself, just relay
from the network, time-bound, just part of the fabric of knowledge-
freighter arrived at zenith. Somebody left at nadir.

Arrival, it said. Arrival within its range and coming—

God, coming fast. He scrambled to bring systems up and listen
Number 17. Number 17, so far as a robot could be, was in a state
panic, sending out a warning. *Collision, collision, collision.*

There was an object out there. Something Number 17 had heard,
it waited to hear—but Number 17 didn't *expect* trouble anymore. Peac
time ships didn't switch off their squeal. Long-range scan on the remo
buoys didn't operate, wasn't switched on these days—power-savin
measure, saving the corporations maintenance and upkeep. Whatever
picked up was close. Damned close.

Maintenance keys. Maintenance could test it. He keyed, a long, lon
way from it receiving: turn on, wake up longscan, Number 17, Number 17

He relayed Number 17's warning on, system-wide, hear and relay
hear and relay.

He sent into the cyberstream:

SANDMAN: *Collision alert from Number 17. Heads up.*

But it was a web of time-stretch. A long time for the nearest authority to hear his warning. Double that to answer.

Number 17 sent an image, at least part of one. Then stopped sending.

Wasn't talking now. Wasn't talking, wasn't talking.

Hours until Beta Station even noticed. Until Pell noticed. Until the
whole buoy network accounted that Number 17 wasn't transmitting,
and that that section of the system chart had frozen. Stopped.

The image was shadowy. Near-black on black.

"Damn." An Outsider didn't talk much, didn't use voice, just the
key-taps that filled the digital edges of the vast communications web.
And he keyed.

Best he could do. The wavefront hadn't near reached Beta. And the buoy that could have given him longscan wasn't talking—or no longer existed. The visual out here in the dark, where the sun was a star among other stars, gave him a few scattered flashes of gray that might be buoy fragments. He went on capturing images.

BettyB went hurtling on toward the impact-point. Whatever was out there might have clipped the buoy, or might have plowed through the low-mass girder-structures like a bullet through a snowball, sending solid pieces of the buoy flying in all directions, themselves dangerous to small craft. The inert, the bullet coming their way, was high-v and high-mass, a solid chunk of metal that might have been traveling for fifty years and more, an iron slug fired by a long-lost warship in a decades-ago war. Didn't need a warhead. Inerts tended to be far longer than wide because the fire mechanism in the old carriers stored them in bundles and fired them in swarms, but no matter how it was oriented when it hit, it was a killer—and if it tumbled, it was that much harder to predict, cutting that much wider a path of destruction. Mass and velocity were its destructive power. An arrow out of a crossbow that, at starship speeds, could take out another ship, wreck a space station, cheap and sure, nothing fragile about it.

After the war, they'd swept the lanes—Pell system had been a battle zone. Ordnance had flown every which way. They'd worked for years. And the last decade—they'd thought they had the lanes clear.

Clearly not. He had a small scattering of flashes. He thought they might be debris out of the buoy, maybe the power plant, or one of the several big dishes. He ran calculations, trying to figure what was coming, where the pieces were going, and he could use help—God, he could use help. He transmitted what he had. He kept transmitting.

FROGPRINCE: *Sandman, I copy. Are you all right?*

SANDMAN: *FrogPrince, spread it out. I need some help here . . .*

UNICORN: *Is this a joke, Sandman?*

SANDMAN: *I'm sending raw feed, all the data I've got. Help. Mayday.*

LOVER18: *Sandman, what's up?*

SANDMAN: *Unicorn, this is serious.*

DUTCHMAN: *I copy, Sandman. My numbers man is on it.*

Didn't even know Dutchman had a partner. A miner's numbers man was damned welcome on the case. Desperately welcome.

Meanwhile Sandman had his onboard encyclopedia. He had his histories. He hunted, paged, ferreted, trying to find a concrete answer on the mass of the antique inerts—which was only part of the equation. Velocity and vector depended on the ship that, somewhere out there, fifty and more years ago, had fired what might be one, or a dozen inerts. There could be a whole swarm inbound, a decades-old broadside that wouldn't decay, or slow, or stop, forever, until it found a rock to hit or a ship full of people, or a space station, or a planet.

Pell usually had one or another of the big merchanters in. Sandman searched his news files, trying to figure. The big ships had guns. Guns could deal with an inert, at least deflecting it—*if* they had an armed ship in the system. A big ship could chase it down, even grab it and decelerate it. He fed numbers into what was becoming a jumbled thread of inputs, speculations, calculations.

Hell of it was—there was one thing that would shift an inert's course. One thing that lay at the heart of a star system, one thing that anchored planets, that anchored moons and stations: that gravity well that led straight to the system's nuclear heart—the sun itself. A star collected the thickest population of planets, and people, and vulnerable real estate to the same place as it collected stray missiles. And no question, the old inert was infalling toward the sun, increasing in v as it went, a man-made comet with a comet-sized punch, that could crack planetary crust, once it gathered all the v the sun's pull could give it.

T_REX: *Sandman, possible that thing's even knocked about the Oort Cloud.*
T_REX: *Perturbed out of orbit.*
UNICORN: *Perturbing us.*
LOVER18: *I've got a trajectory on that buoy debris chunk . . .*
LOVER18: *. . . no danger to us.*

Alarm went off. *BettyB* fired her automated avoidance system. Sandman hooked a foot and both arms and clung to the counter, stylus punching a hole in his hand as his spare styluses hit the bulkhead. The bedding bunched up in the end of the hammock. It was usually a short burst. It wasn't. Sandman clung and watched the camera display, as something occluded the stars for a long few seconds.

"Hell!" he said aloud, alone in the dark. Desperately, watching a juggernaut go by him. "Hell!" One human mote like a grain of dust.

Then he saw stars. It was past him. What had hit the buoy was past him and now—now, damn, he and the buoy were two points on a straight line: he had the vector; and he had the camera and with that, God, yes, he could calculate the velocity.

He calculated. He transmitted both, drawing a simple straight line in the universe, calamity or deliverance reduced to its simplest form.

He extended the line toward the sun.

Calamity. Plane of the ecliptic, with Pell Station and its heavy traffic on the same side of the sun as Beta. The straight line extended, bending at the last, velocity accelerating, faster, faster, faster onto the slope of a star's deep well.

DUTCHMAN: *That doesn't look good, Sandman.*
UNICORN: *:(*
DUTCHMAN: *Missing Pell. Maybe not missing me . . .*
DUTCHMAN: *. . . Braking. Stand by.*
UNICORN: *Dutchman, take care.*
LOVER18: *Letting those damn things loose in the first place . . .*
T_REX: *Not liking your calculations, Sandman.*
LOVER18: *. . . what were they thinking?*
FROGPRINCE: *I'm awake. Sandman, Dutchman, you all right out there?*
DUTCHMAN: *I can see it . . .*
UNICORN: *Dutchman, be all right.*
DUTCHMAN: *I'm all right . . .*
DUTCHMAN: *. . . it's going past now. It's huge.*
HAWK29: *What's going on?*
LOVER18: *Read your damn transcript, Hawkboy.*
CRAZYCHARLIE: *Lurking and running numbers.*
DUTCHMAN: *It's clear. It's not that fast.*
SANDMAN: *Not that fast *yet.**
DUTCHMAN: *We're running numbers, too. Not good.*
SANDMAN: *Everybody crosscheck calculations. Not sure . . .*
SANDMAN: *. . . about gravity slope . . .*
CRAZYCHARLIE: *Could infall the sun.*
UNICORN: *We're glad you're all right, Dutchman.*
SANDMAN: *If it infalls, not sure how close to Pell.*
WILLWISP: *Lurking and listening. Relaying to my local net.*
T_REX: *That baby's going to come close.*

Sandman reached, punched a button for the fragile long-range dish. On *BettyB*'s hull, the arm made a racket, extending, working the metal tendons, pulling the silver fan into a metal flower, already aimed at Beta.

"Warning, warning, warning. This is tender *BettyB* calling all craft in line between Pell and Buoy 17. A rogue inert has taken out Buoy 17 and passed my location, 08185 on system schematic. Looks like it's in-falling the sun. Calculations incomplete. Buoy 17 destroyed, trajectory of fragments including power plant all uncertain, generally toward Beta. Mass and velocity sufficient to damage. Relay, relay, relay and repeat to all craft in system. Transmission of raw data follows."

He uploaded the images and data he had. He repeated it three times. He tried to figure the power plant's course. It came up headed through empty space.

CRAZYCHARLIE: *It's going to come damn close to Pell . . .*
CRAZYCHARLIE: *. . . at least within shipping lanes and insystem hazard.*
DUTCHMAN: *I figure same. Sandman?*
UNICORN: *I'm transmitting to Beta.*
WILLWISP: *Still relaying your flow.*
HAWK29: *Warn everybody.*
UNICORN: *It's months out for them.*
DUTCHMAN: *Those things have a stealth coating. Dark . . .*
DUTCHMAN: *. . . Hard to find. Easy to lose.*
UNICORN: *Lot of metal. Pity we can't grab it . . .*
FROGPRINCE: *Don't try it, Unicorn. You and your engines . . .*
UNICORN: *. . . But it's bigger than I am.*
FROGPRINCE: *. . . couldn't mass big enough.*
UNICORN: *I copy that, Froggy . . .*
DUTCHMAN: *It's going to be beyond us. All well and good if it goes . . .*
UNICORN: *. . . Thanks for caring.*
DUTCHMAN: *. . . without hitting anything. Little course change here . . .*
DUTCHMAN: *. . . and Pell's going to have real trouble tracking it.*
HAWK29: *I feel a real need for a sandwich and a nap . . .*
UNICORN: *Hawk, that doesn't make sense.*
HAWK29: *. . . We've sent our warning. Months down, Pell will fix it . . .*
HAWK29: *. . . All we can do. It's relayed. Passing out of our chat soon.*
T_REX: *Sandman, how sure your decimals?*
FROGPRINCE: *We can keep transmitting, Hawk. We can tell Sandman . . .*
FROGPRINCE: *. . . we're sorry he's off his run. His buoy's destroyed . . .*
FROGPRINCE: *. . . He's got to find a new job . . .*
UNICORN: *They'll be running construction and supply out. I'll apply, too.*
FROGPRINCE: *Use a little damn compassion.*
SANDMAN: *T_Rex, I'm sure. I was damned careful.*

T_REX: *You braked.*
DUTCHMAN: *We both braked.*
SANDMAN: *I've got those figures in. Even braking, I'm sure of the numbers.*
T_REX: *That's real interesting from where I sit.*
FROGPRINCE: *T_Rex, where are you?*
T_REX: *About an hour from impact.*
UNICORN: *Brake, T_Rex!*
SANDMAN: *T_Rex, it's 5 meters wide, no tumble.*
T_REX: *Sandman, did I ever pay you that 52 credits?*

Tinman?

Damn. *Damn!* Fifty-two cred in a Beta downside bar. Fifty-two cred on a tab for dinner and drinks, the last time they'd met. Tinman had said, at the end, that things had gone bad. Crazy Tinman. Big wide grin hadn't been with them that supper. He'd known something was wrong.

He'd paid the tab when Tinman's bank account turned up not answering.

The Lenny Wick business. The big crunch that took down no few that had thought Beta was a place to get rich, and it wasn't, and never would be.

SANDMAN: *Dutchman, you copy that? T_Rex owes me 52c.*
DUTCHMAN: *Sandman, we meet on dockside, I owe you a drink . . .*
DUTCHMAN: *. . . for the warning.*

Dutchman didn't pick up on it. Or didn't want to, having fingers anywhere on the Lenny Wick account not being popular with the cops. Easy for Pell to say it was all illegal. Pell residents didn't have a clue how it was on Beta Station payroll. Didn't know how rare jobs were, that weren't.

The big score. The way out. Unicorns by the shipload fell into that well. And a few canny Tinmen got caught trying to skirt it just close enough to catch a few of the bennies before it all imploded.

SANDMAN: *I copy that, T_Rex. If you owe me money . . .*
SANDMAN: *. . . get out of there.*
T_REX: *Going to be busy for a few minutes.*
UNICORN: *T_Rex, we love you.*
T_REX: *Flattery, flattery, Unicorn. I know your heart's . . .*
DUTCHMAN: *You take care, T_Rex.*

T_REX: . . . *for FrogPrince.* (((*Poof.*)))
UNICORN: *He's vanished.*
LOVER18: *This isn't a damn sim, Unicorn.*
UNICORN: :(
FROGPRINCE: *T_Rex, can we help you?*
UNICORN: *Don't distract him, Froggy. He's figuring.*

Good guess, that was. Sandman called up the system chart—the buoys produced it, together, constantly talking, over a time lag of hours; but theirs wasn't accurate anymore. The whole Pell System chart was out of date now, because their buoy wasn't talking anymore. The other buoys hadn't missed it yet, and Pell wouldn't know it for hours, but the information wasn't updating, and the source he had right now wasn't Buoy 17 anymore.

They all had numbers on that chart. But the cyberchat never admitted who was Sandman and who was Unicorn. It never had mattered.

They all knew who Sandman was, now. He'd transmitted his chart number. He could look down the line and figure that Dutchman, most recently near that juggernaut's path, was 80018.

He drew his line on the flat-chart and knew where T_Rex was, and saw what his azimuth was, and saw the arrow that was his flatchart heading and rate.

He made the chart advance.

Tick.

Tick.

Tick.

SANDMAN: *I've run the chart, T_Rex. Brake to nadir . . .*
SANDMAN: *. . . Best bet.*

The cyberflow had stopped for a moment. Utterly stopped. Then:

UNICORN: *I've run the chart, too, T_Rex. If you can brake now, please do it.*
SANDMAN: *I second Unicorn.*

What the hell size operations had Tinman signed on to? A little light miner that could skitter to a new heading?

Some fat company supply ship, like *BettyB*, that would slog its *v* lower only over half a critical hour?

SANDMAN: *T_Rex, Dutchman, I'm dumping my cargo . . .*
SANDMAN: *. . . I'm going after him.*
HAWK29: *BetaControl's going to have a cat.*
UNICORN: *Shut up, Hawk. I'm going, too.*
SANDMAN: *T_Rex, if you can't brake in time, have you got a pod? . . .*
SANDMAN: *. . . I'm coming after you. Go to the pod if you've got one . . .*
SANDMAN: *. . . Use a suit if not. Never mind the ETA . . .*
SANDMAN: *. . . I'll get there in time.*
FROGPRINCE: *Sandman, go.*
SANDMAN: *I'm going to full burn, hard as I can . . .*
SANDMAN: *. . . Right down that line.*

Button pushes. One after the other. Hatches open, all down BettyB's side. Shove to starboard. Shove to port. Shove to nadir. Sandman held to the counter, then buckled in fast as the scope erupted with little blips.

T_REX: *It's coming. I've got it on the scope. Going to full burn . . .*
T_REX: *. . . It's not getting past me.*
FROGPRINCE: *T_Rex, that thing's a ship-killer. You can't . . .*
FROGPRINCE: *. . . deflect it. Get away from the console.*
FROGPRINCE: *T_Rex, time to ditch! Listen to Sandman.*
T_REX: *Accelerating to 2.3. Intercept.*
UNICORN: *T_Rex, you're crazy.*
T_REX: *I'm not crazy, lady. I'm a friggin ore-hauler . . .*
T_REX: *. . . with a full bay.*
FROGPRINCE: *You'll scatter like a can of marbles.*
T_REX: *Nope. She's coming too close and she's cloaked . . .*
T_REX: *. . . If station can't spot her, she can take out a freighter . . .*
T_REX: *. . . Going to burn that surface off so they can see . . .*
T_REX: *. . . that mother coming.*
T_REX: *((Poof))*
UNICORN: *Not funny, T_Rex.*

Sandman pushed the button. *BettyB* shoved hard, hard, hard.

SANDMAN: *I'm on my way, T_Rex. Get out of there.*
WILLWISP: *I'm still here. Relaying.*
CRAZYCHARLIE: *I'm coming after you, Sandman, you and him.*
SANDMAN: *By the time I get there, I'll be much less mass . . .*

SANDMAN: *T_Rex, you better get yourself to a pod.*
SANDMAN: *. . . I'm going to be damn mad if I come out there . . .*
SANDMAN: *. . . and you didn't.*

Faster and faster. Faster than *BettyB* ever had gone. Calculations changed. Sandman kept figuring, kept putting it into nav.

The cyberflow kept going, talk in the dark. Eyes and ears that took in a vast, vast tract of space.

UNICORN: *I know you're busy, Sandman. But we're here.*
LOVER18: *I've run the numbers. Angle of impact . . .*
LOVER18: *. . . will shove the main mass outsystem to nadir.*
FROGPRINCE: *Fireball will strip stealth coat . . .*
FROGPRINCE: *T_Rex, you're right.*
HAWK29: *T_Rex, Sandman and Charlie are coming . . .*
HAWK 29: *. . . fast as they can.*

Nothing to do but sit and figure, sit and figure, with an eye to the cameras. Forward now. Forward as they bore.

"*APIS19 BettyB, this is Beta Control. We copy re damage to Buoy 17. Can you provide more details?*"

The wavefront had gotten to Beta. They were way behind the times.

"Beta Control, this is APIS 19 *BettyB*, on rescue. Orehauler on chart as 80912 imminent for impact. Inert stealth coating prevents easy intercept if it clears our district. Local neighborhood has a real good fix on it right now. May be our last chance to grab it, so the orehauler's trying, BetaControl. We're hoping he's going to survive impact. Right now I'm running calculations. Don't want to lose track of it. *BettyB* will go silent now. Ending send."

FROGPRINCE: *I'll talk to them for you, Sandman . . .*
FROGPRINCE: *I'll keep them posted.*

Numbers came closer. Closer. Sandman punched buttons, folded and retracted the big dish.

Numbers . . . numbers . . . coincided.

Fireball. New, brief star in the deep dark.

Only the camera caught it. Streaks, incandescent, visible light shooting off from that star, most to nadir, red-hot slag.

The wavefront of that explosion was coming. *BettyB* was a shell, a structure of girders without her containers. Girders and one small cabin. Everything that could tuck down, she'd tucked. Life within her was a small kernel in a web of girders.

Wavefront hit, static noise. Light. Heat.

BettyB waited. Plowed ahead on inertia. Lost a little, disoriented.

Her hull whined. Groaned.

Sandman looked at his readouts, holding his breath.

The whine stopped. Sandman checked his orientation, trimmed up on gentle, precise puffs, kicked the throttle up.

Bang! Something hit, rattled down the frame. Bang! Another.

Then a time of quiet. Sandman braked, braked hard, harder.

Then touched switches, brought the whip antennae up. Uncapped lenses and sensors.

In all that dark, he heard a faint, high-pitched ping-ping-ping.

"Tinman?" Sandman transmitted on low output, strictly local. Search and rescue band. "Tinman, this is *BettyB*. This is Sandman. You hear me? I'm coming after that fifty-two credits."

"*Bastard,*" came back to him, not time-lagged. "*I'll pay, I'll pay. Get your ass out here. And don't use that name.*"

Took a while. Took a considerable while, tracking down that blip, maneuvering close, shielding the pickup from any stray bits and pieces that might be in the area.

Hatch opened, however. Sandman had his clipline attached, sole lifesaving precaution. He flung out a line and a wrench that served as a miniature missile, a visible guide that flashed in the searchlight.

Tinman flashed, too, white on one side, sooted non-reflective black on the other, like half a man.

Sandman was ever so relieved when a white glove reached out and snagged that line. They were three hours down on Tinman's life-support. And Sandman was oh, so tired.

He hauled at the line. Hauled Tinman in. Grabbed Tinman in his arms and hugged him suit and all into the safety of the little air lock.

Then he shut the hatch. Cycled it.

Tinman fumbled after the polarizing switch on the faceplate shield. It cleared, and Tinman looked at him, a graying, much thinner Tinman.

Lips moved. "Hey, man," came through static. "Hate to tell you. My funds were all on my ship."

"The hell," Sandman said. "The hell." Then: "I owe you, man. Some freighter next month or so—owes you their necks."

"Tell that to Beta Ore," the Tinman said. "It was their hauler I put in its path."

CRAZYCHARLIE: *I've got you spotted, Sandman.*
SANDMAN: *Charlie, thanks. Got a real chancy reading . . .*
SANDMAN: *. . . on the number three pipe . . .*
SANDMAN: *. . . think it got dinged. I really don't want . . .*
SANDMAN: *. . . to fire that engine again . . .*
SANDMAN: *. . . I think we're going to need a tow.*
CRAZYCHARLIE: *Sandman, I'll tow you from here to hell and back . . .*
CRAZYCHARLIE: *. . . How's T_Rex?*
SANDMAN: *This is T_Rex, on Sandman's board.*
UNICORN: *Yay! T_Rex is talking.*
FROGPRINCE: *Tracking that stuff . . .*
FROGPRINCE: *. . . nadir right now. Clear as clear, T_Rex . . .*
FROGPRINCE: *. . . You know you *bent* that bastard?*
SANDMAN: *T_Rex here. Can you see it, FrogPrince?*
FROGPRINCE: *T_Rex, I can see it clear.*
WILLWISP: *Word's going out. Pell should know soon what they missed.*
UNICORN: *Or what missed *them*.:)*
SANDMAN: *This is Sandman. Thanks, guys . . .*
SANDMAN: *. . . You tell Pell the story, WillWisp, Unicorn. Gotta go . . .*
SANDMAN: *. . . I'm hooking up with Charlie . . .*
SANDMAN: *. . . Talk tomorrow.*
UNICORN: *You're the best, Sandman. T_Rex, you are so beautiful.*
SANDMAN: *. . . going to get a tow.*
CRAZYCHARLIE: *You can come aboard my cabin, Sandman.*
CRAZYCHARLIE: *. . . Got a bottle waiting for you.*
CRAZYCHARLIE: *. . . A warm nook by the heater.*
SANDMAN: *Deal, Charlie. Me and my partner . . .*
SANDMAN: *. . . somewhere warm.*
FROGPRINCE: *Didn't know you had a partner, Sandman . . .*
FROGPRINCE: *. . . Thought you were all alone out here.*
SANDMAN: *I'm not, now, am I?*
SANDMAN: *T_Rex speaking again. T_Rex says . . .*
SANDMAN: *. . . This is one tired T_Rex ((Bowing.)) Thanks, all . . .*
SANDMAN: *. . . Thanks, Sandman. Thanks, Charlie.*
SANDMAN: *. . . ((Poof))*

Acknowledgments

Sunfall was first published in 1981 by DAW Books, Inc. All original stories
©1981 by C.J. Cherryh.
"MasKs (Venice)" ©2004 by C.J. Cherryh.

Visible Light was first published in 1986 by DAW Books, Inc. All material
©1986 by C.J. Cherryh except:
"Cassandra" ©1978, Mercury Press, first appeared in *The Magazine of Fantasy and Science Fiction.* Reprinted by permission of Gordon Van Gelder.
"Threads of Time" ©1981 by C.J. Cherryh, first appeared in the Darkover Grand Council Program Book IV ©1978, Andrew Siegel.
"Companions" ©1984 by C.J. Cherryh, first appeared in the *John W. Campbell Awards Vol V,* edited by George R.R. Martin, Bluejay Books.
"A Thief in Korianth" ©1981 by C.J. Cherryh, first appeared in *Flashing Swords! No 5: Demons and Daggers,* edited by Lin Carter, Dell Books.
"The Last Tower" ©1982 by C.J. Cherryh, first appeared in Winter 1982 *Sorcerer's Apprentice* by Flying Buffalo.

"The Dark King" ©1982 by DAW Books, Inc., first appeared in *The Year's Best Fantasy Stories 3,* edited by Lin Carter.
"Homecoming" ©1979 by Flight Unlimited, Inc, first appeared in *Shayol* Summer 1979. All rights reverted to author.
"The Dreamstone" ©1979 by C.J. Cherryh, first appeared in *Amazons!,* edited by Jessica Amanda Salmonson, DAW Books, Inc.
"Sea Change" ©1981 by C.J. Cherryh, first published in *Elsewhere,* edited by Terri Windling and Mark Alan Arnold.
"Willow" ©1982 by C.J. Cherryh, first published in *Hecate's Cauldron,* edited by Susan M. Schwartz, DAW Books, Inc.

"Of Law and Magic" ©1985 by C.J. Cherryh, first appeared in a slightly different form in *Moonsinger's Friends*, edited by Susan M. Schwartz, St. Martin's Press.

"The Unshadowed Land" ©1985 by C.J. Cherryh, first appeared in *Sword and Sorceress II*, edited by Marion Zimmer Bradley, DAW Books, Inc.

"Pots" ©1985 by C.J. Cherryh, first appeared in *Afterwar*, edited by Janet Morris, Pocket Books.

"The Scapegoat" ©1985 by C.J. Cherryh, first appeared in *Alien Stars*, edited by Betsy Mitchell, Baen Books.

"A Gift of Prophecy" ©1987 by C.J. Cherryh, first English-language publication in *Glass and Amber*, NESFA Press. Published earlier in Dutch translation.

"Wings" ©1989 by C.J. Cherryh, first appeared in *Carmen Miranda's Ghost is Haunting Space Station Three*, edited by Don Sakers, Baen Books.

"A Much Briefer History of Time" ©1990 by C.J. Cherryh, first published in *Drabble II—Double Century*, compiled by Rob Meades and David B. Wake, Beccon Publications.

"Gwydion and the Dragon" ©1991 by Random House, first published in *Once Upon a Time*, edited by Lester del Rey and Risa Kessler. Reprinted by permission of Ballantine Books, a division of Random House, Inc.

"Mech" ©1992 by C.J. Cherryh, first published in *FutureCrime*, edited by Cynthia Manson and Charles Ardai, Donald J Fine, Inc.

"The Sandman, the Tinman, and the BettyB" ©2002 by C.J. Cherryh, first published in *DAW 30th Anniversary: Science Fiction*, edited by Elizabeth R. Wollheim & Sheila E. Gilbert, DAW Books, Inc.